THE ISAAC QUARTET

The Isaac Quartet

Blue Eyes
Marilyn the Wild
The Education of Patrick Silver
Secret Isaac

Jerome Charyn

FOUR WALLS EIGHT WINDOWS
NEW YORK / LONDON

© Jerome Charyn, 1974, 1976, 1976, 1978

Published in the United States by
Four Walls Eight Windows
39 West 14th Street, room 503
New York, NY 10011

Originally published in Great Britain by Zomba Books, London 1984

Visit our website at http://www.4W8W.com

First printing April 2002.

Cataloging-in-Publication data for this book has been filed with the Library of
Congress.

Text composition by Accurate Conversions, New York

Printed in Canada

10 9 8 7 6 5 4 3 2 1

Contents

Introduction

Blue Eyes and the Barber King

I was drowning somewhere in the middle of 1973, lost in the muck of a new novel, some dinosaur of a book about a barber king and the republic of Andorra, when I discovered Ross Macdonald. I was sick of my own mythologizing and wanted something simple to read. A crime novel, why not? I happened to pick *The Galton Case* and it satisfied right from the start, with its lulling, neutral tone.

The book had a morphology I happened to admire—as if Ross Macdonald were in the habit of undressing bodies to find the skeleton underneath. Nothing was overwrought: landscape, language, and character were all laid bare. But this was no simple-minded accident. It was Macdonald's particular craft, that "wild masonry of laying detail on detail to make a structure."[1]

Wild masonry. That's what Macdonald's work was all about: sad, strange histories that crept between the tight, closed spaces. The lost son who surfaces out of a brutal, murderous past, and then is transformed into an impostor boy whose identity is born in the act of murder itself. And in the middle of all this searching is Macdonald's detective-narrator, Lew Archer, who is neither Marlowe nor Nick Charles, but a kind of deadly angel, the observer with genuine feelings who only invests a portion of himself in the text. Half of him is always elsewhere. Or, as Macdonald says: "Certainly my narrator Archer is not the main object of my interest, nor the character with whose fate I am most concerned. He is a deliberately narrowed version of the writing self, so narrow that when he turns sideways he almost disappears."[2]

This narrowing lens allows Ross Macdonald to deliver both a landscape and a past without the least hint of sentimentality.

---

[1] Ross Macdonald, "Writing the Galton Case," *Self-Portrait: Ceaselessly into the Past.* Santa Barbara: Capra Press, 1981.

[2] Ibid.

Macdonald is able to murder while he lulls us through the book.

I returned to my dinosaur novel, *King Jude*. But things were still rotten in the republic of Andorra. I had nowhere to go with my barber king. I couldn't squeeze him into a narrative that made sense. Not wanting to abandon my barber king, I decided to scribble a crime novel and let Jude the barber boil inside my head. But I didn't have Ross Macdonald's lulling sense of line. My writing was scratchy, secretive as a snake. I couldn't undress bodies with my prose. And I didn't love California the way Macdonald did. I'd lived in California for three years. It held no mythic properties for me. I remembered rocks and redwood trees. I'd have to find my detective hero and bring him to New York.

I'd been a bodybuilder and a ping-pong freak. My sense of the underworld came from pool halls and street gangs in the Bronx. I was something of an extortionist at twelve, but I outgrew the habit and by fourteen I was studying French irregular verbs at the High School of Music and Art. What the hell could I write about crime? I'd have had to go to the library stacks and pull out dossiers on the most memorable thieves of Manhattan and the Bronx, but I didn't want a crime novel that stank of research. So I depended on my one bit of luck. I had a brother who was in homicide. I went out to the wilds of Brooklyn where he worked. I sat with Harvey Charyn in his station house near the beach. I saw the cages where all the bad guys were held. I visited the back room where cops would sleep after a midnight tour. I was Charyn's kid brother, the scribbler, and radio dispatchers flirted with me. I met a detective whose ear had been chewed off in a street fight, another who boasted of all the wives he had, a third who twitched with paranoia, but was reliable in any combat zone.

My brother drove me to the Brooklyn morgue since I needed to look at dead bodies for my novel. The morgue attendant took me and Harvey around. All the dead men looked like Indians. Their skin had turned to bark. I distanced myself from the corpses, pretended I was touring some carnival with refrigerated shelves. It was Harvey who sucked Life Savers and seemed pale. I was only a stinking voyeur in the house of the dead.

But I had the beginning of a history of crime: the sad gleaning of a few Brooklyn homicide detectives. I traveled with them in their unmarked cars, listening to their hatred of the street. They weren't much like the warriors I'd imagined detectives to be: they were civil servants with a gun, obsessed about the day of their retirement. And because I'd grown up with my brother, remembered his muscle tee shirts, his longing to become Mr. America, Harvey seemed the saddest of them all. He's the one who read books at home and I became the writer. He was the artist of the family, but I got into Music and Art and Harvey never did. I'd replaced my brother somehow, bumped him out of the way. I sat scribbling at a university and he had to stare at corpses. He told me about a renegade rabbi who lay rotting in his bathtub for a month, a fourteen-year-old pros who was trampled to death by a gang of pimps because she happened to labor in their territories, the victim of a gangland murder whose arms ended up in New Jersey while his legs were buried in a potato farm somewhere on Long Island. The guy's torso was never found.

I'd watch my brother's face when he told his stories. There was no ghoulish delight. He was delivering the simple facts of his life as a detective. I felt like the brutal one, feeding off his homicide lists. And so I began my novel about a blue-eyed detective, Manfred Coen. This Blue Eyes was an odd amalgam of Harvey and me, two brown-eyed boys. Coen was a ping-pong freak, like I had been. And if he didn't have Harvey's coloring, he did have my brother's sad, gentle ways, a wanderer in Manhattan and the Bronx who dreamt of corpses, like Harvey did. I allowed Blue Eyes a mentor, Isaac Sidel, a honcho in the First Deputy Police Commissioner's office who grooms Coen and later gets him killed. Isaac was the sinister chief, and Coen was his blue-eyed angel, a kind of Billy Budd.

I scribbled a good part of *Blue Eyes* in Barcelona. I was thirty-six and I'd never been abroad. I'd landed in Madrid, wanting to devour every balcony on every street. I saw the Goyas in the basement of the Prado and felt as if my own life was being recast on enormous blood-dark canvases: the giant who devoured his children could have been born in the Bronx. I settled in Barcelona and wrote for six weeks.

I finished *Blue Eyes* in New York and carried it to my agent, Hy Cohen. He looked at the title page. "Who's Joseph da Silva?"

I'd decided to use a nom de guerre after having written seven novels as Jerome Charyn, and all seven sinking into invisibility. I'd invented a tribe of marrano pickpockets in *Blue Eyes* called the Guzmanns. Isaac Sidel is feuding with this tribe, and the Guzmanns become the agents of Manfred Coen's fall. Wanting my own sense of tribe, I'd picked a marrano name for myself, *Joseph da Silva*, hoping that his books might sell better than Jerome Charyn's.

But Hy Cohen convinced me to stay with Jerome. "Kid, you've had seven books. That's something of a feat. If you go with da Silva, you'll be starting all over again. A first novelist is a much more endangered animal than the author of seven books. They'll kill you out there."

So I published *Blue Eyes* without my nom de guerre and returned to *King Jude*. I scribbled on it in Paris, London, Edinburgh, Connecticut, and the upper West Side of Manhattan. The novel thickened to a thousand pages and I still couldn't find a home for my barber king. While I collected pages, my mind seemed to be at work on another book. I was bothered by Blue Eyes' death and needed to revive him. So I started *Marilyn the Wild*, which brought Manfred Coen back to an earlier time of his life. Isaac Sidel had a daughter, Marilyn, who keeps getting married and unmarried and is half in love with Coen. Isaac's ambivalence towards his blue-eyed angel was becoming clearer to me. The old chief resented Marilyn's attachment to Blue Eyes, though he keeps this to himself. He's a coward when it comes to his daughter and won't risk alienating Marilyn the Wild. We can smell the evil begin to build. Isaac is crazy about Marilyn, but she's much too independent for a deputy chief inspector. He can find no means of manipulating her, so he manipulates Coen. And by allowing Coen to get killed, he punishes Marilyn, Blue Eyes, and himself.

I still couldn't put Coen to rest. I had to write another book, one that continued after Coen's death. Isaac has become the chronicler of Coen. *The Education of Patrick Silver* is about Isaac's own self-affliction. Isaac had inherited a tapeworm from the Guzmanns and it flares up soon as Coen dies. He blunders through the city with that worm in him and dreams that Coen is still alive. Coen's death has taken him out of his neat little universe, hooks him with pain. Manfred and Marilyn were his only connection to feelings outside the police. They were Isaac's history. Now he has the worm.

I was hoping I'd finished the story. I had my barber king to dream about. But the Andorran novel stayed dead. It was invention that evolved without a personal myth. I performed magnificent pirouettes on the page. I danced from line to line and was left with boring decoration.

I went back to Isaac and devoted a book utterly to him: *Secret Isaac*. It was the history of Isaac after his fall from grace. The sadder he becomes, the more successful he grows. The worm is eating him alive, but Isaac is now the Police Commissioner of New York. A peculiar thing happens. Isaac begins to cannibalize himself, to feed on his own worm. He's taken Blue Eyes' ghost inside himself. He becomes Coen and barks his own song of innocence and experience.

I thought of other books, a kind of Balzacian series of adventures, with Isaac moving about the country and devouring the United States. What city was a match for him and his tapeworm? But I haven't learned how to be Balzac yet. When I call my brother's precinct, the receptionist says, "Ah, you're Jerome. How's Blue Eyes today?"

I'm the celebrity of Brooklyn Homicide. Captains and lieutenants want me to write their stories. I'm their chronicler now. And Harvey? He begrudges the complications of the last three Isaac books. He prefers the purity of *Blue Eyes*. Manfred Coen came from the Bronx, like him and me. Manfred Coen went to Music and Art. I'm sure he remembers Coen as a weightlifter, but Coen was too busy being wooed by Marilyn to lift weights. Blue Eyes could have come right out of Harvey's precinct. Blue Eyes would have been one of the boys.

But I regard Manfred Coen in another way. Blue Eyes was a ghost long before he was killed. His mother and father were a pair of suicides, and Coen was the orphan from Music and Art who fell somewhere between Marilyn and Isaac and could never get up. His absence, dead and alive, seems to power the four books.

Isaac goes to Ireland in the fourth book, visits Leopold Bloom's house on Eccles Street. He's a police inspector who loves James Joyce, but his pilgrimage is more than literary debt. Isn't Bloom the father Isaac could have been? Isaac had manufactured his own Stephen Dedalus in Coen, but gave him perishable wings. He "makes" Coen, destroys him, and suffers the wounds of that destruction. And why is Blue Eyes drawn to Isaac in the first place? Is he seeking a permanent dad, one who won't abandon him? Or does he know that all dads are destroyers, the good ones and the bad?

What does an author know? For me the four books comprise a vast confusion of fathers and sons. My own dad was a furrier who never spoke. He grunted some primitive language that was more like the call of a disappointed wolf. But I had Harvey to interpret that wolf's call. He led me out of whatever Bronx wilderness I happened to be in. He was father and older brother and a bit of a mum, though he abandoned me before I was twelve, beat me up in front of his latest girlfriend. He had his muscle tee shirts to worry about. He didn't need a skinny kid on his tail.

And so Isaac's worm had been sleeping in me a long time. It grew out of a rift between Harvey and myself, more than thirty years ago. Forget Brooklyn Homicide. You need Sherlock Holmes to uncover the roots of any fiction. I'd come to Harvey to gather material for an uncomplicated crime novel and ended up scribbling four books about him and me and a meticulous tapeworm.

I finally let go of my barber king. Andorra wasn't that magic place where boys and kings can heal themselves. I'd invented a thousand years of history for Jude, a chronology that was filled with wondrous details, but it was spun out of avoidance, a need to hide. *King Jude* is a cold book, mythology without a worm.

Perhaps I'd used more of Ross Macdonald than I'd allowed myself to admit. Macdonald rocks back into his past in *The Galton Case*, weaves a narrative around his own wound, a gnawing sense of illegitimacy. The imposter boy who pretends to be the lost son of Anthony Galton bears a resemblance to Macdonald himself, or, I should say, Kenneth Millar, since Ross Macdonald was Millar's nom de guerre. "My mind had been haunted for years by an imaginary boy whom I recognized as the darker side of my own remembered boyhood. By his sixteenth year he had lived in fifty houses and committed the sin of poverty in each of them. I couldn't think of him without anger and guilt."[3]

Like any fiction writer, Macdonald is "a false claimant, a poor-house graduate trying to lie his way into the castle."[4] I'm another "claimaint," hoping to get into the castle with Isaac Sidel and Manfred Coen.

---

[3] Ibid.
[4] Ibid.

BLUE EYES

PART ONE

ONE

"Shotgun Coen."

The desk lieutenant nudged his aide and winked to the auxiliary policewoman, a blonde *portorriqueña* who worked the switchboard during off hours and had a weakness for detectives; the lieutenant's aide hoped to soften this *portorriqueña* by tweezing the hairs in his nose and trying French perfume, but he couldn't have told you the color of Isobel's underpants, or named one beauty mark above the knee. Isobel preferred the men from homicide and assault.

The five uniformed patrolmen in the musterroom shared the lieutenant's views. They begrudged the privileged lives of the bulls on the second floor: gold shields, glory assignments, the chance to fondle Isobel. They laughed at the war party, a thickfooted regalia of shotgun, cigars, and fiberglass vests. They could tolerate DeFalco, Rosenheim, and Brown, third-graders whose swaggering in stringy neckties was familiar to them. Coen they despised. He earned more than their own sergeant, and he had become a first-grade detective sitting on his rump in some inspector's office and escorting ambassadors and movie stars from the Bureau of Special Services. They were sure Coen was a spy for the First Deputy Commissioner. They prayed he would come back with a hole in his head.

Only Isobel wished him good things. He was the first *israelita* she had met with blue eyes. He didn't ask her to strip on a hard bench behind the squadroom, like DeFalco and Brown. He would take her to his apartment, undress her properly, buy her strawberry tarts, sit in the bathtub with her for an hour, and not rush her into her clothes. She watched him carry his shotgun in a shopping bag. DeFalco stepped between Coen and Isobel. He expected more attention from her. She had unzipped him an hour ago, near the footlockers, just as she was about to begin her tour of duty. He attached the groin protector to his fiberglass vest in front of Isobel. She still refused to look at him. "Where's your boy?" he snarled at Coen.

"On the stoop."

And they tramped out, four Manhattan bulls, past Isobel and the security guard. DeFalco, Rosenheim, and Brown ignored Arnold the Spic, who sat on the steps of the precinct wearing Coen's handcuffs. He was a black Puerto Rican with a clubfoot. He rode with detectives in unmarked cars, near the siren, if possible, and lived with the homicide squad until the commander tossed him out of the house for spitting at male prisoners and propositioning female suspects and half the auxiliary police. Arnold sulked under the green lamps. He wanted to help the bulls collar the taxi bandit Chino Reyes, so he would be allowed to mind the cage in the squadroom again. DeFalco had no pity for Arnold. The Spic was Coen's personal stoolie, and he wouldn't perform for any other detective. Resting on his bad foot, Arnold peeked inside Coen's shopping bag. "I saw the Chinaman, Manfred, swear to God. He was sucking a lamb chop at Bummy's, on East Broadway."

Rosenheim frowned. "Since when does the Chinaman mingle with captains and plainclothesmen? You know who hangs out there. Coen, we take that bar, we'll come out with blood in our eyes."

"Bummy's," the Spic insisted.

"Get in the car," Brown said. Arnold had to lean hard to activate his orthopedic shoe. On the sixth try he cleared the stoop. He sat up front in the clumsy green Ford between Coen and Brown. Being the youngest detective, Brown drove. DeFalco and Rosenheim slumped on the back seat. "Spanish Arnold?" DeFalco whispered. "Want the siren?"

Arnold abused his skin with a handcuff, rubbing until blue lines emerged on his wrist, but he couldn't say no. They ran three red lights, the siren whirling under their knees, Arnold growing stiff. He would have given up humping the grocer's wife for a long ride with the bulls. He made his handcuffs visible to the traffic. His tongue was swollen with spit.

"Hold him. The Spic's gonna fly through the roof."

Coen switched off the siren. "Leave him alone." Arnold wiped his tongue. Rosenheim cackled. Coen slid the shopping bag along his thighs.

Rosenheim saved enough breath to call, "He's right. Coen's right. The biggest brains on the force are out looking for the lipstick freak, and we're stuck with a common Chinese nigger who punches cab drivers in the head. Why didn't they put me and Spanish on the freak? We'd flush him out, chop off his peanut, show him you can't mess with Puerto Rican babies in Manhattan North."

"Rosenheim," DeFalco said, "stop giving Spanish privileged information. He might get the wrong idea. Then we'll have two freaks to worry about. Let him hang on to Chino. Coen and the Chinaman are cousins."

Rosenheim and DeFalco smiled without having to exchange winks; they knew Coen would enter Bummy's first, and they wouldn't grieve if the Chinaman happened to blow him away. They didn't appreciate getting the wonderboy. The First Dep had tossed him into their lap. They preferred a team without Coen. If they needed some face-slapping, or grubby detective work, they could depend on Brown. Coen lost his rabbi in the First Dep's office, and the chiefs couldn't get rid of him fast enough. They bounced him from one detective district to the next. But you couldn't say a word in his presence. Maybe the chiefs were dangling Coen. Only a moron would relax around a man who had come out of the fink squad.

So their expectations bumped in Chino's direction. The Chinaman had promised to fry Coen's brains. Having a Creole father and a Chinese mom, he was peevish about letting a blond detective touch his face. Coen had humiliated him in front of his clients. Chink-town gamblers hired the Chinaman to protect their fan-tan games. He was on good terms with the down-town precincts. None of the gamblers he sat for had ever been raided. But a "kite" came down from the District Attorney's office; a Chinese gentleman in one of Chino's games was wanted for murder in Port Jervis, New York, so DeFalco, Coen and three uniformed men took the game with a sledgehammer, two gold badges, and Coen's shopping bag. They broke through a door at the back of a laundry where the game was held. They frisked all the Chinamen. They scattered fantan beads. They confiscated twelve thousand and eight dollars in cash, Chino smoldering with his arms behind his head. He lunged at Coen, who was busy feeling the Chinaman's pockets. Coen slapped him with a knuckle, and Chino had a split on his cheek. He refused to be fingerprinted at the stationhouse. Coen flopped Chino's wrist over the fingerprint board and stood him inside the cage while DeFalco delivered the gamblers to the interrogation room. Chino spit through the wires. Spanish Arnold, attending the cage before the commander ousted him, offered to sell Chino a pillow and a chair. Chino spit a little higher. Spanish walked around the cage wagging his testicles at Chino. An assistant district attorney peeked at the gamblers through the one-way mirror outside the interrogation room. He advised DeFalco that homicide had booked the wrong chink. The Chinamen

called their bondsmen on the upstairs phone. Chino was on the street
in five hours, but the raid hurt his credibility. Gamblers could no
longer feel immune with Chino in their parlors. He was phoning the
precinct once a week. He wanted Coen. "Tell Blue-eyes Chino Reyes
is remembering him." He began taking off newspaper stands and
taxi-cabs in Coen's district. He hoped to embarrass all detectives this
way. Careless, overeager, he dented a few cabbies' heads. And Coen
carried his shotgun to work in a shopping bag.

They parked on Clinton Street and made Arnold sit in the car.
Rosenheim shook Arnold's handcuffs. "It's dangerous, Spanish. You
don't want Chino to know who fingered him."

Coen felt inside the shopping bag. Arnold couldn't catch his eye.
He moped on the seat and parroted the scratches and bleeps that came
in over the police radio. "Sector Nine Henry, respond to
Seven-oh-five Delancey. Child in convulsions. Advise Central if
ambulance is needed . . . Sector Seven George, suspicious woman
prowling in Battery Park."

Rosenheim walked to the side entrance of the bar and idled
there, cleaning his nails with an emery board. Coen, Brown, and
DeFalco crashed through the front. No guns were drawn, but Coen
had a wrist in the shopping bag. Bummy Gilman saw the three
detectives from his washroom. He rinsed his hands and held them
under the tap. He didn't have to tolerate bulls on the doorstep.
Precinct captains ate with Bummy. Jew inspectors played pinochle
with him at headquarters. And he had a uniformed lieutenant at his
private booth. DeFalco aimed Coen's shopping bag at the floor.
Bummy kept his mean stare. DeFalco approached him.

"Bummy, this isn't my show. Some punk who belongs to my
partner says Chino Reyes was eating lamb chops at the bar."

"I wouldn't hide no crappy chink pistol. Pull your cheap tricks
in somebody else's joint. Your friends stink, DeFalco."

The lieutenant called from Bummy's table. "Bummy, bring him
here." DeFalco remained stiff while the lieutenant brushed his tunic.
"Who told you to come into my yard with a goddamn cannon?"

"We're looking for Chino Reyes."

"Fuck Chino Reyes," the lieutenant said. He was drinking pure
rye. "Who's the glom with the stick in his hand?"   ,

"Coen."

The lieutenant hunched in the booth, his jowls working.
"Manfred Coen?" He sucked on the whiskey. "You talk Chino Reyes,
and you send the First Dep's choirboy down on Bummy?"

"He isn't with the First Dep any more."

"Shithead, the rat squad has lifetime membership cards. They're circulating him, that's all. They plant him on you, then they pull him out. DeFalco, some good advice. Don't bounce too often with the glom. People might think he's married to you. Take him out the back. I don't want to be seen with a rat."

Coen wouldn't go. He ducked the shopping bag under a stool and ordered a sloe gin at the bar. "Woman's drink," Bummy figured to himself, but he didn't ask his barman to close any bottles. Brown had German ale with DeFalco. He only looked once at the lieutenant. Coen walked out the front after his third sloe gin. He stole peanuts for Arnold. Rosenheim was sleeping in the car, a Spanish comic book over his eyes. DeFalco went to twist Arnold's ear. The pout on Coen stopped him. He satisfied himself poking Arnold in the chest.

"Trust a Spic. Who paid you to mention Bummy's? Spanish believes in phantoms these days. He must be sniffing airplane glue."

"Manfred, Chino ate a chop. He had a fancy napkin with Bummy's name on it. He was there."

"I know."

DeFalco slapped a thigh. "Jesus, you take Arnold's word over Bummy?"

They arrived at the precinct without mentioning Chino again.

Humped against a pickle barrel and a pile of table-cloths, the Chinaman had seen Spanish Arnold from the window grille of Bummy's storage chest. He pitied the Spic who couldn't stay alive without sleeping in detective cars and nibbling rust off the squad-room cage. But he wasn't going to allow a stoolie with handcuffs to snitch on him, tell his hiding place to the Manhattan bulls. "Arnold, you'll join your master one of these days. In the cemetery for Jews." He would take Coen and his Spic together, bend their teeth, show them how unprofitable it could be to mess with Chino Reyes. He waited until the bulls left East Broadway, then he slipped out of the closet without confronting Bummy. He was wearing a red mop that he had bought at a trading company on Pell Street and fluffed out with a pair of scissors. He would make no other concessions to the bulls. He wore the mop mostly for Bummy, who entertained assorted captains at his private booth and couldn't afford a fracas in his bar. Otherwise the Chinaman would have pissed on Blue-eyes and his friends.

He crossed the Bowery, avoiding the crooked lanes of Doyers

Street, because he didn't want any of the Chinese grocers to spot him in a wig. He was safer on Mulberry, where the Italians and Puerto Ricans wouldn't be upset by red hair on a Chinaman. He walked under the fire escapes of his old school. A Chinaman with Cuban ways, he had never been accepted by the toughs of P.S. 23 (Chino arrived from Havana with his father at the age of nine). They called him "nigger boy" and outlawed him from all the Chinese gangs. So the Chinaman had to steal fruit and vegetables on his own. He modeled himself after the guinea bloods who loitered on Grand Street, and by the time he was eleven he took to wearing suspenders with his initials on the supports, pants with flares for his knees, and striped socks. At thirteen he delivered shrimp balls and spicy duck to the fan-tan players of Mott and Pell. Soon he guarded wallets and money belts at fan-tan games, and earned bonuses settling fights among the players, until Coen chased him off the street.

He recognized Solomon Wong sitting in a garbage can. Solomon had washed dishes in Cuba for Papa Reyes, and became a *norteamericano* like Chino and his dad. He lived in the yards of certain flophouses off the Bowery. Seeing him in the fall, wallowing inside a ratty spring coat with sleeves that could wrap twice around his waist, Chino was certain the old man wouldn't survive the winter. Then Solomon would appear at the end of March, on a stoop, in a garbage can, or a grounded delivery wagon, his coat rattier than the year before. It was April now, and Chino addressed the old man in Spanish, calling him "tata" (or daddy), with great affection and no snobbery. "Bueno' días, tata." The old man belched a blurry hello. He had trouble pronouncing *s*'s without his teeth. Chino wanted to give him a hundred dollars, two hundred maybe, but Solomon would have been insulted by so munificent a gift. The Chinaman had to learn the art of proportion with this old man. Solomon might accept a loan of five dollars, but only if it was given in the name of Chino's dad. "Tata," the Chinaman said, dropping money in Solomon's cuff. "My father's bones will tear through his grave if you don't accept the fiver."

The Chinaman went to Ferrara's pastry house and ordered three napoleons and one cannoli, and a tall glass of orzata, an almond drink favored by Italians, Cubans, and half-Chinese. A crapshooter from uptown caught him in the middle of a napoleon. The crapshooter was sixty-seven, with bleached hair and uninterrupted moons on his fingernails. His cheeks were wide with agitation. He couldn't keep his hands off the Chinaman's suspenders. "Chino, I want the girl."

The Chinaman started another napoleon. "You hear, it has to be Odette."

"Ziggy, you'd better settle for something less. That girl is off the market."

Unable to operate in Chinatown, Chino was managing a small train of whores for an uptown syndicate.

"Zorro says she's still in business. I'll tell him about you, Chino, I mean it."

"Tell," the Chinaman said.

"Chino, I'm offering you a hundred and fifty. That's clear profit. She doesn't have to take off a garment. I just want to look."

"Ziggy, walk away while you still own a pair of legs. I can't digest the cannoli with your perfume in my nose."

Not all of the Chinaman's problems stemmed from Coen. He was in love with an eighteen-year-old prostitute, one of his own girls. The Chinaman distributed short subjects featuring Odette, the porno queen, to specific bars and stag clubs, he arranged dates for her with serious men who arrived at Odette's apartment on Jane Street with fifty-dollar bills tucked in their shoes, but he couldn't get a finger inside Odette's clothes. She wouldn't fornicate with a Chinaman. Kicking under his pride, he offered to pay. Two hundred dollars. For a girl he was managing. Two hundred dollars for someone who should have admired the soft leather on his suspenders, who should have been grateful for making her rich. Odette said no. "Sonny, I don't get down with triggermen." The Chinaman would have branded her, shaved her crotch, put his initials on her belly, no matter how valuable a property she was, but Odette could control his rages with a few chosen words. "Zorro wouldn't like me with blood on my behind."

So Chino walked the line between Bummy's and Ferrara's, his mop growing a dirty brownish red (he couldn't risk eating at any of the dim sum cafes on Mott Street though he was starving for pork and abalone), until the spit accumulated on his underlip and he tired of almond syrup on his tongue. Then he went looking for Odette. He tried Jane Street, stabbing her buzzer with a double-jointed finger.

"Odette, you home? It's only me, Reyes. I want we should talk. I make you a promise. I won't touch."

Odette's landlady, a woman in hair curlers and pink mules, came to the front door. She wouldn't open it for the Chinaman, and he had to shout through the glass. "Take me to Miss Odette." Her frowns convinced him; he would have to go in around the back. "Hey muchacha," he said, tapping on the glass, "don't wait too long for me." He blustered toward the side of the house, trampling little vegetable gardens, crushing the remains of certain flower pots. The Jane Street alley cats wouldn't move for the Chinaman. He had to unhitch one of his suspenders and whirl it at them before they would give up their perch on the fire escape. Then he grabbed for the bottom rung of the ladder, chinned himself up, and settled outside Odette's windowsill. The window revealed nothing to him. He saw green furniture through a maze of curtain fluff. He forced open the window without splitting any glass. Climbing in, he searched Odette's room and a half, nibbling the miniature sandwiches she kept in the icebox for the clients Chino brought her (crescents, triangles, and squares of black bread with snips of cheese), reminding him of his new livelihood as a pimp. He took stockings out of her hamper, garter belts, soiled brassieres that she wore in her films. He wanted keepsakes, a wealth of underclothes. "Jesus," he said, stuffing his pockets. "She's with her girlfriends." And he went out the front, scorning fire escapes this time, a garter belt dangling at his knee.

He could have charged into Odette's hangout, The Dwarf, but both the lady bouncers were taller than Chino, and he would have lost a sleeve and a shoe before he reached Odette. So he called from a booth across the street. "Odette Leonhardy," he said with a fake lisp.

"Who is this?"

The bouncer had a softer voice than he expected.

"It's Zorro."

"She hasn't come in yet, Mr. Zorro. Can I take a message?"

"Yeah," the Chinaman said. "Tell her somebody raided her hamper. And if she wants her party clothes back, she'd better be nice to a particular gentleman. She'll know who."

"Anything else, Mr. Zorro? Then I'll have to say goodbye."

The Chinaman stood in the phonebooth biting a knuckle and watching the blood rise, his red hair sticky with sugar from all the napoleons he'd consumed. He couldn't decide whether to go uptown or downtown, to meet up with Zorro, Odette, or Coen. He hogged the booth, scattering men and women who wanted to make a call. Finally he trailed a stocking from the top of the booth and walked away from The Dwarf.

TWO

DeFalco, Rosenheim, and Brown despised Coen because he wouldn't live out on the Island with them. He had no family. Only an uncle in a nursing home on Riverside Drive. Coen's wife left him for a Manhattan dentist. She had a pair of new children, not Coen's. He ate at Cuban restaurants. He was a ping-pong freak. He wouldn't allow any of the auxiliary policewomen near his flies. He bought chocolates for Isobel, the *portorriqueña,* and made their own offerings of cupcakes and lemon balls seem contemptible to them. He was the boyhood friend of César Guzmann, the gambler and whorehouse entrepreneur, and they knew that the Guzmanns owed him a favor. After the flop-out at Bummy's, the three bulls drove home to Islip, Freeport, and Massapequa Park, and Coen gobbled black beans and drank Cuban coffee on Columbus Avenue with Arnold the Spic.

The waiters, who couldn't warm to most *norteamericanos,* enjoyed Coen and his ten words of Spanish. They sat him in a privileged spot along the counter. They filled his cup with hot milk. They fed him extra portions of beans. Although they were proud of Arnold's handcuffs, they didn't dwell on the gun at Coen's hip. They accepted him as Arnold's *patrón* without the politeness and fraudulent grins they used on cops and sanitation chiefs. They protected his long periods of silence, and discouraged negligible people from going near him. He sat over his cup for an hour. Arnold read his comic books. Then Coen said, "Leave the Chinaman to me." Deep in his comic, Arnold couldn't hear.

Coen lived in a five-story walkup on Seventieth and Columbus, over a Spanish grocery. He had broken panes in two of his windows. Apples grew warts in Coen's refrigerator. The First Deputy's office woke him at three in the morning. They expected him downtown by four. In the past Coen would have changed his underwear and picked at his teeth with dental floss. But he was tired of their kidnappings. Brodsky, a chauffeur from the office, drove him down. Brodsky was a first-grade detective, like Coen. He earned his gold shield driving inspectors' wives around and grooming undercover agents. Years ago he could buy his friends into a detective squad for a few hundred dollars. He had to discontinue the practice with younger chiefs in power. He rode through Central Park frowning at Coen. "They'll burn you this time." Coen yawned. He was wearing a pale tie over his pajama tops.

"Who wants me?"

"Pimole. He's a Harvard boy. He won't eat your shit."

"Another mutt," Coen said.

He couldn't get clear of the First Dep's office. They stuck to him since his rookie days. Isaac Sidel, a new deputy inspector in the office, pulled him out of the academy because he needed a kid, a blue-eyed kid, to infiltrate a ring of Polish loft burglars who were fleecing the garment area with the approval of certain detectives from the safe and loft squad. Coen wore cheap corduroy for Isaac, and grew a ducktail in the style of a young Polish hood. He hauled coat racks on Thirty-ninth Street for a dummy firm and ate in a workingman's dive until an obscure member of the ring recruited him over a dish of blood salami. Coen took no part in burglaries. He hauled racks for the ring. One day two men in business suits stole Coen's racks and banged him in the shins. Isaac told him these men were county detectives from the District Attorney's office, who were conducting their own investigation of the burglaries and were trying to shake off Coen. "Manfred, how did they make you so fast?"

In a month's time the ring was broken up and the rogue cops from safe and loft were exposed, without much help from Coen. He was returned to the academy. He took target practice with the other probies. In bed before midnight, he followed all the Cinderella rules. After graduation the First Dep picked him up. Coen had a rabbi now. Isaac assigned him to the First Dep's special detective squad. Half a year later Coen had a gold badge. He rose with Isaac the Chief, making first grade at the age of twenty-nine. On occasion the First Dep loaned him out to the Bureau of Special Services, so Coen could escort a starlet who had been threatened by some Manhattan freak. BOSS wanted a softspoken cop, handsome and tough, preferably with blue eyes. He was the department's wonderboy until his rabbi fell from grace. A numbers banker indebted to the District Attorney's office for pampering him after he strangled his wife showed his gratitude by mentioning a Jew inspector on the payroll of a gambling combine in the Bronx. The District Attorney sang to the First Dep. Isaac sent his papers in and disappeared without a pension. The First Dep waited a month before dropping Coen.

Brodsky delivered him to one of the First Dep's ratholes on Lexington and Twenty-ninth. Herbert Pimloe conducted his investigations here; he had replaced Isaac as the First Dep's "whip." Coen sat with Brodsky on a bench outside Pimloe's office. The building was devoted to the manufacture of sport shirts, and Coen compared the design of his pajama tops with the shirt samples on the wall. Brodsky left at five. Coen thought of his wife's two girls. He smiled at the tactics the First Dep men liked to use, sweating you on a wooden bench, forcing you to wonder how much they knew about the fragments of your life until you were willing to doubt the existence of your own dead father and mother. The company watchman arrived on the floor and stared at Coen. "Hello," Coen said. He was getting sleepy. The watchman seemed indignant about having pajamas in his building. Coen straightened his tie and dozed on the bench. A hand gripped his collarbone. He recognized Pimloe by the attaché case and the Italian shoes. Pimloe was disgruntled. He expected his hirelings to stay awake. Coen stumbled into the office. Pimloe closed the door.

"You're enjoying the Apple, aren't you?"

"I can live without it, Herbert."

"Bullshit. You'd fall apart outside the borough. The cunt are scarier in Queens. No one would notice your pretty fingers. You couldn't nod to Cary Grant on the street. I know you, Coen. Take away the Apple, and you'd never make it."

"I'm from the Bronx, Herbert. My father sold eggs on Boston Road."

"The Bronx," Pimloe said. "The jigs own spear factories in the Bronx. Hunts Point is perfect training ground for the tactical units. They could parachute over Simpson Street and kill the Viet Cong. Manfred, you'd freeze your ass in the Bronx. You'd have a shriveled prick."

Coen threaded a hand through the opposite sleeve of his pajamas. "Herbert, what do you want?"

"Change your pajamas, Coen. They stink." Pimloe touched his paperweight, a brass sea lion with painted whiskers. "I need a girl."

Coen forced down a smile.

"Not for me, stupid. This girl's a runaway. She's been missing over a month. Her father thinks some West Side pimp caught hold of her."

Herbert, maybe it was the lipstick freak. Did you try the morgue?"

"Shut up, Coen. Her father's the Broadway angel, Vander Child."

"Herbert, why me? What about Missing Persons or one of your aces over at the burglary squad?"

"Vander doesn't like cops. He'll take to you. I told him you're the man who guards Marlon Brando in New York."

"I never met Brando."

"But you know all the pimps. That's what counts. Vander has a team of private detectives out. They can't find shit. The daughter's name is Caroline."

Coen dug a finger under the pajamas and scratched. Pimloe leered at him.

"She's too old for you, Coen. Sixteen and a half." He scribbled a Fifth Avenue address on a piece of departmental paper. "Vander's expecting you. If you're a good boy, Coen, he'll let you see the view from his windows. Maybe he'll feed you some kosher salami."

Coen turned around. Pimloe kept talking.

"Coen, you're the weirdest Jew I ever saw. Somebody must have put you in the wrong crib. How's Isaac?"

"Ask him yourself."

"All the Jews sleep in one bed. You, Isaac, and Papa Guzmann."

"Your spies are napping, Herbert. The Guzmanns turned Catholic hundreds of years ago."

"Then why do they keep Jew scrolls on their doors?"

"Because they're superstitious people. Now what does Isaac have to do with Papa?"

"You're slow, Coen. Isaac is Papa's new bodyguard. Imagine, the biggest brain we had, whoring for a bunch of pickpockets." Pimloe saved one wink for Coen. "You won't be catching homicides for a while. I'm taking you off the chart. Don't bother with the squadroom. You report to me."

Walking down the stairs Coen put knots in his tie. Brodsky found him dozing on the sidewalk. Coen wouldn't open his mouth until they reached Columbus Circle.

"Why should Pimloe be so curious about the Guzmanns? They can't hurt him much from the Bronx. Papa hates the air in Manhattan."

"It isn't Papa he's after. César's split from the tribe. He's been changing boroughs. But he don't dig the East Side. He cruises on West Eighty-ninth."

"And Isaac? Is Isaac with him?"

"Pimloe tell you that?"

"No. He says Isaac's mooching for Papa."

"Crooks hang with crooks," Brodsky said.

Coen decided to walk the rest of the way. Men stared at his pajamas. He kept his holster out of sight. Remembering Brodsky's allegiance to Pimloe, he cupped his hands and shouted at the car. "Brodsky, you were a mutt before Isaac took you in. He taught you

how to blow your nose. Only Isaac's dentist could cure your bloody
gums."

Brodsky shut his window and fled from Coen.

Herbert Pimloe was a deputy inspector at forty-two. He hated
Coen. He wanted to smear him in Isaac's shit. Isaac had been a DCI
(deputy chief inspector) by the age of fifty, and Pimloe resented this.
He was obsessed with Isaac's career. Isaac had controlled the office
before he jumped into the Bronx, and now Pimloe was in charge of
the First Deputy Commissioner's investigative units, but he didn't
have Isaac's hold over detectives and typists. And he couldn't charm
the First Dep, even though he occupied Isaac's old rooms.

Pimloe graduated magna cum laude from Harvard College, with
a senior thesis on the aberrations and bargaining skills of Hitler,
Stalin, Churchill, Mussolini, and De Gaulle. His friends went on to
law school and medical school and business school and departments
of philosophy, and Pimloe mumbled something about criminal
justice. Having measured the brain power of the chief finaglers of his
time, he developed a singular distrust for colleges and books. He
became a rookie patrolman in the NYCPD. He handled a riot baton
and a Colt .38 Police Special, and escaped the draft. After five years
of walking Brooklyn and Queens, the First Deputy picked him up.
Somebody must have noticed the magna cum laude in his personnel
file. He typed for the First Dep, wrote reports for the First Dep's
whip, Isaac Sidel, did bits of undercover work, changed from a Colt
to a Smith & Wesson. He rose with the younger chiefs of the office,
always a step under Isaac, fumbling in Isaac's shadow until Isaac
disappeared, but there was no easy way to get rid of the Jew Chief.
Isaac could haunt an office.

Brodsky called for him at a quarter to seven. Brodsky had been
Isaac's chauffeur, and although this fact gave Pimloe immediate
status in the eyes of other deputy inspectors, he was suspicious of the
chauffeur; he didn't enjoy being compared to Isaac. Moody, he
wouldn't go home to his wife. "Jane Street," he said. "Find Odette for
me."

The chauffeur laughed.

Pimloe questioned him. "Do you think the glom is hooked?"

"He's hooked. He's hooked."

"Are you sure?"

"Herbert, don't I know Coen? He'll take us to Zorro. You'll see.
We'll throw the tribe on their ass."

The chauffeur couldn't get another word out of him. He missed Isaac. Isaac never moped in a First Deputy car. Brodsky couldn't get comfortable driving for a Harvard goy inspector. He landed Pimloe on Jane Street.

"Herbert, Coen will produce. I swear."

Pimloe dismissed him with a feeble nod. His mind was thick with Odette. He swaggered in her hallway, ringing a whole line of bells. "Cunt," he said, slipping into Isaac's idiom. He couldn't get into the building. Odette's landlady peeked at him from the opposite side of the door. He showed her the points of his deputy inspector's shield. "Official business," he mouthed into the glass, his lips fogging the door. The landlady undid the latch, Pimloe squeezing in. He lacked Isaac's sweet smile, but he could still steal the pants off a Jane Street landlady. "Madam," he said, collecting his Harvard undertones, "is the actress in?"

"She's upstairs."

"Shy about answering her buzzer, isn't she?"

"That's the rules. Is this a breakfast call? I don't allow strange men in my house before eleven."

"Nothing to worry about, madam." He handed her an old Detectives Endowment card. "My number's on the back. You can ring my superior, the First Deputy Commissioner of New York."

The landlady scurried toward her basement apartment, clutching Pimloe's card, and Pimloe went up the stairs. He wasn't scrubbing indoors on the First Deputy account; he was considering the cleavage under Odette's jersey, the dampness of her bellybutton, her manner of frowning at men. "I had to go and fall for a dike," he muttered on the stairs. She wouldn't come to the door until he shouted, "*Odette, Odette,*" into the peep-hole.

"It's me, Herbert. It's time for a conference. Let me in."

Pimloe smiled when the lock clicked, but she kept her chain guard on, and she stared at him through scraps of light in the door.

"We can have your conference right here," she said.

"Odile, are you crazy? This is Herbert Pimloe, not one of your uncle's gloms. I carry a badge with a star on top. I don't whisper to girls in a hall."

"Then talk loud," she said.

Pimloe could have snapped the chain off with his thumb, but he wanted to suffer for Odette. He saw the outline of her nose, slices of her mouth, the startings of a chin.

"Odile, give me a minute inside. I'll hold both hands on

the door."

"Inspector, I'm only Odile to my friends."

Pimloe brushed the chain with a row of knuckles, playing the inspector for Odette.

"Where's Zorro?"

"How dumb do you think he is? César wouldn't come here. But I had another visitor."

"Who?"

"The Chinaman. He stole all my garter belts while I was uptown."

Pimloe could feel the dwindle in his underpants; he'd shrunk with the first mention of Chino Reyes. There was no revolver in his waistband. He kept his Smith & Wesson locked in a drawer, preferring not to be weighted down with a handgun. He hadn't realized the Chinaman enjoyed fire escape privileges at Odette's. He wanted no encounters on the stairs with César Guzmann's pistol. So he wagged his goodbyes with a droopy finger and made the street before Odette could shut her door.

THREE

On Fifth Avenue Coen wore herringbone, and magenta socks. Coming across the park he disregarded the pull of rooflines and burnt stone. Coen dreaded the East Side. During the time of his marriage, while guarding the ingénue of a Broadway musical, a light-headed girl with weak ankles and a list of hectoring suitors, Coen was taken up by the producer of the show. He became a fixed piece in the producer's entourage, appearing at his Fifth Avenue penthouse with and without the ingénue. Coen flexed his muscles, showed his scars and his gold badge, told stories about gruesome child murderers and apprehended rapists, passed his holster around. It took him three whole days to notice that his wife had moved out. She was staying with the young dentist Charles Nerval.

The producer gave Coen use of the maid's room. Coen slept with the ingénue. He slept with the producer's *au pair,* a Norwegian girl who knew more English than Coen. After hints and prods from the producer, he slept with the producer's wife. He got confused when the producer's friends began calling him "the stickman." He shook hands with columnists from the *Post.* Collecting money owed

to the producer, Coen wore the fattest of ties. He missed his wife. At
parties he wrestled with a muscular thief the producer had put in his
entourage. Coen didn't mind the charlie horses and the puffs on his
ear. He drank whiskey sours afterward, spitting out a little blood with
the cherry, and sharing a hundred dollars with the thief. The producer
would advertise these wrestling matches. He gave Coen and the thief
spangled trousers to wear.

The thief, a Ukranian boy with receding gums, hated the
matches and hated Coen. Once, biting Coen on the cheek, he said,
"Kill me, pretty, before I kill you." The boy had not spoken to Coen
until then. Ten years older, with a harder paunch and stronger knees,
Coen could have thrown the boy at will, but he prolonged the
matches to satisfy the producer's guests. During the climax of the
fifth or sixth match, with Coen scissoring the boy, he heard the
twitches of the guests breathing encouragement on him, their bodies
forked with agitation, and he closed his eyes. The boy took advantage
of the lapse to free himself and hammer Coen with his elbows, an
unforgivable act according to the producer's rules. The guests tore
the boy off Coen, booing and launching kicks, the women kicking
with as much fervor as the men. Groggy, Coen leaned over the boy,
slapping at ankles and shoes. He moved out of the maid's room. He
broke off relations with the producer's wife. He cooked at home.
Stephanie, his wife, was suing him in order to marry the dentist
Nerval.

Coen prepared for Vander Child. He mentioned his name to the
doorman of Child's apartment house. The doorman called upstairs.
Coen sat on a scrolled lobby bench with his knees wide apart. The
doorman smiled under the starched blue wings of his dickey and
began to patronize Coen. "I'm afraid Mr. Child doesn't know any
Manfred Coens. State your business, please."

"Tell him *Pimloe*," Coen shouted into the plugboard.
"P-I-M-L-O-E." The doorman let Coen pass.

Child welcomed him in a flannel gown with enormous pockets.
A handsome man with a mole on his lip and a negligible hairline, he
was just Coen's age. Coen found it hard to believe that Child could
have a daughter of seventeen. They stood chin to chin, both of them a
touch under five-feet-eight. Child had greener eyes. He liked the
detective Pimloe chose for him. He mixed Coen a fruit punch with
rum and sweet limes. Child insisted they drink from the same bowl.
Coen felt dizzy by the third sip. On Child's couch each discovered
the other was a ping-pong buff.

"Use a Butterfly?" Child said.

"No. Mark V."

"Fast or slow?"

"Fast," Coen said. "Where do you hit?"

"At home. I hate the clubs."

Coen seemed unnerved. "You have a table here?"

Hugging his gown Child walked Coen through bedrooms, a sitting room, and a hall of closets. A high-breasted girl in another flannel gown swore at Child from one of the rooms. She sat on a round bed drinking punch and jiggling some earphones. "Who's the Sammy?" she said, pointing to Coen. "A new customer? Is he a live one? Vander dear, am I going to perform on trapeze?" She threw the earphones at Child. He ducked and nudged Coen out of the room.

"My niece," Child said. "She has an active imagination. She thinks I live in a brothel." They stopped in a corklined room with soft blue lights and a regulation ping-pong table. Coen admired the luminous green paint on the table. Child put a Butterfly in his hand. He could hear the girl sing a school song. "Carbonderry, my Carbonderry," she said. He hefted the ping-pong bat. Child fed him a fresh ball and volleyed in his flannels. Coen chopped with the Butterfly. Child smirked.

"Who taught you that? Dickie Miles? Reisman? Do you want hard rubber, a pimple bat?"

"No. I'll play with this."

With the ball coming off blue light, Coen had to squint. He wondered when Child would begin talking about his daughter. He had trouble with Child's serves. Swaddled in herringbone he couldn't smash the ball. The necktie was making him gag. Child helped him undress. Coen played in boxer shorts. Uneasy at first, he grew accustomed to the undertable currents on his kneecaps. Child had a greater repertoire of strokes. His loops got away from Coen. His flick shots would break near Coen's handle. Coen slapped air. Child attacked his weak side, forcing Coen into the edge of the table. Twice the Butterfly flew out of Coen's hand. The girl was singing again. "Carbonderry, my Carbonderry." Her mocking, nasal cries upset Coen's ability to chop. The ball made a thick sound against his bat. Child had a lead of 18-2 when the girl came in. Seeing Coen sweat in stockings and shorts amused her. "Darling, isn't this the bloodhound who's going to bring Carrie back? He has cute nipples for a cop." She approached Coen's half of the table. "Did he tell you I'm his niece?" Coen looked away from her open collar. The girl was taller than him, and her bosoms hovered close to his neck. "He really is an uncle, you know. Nobody believes it. Vander doesn't have favorites in his cast."

Child pushed little dents into the Butterfly with a finger. "Shut your mouth, Odile."

"Vander, couldn't you use the bloodhound in a bigger way? He's naked enough. And marvelous with a paddle in his fist. Get him to swish it, darling. I want to see."

Child threw his bat. It struck her on the shoulder, and she shaped a perfect scream with the muscles in her jaw. Her nostrils puffed wide. In pain, her bosoms had a glorious arch. Moaning, her body grew lithe. The girl's physicality astonished Coen. She could shrink a room with any of her moves. She ran out with Child. He heard them chatter in a corridor. Child came back much less interested in Coen. "Odile's an actress," he said. "Don't be taken in by her rough talk. She has pornography on her mind." Child scored three quick points and collected the bats. He brought Coen into his study. "My daughter went to school with Odile."

"Blood cousins?" Coen asked.

"Yes, blood cousins," Child said, scrutinizing Coen. "Odile's the older. She could sway Caroline. They both became involved with a Jew pimp."

"Is he from Manhattan, the pimp? Does he walk, or drive a car?"

"He has a Spanish name, that's all I know."

"Guzmann?" Coen said. "Is it Guzmann. César Guzmann?"

"Maybe."

"How did your girls meet César?"

"You said César, Mr. Coen. I didn't. It might be Alfred, Pepe, Juanito, God knows."

"What were they doing with a pimp, Mr. Child?"

"This isn't East Hampton, Coen. The pimps cruise around Caroline's school every morning looking for fresh tail. They fish pretty hard. Several Carbonderry girls have run off with Spics. The school hushes it up. You can't keep a chastity belt on Amsterdam Avenue."

"You think your daughter's with this pimp then? If your niece was mixed up with him too, she ought to remember his name."

"Odile? You won't get much from her. She's Carrie's conspirator. She plays dumb."

"Still, it can't hurt. I'd like to ask her a few things."

"I'd rather you didn't, Coen. Pimloe can tell you about Odile. He talked to her once. She started stripping for him in the middle of a conversation. She'll steer you wrong, Coen, and try to win you over. Anyway, my own men have questioned her. Detectives from the agency I hired."

"What did she give them, Mr. Child?"

"I told you. Nothing. The little bitch loves to perform for detectives."

Child handed him photographs of Caroline and the detectives' report, which came in a large brown envelope with scalloped edges, the hallmark of that particular agency. The scallops annoyed Coen. He figured the detectives were soaking Child. The girl in the photographs had mousy features and hair like straw. Her neck, her stingy jawline, the bones behind her ears, had little to do with Child. Coen peeked inside the envelope. There were bloated expense vouchers, news of "suspicious vehicles" parked near the Carbonderry School, hints of white slavery. Coen couldn't believe anybody would bother to capture so homely a prize.

"They think she may be in Peru," Child said. Coen smiled to himself. The Guzmanns came from Peru, where they had cousins who were pickpockets, city bandits, and confidence men; these cousins could have swallowed up a hundred New York girls, at Papa Guzmann's request.

"Some money," Child said, drawing six hundred-dollar bills from a wood box. "Pimloe says no cop buys information like Manfred Coen."

"For six little ones I can buy the world, Mr. Child."

"Keep it," Child said, squeezing the money into Coen's palm. "Peru's a lonesome place."

Coen played with the lamp outside Child's apartment. He sat the shade on a chair and passed each of Child's hundred-dollar bills over the bulb. He looked for Pimloe's marks under the treasury numbers. The money was clean.

Child was considering the details of his Harold Pinter festival when he heard a knock inside his dumbwaiter. He dismissed it as a nuisance, rats among the cables, or the superintendent's boy farting in the shaft. Should he open with *The Dwarfs or The Birthday Party?* Should he go with native Americans, or import an English cast? He was fifty thousand dollars shy. He would have to make Odile run a little harder for the money. He wouldn't finance musicals. He would have nothing to do with gauche mystery plays. He resisted vehicles for resurrected movie stars, even though he could have been guaranteed a return of a hundred thousand a year.

Vander was a purist on the question of which shows he would back. He expected to lose his money. His father, also Vander Child, but a richer man, had left Vander II with a taste for croissants and a love for "le ping-pong," which he learned as a thirteen-year-old in a ballroom near the Bois de Boulogne while Paris was flooded with unemployed Czech ping-pong champions after World War II and Vander I was the unofficial New York ambassador to France. After three tiresome years at Princeton, during which he hustled his classmates out of their spending money playing ping-pong with them sitting on a stool, he fell in with a group of impoverished actors, brought a production of Alfred Jarry to New York, and became known as the "Angel Child."

The knocking persisted from the kitchen. Vander opened the dumbwaiter; the Chinaman tumbled out, grease on his bodyshirt, the mop over one eye. Vander prepared to take the Chinaman by a suspender and stuff him back into the shaft.

"Don't," the Chinaman said, his one visible eye trained on Vander. "Another white man touched me before on the cheek, a cop with pretty vines, and he'll regret the wound he made coming out of his mama's belly. This cop has a Puerto Rican sidekick, a cripple. They'll both be eating grass."

"Chino, did you assault any of my doormen? Have you been bruising skulls?"

"Not me. I got in through the basement. I had to find the right dumbwaiter line. Vander, my knees are sore. I'm not used to hugging wires."

"Who sent you? Zorro? You can tell him I'm not taking his money any more."

"Tell him yourself. I don't do business in dumbwaiters. I came for Odette. Where is she? In the tub?"

Vander had to giggle. "You shouldn't mess with her underwear, Chino. She's been promising to scratch out your eyes."

"That's fine with me."

The Chinaman spread his fingers around his chin and shouted at Vander's ceilings for Odette.

"Don't waste your lungs. She's with her sweethearts. She went to The Dwarf."

The Chinaman saw for himself. Raising the shreds of his mop so he could have two free eyes, he tracked across the living room, opened closets double his own height, investigated each of Vander's four tubs. The fineries of perfumed soap in the shape of a yellow egg and abundant robes on a silver hook appealed to him. He fondled the egg, sniffed the robes for traces of Odette. Satisfied she wasn't around, he palmed Vander's doorknob.

Vander got between the Chinaman and the door. "Chino, you'd make me happier if you tried the dumbwaiter again. My neighbors might not appreciate your looks."

The Chinaman moved Vander with a pinch on the sleeve. "Vander, my policy is never go the same way twice. It hurts your luck."

"Then take off that toupee. You'll scare my elevator man."

The Chinaman carried the mop under his arm, his own hair sitting high on his scalp. Vander noticed little improvement; the loss of a toupee only accented the tight lines that went from the Chinaman's ears, over his cheeks, and into his eyes. Grim markings, Vander thought. He couldn't relax until the elevator dropped below his floor. He dialed Pimloe at the First Deputy's office. He rasped into the phone.

"You call that protection, Herbert? He was here . . . not Zorro, the chink. He almost tore my arm. Herbert, I didn't bargain for this. You were supposed to have a man outside twenty-four hours. I've had enough to do with shamuses. Your boy was here. Coen. He couldn't keep his eyes off Odile . . . what? Herbert, I'm not her trainer. I can't shackle Odile . . . Herbert, she hasn't seen Zorro. Wouldn't I know? I'd break her toes if she lied to me . . . Never mind. I don't want Chinamen in my dumbwaiter any more. Attend to him first. Goodbye."

The Chinaman had already wrecked Vander's appetite. He wouldn't have fresh croissants and madeleines brought up from the pâtisserie. He would swallow ordinary bread today.

FOUR

Coen found Pimloe's chauffeur sleeping on Columbus Avenue in a First Deputy car, two doors up from his apartment house. He woke the chauffeur with a knuckle on the head. "Don't get smart, Coen."

"Listen, Brodsky, your boss must take me for a retard. I don't like a fancy goy laying six hundred dollars on me for shit work. Why is Pimloe setting me up? How many clues did he throw Child about the Guzmanns? The schmuck forgot that César doesn't cruise. He can't drive a car."

"If Pimloe's such a schmuck, how come he can slap a uniform on you and make you eat your badge? He owns you, Manfred. Tick him off, and you'll be pulling weeks for some precinct captain on Staten Island. So behave yourself. Just locate the girl."

Coen settled into the car. "Take me to Pimloe."

"No way. You had one audience with him. That's enough. Pimloe can't spare the time."

"Why not? Is he cracking eggs at Gracie Mansion today?"

"He isn't like you, Coen. He doesn't keep shoving ping-pong balls in his pocket." Brodsky smiled. Remembering Coen's knuckle, he bothered to rub his head. "Relax, Manfred. Nobody has to sweat."

"Child doesn't seem all that eager for his daughter. I'll bet she's living on Ninth Street with a professional boccie player. They bowl on the dining room floor."

"Ninth Street? That should make her easy to find."

"Brodsky, take your finger out of your nose and stick it on the wheel. I want Amsterdam and Eighty-nine."

Brodsky dropped him across the street from a blue-stone house with twin flags draped over its front; the flags had exotic lettering, a field of plain stars, and touches of white, plum, and gold. Brodsky was amused by the flags. "What goes? This one of the bordellos you keep hearing about? For African diplomats only?"

"It's the missing girl's school."

"Manfred, should I wait?"

"No. You can tell Pimloe I'm after a white pimp who sits in a Cadillac and provides ugly girls for Peru."

Boys and girls in plum suits marched in and out of the Carbonderry Day School sucking ice cream cones. Pulling on their dark stockings, the girls seemed utterly removed from the voluptuousness of Odile, although several of them walked with a kind of stumpy grace. Coen found no plausible pimp cars near the school; no Mark IV's with soft ray glass; no cream-colored Eldorados; nothing silver; nothing mint green. Plainclothesmen wearing headbands and dungarees passed Coen four times in the same hour. He recognized them by the color of their headbands; on Thursdays the anti-crime boys always wore blue. They were prowling after the child molester who operated exclusively on the West Side. One of the plainclothesmen stopped Coen. "You dig this school, sonny boy? You get your kicks smelling girls' shoes? What's your name?"

Coen stuck his shield under the plainclothesman's teeth. And the plainclothesman, who was timid around gold badges and much younger than Coen, skulked to a different block. More headbands approached. Coen had to give up on Carbonderry or risk a toss by baby cops in dungarees every quarter hour. He decided to visit his uncle Sheb. First he hiked over to a papaya stand on Broadway and watched for a *chileno* in a gypsy cab. It was the *chileno,* cabless today, who wandered into Coen. They drank papaya juice at Coen's expense. The *chileno* got edgy when Coen stayed quiet. He envied the ability of his Blue-eyes to slow himself down, an *agente* with the appearance of a man wanting and valuing nothing. So the *chileno* went to Coen. "I could use a cup of coffee, Manfred. My cab's in the shop."

"A whole cup?" Coen said, establishing the formal bargaining ground of detective and stoolie, without the affection he had for Spanish Arnold. "What do you have that's worth a cup?"

"Try me."

"A white pimp. He tours the neighborhood in a green Cadillac maybe. His speciality is young broads. I want his name."

"White? How white? With blue eyes, Manfred?"

"Figure brown or gray."

"Try Baskins, Elmo Baskins. The chicks call him Elmo the Great."

"Where can I find him?"

"In the street, man. He drives a tan Imperial."

"Blas, I'm only giving you half a cup," Coen said, uncrumpling fifty dollars for the *chileno*. You'll have to blow harder for the other half."

The *chileno* took the fifty, and Coen walked down Broadway. He doubled back to a nut and candy shop, where he bought burnt almonds, dried apricots, and a pound of sesame sticks. He entered Manhattan View Rest armed with paper bags, having to nod to all the old ladies on the green bench outside. He was sure they knew his history. Manfred, son of Albert and Jessica, who put their heads in an oven wearing holiday clothes and made the *Daily News*. Coen picked Manhattan Rest for uncle Sheb because it was without a denomination, and he didn't want to see his uncle plagued by fanatical old Jews for having a brother and sister-in-law who were suicides. Sheb found Albert and Jessica; Sheb brought them out of the oven and screamed their deaths from the fire escape. But he was considered a madman long before this. He sat in Albert's store candling eggs with his prick out. Nobody could sight a bloodclot faster than uncle Sheb. He drank the bloody eggs himself, spitting pieces of shell over the counter. Widows and older wives accepted his remonstrations and bribes of jumbo eggs, and lay with him on his cot near the toilet. It was this nagging sexuality that kept uncle partly sane. He had to dress up for his women and get his hair cut. He had to cackle the right phrases, fondle a kneecap while holding his eye on an egg.

Coming through the bachelor quarters at Manhattan Rest, Coen found his uncle in a small room off the library where gentlemen could reflect in private. Sheb wore Coen's old shirt and Coen's gray trousers from the Police Academy. He was crying and scratching out a letter with a bladderless fountain pen. He dunked the entire pen into a bottle of ink after every five strokes, and pretended not to see Coen, who listened to the scratches and didn't snoop.

"Albert, we don't have the belly for it. Sure, I know men with tits. Not the belly. Jessica has it over us. The superior person is the person who sits down to pee. Always. I'd rather have a hole than a fist in my pants. How many eggs, Albert, how many eggs?"

Ink dribbled on his uncle's trousers, so Coen decided to speak. "Are you writing to Albert, uncle Sheb?"

Sheb took him in with an amazing scorn.

"Albert's been dead thirteen years. Would I write to Albert? Tell me something. What's in your hand?"

"Sweets, uncle. From Broadway."

Sheb investigated the bags. He sniffed burnt almonds, chewed a dried apricot, broke sesame sticks in half. And he bawled Coen out for buying so much. "Manfred, you expecting to shush me with a pound of sesames? Feel it. Isn't it a whole pound?" Coen wondered why his uncle always attacked during his periods of lucidity. "Can't fool me. You blame Sheb. Otherwise you would have come with fewer bags."

"Blame you, uncle? For what?"

Sheb coughed over the sesame sticks. "Why not half a pound? That's a reasonable number. You won't get sick on half a pound. Manfred, did you ever see a belly blow up?" He winked. "Candy has a lot of gas. You're a goner if it travels to your brain. Your ears turn blue." He was crying again. "Your father, God bless him, had big eggs. I wore his pants too. They were tight around the crotch, same as these. Do you hear from Jerónimo?"

"He's with the Guzmanns, uncle. I've been slack about the Bronx. I couldn't find my way on Boston Road."

Jerónimo was César's oldest brother, a boy of forty-three. He roasted marshmallows in the Guzmanns' candy store and created shortages of chocolate syrup. He was thrown out of the first grade thirty-seven years ago because of the prodigious erections he had at the age of six. Jerónimo didn't miss school. He stuck to the candy store or watched Sheb Coen drink bloody eggs.

"Jerónimo's here," she said.

"Jerónimo on Riverside Drive? Uncle, he couldn't tell the streets."

"He visited me last month. We finished three bars of chocolate."

"Was he with César?"

"He came alone."

"Where's Jerónimo staying? Did he mention César's apartment? Uncle, it's important."

"He didn't say. How can you talk with a mouth full of chocolate?"

"Uncle, come. The room's getting dark."

Sheb wouldn't allow Coen to mingle in any of the areas reserved for widows and bachelor women. He was tired of intrigues. He had appropriated his years at Manhattan Rest strictly for contemplation. "Manfred, you wouldn't believe the fucking that goes on inside this place. Only the married couples have it bad." They sat in the common room, Sheb offering nurses' aides, bachelors, charwomen, and cuckolded husbands the opportunity to eat from his bags. He liked to show Coen off to each of his confreres. "The nephew's with the Manhattan bulls. He carries a gun on him could kiss you in your tonsils. I'm only his uncle. No more Coens. My big brother Albert decided fifty years was long enough. He went into the chicken coop with his wife. It was too cold for them on the outside. Jessica, she had delicate skin."

Without warning Sheb pushed down his lip, and he and Coen fell into their old posture of muteness, licking apricots for an hour. A group of widows peeked into the common room, admired the stolid look of the two Coens, and walked out convinced that Sheb was the handsomer one. Sheb finished the last apricot and smiled. There was nothing abrasive about these silences. It was the way of the Coens. Albert and Sheb sat in an egg store thirty years grunting a few words every day. Even the worst cuckold at Manhattan Rest could appreciate the current that passed through Sheb and Coen. They galvanized half the population in the common room before Coen left.

Coming down Columbus Coen thought a man with red hair might be following him. He stalled in the window of a drugstore reading a display about the circulation of the blood. A machine at the bottom spit purple water into the kidneys, heart, and brain along a system of branched tubes. Coen's man went into a Cuban coffee shop. Coen watched the tubes. His telephone was ringing when he got home. He could hear the disaffection in Isobel's voice. Coen had neglected the *portorriqueña* from the stationhouse doing Pimloe's chores. She didn't scold. She had a message from Spanish Arnold. Arnold tripped and lost his orthopedic shoe.

"Did they take him to Roosevelt, Isobel?"

"Arnold hates hospitals. He's in his room."

"Who swiped Arnold's shoes?"

"Chino Reyes."

Coen remembered his man from Columbus, high cheeks under a red mop. He called himself prick, prick, prick, prick, prick. The *israelita's* going crazy, Isobel decided, and she hung up on Coen.

Isobel had to keep the desk lieutenant from crawling up her skirt. "The captain wants his milk," she said. But she didn't go upstairs. She would have been waylaid by the homicide squad. Isobel still had sores on her elbows from scraping Detective Brown's locker-room bench. And DeFalco had ripped her mesh pants after coming off his late tour. So she sneaked behind the lieutenant without signing the attendance sheet, she smiled at the security man, motioned to one of her girlfriends typing near the musterroom, and took an early lunch break. She missed the *israelita*. Brown and DeFalco were rough with her. The *israelita* had soft hands. And he knew how hard to bite into a nipple. She was having less fun at the stationhouse without Coen. She was tired of being scratched by house bulls. She didn't care for the whiskers on Brown. Flirting with a Puerto Rican cabby (Isobel didn't encourage his leers or the clicks he made with his tongue), she was on Coen's stoop in under nine minutes.

She caught the *israelita* in his coat. He was leaving for Arnold's hotel. She wished the Spic had been able to hold on to his shoe. Coen hesitated removing his coat but he welcomed her in.

"Isobel, they've been running me uptown and downtown," he said. She liked the nasal touches to his voice. DeFalco couldn't speak without forming bubbles on his lip. And Brown had his orgasms too close to her ear; his growls could make you deaf.

"I'm not complaining, Manfred. You want to see Arnold? I can visit another time."

But they were on Coen's day bed beginning to thrash although Coen didn't leave spit on her arm like DeFalco or scar her buttocks with a yellow toenail like Brown. He wasn't a hungry man. He didn't own a Long Island wife, come to Isobel straight from his marriage bed. He had no baby pictures and candid shots of a lawn or a family sofa to hurt her with, remind her that she was only a *portorriqueña,* an auxiliary at the mercy of the bulls. And he wouldn't single out her sexual parts, inventing praises about the folds of skin on her clitoris until she felt like a police lady with kinky genitals. The *israelita* didn't pry. He never peeked at her from the corners of the day bed. He eased her into nakedness, accepting the holes in her underpants and the milky stains on her strapless cocktail bra. But she couldn't get below the nicks in his eyebrows. The *israelita* told her nothing about himself (she learned from Brown and the Spic that he lost his wife to a tooth doctor and had been orphaned at the age of twenty-three). She wanted to reassure him, tell him her own losses, a husband who raped her sister and rode cross-country to the Great Salt Lake, a father who died of tuberculosis, a brother who chased a pigeon too far and fell off a Brooklyn roof, but she could sense the *israelita* had Arnold in his head, and she would prevent him from concentrating on the boot. So she stayed quiet and did nothing but remind him of the hour.

"Manfred, you don't have to run the tub. I'm on call at one o'clock."

But he made her soak. She hadn't met another cop who could be so gentle in a tub of water. He washed her breasts without measuring them or reading her beauty marks. He wasn't squeamish about the sweat under her arm. He didn't count the creases in her belly (Isobel attributed these to the abortions she'd undergone). She was late, and she had to shake her hair on Coen's rug and fit the bra over wet skin. Coen tried to dissuade her.

"Isobel, the captain's man will wait. He's got all afternoon to collect his Coke bottles."

"Manfred, you live upstairs in the squadroom. You solve your mysteries. You come and go. You don't appreciate the boys in uniform. They'll piss inside my bloomers if I'm not there to nurse their precious switchboard and fetch coffee for them."

"I wore the bag once, Isobel. At the academy. Grays instead of blues. I wouldn't mind giving up my detective shield. I can survive in a bag."

Rushing, she could no longer argue. She flattered him instead. "You're cuter in pinstripe." But she would have liked this one, this *israelita,* even in a blue bag. She kissed him on the side of his mouth, her tongue behind clamped lips (she couldn't have left otherwise), and searched for a cab in the street. A hand pushed her toward the sidewalk but didn't allow her to fall. She saw pits of black through a red wig. The Chinaman was grateful to Isobel. She had fed him water and Arrowroots in the detention cage when Coen brought him into the house to be fingerprinted. He wouldn't assault a *portorriqueña* on Columbus Avenue; he meant only to remind Isobel of his obligation to her. He was holding a shopping bag in his other hand.

"Is that where you keep Arnold's boot?" she said.

The Chinaman showed his teeth. "What's the matter? Doesn't Blue-eyes take a shopping bag to work?"

"Chino, are you following Manfred?"

"Never," the Chinaman said. "The cop didn't buy this avenue. I'm hunting for bargains."

"What kind of bargains?" Isobel asked.

"All kinds."

"Chino, give me the shoe. I won't tell Manfred where I got it. I'll say it was in the sewer."

"The Spic has to suffer," he said, holding the shopping bag out of reach. He put Isobel in a cab.

"Make him fast, Isobel. Blue-eyes is going to have a short life."

The Chinaman took no pleasure in Isobel's puffy eyes; he had misjudged the extent of her loyalty to Coen.

"Don't worry," he said. "I'm the Blue-eyes' angel. With me in Manhattan what harm can come?"

Isobel arrived at the stationhouse while the foot patrolmen were turning out. Some of them marched with night sticks between their legs, aimed at Isobel's groin. "Coen's lady," they said. "The bride of Shotgun Coen." And they poured out of the house, bumping Isobel along until she broke free of their crush. The captain's man, who was minding the switchboard in Isobel's absence, laughed so hard he forgot to scold her. He couldn't complete his afternoon's assignments with Isobel away from the board. He had to locate a particular brand of cigars for the captain's brother-in-law, and chauffeur the lieutenant's wife to a beauty parlor in Queens. Isobel didn't object so much to his wandering thumbs. The captain's man was too

preoccupied with his chores to dig very hard. And Isobel was
thinking of Coen.

FIVE

Coen had to sing his name twice before Arnold would allow him in.
Arnold hobbled over to his couch. He lived in a hotel on Columbus
Avenue for single-room occupants, or SROs. He kept a cocoa tin on
the radiator with all his kitchen supplies. Outside his window was a
dish for American cheese. He had blue scrapes on both sides of his
nose. He was holding a Japanese sword.

"I'll kill the Chinaman, he visits me. I'll teach him fan-tan. I'll
write a checkerboard on his stomach."

"Arnold, what happened?"

Arnold hit his crooked foot with the blunt edge of the sword.
"He jumped me, Manfred. On Amsterdam. The cholo put a shopping
bag between my legs. He stole my big shoe."

"Was he wearing a red mop?"

"I can't tell. He moved too fast."

"Are you sure it was Chino?"

Arnold made a bitter face. "I know the Chinaman's style. You
can't hock a shoe. Only a cholo would think to grab it off a cripple.
He talked to me, Manfred. He said regards to Baby Blue-eyes."

"I'll handle him, Arnold. You rest."

Coen sat on the couch. Arnold watched him fidget. His *patrón*
was being polite, respecting Arnold's sores. So Arnold unburdened
him. "Manfred, tell me what you need?"

"Nothing," Coen said.

Arnold wanted to catch him before Coen went utterly quiet.
"What can I buy for you? Manfred, play fair."

Coen bent his head. "A white pimp named Elmo, Elmo the
Great. He trails little girls. Where can I find him?"

"Lend me a dollar." Arnold launched himself using the sword as
a crutch. The sword left nips in his rug. He went to a prostitute next
door. The pros worked the garment area and most of the West Side.
She was beholden to Arnold. Before the squad commander flopped
him, Arnold provided little amenities for her at the stationhouse
whenever the plainclothesmen from Coen's district came down on
the girls. Through Arnold Coen could connect with any whore at the

hotel. He listened for sword clunks in the hall. Arnold gave the dollar back to Coen.

"Betty says Times Square. She won't take money from you. This Elmo parks outside the Port Authority. He's a tough customer. The nigger pimps give him plenty of space. He clips country girls right off the bus. You know, runaways up from the South. Black and white, eleven and over. Manfred, he won't scare."

"He'll scare," Coen said, getting off the couch. Arnold tilted the sword, pursuing Coen.

"I'm going with you. Manfred, you won't be able to take him without me."

"I'll flake him. Did Betty say anything about his car? Is it a tan Imperial?"

"She says Apollo. Buick Apollo in some muddy color."

Coen pulled on his chin, a habit he picked up from his father, who would go for days without selling an egg. "I can't even make the pimp's car."

"Manfred, what do you want with such a geek?"

"I'm doing favors for the police department."

Coen stepped over Swiss-Up bottles in the hall. A few SROs whispered to him from their rooms. "Hey man, what's happening?" They didn't need Spanish Arnold to tell them about Coen. They knew him from Schiller's ping-pong club, which was located in the basement of the hotel. When they grew tired of staring at walls and drinking rotten wine off their windowsills, they went down to Schiller's, where they could convene on a bench and watch ping-pong balls fly under soft lights. They were particularly fond of the hours. Schiller's never closed. Schiller, a bearded gnome who lived in a tiny parlor behind his tables, scorned his fancier customers to sit with the SROs. He shared his pumpernickel bread. He baked vegetable pies for them. But he was a man of variable moods. And if the SROs hogged him too much or threw lumps of bread at the players, Schiller cleared the bench. Usually it took a week before the SROs forgave Schiller enough to sniff horseradish with him and eat his pumpernickel. They also hated the Spic. Schiller wouldn't chase Arnold out along with them. Arnold had the chair opposite the table reserved for Coen. They felt beneath him because of the handcuffs Arnold owned and because of Arnold's proximity to the Manhattan bulls. So they belched out Arnold's secrets. They mimicked his walk. The foot comes from inbreeding, they said. A father fucks his daughter, and Arnold arrives with stuck-together toes. How else do you find a mama who's only twelve years older than her boy? It was common knowledge that Arnold's father was a gravedigger in San Juan. The Spic, they liked to say, came from Rico with his sister-mother-aunt at five to help her career as a *prostituta* in nigger Harlem. The little scumbag painted his bad toes in Easter-egg colors and limped through Harlem bagging Johns for his mother. He had to be a mutt, no? Only a reject would suck up to a blue-eyed Yid.

Coen was tempted to stop off at the club (Schiller kept Coen's bat, sneakers, towel, and trunks in a closet filled with shoes). If he entered Schiller's he would spend the afternoon slapping balls and there would be little energy or enthusiasm left for the Port Authority pimps. So he flattened the crease in his trousers and hiked to Times Square. Coen was one of the last detectives in New York who didn't have a car. Occasionally he borrowed a green Ford from the homicide pool and chauffeured himself around the precincts. But he preferred the subways or his own feet. Sitting behind the wheel he would recall his father's eggs, Jerónimo, his wife's two girls, and his attention would drift away from the road. The bulls from his squad thought Coen had a secret driver, someone from the First Dep's office to take him around, which convinced them all the more that Coen was a rat and a shoofly for the chiefs.

He took Ninth Avenue down. He sucked an orange on Forty-seventh Street. He browsed in the spice markets. He bought a Greek doughnut, pleased with his choice of Ninth Avenue over Eighth. The sidewalk porno shows, the fake leather shops, the night club barkers in fedoras and duck suits would only depress him. Coen, who had seen murdered babies at the morgue and smelled crispened bodies after a fire, went from the academy to the First Dep, from the First Dep to homicide, without having to raid a pornographer's shop. He circled the Port Authority building, noticed black pimps in Buicks and Cadillacs on the opposite streets. They waved to him as he poked his head, shooting their power windows up and down, so Coen couldn't peek at their faces. The pimps were alone. No country girls with torn satchels were in the neighborhood. Coen stepped into a beige Sedan de Ville squatting between two taxicabs on the Ninth Avenue side of the terminal. He couldn't find any other white pimp. "Elmo Baskins?"

Elmo wouldn't give him sitting room, and Coen had to lean against the window. He was polishing the vamps on his platform shoes with a dry finger when Coen arrived. He wore pinkie rings and wrist straps studded with glass. "Who wants me?"

On a hunch Coen said, "Vander Child."

Elmo laughed into his wrist straps. "Child's gun? You'll rip my belly off with stuff like that. You must be Coen, the little cop who owns Manhattan."

Coen slumped down and tried to intimidate the pimp. "You can speak to me, Elmo, or you can cry to the DA. Stealing girls out of private schools isn't going to increase your popularity." He plucked three of his fingers. "That's sodomy, rape, carrying minors over the state line. Nobody loves a kidnapper."

Elmo wasn't buying the bluff. "Here, man, I'll help you make the collar. I'll drive you. Take me in."

"Elmo, how's the slavery business? Where'd you put Child's girl?"

"Go to sleep, man."

They sat without touching, maybe three inches apart, Elmo blowing on his rings, Coen wishing he could forget Pimloe and catch homicides again, until Arnold arrived from the left and bumped Elmo into Coen. Elmo raged. "Bringing Puerto Ricans into my bus?" Arnold had already dropped a two-dollar bag of heroin into Elmo's ashtray (the shit came from Betty). He waited for Coen to move on the pimp. Arnold wasn't jittery. He had dirtied Cadillacs before. Elmo chewed his own spit. He hated scrounging between a cop and his stoolie. He snarled first. Then he saw Arnold's sword. Coen was amazed. The pimp couldn't control his knees. Only a crazyman would carry a sword on Times Square. Elmo wasn't safe around such dudes. They were capable of slashing his seat covers. "Guzmann's the one you want."

"Why Guzmann?"

"He's feuding with Child."

"Vander says he never met César."

Elmo lost a little respect for the sword. He played with his spit. "How long have you been working for him?"

"You think César snatched the girl?"

"Not César. But he could tell you where she is."

"Peru?" Coen said.

Elmo sneered openly. "There's no trunkline to Peru."

"Give me César's address."

"I can't, Coen. I swear. He has a string of apartments. For his crap games. He floats with the games. That's why you can't pin him down."

"Are you stalking the Carbonderry School for César? The place on Eighty-ninth."

"Eighty-nine? Man, you won't find me up that far."

"What about Child's niece? Odile. You know her?"

"The chick with the long legs and the narrow crotch? She's into cat flicks. She goes to The Dwarf a lot. It's a gay bar on Thirteenth. Strictly for the girls. Coen, you'll need a pass to get in. The lady bouncers don't honor a cop's badge."

"I've been inside The Dwarf, Elmo. Tell me, are César and Child feuding over the rights to Odile?"

"I'm not sure."

Arnold sulked in the taxicab going up to the seventies with Coen. He wished he could have questioned the pimp. He was wearing three socks and a broken slipper over his bad foot. The sword lay across his knees. "Manfred, you should have asked him more." Arnold nagged him every five blocks. Coen was grateful anyway. He couldn't have opened Elmo by himself. They stopped at Arnold's single-room hotel. "Manfred, take me to The Dwarf."

"Spanish, I'm not going to The Dwarf today. I'll take you if I go. I've had enough."

Arnold limped into the hotel. Coen shouted after him. "Spanish, should I bring you some gypsy pudding?"

"I'm not hungry," Arnold said from inside the stoop.

"Do you want to watch me hit at Schiller's?"

"Not today."

Coen was no longer in the mood for ping-pong. His thighs would get cold in his navy trunks. Schiller would remind him how many times Coen's table had to be scrubbed. And he didn't want to touch The Dwarf, no matter how much Odile could help him. Three years ago Coen had staked out The Dwarf from a panel truck that belonged to the First Dep. He had even taken pumps, skirts, and hair out of the surveillance closet to get inside the place. Smelling a cop, the bouncers frisked him at the door. Coen had left his holster with Isaac. He was clean. He danced with a librarian out of Brooklyn. The librarian had lovely bosoms and a hand that could relax the bumps along Coen's spine. He clamped his legs to keep his erection down. He was already half in love. He agonized over telling the librarian he wasn't a girl. She would spit at him. The bouncers would tear out his arms. Both of them were burly girls. His throat had grown hoarse from having to whisper so often. The librarian counted on his infatuation. She expected money from Coen. She was on salary at The Dwarf. Coen pressed Isaac for a raid. Isaac dawdled with him.

Coen went back to the panel truck. Finally Isaac told him the raid couldn't go down. A deputy commissioner had queered it for them. Some big fish in the Mayor's party had a twin sister who practically lived at The Dwarf.

Coen decided he would visit his remarried wife. So he walked over to Central Park West. The doorman told him Stephanie wasn't upstairs. "I have her key," Coen lied. He opened Stephanie's lock with the set of burglar picks Isaac gave him, fumbling in the hall for the right pick. He snacked out of the icebox, spreading fancy Dijon mustard over a soda cracker and drinking a glass of Portuguese wine. Charles Nerval, Stephanie's other husband, had grown rich in the East Bronx exaggerating Medicare claims at his dental clinic. Coen got out of his pants, put his holster aside, and found one of Charles' woolly robes. He had gone to the High School of Music and Art with Stephanie and Charles. Coen, who could trace an egg and draw his father's knuckles, got in because the school was desperate for boys. Charles, whose father was a ragman, played the violin. Stephanie played the flute. The prize of older boys, she seldom talked to Charles or Coen. She went on to Oberlin, lived with the dean of music after her degree, raised tulips in Ohio, had an abortion, came home to New York, met Coen in the street, married him. Coen relaxed in Stephanie and Charles' tub, his wineglass on the sink. He tried Charles' Vitabath, and sat in foam up to his jaw. He didn't hear Stephanie come in. "Bastard," she said in front of her girls—Alice, three, and Judith, four—wearing identical gray jumpers. "Who gave you permission to break in here?"

She was pleased to see Coen and ashamed to admit that the girls liked him better than Charles. He frowned and begged kisses off Judith and Alice. If he hadn't been preoccupied with Elmo, he might have raided the five-and-ten for the girls, escaped with licorice, orange slices, and peppermint lumps. Stephanie set towels for Coen. A fecund girl, she had wanted children with him. Coming off the peculiar death of his mother and father, Coen shied away from long families. Now, removed from Stephanie, he loved the two girls and wouldn't allow them to call him uncle, only Dad or Freddy Dad. These devotions to the girls also drew Stephanie to Coen. She had never gotten over the pure coloring of Coen's eyes.

"Freddy, the girls shouldn't see you naked like that."

"Who says? I'm under the suds. Don't they peek at Charles?"

She gathered up Judith and Alice, took them to their room, turned the humidifier down to low, pulled out their toy trunk, and came back to Coen. He was busy toweling his buttocks. Stephanie admired the curled lines his abdominals made with every sweep of the towel. The hair over his belly dried in the shape of a tree.

"Why aren't you out looking for that maniac who mutilates little boys?"

"I'm not very popular, Steff. The chief who's carrying the case probably wouldn't want me around. I might contaminate his men. They can't forgive me for being Isaac's pupil."

"How is that lonely son-of-a-bitch?"

"Isaac? The First Dep's new whip claims he's working for the Guzmanns. A schmuck by the name of Pimloe. He's been jerking me off the last few days."

It was this surly cop talk, exactly this, that had helped turn Stephanie off Coen; Charles had shallower eyes, he was awkward around his own girls, he had soft abdominals, but he didn't scowl or curse out of the side of his mouth. Most of Coen's vocabulary came from Isaac. But she no longer had to live with him, so she could be less of a scold. She touched his collarbone. Coen fetched her with the towel. They kissed against the shower curtains, his tongue in her throat. Charles didn't know how to kiss. He would cuddle her for a minute, snort once, and fall into the pillows. With one lousy finger Coen could pick all the sensitive places from her wings down to the middle of her thighs. But she didn't cling to him on account of expertise. In his grip, removed from her babies, her husband, recollections of her flute, she could feel the sad pressure of a man crazied by the loss of mother and father, a man beyond the pale of detectives and supercops.

Later, feeding Charles, Alice, Judith, and Coen, Stephanie felt embarrassed about the blush lines on her neck. She served the largest portions to Charles. Coen grew moody opening the jacket of his potato. He wouldn't be hunching over a baked potato if Charles resented him more. He, Coen, couldn't have tolerated an old husband in his midst. But with Coen around, Charles was less money-minded, more boyish, aware of his girls and his wife. He turned Judith's napkin into a hat. He tasted Alice's spinach. He called Stephanie "Mrs. Coen." Coen had watched over him in high school, discouraging neighborhood boys from poking fun at Charles' fiddlecase. Even then Charles was amused by Coen, who smelled of eggs and couldn't draw. Despite his blue eyes and blond features, Coen was the shy one around girls. It was Charles who carried prophylactics in his rosin bag, Charles who could unhook a bra with the end of his bow, Charles who grabbed a wife away from Coen.

"More carrots," he grunted. "More peas. Manfred, do you ever use the pistol range at Rodman's Neck?"

"No. I play ping-pong instead."

Judith bit her ice cream spoon. "What's ping-pong, Daddy Charles?"

"Ask your Daddy Fred."

Stephanie brought the coffee mugs and volunteered to tell Judith.

"It's for mutts," Coen said. "For people who hate the sun. We hit little balls on a green table with rubber sandwiches."

Coen went down the elevator with an apple in his hand. He saw some red hair in the bushes across the street. He ran into the park. "Chino," he hollered. "Come on. Show your face." Nothing came out of the bushes. "You keep shadowing me, I'll kill you, Reyes." Wagging his pistol Coen blustered deeper into the park. His apple got lost. He was behaving like a glom, chasing wigs in a bush. He put his pistol away.

The Dwarf's senior bouncer, a former handwrestling queen at the Women's House of Detention called Janice, made herself Odile's churchwarden and benefactress. She cut in soon as Dorotea placed a hand near Odile's crotch. She wouldn't allow hickeys or dry humps that close to the bar. None of the regulars, short or tall, could dance with a face in Odile's chest. Sweeney, a slighter girl, and the bouncer's partner and cousin, tried to soften Janice's stand. "Sister, aren't you coming down a little too heavy? Pick on somebody else. How come Lenore can kiss in the front room, and Dorotea can't?"

"Lenore isn't dancing with Odile, that's how come. Odile draws the sisters like flies in a sugar pot. I won't tolerate it when I'm on call."

"You're jealous, that's the truth. You want Odile sitting down where you can watch her all the time."

"Sister, you shut up."

And Sweeney had to concede; her cousin owned the biggest pair of brass knuckles in New York. She could afford to back off from Janice without compromising her position at The Dwarf. Anyway she had news for Odile.

"There's a man outside looking for you, baby. A pimp with a funny shoe. I'd swear he's that Chinaman who pesters the girls, only there's something different about him today."

"Shit," Odile said. "Shit." She might have used stronger talk in describing the Chinaman if Janice hadn't forbidden swearwords in the front room. Still, she broke from Dorotea to catch the Chinaman through a slice of window between the curtain and the curtain-rod. She had to control her laugh or deal with Janice's sour disposition. The Chinaman was wearing an enormous shoe on his left foot, a crooked coffee-colored shoe, a shoe with a hump in the back and the thickest sole she had ever seen; it had wrinkles on both sides along the leather, ugly tan laces with plastic nibs half eaten away, and it climbed to the middle of the Chinaman's calf, where it bit into the trousers and ruined the line of his cuff. He also had some ratty hair in his eyes. He swayed on his hip, pivoting off his plainer, lower shoe. Odile moved over to the door, near enough to Sweeney at least, and spit warnings in the Chinaman's direction.

"Chinaman, you ever rip me off again, you come through my window once more, you toy with my garter belts and my movie clothes, you touch my sandwiches, and you'll need a special shoe for your other foot."

The Chinaman lost his sway; he had hoped to charm Odile, show her the intricate turns he could accomplish with Arnold's boot for a rudder.

"Odette, I thought you'd like it. I stole it on account of you. It belongs to a Puerto Rican stoolpigeon."

Odile was affected by the Chinaman's droop, by the desperation in his posture, but she wouldn't go outside. And when the Chinaman hobbled toward her, she hid behind Janice and Sweeney. "Don't you come close," she said.

The Chinaman saw Janice take the brass knucks out of the pocket of her doublebreasted coat. Sweeney was smiling too hard. She cooed at the Chinaman. "Just step over the doorpiece, Mr. Reyes. The threshold isn't high. Come on, Chinee. Cousin has some hors d'oeuvres for you."

The Chinaman would only address Odile. "There's business between us, Odette. Customers. Mr. Bummy Gilman. A few other Johns."

"Then call my answering service," Odile said, peering around Sweeney's shoulderpadding. "Leave names and dates with the operator. And make sure you quote the price. I'm not getting down with those goofballs for less than seventy-five."

"Zorro isn't going to dig all this sudden shyness. Since when are you handling your own fees?"

"That's for Zorro to know, and you to guess. What's between me and César isn't any Chinaman's affair."

Dorotea, Nicole, and Mauricette, Odile's three steadiest dancing partners, arrived at the door to gloat over the spectacle of a Chinaman with one high shoe. Janice pushed them back inside The Dwarf, Dorotea taking Odile by the hand and leading her to the dance floor, six square feet of splintered boards between the jukebox and the bar. Janice controlled the music; the girls had to dance to Peggy Lee and Rosemary Clooney or retire to the back room, where they could sip rum Cokes, study the divinations in the *Book of Changes,* or soulkiss over parcheesi boards (the cousins wouldn't permit any other show of passion).

Odile was abrupt with Dorotea; she didn't need a tongue in her ear while she was considering the Chinaman; she could still see his absurd hair under the curtainrod. She remembered what Janice could do to a drunken male who stumbled into The Dwarf by mistake, or a huffy police officer who tried to take the bar without proper papers— a broken finger, a wrenched armpit, a cheekful of blood—and Janice would be remanded to the Women's House for her zeal at The Dwarf. Odile couldn't explain why, but she didn't want the Chinaman hurt. Perhaps it was his chivalry in wearing the boot. The Chinaman knew what could please her; not gifts of perfume, not mink stoles which any furrier could produce, but a freak shoe. Dorotea switched from the left ear to the right. "Sis, why don't you explore Nicole?" Odile said. "Leave my roots alone." She followed Sweeney into the back room. Sweeney was the only one who didn't paw her, who didn't lick her ears when they danced. A pair of parcheesi players, noticing Odile and Sweeney, moved to another location. Sweeney had the darkest corner in the place for Odile.

"Having man trouble, baby? You could always come live with me. You wouldn't starve. And you wouldn't need pig money either."

Odile was humming Peggy Lee. She couldn't get off the Chinaman. She hissed Chino Reyes, Chino Reyes, between refrains of "Golden Earrings," Peggy's 1947 hit. She wasn't going to sleep with a yellow nigger, one of Zorro's employees. Was she responsible for the stolen shoe? How could she stop a Chinaman from being crazy about her? She pushed away the parcheesi men, yawned into a fist, and slept against Sweeney's shoulderpadding.

SIX

Along Columbus Avenue he was known as the supercop. They badgered him about a lost monkey, a stolen television set, cousins who had been shaken down by the local police. After seeing a First Deputy car outside his stoop so many years (Isaac developed his best theories playing checkers with Coen), they figured Coen had an ear to the Commissioner. The woman who lived over him, a widow with a young Dalmatian, was worried about the safety of her dog. There had been an epidemic of dog poisonings in and around Central Park and Mrs. Dalkey wanted Coen to catch the poisoner without fail. She offered him fifteen dollars for his troubles, coming down to his apartment every morning with Rickie the Dalmatian to keep him abreast of the most current poisoning. Coen couldn't abide the dog. He was a sniveler, spoiled by Mrs. Dalkey, in the habit of leaving pee drops on Coen's doorsill.

"Detective Coen, Detective Coen."

Coen slumped to the door in pajamas. He could hear Rickie scratch the walls and chew paint. The dog nosed his way in. Coen expected pee on his furniture. He offered Mrs. Dalkey cherry soda and Polish salami. He had to provide for the dog before she would tell him anything. Rickie tore salami and drank out of a long-stemmed cup. Mrs. Dalkey couldn't eat so fast. "Convulsions," she said. "Mr. James' poodle. Fredericka went off the leash. That killer infested the rock garden on Seventy-second Street. Fredericka coughed up stones. She dropped dead trying to chase her tail. Mrs. Santiago thinks she saw him. A small Puerto Rican who gives candy to infants. He lives at the welfare hotel. I'm positive. He could also be the lipstick freak."

"Why Mrs. Dalkey?"

"Because a man who hates dogs is more likely to hunt little boys. Poisoners and sex criminals have the same mind."

Widow's tale, Coen told himself. He thanked Dalkey for her ideas and cleaned up after the dog. He rode the IRT into the Bronx. There had been too many mentions of César Guzmann, too many mutts running around with César in their heads. He would go to the source, Papa himself, for César and Child's girl. Papa might be planted on Boston Road but he had access to his five sons.

Moisés Guzmann reached Boston Road by way of Havana with a brood of small boys and no *mujer,* or wife. This was 1939. For sixty years Guzmanns had squatted in Lima, Peru, adopting the religion of the *limeños*. They were peddlers, smugglers, pickpockets, all citified men. They kept Hebrew luck charms in their catechism books. They prayed to Moses, John the Baptist, and Saint Jerome. Regular churchgoers shunned them. Others looked away. The Guzmanns considered themselves Hollanders, though they couldn't speak a word of Dutch. Before the Americas the family drifted through Lisbon, Amsterdam, and Seville. The Guzmanns of Peru had no memory of these other places. Moisés ran from Lima because he murdered a cop. Alone with five boys, he became "Papa" to the *norteamericanos*. He bought a candy store and moved into the back room. He sacrificed his love for guavas and pig knuckles, and taught himself to make the watery coffee and sweetened seltzer that the gringos adored. Occupied with his candies and his boys (in 1939 César was under two), Papa took seven years to establish a North American pickpocket ring. Cousins arrived from Peru. During one period fourteen men and boys lived in Papa's candy store. The cousins married, plunged into Brooklyn or New Jersey, and Papa had to retrench. He acquired permission from the Bronx police and the five main Jewish gangs to establish a policy operation in the store. The five gangs destroyed themselves and left Papa the numbers king of Boston Road.

Coen's train creaked out of the 104th Street tunnel, pushing toward the elevated station at Jackson Avenue in the Bronx. At the spot where the train first touched light the tunnel walls were clotted with a hard gray slime that had frightened Coen as a boy and still could bother him. That movement under ground, from the Jackson Avenue pillars into the flats of the tunnel, walls closing in around the subway cars, made Coen seasick on the IRT, and he would arrive nauseous at Music and Art, hating the egg sandwiches in his lunch bag. The stops from Jackson to Prospect to Intervale to Simpson to Freeman Street numbed Coen, drove him into his own head. From the Simpson Street station you could almost pick carrots off the windows of the Bronx Hotel; twice he had seen colored girls undress; he recalled the torn matting of his seat, the underpants of the second girl, the specific angle the train made with the window ledge, minimizing Coen's view, forcing him to hold his neck at an incredible degree or lose all command of the window.

He came down from the subway at 174th Street, where Southern Boulevard bisects Boston Road. He didn't go straight to Papa. The candy store was a main policy drop, and Coen might frighten off a few of Papa's runners. So he gave the store enough time to react to a

foreign cop in the neighborhood. He stayed across the street, near the
Puerto Rican social club which served as a lookout for Papa. The
club members eyed him from their curtainrod. Coen revealed a piece
of his holster. He wanted the Puerto Ricans to make him. He felt
relieved when they signaled to the candy store by flapping bunches of
curtain. They leered at him and mouthed the Spanish word for fairy.
Coen smiled. Then he moved into the store. Papa's runners and
pickup men were concentrated at the shelves devoted to school
supplies. They were tallying policy slips with their backs to Coen.
Nobody stirred for him. Papa was behind the counter preparing
banana splits for a tribe of cross-eyed girls sitting on his stools. The
girls, with thick glass in their eyes, must have been sisters or cousins
at least. They thumped the stools and wailed with pleasure when Papa
brought over a big jar of maraschino cherries. Being a fat policy man
didn't get Papa to neglect his ice cream dishes. He wouldn't look at
Coen until he satisfied every girl. "Sprinkles, Mr. Guzmann. Marietta
expects another cherry."

With the girls rubbing their bellies and wearing hot sauce on
their cheeks, Papa came out from the counter to hug Coen. They
embraced near Papa's Bromo-Seltzer machine. He wasn't timid about
showing affection for a cop. He could kiss Coen without
repercussions. No one but Papa controlled the candy store. He stayed
king because of this. He squatted over his provinces with one finger
in the chocolate sauce. Every individual runner, pickup man, and
payoff man had to report to the candy store. Papa's three middle sons,
Alejandro, Topal, and Jorge, ran for him when they weren't fixing
sodas or frying eggs. His other collectors were South American
cousins, retired Jews, busted cops like Isaac, or *portorriqueños* who
owed their livelihood to Papa. Any runner who grew independent and
bolted with the day's receipts had twenty-four hours to redeem
himself; after this period of grace he was ripe for Papa's dumping
grounds at Loch Sheldrake, New York. Whoever accompanied the
reprobate to Loch Sheldrake would say, "Moses, I'm working for
Moses." In matters of business Papa demanded that his code name be
used.

"Papa, where's Jerónimo?"

"Ah, that dummy, he walked into the next borough to be with
his brother. He can't swallow a marshmallow without César. I'm only
his stinking father. I bathed him forty-three years. Manfred, you
remember how Jerónimo went gray at fifteen? Imbeciles worry more
than we do. Their arteries dry fast. They don't live too long. You ask

me, he's smarter than Jorge. Jerónimo counts with his knuckles, but he counts to thirty-five. Jorge can't go over ten without mistakes. They're good boys, all prick and no brain. Am I supposed to make fudge the whole day and forget Jerónimo? César won't bring him back."

"Should I collect him for you, Papa? Tell me where César is. I need him for something else."

"He keeps ten addresses, that boy. So who's the moron? Manfred, he's a baby. He had to fly from here. They'll cripple him in Manhattan."

"How did Jerónimo find him, Papa?"

"With his nose. You develop your smell living around sweets. What do boroughs mean? Sweat can carry across a river."

"What about Isaac? Where's Isaac?"

Papa stared at the banana splits. "Which one? Isaac Big Nose? Or Isaac Pacheco?"

"My Isaac," Coen said. "The Chief."

"Him?" And Coen had to face the wrath in Papa's yellow teeth. He'll curse his family with devotion, Coen thought; not strangers or cops. "I leave the bones for Isaac. He picks my garbage pail."

"Papa, since when are you so particular about one busted cop? You have pensioned detectives fronting for you, you keep old precinct hands on the street. You should use him, Papa. Isaac has the biggest brain in the five boroughs."

"So smart he got caught with a gambler's notebook in his pocket."

"Somebody stuffed him. I can't say who. Isaac won't talk to me."

"I say he's a skell and a thief. I took him in because I'm ashamed to see another Jew starve on Boston Road. The city has charity. I have charity. No one can tell me Moses doesn't provide. Manfred, how's the uncle?"

"Papa, he looks fine. He can't stop thinking about my father."

"I mean to visit. I'm not comfortable away from the store. But I owe it to Sheb. He was kind to Jerónimo. You remember how your uncle could paint an egg. Him and César, they were the only two could take Jerónimo's mind off chocolate and the halvah."

The girls screamed for Papa; they wanted second helpings. Papa hissed back. "Quiet. You're at the mercy of the house. Free refills come to Papa's convenience." He asked Coen to stay.

"Can't," Coen gagged; the aromas off the counter had begun to

take hold. He was incapacitated by the imprint of Jelly Royals under
sticky paper, lollipop trays, pretzels in a cloudy jar. Papa couldn't
have changed syrups or his brand of malt in thirty-five years; the
sweetness undid Coen. He saw Jerónimo go gray. His throat locked
with thick fudge. House, house, is Moses in the house? If César could
steal pretzels, so could Coen. In twenty years of patronizing the store,
Coen stole no more than twice. He had a fierce respect for the old
man. It was Moses who wired him the money to come home from the
barracks at Bad Kreuznach after his mother and father died. And it
wasn't Papa's fault it took three weeks for the money to find Coen.
Sheb knew where he was. But Sheb wouldn't open his mouth.

"Manfred, why do you need him?" Once behind the counter
Papa had to shout to hear himself over the girls. "César."

"Information, Papa. César can help me find a runaway girl."

"A goya or a Jew?"

"A goya, Papa."

"Manfred, you know the dairy restaurant on Seventy-third near
Broadway? Go there. Maybe eight, nine at night you'll see the old
cockers with boutonnieres. Pick up a flower and wait. It's a
dice-steering location. Get in the car with the old men. Give my name
to the steerer. Say Moses, not Papa. That's the closest I can get you.
Manfred, you won't forget Jerónimo? You'll tell me if he likes it with
his brother?"

"Papa, I will."

Coen avoided his father's egg store, south of the Guzmanns on
Boston Road. He didn't want to dream of eggs tonight. Now a
pentecostal church, painted sky blue, it was another Guzmann policy
drop. Coen met Jorge outside the candy store. The middle-most of
Papa's five boys, stupid and uncorruptible at thirty-nine, with few
attitudes about his brothers, and wifeless like them, he was carrying
quarters in his pockets and in his sleeves; because he was poor at
arithmetic and could get lost turning too many corners, Jorge walked
the line of Boston Road accepting only quarter plays. Papa bought
him shirts and pants with special pockets, but by the afternoon Jorge
had to store quarters in his shoes. Weary in his overalls, weighed
down to his heels, Jorge had no appetite to chat with Coen. He
grunted his hellos, and tried to pass. Coen held on.

"Jorge, where's Isaac? Please."

Still grunting, he twisted his chin towards the electrical
signboard of the Primavera Bar and Grill on Southern Boulevard and
174th. Not knowing how to thank him, Coen jerked Jorge's sleeve,

then he jumped between traffic and entered the Puerto Rican bar. He recognized a bald man at the last stool with gray curls around the ears. The man climbed off before Coen could say "Isaac" and locked himself in the toilet. Coen could have flicked the latch with his Detectives Endowment card. He called into the opening.

"Isaac? I'm wearing your burglar picks. I could pull you out if I want."

Either Coen heard the toilet flush, or the man was weeping inside.

"Isaac, are you front man at the bar? I'm stalking for Pimloe. Can I trust him, Isaac? Is he wagging my tail? Chief, could you use some bread?" Coen put twenty dollars under the door from the boodle Child had given him. He couldn't tell whether Isaac was scraping up the money. The bartender glared at Coen. "No more checkers, Isaac? Nothing." He wanted to clarify his involvement with Child, his perceptions of Odile. Coen had little to do with other detectives. He could only talk shop with Isaac. After Isaac's disgrace Coen sleep-walked through detective rooms in Manhattan, Brooklyn, Staten Island, and Queens, shuffling from one homicide squad on his way to the next. He was Isaac's creature, formed by Isaac, fiddled with, and cast off. He made no more overtures to the door. He tied the boodle with a rubberband and went over to the IRT.

The rookies Lyman and Kelp were cruising the Bronx in an unmarked Ford, complaining about the policewomen who had been in their graduating classes. They belonged to a new breed of cop— enlightened, generous, articulate, with handlebar moustaches and neat, longish hair and an ironic stance toward their own police association. Lyman was living with an airline stewardess, Kelp had a stock of impressive girlfriends, and the two rookies were taking courses in social pathology and Puerto Rican culture at the John Jay College of Criminal Justice.

"Cunts in a radio car," Lyman said. "Man, that's unbelievable."

"Alfred, you expect them to type all day in the captain's office? Imagine all the hard-ons they'd generate."

"Listen, when the shit begins to fly, when it gets hairy over on Seventh Avenue, the junkies poking antennas in your eyes, the transvestites coming at you with their sword canes, these stupid cunts lock themselves in the car, and they won't even radio for help. And control thinks you're banging them in the back seat. Unbelievable."

The rookies had just been reassigned; they were snatched away from their precincts and picked up by Inspector Pimloe of the First Deputy's office. It was no glory post. Instead of undercover work, with wires between their nipples and a holster in their crotch, they chauffeured inspectors from borough to borough in a First Deputy car. They would have cursed Pimloe on this day, called him a high-powered glom, but the DI (Pimloe) had put them on special assignment; they were going to meet the First Deputy's old whip, the legendary Isaac who had disgraced himself and left a smear on the office. But the investigators attached to the First Dep were still devoted to the Chief; through them Lyman and Kelp had heard stories of the old whip. These investigators demurred over Pimloe; they remained "Isaac's angels."

"Alfred, how much do you think Isaac took? Half a million?"

"More, much more. Why would he fuck his career for anything less?"

"Shit, we get Pimloe, and we could have had the Chief."

"Man, he should have waited a few years before going down the sink with a bunch of gamblers. Can you imagine being on a raid with Isaac? Shotguns coming out of your ass. Unbelievable."

Their checkpoint was a mailbox on Minford Place, two blocks down from Boston Road. The man at the mailbox didn't bother signaling to them. He wouldn't sit in the back, on the "commissioner's chair." He climbed up front with them. They weren't put off by his rags; Isaac was a master of disguise. But his stench was overpowering. Lyman, the man in the middle, had to sit with his nose upward. Kelp, who lived in a flophouse once doing field work for a course at John Jay, had more experience with unwashed men. He volunteered the first question.

"Chief, am I driving too fast?"

Isaac growled at him. "Don't call me Chief."

"Should I slow down, Inspector Sidel?"

"I'm Isaac. Just Isaac. Drive the way you like."

Kelp turned the wheel with smug looks into the mirror; the investigators had exaggerated Isaac's reputation. He was only a fat man with unruly sideburns and a balding head. A dishonored deputy chief inspector going to pot from his exiled station in the Bronx. Kelp was glad now he had never been given the opportunity to be one of Isaac's angels. Pimloe began to flush out with esteem in Kelp's mind. Pimloe had manners. Pimloe had a Harvard ring. Pimloe didn't own layers of fat behind his jaw. Pimloe showed respect for a rookie. He wouldn't humiliate you by sitting up front.

They crept toward Manhattan in a silent car. Unbelievable, Lyman thought, afraid to mutter a word. The stink drove his face into Kelp's shoulder. Kelp welcomed Isaac's reserve. He didn't want to discuss tactical matters with a double-chinned cop. He watched this fat man in the glass. Let him swallow his lip. Near the Willis Avenue Bridge Isaac opened up. "How's Herbert?"

"Pimloe?" Lyman mumbled under Kelp's arm. "He's fine. The whip said we should take care of you. He sends his regards."

"Did he scratch my chair?"

"What?" Kelp said.

"The chair he sits on. In my room. Is it scratched?"

"Isaac, I didn't notice."

Kelp was pleased with his response; he was standing up to the Chief. Kelp had the badge now, not Isaac. He would tell his rookie friends: He's nothing, this Isaac. I blew in his face, and he didn't blow back.

They drove the Chief to an apartment house on East Ninety-first with two doormen and a glass canopy. Isaac went past the doormen in his rotten clothes. He hadn't even thanked the rookies.

"What a personality," Lyman said, able to breathe again. "The guy goes anywhere in a beggar's suit. Unbelievable."

Kelp had less charity for Isaac. "Good riddance. He's a glom, can't you see? That smell was no cover-up. Alfred, it's for real. He's nothing but piss and scabby ankles."

"Isn't this the First Dep's house? Would the First Dep invite him in if it's only piss? Use your brain. How are we going to earn the gold shield? The First Dep must be fond of Isaac. Maybe he's going to repatriate him, bring Isaac back. He wouldn't waste his time on a reject."

"Let Pimloe worry."

Kelp headed for the East River Drive; if he watched the speedometer they could cruise downtown at a walk and make the office while Pimloe was out to lunch; it would be malteds for them, feet on their desks, telephone calls to their sweethearts from inside their own cubicles.

"Unbelievable."

SEVEN

At the dairy restaurant Coen wore his "gambler's coat," a red jacket with green piping under the pockets; he had once seen a reputable crapshooter in a similar coat. He picked his father's favorites off the menu in the window: broiled mushrooms on toast, split pea omelette, chopped Roumanian eggplant, prune dumplings, and a seed cake called mohn. All the Coens were confirmed vegetarians, father, mother, and uncle Sheb; only the son was spared. Coen had fewer meatless days than any of them. A growing boy needs a little chicken in the blood, his father pronounced, so Coen had to eat chopped turkey, chopped liver, and chopped chicken in his lettuce hearts. At thirty-six Coen still gagged over the sight of lettuce being washed. The odor of chicken livers depressed him, and the stink of turkey made him cross.

Old men were coming out of the restaurant with roses in their lapels. They were dressed in baggy tan or gray, with stockings bunched over their ankles and scuff marks on their shoes. César couldn't have found his calling in Manhattan if he catered to these fish. Coen worried about a boutonniere until he noticed a stash of pink, short-stemmed roses for sale near the cash register. He smiled at the thoroughness of César's operation: the restaurant provides the roses. But he had trouble buying one. The cashier claimed they were for her regular customers. She gave in when she saw Coen's eyes go slate blue, an inhuman color according to her. He walked away sniffling, with the boutonniere oversweet in his nose. He stood near the old gamblers, giddy from all the fumes. Ignoring him, they played with their buttonholes.

The steerer arrived in a twelve-passenger limousine, counted roses, and allowed Coen to get in. The gamblers occupied eight of the seats. With Coen among them, they were in a foul mood. The steerer tried to shake off their long faces. He was a fattish man in a silk girdle-vest; the vest gave him bumps along both sides. "Julie Boy, would I hit you over the head? Boris Telfin doesn't lead his friends to a poisoned game." Coen didn't like the steerer's glibness, his winks, his habit of pulling the buckles on his vest. He mumbled three words.

"Moses sent me."

The steering car shot uptown, turned east, dawdled at the top of the park, then crawled to a second location a few blocks north of the dairy restaurant. Five of the gamblers climbed out and waited in front of a launderette. The steerer deposited a sixth gambler at a shoemaker on Amsterdam. The final two gamblers were humming now. "Boris, will the sky hold up? It looks to be rain." Coen was the one with the long face. The steerer went south. His limousine was equipped with a police-band radio, and on the ride downtown Coen could hear a dispatcher from his own district summon a team of burglary detectives back to the house. The steerer was showing off. He wanted Coen to know that César had his finger on the Manhattan police. He switched frequencies and jumped on a citizens'-band. Two men were screaming out the merits of alpha and beta waves. The gamblers sat with dumbfounded jaws.

—Did you or didn't you *succeed* at alpha?

—I'm not so sure.

"If you cover your eyes with half a ping-pong ball, you can have a white-out in under twenty minutes," Coen muttered into his sleeve. The gamblers figured he was another moron from the Bronx; they knew the case histories of César and his brothers; the tantrums, the bouts of forgetfulness, the swollen eyes. But Coen didn't have the look of the Guzmanns; he was only talking to the radio. Isaac had introduced him to the idea of brainwaves. At checkers with Coen, Isaac would slice a fresh ping-pong ball with Coen's scissors, cup each eye, squeezing the halved ball into place with his cheekbones, sip Coen's lukewarm tea, and "go into alpha" while Coen washed the dishes and waited for both halves of ball to pop out of Isaac's eyes. This meant Isaac was coming out of alpha to trounce Coen in checkers and solve whatever police mystery had been plaguing him on that day. Coen himself had little success with the ball; he could sit for hours with his eyes shuttered up and experience nothing but a cramp in his neck and a burning sensation where the ball kissed his cheek.

The steerer made East Broadway and stopped at Bummy's, where Coen had searched for Chino Reyes. He sat alone in the car, the gamblers accompanying the steerer into Bummy's. Coen wondered how long they would keep bouncing him. He might get to see Staten Island or the best Brooklyn wharves. Two mutts from Bummy's climbed in with him; Coen recognized them as drifters who hired out at thirty dollars a day. It had to be hard times for César. They squeezed Coen into the upholstery. He wasn't surly. He knew they would have to feel him up; the steerer must have warned them to be sure he wasn't carrying a wire. "Monkey," the first one said, "who sent you?"

"Moses."

"Sherwin," the second one said, "he's a monkey all right. Should I touch up his face?"

"Monkey, are you after Jerónimo?"

Coen shrugged his head. "I'm looking for César Guzmann."

"Monkey, who are you?"

"Detective Coen, Second District Homicide and Assault Squad."

"Sherwin, I told you, he's a monkey with a badge. He wants to sink Jerónimo."

"I went to school with César," Coen said. "I drank malteds with Jerónimo. What would I want with him? Just get César on the phone. Tell him Manfred's here. In his car."

The two drifters made faces over Coen, conferred, warned Coen not to move, and brought the steerer out of Bummy's. The three of them fussed over Coen's shield. They bounced him east and west before they drove him to a parking lot on Hudson Street. Coen was desperate to pee. They allowed him to go behind the watchman's shack. They giggled at the crackling of the boards. These giggles made Coen pee in spurts. He shook off most of the drops and returned to the limousine. He couldn't find the steerer or the two mutts. Then the mutts began to whine. "How can we tell? He says classmate, he says school. What do we know about a badge?" They had to be behind the shack now with a fourth party. The second mutt emerged holding his cheek. The steerer skulked around to the opening in the shack. The first mutt approached the limousine and held the door for César. Coen couldn't be sure if César had come to murder him or give him a hug. He was the most volatile of all the brothers, craftier than Alejandro, stubborner than Jorge, the youngest, the skinniest, the shrewdest, the one with the nerve to break out of Papa's fist. His code name had been Zorro the fox before he eloped to Manhattan. This was how he was known in the heaviest policy circles. He wore suspenders this evening, a mohair shirt, and narrow boots. He snarled his greetings to Coen. "If I wanted you, Manfred, I'd sit and wait on your stoop. Why do you come to me using Papa's name?"

Coen decided to play the fox. "I'm looking for Jerónimo."

"Ha-ha. More jokes like that, Manfred, and you'll bleed between your legs."

They had been inseparable as boys, protecting Jerónimo from rock throwers and the thieves of Southern Boulevard, undressing the Loch Sheldrake monster scarecrow across the road from Papa's summer farm, sniffing laundered brassieres on country clotheslines, shoveling snow outside Papa's candy store, stealing sour pickles for Jorge and Jerónimo, practicing certain blood rites (they pricked their arms with safety pins), following *prostitutas* in the street. When his mother and father went on an egg-buying trip, Coen slept with César and Jerónimo in Jerónimo's bunk. César would kill for his father and his brothers, and once he would have killed for Coen. At fourteen they grew apart. Coen ran around Manhattan with bohemians and bagel babies from the High School of Music and Art. He neglected César. A convert to Manhattan, he felt superior to the Guzmanns of Boston Road. He brushed his teeth in Manhattan water. He ate his mother's egg sandwiches in parks and museums. Realizing his own snobbery at fifteen and a half, his discomfort around the bagel babies, his nervousness in museums, he couldn't get back to César. Inscrutable by now, assuming Jerónimo's silences, César had nothing for Coen but mute hellos and goodbyes. Papa could forgive the high school boy, serve him extra balls of ice cream, seat him next to Jerónimo; César couldn't.

"Manfred, I may jump in and out of closets, but I don't miss too many of my father's songs. How bad do you want the Child girl?"

"You talked to Papa?" Coen said.

"Tell me, how bad?"

"I'm in a hole unless I bring her in. I'm still attached to one of the commissioners. And they can drop me anywhere they please."

"She's in Mexico City."

"I thought Peru," Coen said. "César, can I get in?"

"Not alone. You'll need somebody. But you may not like him. The girl's with some mean characters."

"Did they buy her?"

"Never mind. Meet me in an hour. The steerer will give you my address for tonight."

"César, why were your boyfriends over there babbling about Jerónimo?"

"Don't question me, Manfred."

"Maybe I can help."

"Sure. The biggest gloms in your department are trying to sink my brother, and I suppose you're ready to stop them. Manfred, go away."

"Sink Jerónimo? For what? Walking in the street? Tickling his prick? That's crazy."

They want to make him into the lipstick freak. That's the word coming down. And I don't throw hard money around for stale information."

"César, I saw the sketches the police artists made, sketches of the freak. It's nothing like Jerónimo."

"Don't worry. If they get their fingers on him, they'll change the sketch."

The steerer drove Coen uptown. In the old days, when Coen still lived on Boston Road and worked for Isaac, he once rescued Jerónimo from a station-house in the Bronx. Selma Paderowski, thirteen, and a drinker of chocolate sodas, squinted at Jerónimo's woolly gray hair and decided to be in love. Proving her affection she tossed rocks at him, tore pieces off his shirt, dared him to peek at her crack. Because her craziness was undisguised, the Guzmanns tolerated these overtures to Jerónimo. Thus encouraged, she caught him near a fire hydrant, alone, without César or Alejandro, coaxed his thumb inside her skirt, and screamed until a foot patrolman arrived. Coen was sitting on his fire escape. He clumped down the steps, hopped off the ladder, and took the patrolman aside. Sheltered by Isaac, a newcomer to the police, he fumbled with his detective badge. "Civil problem," he said. "I can handle it." The patrolman told him to flake off. "This is my collar, friend." Papa, César, Topal, Alejandro, and Jorge were hunched around the johnny pump feeding water to Jerónimo and watching Coen. César wanted to leap on the patrolman's back. But Papa kept him behind the johnny pump. Still, he was terrified, more terrified than his sons. Coen remembered Papa's sag; a North American for almost a quarter of a century, he had the stance of a foreigner, a *peruano* in the Bronx. The patrolman left with Jerónimo. "Papa, I'll help," Coen shouted. He assumed the patrolman belonged to one of Papa's rivals. He ran to the drugstore and telephoned Isaac. Isaac intercepted the patrolman, got him to alter a few words in his complaint book, and gave Jerónimo to Coen. Jerónimo went straight to the candy store, drank half a gallon of chocolate milk, ruining three paper cups, and Papa swore his gratitude to Coen and promised to memorialize Coen's Chief on his Jewish-Christian candlesticks.

Coen showed up too early at César's West Eighty-ninth Street address, and he loitered outside the building. A man came out of a panel truck across the street with a large metal box that said "Telephone Repairs," went into the building, chatted with the night doorman, shook his hand, and proceeded toward the elevators. Coen didn't like the smug way the doorman watched himself in the mirror. Some money changed hands, he had to figure. The doorman was opening his wallet when Coen asked him for apartment 9-D.

"Who you looking for?"

Coen was reluctant to say Zorro. So he became secretive with the doorman. "Ring him. Tell him Coen's here."

The doorman backed off. "Is the gentleman expecting you, sir? Go straight up."

Coen went down to the cellar. He found the repairman sitting on his box near the telephone lines with a notebook in his lap; he was wearing headphones and jumping onto somebody's wire with a pair of alligator clips. What annoyed Coen most was the pleasure the man took in his work, chuckling silently over everything he picked up with the headset. Coen pulled the box out from under him and dragged him around the room by his shirt.

"Fast," Coen said. "Who's paying you?"

"Let's talk," the man said. "I'll play, but let's talk."

Coen relaxed his grip and stuck the man in the belly with the butt of his off-duty .38. The man cooed at the sight of Coen's gun.

"That's a Police Special, isn't it? Christ, you scared me. I thought you were some kind of gorilla. Listen, give me your badge number, and I'll fix you up. My people are in with the brass."

"Prick, you're going down. You'll have bedsores on your ass for the next ten years. Tapping wires is no joke."

The man slobbered into his notebook. "Wait. I'm a private operator, Jameson. Take my card. It was nothing, I swear. I was going to get right off."

"Who's paying you?"

"Child."

Coen tramped on the headphones and kicked Jameson out of the cellar.

César was waiting for Coen in pajamas with ventilated sleeves; the pajamas improved his disposition. He smiled, hugged Coen at the door, had a pitcher of sangría prepared with fruit at the bottom. He stirred the fruit and tested the sweetness with his finger. He sucked his finger in the style of the Guzmanns, sticking a knuckle in his mouth. Satisfied, he poured for Coen, who couldn't shake off the gloom after his encounter in the cellar.

"César, why bother with all the apartments? I caught Child's man downstairs sitting on your wire. What's between you and Child?"

"He makes home movies, and he accuses me of trying to muscle in."

"Are you, César? Are you crowding him? Are you moving in on Child?"

"Never happen. Vander deals in shit."

"Is his niece the star?"

"Who? High tits? Odette? Odette Leonhardy?"

"Isn't she Odile?"

"Odette, Odile. The girl's crawling. She's diseased. She takes them ten at a time."

"César, did she ever work for you?"

César dropped his nose in the sangría and sniffed. "Manfred, my line is dice. You met the steerer. I provide the furniture, that's it. My customers make their own accommodations with the broads. Maybe she can advise you how often she gets down with crap players. Am I responsible for Odette?"

"Who put Carrie Child in Mexico?"

"Search me?"

"Try a little harder, César. If you can locate her so fast, you must know who took her out of Manhattan."

"Ask Isaac," César said, his nose moist from the pitcher. "Ask the brain."

Coen was about to have a fit. "I suppose Isaac's into white slavery. I suppose he carries a whip for your father. Nothing would surprise me."

They both crunched ice and nibbled on the rinds. They nibbled while the doorbell rang. Coen coughed up ice when he saw a switch of red hair against César's door. César laughed at the spectacle of Coen and the Chinaman stalking one another with holsters sticking out of their coats. "Put your pieces away," César said, disgusted by the obscene tilt of the holsters. None of the Guzmanns owned a handgun. Papa didn't trust the validity of mechanical things. He was afraid his sons might shoot their peckers off. This is why Papa and the Marrano pickpockets couldn't succeed in Peru. Every other smalltime crook and policeman wore his *pistola.*

"César," Coen said. "Is this the shark you got for me? Forget it. I'll make Mexico on my own."

"Manfred, you're asleep. They'll swallow you alive in Mexico City. Chino can get you in. Chino knows the hombres and all the streets."

The Chinaman took off his wig. "I'll fix you, Coen, you blue-eyed fuck. I gave César my promise. So I'll help you first." He turned on his hip to pluck Coen's right ear (he'd left the humpbacked boot downtown). They began to wrestle in their coats. He threw Coen into César's bookcase. "You think this is the station-house, eh cop? You like to touch my face with the bulls standing around. We come back, man, I'll finish with you."

César pulled books off Coen. The Chinaman squatted down and pretended to wipe himself. "Here Coen, take my fingerprints now."

Coen came up growling, and César had to make the peace. They settled on the date, the proper hotel, and the means of recouping Caroline Child. César didn't offer the Chinaman a drink out of the pitcher. Coen found the Chinaman a glass. Chino wouldn't drink without a nod from César. And Coen felt like a reptile. He couldn't decide whether César was following the turns in his father's Marrano etiquette. Maybe the Guzmanns weren't supposed to drink with the pistols they hired. But the Chinaman got the nod, and he said "Salud" before he licked the sangría. Coen smiled. His head was stuffed with sweetened alcohol.

"Vander will pay for the whole trip," he said.

César's cheeks flared little puffs of annoyance. "Manfred, you pay for yourself. I'll take care of Chino and the girl." Then his cheeks grew shallower, and he nibbled rinds again. "That's my present to Vander." He gave Coen one final hug. "Manfred, I'm no goody boy. You ask me for the girl, you'll get the girl. I want something in return. A favor."

Coen didn't break the hug.

"Jerónimo's in Mexico." César felt Coen's shoulders slacken with surprise. "He's staying with our cousin Mordeckai. He'll be glad to see you. I don't want my brother with strangers all the time. Go to him, Manfred. Sit with him in the park. Chino will show you where. If he's too thin, if my cousin takes advantage, if they don't give him enough, you talk to me. Only don't repeat what I said. Nobody should find out about Jerónimo. Not Isaac, nobody."

"César, I never see Isaac. But why are you so afraid? Isaac works for your father."

César stared at him. "He's the one who put the pins in Jerónimo."

"César, are you telling me Isaac's a rat? They threw him off the force. Why would he help them? He wouldn't bury Jerónimo."

"I don't care. He's the one."

Coen went out the door with a buzz in his head.

The Chinaman had to interrupt his siege of The Dwarf to satisfy Zorro and come to terms with Blue-eyes Coen. He would take the cop to Mexico, but he wouldn't wear his high shoe above Fourteenth Street. He no longer thought of it as Arnold's boot. He hadn't changed the laces or smoothed the wrinkles out. He didn't want a fancyman's shoe. No cop in the world could make him give it back. Not even the great Isaac, who was washing nickels in Papa Guzmann's sink. The Chinaman could have rushed The Dwarf with his pistol, a Colt Commander .45, which he would bury in a lot on Prince Street before his Mexican trip. He could have left some smoke on the lapels of the bouncer girls, Janice and Sweeney. But he would have frightened Odile. So he approached the door with his gun hand free, the Colt .45 tucked inside the quick-draw holster sitting over his heart. The Chinaman had only two hours to spare; then he would have to ditch the gun and find Coen at the airport.

Odile watched him from the curtains. She hadn't left The Dwarf in thirty-six hours. Even when the Chinaman disappeared from time to time, she suspected he was pissing in a hallway down the block or buying cans of beer. Janice woke Sweeney, who had been snoring comfortably in a cot behind the bar. "The Chinee's coming," Janice said. "He's crossing over." The cousins had a gleam on their chins that didn't suit Odile. She could sense the battle lines. The Chinaman would never be able to dodge Janice and Sweeney wearing that wicked shoe. He was foolish to rile the cousins. "Chino Reyes," she screamed, "I'm not getting down with any of your customers if you don't step back."

They snatched him up by his arms, lifted him over the doorsill (he was only a bantamweight, one hundred and seventeen pounds), and hurled him against the bar. Janice cupped her fist into the finger grooves of the brass knucks. The Dwarf was empty at six in the morning, and she could have the Chinaman at her own leisure, play cat and mouse with him first. Sweeney tore the holster off his chest, threw the gun into an ice pail. She held the Chinaman down while Janice nipped his ear until the blood came. Sweeney cautioned Odile. "Baby, close your eyes. It's better if you don't watch."

But Odile was already slapping at the brass knucks, dents in her palm from contact with the metal. "Sweeney, get her to stop. The Chinaman's my problem."

"Not when he invades the premises," Janice said. "Then he belongs to us." She was having too much fun to heed Odile.

"Sweeney, I'll stay out of here for life. One more mark on his ear and that's it."

"Don't listen to the bitch," Janice told her cousin. "She'll come crawling."

Sweeney was terrorized of having to work. The Dwarf without Odile. She raised the Chinaman to his feet. He hung like some rag doll with one raw ear and a high-climbing shoe, his neck under Sweeney's elbow. Odile catapulted him out of The Dwarf, hooking onto his suspenders with both hands, convinced that such a feather couldn't have survived one of Janice's attacks. She was pleased with the Chinaman although she didn't intend to show it. "Moron," she said, "you can lean on me if you want."

"Don't stretch the suspenders," was all he cared to say. No man or woman had ever tattooed the side of his face with brass knucks; he heard howlings in his ear. He sucked bits of red mop to preserve his sanity around such noise. Odile began to wonder why he was wetting his wig.

"Chino, I could carry you better without the boot."

But the Chinaman refused. He wasn't going to leave his high shoe in the gutter no matter how deaf he became from the blasts inside his head. Odile brought him to her house. She soaked his ear in an iodine solution and dressed him in little cotton bandages. The howling stopped but the iodine sting caused him to bite into the wig. Odile undid his collar and washed the signs of blood off his neck. She saw the tension in his ribs. She insisted on taking his temperature. The Chinaman mumbled with Odile's thermometer in his mouth. He was lying in her mattress, propped against scatter pillows. "I have to be in Mexico, Odette."

She put more pillows on his knees. Being a far-sighted girl, she couldn't read the thermometer (Odile didn't own a pair of eyeglasses). So she faked a reading. "A hundred. A hundred and a half. Jan must have given you the flu."

The Chinaman forgot about his burning ear. He couldn't afford to disappoint Zorro; he had promised to be Blue-eyes' chaperon. He snatched the thermometer away and investigated the markings. He frowned through the glass. "Odette, it's a rundown tube. The mercury's gone."

"Liar," she said.

He snapped the thermometer over Odile; no mercury balls fell into her hand. The Chinaman smiled at his victory. Odile was miffed.

"Chino, button your collar. I don't like a naked man in my bed."

The Chinaman was less groggy; his ear had quieted down, and he didn't intend to be bullied by a girl who worked for him but would take nothing more than his telephone calls, who sent him cash in perfumed envelopes from the customers he supplied but treated him with disregard. The Chinaman had his advantage now: he occupied a favorable position on her mattress. He didn't claw. He didn't ruffle her material. He used logic with the porno queen.

"Anybody who goes down for Bummy shouldn't be so choosy." He huffed out his pigeon breast. "I'm better built than Bummy any day of the week."

Odile was tempted to take off his clothes. He had a delicious bump under his bodyshirt. But she didn't care for his argument.

"I never got down with Bummy Gilman," she said. "He pays me to soap his hernia. A hundred—no, a hundred and a half every single wash."

The Chinaman was relieved the bouncers hadn't gone through his pockets; he drew a nest of fifties from his money clip. "I'll pay. Call it a cash sale. What's four hundred to me?"

"Chino, I can't accept gelt from you," she said, making him drop the money clip into his pocket. "You're too close to Zorro. He'll kill me if he ever finds out."

She pitied the Chinaman's glum face, the palpitations of his chestbone, his cottony ear, the bend in his triggerfinger, and she was charmed by the display of his money clip; no man had offered her four hundred dollars yet for her simple tricks. She soothed him, put her hand over the palpitations. His chestbone beat against her touch. "We'll play," she said. "Only pants and shirts have to stay on."

The Chinaman didn't know how many embargoes Odile would place on him; he couldn't bring her down to her garterbelt. He should have been more humiliated, but he wanted her hand on his chest. He kissed her, felt the rub of her teeth, and his head was smoking all over again.

"Chino, are your feet cold? Why are you shivering?"

"Caught a chill in my ear, Odette. It's nothing."

And he had to restrict his hands, keep from brushing her skin too fast, or the pressure points behind his ears might swell and clog his adenoids; that's how much Odile could bother him. The Chinaman was no crappy fetishist. He could have managed five more girls, *cubanas* and *negritas* with rounder bottoms and fatter thighs, or a Finnish beauty who needed Chino's *pistola* against her navel to enjoy a proper climax. The Chinaman preferred Odette. It wasn't a matter of height (the Chinaman would only allow himself to be ravished by a tall girl), or the loveliness of Odile's long bony fingers, or the perfect span of her chest (he could have given up an hour following the line of Odile's bosoms, the curve from nipple to nipple, the wrinkles produced by the tug of an armpit). Her haughtiness appealed to him, the tough protrusion of her underlip, the amounts of scorn she seemed to blow into a sentence. If he had his own way with her, he would shove Odile out of pornography. He would put Janice and Sweeney in a bottle, close The Dwarf to Odette, hold her at Jane Street, deny Bummy Gilman visiting rights. She wouldn't have to wash that man's balls for a living. But the girl belonged to Zorro, and not to him. And if he defied the Guzmanns, he would have to take off taxi cabs again, and dodge shotguns in a shopping bag. The Chinaman was depressed.

Odile shucked off his mop, fondled the dark roots of his scalp, and the Chinaman wasn't so morose with lovely fingers in his hair. He dove into the pillows, caught Odile by one leg, reached under the stirrup of her ski pants, worked an arm into the hollows at the back of her knee, climbed half a thigh, worshipping the gooseflesh and thighdown (not even the beautiful Finn had hairs quite so fine), felt her erect nipples with the nubs of skin on his forehead and the depressions of his cheek, and came against her other hip, his screams muffled by the proximity of her jersey to his mouth. Odile liked his knobby head in her bosoms. She wanted to maintain the exact location of their hug, but the wetness in his pants troubled the Chinaman. "Mexico," he blurted, getting off her chest.

"Chino, where are you going with that sick ear of yours?"

He couldn't remember having such a sticky groin since his lurchings at Mott Street movie shows during the eighth grade (the Chinaman was always a year behind at school). He covered the bad ear with some furls of the mop. He was too distracted to kiss Odile right now. "I'll bring you charms from Mexcity," he said. "Something Zorro won't be able to identify."

She thought he was hallucinating. "Chino, get into bed."

He pulled the kinks out of his suspenders in the hall. Odile's landlady passed him on the stairwell. She frowned at his bandage and the rumpled state of his bodyshirt. The Chinaman was immune to landladies. He found himself a cab at Abingdon Square. "Prince Street," he shouted. "Make it quick."

The cabby Quagliozzo, an alert Queens man of forty-five with a billy club near his money box for take-off artists and unwelcome guests, wasn't fooled by the red mop. He had a circular stuck to his dash-board advertising the taxi bandit Chino Reyes, with a reward of $1,000 from independent fleet owners for the Chinaman's arrest.

Quagliozzo (his friends called him Quag) recognized the cheekbones behind the manufactured hair, only there was nothing in the circular about a clubfoot. The cabby reasoned that no professional bandit could flee fast enough from a job in a high shoe. The garagemen, who had their own connections with petty crooks, informed him that the taxi bandit was masquerading as a pimp to throw off the Manhattan bulls. So Quagliozzo decided to test the Chinaman in his cab. He wouldn't keep a glass plate between him and his customers like other security-crazy hacks (how could he chat through such a barrier?); accordingly he drove with a hand on the club.

"Mister, I hate them lousy pimps. They take advantage of white girls. They shellac their hair. They sit in fucking Cadillacs. If I had a pimp in my car, I'd murder him."

Quagliozzo couldn't get the Chinaman to raise a cheek. "Mister, what's your opinion?"

"Prince Street," the Chinaman said, and he motioned for the cabby to pull over near a lot. "Wait for me." He walked to a row of garbage cans inside the lot. Solomon Wong, his father's old dishwasher, was sitting on the northernmost can.

"Salomón, que tal?"

Solomon gathered the many skirts of his coat (it had once belonged to Papa Reyes), and removed a cloth traveling bag from inside the can. The Chinaman changed shoes, putting Solomon in custody of the boot, and shoved the mop under Solomon's coat; he wasn't going to be stuck with red hair in Mexico City.

Quagliozzo was restless when the Chinaman returned to the cab. "Mister, where should I go now?"

"Drive," the Chinaman said. "I'll tell you later."

Quagliozzo had sufficient proof to sink the taxi bandit; without his mop and high shoe he was exactly the man in the circular. Smart, smart, Quagliozzo reckoned. He uses a garbage can for a drop. That's where the cash goes after a steal. Quagliozzo had more respect for the Chinaman.

"Mister, I gotta take a dump."

He stopped at a cafeteria on the Bowery, brought his money box inside to the shithouse at the end of the counter, then doubled back to the telephone on the wall. He dialed the police emergency number. He walked out chewing sticks of gum. The Chinaman wasn't in the cab. Quagliozzo blamed himself. "I shoulda used the club on him." He joined the three radio cars that responded to his call, steering them to Prince Street. They couldn't find Solomon in the lot; they overturned every can, mucking through the garbage, but nobody came up with the Chinaman's shoe.

EIGHT

Because he could see himself getting raked on every side (by Pimloe, by Papa, by Vander, by Isaac perhaps), Coen mentioned his trip to no one. He would leave the country without notifying the First Deputy's office or the Second Division. Pimloe would go berserk if he knew Coen was traveling with a Chinese taxi bandit. Homicide would nail him to the wall. The First Dep would pray for the return of Isaac. Coen still had Vander's boodle, and he intended to blow the remains of it in Mexico, on Jerónimo, himself, and cousin Mordeckai. He would travel incognito, without badge or gun.

Leaving for the airport he found a swollen paper bag outside his door. The aromas were unavoidable. Coen smelled Papa's sweet-meats through the bag; black halvah, jellies, overripe chocolate, bitter sucking candy, light and dark caramels, for Jerónimo. César must have ordered one of his brothers to empty Papa's store. Or did Papa himself learn Jerónimo's whereabouts? Coen had no more time for crude speculations. He took the candy with him and met Chino outside the Aeronaves terminal. He said nothing about the black lumps on the Chinaman's ear. They both walked under the bar of the metal-detecting machine. But first the Chinaman laid his money clip and his cigar case in one of the baskets. He seemed annoyed when Coen didn't take a basket for himself. "Cop," he said, "where's the cap pistol? Where's the badge?"

"I left them home," Coen said. "In a stocking under my bed."

"Imbécil," Chino muttered. "We have to go against the punks without police toys? I never figured on that. Zorro told me you had a little water on the brain. A bull with a soft head. The badge is priceless, and you cuddle it in a stocking. Imbécil." He rattled at Coen up to the departure gate and into the Aeronaves jet. Coen yawned. He would have to sit for hours side by side with a spitting Chinaman from Havana. So he thought of the menu. He figured they would serve him tostadas and refried beans on a Mexican plane. He clutched his safety belt until they were well off the ground. He had flown only twice before, on Army transport planes, in and out of

Germany, thirteen years ago. Chino was the veteran rider, taking Caribbean holidays and flying for César. He had come from the *barrio chino* (Chinese quarter) of Havana, where his father owned a bakery and a restaurant until 1959. He was twenty-four years old and despised the *fidelistas* whose presence in Havana had frightened his father into selling the bakery and closing the Nuevo Chino Cafe. Away from Cuba his father's bones shrank, and he coughed out his blood on Doyers Street. Chino taunted Coen for the politics of the Jews, which, he was convinced, had put the *fidelistas* into power. "Coen, your papa alive?"

"Dead."

"Me too. He loved Stalin, your papa, no?"

"He was Polish," Coen said. "The Poles hate the Russians."

Chino allowed his elbow to settle nearer to Coen. He had never worked with a cop. "Coen, don't worry about the badge. I know a tinsmith at the Lagunilla market. He'll fix you up with beautiful badges." Still, he had to punish this Jew when they got home. Too many people had talked about the cop who slapped Chino Reyes. Coen had to live without refried beans. They fed him deviled ham and potatoes au gratin, and a slab of lemon pie.

Coen felt giddy in Mexican sunlight. He looked for exotic plants around the airport. Chino walked him through customs and then commandeered a taxi. He haggled with the driver, offering a fixed price with his fingers, and pushed Coen inside. They drove through a neighbourhood of shacks and seedy condominiums, Coen staring at faces and holes in the sidewalks, and went up Insurgentes Sur into the Reforma, where they came upon a fairyland of monuments, *glorietas* (traffic circles), and high pink hotels. The Chinaman pointed out at the boulevards. "Like Paris, no? The Campos Elíseos."

"I haven't been to Paris," Coen said, intimidated by all the *glorietas* and the crisscross of traffic.

"Me too," the Chinaman said.

They stopped at the Hotel Zagala across from the Alameda park, Chino paying the driver in US coins and summoning a bellboy with the shout "Mozo, mozo." Coen had his luggage swiped from his hands by a thin old man in a monkey cap who could hold six suitcases at a time. They were put on the third floor, in a narrow room that faced the wall of another hotel. Coen was ready to lie down but Chino wouldn't tolerate the room. He screamed into the telephone, berating the manager, the manager's wife, and the third-floor concierge. "You have to stick them in the head," he assured Coen, "or you'll rot behind a wall." They were transferred to a narrower room on the eighth floor, with a huge porcelain *bañadero* (tub) that overlooked the park. He dismissed the *mozo* with a pat on the shoulder and three dimes. Then he grew kinder to the old man and gave him a hat and a scarf out of his suitcase. "Coen, don't tip too hard. Otherwise they'll know you for a sucker."

"Chino, you gave him a fifty-dollar hat."

"That's nothing. I liked the size of his head. But no money."

Sitting inside the great *bañadero*, with a bar of hotel soap on his knee, the Chinaman taught Coen a formula for changing dollars into pesos. Coen stalked the bedroom trying to memorize this formula. He was getting fond of the Chinaman. "Chino, what's your regular name?"

"Herman," the Chinaman said, without hesitation. "Only my father could call it to me. You call it, I'll bite your face off. I promise you."

Coen was anxious to deliver Jerónimo's candy but the Chinaman slept for an hour after his bath. He put on an embroidered shirt, tweaked his suspenders, tucked a fresh scarf into his pocket, and ordered strong tea in the lobby. Then they crossed the Alameda into an older part of town and went looking for Jerónimo. Chino passed up the taco stoves and the coconut vendors to buy Life Savers from an Indian woman in the street. He wouldn't let Coen watch two boys stamp out tortillas at a sidewalk factory. "Hurry," he said. Away from the boulevards Coen felt the temperatures of the street bazaars, the vendors, and the press of faces near the curbs. Resisting Chino he ate cucumber slices (dusted with chile powder) on the fly. He goggled at shop signs—*Tom y Jerry; La Pequeña Lulu; Fabiola Falcon*—and bakery windows. Chino frowned at the bag Coen was holding for Jerónimo. "Fish?"

"Halvah. From Papa."

They passed *pulquería* after *pulquería* (sidewalk taverns) along San Juan de Letran, the men inside staring at the chino and the blondo walking together. Coen saw fewer and fewer women in the streets. The Chinaman turned up Belisario Dominquez and stopped at a house with a grubby balcony and an inner court. "The chuetas live here," he said. "The porkeaters. The Christian Jews."

"Marranos?" Coen asked. "Is this a Marrano neighbourhood?"

"Chuetas," the Chinaman sneered at him. He entered the court, his body sinking into grayness after five steps. Coen stayed under the balcony. Accustoming himself to the soupy light between the walls he detected two smallish boys in nightshirts playing pelota near a bend in the court. They played with closed mouths, the thunks of the pelota the only noise coming from the walls. Coen couldn't make any sense to their game. They slapped at the ball like old men, prim in their nightshirts, stiff at the waist, with no energy to spare. He wondered whether all Marrano boys were born with tight knees. On Boston Road César and Alejandro kicked a pink ball with a fever, a twitch in their legs. Even Jorge, who couldn't stoop because of the quarters he carried for Papa from ten on, and Jerónimo, whose mind was occupied with sweets and the dying pigment in his hair, had more animation than these two boys. Just when Coen began to feel his abandonment, the Chinaman emerged with cousin Mordeckai, a fatter Guzmann in a nightshirt, with Alejandro's features and Jorge's disjointed eyes. Coen was introduced to Mordeckai as the Polander, "el polonés." Mordeckai seemed pleased with the name. Chino wanted the candy from Coen. Mordeckai thanked "el polonés." Then he went back inside. "Come on," Chino said.

"Where's Jerónimo? Is he bringing him down? Didn't you see him?"

"The baby? No." The Chinaman walked toward San Juan de Letran. "Imbécil. You can't meet here. The chuetas are crazy. They're superstitious about blue-eyed people. They're afraid of blond hair. Don't worry. It's been arranged. Jerónimo will come to you."

He stationed Coen at the north end of the Alameda. "Wait. I'm going to get the hardware for tonight. Smile, Coen. I said the baby will show."

At forty, thirty, twenty, fifteen, Jerónimo had been *the baby*. Papa stuffed spinach sandwiches down his throat, Topal cleaned his fingernails with a safety pin, whoever found him in the street had to tie his shoes. The five other Guzmanns took turns bathing him; no one could trust him alone in a tub. Yet Jerónimo had an infallible sense of direction, the ability to read red and green lights, the acumen to avoid the harsh yellow paint of the taxicabs, the boldness to clamp money into a busdriver's fist. He could sing louder than Jorge. He swallowed caramels faster than Topal or Alejandro. He consumed more chocolate than a covey of schoolgirls. He mourned the plucked chickens in butcher windows, his eyes following the hooked line of strangled necks, pitying the lack of feathers more than the loss of life. He had profounder silences than any of the Coens. Among the Guzmanns he had the strongest grip. He loved César best, then his father, then Topal, then Alejandro, then Jorge, then uncle Sheb. He

missed the egg store, the blue-white aura of the candling machine, the
pea soup of Jessica Coen. He was a manchild fixed in his devotions,
his manners, his fears. He wouldn't step under a ladder but he could
kiss the wormiest of dogs. He tore off chunks of halvah for toothless
abuelitas (grandmas) and desperate nigger boys, not for young wives.
He was kind to squirrels, mean to cats. He would climb fire escapes
to mend a pigeon wing. He ignored birds with bloody eyes.

Coen saw him cross the park from Hidalgo Street, his shoelaces
dragging, his trousers filled with candy, his forehead pocked from
bewilderment; he hadn't spotted Coen. The marks deepened on his
face as he searched the park. He pulled an ear out of frustration. Coen
shouted, "Jerónimo, Jerónimo." And Jerónimo went fat around his
eyes. The webs disappeared. He ran to Coen, his fists slapping air.
Coen tied Jerónimo's shoes. Then they embraced, Jerónimo
squeezing Coen's ribs with an elbow. He had thick gray sideburns.
The hairs in his nose were also gray. On his knuckles the color was
Guzmann black. He wiped spit before he could talk. He mumbled
Coen's first name, saying "Manfro." He seized Coen by the hand and
took him out of the park. But he wouldn't let Coen cross over until
the traffic light switched to "Pase." Then he led Coen straight to an
ice cream parlor in a huge drug-store on Madero. He ordered hot tea
for himself and a chocolate sundae for Coen. He crumbled halvah
into the tea and softened his father's caramels with a heavy thumb
(the baby had incredible fingers). The ice cream tasted like cheese.
On tall stools with their thighs in a confidential position, Coen meant
to pump the baby about Mordeckay, César, and the Mexican
Marranos, and the trip from Boston Road to Belisario Dominquez via
Manhattan. But he couldn't use his guile on Jerónimo, so he resigned
himself to the sour chocolate in his sundae cup.

Walking with the baby up Madero, Coen sensed the incongruity
of a Bronx boy in Mexico. His hand in Jerónimo's three-fingered
grip, both of them with their eyes down, watching for puddles and
cracks in the sidewalk, they could just as well have been on Boston
Road. The baby turned left at the Zócalo, the main old square, and
brought Coen into a district of bazaars. Jackets belonging to the
house of Juan el Rojo hung inches from Coen's head. *Salons de
belleza* (beauty parlors) and radio schools coexisted in the street.
Stalls hugged the Avenida 5 de Fabrero from end to end. Jerónimo
and Coen stopped at a *pastelería*, where they collected a pair of metal
pinchers and began loading cakes, buns, and rolls on a tray. Jerónimo
operated the pinchers with his tongue out. Emulating the other

patrons, Coen gripped an enormous wood shaker with a rounded head and sprinkled a polite amount of confectioner's sugar on Jerónimo's cakes but Jerónimo wanted more. So Coen dunned the rolls. He payed under five pesos (the equivalent of thirty-nine cents) for the sixteen pieces on the tray. They popped rolls into their mouths, ending up swollen-cheeked at the Zócalo, each with a moustache of sugar. Finally Coen said, "César worries about you, Jerónimo. Do you have enough? Are you close with Mordeckai?"

The baby flicked sugar off his lip.

"Jerónimo, what should I tell César?"

Jerónimo kissed Coen above the eyes and led him to the borders of the Alameda.

"Baby, should César come and get you?"

Coen tried to go above the park with Jerónimo, but the baby held his wrist and prevented him. "House," he said, pointing beyond Madero Street. He walked away from Coen with the remains of the rolls in a stringed-up bag the woman at the *pastelería* had given him. He didn't wave. He didn't smile to Coen. He was absorbed in traffic signals. Crouching in the direction of San Juan de Letran, he picked at seams in the gutter with a shoe. Coen watched his crooked strides, thinking Jerónimo could make his Boston Road on Hidalgo Street. The halvah was a simple gratuity. The baby survived without the candy store.

Coen berated himself inside the lobby of the Hotel Zagala. He had forgotten to check Jerónimo's fly. He was so gloomy in the elevator, the *mozo* had to remind him of his own floor. He had no news for César. The baby was privy to secrets that Coen would never discover. He couldn't get between Jerónimo and Mordeckai; the Guzmanns were a close-mouthed people, sly, with vast, puckered foreheads and a reticence that was centuries old. They had played dumb in Lima, Peru, putting on the official uniform of beggar mutes to snatch a money pouch or burgle the summer homes of the *ricos*. Before that they mumbled Christianlike prayers in Holland, Portugal, and Spain, the quality of their voices depending on the season, the climate, and the local affinity for Marranos and other converts. Only Papa loved to talk, but he gave away nothing of himself in his blistered stories about raising five "pretzels" in America.

The Chinaman found Coen slouching on the bed. He opened his traveling bag and dumped out two 9mm. automatics with long, oily noses, two leather truncheons, a variety of badges, and a box of shells. Pleased with his loot, he walked around Coen with his knuckles in his sides. Coen wouldn't look at the badges or the guns.

"Why didn't Mordeckai come with Jerónimo? Can't he sit in the Alameda? Drink tea at a counter? Is he frightened of American cops? I wanted to talk to him about the boy."

Chino dismissed Coen's bile with a flip of his hand. "The chuetas never leave their homes. Mordeckai is married to his porch. I promise, he couldn't tell you where the Zócalo is. No pigeater sits in the park. Who would watch the pork on their stove? Don't be scared for the baby. He has his address pinned to his shirt. He can't get lost."

"Somebody ought to tell César about Jerónimo's solo walks. I thought the boy is supposed to be in hiding."

"Hombre, you can't tell Zorro what Zorro already knows." He herded the badges into Coen's lap. "We have other business here. I didn't come to mind the baby. Which one do you want? The Texas street cleaner's badge? The fireman's star? The hospital attendant? That's the shiny one. The park ranger? It doesn't matter. Just so it's in English. The cholos can't read. Imbécil, will you choose?"

"The fireman," Coen said.

Now Chino could ignore him and attend to his own needs. He hefted both automatics, closed an eye over each barrel, and proceeded to fill the magazines. Coen saw the bullets pass between the Chinaman's fingers. With the hump of his palm Chino fed the loaded magazines into the hollow butts. Then he swabbed his ears with a damp cloth, changed his undershirt, and rubbed scented oil into his collarbone and his neck. Coen had met take-off artists in perfumed vests and tapered calfskin, but he hadn't expected the Chinaman to prepare himself so fine for an ordinary piece of work. The Chinaman wore a garter on his calf for one of the truncheons. He gave a similar garter and the other truncheon to Coen, who tried them on more out of amusement than anything else. But he wouldn't accept a gun.

"Blue-eyes," Chino said, "you're going to walk into these gorillas, steal their wife, without a stick?"

Coen said yes. Then he quizzed the Chinaman. "Wife, what kind of wife? Chino, did they buy the girl off César? Does he doctor up marriage certificates in Mexican? Did you bring the girl here?"

"Come on," Chino said, and he stuck both automatics into his belt. Buttoning his wrinkleproof jacket at the bottom, he walked without any bulge. Coen followed him into a sidewalk cafeteria on Juarez. The bulb in the window twitched out "Productos Idish" in bright green. The Chinaman ordered a bowl of sour pickles and hot pastrami on a plate. Coen had chicken soup.

"Not bad, eh Polish? They fly in the salamis from Chicago."

"Who told you?"

"Zorro."

"Christ," Coen said. "César eats here too? Nobody but César orders pickles out of a bowl."

"Schmuck," the Chinaman said. "I can't learn? Shut up about César. You're messing with my appetite."

They took a two-peso cab at the Reforma, riding with a party of Mexicans in shortsleeved shirts. "Bueno' noches," Chino said, beguiling the Mexicans who were anxious to hear a Chinaman talking Spanish like a *capitalino*. "Noches," they said. Sitting four in a row at the back of the cab, with their knees in a huddle, none of them noticed the gun butts under Chino's pockets or felt the truncheon at his calf. A flurry of introductions carried from seat to seat. "Hermano Reyes," Chino said, using his Christian name for the Mexicans. He glowered at Coen, pinching him along the heel for being silent so long. "Noches," Coen said. Chino introduced him as "un gran hombre," Detective Manfredo Coen. The Mexicans blinked with respect when they discovered that Coen was a homicide man from New York. They wanted to know more about the Chinaman. He told them he was a merchant, a trader in horse meat and other perishables, and a specialist in the operation and maintenance of taxi-cabs. From the tight look on their faces and their attention to the Chinaman they must have considered horse-meat and taxicabs more interesting than homicides. At the Mississippi circle they shook Coen's hand and assured the Chinaman that their city was *su casa* (his house). The Chinaman wanted some sucking candy before he would go for the girl. So they followed the boulevard to a hippopotamus drugstore made of tiles and glass. Coen saw a horde of blondish girls and boys in bleached outfits gabbing at one of the counters. He couldn't place their voices, their accents, or their stiff rumps. With their trunklines unbroken and their fingers in their pockets, they seemed to be posing in the drugstore. Coen didn't mention them until the Chinaman decided on his sour balls. Then he whispered, "Who are they? Pale freaks?"

"Kids from the American colony," Chino said.

"Can't they bend? Don't they have a waist?"

"Ah, don't worry for them. They're out of it. The gringo babies. They live off the covers of the record albums. They take technicolor shits. They drink with a straw. Like Jerónimo. They're worse than the pig-eaters. At least Mordeckai sits at home." Then he softened to them. "Polish, it's not their fault. They didn't send their papas into Mexico. How you think I looked when my papa brought me to New York? I wore earlaps summer and winter. I put sugar on the corned beef. I lost my hat in the toilet bowl. Don't sit on my hand, Polish. Come on. The cholos might not like the time we picked to steal their little gringa."

He led Coen up Mississippi Street and across the three tiers of Melchor Ocampo to an apartment house in pink stucco on Darwin Street off Shakespeare. It was hard for Coen to associate grubby hoods and a shanghaied girl with the striped awnings over the windows and the gold knockers on the main door. They rode a tiny elevator with an inlaid ceiling and hammered walls up to the fifth floor. Coen kept scratching his knuckles but the Chinaman didn't fidget once. He lifted the tails of his jacket to air his pistol butts. He stepped onto the landing, opened a door, and walked in without announcing himself. There were four Mexicans in the sitting room. All of them had on ties and laundered white shirts. They wouldn't budge for the Chinaman. Coen figured they were brothers because they each had a chubby face with an irregular eyeline that gave them a permanent scowl, only one of them wore a moustache. They cursed the Chinaman, using his pet name. They also mentioned the Guzmanns and Zorro. They sneered at the Chinaman's automatics and they showed him some kind of receipt.

The Chinaman turned to Coen, who was still in the doorway. "Polish, they say the little gringa's their wife. And they have papers to prove it. Imagine, a legal shack job, split four ways." He shoved Coen into the sitting room. The Mexicans backed off. "El Polonés," they whispered, pointing to Coen. They looked away from his eyes. "El Polonés." They grabbed their belongings and flitted past Coen, crowding into the fancy elevator.

"What the fuck?" Coen said.

"Polish, you made your rep. Mexico's yours. They won't be home for a week." He cracked a sour ball and stuck the pieces under his tongue.

Coen began to fume. "You scumbag Chinaman, did you run around the city in the afternoon planting stories about me? Have you been dropping kites all over the place? Am I supposed to be Zorro's new pistol? A special hand at strangle jobs. Do I blow people's mouths away?"

A girl came out of the bedroom in a prim olive robe. She had crust in her eyes from sleeping too hard. "Where's Miguel? Where's

Jacob the Red?"

The Chinaman shrugged off the names. "Can't tell you, sweetheart. They left in a big hurry. Jacobo, he said, 'take care of my wife.' "

Still drowsy, the girl stubbed her toes against the Mexicans' fat-legged couch. She hopped near the Chinaman, holding one foot, trying not to fall on Coen. The hopping must have ended her sleepiness. She hissed for a while when she discovered a badge on Coen. "You're the dude who works for my father. Odette warned me about you. The Yid cop who goes down for millionaires." Then she inspected the badge and saw Coen was wearing an Acapulco fireman's star. She ignored him and laughed in the Chinaman's face. She had to sit on the floor to control the heaves in her belly. The Chinaman enjoyed how her calves could swell.

Coen squatted over her, hands on his kneecaps. "Carrie," he said. "Caroline. Please get up." The Chinaman thought Coen shouldn't placate her so much. He would have taken her by the hair and shown her his worth. He didn't value rich little gringas, the ones that spit at you and ran behind their papa's knees. But he had to mind himself. He couldn't offend Señor Blue-eyes.

"Don't be fooled by the star on his shirt, Miss Child. He's the legitimate article. Detective Coen. Me and him, we can't stand to see you living with cholos."

Caroline took off her four wedding bands and hurled two at the Chinaman and two at Coen. "I'm not going anywhere with you. Where's Miguel?"

Careful of Coen, he lifted her by the elbows and walked her toward the bedroom. She was crying now. "Where's Miguel?"

"Chino," Coen said. "What are you doing?"

"Let me talk to her, Polish. In there. I'll convince her. Soft, soft."

Coen listened through the bedroom door. He heard her say, "Daddy has all the clunks." She came out with Chino in a simple cotton dress, a seventeen-year-old with plain hands and a bony face, no more the mistress-wife of Darwin Street. Coen pitied her and loathed his own part in playing the shepherd for her father. The Chinaman tried to amuse him. "Polish, she didn't change her clothes before I shut my eyes." He held her arms for Coen. "Look at those marks. The cholos put her on horse."

"He's crazy," Caroline said. "They're allergy shots. Miguel paid for them. My nose would run without injections."

"Horse," the Chinaman said.

They sneaked her past the concierge at the hotel. Coen paced the bathroom. "How do we get her out? She needs a tourist card, something to prove she's a citizen."

The Chinaman smiled. "Don't worry. Zorro fixed it." He removed wrinkled papers from his wallet, tourist card and birth certificate in the name of Inez Silverstein, Mordeckai's North American niece.

Caroline slept on Coen's bed. Coen sat beside her. "Carrie," he whispered, "who brought you to Darwin Street?"

The Chinaman scolded him. "Jesus, you'll wake her." He prepared bunks for him and Coen under the footboards of the two beds. Coen undressed in the bathroom. The Chinaman mumbled "Noches" and immediately began to snore. Coen went to bed in his underpants.

Caroline preferred the Chinaman's even snores to Coen's thick breathing. She wished she could be with Jacobo the Red. Jacobo wouldn't hide under a hotel mattress with his toes sticking out. If she had the choice, she would have taken the Chinaman into her bed. Coen's ears were too sharp. They had the fix of a bloodhound. And she disliked cops in pointy shoes. The Chinaman had cuter eyes; he didn't represent her father, like Coen. She owed a certain allegiance to the Chinaman; he brought her into Mexico, together with that grey-haired boy, an imbecile who had erections on the plane. The Chinaman introduced her to Jacobo, Chepe, Dieguito, and Miguel, borrowed the wedding bands off an old Jew in another barrio, a certain Mordeckai, and now he was conspiring to take her back. This cop had some power over him, probably.

Caroline wasn't a spoiled girl. The Carbonderry School hadn't made her cross, like Odile. She held few illusions about her worth as a seductress. Jacobo had gotten her for free; in deference to her cousins, he was sharing her. This arrangement satisfied Caroline. She hated her father's devotion to high art, his smug promoter's life, his superiority to anything natively American, his Pinter festivals, his Beckett weeks, his Artaud happenings (little events where benches would be destroyed, girls in the audience would lose pieces of blouse, though never Caroline), his English teas, his croissants, the rococo games in his ping-pong room, none of which Caroline was permitted to join. Bereft of her father's pleasures, Caroline paid cousin Odile three hundred dollars, saved from an allowance of thirty a month, to smuggle her out of the country. She might yet have stuck with her daddy if he had been able to look her in the face. Vander was a collector of beauties; he surrounded himself with Odile and the hypersensitive creatures of his Bernard Shaw revivals (girls with flawed noses and fabulous chins). Recognizing her own plainness, Caroline had to show daddy Vander that a man could desire her, even if it was only Jacobo the Red.

She kept her eyes on the Chinaman now. She wanted more of him than the whistles coming up the side of her bed. So she reached a leg down and scratched him on the arm with a painted toe. The Chinaman woke stiff as a knife. He acknowledged the foot hovering over him.

"Missy, get them toes back upstairs and keep them there."

"No," she said, trying hard to whisper. "Chino, are you sleepy? If you can't come up, I'll come down to you."

"Are you crazy?" he said. "What about the Polish boy under the other bed? That cop, he's a scrupulous man. Don't kid yourself. He'd know if we used the same toothbrush."

Caroline began to pout; the nightshirt Chino had given her to wear halted at her kneecaps, and she couldn't get the hem to rise. "Oh, bother with him! He's just a silly cop. I don't care."

"Missy, I do." The Chinaman crept away under the bed; he had Odile to reckon with; that girl had made him wet his own pocket. He should have followed César's maxims; never fall for a *prostituta*. But his fingers itched from having climbed up the leg of somebody's ski pants to touch silky hairs on a scarred knee. And with Caroline jostling over him, putting crinks in the mattress, the Chinaman was afraid he would be denied all the benefits of a snore.

The *chueta,* Mordeckai Cristóbal da Silva Gabirol, had come to Mexico from Peru. His forebears were mostly Portuguese. Crypto-Jews who converted to Catholicism to preserve the wholeness of their skin, they became priests, sailors, and ministers to the kings of Portugal until the Inquisition struck and pushed them into Holland and the Americas. The da Silvas underwent five smaller Inquisitions before landing in Peru. Having already been reduced to penniless scratchers, they attended church (which they called El Synagoga), and mumbled secret prayers at home, cooking vast amounts of pork outside their doors to mislead their Christian neighbors and protect themselves from future Inquisitions. Thus Mordeckai inherited his role as a cooker and eater of pork. There was no longer an external need to fool the Christians (no da Silva had burned since 1721), but the *chuetas* couldn't give up their secretiveness. Like his fathers, Mordeckai had a predisposition toward gloom. Never venturing outside his own *colonia* (or district), he knew nothing of Mexico City. He lived between walls, accepting the conduits and *galerías* inside Belisario Dominquez, and hating the noise and brutal light of the street.

He performed a few specific services for his cousins from North America in the Bronx, for which he was adequately paid. He sought no other employments, spending his hours praying over his pots of boiling pork. Mordeckai had prayers for the da Silvas, living and dead, for his Bronx cousins and *chuetas* everywhere, for El Dia del Pardon (the Day of Atonement), for the pigs that were slaughtered so that the da Silvas could survive, for the darkness that protected the *chuetas,* for the Portuguese language that had succored them, for the Spanish they spoke in America, and for his own apostasy, his forced departure from the laws of Moses. He worshiped Cristóbal Colón (Christopher Columbus), whom he considered a *chueta* out of Portugal, and Queen Esther, who married a Persian King to save the Jews, becoming the first Marrano in history. The *chuetas* had holy obligations to Santa Esther; on her feast day they were forbidden to spit, urinate or consume pork. Mordeckai would only eat spinach for Esther's day. And no matter how hard his kidneys throbbed, he wouldn't pass water until sundown.

Mordeckai was uncircumcised. Centuries ago the *chuetas* couldn't afford to have their glans removed for fear of the Inquisitors, who would have spotted them instantly as Jews; the current *chuetas* persisted in this habit with these old Inquisitors in mind. They couldn't break a five-century bond. So they kept their foreskins and prayed to El Señor Adonai for forgiveness, crossing themselves and spitting in the direction of the devil. "Forgive me, Adonai," Mordeckai would recite every morning in modern Portuguese, "forgive me for trampling on your laws, for ignoring the mandate of circumcision. I am unclean, Father Adonai. I am made of pestilence, and I have unpure seed. For this reason, Adonai, I have chosen never to marry. Last year, Adonai, a rabbi came from North America with a special man to circumcise the conversos of my district. I refused, Lord. I could not betray the trust of my family. At thirteen, Adonai, our fathers revealed to us the truth of our heritage, and swore that any one of us who submitted to the ritual wound could not remain a da Silva. So I closed my legs to the rabbi's knife. What I did, Adonai, my ancestors have done. I could not exist otherwise. Forgive me,

Adonai, and send me books about your laws in Spanish or Portuguese. It is my hope and prayer that the spies of the afternoon will not discover where I live, and that only your angels, Lord, the angels of Adonai, follow me into the safe, dark porches of my home."

As part of his obligations to the Bronx, Mordeckai inherited Jerónimo. Meeting the baby at the airport (for the Guzmanns, and the Guzmanns alone, would Mordeckai leave his *colonia*, and only in a chauffeured car with shades on the windows), Mordeckai brought him to Belisario Dominquez. But the baby couldn't sit still. So Mordeckai had to accompany him to the edges of the Zócalo and the clutch of *librerías* (book-shops) on the near side of the Alameda park. He couldn't keep up with Jerónimo's terrific pace, and he would be forced to occupy a bench in the Alameda and suck air between his ribs if he wanted to arrive at his *piso* (flat) with a workable lung. Still, Mordeckai maintained a closemouthed loyalness and a delicacy of feeling that were rare even for a *chueta*. He never asked his cousins why they had saddled him with a *subnormal* who couldn't survive without a lump of caramel in his mouth. It didn't matter that he also loved the boy. He would have surrounded him with an equally fierce devotion whether or not he despised those sticky caramel cheeks.

Only once had he mixed into the affairs of his Marrano cousins. This was eighteen years ago, on a visit to the Bronx at Moisés Guzmann's request. Mordeckai went by ship. His freighter took him through the Tropic of Cancer in the Gulf of Mexico, around the Florida Keys, up the bumpy Atlantic into the Port of New York. The Guzmanns greeted him at dockside in sweaters and earmuffs, icicles forming on their syrup-stained trousers. Mordeckai was wearing a madras shirt, appropriate for the Mexican winter. They bundled him in sweaters and earmuffs, and escorted him out of Manhattan, with a neighbor, Mr. Boris Telfin, at the wheel of the family car, a '49 Chrysler sedan (no Guzmann would ever learn to drive). Mordeckai admired the roominess of this vehicle.

"Moisés," he shouted, in a mixture of Spanish and Portuguese, so that the Guzmann boys wouldn't fully understand, "are we going to your *judería?*"

Papa laughed. He told Mordeckai that the *judería* (Jewish quarter) of the Bronx lasted from one end of the borough to the other.

Mordeckai was hit with a definite wonder. He had never heard of a *judería* so big that it could swallow whole boroughs; not even the great *judería* of Lisbon (before the expulsion of the Jews) could have rivaled the Bronx. He remained in a stupor until he was pushed from the Chrysler to the candy store with five swaying Guzmanns. They introduced him as "Primo Mordeckai," their Mexican cousin. He had no bed of his own, migrating from bed to bed at the rear of the store, sleeping with Jerónimo one day, and with Topal the next. He was given sets of long underwear, a wormy toothbrush (formerly Alejandro's), and a pot to defecate in should the toilet be stuffed (Jerónimo had his best dreams on the Guzmann's communal chair).

The calendars of Mordeckai and Papa weren't strictly the same, and when Mordeckai announced that he had to bake his *pão santo* (holy bread) in midwinter, Papa stormed. "Cousin, this isn't the time for *Pascua*. Wait for us. We bake bread in July."

Primo Mordeckai refused, and Papa had to relinquish his oven for the brittle sheets of *pão santo* (sheets that wouldn't rise), which were bitter on his tongue and gave him heartburn. Nevertheless he forced his sons to digest Mordeckai's bread. But he wouldn't allow Mordeckai to bully him into observing Saint Esther Day.

"Cousin, we don't worship women here."

"Moisés," the cousin said, his face flushed with heavy red marks of shame, "not even the limpios"—Christians of the purest blood— "would insult the virtues of Santa Esther. I cannot sit in your house."

And Papa, who could squash a man's nose between any two of his knuckles, decided to be gentle with Primo Mordeckai. He didn't want this cousin of his to disappear into the black dust of Belisario Dominquez without a taste of the Bronx. So he held his piss in on Esther's day until the blood beat thick in his head and he suffered double vision (the Guzmanns usually peed every hour because of the number of sodas they swallowed). He denied pork to his boys and fed them spinach at Mordeckai's command. This was how he honored his cousin, the primo who recited longish prayers to Adonai and trafficked with female saints (a horrific act in Papa's eyes).

Mordeckai, in turn, paid his respect to *los negocios de Moisés* (Papa's occupations). He became part of the Guzmann machine, a conspiracy of runners, collectors, and bankmen who handled small denominations. Mordeckai didn't see North American paper money larger than *cinco dolares* (five) in his time with Papa; *chuetas* from Bogotá, Lima, and Palestine, mental deficients, disgraced policemen, and homeless *portorriqueños* ran for Papa, dropping and picking up silver pieces, scratching words on toilet paper, in a game Mordeckai couldn't quite understand. He fell into companionship with one of Papa's runners, a cousin from Palestine. (The *chuetas,* who passed their lives in various stages of dispersal, who could only breathe in an alien culture, who were as much Muslim and Christian as Jew, wouldn't accept the sovereignty of a temporal Jewish state, and thus they avoided the mention of modern Israel, their "Israel" being a condition of the head, a drowsy place with no fixed boundaries, a place Santa Esther might have concocted in the bed of her Persian king.) This *palestino* had gone from Bogotá to Tel Aviv because he wanted a short vacation from the rigors of dispersal and was curious to know a city governed by Jews, but he fled *La Palestina* to avoid a chief rabbi who hoped to have him circumcised and bring him into the synagogues. The *chuetas* couldn't enter a synagogue; they prayed at home or in a proper church.

Mordeckai made a shawl for the *palestino* from the linen of a barber on Boston Road; they crept under the striped shawl around noontime and wouldn't come out until after six, when they finished celebrating Santa Esther, Santa Teresa of Spain, the Christian and Marrano martyrs, the Turks who once loved the Jews, each of Moisés' sons, and the angels of Adonai. In addition to his holiness, the *palestino* was a thief. Papa might have overlooked slow, dwindling revenues, but the *palestino* (his name was Raphael) robbed Papa with both fists. Before planning the *palestino's* grave-site, Papa consulted Mordeckai.

"Cousin, this Raphael injures me. If I don't fight back, others will learn from him. Mordeckai, he'll have to go. I could bury him in Queens with the *católicos*, or on my farm. You make the choice. Don't worry, I'll put crosses on his stone."

Mordeckai shivered for the *palestino*, and his cheeks mottled blue and red at Moisés' barbarism. "Reprimand him, yes. Moisés, I don't ask kindnesses for a thief . . . but take blood from your own family? He's your cousin, Moisés. God forbid." In the teeth of Papa's stubbornness, Mordeckai turned to prayer. He crossed himself, kneeled under Moisés' leg, and summoned his favorite saint. "Queen Esther, intercede. Protect your sons, the chuetas. Show my cousin the harm he will do if he hurts one of your own."

The fates were on Papa's side. The *palestino,* who had been seducing the wives of Papa's runners, was murdered by an angry husband. Papa had the body shipped to a Puerto Rican funeral parlor at his own expense. Then he summoned Mordeckai and his five boys.

"Children, the *norteamericanos* will mock us if I don't move fast. Moisés Guzmann does not allow cuckolds to do his work. If I couldn't slap Raphael while he was alive, we'll slap him dead."

Mordeckai mumbled something about the differences between

holy and unholy revenge, but he had to go along; to resist the family
that was housing him would have been an unconscionable act. At any
rate he was swept up to the doors of the funeral parlor by the strength
of Jorge and Alejandro's shoulders. Mordeckai removed his earmuffs
and his hat. Guzmanns poked everywhere; finding the correct chapel,
they interrupted services for Raphael. There was only a smattering of
people in this particular room; a *chueta* here and there, the wife of the
angry husband, the janitor of the chapel, and a priestlike man in
cassock and wool sweater. Papa approached the coffin. He raised the
palestino's head (it had been painted and waxed by a shrewd
undertaker so that Raphael could hold half of a smile), kissed the
eyes, mourned the loss of a cousin with two ear-splitting wails, and
slapped both cheeks. Jorge, Alejandro, Topal, César, and Jerónimo
followed the same procedure, their wails as loud as Papa's.
Mordeckai was crying when he reached the bier; the *palestino's* face
was discolored from all the slaps, and one cheek had already
dropped. "Adonai, forgive me for desecrating one of your angels. I
promise to learn your laws. I will pray harder and longer at the next
Queen Esther."

He slapped.

Mordeckai's fingers came up powdered blue; the cheek (the
undropped one) wobbled from the force of his hand. He ran out of the
chapel.

"Papa," Alejandro whispered, "should I bring him back?"

"Leave him alone," Papa growled.

By the time Papa and the boys returned to the candy store,
Mordeckai was in his madras shirt. He begged Papa to release him
from his obligations to the Bronx. Papa couldn't force a cousin to
stay; such a prayerful man was unsuited for Boston Road. He kissed
Mordeckai on the forehead. Mordeckai thanked the boys for
tolerating him in their beds, and he got on a Mexican freighter with
earmuffs in his pocket.

PART TWO

NINE

The occasionals, the once-a-weekers at Schiller's ping-pong club were amused by the cop who wore his badge and his gun to play. They enjoyed the sight of a holster on blue shorts. And they took bets among themselves, gentlemen's bets, nothing over a penny or half a cigarette, that the cop couldn't smash the ball in his artillery. Schiller disapproved of these bets. He didn't want his club to deteriorate into a circus. So he kept the once-a-weekers away from Coen. But he wasn't a hypocrite. Not even Schiller could ignore the peculiar bite to Coen's uniform: the yellow head-band, the wriststraps, the Police Special, the blue jersey and shorts, the gold shield, and the Moroccan sneakers gave Coen the aura of a man with formidable concentration, a craziness for ping-pong.

It was Chino who forced the gun on Coen. With the Chinaman on the loose, marauding taxicabs, abusing Coen's name in the Second Detective District, shadowing him later in a red wig, he couldn't afford to walk into Schiller's without a gun. First Schiller himself or Spanish Arnold held the holster, and Coen played at the end table, where he commanded a view of all the exits. But it upset him to have Schiller and Arnold become his watchdogs. Why should they be burdened with sticking his gun in the Chinaman's face? So Coen put the holster on. And because he was self-conscious in gym shorts, and he wanted to be sure no newcomer mistook him for a Columbus Avenue hood, he also wore the shield. Schiller seemed to have two minds about the whole thing. Although he hated the idea of firearms in his club (he was a pacifist vegetarian Austrian Jew), he felt much safer with Coen inside. None of the punks from middle Broadway would dare come down and disturb his benches, his tables, and his coffee pot.

After Mexico Coen stopped worrying about Chino Reyes but he forgot to change his uniform. The gun became a habit. He needed the weight at his hip to make his best shots. And he would rub the badge whenever he missed an easy return or couldn't cross over to his

forehand fast enough. He was playing regularly again, six times a
week. He had imposed a vacation on himself. He delivered the girl to
Pimloe's chauffeur instead of Child (Isaac taught him years ago how
to stroke the egos of his superiors), but Coen hadn't reported to his
division yet. He was tired of poking around in the field. So he washed
his headband periodically and hit the balls at Schiller's with his Mark
V.

   Coen had played ping-pong in Loch Sheldrake with the
Guzmann boys at ten, eleven, and twelve. He was lord of the country
tables, beating farmers, bread deliverers, bungalow colony men,
Jorge, César, and Jerónimo with a borrowed sandpaper racket or
César's fancier pimple rubber bat. Nobody could cope with his bullet
serves and his awkward but deadly scrape shots off the sandpaper. An
outdoor player he could push the ball into the breeze and make it die
on your side of the net. The Guzmanns would grit their teeth and
swear that Manfred was fucking with the wind. Jerónimo only played
with him on the sunnier days. César learned to cash in. He taunted the
farmers and bungalow men and offered them five to twelve points
with Coen, depending on their ability and Coen's moods. Before
Coen was thirteen his father stopped sending Sheb, his mother, and
him to the Guzmanns' summer farm. He forgot ping-pong and
concentrated on a portfolio for Music and Art, sketching Jerónimo in
charcoal and also his father's eggs. During the following summer he
minded the store with Sheb and thought about the Loch Sheldrake
scarecrow. He was eight weeks into Music and Art when César came
home from the farm. Estranged from the Guzmanns for half the year
(Papa pulled César out of school in May and didn't return him until
October), Coen walked Boston Road with an M&A decal (maroon
and blue) on his shirt and stayed clear of Papa's store.

   After his wife went to marry dentist Charles, Coen wandered
into Schiller's. In his dark square coat and high trouser cuffs Coen
was unmistakably a cop. But Schiller took him in. He respected the
primitiveness of Coen's needs. Gold shield or no, nothing but a
lonely man would gravitate toward a ping-pong club. Schiller had a
theory. Ping-pong was a "heimische" game. It encouraged gentleness
and other virtues. So he put a racket in Coen's hand, sponge and soft
rubber, his best, a Mark V. And Coen played. With Schiller himself.
He had never touched a bat like this one. The ball sank into the
sponge and hopped off in crazy directions. He couldn't hear the
familiar *pok* of hard rubber or the shriller sound of sandpaper. The

ball seemed to moan against the sponge and make a squish. And soon he couldn't live without this noise. Playing indoors, without the benefit of wind or sun in your eyes, he had to give up his old sharpster's habits and learn to temper the racket's wicked pull. Schiller could fake him out with soft low cuts that Coen couldn't push over the net. Schiller refused to pamper him. Coen glowered for a week. Then he watched the flight of the ball. His lunges were helping Schiller, not him. By getting his racket under the ball without slapping or turning his wrist he could break Schiller's spin and lob the ball over the net. He developed a serious counterspin. He returned Schiller's forehand drives. Standing close to the table he took Schiller's balls right off the hop and fed them into the corners, sending poor Schiller on a dizzy run. "Emmanuel, where was all the sponge when I was a kid?" Coen said, swabbing the Mark V with a paper towel. "It wasn't fair to make me play with sandpaper. I could have been a phenomenon with the sponge, a five-star player."

"Sure," Schiller said, cutting into Coen's euphoria. "They didn't have soft bats then in the United States. We caught the habit from the Japanese. We gave them a taste of the atomic bomb, they gave us the sandwich bat. Which is the rottener weapon, I can't say."

With Schiller exhausted and a little chagrined by a pupil who could outgun him so fast, Coen proceeded to the bottom layer of regulars at the club, those ping-pong freaks who had been suckled on hard rubber and were reluctant converts to sponge. Coen embarrassed them with his drop shots and the variety of his spins. He found his mettle among the middle range of freaks, winning, losing, discussing the properties of the various rubber sandwiches and wooden grips. But the ultimate players, the superfreaks who changed rubber the minute a splinter appeared, who used only balls from the China mainland, and practiced their strokes on empty tables, were in a different hemisphere from Coen. They were the ones who could loop the ball, slide it off the face of their bats with a pure upward thrust, so that it formed two perfect camel humps coming over the table and bounced into your fist or bobbled off your rubber. Schiller made his living off these superfreaks but he didn't enjoy their company. They were bitchy and aloof, condescending to weaker players, and jealous of one another's strokes. Schiller gave them the two front tables and wouldn't let them near his coffee pot. They were more familiar with Coen than with the other, lesser freaks on account of his detective shield but none of them showed him how to loop. And whenever three or four of them got together they sniggered privately at his uniform and they asked themselves where the detectives could be with Coen on board.

He played so often now and with such concentration that he kept scraping the bat against the side of the table; pieces of rubber chipped off near the handle. Coen treated the bald spots on the edges of the sponge with red nail polish, which prevented further wounds, but he would have to peel the rubber off pretty soon and buy a new sandwich kit. He resented the delicacy of the bat, its profoundly short life, and he told Schiller so. "Then play with the pimples," Schiller said, and Coen shut up. Looking over the span of tables he saw Vander Child coming toward him, in sneakers and duck pants, with a tote bag under his arm. "Buenos días," Child said, aping Coen's bit of Mexico. Schiller disliked him from the start; only an unprincipled man would arrive for ping-pong in a pair of white pants. And he went to his cubbyhole behind the tables to bake an asparagus pie. Schiller's coolness sobered Child. "I'm sorry. You wouldn't drop over. And I wanted to thank you . . . so I thought we could hit a few. Okay? I didn't mean to occupy your territory. Should I go?"

"Let's hit," Coen said, and Child unwrapped his Butterfly.

"I picked a boarding school for Caroline in Vermont. She won't run far. She'll have great stories to tell the girls. I doubt that any of them ever set up house-keeping in Mexico City. Manfred, I'm grateful to you. Without you Pimloe would still be smelling the ground."

"I'm not so sure," Coen said, delivering a lob serve that caught Child with his feet pointing away from the ball. He congratulated Coen.

"You've gotten sneakier since we played in my den."

"It's not me," Coen said. "It's the bat." And he dropped a serve into the other corner. Child made a clumsy swipe, the Butterfly like a claw in his hand, and the ball slapped his knuckles. Coen didn't appreciate Child's bearishness. He knew the margin his serves ought to bring. They shouldn't have given Child that much trouble. The next time he put nothing on the ball. It drew knuckles again. He pushed two more serves past Child and lost all interest in him.

"I don't forget the man who does me a favor. I told Pimloe exactly how I feel. I said, "You're underplaying this Coen. He belongs higher up." Manfred, you can't be that far from retirement. If the bastards manhandle you, you can always come to me."

"Hit the ball, Mr. Child."

Child wooed Coen between serves. "I wouldn't be stingy with a man of your scope. You could keep Caroline out of the potholes, away from the bog. Are you listening, Manfred?"

"You don't owe me, Mr. Child. You owe César Guzmann. He found your daughter, him and a taxi jumper named Chino Reyes. I was in the middle, that's all."

"Tush," Child said. "Carrie wouldn't have come home with those palookas. It had to be you." Coen stopped counting points.

"She wasn't too anxious to come. The Chinaman persuaded her. What's going on between you and Guzmann, Mr. Child? I'm not crazy about monkeyshines. You swore to me you never heard of César."

"Business ethics, Manfred. Nothing more. I don't like to mention a rival. Especially when he's such a pest. Besides, there's no harm done. Carrie's back, and you're in the thick with Inspector Pimloe. He's your rabbi. Isn't that what they call it in the stationhouse? Somebody to snatch you up."

"My rabbi's gone," Coen said. "He's fishing in the Bronx."

Unable to budge Coen, to align him properly and sweep him under his cuff, he picked right now to mention the badge and the gun. "Trussed up today, aren't you, Manfred?" Coen still refused to perform for Child.

"Force of habit," he said. "I can't even piss with my holster off."

Child couldn't reach such a dumb cop. He was ready to slap Coen with the Butterfly, bite him in ping-pong, jerk him from corner to corner, punish him for being intransigent, for not realizing he had missed his chance with Vander Child, but Coen put no energy into his returns, and Child couldn't play off a dead bat. So the ball moved between them in a dull floating line that wouldn't vary. Stubborn, they hid their resentment behind a series of prettier and prettier shots. They swayed on either hip, tossed their shoulders in a perfect arc, and huffed politely without affecting the line of the ball. Spanish Arnold thought two *maniacos* were at the table. He didn't like to interrupt Coen's ping-pong matches but his face was growing chalky from watching the ball, and the First Deputy's man wanted Coen. He twiddled a finger at Coen's eye. He mimicked the chauffeur's Neanderthal slouch. He spit into his hands. Coen wouldn't look at him. Arnold mumbled "Crazy." The *maniaco* would go on slapping the ball unless Schiller took the table down. Arnold resorted to sneakiness. At Child's next return he jumped out to whisper to Coen. "Brodsky's waiting for you."

The ball crossed the net twice before Coen said, "Shit."

"Manfred, he's outside."

Coen entrusted his bat to Arnold, made apologies to Child, and passed Schiller's cubbyhole on the way out. The chauffeur cursed him and belittled his ping-pong clothes. "If you're going to live in a cave, couldn't you call in? Pimloe wants you. Come on."

Coen expected Pimloe's downtown dungeon but Brodsky took him to a supermarket in Washington Heights. Pimloe tightened around the mouth when he saw Coen. Then he turned on Brodsky. "Couldn't you bring him in something decent? Lend him your coat, for Christ's sake." Coen smiled at the groceries in Pimloe's cart; jumbo-sized boxes of farina, different toothpastes, grapefruit sacks piled high to keep him out of sight. Serving with Isaac had crippled his Harvard upbringing, and he couldn't talk without Isaac's mannerisms and Isaac's slurs. "Coen, you've been on tit jobs too long. I'm taking you off the tit. Cooperate, or you'll be watching nigger eyes on Bushwick Avenue."

"You'd be doing me a favor. They hate my guts at the Second Division. They think I'm your private rat."

"Just mind my store, Coen, and you won't have to catch homicides with those gloms from the Second."

"Herbert, who are you going to make me tickle?"

"Nobody. I want you to stay close to César and all the Guzmanns."

"Brodsky," Coen said. "Tell him he's a funny man."

"Manfred, he knows you grew up with the tribe. He's not asking you to bury them, only sit with them a while."

"I suppose César's going to kiss me and give me the lists of the whorehouse chain he intends to open. Maybe I can nail chickens and dicemen for you."

"They're not into whorehouses," Pimloe said. "They're into something else. Anyway, you don't owe them."

"Herbert, why are you so sure?"

"They killed your mom and dad."

The holes in the grapefruit sacks twitched green for Coen. He was calm otherwise. The farina labels remained perfectly clear.

Pimloe stayed behind the cart; even before his own ascendancy he had questioned Coen's worth to the department, this boy with the beautiful cheeks who could play a woman or a man with equal facility but had a cold, hard nature and a thick skull, and an utter disregard for concepts. So he turned away and let the chauffeur have Coen.

"Manfred, the Inspector's right. The supermarkets murdered the little stores. Your dad took bread from the Guzmanns to keep alive, and when you went into the service, when you wore the uniform, mind you, and saved Papa's Bronx from the Reds, Guzmann put the bite on your dad, made unreasonable demands, wanted his money back in one small bundle, and your dad lit the oven rather than face the thought of losing his store."

Coen pushed the farina boxes out from in front of Pimloe's head. "Who told you?"

Pimloe tried to wheel the cart into another aisle but Coen stuck a foot in his path. "Who told you?"

The chauffeur answered, "Isaac."

Pimloe clamped his teeth. "I swear. It was Isaac." He was afraid for his life. Bare knees and a blue jersey might be contemptible on a bull in a supermarket, only Coen was the one with the gun.

"Manfred," the chauffeur said. "We knew it for years. About your father and the Guzmanns."

Coen's legs were chilled. The refrigerated air ate underneath his woolen socks and stormed on his ankles. He had to speak low. "Brodsky, take me to Schiller's."

Brodsky looked to Pimloe.

"Take him," Pimloe said. "Then come back for me." With Coen in a stupor, Pimloe could afford some charity. He upended the farina boxes and refurbished his plans for Coen. "Remember, Coen, remember, pull on César's tail." Secured behind the cart he could squall again. "Brodsky, reassure him. Tell him I'm not his enemy. Tell him we want the same things. Guzmann in the can."

Brodsky got him to the car. Coen rubbed the chill off his ankles. He removed wriststraps and sweatbands and stuffed them in his pocket. Brodsky wasn't sure where the recriminations would fall. He braced his shoulders and his neck.

"Manfred, I know it's shitty telling you now, but the Inspector needed the leverage. He doesn't have Isaac's charm. Manfred, it was my idea to hook you into this. Forget the whores. César's running a goddamn marriage bureau, a lonelyhearts club for middle-class Mexicos. He'll supply you with all the bribes you want. The package comes guaranteed. If you don't like her, he changes brides. How he smuggles them in is nobody's business. Where he gets the raw material, that's what I'd like to know. He specializes in young stuff."

"Port Authority," Coen volunteered.

"What?"

But he wouldn't open his mouth until the chauffeur dropped him on Schiller's basement steps. "Pimloe blows his nose too hard. Isaac could have stopped any lonelyhearts club in a week. They nab stray girls outside the bus terminal. That's the central chicken coop. Now you tell me what's in Pimloe's head. Why does he want to hurt Jerónimo?"

The chauffeur shrugged. "Who's Jerónimo?"

Coen followed him up the street kicking fenders on the First Deputy's car.

"Manfred, stop, please . . . I can't tell you about Jerónimo."

The fruit sellers along Columbus were fond of Coen. They waved to him while he kicked.

"Manfred, I never talked to Jerónimo in my life. Ask Pimloe yourself. Pimloe wouldn't lie."

He walked into Schiller's. Arnold was still at Coen's table with Vander Child. They saw the pale markings on Coen's cheeks, the swollen blue under his eyes. "Manfred, what's wrong?" Alone with Arnold, Child learned to appreciate Coen's habitat. He didn't say one smug word about the knotted rag Arnold wore on his foot. (The Spic wouldn't suffer the indignity of being fitted for another orthopedic shoe; he was waiting long enough for Coen to win his old shoe from Chino Reyes.) And Child was startled by the devotion Coen could command from a gimp. "Manfred, what's wrong?"

"I'm tired, Arnold. I'll rest in Schiller's room."

Child wrapped his Butterfly. "Manfred, I hoped we could settle all the mysteries . . . play a decent game . . . no phony spins, carnival shots . . . without this César fellow."

"Later, Mr. Child. Maybe later."

He bundled up his tote bag and walked out in white ducks. Schiller wouldn't say goodbye. Arnold found pillows for Coen.

With Coen wiped out, retiring to Schiller's tiny room in gym pants, Arnold went upstairs to the singles hotel. He had some trouble on Schiller's step because he needed to clutch the banister with two hands and hop with his bad foot in the air; the rags on his foot unwound, and Arnold had to make another temporary shoe with old newsprint and string from Schiller's cellar. He hobbled this way to the second story of the hotel, dogs and babies in the shit-mobbed hall admiring his paper boot. The SROs knew Arnold was a common snitch, a stoolie for Coen; he enjoyed a certain prestige nevertheless, on account of his handcuffs and the expired Detectives Endowment card (Coen's) he carried in his wallet.

Arnold was the hotel's unpaid sheriff. He policed the halls, keeping out the junkmen from other singles hotels, guaranteeing the safety of prostitutes inside and outside their rooms, returning stolen food stamps and welfare checks to gentlemen retirees who were vulnerable to the more ambitious young dudes at the hotel. The Spic had no power other than the visibility of his handcuffs. Any of the dudes could have broken his feet, the good one and the bad, but they were conscious of how Arnold acquired the handcuffs, and they didn't want to mess with Coen. They had heard of "the Isaac machine" at the First Deputy's office, men with eyes bluer than Coen's, who could pop your nose with a thumb and shoot notches in your ear with a Detective special. Still, Arnold was hindered in his work by the loss of his shoe.

He visited the winos who congregated on the landings with their bottles of Swiss-Up. He cautioned them to remove empty bottles from the stairs.

"Amigos, you'll cripple the dogs with that glass. You can thank Jesus no kid has swallowed a jug handle yet."

The oldest wino, Piss, an ex-vaudevillian who had crimps in his skull from all the headstands he had performed on stage, talked back to the Spic. "Spanish, we don't need advice from a man what can't hold on to his shoe." He rallied the other winos, getting them to surround Arnold and push him into the wall. "Some tribute, Spanish. Pay us now, or you'll go down the flights head first."

Arnold didn't shake against the wall; he'd outfoxed these winos before. He had to learn their qualities, or he couldn't have survived as sheriff.

"Piss, I'll come back dead and climb up your shoulder. I'll take blood out of your neck. I'll turn your eyeballs white."

Piss released the winos from their obligations to him; he wouldn't accept tribute from a ghoul.

Arnold went into Betty, the pros who lived next door to him. She usually shopped for the Spic, claiming him as a husband on the government papers she signed; she couldn't qualify for food stamps unless she had the semblance of a family.

"Arnold, there was a run on brown eggs this morning. I bought us three dozen."

"Betty, you know eggs give me a rash if I have more than one a week."

"Honey, that's all right. They'll last."

Arnold carried his share of the eggs to Rebecca and George, an old couple who had to live across the hall from each other since the hotel rules stipulated that there could only be one occupant to a room. George might have gotten around this "single body" rule if he'd had enough cash to bribe the security guard. Babies were also "illegal" here, but the hotel was packed with unwed mothers, each of whom paid Alfred (the security guard) a dollar a week for the rights to her child. The same dollar could be applied to any man or woman with a dog. But Alfred canceled such privileges if a dog yapped at his hand or shit under his chair.

To offset Alfred, the Spic put a couch in the hall for Rebecca and George. The couple spent most of their time on this couch, leaving it only to boil an egg or comply with the midnight curfew. They thanked Arnold for the eggs. He couldn't chat with them. He had his chores to do.

He passed the group of unemployed actors (men without jobs for fifteen years), who played Monopoly with matchsticks and odd buttons which Arnold supplied as best he could. He was without buttons today. "Amigos, you'll have to wait. Schiller downstairs promised me a fresh batch. Adios." He signed compensation forms for Cookie, the blindman in 305. He fed Miss Watson's baby, Delilah, a girl of two. He was saving the dollmaker for last.

Ernesto had arranged puppet shows for the sons and daughters of a sugarcane magnate in Santiago de Cuba. He couldn't find work in the United States. The *norteamericanos* had no love for Ernesto's dolls; they were creatures with big hands and bulbish leering faces; some of them wore tails. The *cubano* wouldn't name his dolls. He couldn't alter their costumes if they had fixed personalities. He owned an assortment of lipsticks and rouge, which he would smear on the dolls, then wipe off. Arnold pitied Ernesto's unemployability; the *cubano* was lacking in friends at the hotel. He spit on the dogs, whom he believed were conspiring to chew his dolls. He wouldn't gossip with prostitutes, winos, or unwed mothers. Occasionally he prowled the streets, returning to the hotel with tar on his sleeves or mud in a shoe. The *cubano* had picked up scraps of English from the children of the sugarcane man, but he wouldn't speak this language inside the hotel. He was intolerant of Puerto Ricans. He gave the Spic a hard time. Arnold could ignore the *cubano's* irritable looks. He brought Ernesto gumdrops and Spanish comic books; mostly he came to visit the dolls.

He took pleasure in the lines Ernesto used to articulate a knuckle; these joints were frighteningly real to the Spic. He couldn't afford to settle too long on any doll's face. The face might disappear by the next visit, and show up in Arnold's sleep. He picked out isolated features, rouge on a flat nose, burrs over an eye, then progressed to a new doll. Arnold swore that he had seen identical dolls as a boy, during witching ceremonies outside San Juan. He stayed with Ernesto five minutes, no more.

The security guard accosted him in the hall. He held his billy club high, and wouldn't let Arnold go around his chair. He sat under a lightbulb wearing shades.

"Brother, you owe me a piece. You been collecting from dudes on every floor. The blindman give you a quarter for copying his signature. How much you gross pimping for Betty?"

"Alfred, look again. You're mistaking me for one of your dollar-a-week customers. I'm not hiding babies in my pants."

Arnold might have been harsher with the man, but he didn't have a lease, and Alfred was in direct communication with the owners of the hotel.

"You're my competition, Spic. This place can't hold two sheriffs. Watch yourself on the steps, hear? I'd have to write me a report if somebody put a stick up your ass and sent you to China."

"I'm grateful for your worrying, Alfred. A First Deputy man's coming tomorrow to investigate the dude that's been selling rotgut wine mixed with wood alcohol."

Alfred's rump crept along the seat of his chair, the billy going slack in his hand.

"There's a badge in my pocket. I ain't afraid of no supercop."

Arnold took advantage of this lapse to hobble over the billy club before he could be tripped. Alfred lunged for the handcuffs. Arnold reached his room. The newsprint on his foot was shredded in spots from the amount of dragging he had done. He took more socks out of his closet (donations from Betty), and made another temporary shoe.

TEN

He couldn't fall asleep in Schiller's back room. It wasn't the odor of asparagus that kept him up. Coen had snored through other bakings and fries. Arnold had once shown him the way to exorcise an enemy by spitting on a wall until your lungs pounded and your face went dark, and Coen might have tried some of this, but he didn't have murderous feelings today. The Guzmanns weren't on his mind. He was thinking about uncle Sheb, and a question that had been nagging him these thirteen years. How come Shebby stayed alive? Coen understood his father's narrow logic. Albert wasn't a neglectful brother. Whatever his madness, no matter how many Guzmanns plagued him or the number of eggs he stood to lose, he wouldn't have gone through the trouble of getting out of this world and not take Sheb along. The Coens were fastidious people. They went into the oven with starch on their clothes. What did Shebby put on when he climbed out the fire escape to sing Albert's (and Jessica's) death? A neighborwoman found him in Albert's old smock, store clothes, with bloodclots on the sleeves and the smell of eggs. Jessica wouldn't have tolerated such a garment inside her house. She was in charge of grooming Sheb, plucking ratty scarves and underpants out of his wardrobe, so he could smile at widows and stray wives. Albert and Jessica didn't throw Sheb at the customers. Uncle's successes came on his own. But they wanted to drape his odd behaviour, to remind Boston Road how handsome Sheb could be, even if he stopped and made bubbles with his teeth. And what about an uncle deprived of Albert's eggs? Avoiding the oven didn't cost Sheb. Coen grew permanent lines, scatter marks, along his cheeks, his knuckles ached in rotten weather, his blondness was dulling fast, but Sheb hadn't aged in thirteen years.

Should he dispatch himself to the rest home and question uncle Sheb? He couldn't go. Try Isaac's techniques on his uncle? Quiz him? Bully him? Make him cry? What could Shebby say about money matters? Albert never trusted him with anything over a dollar. And Sheb couldn't have gotten between Albert and Papa Guzmann. There were certain chivalries on Boston Road. Papa, who raised Jerónimo by himself and knew what it meant to have a slowwitted boy, wouldn't have used Sheb to frighten Albert out of his egg store.

Coen had no inclination to ride into the Bronx and settle on Papa's door. What would the Guzmanns admit to him now? He changed into street clothes, finished with his nap. He would go Isaac's way, roundabout.

Observing Coen's concentration marks, Arnold didn't bother to wave. He had his feelers on Coen; the cop was into something personal. And Coen took the No. 10 bus down to this girls' bar, The Dwarf, to wake Odile. He couldn't say why. Maybe he was in a downtown mood, and he thought he could find César under Odile's skirts and get to Papa from there. Or maybe he was hungry to see girls dance. But this time Coen wasn't working for the First Deputy in drag. And the bulldikes at the door, huskier than him and with wider shoulders, peered down to scorn at his maleness and ask him for his membership card.

"I'm a guest," Coen muttered into the piping on their double-breasted suits.

The girls, cousins Janice and Sweeney, weren't fooled by any Coen. "Who would invite a thing like you?"

"Odette. Odette Leonhardy," Coen said, recalling Odile's professional name.

But the cousins still wouldn't buy him. "Odile knows the rules. She isn't supposed to solicit in here."

Coen was going to test his stamina against the girls on stiff ping-pong knees when Odile poked her nose through the curtain. She recognized Coen, and she tried to soothe the cousins. "Sweeney, this one's mine. Belongs to my uncle Vander. He's a regular firecracker. He pulls girls out of Argentina. He takes starlets to the movies. He's a very particular cop."

The cousins divided on Coen. Sweeney would have taken him in if he promised not to dance with Odile, but Janice, with all her seniority at The Dwarf, refused to have him around. So Odile took him to Jane Street. They sat in her room-and-a-half, Odile in plain cotton, a highcheeked girl with gorgeous fingers and a sturdy profile, and she asked him what he wanted of her. "Straight talk," he said.

"Oh, the ambitious little cop. First we have some breast beating, confessions from Odette, then a seduction number, with your pants on my chair. Mister, I'm not so crazy about men this season."

"Don't tense up on account of me, Odette. I'm not much with the girls any more. I get most of it off on the ping-pong table."

"Odile," she said. "I'm Odile. Odette is for the hard-ons. I remember the ping-pong. You played Vander with your tie off. Why'd you come?"

"Because I'm getting bullshit in both ears, and maybe the same people who are fucking my brain are also fucking yours."

She decided he was no great shakes of a cop, and she warmed to him considerably. She mashed two lemons and made him a hot buttered drink in a tall glass. She opened her icebox for him, spared him the canapés of luncheon meats and triangular party breads, which she served to male clients and Vander's friends, and fixed him one huge, unnatural pancake with primitive utensils and her own private awkwardness. It was the pancake, filled with egg fluff and clotted bits of sugar, that galvanized Coen's affections, fastened him to Odile. He would have a hard time questioning her now. And Odile, used to acrobats on a couch as the nimble Odette, playing nymph for uncle Vander's movie company since her sophomore years at high school, smearing herself with jelly in front of Child's cameramen and grips, felt nervous with this Coen. He wouldn't leer at her, wink, or force her to sniff his cologne. He wouldn't say *baby* and lick around with his tongue like the other cops she had known. She couldn't figure out such a serious man. She fed him one more pancake. Her arm was sore from shaking the pan. She wanted to tell him off, advise him to scratch elsewhere. He had a vein under his eye with the thickness of a scar. The vein splintered on his cheek, spilled sudden blue lines. She wished she could blanket him, put him to sleep, and measure the splits on the side of his face. She wouldn't have dared touch an unsleepy Coen. He was even prettier with an open mouth.

"Odile, do you work for Vander or César Guzmann?"

"Both."

The vein twitched on his cheek like a finger stuck under skin. She didn't know what to say. But she'd go on deviling him like this if she could make more veins come out. "César was my boyfriend for a while."

"How did you meet him?"

"Through uncle Vander."

"Bastards," Coen said, his face dug with blue. "What have they pulled you into, Odile?"

"Cat films," she said. "Uncle's the producer, César's the distributor, and I'm one of the stars." Weary of her own confessions, she got kittenish with him. "You saw uncle's studio, Mr. Coen?"

"Where?"

"His ping-pong room. The table's just for fun. The lights are in the closet."

"It figures," Coen said. "What about César's marriage bureau?"

"Oh that." Odile puffed disapprovals through her nose. "The bride shit, you mean. The little novias."

"How did they get the brides into Mexico? César's too hairy-looking to do it himself. And his trigger, Chino Reyes, isn't much of a chaperon."

"Vander flew with them. Sixteen to a plane. He dressed them in schoolgirl clothes. Pretended he was on an archaeological trip. Taking young ladies to the pyramids. A Jewish man met them at the airport with the rings. César arranged for a cockeyed wedding ceremony."

"Mordeckai." Coen muttered. "The name of the marriage-broker is Mordeckai."

"César didn't say. Vander collected from the brid-grooms and took off. But he was getting into heavy stuff, and he wanted out."

"So César stole Caroline off Child to keep him in line."

"No. That was my idea. César was doing me a favor. His Chinaman put her on a plane."

"You sold Carrie to the Mexicans? Why?"

"It was only temporary. I had to move fast, Mr. Coen. She was getting itchy to be in her daddy's films. And Vander might have obliged her."

"Prick father," Coen said.

"Vander's not so bad. He spoiled Carrie and me. I'm the one seduced him, rubbed his nose in incest."

Coen sat on his fist, contemplating in a green shirt. His father and mother may have been oven-minded, his uncle might hold secrets under a dirty smock, but the Coens had simpler ways than the Childs. "Odile, if your Uncle Vander's involved up to the tit in César's marriage bureau, why does he pal around with police inspectors?"

"Because he wants to preserve his own skin when it's time for César to get squeezed."

"Is Vander working for Inspector Pimloe?"

"Not Pimloe. There was a second man."

"Isaac?" Coen said. "Chief Isaac Sidel? A short man with sideburns."

"I don't know."

Coen slumped in Odile's long chair, his nostrils wide with

frustration, and Odile risked a touch on the face before he had the chance to recover. With fingers on his cheek she expected him to cry something and push over the chair. He didn't move. She followed the curve of his eyebrow, tracked him from his ear to his lip, thinking love bumps, a cop with a sinuous face. And Coen let her explore. He had never been so passive under the sway of a finger. He felt like some grateful old dog. Seeing she could have her way with him, she got reckless and bit all the furrows in his cheek. They sank into the chair nuzzling hard. They swam in pieces of underwear. Having her fornications mostly in the studio, with cameras grinding in her ear, she was suspicious of foreplay. So she took a prophylactic out of a box and told Coen to put it on. The cold skin gave him the twitters. Both of them struggled to fit Coen. He hadn't worn a rubber in eighteen years, not since his last fumblings as a senior at Music and Art. "Stupid scumbag," he said. And Odile, who was nonchalant about her acting career and swore she couldn't feel a man inside her (none of her girlfriends at The Dwarf had ever been below her waist), quivered and felt thumbs in her belly when Coen had his climax and dropped spit on her neck. She didn't know what to do about his shriek. Her studio lovers had grunted once and climbed off. "Coen," she said. "I lied to you before. César isn't anything to me. The Chinaman asked me to be his old lady. I said no. César warned him not to sniff."

She found her pants in Coen's pile. She dressed before he did. Odile didn't appreciate nakedness out of bed. She accepted occasional clients from César, setting a half-hour limit (Odile supplied the prophylactics, party bread, and cordials), but she hadn't spent the night with any of these men, and she wouldn't break a habit for Coen. She slept with a furry animal, an old bear from Vander, with shallow paws and buttons for eyes, Odile in simple headdress (she hated sun on her face) and two full gowns. She scratched around on the chair, having no idea how to kick Coen out. She pulled her mouth into a yawn. He wouldn't leave.

"César wants to keep me single," she said, pouting hard. "He looks after my interests."

Coen fiddled with his shoe, digging for the tongue. "Odile, does César ever mention me?"

"Hardly ever."

"Did you meet Papa Guzmann?"

"Once or twice."

"What about Jerónimo?"

"The baby? He stayed here a week. The Chinaman got him into Mexico with Caroline. She fixed his menu on the plane. Ordered extra sodas for him."

"Did you hear the name Albert from Papa or César? Albert and Jessica?"

"No. But Jerónimo said, 'Sheb Coen, Sheb Coen.'"

"What else, Odile? Please."

"I can't remember. Something about a head in the fire."

His crumpled cheek aggravated Odile again, and she took him into her bed. Coen stared at the wall. Sheb got out of the fire. Did Jerónimo find him, bring him to the candy store? Did the Guzmanns undress him, hide his Sunday clothes, sneak him back upstairs in rags, point him to the fire escape so he could sing his death songs for Boston Road? Odile had to duck her head under his armpit to find a piece of Coen. She couldn't get comfortable with so contrary a man. She slept against a shoulderblade, listening to the beat of Coen's ribs. She longed for the bear.

Sweeney, the number-two bouncer, lived over a dress factory in SoHo (off Broome Street), when she wasn't on call at The Dwarf. She had three miserably lit rooms with the feel of a rabbit hutch; tiny, thinwalled, with crooked floors and low, low ceilings. Hot air from the pressing machines downstairs smoked through the walls and warped Sweeney's woodwork. Short of labor, the factory employed retarded girls bussed into SoHo from an institution near White Plains. The girls wore blue cotton uniforms and highbacked shoes in neutral brown; they hunched over their sewing machines like monkeys with mottled blue skin. Sweeney fell for these girls, and she would sit with them in a Greene Street luncheonette during the half hour they were free, telling them stories about the iron buildings of SoHo, and the rats who lived in the buildings and could take metal into their systems until they died from the rust that clogged their ears. Sweeney had to tolerate the mistress of the girls, a contemptuous woman who interrupted the stories to frown at her and drive the girls out of the luncheonette and into the factory. Otherwise Sweeney existed at The Dwarf.

She was in love with Odile. The bartendresses knew this. Girls who danced regularly at The Dwarf would laugh into the sleeves of their denim shirts watching Sweeney moon over Odile. Sweeney had

a seriousness about her that Odile's partners couldn't understand. She
didn't clutch Odile's bosoms in the back room, like Dorotea, like
Nicole, or nip Odile behind the ear, like Mauricette. Nicole and
Mauricette came to The Dwarf to taste Odile, not to goggle. They
would pair off with fresh "sisters" if Odile wasn't around. Dorotea
had more of a devotion to Odile, but even Dorotea grew weary of
Odile's fixation on men. It was Sweeney who endured Odile's
wavering attitudes, her defilement with male customers, her reticence
at The Dwarf. Odile was still "chicken bait" to all the sisters. Those
swiny men didn't count. Odile might perform for a swat of little
gangsters from the Bronx, but she hadn't slept with Dorotea, Nicole,
or Mauricette. The sisters were more careful than Sweeney. They
could worship Odile, but they kept girlfriends on the side.

She was born Abigail, Abigail Ruth McBean, and she remained
Abigail until her eleventh year, when she took the name Sweeney
from a tavern in Providence, Rhode Island, where her father worked
and played the pianola; none of the regulars at The Dwarf came from
Manhattan, except for Odile. Her cousin Janice was a refugee from
Montauk; Nicole and Mauricette were Connecticut girls. Sweeney
would be thirty in a month. She meant to celebrate her birthday with
a present for Odile. But she anticipated certain difficulties. Odile
wouldn't wear clothes from Spike's or one of the huskier leather
shops. Sweeney would have to go to Bergdorf's or Henri Bendel,
where the sales-people were too high-minded to be simple cashiers,
and they would only handle your money long enough to stick it in a
wire cage for some invisible teller (checks were better than cash at
Henri Bendel's). The store frightened Sweeney, who seldom went up
to Fifty-seventh Street. She would have to enter Bendel's in an Army
field jacket, the cold weather type that could button around your ears;
this was the one coat she had (unless she borrowed Janice's
chesterfield).

Wednesday being her night off, she brooded past four a.m.,
preparing herself for the trauma of uptown fashions. She had eighty
dollars to spend, the yearly dividend from a policy her father had
opened for her at the age of seven and wouldn't fully mature until
Sweeney was forty-five. The doorbell rang. She wanted no visitors to
clog her lines of thought. "Go away," she said. "Piss on someone
else's door. I'm through collecting for the March of Dimes. If you're
the Heart Association girl, I'm not here."

Sweeney was in her cups, the Irish coffee she'd drunk to keep her mind on Henri Bendel was causing her to hallucinate. She wouldn't go near the door.

Then she swiped at the knob, her confidence shot; she could recognize the squeaks of Odile. "Baby," she said, "why are you cruising so late?"

Odile knocked dust off the crepe rubber heels of her platform shoes. "Sweeney, there's a man in my house. A curly man."

"That cop you were with? That blond fish? Odile, you must be slumming tonight."

"Sweeney, he wouldn't go. The cop wouldn't go. He fell asleep on me. I couldn't breathe. I had to bypass Janice. You know the music she lays on us this time of night. Fox trots and Nicole's hands on my boobs. Not the state I'm in. I didn't even wash his smell off me. I came to you, Sweeney. I had nowhere else."

"You don't have to explain." And the image of Henri Bendel, wire cages bumping through the ceiling, stuffed with personal checks, disappeared for Sweeney. She could forget presents, figures on a policy, the dress factory underneath. "Baby, I'll make your bed."

She wouldn't allow Odile to sleep on the foldaway, a lousy kitchen bed with moldy springs and other works. Odile had to accept Sweeney's own "honeymoon" mattress with springbox and high wooden pegs. She was given cocoa to drive out the cop's taste. She wore Sweeney's corduroy pajamas. And Sweeney tolerated the kitchen bed like a happy dog. She turned off refrigerator drones, and the mousies in the wash-tub She would sweep up the pellets of mouseshit before Odile awoke. She wouldn't have to eat with retarded girls at the luncheonette. She would cook a SoHo breakfast, sausages and symmetrical pancakes in brown sugar syrup, for both of them. She would stay clear of white flour. She wouldn't feed Odile that luncheonette garbage with the papery flavor. She would squeeze the oranges with her own fist.

The springs of the foldaway clawed into her back. She felt a tug in her kidney. She would lie awake for the rest of the night thinking she had to pee. She'd had those spells before. If she sat on the pot, she wouldn't pass any water. And she might disturb Odile. She'd had too many fights at The Dwarf, too many cousins to confront, too many boisterous hens to throw out, too many drunkards with a hatred for women in a man's suit, too many blows to her groin, too many fingers in her eye. She prepared breakfasts in her head over and over again to numb that kidney until some light crept through the fractures in the kitchen blinds so she could begin to cook for Odile.

ELEVEN

Coen got up from a dreary sleep without Odile. She's fled to her club, he imagined, César's girl. She'd left him a bun on the table and a potful of smelly tea. Coen walked uptown, fire escapes in his head. Hearing his uncle's songs he went narrow in the chest and had to blow air on Sixth Avenue. He was so truculent at the crossings, other early morning walkers avoided his lanes. He marched into the park and arrived at Schiller's with gaunt markings on his face. These were the voodoo hours for Schiller, when most of the ping-pong freaks were in bed, and refugees from the game rooms of certain New York mental institutions would drift in with sandpaper rackets clutched in their hands and volley among themselves, aiming at one spot on the table with a precision that confounded Schiller and drove him into his cubbyhole. He had to close his eyes to them or give up being an entrepreneur. Having nowhere else to go, they played at Schiller's for free. But they weren't allowed near the end table, which served as a message board while Coen was away. Coen found a note stuck in the net; Arnold wanted him. So he went upstairs to the SROs. He climbed over mattresses in the hall. He intercepted an argument between an old wino with crooked lines in his scalp and one of the young bullies at the hotel, a stocky boy in a velveteen undershirt, a head taller than Coen. The boy was crowing for his admirers, who wore similar undershirts and urged him to slap the old man. "Piss," he said. "Pay me a dollar." With that first slap the old man's teeth jumped out of his head. Coen clawed the boy on his velveteen. "Lay off," the boy griped, stupified that any man small as Coen would dare finger him this way. But the boy had an instinctive feel for cops, even blond ones, and he preferred to disappoint his admirers rather than face up to Coen. "Mister, what's Piss to you?"

"He's my dad," Coen said. He liked the bumps along the wino's skull. Mindful of his benefactor, the old man scrounged on the stairs for his teeth. He was sure he could pluck a dollar out of Coen.

"Miserable," he said, smacking his gums. "I could get ham and cheese at the deli for a little cold cash."

And he walked on his hands near Coen, astounding the boys in velveteen with his system for producing hunger pains; he barked with his stomach while he groveled and slimed on his jaw.

These contortions sickened Coen. He abandoned the old man in the middle of his crawl. "Hey," Piss said, realizing he would be smothered in velveteen without Coen. "Don't leave me here." But Coen was only a step away from Arnold's room. He closed the door on Piss.

Arnold paraded his orthopedic shoe. He would have worshiped Coen if Coen had allowed it. "Manfred, you did it, you did it. You made him bring it back."

Coen stood against the door scrutinizing the polish on Arnold's fat shoe.

"Manfred, he was here, the Chinaman."

"When?"

"Maybe two hours ago. Lucky for him he wanted peace. I had my sword in the hamper."

"What did he say?"

"Look, he shined it himself. With an expensive cloth."

"Arnold, what did he say?"

"Nothing. A few crazy words. He smiles, he puts down the shoe, he says, 'Spic, tell Blue-eyes regards from César and me.'"

Coen already figured César had to be involved in the return of the shoe. The Chinaman didn't give up his trophies so easy. Coen understood the Guzmann way. Papa would hug you, feed you, open his farm and his candy store to you, lend you Jorge or Alejandro for the day, but he wasn't careless about any of his gifts. Perhaps the Marranos who had been shorn of their possessions in Portugal and Spain developed a residual language in the give and take of worldly goods. Coen couldn't tell. But if Papa gave you anything outside his own natural affection, there had to be malice in it. César was the same. Coen would have to determine what he had done to deserve the shoe. Had he corrupted Jerónimo inside the Alameda Park? Did he wrong Mordeckai? Odile? Odile must have squawked to César about his visit to Jane Street.

"Manfred, should I take off my shoe?"

"No," Coen said. "But don't give away your sword."

"Manfred, does the Chinaman still hate our guts?"

"Not so much. Maybe it's César Guzmann. Or his Papa. Or both."

They ate American cheese from Arnold's windowsill, Coen moistening the thick slices with some grape water that Arnold kept under the sink. Soon the blondo would fall into one of his silences, and Arnold would have to scour the room for specks of cheese. Spanish had his own ambitions. He didn't want to remain a simple police buff in a charity hotel for the rest of his life, chasing ping-pong balls and gobbling American cheese. Although he said nothing to Coen, Arnold admired the Chinaman's cool and the fringes on his bodyshirts. If he couldn't be a cop on account of his foot (he was also nearsighted and shorter than Coen), Arnold wouldn't mind serving César or another Guzmann. Like most buffs, he was wise to the special rhythm that always seemed to mark the seesaw dance between the cops in a neighborhood and all the crooks. He could no longer respond to ordinary citizens, the "civilianos" who frowned at the cops and isolated themselves from the punks and the SROs. Once he had come to love tending the squadroom cage, he couldn't sit on neutral ground. The civilianos were his enemy, and he either danced with the Guzmanns, the Chinaman, and the cops, or he danced alone.

Coen left him there with his knees out, dreaming the Chinaman's shirt. "Arnold, I'll catch you later. Goodbye."

He found the wino groaning on the stairs. The old man had new lumps along his scalp and red flecks in the slime on his jaw. But he wasn't disconsolate enough not to pose. He walked with his rump in the air, his arms around the railing. Deprived of an audience of velveteen boys, his shufflings seemed miserable to Coen. "Dollar for bandages and coffee," the wino said. Coen gave him the dollar and put his rump where it belonged, on the stairs. He panicked outside the hotel, blamed himself for the death of his mother and father. He had abandoned Albert and Jessica (and Sheb), allowed the Army to plunk him into Germany. They wouldn't have chosen the oven with him in the Bronx. An only child, he ought to have been shrewder about his father's closefisted nature, the instability behind the calm front. Coens had to lean on Coens to keep the eggs intact.

He walked to Central Park West, to the playground opposite Stephanie's apartment house, where Stephanie passed her mornings with Judith and Alice, away from wealthy neighbors and the auras of her husband's dental clinic. She would sit behind one particular tree, everything above her hips in deep shade, Judith and Alice occupied with sand. Coen wanted the girls. Burdened with Albert and Jessica and losing his wits over Arnold's shoe, he needed to rub against an old wife's family, claim some daughters for himself. Whether Stephanie preferred being untroubled at nine o'clock (she had jars of milk for her and the girls), she didn't begrudge Coen. She recognized his stoop from the opposite end of the playground. The truculent cop walk irritated her but that coarse handsomeness, all the pluck on his face, could make her disremember the bad Coen, his obsequiousness before Isaac, his muteness with her, the confusions in his head. Coen was the one who stalked her, continued his brutal, disconnected courtship. He would break into her apartment, rut her against the bathtub, smolder over Jello with Charles, then disappear for weeks. Still, roosting behind her tree, the milk jars wet in her lap, she was glad he had come. The girls climbed out of the sand-box. "Daddy Fred. Daddy Fred." He hoisted them over his shoulders with a firm buttocks hold, mouthing the word "shit." He always arrived emptyhanded, visiting them at the wrong hours, when the nut shops and the five-and-dime were closed. Stephanie had to smile. He carried her girls with such devotion in his grip, she couldn't shut him off. "Freddy, a glass of milk?"

So he had his second breakfast, animal crackers and bloodwarm milk, Arnold's cheese sitting in his craw. Nervous, he could think to ask her only about Charles. She wouldn't entertain him with clinic stories. "He flourishes," she said. "He comes out of the Bronx a few times a week to look at his daughters and fondle me. Freddy, who's your longhaired friend?"

Coen munched an animal cracker. "What do you mean?"

"The man who's been following me around the last few mornings, blowing bubbles for the girls. He calls me 'Mrs. Manfred.'"

"Steffie, did you see him today?"

"Yes. A half hour before you."

"Is he a chinkie sort with a red mop?"

"I think so. Part Chinese."

Coen put down the girls. "Son-of-a-bitch." He talked with a knuckle in his mouth. He kicked at his heels. "Fucking César."

Judith put her fingers on Stephanie's thighs. Alice stuck to Coen. "Freddy, what's wrong?"

"Nothing," Coen said. "Chicken stuff." He kneeled in front of Alice. "Don't take bubbles off that Chinaman." He held Judith's ankle, touched the baby scruff around the bone. "Honey, it takes a runty man to bother your mother and you. I know how to find him." He hustled from the playground with milk on his lips, yelling from the crook in his shoulder. "Steffie, don't worry about it. You're free.

The Chinaman won't have his bubble pipe for too long. I'll strip him and his boss." Stephanie wanted to hail him back, assure him that she wasn't afraid of Chino Reyes; the Chinaman had been gentle with the girls, picking sand from beneath Judith's toes, and polite to her, confessing his admiration for "husband Coen." But she had been slow in trying to recall him.

Coen was already out of the park. Too anxious to plod downtown in a bus, he rode a gypsy cab straight to Bummy's. Bummy Gilman was known as a good cousin at the stationhouse; he delivered his "flutes" to the captain's man (Coke bottles filled with rye), and he didn't expect to see rat bastards like Coen in his establishment, snoops who annoyed his customers and made everybody unhappy, civilians and regular cops. "Mister, one schnapps on the house, and then you go. And don't sip. Three swallows is all I'm allowing."

Coen wouldn't answer him. He walked the line of Bummy's stools, poking for the Chinaman. Bummy had the sense not to bother Coen's sleeve.

"I could call the precinct, Coen. Who are they going to protect? Me or you?"

Coen rasped at him finally. "Bummy, get off my back."

Bummy couldn't negotiate with a crazyman; he let Coen pass, swearing he would register his complaint to the captain's man. He wasn't providing flutes for nothing. Bummy had an investment in Chino Reyes; Chino supplied him with the films that he showed in his kitchen to nephews and cop friends on Saturday nights, and arranged his half-hour appointments with Odette Leonhardy, who could make his tonsils crawl with one of her colder looks. He loved to be swindled by this girl. He got five minutes of skin from Odette, and twenty minutes of sandwiches and frowns. In addition to which, he owned a piece of the films and had an interest in César's Mexican affairs. So he catered to the Chinaman, allowed him to sit at a booth so long as he wore his wig and didn't mingle with too many cops.

The Chinaman spotted Coen at the door. He wasn't apprehensive. He finished his second Irish whiskey of the morning and watched Bummy mix with Coen. He couldn't figure why Bummy had such a swollen face. He had gotten fond of Coen in Mexico (because of his loyalties to Jerónimo, his quiet, Polish ways), and the fondness stuck. The Chinaman was brooding over his failures with Odette; he couldn't find the porno queen. He led Coen over to his booth. "Chino, what's happening?"

Coen leaned into the Chinaman, pushed his nose against the wall so that the Chinaman couldn't breathe. "I'll kill you, you mother, if you ever go near my wife and her babies again."

Coen brought his hand away. The Chinaman gagged but he didn't get up or make a move for Coen.

"Polish, that's the second time you touched my face."

With the booth between them, they had a huffing war, blowing air around in great sulks. The Chinaman's coloring came back once he conceived a plan. He would smile now, then lay for Coen, catch him by the neck. He couldn't afford to wrestle in a public place. He would lose his standing with Bummy and bring the cops here. So he clawed the inside of the booth, crossed his feet, and talked to Coen.

"Polish, it was a social call. I didn't scare the wife. She has lovely kids." He saw Coen's hand curl, and he protected his nose, bedding deeper into the booth. "Didn't I reward the Spic? He'd be limping with sores on his feet, if not for me. I mobilized him, Polish, don't forget."

"Chino, keep Arnold out of it. He doesn't need your gifts. And if César wants to signal me, let him do it himself."

The Chinaman had signals of his own for César. Maybe Zorro was hiding the queen. Or telling her to avoid her usual lanes. He hadn't been able to catch Odile at Jane Street or The Dwarf.

Calmer after having had some flesh in his hand, after squeezing the Chinaman, Coen could sit on a bus. He stopped at the dairy restaurant on Seventy-third and waited for Boris the steerer, the man in the three-button vest. Coen kept aloof from the gamblers who licked almond paste on their pignolia horns and flicked their boutonnieres in the window. He couldn't tell if the steerer made any morning calls. He wouldn't buy a flower. The steerer passed him in a feathered hat. "Boris?" Coen hissed.

The steerer frowned at him and walked a little faster. Coen seized him up by the coattails. The steerer swayed on his legs.

"Boris, tell César, and tell him good. No more pranks on any of my people. This is Manfred Coen talking to you. I can take your whole operation off the street. I can sit you down in the detective room. I can send all the old cockers with flowers in their coats into the judge. So Zorro better get to me in a hurry."

The steerer was mortified to find someone taking liberties with his clothes in front of the restaurant. He smoothed his coattails the

first chance he had. And he tilted his head to the boutonnieres in the
window to prove that he was in command. "Mr. Coen, only Zorro
knows where Zorro is," he said, biting his cheek cryptically and
rushing indoors. But he dropped his hat on the sidewalk, and Coen
had to straighten the feather for him. "That swine isn't pure enough
for my boss," he whispered to the boutonnieres. "He once had an
unkosher wife."

In five minutes Coen was sitting on his bed, his ankles itching
from the number of confrontations he'd had. He smiled when the
phone rang. César called him prickless and gutless. "Manfred, you
don't have to pull on Boris to find me. Why shame a man in his own
territory? He won't enjoy his blintzes any more."

"Zorro, you shouldn't have made the Chinaman bring back
Spanish's fat shoe."

"Crazy, do I interfere with the chink's personal business? He has
a mind. And since when am I Zorro to you?"

"You're the one who wants me for an enemy. Why are you
dogging my wife? César, I promise you, that Chinaman shows up at
her playground one more time, I'll kick you as far as Boston Road.
What's the matter? You can't stand me fraternizing with Odile?
Don't worry. I didn't taste her sandwiches."

"Look who discovered America," César mumbled into the
phone. "She's wide."

"What?"

"I said she's wide. The virgin queen. She puts it in your face,
and runs to Vander Child. I couldn't care a nigger's lip how much
you're getting from Odette. Schmuck, she works for me."

"Then what's bugging you, César?"

"You know, you miserable shit. Papa gave you the farm. He let
you sit on his own toilet seat. You took his food. You burned his
candles on the holidays. He trusted you with Jerónimo. He put you
next to him, on his left side. He forgave you for being a Coen. I could
see you turn. Manfred with his sketching pad. The boy from the
Manhattan high school. With his fancy report cards. I told Papa to
throw chocolate syrup in your eyes. But Papa liked you, so he blinked
the other way."

"That's twenty years ago. What's it got to do with planting the
Chinaman near my wife?"

"Ask your sweetheart, your old Chief."

"Isaac? He's your Papa's man."

"Baloney. Boston Road's one big wire, with plugs going from our mouths to the Chief's ass. Isaac doesn't miss a word."

"So why did Papa take him in?"

"Because if a rat comes sniffing around it's better to keep him where you can find him, so he won't feed off your guts in the dark."

"César, the last time I was in the Bronx Isaac put the wall between me and him. He closed the toilet door in my face."

"We showed you Jerónimo, we showed you Mordeckay, we got Vander's kid for you, and you turned around and went to the Chief."

"I've been nursing a ping-pong bat since I'm home. Nothing more."

"That's not how Isaac tells it. He taunts Papa with your name. You're his 'principal bait'. You dangled yourself on Isaac's line. Manfred, you got to be a cunt-face and a snot from your mother. She took sunbaths in Papa's orchard, she made sure Jerónimo could see her from her nipples down, and then she complained that the baby was spying on her."

Coen remembered the orchard table, Papa's hump-backed trees, Jerónimo playing with a bow too weak to hold an arrow, Albert and Sheb off the farm looking for country eggs, jumbos to take with them to the Bronx, Coen with his mother on the table, begging her to wear a blanket, walking around the table like some scarecrow with stretched arms whenever Jerónimo blundered near them trying to retrieve the arrows that spilled off his bow.

"César, my mother's not here. Ask Papa how much my father owed him before he died? Tell me why it took so long to locate my address in Germany? Did you all add my father's bills up to the penny? How much was the egg store behind?"

"Manfred, wake up. Papa could have carried the egg store on his finger. Why should he need your father's little grubs?" And he hung up on Coen, who couldn't get the whiff of strawberries out of his nose or forestall the image of his mother stooping in the fields, putting strawberries in the bandanna that ought to have been on her chest. Did she ever strip like this with Albert around? Was she defying the Guzmanns or showing off? Who else peeked under the bandanna? Is that why Albert wouldn't send them to the farm any more? Coen stuck a pillow on his head and chewed near the wall.

Boris Telfin, *the* Boris Telfin of cherry blintzes and quarter cigars, was a dice steerer, a man who sat for gamblers, not a message boy. It was bad enough that he was owned by Marranos, a family of pig-eating Jews, the Guzmanns of Portugal, Lima, and the Bronx, who mumbled paternosters into their chicken soup, who put crosses on their graves, who were Christians 80 percent of the time; but he didn't expect to be a permanent liaison between Zorro (the most variable of his masters) and a Chinaman. Still, it wasn't entirely César's fault. The First Deputy men were keeping him indoors, patrolling his dice cribs (the apartments where the games were held) in green cars, and César couldn't risk a ride into the Chinaman's territories. So Boris had to go.

He met the Chinaman in a lot on Prince Street. The fool wore suspenders that could have marked him a mile off. Boris couldn't get familiar with such a person (at least the Marranos had a distaste for violence and open warfare). He knew about the Chinaman's career, the skullings of cab drivers and other chauffeurs. No hackie could be safe around this chink.

"Sweetheart, tell Zorro I dumped the shoe. It was my choice. It's a whore's boot. It was bringing me hard luck."

"Mister, that's old news. I mean about the shoe. Zorro asks you a favor. Concerning the gentleman Coen. Enough is enough. Personally I wouldn't mind a little brain damage. His head could use a few more holes. But that ain't César's wish. He wants you to lay low. Madam Coen is free to think her Christian thoughts unmolested in the park."

"Boris, he touched my face. Twice. Once at the stationhouse, once at Bummy's. He gets blown away for that, but I'll pick the hour."

"Mister, he touched me too. He pulled my coat. Imagine, he molests you on the street, the tin cop. All my brother-in-laws were watching."

"Boris, I'll remember him for you. I promise."

The steerer was getting to like the Chinaman. "Chino, you have my approval, but please, don't mention it to Zorro. He'll pack me to Queens, in a box."

"I'm no fink," the Chinaman said.

"Chino, what can I do for you? Just ask."

"Boris, there's a man, Solomon Wong, he used to scrape plates for my father in Cuba, an old man, I want him protected. He won't take money from me."

"How much of a cosh?" Boris asked, being practical.

"Maybe ten a week." The Chinaman went for his money clip. Boris shook his head.

"Ten a week? César will pay."

"No. It's gotta come from me. Else it won't work."

Boris accepted the Chinaman's money. He was ready to drive off. The Chinaman grabbed on to the limousine.

"Don't you want to know where to find him?"

"Who?"

"The dishwasher. Try the other lots. Or the flop-houses."

"Mister, how many Solomon Wongs can there be?"

Chino let go of the car. He was hurting for a gun. The bouncers at The Dwarf had his Colt. They'd dropped it in a water pail when he rushed the joint for Odile. He would slap those two huskies after he finished with Coen. He couldn't buy a gun off of his regular suppliers. The market was drying up with police agents everywhere; only the niggers would sell you a piece, and he couldn't go uptown that far. He missed his shoe, that humpbacked strip of leather. But he'd been getting touchy pictures of his father lately in his head each time he wore the shoe. The Chinaman was a believer; he had no compunctions about the credibility of ghosts. He was accountable to them, for sure. His father had mud in his scalp (a sign of unrest). To appease the ghost Chino hoped to make provisions for Solomon Wong. Perhaps his old father was destined to walk with a muddy head until Solomon, alive in this world, could be rescued from the lowly state of dishwasher and bindlestiff (a Cuban *vagabundo*), and given a definite income, no matter how small. But he couldn't locate Solomon these days. And the ghosts had to be fed. So he got rid of the shoe. Heeding the growls in his stomach, he marched to Grand Street for canoli and Sicilian almond water. Blue-eyes would come, only not this afternoon.

TWELVE

His ring-around-a-rosy with César and the Chinaman must have puffed out his heart. Coen, who swore he never dreamed, was dreaming three times a night. The dreams didn't involve the Guzmanns, the egg store, or the farm. Most of them were about his marriage, Coen redraping his fights with Stephanie, tucking under her crying spells and his tightmouthed, mummied looks with nothing more durable than spit, love-making spit, Coen crazied with the notion that if he penetrated his wife long enough their differences would dissolve. But the last of the dreams drifted off Coen's marriage and occurred in the stationhouse. Coen, a bachelored Coen, was called into the long and narrow yard at the side of the stationhouse (such yard serving as an outdoor gym, a mustering place, and a temporary morgue), to identify two bodies found on precinct turf. The bodies were housed in makeshift coffins (wicker baskets from a hospital laundry room padded with old blankets from the horse patrol). Coen recognized the baby fat through the wicker plaits. The girls had blue disfigured chicken necks and thickened tongues. The wickers had creased their flesh. Their eyes were swollen over with brown lumps. They bled from their teeth. The captain's man must have crossed their fingers and bent their legs together; they couldn't have died in such a benign position. Coen touched Judith first. He didn't want a scrubby horse blanket on his girl. There were bugs in the basket, water beetles. Coen injured them with his thumbs, but he couldn't go far enough, and the beetles turned over on their backs and made disgusting noises through the cracks in their shells. Coen undressed in the yard. He put his coat under Alice, and stuffed Judith's coffin with trouser legs. The morgue wagon arrived, purring gas. Coen still hadn't determined who called him into the yard. The squad commander? Brodsky? Pimloe? Coen's sometime partner, Detective Brown?

He woke spitting Isaac's name. His nose was stiff with mucus. It was three in the morning by his own clock. He got out of bed in a shiver, with unreliable knees. He had involved Stephanie in his own dreck. But he couldn't slap the Chinaman again on account of one lousy dream. He wore his detective suit (herringbone, gray on gray), shaved the pesty hairs under his nose, and went to Stephanie's block. He badgered her night doorman, sticking him in the ribs with his gold shield. "Mrs. Nerval needs me. I'm a relative of hers and a cop." The doorman didn't like cops in his building after midnight. He dangled the plugs of the intercom with a nervous fist. He got Charles. "Dr. Nerval, sorry Dr. Nerval, a gentleman here, says he's connected to your wife. He's holding a badge on me."

Coen heard Charles sputter through the plugs. He put away his shield. "I want Mrs. Nerval, not him."

"Dr. Nerval, the gentleman asks for your wife."

Coen stuck his mouth near the wires. "Charlie, don't be such a shit. It's important. Let me up."

"Coen, it's four o'clock. You think dentists never sleep? I have two girls in the other room."

Charles wore his slippers for the cop. He wished Coen would chase his wife during proper hours. He was in love with both of his dental assistants, Puerto Rican girls with delicate moustaches and narrow waists. But Charles was too shrewd to shake up the equilibrium at his clinic. He wouldn't pursue Rita or Beatriz until they left him for a better job. He confined himself to hurried squeezes of a thigh whenever his patients, mostly old men, fell asleep in the dentist chair.

Stephanie came out of her bedroom in a clumsy wraparound showing a good deal of skin. She had enough sense not to fool with Coen. "Freddy, sit down." Charles looked once at a pocket of veins on Stephanie's thigh and considered how lucky he was to have Rita and Beatriz.

"Steffie, wake up Judith and Alice, please."

Charles clutched his pajamas. "The captain's giving orders. Stephanie, meet your men friends outside the building from now on. The guy downstairs will call us gypsies soon."

"Charlie, let him finish. Make some toast for us or go to bed."

Coen tried not to stare at his old wife; it was the crooked fall of the wraparound, the puffs of cloth, that roused him, not the bared skin. "Take the girls to Charlie's mother. Get them to Connecticut. Right away."

"He's simple-minded," Charles said. "He's demented, that's what he is. He thinks we run a shuttle for little girls. Stephanie, tell him to find other people to annoy."

"Fred, does it have something to do with that Chinese boy?"

"Chino Reyes was hired to do a tickle job. I offended his master. The Guzmanns say I'm a spy."

"Is Isaac in the middle of this?" Stephanie said. She still had a grudge against the Chief; Isaac was the one who had stepped into their marriage, manipulated Coen, masterminded plots that kept him away from her.

"Who's the China boy?" Charles said. "Why can't the girls sleep in their own beds?"

"The Chinaman has funny rules. He'll slap anybody who's close to me. He's been sneaking looks at Judith and Alice in the park."

Charles wandered around the parlor, grim-faced, his teasing

manner gone. "It's Coen's fault. A cop who lies down with crooks. Stephanie, why'd you divorce him if you meant to bring him home? He'll get the babies killed. I'm going to call the police."

"Charlie, you're looking at the police."

"You? You're no cop. I know about Isaac Sidel. He dressed you, he made you up, and left you with your finger in your ass. You can't cross the street without Isaac. I hear it plenty from detectives in the Bronx. You were perfect for wagging a chief's tail. Stephanie, bundle up the girls. I'll drive them to mama. Coen, do me a favor. Don't come back."

"They'll only be in Connecticut a few days," Coen muttered. He was ashamed to tell Stephanie that all his suspicions came from a dream. But the image of Judith and Alice in straw coffins seemed perfectly valid to Coen. There was too much pulp in the wickers for him to ignore. Charles fixed Alice but Stephanie lingered with Judith's sock so she could talk to Coen. "Be careful, Freddy. Make peace with the Guzmanns, and get out."

She hugged him in front of Charles and the girls, held him in a wifely way, without shifting her tongue, and Coen felt his nervousness go but he couldn't get rid of his dread; lost father, lost mother, lost Coen. Stephanie perceived the animal sharpness of his body, the twitches in his chest, and she wished she could have two husbands instead of one. Charles began to nag. "Coen, she'll continue the massage tomorrow. Damn it, Stephanie, can't you hate him, just a tiny bit, for bringing your daughters into his stinking life? I'm only their father. I don't count."

Hunching past the doorman, Coen made the street. He walked with his eyes deep in his head, spooking cab drivers on Central Park West; they saw a herringbone man with a hard stare. Now, facing Columbus, five blocks down from Stephanie and Charles, he could consider how relieved he was to find the girls still alive. Coen wouldn't attribute any wizardry to his dream. But the straw coffins outside the stationhouse shoved him closer to his father's oven, made him peek into the stove. Stuffed with Albert, it was easy for him to credit Judith and Alice with chicken necks. Approaching his corner, he had to choose each of his steps to avoid a tangle of elderly women and men. They were pummeling a *cubano* into the ground, an SRO from Spanish Arnold's hotel. Coen recognized their leader, the Widow Dalkey, his neighbor, who was also the captain of the block. The *cubano's* arms were covered with fists and claws. He was hugging something against his belly. He had scratches around the eyes. Coen pushed himself into the war party. He took Mrs. Dalkey's fist off the *cubano's* cheek. She wailed and spit until she saw it was Coen. A Pomeranian with blood in its nose dropped between the *cubano's* legs. Mrs. Dalkey blew hot air at Coen. "We caught him, Detective Coen. We caught the filthy bum. He won't murder dogs no more." She pointed to a cracked dish near one of the trees that she had planted for the block. "He fed Mimsey poison in a lump of steak." The Pomeranian could no longer raise her head. Her nipples had begun to swell.

Coen stood between the *cubano* and Dalkey's people. He didn't have enough ambition to march him to the nearest stationhouse with Dalkey on his toes, petting the dying Pomeranian, and holding it as evidence. The *cubano* could answer "Yes," and "No" in English, and nothing more. He shivered up against Coen, preferring to show the side of his face to a few old men rather than Mrs. Dalkey. He was wearing stale perfume. "Beast," Mrs. Dalkey hissed through the wall of old men. When she decided that Coen couldn't satisfy her, she summoned a rookie cop from Broadway. The rookie was thick in the pants with paraphernalia; handcuffs, holster, club, cartridge belt, memorandum book, and pencil case. His name was Morgenstern. A pin from one of the fraternal orders of Jewish cops was tacked to his blouse. Coen had the same pin, but he never wore it; during the time of his marriage the Society of the Hands of Esau had informed him that it could not provide burial space for non-Jewish wives. Coen and Stephanie would have to lie in different cemeteries, according to the society's bylaws. Coen turned over his future grave to an indigent Jewish cop who hadn't kept up his premiums and wanted to be buried on the society's grounds.

"You take the collar," Coen said. "It's your beat. But be sure these ladies and gentlemen don't tear him to pieces before you get to the house."

The rookie insisted on shaking Coen's hand. This was only his third arrest. The bulls at his precinct were much stingier than Coen. They didn't give "collars" away. And they wouldn't talk to him on the street.

"Officer Morgenstern," Mrs. Dalkey said. "He's the lipstick freak, I bet. I can tell a pervert by the sweat in their eyes."

The rookie dug for his memorandum book. His pencil snapped on the "f" of freak. He got one from Mrs. Dalkey with a better point.

Coen shouted his telephone number. "Call me after they bring him upstairs."

"What should I do with the dog, Mr. Coen?"

"Give it to Dalkey. And don't forget the dish."

The rookie had to be content with second place behind Mrs. Dalkey, who gathered her people, the dog, and the dog dish. Coen couldn't reach his building without walking through her procession. The rookie called him in under two hours.

"They broke him, Coen. The lady was right. He used to be a dollmaker. He hasn't worked in years. He coaxed those kids onto the roofs. He used an Exacto knife on them from his doll kit. He has play dresses at home. For old dolls. The freak tried to fit the dresses on the kids. He marked them up with his grease pencils. He gave each of them a new set of lips. He couldn't fool the bulls."

Coen turned around on his bed. "Morgenstern, they must have some pretty sharp heads over there. That *cubano* couldn't even speak his name in English. Did they find any doll dresses on him? And why does he poison dogs?"

"I don't know."

Coen figured Morgenstern might be less jubilant by the middle of the afternoon. The bulls would probably erase him from their report. Having a rookie put his fingers on the lipstick freak could take away from their prestige.

Irene, alias the Widow, alias Dalkey, couldn't have been widowed, because she'd never been a wife. She was born in a foundling hospital on Delancey Street, and was given the name Irene by a hospital nun. The plumber Frankensteen and his wife, a petulant woman unwilling to suffer through a childbirth of her own, adopted Irene and brought her to Frankensteen's cellar shop, where they also had their living quarters. As soon as Irene learned all the habits of speech (around the age of three or four), Mrs. Frankensteen confounded the little girl over the state of her birth, telling her she was an "elf child," a changeling dropped on the stairs of the hospital by some rich uptown woman who didn't want the nuisance of being a mother. Thus Irene became aware of her illegitimacy. At P.S. 23 on Mulberry Street (fifty years later the Chinaman would attend this same school), Irene began to ponder the doubleness of her life; rich lady's girl fobbed off to the Frankensteens. She fell behind in her studies and was taken out of school to serve as a laundress (Irene was under twelve). Boys and older men fumbled with her at the laundry, undoing the strings of her apron while she soaped table linen from a Twenty-third Street mansion and continued to ponder the possibilities of another life.

At fifteen she ran off with a broom salesman who came to the laundry once. The salesman called himself Mr. Dalkey. Owning a wife and three sons in Hartsdale, New York, he installed Irene on Columbus Avenue, then a neighborhood of stores and dumpy apartments for carpenters and grocers who served all the mansions near the park. The salesman visited his Columbus Avenue "missus" maybe twice a month. The Missus Dalkey, Irene, threw him out after nine years and became the Widow Dalkey. She was twenty-four and a laundress again.

The Widow had a succession of dogs, Everett, Stanley, Chad, Noah, Raoul, before her current Dalmatian Rickie. She took no more beaus. Men were only a trifle short of being monsters in the Widow's eyes. The salesman wasn't part of this scheme; he didn't even enter the Widow's visions of herself. She was thinking of the man who had ruined her mother, the rich lady, compelling her to turn her own baby into an elf child.

She watched the neighborhood deteriorate as the grocers screamed for more money and the mansions could no longer support a whole battery of slaves. Hotels became rooming houses. The grocers sold out to hardware stores. Jews crawled uptown from the Bowery, blacks moved in, then Puerto Ricans, and finally the *cubanos*. Dalkey resisted these petty immigrations as best she could. She became the captain of her block, fighting for high-intensity lamps, church attendance, curb space for dogs, tree plantings, and the return of the white grocers. Until Coen sided with the *cubano*, she could forgive his Jewishness. She liked having a detective in the house. But she wouldn't accept favors from Jews any more. Dalkey was serious. She instructed Rickie to pee on Coen's door.

The evening of the *cubano's* capture she saw a black man through her peephole. He had a badge in his hand. Dalkey panicked. She wished Coen hadn't abandoned her. She might have summoned him from her fire escape. She looked through the peephole again. It was hard times when a nigger could carry a badge. She wouldn't answer the man until she propped Rickie against the door. "Speak your business. Who are you and what do you want?"

"Mrs. Dalkey, I'm a detective from the hotel up the street.

Alfred, in charge of security over there."

The mention of the hotel frightened Dalkey; she wondered if the *cubano* had influential friends. "Well, what is it you expect of me?"

"My boss, Bogden, Smith, and Liveright, the company that runs the hotel, asked me to thank you, Mrs. Dalkey. There's a reward coming. Can we talk? Inside, Mrs. Dalkey?"

Mrs. Dalkey sprang her locks, keeping Rickie between her and the nigger. Alfred didn't take to the dog. He would have scratched Rickie's nose with the eye of the badge if he hadn't been on an official trip. Dalkey led him into the foyer, but she didn't offer him a chair.

"Mrs. Dalkey, I have fifty dollars if you promise not to advertise where the freak comes from. You know the city, ma'am. They shove the welfare people in on you, and you're stuck with them. If not we'd have a first-class clientele. This Ernesto, he's a retard. We knew it. But does the government care? They protect all the sissies. I caught him licking them dolls of his. Voodoo stuff. He sits them down with wet cheeks. Should have flinged him off the stairs. But the government's looking after his rights, and my badge isn't special enough. What do you say, Mrs. Dalkey? Are you with us? Will you help the company?"

The Widow threw Rickie into Alfred's knee. "I don't trust a company man," she said. "You can tell your employer that Irene won't accept their bribe. It's blood money. I hope your hotel falls to the ground."

"Kiss my ass," Alfred said, going out the door. He put on his shades, spit at the lightbulbs in the hall. "Kiss my ass. Kiss my ass."

Dalkey was clicking bolts. She trembled into the door, Rickie whining at her different shapes. "Shut up," she said. "Why didn't you massacre him?" She wouldn't feed the dog. She drugged herself with swipes of honey in black tea. She crossed her knuckles over her heart. Dalkey was seventy-four. She vowed to destroy the singles hotel in her own lifetime. But the nigger hotel detective had made her grumpy. She refigured the routes of her girlhood, her sofa bed in a cellar shop, both Frankensteens, the ignominy of living so close to a plumber's shit-stained boots. Dalkey began to cry. She had no husband to protect her, only a sniveling dog. Her history seemed to unwind like kitchen paper on the spindle over her sink; useless crinkled throwaways. Why should she have to absorb the horrors of a neighborhood? Let the housewives woo back the white grocers.

Dalkey was finished. She would resign her block captaincy. She wanted her rightful mother, not Mrs. Frankensteen. She was tired of being the Widow. Rickie buried his head in Dalkey's underskirts. Now she could pity the dog. "Rickie, do you remember your dad? We're orphans, dear. We've fallen out of the bag. Elves' children, that's what the missus said." She rubbed the bald patches on Rickie's skull. She peeled crust off his eyes. She fed him carrots, salmon, and liverwurst. Dalkey was herself again. She would plot a new campaign for trees.

THIRTEEN

Coen dialed the First Deputy's office after his morning tea.

"Give me Isaac Sidel."

The receptionist asked him to spell the name.

"We have no listing for Sidel," she said.

"Look for him in Herbert Pimloe's private book."

"Who's calling, Sir?"

"Manfred. M like Monday, A like Athlete, N like Neglect, F like Fishingpole, R like Ruler, E like End, D like Dollar."

Pimloe's chauffeur got on the line. "Coen, what do you want?"

"Brodsky, tell Pimloe I want to sit down with Isaac. Make it Papa's stoop, my apartment, anywhere Isaac suggests. If he won't sit with me, Brodsky, I'm going to play a little pinochele with the Guzmanns."

"Stay with ping-pong, Coen. Pimloe doesn't need you any more. Your buddies at homicide have been asking for you. Coen, you're back on the chart. You should be catching stiffs by tomorrow."

"If Pimloe wants me in the squadroom, he'll have to drag me. I take my orders from Isaac."

"How many times do I have to tell you, glom? Isaac doesn't work here."

"Then maybe I'm not Coen. The Guzmanns never left South America, and Boston Road isn't on the map."

He went across the park in smelly trousers and a shirt with missing sleeves. Child's doorman mistook him for one of the painters who were crawling through the apartment house. He was told to use the service entrance next time. Child was having a demitasse with croissants. He sat Coen down at the table and wouldn't let him wolf his croissant dry. He spread blueberry jam for Coen with a thin silver knife that could have fit inside Coen's index finger. Child assumed Coen had come around and would now work for him. But Coen wasn't smiling, and he wouldn't move his chin further than his coffee cup. "Vander, are you Pimloe's stoolie, or Isaac's?"

Child finished both wings of his croissant. He pushed crumbs off his face with the edge of his napkin. When he tried to sip coffee, Coen put his hand over the cup. "Vander, you've been jobbing me all along. You wanted your daughter out of the country so you'd have more room for your porno shows. Why'd you run César's brides into Mexico? Did you get a kick out of delivering the girls? Scumbag, how much did you pay the pimps at the bus station? Twenty dollars a head? Or maybe you clipped the girls off the bus yourself to save on shipping expenses. Whatever deal you made with Isaac might not go down. No judge in America would appreciate a Fifth Avenue man who gives away underaged brides."

The table rattled across from Coen, so he put the cup to Child's lips. "Drink, you bastard."

"Money," Child said, his mouth thick with coffee. "I was in a bind."

"You're supposed to be the big Broadway angel. Why would you need César's crumbs? You know where his father lives? In a candy store. Papa Guzmann mixes ice cream sodas. A hundred a day. He has two sons who aren't totally there, and two more on their border line. César's the youngest and the brightest, but you could have done better than that."

"Coen, I lose a hundred thousand a year backing Broadway shows. The apartment costs me another thousand a month. I have a wife in Florida, and a limousine to support. I couldn't invest a nickel without those films. Coen, who kept Harold Pinter in New York? Who revived George Bernard Shaw? Who paid to translate Gorky?"

"Vander, I never saw a play in my life except when I escorted ambassadors' wives for the Bureau of Special Services. And all of them were musicals."

Coen recognized Odile by her tittering. She joined them at the table in a towel robe and immediately stuck her bare feet on Coen's double-tone shoes. She wouldn't stop scowling.

"The classic confrontation," she said. "The culture freak takes on the caveman cop. Both of you make me puke."

Coen licked jam off his fingers. "Odette, you don't look all that pure from where I sit. You helped smuggle Carrie into Mexico for your own sake. None of you figured I'd ever get close enough to César to bring her back. Meantime you could have your little circus in Vander's apartment and keep another room downtown. Maybe Carrie didn't like smelling you all over her father."

"Uncle, shut him up. He's a fat liar. He tours girls' bars so he can catch a free nipple. He sleeps with a gun on the couch."

Vander washed the cups, the knife, and the coffee spoons. Odile tangled herself in Coen's legs without remembering what she had done. She hated the cop, she wanted to float jam in his eyes. She had missed his stringy body in her bed after having been with him half of one night. She didn't want to be beholden to any man. She could parry with her uncle, push him around like her toy bear, because he was still afraid of César Guzmann and she was one of César's girls. But she couldn't lead Coen by the nose. He didn't gawk at her like the Chinaman did. He didn't show her his tongue. He was more like César, who wasn't a fairy exactly but didn't have much need for a woman more than once or twice a month. She had even slept with Jerónimo, seduced him while he was in hiding on Jane Street, because she thought this would please César, and the baby had the same scornful expression on his yellow face before he dropped his sperm in her, a mouthful of teeth, that independence, that hard, motherless look. She wondered if a woman had ever touched Jerónimo's eggs before her. But she was too frightened to ask César. And now she had Coen. In bed he screamed a little like Jerónimo, short and dry. She couldn't understand what thrust her toward such a sullen tribe of men. She tried to get up from the table but she was stuck to Coen.

"Get off my feet," she said.

Coen reached under the table and pushed her ankles free. Child didn't offer him another demitasse, and Odile gobbled crumbs off the croissant dish without looking up, so Coen disappeared. He took an irregular route across the park and landed high in the eighties. Coming down the street he saw a head of thick gray hair, big as a cabbage, shooting toward Columbus. The head moved at an incredible rate, bobbing over car roofs, missing lampposts by an inch. Coen didn't have to calculate. No one but the baby could carry his head around with so much accuracy. And with Isaac in the city, after Guzmann blood, he worried for the baby's life. "Jerónimo, why did César bring you home so fast? Did Mordeckai eat up all your candy?"

Coen breathed hard but he couldn't run with the baby. He lagged a
block behind. He knew where the baby was going. To visit uncle
Sheb. They used to sit for hours in the Bronx and pick each other's
gray hairs. Coen was lucky to slow down. He might not have noticed
that the baby had a tail. Brodsky was following him in a First Deputy
car. Coen let himself in at the next light. "Brodsky, tell me again you
and Pimloe aren't married to the Chief. Didn't you say you never met
the baby?"

"Coen, out of the car, fast, or I'll run you over to the precinct.
You won't be too happy sitting in the cage. They'll throw peanuts at
you, Coen. That's how much they love you over there."

"Lay off the baby, Brodsky. He gets along fine without a
shadow. Cruise somewhere else. I swear, I'll ground your car into the
window of the First National Bank."

"You're an animal, Coen. They ought to give you to the zoo
patrol. You don't belong in the street."

Coen twisted Brodsky's key and stalled the car. "What does the
First Dep want with Jerónimo? The gloms from the Fourth Division
already found the lipstick freak. Didn't you hear? He's a dollmaker at
the singles hotel where Arnold lives. He also poisons dogs. What's
the matter, Brodsky? Can't you check it out? Is the Detective Bureau
holding out on the First Dep? Are they feuding again? Then Isaac
must be in his old chair."

Coen stood outside Manhattan Rest. He didn't want to interrupt
the baby's communion with Sheb. He bought dried pears for his
uncle and finished half of them waiting for Jerónimo. The baby tried
to swerve past him on the stairs. He had no greeting for Coen.
Indentations appeared on both his temples after Coen blocked his
path.

"Jerónimo, where are you coming from?"

César must have warned him not to talk with Coen. Did he stick
it in the baby's head that Coen was Isaac's rat?

"Jerónimo, please, don't visit Shebby during the day. The nurse
will take you up to him at night. Here, I'll write you a note for her."

The baby tore the note and chewed the pieces of paper. The
veins stuck out like knuckle joints on his head. Coen didn't want the
baby's brains to spill. He had to let him go.

"Jerónimo, take the side streets. Don't stop for anybody in a car.
There's a man with sideburns looking for you."

The baby was on a different block before Coen could finish his shout. He watched the cabbagehead turn a milky color. Then he walked upstairs to Sheb.

They munched pears in the dormitory. Shebby could tell something was wrong from the bites Coen took. The nephew didn't bother to suck his pears. Shebby pulled his blankets up. He was glad there were other men in the dormitory so he wouldn't have to listen to these bites all alone. He offered around the last sticky pear. The nephew was crazy; either he brought too little or too much. Couldn't he figure the number of pears to feed a dormitory of four constipated bachelors and widowers?

"How's the baby, uncle Sheb?"

Sheb squinted at Coen. He stuffed the two dollar bills he had through the hole in his pocket. The nephew wouldn't search an uncle's pissy pajamas. Then he forgot why Jerónimo always brought him two singles wrapped in toilet paper.

"Uncle, what did Jerónimo say?"

"He said the walls stink in Mexico. The ice cream has straw in it. Flies sit in the cakes. He didn't have enough centavos to buy a decent stick of gum."

The dollars fell through Sheb's pajama cuffs. He swatted his waistband and tried to flatten them against his stomach. Coen wouldn't mention the dollars no matter how hard Shebby rubbed.

"Manfred, how much is twenty-four dollars times thirteen years?"

Coen picked old raisins off his uncle's pillow. A foot from Shebby's pajamas he lost the power to accuse. How many uncles could a cop have? The Guzmanns had relatives to spare, Papa could tweeze them like hairs out of his nose, trade a cousin for a cousin, but they were the only two Coens.

"Sheb, I could bring you nuts tomorrow. The pears have been in the window too long. They taste better when they're not so bleached."

Shebby wouldn't consider the disadvantages of sunbleached fruit. The nephew stumbled uptown to be with him maybe eight, maybe nine times a year. If he offered to come again tomorrow, it couldn't be out of simple love. So Sheb cleared the dormitory. "Boys, go sit with the mademoiselles. The nephew and me have to talk. Morris, pick up your ass. It's dragging on the floor. Sam, you listen through the keyhole, I'll plug your big ears with a fig. Irwin, I want private, I want alone." And with his roommates gone, Sheb's tonsils began to sweat. He could get by without a nephew. All he needed was two dollars a month, and enough toilet paper in his fist. He sneezed.

"God bless you, uncle Sheb."

"Who taught you that? Your mother? She was careful about a sneeze. Your father took a holiday, Manfred. He went to sleep in his vest. They made me comb their hair."

Coen held Shebby's knuckle.

"Manfred, only two heads could fit at one time."

"Uncle, I know. You don't have to tell."

Coen wobbled near the bed. He had to grab his own knee or fall into the pillows with uncle Sheb. He didn't want to hear the dimensions of his father's stove. But Sheb wouldn't let him free.

"My brother, my lovely brother, he wanted me to go into the coop with his wife. So he could turn the knobs and poke us with his thumb and see how we cooked. Then he would take us out careful, careful, make room for himself. But Jessica said no. She wouldn't share the coop with me. She wanted to swallow gas holding Albert's hand."

Sheb took Coen by the calf and brought him into bed. They sat hunched over, with a slipper, a washcloth, and a pillbox between them.

"Your father Albert had chicken soup in his blood. He left me to turn the knobs."

Coen fit his hand into Shebby's slipper: all the Coens had little feet.

"Shebby, was it Albert who gave you the smock to wear, the smock from the store?"

"Smock?" Shebby said. He couldn't think without swishing his tongue and working spit through his teeth. "It wasn't Albert. It was Jessica. She didn't want me dirtying my shirt. I was supposed to change when I fished them out of the coop. Piss on them. I wasn't going in after Albert. I had nobody to hold my hand."

He dug his fingers into Coen's arms and shook him. "Call that a brother? He planned and planned, and I ended up the oven boy, hugging knobs for them."

"Uncle, where were the Guzmanns? Who put their fat toes in the egg store? How much did Albert borrow from Papa?"

"I talk my heart away and he tells me about the Guzmanns. Did I count Papa's dimes? Manfred, you have your mother's temperament.

She couldn't look at you without slanting her mouth. Jerónimo brings me dollars. Who remembers the reason?"

"Did they pay you to forget my address in Germany? Did they want me out of the country long enough to clean smoke off the oven?"

"Two dollars for all that? I must have a rotten sense of money. Why shouldn't they keep paying me? It's only Albert's twelfth anniversary. Can you find another brother in thirteen years? Manfred, you're wet. They paid me before the Coens took gas. I'm nobody's pauper. Papa opened a savings account for me and Jorge. But I lost the book. Manfred, I didn't need your mother's charity. I could have ironed my own three shirts."

Sheb sat with his thumb in his nose, his eyes off Coen, focused on the pillbox, his feet nibbling at the slipper. Coen called for Shebby's dormitory mates. His uncle, who had to have his bananas mashed at home before he would take a bite, who wore discards and never learned to part his hair, was the headman of Manhattan Rest's north wing. Coen had minimized Sheb. Out of the Bronx, away from Albert's jumbos and Jessica's hand, the uncle thrived. He had educated himself on the dials of a stove. Coen, the homicide man, had seen DOAs (dead-on-arrivals) with their tongues in their necks, fire-scarred babies, a Chelsea whore with a curtain rod in her crotch, a rabbi from Brooklyn with lice where his eyes should have been, a drowned pusher with tadpoles in his pubic hair; he had been on official business at the morgues of four boroughs, he had touched skin thicker than bark, he had watched medical examiners saw into the tops of skulls, but he hadn't lit the oven for his father.

What did he know about Albert and Jessica? How deep could you sniff into a bowl of vegetable soup before your face burned? Other boys found prophylactics in their father's drawer. Why not Manfred Coen? How come Jessica only took off her brassiere, fat cups with a full inch of stitching between them, after Albert went to the store? Did they kiss with their mouths open? What was the point of living along the same wall if you couldn't hear your father's comes? At least he had caught Sheb with his prick in his hand. Nothing more. The Coens weren't a licentious race. He had to wonder now if his father owned a prick. Where did his mother's bosoms go with Albert scratching chickenshit off his jumbos? Could he name another father who sold nothing but eggs?

He remembered scraps, the color of Albert's change-purse, the slight deformity of Albert's thumb, the odor of vinegar in the house, the grooves in the handle of the salad chopper, the bonnet Jessica wore to keep flour out of her hair, the hump in Jessica's neck, the creases in her smile, the mothballs hanging like disintegrated berries at the bottom of the hamper, Albert's razor, Jessica's comb, the pattern on their bedspread, their hats, their shoes, but nothing that would allow him to claim them as his mother and father. He might as well have been born a Guzmann than a Coen.

Sheb was too busy with Morris, Irwin, and Sam to notice that Coen wasn't there. He had no more pears to give them. He could have finished off the morning cracking knuckles beside them, but with two dollars in his pajamas he was more ambitious. He challenged the richest furrier of the south wing to a game of cutthroat pinochle, Morris and Sam to be witnesses and money handlers. He gave up his two dollars in one deal of the cards, and owed the furrier a dollar more. Promptly at eleven o'clock he had recollections of Manfred's visit. He asked Irwin to look under the beds because he couldn't recall sending the nephew home. He was crabby the whole afternoon.

Odile wanted her revenge. She could have asked Sweeney to break the cop's back, or crush a few knuckles so he would never play ping-pong again. But decided not to involve Sweeney in the undoing of Coen. Friends had too much brio; they betrayed your interests with overdevotion. Odile preferred professional work. The cop had humiliated her in front of Vander, accused her of conspiring to get Carrie out of the way in order to expedite a little incest—as if she had the urge to jump in Vander's lap! She'd rather sleep with the Chinaman, become his mama, for God's sake, than park on Fifth Avenue with that uncle of hers. All Vander Child cared about was the shine of her skin under his lamps. She called him from Jane Street.

"Vander, where can I find a ping-pong pro? A hustler who operates downtown?"

Vander was curt with her. "Forget it, Odile. Your complexion isn't suited for a green table. Try a badminton sharp. You'd be exceptional stuck inside a net."

"The hustler isn't for me, uncle. I'd like to shit on Coen."

"Why go so far? Coen's no good. I could make him eat the ball. Hire me."

"I can't. You're a sentimentalist. You're liable to cry on Coen's paddle. I'll do better with strangers."

She could hear Vander go stiff; he was proud of his finesse on the table. He could volley with an elbow, a hand, or the top of his head. But Vander was useless to her.

"Go to Harley Stone at the health spa on Christopher Street. Ask for the ping-pong room. He'll be there. Harley took the Canadian Open a few years back. He has the best strokes in New York."

"Uncle, you don't understand. I'm not interested in strokes. The tournament boys are too pretty. I need a money player, a guy who won't freeze with two hundred dollars sitting under the table. I want Coen to lose his pants."

"Then you'll have to depend on a Spic. Sylvio Neruda. He can make a shot off Coen's eyeballs. But he's a tricky son-of-a-bitch. He won't produce unless you catch him in the right mood."

"He'll produce," Odile said, and she ran to the health spa, which was open only to men. The beadle let her through when she whistled Vander's name. She passed the volley ball room, the badminton room, the shuffleboard room, the quoits and horseshoe-pitching room, naked men hissing at her, lurching for a towel or hopping with their genitals in their hands. "Holy shit," Odile had to mutter. "It's a fags' house." Vander might have told her that Sylvio was the porter of the ping-pong room. He sat hunched on a stool at the end of the room, a mop between his legs, snoring and jerking a shoulder to the clack of the balls. The room's five tables were occupied, and Odile marched around the players to get to Sylvio, the ping-pong shark. He had stubble on his cheeks. He looked at her slantily after she woke him with a tug of the mop. "Mama," he said, "what you doing here? They don't allow any ladies. You fuck with my job, I burn your ass."

"Sylvio, I came for you. With a recommendation from my uncle. Vander Child."

Sylvio, who was something of a Christian, believed in epiphanies; he couldn't reconcile the contours of Odile's face, the sharp angles in her nose, under fluorescent light. He figured she might be one of the saints from his catechism book, come to bother him.

"Vander Child don't play here. Girlie, what's your name?"

"Odile. I need your paddle, Sylvio. I'd like to borrow you for an hour. I'll give you a hundred dollars if you can beat an uptown man."

Sylvio began to mumble out a few of his saints. "Lucie, Teresa, Agnes." He was staring hard. "Who is he, your hundred-dollar boy?"

She told him.

"I never heard of Coen. Where does he hit? At Morris' or Reisman's place?"

"It's Schiller's. On Columbus." And she showed him the address.

Sylvio laughed into the handle of his mop. "Mama, the clowns go there. I don't take money off cockroaches. Reisman's, all right. Schiller's is a hole. I'm losing sleep because of you. So long."

Odile wouldn't let him nod off.

"Coen's a killer, a killer paid by the City of New York. He belongs to an elite band of detectives. They persecute idiot boys, run them down with cars."

Sylvio swiped a leather pouch from under his chair. "A ping-pong cop? Girlie, I'm coming."

He pulled her toward the IRT, but Odile wouldn't go into a tunnel; she had never been on a subway in her life. She got him into a cab, closed the door. He sulked. "Mama, I don't dig the outdoors." He gave her his pouch to hold; she could feel the imprint of a bat. He settled into a corner, dropped his chin down. Odile had to poke him when they arrived. He wouldn't go first, so she took the plunge into the cellar, Sylvio at her heels, falling away from the banister. The shock of foul air, crooked light coming off the walls (Schiller's was notorious for its spots of shadow), the irregular throw of tables (most of them with at least one hobbled leg), and the SROs leering from the gallery, disturbed Odile, who had gotten used to the quiet life and gentlemen players of the health spa. But the SROs did appeal to Sylvio; he hadn't expected this many *portorriqueños* at Schiller's club. "Friends," he said, speaking English on purpose, "the lady, she brought me for your star. Coen the cop."

The SROs were twittering now, and Sylvio lost his edge with them; he groped for the pouch in Odile's hand. She was already halfway to Coen. She had seen him sitting in street clothes at the end of the gallery, with Schiller. Coen wouldn't get off his rump for Odile; Schiller had to move him. "Manfred, I think the girl is talking to you."

She stuck a hip out at him, presented the details of her profile, only she was at a disadvantage in the harsh, uneven light.

"Coen, I'm putting a hundred dollars on my man. I say he can trim you in your own sport. He's Sylvio Neruda from downtown."

Schiller whispered to Coen. "Manfred, don't play him. He'll

steal your shoelaces. That's the kind of guy he is. He's fierce when it comes to money. Otherwise his reputation wouldn't have spilled uptown."

"Schiller, lend me a hundred."

Coen undressed in the back room while Schiller counted singles and fives from his money box. He would have groaned louder, but he couldn't disappoint the cop. He called into the changing room. "Manfred, should I send for Arnold? Arnold brings you good luck."

"No."

Coen came out in his ping-pong suit, the holster clipped to his shorts. A weirdo, Sylvio figured, but he wouldn't give Coen the satisfaction of a smile. Sylvio had played with loonies before; he wasn't delicate about taking their money. Odile put her hundred dollars under the table; following the tradition of ping-pong sharks that Vander had explained to her once, she crumpled the bills. No hustler would perform with money lying flat on the ground; crumpled bills were a lucky omen; also, it was easier to grab the whole pot, if the bulls should decide to invade the premises. Schiller dropped Coen's hundred in a coffee tin, sliding it deep enough between the legs so it wouldn't distract Sylvio or Coen. Then he went for the balls.

"I have a box of Nittaku's. They're fresh."

But the shark wouldn't play with a Japanese ball. "Too heavy," he said. "They have unreliable seams." He dug into his pockets and brought out two "Double Happiness" balls, which came from China and were hard to find in Manhattan. He blew on the balls, rotating them in his palm. "Okay with you?" he asked Coen.

"Test them, Manfred," Schiller said. "They could be warped on one side. They'll take away your control, and give him extra spin."

Coen wouldn't listen. "Sylvio, where's your bat?"

The shark could afford to smile; he unzipped the pouch and removed the fattest paddle Coen had ever seen; it was a Butterfly with a superfast face, five millimeters of rubber and sponge on each side, more than was allowed in tournament play. Coen's Mark V was a puny weapon compared to that.

Schiller complained. "Manfred, he's got a club in his hand. You'll never make it."

"Sylvio, throw up the ball."

They volleyed for two minutes, Sylvio using his most languid strokes, testing Coen's backhand; like most sharks, he wouldn't reveal his best serves before the game; he didn't want Coen getting too familiar with the hops off his bat. Sylvio preferred the "penholder" grip, clawing the Butterfly with his palm full on the rubber so that he could play backhand and forehand with one side of the bat. Coen was a "handshake" man; with the handle in his fist and only a finger on the rubber, he was forced to turn the bat when he switched from forehand to backhand, slowing his response to the ball. Sylvio could hug the table, scooping up every shot. Coen had to play further back.

Returning the ball, Sylvio flitted past Odile, stopping close to her ear. "Mama, you can't lose. This cop doesn't have the strokes."

He returned to the table. "Coen, we'll play a set for the hundred, okay?"

"No sets," Coen said. "One game."

Sylvio winked to Odile. "He's a joker. He won't see my serve in one game. It'll spin past his nose. Coen, I'll make it fair." He pointed to Schiller. "Why should I rob his old man? How much of a spot do you want? Six points? I can give you more."

"No spot."

Sylvio put both hands under the table; Coen had to guess which hand had the ball if he wanted the serve. "Left," he said.

Sylvio brought the ball up in his right palm. "Coen, you dropped your luck in Schiller's room."

Schiller wagged his head. Crouching, with his ass near the ground and his bat belt-high so Coen wouldn't be able to determine the direction of the spin, Sylvio drove five wicked serves, all exactly the same, into Coen's fist; no wood or rubber touched the ball from Coen's side; he had nothing better than his knuckles to offer Sylvio. The ball plummeted off the table every time. Sylvio caught him five-zip.

Using a simple lob serve. Coen got two out of five. Because he took his eye off the ball to peek at Odile, Sylvio faulted once, making four of his next five serves. Coen played with his knuckles again. He couldn't solve Sylvio's spin. The score stood twelve to three, Sylvio.

"How about another hundred, Coen?"

"Schiller," Coen said, "get your money box."

Sylvio watched the cop. "It's a joke. I don't change stakes in the middle of a game."

Coen got one lob past Sylvio, then volleyed home two out of four, meeting Sylvio's slices with little push shots, surprising the shark. Sylvio had expected him to crack by now. He rubbed his lip with the top of the Butterfly.

"Coen, you'll have to take off the holster and the badge. They're fucking with my concentration."

Schiller began to protest. "Where is it written that the gun has to go? Did you sign a contract with him?"

"Balls," Sylvio said. "That man's trying to ruin my eye. Why else would he wear gold on his chest?"

Odile was even more adamant than the shark. She couldn't get a rise out of Coen, whatever the score. She suffered near the table. The shark had revealed something to Odile; there was no way to humiliate Coen with a ping-pong paddle. She wallowed on her platform shoes; a tall girl without the shoes, she was over six feet in her creped heels and soles, which allowed her to fully dwarf the others at the table, Schiller needing to stand on the point of his slippers to remain in communication with her. Coen clipped off the holster and the badge.

He was a man with nothing to lose. Sylvio could trip him twenty-one points in a row, and Coen would have given up the money in the coffee tin without a peep. He had no mother, no father, to provide for; the First Dep's office might disclaim him, but they couldn't swipe his pension so quick. It was Schiller who poked his head outside the range of Odile's shoulders to have an eye on the door. Coen didn't flinch. If the Chinaman arrived while Schiller clutched the holster in his lap, Coen could wear his bat like a chest protector or meet the Chinaman frown for frown. He missed the feel of leather on his hip, the slide of the holster when he stretched for the ball, but he couldn't be hurt by Odile's shark. He took Sylvio's cut serves on a higher bounce, with his knuckles out of the ball's path. He showed more rubber now, and the ball remained on the table. Overcoming the trickiness of the serve, he could deal with the flaws in Sylvio's style. The penholder grip gave Sylvio less of a stretch than Coen because he clawed the bat and had to swing in a narrower arc, leaving him vulnerable in the corners. So Coen angled his shots, striking deep into the sides of the table.

"The ball's flat," Sylvio griped. "There must be a split somewheres."

"Nine serving sixteen," Schiller said, handing Coen the other "Double Happiness" ball. Odile didn't need a bearded, slippered gnome to repeat the score. The game was inconsequential. Unable to count on the shark, she interposed herself, kicking off the crepes and

stepping out of her skirt. She would *make* Coen look at her, force him
to comment on her nakedness, upset his strokes if she could. Odile
wore no underwear on this day, and Schiller, who admired the precise
swell of her bosoms in a shirt from Bendel's, was astonished that her
breastline didn't change without the shirt. A cultured man, a polite
man, he was ashamed of the erection in his pocket. This Odile had
the firmest chest in the country, Schiller believed. He was too
distracted to reckon with the silk in her pubic hair. Coen was busy
lobbing the ball. He saw the fallen skirt, but he wouldn't inhibit the
sweep of his bat for Odile. The SROs screamed from Schiller's
gallery. "Sweetheart, do the turkey trot." They clucked with their
tongues, climbing over the gallery wall; they would have gone
further, but they realized the cop owned a gun in Schiller's lap. Odile
put her shoes back on, so she could annoy Coen from a higher level.

The gallery screamed, "Sweetheart, sweetheart."

This noise finally caught Sylvio in the head; he'd been brooding
over the collapse of his game (the shark still had Coen eighteen to
twelve). He turned around, noticed Odile in her shoes. Coen pushed
three points past him. Sylvio gripped the Butterfly with his pinkie in
the air. No breastline or Venus hair could have disconnected him so.
Sylvio wasn't taking a sexual stance (others had tried to tempt the
shark during a game, and failed). It was the porous nature of the light
in Schiller's club that undid Sylvio; the shark suffered a religious
manifestation, an epiphany of sorts. Naked in the muggy light, with
dark streaks coming down her chest like so many wounds, and her
profile punctured by the shadows flying off Coen's bat, the girl
became one of the great martyrs for Sylvio, *Santa Odile*. His fingers
numbed on him, and he lost all the advantages of the penholder grip;
he couldn't scoop up the ball. He might have beaten Coen anyway;
even in a crisis, the shark was better than a cop. But Odile had gone
for her clothes. Crying, bitter at Sylvio, bitter at Schiller, bitter at
Coen, she stuck a leaden arm into the Bendel shirt. She passed the
gallery with one buttock showing. Sylvio followed her out, his neck
twitching in Coen's direction. "Cop, I be back. Next month. I shave
your ass sitting on a chair. I spot you twenty, man. You play like a
cunt."

The shark forgot his pouch and his "Double Happiness" balls,
and Coen had to fling them at him. He didn't want the money. "Give
it to the welfares, Emmanuel. Let them buy ice cream and cake. They
can feast the whole fucking hotel. Everybody eats. But save a few

dollars for Arnold." He had nothing to gloat about; he couldn't cherish Sylvio's retreat the way Schiller did. Schiller rattled the money tin.

"Manfred, that's another hustler who'll think twice before annoying us. He won't dare bring the bat into a public place."

Coen had the urge to run after Odile, an urge which he suppressed; she came with the shark, she could go with him. He wondered what deal she'd made with Sylvio: cash or bedwork? The cop was growing jealous. He was fond of her, in spite of her waspishness. She had a stylish walk in her big, gummy shoes. He muttered to himself once Schiller was out of earshot. Odile, you figured wrong. I'm the real hustler, not Sylvio. I was playing money games for Zorro before the kid knew what a paddle was. Manfred Coen of the Loch Sheldrake ping-pong school. I was terrific with sandpaper.

Odile made the stairs with her cheeks on fire. She wouldn't look at the shark. Her hems were crooked. She came out of the cellar only partially dressed; she couldn't get her fingers through the sleeve. Sylvio guided them for her, feeling the luxury of knucklebone.

"Don't touch me," she said. She pressed a hundred dollars in his hand. "You're paid. Now disappear."

Sylvio kept two feet behind Odile, varying his speed according to hers. His pupils had shrunk, and all Odile could see of him were dirty eyewhites. He reminded her of the junkies who punked around in the hallway opposite The Dwarf, their faces a bloodless gray without proper eyeballs; that's how much he had deteriorated after dueling Coen. "I gave you carfare," she said. "Now go and scratch." He dropped behind one more step. She fetched a cab for herself and locked the door on him. Going down Columbus she had a change of heart. She told the cabby to circle around the block; his meter ate thirty cents finding Sylvio. "Get in."

He slumped with his knees higher than his head. He didn't dare touch Odile again. For comfort he rubbed up against the upholstery with the small of his back. Odile hadn't meant to beleaguer him.

"My uncle picks the winners. Some shark you are."

"Mama, I'm wiped out. You know what it is playing a dead man? I counted his blinks. Two blinks in thirty shots. That's not human. A human man I could squash. Ask around. Ask when the last time was Sylvio Neruda left money under a table."

She said, "Shut up," so he crossed his arms until Christopher

Street. She wouldn't let him off without clutching him. Her tongue licked the flats of his teeth. Even the cabby was suspicious. He wouldn't believe such kissing could exist in his own cab.

"I'm sorry," Odile blew into Sylvio's ear. He liked the heat of a moving lip. "He's icy, Coen. Very icy. Some big shit called Isaac trained him to be like that."

The shark waddled into the health spa. Sitting with Odile must have activated the crazy bone in his knee. How could you evaluate the kiss of a mama saint? The girl had a bitter tongue, that's the truth. She took the strength out of his legs, Santa Odile. He wouldn't accept women backers any more. He reached the ping-pong room huffing, his eyes off the players, thankful for the clean grace of fluorescent light.

PART THREE

FOURTEEN

Just when Coen was ready to go to Papa, to warn him at least of the
tail on Jerónimo, to chide him about the hush money for Sheb, to
curse him maybe for monkeying with the finances of his father's
store, Papa came to him. Coen knew the tribe was around his door the
moment he spotted an oversize head under his fire escape. It was
Jorge eating a Spanish jellyroll. The boy couldn't decipher street
signs but he was the only muscle Papa would ever need. He could
poke your eye with a finger, climb on your back and lock your neck
in his jaw, grab your testicles, or skewer you with a kitchen knife.
Papa wouldn't have come out of the Bronx for a trifle. So Coen
didn't idle near the door. He sent Papa into the living room, while
Jorge remained in the street, remembering faces along the perimeters
of his eyes. Jorge was meant to whistle if he saw a cop in plainclothes
or a goon belonging to Isaac. He held the jellyroll close to his mouth.
His nails were a fine pink from the number of chocolate milks he
drank.

Coen offered Papa peach liqueur or a Bronx snack of cherry
soda and pretzel sticks. Papa declined. He had given Coen a
perfunctory kiss and went to sit in a corner chair. He was dressed in
his store clothes, an old twill jacket with clots of syrup on the sleeves.
Papa would sneeze into the shoulder padding from time to time. He
hated the North American passion for super-hygiene. When he
couldn't leave his counter he pissed in his shoe. He would never
bathe his boys more than once a week. He left the bugs to swim in his
syrup tanks. No one ever died of a Guzmann "black and white." He
couldn't swallow the thin homogenized stuff from the Bronx dairies
that wouldn't even leave a proper moustache on your face. Papa
drank cream from a can. His eyes were puffy today, and he had to
pinch his cheeks to get the twitches out. Coen couldn't believe that
Papa had money or policy slips on his mind.

"Manfred, I want Jerónimo safe. Go to your Chief—tell him
Papa will give up five of his runners and his wire room on Minford

Place if he agrees not to touch the boy."

"Papa, I already told César. I'm not working for Isaac. I'm playing the glom these days. Papa, ever since Isaac resigned, they've been throwing me into all the boroughs except one. They wouldn't let me catch homicides in the Bronx. Why? Because I might step on Isaac's toes and prevent him from watching the candy store."

"Manfred, he got nothing but bellyaches from me. He had to scrape the floor to collect a penny. Isaac lived on fudge. I spit inside every sundae I made him. I would have brought him up to the farm in a basket and shoveled dirt in his mouth, but this is the United States. You can't wipe off a big *agente* like Isaac and expect to stay in business. The cops would mourn for him all over Boston Road."

"Papa, why did Jerónimo come back from Mexico? You should have kept him with Mordeckai."

"The boy was lonely. He couldn't adjust to the Mexican traffic lights. A cousin isn't close enough. How long would he survive without seeing his brother's face?"

"If you hadn't opened your marriage bureau, Isaac might have left you alone."

"That's César's trade, not mine."

"Please. César wouldn't have moved into Manhattan without the nod from you. And I don't believe Mordeckai became a rabbi just for César. Papa, you okayed the brides. But Isaac's going to have to chew his own warts for a while. They caught the lipstick freak at the Fourth Division, so he can't lay that trick on Jerónimo."

"He'll find something else. There's always a loose freak running around."

And Papa sat with his thumbs under his chin, an old habit from Peru, when he had to wait for hours at the market of San Jerónimo for a tradesman with pockets fat enough to pick. He had loved Coen the boy, had opened the candy store and the farm to him, had mixed him with his own brood, but he was suspicious of the man. You couldn't traffic with Isaac for twelve years and go unspoiled. So he trusted Coen only by degrees. Whatever Coen was capable of doing to him and César, he didn't think the cop would hand Jerónimo over to Isaac.

"Manfred, I could offer him cash. I could set him up in the south Bronx under a code name. Abraham. It's stinkproof. No commissioner has a nose that good."

"You can't make Isaac like that. Best thing, Papa, is chain

Jerónimo to the candy store, or give him ten blocks on Boston Road for his hikes, with Jorge and Alejandro at the other end of his pants."

"Manfred, I've dealt with those *agentes* before. They could kidnap Alejandro. They could give Jorge a permanent headache with their clubs. They could run Jerónimo down with a car. I'm superstitious, Manfred. I don't want any of my boys to die before me."

"Papa, I'm superstitious too. I didn't know my mother and father would pick the oven when I went into Germany."

Papa brought his thumbs out from under his chin and crossed them over his nose.

"Why did you hound Albert for money? Papa, couldn't you have waited until I got back?"

"Manfred, who's been fucking you in the ear? Did you bribe your uncle with chocolate bars?"

"No. Isaac told Pimloe, and Pimloe told me. He thought I'd be anxious to spy on César if I knew."

"Pricks," Papa screamed, and put his thumbs in his pockets. "Hound your father, you say. I kept him alive. He couldn't have fed a weasel on the eggs he sold. My cousins from Peru had to suck four eggs a day because I wanted to satisfy the Coens. I won't hedge with you, Manfred. I'm a policy man, not a charity house. Your father, your mother, and your uncle Sheb did small favors for me. I stored some of my account books in their egg boxes. I sent your uncle on errands so he wouldn't lose his self-respect. I gave them a free bungalow in Loch Sheldrake, but your mother was too refined. She didn't want your father getting contaminated by me or my boys. She was a cultured woman, that Jessica. I enjoyed having her on the farm. She told your father I flirted with her. Manfred, I swear on Jerónimo's life, I didn't do nothing but touch her once on the knee. She should have walked in my orchard with more clothes."

"Papa, that still doesn't explain why they preferred gas?"

"Manfred, every month your father sold less and less. I could have choked an army with the eggs I took off him. I couldn't carry him forever."

"Then you should have closed him down before I went on maneuvers. How could I clear Albert out of the store from a post in West Germany?"

"They had it in their heads to die for a long time. Your father had too much gentility. You can't exist on Boston Road with his diet.

The Coens would have been better off if they ate meat instead of grass."

"Explain to me, Papa, why Sheb has been collecting premiums from you for so many years?"

Papa scowled in Coen's chair. "What premiums?'

"Two dollars a month from Jerónimo's hand."

"Manfred, don't stick me too hard. There's some blood under all my freckles. After he prepared the oven for Albert your uncle was a maniac. Jorge found him on the fire escape laughing and screaming, with piss everywhere. César climbed up and wanted to bring him down. But he would only go with Jerónimo. So the baby went up there and held Shebby's fingers. That's how we got him into the candy store. The boys washed the piss off. He slept with Jerónimo, he ate off Jerónimo's dish. And I gave him an allowance same as the baby. Two dollars a month. We lent him Jorge's coat for the funeral."

"Papa, somebody should have thought about inviting me. I had the right to throw a little dirt on my father's box."

"Manfred, César wrote the Army. They didn't write back."

Coen lost his inclination to dig. He couldn't turn Papa's head, force him to look at Coen outside Guzmann lines. So he slouched against the wall. Papa got up. Worrying about Jerónimo gave him a squint in his left eye. He had more gray hairs on his neck than Coen could remember. His knuckles were humped from fixing ice cream sodas. He gave Coen a better kiss than before.

"Manfred, be careful. You shouldn't touch César's Chinaman in the face again. He's been speaking your name."

Coen watched the Guzmanns from his windowsill. Papa couldn't bend like Jorge. He had a stiff-legged walk from standing behind his counter seventeen hours a day. He put his hand in Jorge's pocket and led them both across the street. His shoulders wouldn't get warm in Manhattan. Jorge was growling for food. So they had barley soup at the dairy restaurant before César's man drove them to the candy store. Papa couldn't fill his stomach without beef or pork. But Jorge seemed fit. He belched through his fist in the steerer's car. Papa didn't like to think about the dead. The living gave him plenty to do. But Albert's wife still had the power to sting him in the ass. Nipples didn't move him so much. He could have listed on a sheet of policy paper a hundred nipples fancier than Jessica Coen's. But he couldn't get underneath her smile. Albert he pitied. Manfred he loved. Jessica could only bother him. She brought pimples on his

arms. Instead of salting twenty-dollar bills in the chimneys of his
farmhouse, he would watch Jessica from behind a tree, her face stiff
in the sun, while his boys clumped around the orchard in country
shoes. Nothing could make her put on her halter or hurt the
confidence of that thick smile. Did she want all six of the Guzmanns
to pay for Albert's ineptness, his inability to provide?

Papa had only a narrow fondness for women. He had a habit of
changing *queridas* after pregnancies were over. They would bear a
child for Papa and move to another pueblo. He took pride in the
knowledge that every one of his boys had a different mother. He
expected simple fecundity from a *mujer* and would tolerate nothing
else. Alejandro's mother was a beauty with eleven toes. Topal's was
a straightforward market slut. Jorge's had becoming moles on her ass
and could prepare a remarkable fisherman's soup. He might have put
up with her for a while longer if she hadn't been jealous of his older
boys. César's was a mestizo with slim hips. Jerónimo's he couldn't
remember. All the *mujeres* accepted Papa's crazy calendar. Ever
since their time in Portugal, when they had to conduct the Marrano
services in a wine cellar under the feet of the civil guard, Guzmanns
have celebrated Christmas in July and Pascua (the Marrano Easter) in
the fall. The *mujeres* worshiped Moses, Abraham, John the Baptist,
and Joseph of Egypt. They depreciated the value of the Holy Virgin
(no Guzmann would ever pray to a woman), they soaked the Marrano
pork in hot oil, they washed the genitals of Papa's boys. Papa sacked
them anyway, one by one. Yet he couldn't rid himself of that other
mujer. He would rinse a glass, scrape off the remains of a banana
split, and see a nipple in the sink. He was no better off on the farm. If
he sat in his own orchard too long without one of his boys he smelled
Jessica near the strawberry patch.

Jorge fell asleep in the car. Papa's disposition changed once the
steerer took him over the Third Avenue bridge. The water smelled
different on the Bronx side. His shoulders baked. He could tickle his
brain without terrorizing himself. Papa had learned to play cat's
cradle with other Marrano boys in the flea markets of Peru. No
proper *limueño* could revive a dead piece of string like the Marranos,
who had to spend their lives bundling and unbundling their goods. If
a boy had no intuition in his fingers and couldn't feel his way through
the constellations of the game, if he knotted his thumbs when he tried
to get beyond "the scissors" or "the king," Papa, who was called
Moisés then, would dig around the thumbs and perform surgery on

the string. His own boys couldn't catch on to the game. Jerónimo's abilities ended after "pinkie square." César had the fingers but no patience. Jorge, Topal and Alejandro bungled on the first constellation. They couldn't even fit the string. The *norteamericanos* had their own games. None of the farmers at the lake or the merchants of Boston Road could play with him, nobody but Jessica Coen. Who had blessed her fingers? Papa couldn't vex her with his constellations. She tilted the string with her thumbs turned in, and got out of Papa's snares. It was curious lovemaking. Four hands in a pie of string. How many times did he graze her bosoms going from "the diamond" to "pinkie square?" And he'd hold her cups for a second while she stood against him taking a constellation off his fingers. She didn't approve or disapprove of Papa's caress. He only saw the teeth in her face and her jumbo eyes. She always had the boy with her. Was he concentrating on the hands inside or outside the string? Because Manfred could make "the butterfly" almost as fine as Papa.

His boys had an uncommon knack. Jorge snapped awake a block from the candy store. Papa's stools were filled. The girls were waiting for their ice cream The hard smudges under their eyes, all their piggy looks, told him he'd better not dally with the steerer. So he sent the car back to the dairy restaurant with one slap of the fender. And he had the girls in their plates, breathing hot fudge, before Jorge could count the quarters in his pockets.

"Isaac, Isaac the Prick."

DeFalco, Rosenheim, and Brown, snugged up in fiberglass vests, were berating Coen's old Chief; they couldn't understand why their own squad commander had surrendered them over to Isaac. Brown and Rosenheim carried riot guns from the borough office. The pump gun that DeFalco was cradling belonged to Coen. DeFalco had snapped open the door to Coen's locker with a common pair of pliers, but he wouldn't take Coen's shopping bag along.

"Why doesn't Isaac get the rat squad to chauffeur him around?" DeFalco snarled; none of them was anxious to ride shotgun for the First Dep.

"Maybe he knows what shitty work they do, all them blue-eyed gloms," Brown said. "He wants a decent team."

"Bullshit," Rosenheim said. He had more cunning than the other two. "It must be a cover. Isaac can't be seen with First Deputy boys."

They saluted their dispatcher with shotguns and trundled down the stairs; outside their own offices they walked with a pronounced slump. Their backs curved more on the ground floor, inside the territories of the uniformed police; they were contemptuous of all the hicks in blue bags. Brown stopped at the switchboard to bother the *portorriqueña* Isobel; she had been subtle with him this past week, refusing to crouch in the lockerroom, near his fly.

"Isobel, we're going to blow on Shotgun Coen. He's sleeping with César Guzmann—you know, the nigger Jew, and if we catch them together, it'll be their last embrace in a while."

Isobel wouldn't play. She was worried about Coen; and she couldn't satisfy Brown with the *israelita* in her head.

"O boy," Brown mumbled, rolling his eyes in memory of Isobel's knobs and the warm spit between her teeth. He would have crashed into the desk if Rosenheim hadn't steered his elbow another way. The three bulls pushed through the door.

"Where's Arnold?" DeFalco laughed, looking at an empty stoop. "Where's the little rat?"

"Fucking ungrateful crip," Brown said. "Didn't we throw him a dime for every coffee he brought up? I'd like to piss on his gimpy toe."

"It's true," Rosenheim complained to himself. "I had softer bowel movements with Spanish around."

DeFalco was snarling again. "Blame Isaac. The Chief owns the Puerto Ricans. Didn't he recruit Arnold for Coen? How many spies do you think Isaac used to run? Maybe a hundred, I swear."

"Bullshit," Rosenheim said. "The man's lucky if he had ten guys working for him, all rejects."

They noticed Isaac sitting in their Ford.

DeFalco hefted the stock of Coen's pump gun; he could sense the imperfections in the wood. "The prick's waiting."

"Let him starve," DeFalco said. Close to the car his snarl disappeared. The bulls shook politeness into their fiberglass vests. They ate their own teeth wearing rubber smiles. They prayed Isaac would adopt them; no detective was feared like one of Isaac's angels.

They piled into the front seat, Isaac squinting at them from the rear. None of them volunteered to sit with the Chief. But Rosenheim and DeFalco moved to the back when they saw Isaac step out of the car. They were afraid to risk Isaac's displeasure. Hunching under the range of the mirrors, DeFalco slapped Rosenheim's hand. They smiled; Brown had Isaac to himself. They hoped he enjoyed the glom. Brown felt prickles on his neck. He couldn't drive without orders. "Where we going, Isaac?"

"Touch the handbrake," Isaac said. "You're burning rubber." Then he relented a bit. "Bummy's. We're going to Bummy's."

"Are we wasting him, Isaac?" DeFalco said. He was nervous. The First Deputy men were supposed to be shotgun crazy.

"No. I'm looking for the Chinaman."

DeFalco began to leer. "Can I break one of his legs, Isaac?" He had misjudged the Chief; Isaac was pure genius, the First Deputy's sweetheart, disgraced or not.

"I expect to jump on his tail," Isaac said. "We'll follow him uptown. See where he lands."

"Could be he'll marry up with Zorro somewhere in the seventies or the eighties," Rosenheim said, anticipating the Chief.

Brown was unconvinced. Isaac didn't act like a man who had given up any of his glories. Certain Bronx detectives told him Isaac had grown too fat in the Guzmanns' candy store, that Papa had scarred him for life. Where were the signals? His coat wasn't shabby. His famous sideburns cloaked portions of his ears. Brown and his partners were the shabby ones. They didn't have Isaac's feel for a good piece of cloth. They were only detectives with chubby fists. None of them could have survived Isaac's fall.

"Where's Coen?" Brown sputtered, his thoughts jumping ahead. Why isn't his wonderboy with him?

"Coen's asleep," DeFalco answered for Isaac. But Brown wasn't pleased with this remark. The Chief wouldn't commit himself. Maybe Coen got stuck with the Guzmanns in Isaac's spot, Brown was moved to speculate. This shotgun party made no sense. Why so much firepower for one smelly chink? Brown could have taken the Chinaman apart with his thumbs. He pressed a finger into his own cheek.

"Isaac, you sure Chino will run uptown?"

DeFalco answered again. "I know all the bandit's moves. He gets lonely on the Bowery. He'll run."

Brown parked across from Bummy's, DeFalco and Rosenheim edging toward their door. Isaac didn't move. "Stay put," he said.

The caper was perplexing Rosenheim. He wouldn't mind being a hammer for the First Dep, but he couldn't tell where he stood with Isaac. "Chief, don't you need an advance man, somebody on the point, who can coax the Chinaman out of the bar? A handy broom."

"Don't call me Chief," Isaac said.

Rosenheim shifted the riot gun to his other thigh. "What?" He wasn't taking guff from a dropped inspector, one who came begging for shotguns from the homicide boys because he couldn't be seen with his own squad of angels.

"I'm not your Chief, and the Chinaman isn't in there."

Rosenheim couldn't back off. Fuck the brass. Fuck the squadroom. Fuck Isaac. Fuck Coen. "Honest to God, *Inspector Isaac?* The Chinaman isn't eating kreplach with Bummy?"

DeFalco sat on his partner's riot gun; he wanted to avoid a showdown in the car. "Isaac, are you saying you spoke to Bummy? The bar is minus a chink at the moment?"

"That's correct."

DeFalco wished he had been more tolerant of Coen's shopping bag; he might have snoozed with the bag over his brains. "Wake me when the Chinaman shows."

The Chinaman was three doors down, enjoying a mocha egg cream in a candy store owned by Roumanians. He also had a woolly head from being deprived of Odile. His tongue began to labor after the third or fourth sip. He spit the dark water over the Roumanians' counter. "Ansel, who told you you could fix an egg cream?" He squeezed up his eyelids. "This is mocha? Papa knows egg creams. You know shit. You should take lessons from the Guzmanns, Ansel, no lie."

The counterman wiped Chino's egg cream spit with a dishrag. "I'm sorry, Mr. Reyes. It's the syrup. They're using synthetics. They color the water, yes, but they can't duplicate the mocha."

The Chinaman stole halvah off the counter, and gave up in one chew. Stale. The candy store was a grave for stale goods. Slapping Ansel wouldn't get him where he wanted to go. He had to slap another Jew, Coen. And he didn't have slapping tools. The sink's gone dry. If he'd known there would be a shortage this season, he might have stocked up. He could get bombs, sledgehammers, ice picks, no Colts. He was Zorro's triggerman, a pistol without a gun. "Ansel, goodbye."

He left the candy store doing the Chinaman's strut, a bowlegged walk he'd developed on Mulberry Street twelve years ago when he hunted for *sicilianas* from the seventh grade, with a pinkie curled around each suspender. It was time for his *comida* at Bummy's, black coffee, sugar, rye whiskey, and whipped cream in a heavy bowl. DeFalco, Rosenheim, and Brown laughed at the grinding knees and other peculiar notions of the Chinaman's strut. The wig didn't fool them; they recognized Chino once he hit the street. They grew shy in Isaac's presence; now they could appreciate the hard brilliance of Isaac's technique. "Isaac," DeFalco said, "how did you figure out his schedule? You tracked him to the nearest second."

Brown strummed the barrel of his shotgun. "Isaac, should I lay one in his ear? The charge will straighten the bends in his ass."

Isaac wouldn't give in to their jubilation. "We'll wait for the man. He won't hold us long."

The Chinaman greeted Bummy's Italian barkeep with the two-fingered salute famous in SoHo. Unable to penetrate the surface chill of uptown North America, the Chinaman considered himself a proper Sicilian from Mulberry Street. He might have been even more of a polyglot if he'd had a less active life (pistols weren't paid to spit foreign verbs). Aside from Spanish, Italian, Manhattan English, and Cuban Chinese, he could jabber phrases in Yiddish and creole French (one of his father's native tongues). His loyalties were singular; he respected no other holiday than the feast of San Gennaro, which spilled into the northern tip of Chinatown and fattened him with sausages and smooth cottage cheese. A precinct captain, familiar to the Chinaman, was snoring at Bummy's table. Chino didn't have to muffle his steps; waking or sleeping, this captain accepted the Chinaman's red hair. He wasn't going to cooperate with a squad of midtown detectives and nab Chino in Bummy's place, so long as the taxi bandit didn't operate in his precinct. The pretty boys from homicide and assault could do their own stalking. The captain slept better with his gun on the table, otherwise his paunch interfered with his nap, the holstered Police Special rubbing his kidney or his groin whenever he snored too loud.

Chino hadn't been this close to a piece of hardware since Mexico City. He imagined how Coen would look staring down the bore of a captain's gun. The Jew's face would crumple into piss-colored dots. Either Coen begged Chino's forgiveness or he'd get his fingers shot off. The Chinaman had to afford this mercy because the Jew was once a friend of Zorro's. Still, the Chinaman stalled at the table, weighing his choices. If he swiped the gun, Bummy would lock him out for the duration. Yet if he didn't punish Coen by the end of the week, he'd have to admit that a Polish, a blond Jew, *could* touch his face. The Chinaman leaned on one heel. Already his ankles were growing numb. The gun slid out of the holster with a simple crush of leather and a delicate whine. The captain chewed his gums.

DeFalco timed the Chinaman's stay; six minutes and eleven seconds. Brown was working the clutch. Isaac placed a leg over Brown's. "Don't. Give him half a block. He'll smell us from here. Green Fords are a giveaway."

"Isaac," DeFalco said, "how did you guess he'd come out so fast?"

Brown wagged his head. "He's got pins in his ass, that Chinaman. He can't sit too long. Isaac knows."

Rosenheim settled into the car, resigned to his job; he'd bounce wherever the Chinaman took him, but he wouldn't join in any celebrations of Isaac.

FIFTEEN

Coen expected Isaac. He tried to figure the route his Chief would take. Isaac was fond of fire escapes. When he wanted to visit Coen unannounced, he'd come in through the window wearing gloves and a scarf to protect him from the draft in Coen's alley. On formal occasions he'd leave a note with Schiller or have his chauffeur (Brodsky, of course) ride around the block until Coen recognized the car. Isaac never telephoned. He couldn't guarantee who else was sitting on Coen's wire. Coen felt sure Isaac wouldn't make any cheap entry. Isaac didn't have Pimloe's flashy tastes. He wouldn't have met Coen in a supermarket, with sacks of grapefruit between them. It would have been Arnold's room or the ping-pong club. Isaac had a certain amount of affection for the Spic. It was Isaac who first pulled Spanish Arnold into the stationhouse, made him a stoolie and a buff. Whatever sources of information Coen had, disgruntled pickpockets, unemployed triggermen, marginal pimps, came through Isaac. Coen would have humped dry air without the Chief.

Isaac didn't show. Coen put on his trousers and went into the street. Mrs. Dalkey was sitting on the stoop with Rickie, her Dalmatian. Coen couldn't get around the Widow's knees and the dog's thick jowls. Smug with the knowledge that she had trapped the lipstick freak, Dalkey wouldn't even look at Coen. She had no use for a detective who pampered dog poisoners and befriended Puerto Ricans from the welfare hotel. So Coen stepped over her knees and brushed Rickie's two chins. Dalkey growled. Coen excused himself. He didn't want tallies against him on the block captain's sheet. He'd have to dodge all his neighbors or go live in some garage.

"It's a kind night, yes Mrs. Dalkey? How's the poodle?"

She swabbed Rickie's ears with a Q-tip, and Coen walked uptown. The fruitmen gestured at him with cantaloupes, which were coming into season. The waiters at the Cuban restaurant knocked their hellos on the windows. Coen stepped around some dogshit and smiled into the restaurant. He was hungry for Cuban coffee but he wouldn't eat without Arnold. The gay boys were wearing their summer outfits (it was only the fifth of May), jerseys with low necks that revealed the split in their pectorals; they sat in a long file at the drugstore adjoining the Cuban restaurant and watched Coen's blue eyes. There had been friction over the winter between the *cubanos* and the gays, and the boys could no longer pick fellows off the street under the Pepsi-Cola sign. They rode the stools, winking at Coen and angling themselves so that their wings and pecs could be seen in full. "Hey blondie. Look over here." They knew he was a cop. But this one wouldn't come in and catch their genitals under a stool with handcuffs or spill soup down their jerseys like some of the bulletheads from the precinct. He didn't make war on fags. So they hooted in appreciation, they thanked him for leaving their fellows on the stools. A woman holding a tiny purse made of antelope skin waylaid Coen at the end of the block. She swore the subways had run out of tokens. There was more than meanness in the temerity of her grip. She had mousy eyes that roamed over Coen's shirt. Only half her mouth would close.

"I'm a mother," she said. "I'm a citizen. I raised boys for the Army. Why shouldn't I be able to pass through a turnstile?"

Coen tried to give her a subway token but she wouldn't accept favors from strange men. So he had to sell her one and curl his hands to receive the pennies that she shook out of the antelope purse. A few of the single boys outside the SRO hotel spotted the transaction and they reviled Coen for taking pennies off an old lady. He ducked under the stairs and emerged in the damp vestibule of the ping-pong club. It was Schiller's rush hour. Coen got bumped with hot air off the tables. The freaks were hitting balls without mercy tonight, gearing themselves for a tournament at the Waldorf Astoria. They wouldn't nod to Coen or recognize that he was alive. They had no time for cops. They were perfecting their loops and taking the kinks out of their other shots. So Coen avoided their playing zones and took the long way to Schiller's frying pan. He had scrambled eggs, clutching an onion in his fist like Schiller, and gnawing into it. "Emmanuel, any messages for me?"

Schiller had never trifled with Coen's correspondences. "Mister, do you have a note on your table? The net's clean."

"Sorry, Emmanuel. I thought Isaac might get in touch. He owes me a visit."

"Isaac's with the dead. He wouldn't have missed my omelettes otherwise. That man knew how to eat an onion with the peel."

"Emmanuel, your onions improved his nose. He's been so busy smelling for Guzmanns, he forgot who we are."

"You're misjudging him. Isaac isn't a forgetful man."

Coen retired to Schiller's closet. In half an hour the tables began to clear, and Schiller found a partner for Coen, a Cuban dishwasher named Alphonso, with a raw, unorthodox style that made trouble for you in the corners. With the freaks gone, Coen came out of the closet in his ping-pong clothes. Alphonso wasn't intimidated by the shield and the gun butt. He had played this chico with the yellow headband once before. Both of them dusted their Mark V's with a rag that Schiller provided. They warmed up with a house ball, then switched to a heavier, three-star ball that wouldn't pucker under the pressure of their thick-handled bats. Coen might have hugged the table with eggs on his mind, but the *cubano* wouldn't allow it. He had Coen cracking at the hips, and forced him into the game. So Coen put away the morbid turns of his past, mother, father, Papa, Isaac, Sheb, to contain Alphonso. He served the ball off the side of the bat, showing Alphonso only negligible amounts of rubber and sponge. His push shots traveled so close to the teeth of the net, Alphonso couldn't return them without scraping the elbow of his playing arm. "Maricón," he cried at the ball. "Bobo." But he gave it back to Coen. Lunging for a corner shot, the cop would stab his holster against the edge of the table and lose the point. He might have untrussed himself, leaned the holster on a chair, but he didn't want to change his style on account of Alphonso, who would have sucked the ends of his moustache with great satisfaction if he had made Coen undress. Alphonso saw the fresh white scars in Coen's holster, and he played with half a moustache in his mouth. Coen had to work. He was pushing the *cubano* into the gallery with his wrist slams, setting him up for a lob that would have landed Alphonso's nose on the table, when a thought stuck in his head. He couldn't finish the point. He walked around the table to Schiller's cubicle and destroyed Schiller's nap. "Emmanuel," he said, poking him with the bat. "I never kissed my father."

"So what?" Schiller grumbled in his good-natured way.

"I can't remember touching his shoulder, shaking his hand, nothing."

"Manfred, it happens to lots of boys. I had a father who slapped you on the chin if you forgot to call him 'Sir.' "

"Did you kiss him?"

"Maybe once in my life. It tasted horrible. Like wet paper."

Alphonso shouted from the table. "Hey man, don't bullshit so much."

He toweled his moustache before he would play with Coen. He dusted the ball with his undershirt. He gave Coen trouble in both corners. With the *cubano* smacking the floorboards, it took Schiller minutes to locate his natural sleeping position. And he inherited nightmares from Coen, feeling the press of a bony hand on his forehead. He groaned, rubbed the wall, kicked the frying pan off its hook, and the *cubano* swore that he wouldn't pay for his time with Coen if Schiller didn't learn to sleep quiet. Alphonso reproached himself for having dusted the ball. The cop was eating up his serves. Ever since Coen stalled their game to chat with the house about father kisses, Alphonso couldn't get his momentum back. He smiled, thinking maybe Coen and Schiller were fairies together, but he still did nothing with the bat. Coen jockeyed him away from the table, caused him to stumble in his combat boots and swing under the ball.

Chino Reyes stood at the front table with his Police Special, a snubnosed .38. He had come uptown to humiliate the cop, make him beg for his life. But watching Coen in little Morrocan sneakers, he forgot whatever plans he had. His eyeballs hung on the patterns of Coen's feet, those bends to the side, the red sneeze of the bat, the power Coen had over the ball. He liked Coen's blue shorts, the vulnerability of his bared knees. The holster didn't frighten Chino. He could have popped Coen in the head before that holster went into play. He passed Schiller's bench, got within yards of Coen. Alphonso saw the gun first. He was close enough to the line of fire to lose a cheek or a hand. Chino motioned to him with the gun. "Vamos, muchacho. Out of here," But Coen was waving his Mark V.

"Finish the game, Alphonso."

Caught between two locos, a copy with a queerness for ping-pong and a Chinaman who liked to point guns, Alphonso decided to heed Coen. He was more afraid of the snarl on Coen's lip than the Chinaman's piece. So he served high, into Coen's bat, amazed by the sureness of his own reflexes and the cooperation in his knees. The routine flights of the ball infuriated the Chinaman.

"Coen, why are you bringing the cholo into this? Send him home. I don't have quarrels with a Spic."

"Chino, you're going to eat that pistol after the game is over. I told you keep away."

Alphonso felt his ankles give. He leaned hard into the table and returned Coen's chop but he couldn't get the Mark V to bite. And Coen smashed the ball into his armpit. It stuck there, befuddling Alphonso who had never carried a ball in his armpit until now. Then it spilled onto the table. Alphonso pushed it back to Coen. Chino spit between his legs. He wasn't going to tolerate another volley with that ping-pong ball.

"Coen, you bother me too long for one night."

He aimed at the net. He wanted to blow all of Coen's securities away. But the gun had too much kick. And he splintered Schiller's wall, leaving cracks around the bullethole. Alphonso crawled along the tables and hid in the vestibule. He might have run further if his ears weren't whistling so loud. Schiller woke with dust in his mouth and the bench on top of him. He thought the hotel had fallen through the ceiling until he swallowed a little dust and figured who the Chinaman was. The taxi bandit had come to shoot up Coen. Schiller wasn't worried about the splinters. The Chinaman could pick off every wall in the place, dear sweet God, provided he continued to miss. Schiller meant to shout instructions, warn Coen not to be hasty, advise him to speak slow and curry the Chinaman if he could, but only a few dry squeaks came out. The dust had reached into his throat. And his arms were dead. He couldn't raise the bench off his feet.

All the Chinaman got from Coen was grief. "Draw on me, Polish. Show me who you are. You have a trigger. Just move your right hand." Coen held on to the Mark V. He smiled into the Chinaman's face. Measuring Coen's smile, the Chinaman understood that there would be no satisfactions for him this far uptown, and he gripped the Police Special with both hands, conceived a target in his head a good three feet around Coen, and fired into the target. The bat jumped over the Chinaman's ears. Coen felt a crunch from his teeth down through his groin and into the pit of his legs. He tasted blood behind his nose. His shoes were in his face. He couldn't determine how he had gotten from the table to the wall. He was thirsty now. He remembered a peach he had bought during maneuvers in Worms, a giant red peach, a "colorado" for which he paid the equivalent of fifty cents, because the fruitman swore to him in perfect English that the "colorado" had come from South America in a crib of ice. Coen scrubbed the peach in canteen water, his fingers going over the imperfections in the red and yellow fuzz. He cut into the fuzz with his pack knife, finding it incredible that a peach, whatever its nationality, should have wine-colored flesh all around the stone. He ate for half an hour, licking juice from his thumbs, prying slivers of fruit out of the stone, savoring his own sweet spit. There was blood in his ear when he tried to swallow. His eyes turned pink. His chin was dark from bubbles in his mouth. Only one of his nostrils pushed air.

Isaac arrived with his war party after the second shot. Coen's partners, DeFalco, Rosenheim, and Brown, barreled into the vestibule wearing shotguns and shiny vests. Alphonso had to get out of their way or risk being trampled. It was too dark for him to notice the gold badges clamped to the three bulls, but he couldn't mistake the importance of these men. Nobody but supercops could bust into a ping-pong parlor so fast. The Chinaman was at the middle table by the time he heard the commotion in the vestibule, the cocking of shotguns, the pulsing of shoe leather. Coen's bloody ears didn't comfort him. He had meant to crease the Blue-eyes a little, not bend him in half. "Polish, you should have been nicer to me." Even as he looked between shotgun barrels and recognized Isaac, whom he had met in the Bronx and knew to be a heavy police spy, he couldn't understand what the bulls were doing here with so many cannons. He should have been out searching for Odette. Next time he wouldn't drip in his own pocket. He'd undress the queen, make her feel the bump in his chest.

DeFalco, Rosenheim, and Brown saw the blood leak from Coen, saw the Chinaman dangle the .38 (it was pointing nowhere), and they opened up. They ripped the woodwork, shattered three of the nine tables, brought a fixture down, left a mess of glass, and wasted Chino in the process. Rosenheim was the first one out of the vestibule.

DeFalco and Brown rushed the tables. They needed no evidence about the Chinaman's condition. But Brown squatted over Coen. "He's dead." Toeing through the glass DeFalco stumbled onto Schiller. He pulled the bench off Schiller's feet, helped him up, and took the bits of plaster away from Schiller's eyes. DeFalco couldn't tell if Schiller was sobbing or trying to cough. He figured something had to be wrong with Schiller's tongue. "Pop, what are you trying to say?"

Spanish Arnold was curling his sideburns in preparation for dinner with Coen when his jars and drinking cups fell off the windowsill. He hopped downstairs in his undershirt, without the orthopedic shoe. He got around Alphonso and took in Isaac, Schiller, Coen, the three detectives, and the Chinaman's remains. His head bobbed in Isaac's eye. "Cocksucker, you set him up. You couldn't catch Guzmann's tail, so you let the chink have Manfred, and then you got the chink."

DeFalco answered for Isaac. "Spanish, it wasn't like that, I swear. It was supposed to be routine. The Chinaman went to Mexico with Coen, didn't he? They slept in the same room. So why can't they have a talk over a ping-pong table? We're sitting outside in the car, so help me, joking about where the Chinaman's going to take us next, and a report comes in over the radio five minutes ago that the chink walked out of Bummy's with this captain's gun. Arnold, we were in here like a hurricane after that."

"Routine?" Arnold had to hold his lip so he wouldn't cry in front of Isaac and the bulls. "Then why'd you come uptown with shotguns?"

"Arnold," Rosenheim said, "you know what the Chinaman can do when he's on one of his mads. We couldn't predict his mood. We had to be ready for him."

Brown was still squatting over Coen. He had no love for Isaac. How much of a rat could Coen have been, if his own Chief couldn't save him? Isaac had an unnatural gift for pulling himself out of his own debris, for surfacing whenever he chose, and Brown could no longer be sure what was legitimate and what was sham with Isaac in the area. True, half the district (including himself) hoped the Chinaman would grab Coen's balls, but Brown wasn't so eager to rejoice. He could have pissed into Chino's skull, wasted another Chinaman tomorrow; he wasn't going to shame a dead cop. Perhaps he could read some of his own features in Coen's bloody face.

Perhaps there was a fondness in him for Isaac's baby under all the rancor. Brown couldn't say. He covered most of Coen with Schiller's pink towels and waited for the morgue wagon to come.

All the little shufflings at the First Deputy's office were completed by the time Coen was put into the ground (the Hands of Esau took charge of the body at the request of a certain Manhattan chief, even though Coen had been delinquent in paying his dues). Pimloe suffered the most. He lost his chauffeur and had to vacate his front rooms overlooking Cleveland Place for a closet in the back. The lower-grade detectives who made up the bulk of the "rat squad" (they infiltrated police stations and spied on cops for the First Dep) could barely disguise their joy over the move. They had been trained by Isaac, and they respected the unsmoothed lines of Isaac's theories, his avoidance of textbook procedures, his fanatical devotion to the *modus operandi* of criminals and crooked cops. He wasn't the DCI to them (deputy chief inspector), somebody to avoid. He was Isaac, the master, the only Chief. And they didn't have to cater to an ordinary DI like Pimloe. Isaac had come home.

He sat in his office brooding over the congratulations he received for quieting Chino Reyes and closing one or two of César Guzmann's dice cribs. The stenciler was outside scraping "Herbert Pimloe" off the door. His handgrips, his teapot, his honor scroll from the Hands of Esau, his bottles of colored ink, stored in the basement for months, had been returned to his rooms. His subordinates were overly polite. No one would mention Papa or Coen to him. Isaac had meant to have all six Guzmanns in his pencilcase (he would institutionalize Jerónimo rather than indict him) and Coen near his door when he returned from the hole (Boston Road). He hadn't grubbed on his knees delivering nickels for Papa, gorged himself with sweet sodas, gotten pimples on his butt riding barstools, to come up with a Cuban Chinese refugee, a bandit he had helped to create. It was Isaac who queered Chino's gambling operations on Doyers Street, sending kites to the District Attorney's office about the fan-tan games under the Chinaman's wing; it was Isaac who forced him uptown, reduced his options until he had to hire himself out to César or starve, because Isaac was bumping his own head in the Bronx and couldn't find any gambits better than the Chinaman. He considered Chino Reyes sufficiently stupid to lead him through Guzmann lines, expose César's marriage bureau, so he could catch a few Guzmanns with the brides. Only the Chinaman brought him nowhere but to Coen.

Isaac might never have started with the Guzmanns. Papa's numbers mill didn't disturb him. As lodge brother and information minister of the Hands of Esau, he was ashamed to admit that a family of Jews could monopolize a portion of the Bronx, but he consoled himself with the knowledge that the Guzmanns were false Jews, Marranos who accepted Moses as their Christ, ridiculed the concept of marriage, and ate pork. Then stories, rotten stories, filtered down to Isaac by way of his Manhattan stoolies that a policy combine in the Bronx was moving into white slavery, that its agents at the bus terminals didn't even have the character to distinguish between gentile runaways and Jewish ones. The Guzmanns were no longer quaint people, retards with policy slips who worshiped at home in a candy store; they were "meateaters" (buyers of human flesh), a family of insects praying on Isaac's boroughs. He sent his deputies into the terminals without telling Manfred, who had been raised on Guzmann egg creams and might blow the detectives' cover (most of them were in women's clothes). The deputies came back with potato chips in their bras. They couldn't link the Guzmanns to terminal traffic. The pimps working the bus routes had to ask, who's César, who's Papa, who's Jerónimo? And Isaac was made to realize that he couldn't trap the Guzmanns with old coordinates and shitty spies.

He swayed the First Deputy, an Irishman with an aquiline nose, a gentle person who deferred to the brainpower of his Jewish whip, and was terrified by Isaac's picture of six Guzmanns swallowing young girls. Isaac plotted his own doom. He paid an informant to squeal on him, implicate him far enough into the lives of Bronx KGs (known gamblers), so that he would have to send his papers in, give his badge to the property clerk, lose the rights to his pension, and resign from the Hands of Esau. The detectives under him trudged through the office, their eyes bulging with remorse. "Isaac fronting for gamblers? Bull. Somebody wants him stung." Only Isaac could appreciate the full symmetry of his fall; within a week of clearing his desk he had offers to join gambling combines in Brooklyn and Queens. Isaac decided to starve. He was forty-nine, with a swimmer's pectorals, bushy sideburns, and a boy's waist, and he had a married daughter and an estranged wife who was rich without him. He moved from Riverdale to Boston Road. He sat in cheap bars waiting for Papa to bite. He taunted foot patrolmen, but they had heard of Chief Isaac, and they didn't have the gall to hit him with their sticks.

Papa took him in but there were no preliminary hugs. If Isaac had known the habitat of the Guzmanns, he might have understood the queerness of this and crept with his tail in his hand back to the First Deputy. The Guzmanns never hired a runner without hugging him first. Papa was following the customs of his fathers in Peru. For the Marranos evil had a discernible stench from up close. Their hug was only a subterfuge, the chance to sniff how much harm they could expect. Not to smell a man was to show him the greatest contempt. Isaac sucked the liquid out of Papa's cherry candies and ate with Jerónimo's spoon. He carried quarters from Jorge's overflow, he formed a chain with Topal and Alejandro to load five-gallon syrup jugs into the cellar, he was given all the nigger accounts to play with. Papa had no salary for him. He lived on the pennies he collected, without seeing a dollar bill unless he brought his loot to the bank. No matter how far he toured Boston Road, he couldn't find any smudges of César or the marriage bureau.

So he washed pennies in his tub, learned the aromas of white chocolate from Jerónimo, shaved every third day, slouched like a Guzmann, grunted like a Guzmann, picked his nose, and arrived at the First Deputy's office with sticky sideburns, a scratched face, and penny dust on his fingers. His former deputies could only goggle. They knew Isaac was floating in the Bronx, but they hadn't expected such deterioration. Isaac, they remembered, was an immaculate man. Pimloe sneered together with the other DIs. They wouldn't associate with an unfrocked inspector. And Isaac, who had been using monosyllables on Boston Road, penny talk, gesturing to Jerónimo, mooing at Jorge, saw he couldn't explain himself to these men. The First Deputy rescued him, clarifying Isaac's mission to the DIs and detectives from the rat squad. The DIs shook Isaac's fist (they realized he would be the next First Dep). The detectives goggled anew, their faith restored in the master's technique; no one but Isaac could have watched Papa Guzmann through the stem of an ice cream dish.

Of all the Guzmanns Isaac preferred Jerónimo. They would break the hump of an afternoon leaning against Papa's comic book racks, playing tic-tac-toe on a magic board (the baby generally won), finishing a gallon of chocolate soda between them. But Isaac wouldn't allow fondness to muddy up the logistics in his head. Jerónimo was the Guzmanns' weakest point. The baby couldn't have

wiped himself without the toilet paper Papa stuffed in his underpants
to remind him where to look. He had to pause at most corners,
rethinking the concepts of green and red. Still, Isaac might have gone
after Jorge, who lacked Jerónimo's social graces and could get dizzy
walking a straight line, if Jorge hadn't been so articulate with a
fingernail and a knife (Isaac had seen Papa's middle boy carve a
runner for chiseling the family out of fifty cents). So he had
detectives in unmarked cars ride behind Jerónimo in the street, bump
him at five miles an hour. It didn't take Papa more than a week to
catch the drift of Isaac's cars. He sweetened Isaac's sodas, gave him
phantom accounts to chase. Only then would he say, "Isaac, I don't
want bruises on my boy. If Alejandro finds a fender in his ass, that's
one thing. He knows how to spit through a window. Isaac, listen to
me, that man who harms Jerónimo, black or white, will go out of this
world with a missing pair of balls. Don't be misled by the malted
machines. I was raised in Peru."

And Isaac, who had taken overeager triggermen out of
circulation, who had destroyed all the straw dummies in the
policemen's gym perfecting his rabbit punch, could only wag his
head. "Papa, I never touched the boy. Those are somebody else's
men. I can't direct traffic from a candy store."

Papa didn't have to rely on Isaac's generosity. He took Jerónimo
off the street. The boy had to confine his hikes to the spaces between
Papa's stools. He grew miserable dodging the leather bound seats
with chocolate in his mouth. Isaac was waiting for the Guzmann
machine to collapse under the strain of Jerónimo's sad eyes when the
baby disappeared into Manhattan. Restless, with Papa on his back,
Isaac learned to hate that other baby, Manfred Coen, who had been
reared with Jerónimo, Jorge, and César. Coen suffered from syrup on
the brain (like Jerónimo), chewed from the same lamb's bone during
the Marrano Easter, and Isaac resented this. He had pulled him out of
the academy because he needed a boy with a pliable face, a blue-eyed
wonder who wouldn't look outlandish in a brassiere, who could chase
a felon in women's shoes, wear a false nose, become a swish for half
a night. And Isaac got his plastic man. Fatherless at twenty-three, a
rifleman out of Worms brought into passivity by a Bronx oven, Coen
was ready to have his chin thickened with putty. Isaac had found the
ultimate orphan, a boy with a squashable self. Steered by Isaac, Coen
made detective first grade impersonating bimbos, Polacks, fingermen,
and lousy cops. Coen picked up a wife somewhere, a girl who took

him to concerts, deprived him of his orphanhood little by little, and threatened his usefulness to the police. So Isaac began lending Coen to the Bureau of Special Services, and the wonderboy escorted other men's wives, slept on Park Avenue, drifted out of marriage, and jumped into Isaac's lap.

Isaac hadn't taken advantage of Coen's prettiness, turned him into a herringbone cop, simply out of love for his own department. He figured Coen would be better off without a wife. When the deputy inspectors under him got on his nerves, he would climb Coen's fire escape, sit with the cop over checkers and strong tea. Coen encouraged Isaac to come through the window. He was a boy without ambitions. The double and triple jumps he gave up to Isaac weren't meant to flatter the Chief. Coen had no head for strategies on a board. And Isaac could appreciate an hour away from whining inspectors. He trusted the boy enough to take off his shoes and nap in Coen's presence. Brodsky would honk at him from the street if any emergency arose. And Coen would rouse him with a finger. "Isaac, get up. They can't survive without you." Nudged out of sleep, Isaac had the comfort of a smile, blue eyes over him, a boy with a gun near his heart, one of Isaac's deadly angels (most of Isaac's deputies were marksmen with good manners and sweet faces).

The longer Isaac scrounged in the Bronx, the more bitter he grew about Coen. The boy was as much Guzmann as cop. Isaac had bottled Coen, restricted him to homicide squads in the southern boroughs, because he didn't want to compromise his angel, force him to choose between Papa and the First Dep. Then Isaac reversed himself. Humiliated by Papa, licking syrup in a dark store, he threw Coen at the Guzmanns, pushed him into the middle of César's marriage bureau, pointing him toward Mexico, Fifth Avenue, and Vander Child. The boy irritated the Guzmanns, but he couldn't harm them. Instead of luring César out of the closet, he got a bullet in the throat. And Isaac sat in his office, repatriated, his minor sins absolved by the Hands of Esau, the letters of his name moving across the door (it took the stenciler a whole hour to scratch out Pimloe and complete I-S-A-A-C), his handgrips in their old place on his desk, his locks and fountain pens restored by the property clerk, his deputies milling in their cubicles, waiting for the word, his office toothbrush on the sink, his stockings gartered, his suspenders tight, but without César, without Papa, without Coen.

PART FOUR

SIXTEEN

Schiller lived amid the rubble. He wouldn't clean. His voice came back after sucking lozenges for a week but he had little to say. The freaks might have remained loyal to the club. The first three tables were unharmed, and Schiller was too distracted to collect more than a few pennies from them. But the lights buzzed in their eyes, the walls began to sweat, and they were worried about getting glass in their sneakers. So they went to Morris' on Seventy-third, where the ceilings were low and the wire cage around every bulb left shadows on the ball, or else they played at Reisman's on Ninety-sixth, which was roomier and better lit but cost them a quarter more per hour. If they did think of Coen, it was only to remind themselves that such an odd cop deserved a ping-pong grave. And they would advertise to their relatives how they had seen the Chinaman's bullet land under Coen's neck, carry him eight feet, rupture an artery, and squeeze blood through his ears, although not one of them had been inside the club when the Chinaman shot Coen.

Arnold lost his ambition to move out of the singles hotel. He added marmalade to the jars on his window and put a coat of yellow shellac on his orthopedic shoe that was guaranteed not to eat leather or melt the foam in his arch. He couldn't blame the Chinaman. In his mind Isaac and the Guzmanns murdered Coen. He received an invitation from Rosenheim, DeFalco, and Brown (countersigned by a borough chief) to reenter Coen's district and preside over the cage in the squadroom, but Arnold declined. He had no tolerance for detectives without Coen. Schiller gave him Coen's bat and headband (the shield, holster, and gun went to the First Deputy's office). Arnold wore the headband in his room. He took the Mark V with him on his walks around the block, the handle under his strap, rubber against his ribs. The bat gave him a certain prestige among the SROs, who couldn't worship Coen until after he was dead, and the Cuban waiters, who had been fond of the *agente* with the *blanco* complexion. He would descend the steps of the club, his big shoe pointing into the rails, clear the vestibule in twenty swipes, find Schiller, and say, "Jesus, open your lungs. Hombre, go upstairs." Schiller wouldn't move. Maybe Arnold had a candy bar for him, or yesterday's newspaper. They sat together on Schiller's bench, not knowing what to do with their thumbs. Arnold couldn't breathe glass and live near wall dust without having to sneeze. He would touch Schiller goodbye, most likely on the knee, make it to the vestibule, and start the climb with both hands on the rail and the shoe pointing north.

Even with César scarce and the Chinaman dead, Odile didn't have to sacrifice any of her routines. She traveled in a triangular sweep from The Dwarf to uncle Vander to Jane Street to The Dwarf again at least twice a day. She danced hip to hip with her girlfriends at The Dwarf but wouldn't kiss them on the mouth. She balanced dessert spoons on her labia to satisfy Vander's cameramen, had climaxes off the edges of spoons. She didn't need the Chinaman to solicit for her. Bummy Gilman came to Odile of his own accord. She washed him in a milky solution (89 cents at the drugstore) with all her skirts on and collected a hundred dollars. It was here, shampooing Bummy's genitals, rinsing down his thighs, that she appreciated Coen. The cop hadn't itemized her, hadn't inspected her longish nipples and the moles on her back, hadn't asked her for tricks with her labia or white shampoos. Odile believed in fatalities: Coen had to die this year, but she wished he would have avoided the Chinaman one more month. She might have lured him to Jane Street then, studied the scowl bumps over his eyes, made a hollow for herself under his arm, slept there an hour, and still have gotten up in time to dance with Dorotea at The Dwarf.

Odile would be nineteen in June. She had starred in eleven features and thirteen featurettes, she had worn vaginal jelly for a hundred and five men, not counting Vander, whom she seduced while she was twelve; Bummy, who hadn't been inside her clothes; the Chinaman, who had gone no further than to dribble sperm on her left thigh; Jerónimo, who had her with his eyes shut; César, who owned her more or less and didn't need invitations to Jane Street; the four remaining Guzmanns (Topal, Alejandro, Papa, and Jorge), or Coen. (Odile, who had seen Jewish men in their nakedness, men like Bummy and the cop, still couldn't understand why all six Guzmanns had to be burdened with pieces of skin on their pricks. She got no explanations from César. She had to figure that the Guzmanns made poor Jews.) She began lighting the green memorial candles César gave her after her dog Velasquez choked on a wishbone. But she forgot the prayers that went with the candles, and she wouldn't saw them in half with a butterknife the way the Guzmanns did. So she ran out of her short supply and stopped bothering with Coen.

Convinced that he was under a benign form of house arrest, Vander hoarded his croissants. The First Deputy's office had advised him to sit in Manhattan. He was supposed to maintain contact with the Guzmanns, but Zorro wouldn't nibble. He had no misconceptions about his value to the chiefs. When his usefulness plunged deep enough, he would be fed to the grand jury like a vile animal. Isaac had fingered him at the airport in January coming home from Mexico with vouchers from Mordeckay on the brides (most of them were in a Marrano code and couldn't be deciphered). It took Isaac under an hour to turn the Broadway angel around, and Vander left the airport a spy registered to Deputy Inspector Herbert Pimloe (Isaac wouldn't accept informants in his own name). Hurrying to dismantle his cameras and liquidate his production company, Vander discovered that being a spy gave him immunity from the local police. He could operate as a pornographer without fear of a raid. He was untouchable for the moment, on the First Deputy's rolls. And if he couldn't make Spain this year to collect pesetas from his investments in Castilian construction firms and visit his favorite Goyas in Madrid, he could walk Odile through a film a month. He remembered nothing more of Coen than their ping-pong. He assumed that the Chinaman's death prefigured the collapse of the Guzmanns. But there was no evidence of this.

César didn't neglect Isaac's restoration. He juggled his addresses, hopping from Eighty-ninth Street to Ninety-second to a room over the dairy restaurant on Seventy-third, where he used the name Morris Shine. He had a fuzzy attitude about Coen's death. He missed the Chinaman more. One of his Bronx cousins claimed the body from the morgue. He buried Chino in the Guzmann plot, outside city limits, with a Marrano crier in attendance, Papa, Topal, and Jerónimo wearing the gray Marrano death shawls, Jorge guarding the entrance to the cemetery, a spike in either hand.

The smell of barley soup and mushroom pancakes came up

through the woodwork to badger César. Coen was the dairy boy. César was a porkeater, and the memory of his meals with the Chinaman, stringbeans and minced pork, pork rolls, five-flavored pork, pork and Chinese cabbage, made him spit into the toilet with anger and spite. César rang downstairs (he had a special line hooked into the cashier's stall at the dairy restaurant). "Get me Boris Telfin. I want his bus outside in eight minutes. Lady, this dump stinks."

The cashier said, "I'm sorry. He isn't at his table, Mr. Shine. What should I do?"

César muttered whoreboy, whoreboy, until his steerer came on the line.

"Zorro, I was in the men's. I can have the car. But where's the rush? You know how many eyes this Isaac has? He carries binoculars in both tits."

"Boris, you told me a room with a first-class view. You forgot to mention that it's choked with kitchen pipes. Get the bus."

César rode to Jane Street. He was wearing a winter coat in May, with the collar up around his ears, and a seaman's cap pulled against his eyebrows. Odile recognized him under all the baggage. She couldn't tell whether Zorro had come to kill her or maim her limbs because of her alignment with Vander, but she had to let him in. Her belly tightened as he passed her in the hallway. Her heart thumped into her ribs. Would he undress her before he snapped her neck? Would he have her perform disgusting tricks? She saw his pallor when the hat and coat came off. He collapsed into a soft chair. Odile felt a mild rage against César; he wasn't going to make any overtures at all.

"Zorro, would you like a snack?"

"None of your sandwiches," he said. "Save them for the Johns. Who are the green candles for?"

"They're for Coen."

"I should have figured you'd be mourning Isaac's boy."

César wouldn't stroke her with pieties. Twenty years apart had deadened him to Coen. He had his brothers and his whores and one Chinese pistol. César reformed the taxi bandit, deflected his violent streak by giving him a string of whores to supervise, and took him into the Bronx for Marrano wine; he couldn't distrust a man who loved pork. César regretted losing Chino (he should have realized the Chinaman would kiss himself into the ground chasing Coen), and he worried about Jerónimo's new hideaway (with Isaac sitting on

Manhattan, César had to cancel his trips to the baby), but he had no trouble sleeping in Odile's chair. César snored like his brothers, and slept with a hand on his balls. Getting nothing from Zorro, Odile wanted to run to The Dwarf, dance with whoever was on call, feel a hipbone in her groin, but she didn't dare leave the room. César had strict habits. He would send his brothers to smash up The Dwarf if there was no Odette when he woke. So she had to be content eating wax off the bottom of a green candle and watching Zorro blow air.

Papa was preparing to shut the candy store. He never fixed sodas beyond the second week of May. Alejandro would remain in the Bronx. He would move into a bowling alley for the summer months and preside over Papa's accounts from there. If Papa's better customers preferred to do business with the nigger banks while Papa was out of town, it didn't matter too much. Papa would get them back in the fall. He wasn't going to sacrifice Loch Sheldrake for a pile of ten-dollar bets. He had his orchard to think about, his garden, the strawberry and blackberry seasons, and the safety of his boys. Jerónimo couldn't get run over in an orchard, and Jorge could survive without being plagued by street signs and traffic lamps. Papa burned candles for the Chinaman and Coen on the shelf above his malted machines. He prayed to Moses with a dishrag on his skull, spit three times according to Marrano law, so Coen and the Chinaman might be able to rest in purgatory. Still he had only a passing confidence in the efficiency of his prayers. He didn't believe one solitary man could heal the miseries of the dead. Papa was no moneygrub. He could have hired professional mourners to trick the three judges of purgatory (Solomon, Samuel, and Saint Jerome), with powerful cries from the lungs. These mourners had sensible rates. They could tear through walls with a cry for anyone who could meet their price. But to Papa cries weren't enough. The dead needed whole families to intercede for them, brothers, sisters, fathers, nephews, mothers, sons, to wear dishrags and shawls, to offer pennies to the Christian saints, to appease Moses with a candle, to recite Hebrew prayers transcribed into sixteenth-century Portuguese; Coen and the Chinaman were familyless men without the Marrano knack to survive. Papa discarded any notions of immortality for himself. He had lived like a dog, biting the noses of his enemies, smelling human shit on two continents, sleeping in a crouch to safeguard his vulnerable parts, and he expected to drop like a dog, with blood in his rectum, and somebody's teeth in his neck. But Papa didn't intend to die from an overdose of Isaac, or offer his sons to the First Deputy's shotgun brigade. He believed Isaac was more than a simple son-of-a-bitch. What cop would want to erase six Guzmanns, almost an entire species of men? Isaac had to be one of those destructive angels sent by the Lord Adonai to torment pigeaters, the Marranos who had slipped between Christians and Jews for so many years they could no longer exist without Moses *and* Jesus (or John the Baptist) in their beds, and had defied the laws of Adonai with their foreskins and their rosaries. Unable to snatch a Guzmann, Isaac settled for a blond Jew and a creole with Chinese ancestors.

So Papa wailed. The dishrag surrounded his ears. He screamed for the Chinaman in English and fine Portuguese, but he screamed louder for Coen. Papa had fattened himself in North America after sitting on his rump in Peru. He owned earth, a farm with Guzmann berries, and fixtures in the Bronx. And in Papa's head all four Coens, father, mother, lunatic brother, and son, came with the fixtures and the berries. The Coens were Papa's North America. Papa didn't have to scan outside Boston Road; he could measure his strides against the cracks in Albert's eggs. When he wound the Marrano phylactery— tiny leather box containing Spanish, Dutch, and Portuguese words from the books of Moses—through the opening in his sleeve, he prayed first for the health of his boys, then for the maintenance of the Coens. He couldn't discount Jessica, who gnawed at his guts with her independent smiles, who must have understood Papa's game; Papa needed a stumbler like Albert to add some bulk to his own success. But it wasn't plain exploitation. Papa loved the Coens. He might have been disgusted by their vegetable meals, but he admired Albert's gentleness, he pitied Sheb for his swollen brains, he was attracted to Manfred's blond demeanor (the Guzmanns were a hairy black), and he was bothered by Jessica, terrified of the scorn she could produce with a smile, and adoring the ambiguity in her face. So he wailed. Not because he had turned three Coens toward their graves and left the fourth to rot in a home with a river view, by compromising Albert and romancing Jessica with a piece of string, by keeping them prisoners in an egg store with his small loans, by letting Manfred stumble into a war zone meant for Isaac and the Guzmanns, and fanning Sheb's isolation with dollar bills. Papa had wiggled too hard staying alive to be deformed by a sentiment so unprofitable as grief. But he was bound to the Coens, in the Bronx, Manhattan, or purgatory, and his wails only reminded him that he could never get clean of them.

The steerer was holding Jerónimo until the strawberry season when he would drive the baby to Loch Sheldrake together with Papa, Jorge, and Topal. There were too many sharks on Boston Road (police cars under Isaac's control) to satisfy Papa. So Boris Telfin sat with the baby in a rented room on Ninetieth Street with a steampipe that would knock through July, and made no more than one or two trips per day to his window seat at the dairy restaurant. He suffered from the loss of spinach pancakes and bean pie. And he was frightened of César. With his crazy Guzmann head Zorro could intuit if Jerónimo had an insufficient supply of chocolate or a grease spot in his hair. Boris groomed the baby, evening his sideburns with a pair of scissors, and cursing Zorro while he shampooed Jerónimo's scalp.

The baby demanded more. He ripped through the steerer's pockets in search of Brazil nuts and black halvah. Boris had to endure fingers in his pants. And if he didn't acquiesce to the baby's walks, he would have gone to the dairy restaurant with long scratches on his face. "Jerónimo, look before you cross, This is Isaac's village. If they kidnap you, I won't need burial insurance. Your father and your brother will treat me to a stone." He dressed the baby in slipovers, peacoat, and earmuffs. "Better warm than cold. The weather can change. And the dicks won't expect you in such a bundle." Boris felt for his wallet and patted nothing but cloth; the baby had already picked his side pocket. Just like monkeys, Boris concluded. A family of thieves. But the baby hadn't stolen money from him before. "Two dollars? Jerónimo, why two dollars?" Boris didn't quarrel with the steal. The Guzmanns were paying him a hundred a week for the baby's room and board, and he could deduct two dollars from his profits without getting hurt. "Jerónimo, the key's under the garbage pail in the hall. It fits the top lock. Not the bottom. Turn it with both hands. You'll lose your grip otherwise."

The baby left first. He picked his way through bundles of newspapers on the stairs, testing for solid ground with one shoe, keeping the other shoe flat. The janitor misinterpreted the off rhythms of Jerónimo's moves, thinking a hare-brained cripple lived on the second floor. Jerónimo rejected the musty odors of the janitor's hall for the more natural stinks outside. His skin pinkened in the street. He had a dark blush around the eyes, the color spreading into a definite blotch behind the ears. Half a block from the steerer's place his knees began to pump higher than his belt. His earmuffs climbed with every step. The citizens of Ninetieth Street weren't accustomed to such stupendous walking. The baby could avoid tricycles and wagonettes without shifting a heel. His head maintained a regular line. Roughened alley cats, some with scars in their whiskers, dropped chicken wings and ran from the baby's staggered sounds. He was over Broadway and on the stoops of Manhattan Rest in under three minutes. The nurses made allowances for him. They knew he was the gray-haired boy who visited Sheb Coen. Jerónimo laid the two sticky dollars and a clutch of toilet paper in the elbow of Shebby's pajamas. They kissed in front of neighbors (men and women from a lower floor), the blotch disappearing from Jerónimo's neck. The neighbors didn't take Shebby to task for kissing in a public dorm. None of them was fooled by the bushy gray hair, or Jerónimo's chubbiness in the peacoat. He had all the marks of a Guzmann; tight cheeks, knobs in the forehead, deep sockets for the eyes, lips that curved into a fork under the jaw. Shebby's neighbors wanted to undress the boy. They pulled at his sleeves, tried to get under the muffs. Shebby howled in his bed. "You bitches, let go. That's all-weather clothes he's wearing. I'll mangle you, you play with his ears. Jerónimo, he's like a sister to me, better than any nephew or brother boy. Brings me dollars and no unkind news."

Sheb had to throw bookends and medicine bottles before his neighbors would desist. Jerónimo remained with one earmuff over his mouth, and his sleeves puffing like elephant trunks near the floor. Sheb fixed the baby, bundling him with clawed hands. The neighbors scattered elsewhere, and now Sheb had his own dorm mates to reckon with. "Bitches, make room for the boy."

Without prologues or explanations Sheb and the baby locked wrists and began to weep; these loud sniffles alarmed the dorm mates, Morris, Sam, and Irwin, because they couldn't locate any genuine cause for such spontaneous commotion, and they had no chance to realize that Sheb and the baby were given to long cries, that they had behaved like this in the egg store, under fire escapes, and on the farm. They were crying for their sustained infanthood, for the white patches that had sprouted on Jerónimo's scalp early in life, for the little indignities that had swelled their knuckles and shortened their necks in the Bronx, for their inadequacies in matters concerning the making of money, for their dependence on brothers, fathers, and a sister-in-law, for their heavy drugged sleep in which they dreamed of winter storms, sewer floods, collapsing fire escapes, burning roofs, Bronx volcanoes, for the fright they carried with them during the hours they were awake. Sheb broke the wristlock and wiped the baby's eyes with a pajama cuff. Morris winked to Irwin, Irwin winked to Sam. "Kookoo." The baby prolonged his goodbyes, exploring under Shebby's sleeve with half a knuckle. Sheb understood the implications of the gesture; the baby wouldn't be back until the fall. "Jerónimo, watch out for dead branches. Don't come home with a splinter in your ass." They kissed for the last time, Sam sticking out his lip and becoming Jerónimo for the benefit of Irwin and Morris. "Put your face where it belongs," Sheb told Sam after he sent the baby off. He gave the dollars to Morris (the toilet paper he kept). "Find your teeth and go to the corner. Get us a mixed assortment. Some apricots, some pears, some prunes."

"And dates," Irwin said.

"And dates," Sheb confirmed. "The man can't shit without his dates."

Jerónimo whisked through the nurses' station. The old men standing in the hall with their robes on caught the bobbing earmuffs and a navy blue cape. They wondered what mischief a walking blue coat could bring. The baby saw Isaac and his chauffeur at the bottom of the stairs. Brodsky was grinning and dangling his handcuffs at Jerónimo. Isaac was carrying a fat cardboard box.

"We got him," Brodsky squealed, his lungs thick with anticipation. "Chief, should I go for his arms or his legs?"

Brodsky blocked the stairwell, and the baby would have had to climb over the chauffeur's head or run up to the roof. He crouched on a middle step. Isaac made Brodsky lower the handcuffs.

"Jerónimo, come down."

Brodsky whispered to the Chief. "Isaac, don't be strange. Put a bracelet on his leg and he'll lead you to Zorro. I've dealt with dummies before. I know their shtick."

"Brodsky, get out of his way."

The chauffeur humped himself into a corner, regret ballooning out on his face. Brodsky had taken up Isaac's cause with so much vehemence, he couldn't let a Guzmann go free and not damage some of his own tightened parts. He developed a cough on the stairwell. Isaac wouldn't console him. The baby edged down a shoulder at a time and slipped between Isaac and his man without rubbing either of them (a remarkable feat considering the narrowness of the stairs and the chauffeur's hefty proportions). Isaac had to shout fast or lose him completely.

"Jerónimo, tell your father he may have some frozen berries on his hands this summer. I'll be looking for him. There's no China wall between here and Loch Sheldrake. Jerónimo . . . "

The boy was out of reach, so he pointed Brodsky up the stairs and away from Jerónimo's tracks.

"I can catch him on the run, Isaac. He won't dodge my bus so quick."

"We came for Shebby, not the boy. I'll have my day with Zorro. I don't need a baby for that."

They passed the nurses' station flicking their shields and went to Shebby's dorm. Morris, Sam, and Irwin had never been entertained by a deputy chief inspector. They crowed for Isaac and hid the egg stains on their pajamas. They assured Isaac's man how satisfied they were with the police. "No bums can get up these steps," Morris chirped. But Shebby wouldn't commit himself. He focused on Sam, whose face happened to be in view, and scowled at him for his readiness to become Isaac's pansy. Sheb was a harder man to buy. He hadn't candled eggs on Boston Road for nothing. Sitting in the dark of Albert's store he was always the first to hear the thump of bookmakers and other fancy men who fell off the roofs for shifting their allegiances a little too often. Sheb couldn't kiss Jerónimo and then be comfortable with Isaac. As next of kin he was entitled to the private belongings of Coen's police locker, also to Coen's wallet, and to the short pants, blue shirt, and sneakers Coen had died in, all of which Isaac removed from the cardboard box and presented to Sheb. Irwin was awed by the blood on the sneakers and the shirt. Morris and Sam settled on the shoehorn from Coen's locker.

"Poor bastard," Brodsky muttered sufficiently near the Chief, then apologized to Sheb. "Sorry, Mr. Coen. But your nephew was some cop. They feared him out there, they really did. Ping-pong, that's how they got to him. He was too tough on the street."

"Don't I know who he is?" Shebby said. "Why did you bring me his stinking clothes?"

"Keepsakes," Brodsky said, proud of his vocabulary. "Mementos. What's wrong with you? You should have respect for a dead man's stuff."

Shebby poked through the wallet. He found certain insurance

cards, pictures of an old wife's girls. He ripped open all the flaps. "Where's the money?"

"That's more complicated, Mr. Coen. The property clerk has it. Don't worry, it'll get to you. Maybe four dollars in change. But what's four dollars to you? You're a rich man, Mr. Coen." Brodsky nudged his Chief for some cooperation. "Isaac, show him Manfred's policies."

Isaac had been staring at the shoehorn, the sneakers, the filthy drinking cup, the razor blades, the shaving glass, the bent spoon, droppings of a sorry man, and he felt mean and grubby for having the urge to glorify Coen, dress him up in front of Sheb and his three companions. Sheb didn't need beatitudes from Isaac. So he restricted himself to the policies in paper jackets that he took out of his coat, intoning on insurance coupons, death benefits, and fiduciaries, and after adding up the sums, he told everybody in the dorm that Sheb would receive fifteen thousand dollars in a matter of five years. Sam rolled his eyes in deep respect. "Fifteen thousand?" Morris went numb with envy. Irwin studied the policies in their jackets. "Shebby, we'll be kings here. No more black and white. We can afford the color television."

Sheb wasn't taken in by enormities. "Never mind the fifteen thousand. Just give me the four dollars that belongs to me."

The Chief couldn't function in the middle of such intransigence. Brodsky had to remind him of the medal in his pocket. "Esau," Brodsky said. And Isaac fished with a whole hand. The medal had a silver backing, a ribbon in blue and white, and Coen's name and dates of service on the front, under a ram's horn. Isaac pinned the medal on Sheb's pajamas, pricking his finger in the act. He took one long suck at the blood, delivered a citation from the Hands of Esau outlining Coen's bravery in getting killed and mentioning his place of honor among gentiles and the Jews, then he clasped Shebby's hand, withholding the finger with the blood, and walked out, Brodsky behind him.

Sheb had chewed half the ribbon before Sam and Irwin could pull the medal away; the clasp broke off in the struggle, and Morris searched for all the pieces. Sheb had blue and white threads in his mouth, Irwin lectured him. "Moron, that's no way to treat a medal."

Sheb was crying without making a sound; only his throat moved. The boys didn't know what to do; they had just learned to tolerate his thick wet cries with Jerónimo. They couldn't find a tear

on Shebby's body. Morris waved his paws over Shebby's eyes.
"Sheb, do you hate your nephew so much?"

"Talk to us," Irwin said. "Shebby, be fair."

"Morris," Sam said, "go get him his dried fruit. Maybe an
apricot will moisten his tongue."

The threads began to curl under Shebby's lip. Sam didn't dare
pick them off. He signaled to Irwin and waited for Morris to get back.
They fed him apricots, pears, dates, and prunes out of an oily bag.
Shebby didn't spit apricots. The food went down. He swallowed
dates and threads. He strained to belch. Morris had to slap his ribs for
the belch to come. But his crying was the same. They could squeeze
no more noises out of him. So they retired to their own beds. Irwin
passed the bag around. They ate whatever fruit was left. The apricot
bark was tough. They kept spitting out the skin. Sheb looked at the
wall.

"Short pants," he said.

"Shebby, say what you mean."

"What detective dies in short pants?"

"Shebby, he was doing his ping-pong. It was only circumstance.
Would you be any happier if your nephew ruined a good pair of
slacks?"

Shebby still wouldn't wear the medal. "They took Albert's boy
and turned him into a swan."

Sam shrugged his head. Morris and Irwin exchanged cockeyed
stares. What could you do with a man who begrudged insurance
policies and wanted to eat a medal? Sheb was busy eradicating Coens
in his head. He had been doing fine, moving his bowels without
anybody's help, getting by on Jerónimo's visits until Isaac brought
him pants and sneakers in a box, and woke him to all the incapacities
of the Coens. They could sing to him about badges and medals and
bloodrags; the boy had no business being a cop. When he saw that
rookie suit for the first time, the satchel with the nightstick poking
out, the probation grays, Manfred smiling under the bill of his cop
hat, Shebby should have bitten through the sleeves, held Manfred by
the calf and proved to him the folly of a Coen in such a hat. The
nephew presented Sheb with his gray pants after graduating from the
Police Academy. Sheb wore them without having to lower the cuffs.
So who's the fool in cop pants? Who's the angel-eyed boy? Sheb the
candler winked at bloodclots thirty years, a boarder in his brother's
house, and ended his long sit with the Coens pampering an oven for

Albert. Kill a brother and inherit his son's pants. That's the logic of the Coens.

Sheb smelled fire in the walls. He picked on Sam who occupied the neighboring bed. "Run for your life. The roof's burning."

Sam deferred to Morris and Irwin, younger men, men with broader chests. They surrounded Sheb with blankets. This was the third fire Sheb had smelled in a week. Sam figured he might be agitated over the medal. "Should I call the nurse?"

"No."

They stuffed the blankets on him, covering him up to his ears. He would stop smelling fires if they could make him sweat.

"Shebby, are you warm?"

They put stockings on his hands and feet. Morris traced a finger around Shebby's ears. They didn't smile until the finger came off wet. They allowed him to bake another minute before returning to their beds.

The DI, Herbert Pimloe, watched the young smart deputies shuffle from their cubicles to Isaac's rooms. These "angels" were grooming themselves for their own inspectorships; they smiled for no one but Isaac. He, Pimloe, could never be an Isaac man; his eyes weren't blue enough, and he wouldn't wear garters in the field (or a padded bra). He had dropped eleven pounds since Isaac rose out of the Bronx to occupy Pimloe's chair. The DI wasn't an ingrate; he recognized elemental truths, that he'd inherited this same chair from Isaac himself. But the loss of a view from his windows on Cleveland Place, the usurpation of his chauffeur Brodsky, and the indignity of his new quarters (a poorly ventilated closet)—such things debilitated him. The office was Isaac's roost, and Pimloe could scratch himself or get out.

The DI had certain options. He wouldn't apply to the First Dep's car pool for another chauffeur, but he could wheedle a job with the District Attorney, or pack in police work and become head of security at one of the Islip shopping centers. He resisted these moves. Hating Isaac couldn't make him disloyal to his office. Pimloe was a First Deputy man. He would have to ride through Isaac's redemption. So he scratched. And scratched. And scratched.

Isolated in his closet, a perpetual dampness in his nose (not even rain could penetrate the air shaft behind Pimloe's wall), he went looking for Odile. The DI was partial to three-piece suits; he tried

The Dwarf wearing Scottish wool and made a strong impression on one of the bouncers. Sweeney was harsh with him out of jealousy. She refused to accept that Odile could have a boyfriend so refined. She preferred Jew pimps and China trash with Odile, men she could openly despise. The DI's sadness was hard to overcome. She could taste his damp wool. "Cuntface," she said (meaning Pimloe), "the queen's at home. She attends the sick on Thursdays and Fridays. Knock soft on her door. You can't tell who you're liable to find."

The DI didn't follow Sweeney's cautions; he rang Odile's downstairs bell without disguising his voice. "It's me, Herbert," he sang into the intercom. "Don't be scared. It's a social call." He expected arguments from Odile, but the door buzzed, and he stepped into the house.

Odile was in a panic upstairs, certain that Pimloe had come with Isaac and a raiding party of First Deputy men. She had Zorro with her, and she was pushing him into his clothes. He'd been inside her apartment for three days, mourning Coen and the Chinaman, and God knows how many more. He wouldn't talk. She'd shaved him and scrubbed him, afraid to touch his genitals or leave the house. They'd fed on saltines and sour beer. Now she had to fit his seaman's cap on his skull and get him out the fire escape before Isaac's angels surrounded the block. She propped him over the windowsill, aimed his feet at the iron stairs. She couldn't hide the affection in her shoves: Odile was cuckoo for all the Guzmanns. She began to cry. "César, watch yourself. This Isaac shows up everywhere. I'll bake cookies for Jerónimo, I will." She kissed him on the mouth, felt the strength of his lip (was he chewing or kissing back?), and closed the window on him. She couldn't stall the DI.

Pimloe was amazed at how fast he got through Odile's chain guard. His mouth puffed ready to speak, ready to explain himself, and Odile had him in her room, the door locked again, the peephole back in place. Playing hostess she patted his trousers for a gun, eyed him down for suspicious lumps, and came away from him with a befuddled look; the DI was pistolfree. Still, Zorro needed time to walk the fire escape, so she offered to mash some lemons in Pimloe's drink.

"Thanks," he said. "I don't want a highball."

She would have undressed without any signals from him (she was wearing a flimsy shift without pockets), coaxed him toward her mattress, suffered his policeman's body on hers, for Zorro, but the dark, unhealthy lines of his face, the sag in Pimloe's cheeks, intimidated her, made her keep her shift on. That smelly wool on him had a certain power over Odile. At least one of them ought to undress, that's how she figured. "Get comfortable, Herbert. You must be itchy in your suit."

He was obedient with her, and she hung vest, coat, and trousers in her closet, clamping the door shut. She smiled; she had him down to his underpants, and he couldn't chase Zorro this way. He was making spit with his tongue.

"Herbert, what's your trouble?"

"I got kicked in the teeth. They've been shunting me like a dirty head of cabbage."

"Who, Herbert? Who's that? I thought you were solid at the office."

"I was. It's Isaac, Isaac and his flunkies. He's left me with my own nuts in my hand."

Odile couldn't explain why the DI should be attractive in his misery, as if a mouth could be more sensual under the threat of pain. Cops and crooks, cops and crooks, she swayed between them. The DI didn't even see her nipples harden under the shift. She liked the style of his underpants: blue diamonds on a red field. "Herbert, do you want to rest your toes?"

They sat on her mattress, their knees coming together in a dignified position.

"I dangled Coen, and they dangled me," Pimloe said. "My own chauffeur ratted me out. He went back to Isaac so he could snub me in the halls. They'd be happy if I choked on my badge."

Odile wouldn't listen.

"They were looking for a temporary whip, a sweetheart who'd warm the head stool while Isaac was jammed up. I'm a bigger glom than the Chinaman."

She brushed his ears with a finger, confronted him knee to knee.

"They banged me in the ass," Pimloe said. "Total and complete."

Odile had a better hold on his neck. Caressing the bones in his scalp, she lowered him down to her chemise. She didn't have to instruct; Pimloe chewed the little puffs of cloth over her nipples. Her bust was growing wet. Odile moaned once. Her elbows buckled over. It was no longer Zorro she was thinking of.

MARILYN THE WILD

PART ONE

ONE

"Blue Eyes."

She was indebted to the gouges in his face, high cheeks that could blunt a scary color. The specks in his eyes might harm any girl who had just run away from her husband. She didn't want to be snared again. She had come to him for Russian tea, firm pillows, and the comforts of a temporary home.

"Marilyn," he said, with a nasalness that made her twitch. He had her father's voice. And she refused to wrestle with Isaac on Coen's bed.

"Marilyn, shouldn't you talk to Isaac?"

"Screw him." She had unpacked an hour ago. Her suitcase was under Coen's laundry bag. She intended to mingle her dirty underwear with his. She would rinse them in the bath-tub together, with the Woolite she had brought, after Coen went to work.

"Marilyn, suppose he finds out? I'm not too good at lying."

She held his collarbone in her teeth, made perfect little bites that were meant to arouse her father's man. She would tolerate no protests from him. She dug her nipples into his chest. She worked spit under his arm. But she'd trap herself, fall victim to Coen, if she couldn't get around his eyes.

Whenever she weakened and let his infernal blue peek out at her, she would lower her head to lick the scars on his back (souvenirs Coen had acquired in the street), or stare at the holster on his desk.

She straddled him, rubbing his prick with a wet finger. The blueness couldn't hurt her now. Coen's eyes were thickening with impure spots. She pushed Coen inside herself, milked him with the pressure off her thighs, until she lost all sense of Isaac, and that husband of hers, a Brooklyn architect, and responded to Coen's gentle body.

Twice divorced at twenty-five, she could chew up husbands faster than any other Bronx-Manhattan girl who had bombed out of Sarah Lawrence. Isaac had always been there to find husbands for her, genteel men with forty-thousand-dollar jobs and a flush of college degrees. Her father sat at Headquarters behind the paneled walls of the First Deputy Police Commissioner. He'd been invited to Paris, she heard, as the World's Greatest Cop (of 1970-71), or something close to that. And Coen was Isaac's fool, a spy attached to the First Dep.

She gulped through her nose, smelling Coen's blond hairs. She came five times, her tongue twisting deeper into her mouth. She could beg him now.

"Come in me, Manfred, please."

She saw the hesitation in the pull of his lip. He was frightened of knocking up Isaac's girl, and imposing a grandchild on his Chief, a baby Coen. But Marilyn was a stubborn creature. She soothed the bumps in Coen's jaw with the side of her face. She understood the depths of her father's cop. He was a shy boy, a Jewish orphan with a handsome streak that fed itself on Bronx sadnesses: both his parents were suicides. She softened the points of tension in his throat with the flesh of her shoulder and the powerful membranes in her ear.

Marilyn hadn't reckoned on the telephone. Coen was out of her before she could kick the receiver under the bed. "Fuck" was all she could think to say.

She crouched against Coen so she could listen to her father. He was calling from Times Square. "Manfred," he croaked, "Marilyn's left her husband again. Has she been in touch with you?"

"No," Blue Eyes said. Marilyn was grateful that he didn't lose his erection under duress from her father.

"Stay put," Isaac said. "She always comes to you."

Coen returned to bed without a prick. Marilyn couldn't hold a grudge against the cop. Her father had half of New York City by the balls.

"Isaac's smart," she said. "He's got me mapped in his head like a Monopoly board. He knows all my resting places, that father of mine. Every water hole."

"Don't goose him too hard, Marilyn. He worries about you."

"Wake up, Manfred. You're just like me. We're on Isaac's casualty list. Aren't both of us divorcees?"

And she made the cop laugh. She'd fall in love with him, maybe, if he had the nerve to crumple his shield and spit in Isaac's face. But she shouldn't be harsh with him, strangle him with fantasies and expectations. Coen was Coen.

Isaac hadn't been cruising Times Square, nesting in ratty bars, peeking into pornographers' windows, for the First Deputy's office. He was on a personal mission. He pushed in and out of his car with a photograph in his fist. He had the First Deputy's private sedan at his disposal, a big Buick with bullet-proof windows. But he wouldn't use the First Dep's chauffeur. Isaac had his own man. Fat Brodsky, a first-grade detective with piggly eyes, was Isaac's toad.

"Who's the girlie, Isaac? You say you haven't seen her since she was five. How are you gonna recognize her from a dumb photograph?"

"Never mind," Isaac said. He found a girl with a thick nose and a high, summer skirt (it was February) near Forty-sixth Street. He opened the door for her. "Honey Schapiro, get in."

The girl had welts on her exposed kneecaps. She growled at Isaac. "I'm Naomi, Mister. Who are you?"

He lunged at her and installed her on his lap, but he couldn't shut the door. Honey was kicking too hard. Isaac had to keep her from biting his ears.

"What is this? You don't belong to the pussy posse? I know all them guys."

She began screaming for her protector, a dude named Ralph, who rushed over from Forty-fifth Street in his leather coat. Brodsky upset him more than Isaac. The chauffeur was pointing a holster at Ralph's groin.

"Hey brother," Ralph said, with a nod for Isaac. "Speak to me." Ralph didn't reach for his money clip. The Buick made him cautious; ordinary house bulls wouldn't have come to him in so conspicuous a car.

"You bringing her down?"

"No," Isaac said. "She's going home to her father."

"Cut the shit, man. You asking me to buy you a hat? I'll buy, but I ain't supplying the feather. Fifty is all I'm giving today." Then he saw the blue teeth on Isaac's badge. He shuddered under his coat. Ralph was wise to the nitty-gritty of Manhattan station-houses: no detective carried a badge with blue teeth.

Isaac spoke through his window. "Forget about Honey Schapiro, you understand? If I catch her above Fourteenth Street again, I'll personally break your face." He signaled to Brodsky, and Ralph waved goodbye to the Buick on jiggling knees. He didn't like to be swindled. If he'd known how Honey was connected, he wouldn't have battered her legs. He'd have rewarded her with a better corner, and a cleaner clientele. That ugly Jew broad had her hooks into the police.

Brodsky laughed on the ride downtown with Isaac and the girl. "Boy, you can scare nigger pimps. Isaac, did you look at his eyes?"

"Shut up," Isaac said. And Brodsky was satisfied. He loved to be scolded by his Chief. A slur from Isaac made him vigorous and alert. Brodsky could have farted on every cop at Headquarters, including the number one Irisher, First Deputy O'Roarke. The chauffeur swore himself to Isaac. Isn't he going to Paris, France, Brodsky reasoned. What other cop travels four thousand miles for a lecture?

The girl moved off Isaac's lap. She panicked at the benches and frozen grass of Union Square park. Second Avenue curled her chin into the padding under the window. With glum, bitter cheeks she watched Isaac's descent into the lower East Side.

Brodsky became aware of the girl's worsening state. "Honey, would you like a gumdrop?"

"Leave her alone," Isaac said.

They parked in a lot behind the Essex Street housing project, Isaac sticking his Deputy Chief Inspector's card over the dashboard. The smell of urine accompanied them to the back doors of the project. Brodsky was about to comment on the smell when he noticed Isaac's glare. He displayed his badge to the housing guard, who had a disfigured nightstick and stubble on his face. He read the graffiti in the elevator car with obvious contempt. Essex Street had the musk and corrosive charm of a zoo. Brodsky lived in a house on Spuyten Duyvil hill. He came to Essex, Clinton, and Delancey to buy horseradish and squares of onion bread that were unknown in his section of Riverdale.

Isaac and the girl lost their winter flush in the overheated halls of the ninth floor. They drifted into an apartment with mousy green walls. Brodsky was the last one inside. A man in silk pajamas, without a tooth in his face, hugged the girl and cried into his sleeve. Sensing Brodsky, a stranger to him, he recovered himself. "Isaac, I search for months, and you find her in an hour and a half. You're a magician, Isaac. She was a baby the last time you saw her."

"I had her picture, Mordecai. It was nothing."

"Nothing he says. The police force would be poking in a ditch without you."

"Mordecai, I have to go." The Chief kept his eyes on Honey; she couldn't relax in her father's grip. She had the waxy features of a bloated doll.

"Isaac, one more thing. Philip is looking for you."

Isaac headed for the door; he didn't want to be sucked into another family dispute. He had his own troubles: a wild, uncontrollable daughter who shed husbands in the middle of winter.

"I'll catch him later, Mordecai. Not now."

Brodsky climbed into the elevator with Isaac. He could hear shouts and cries coming from the apartment, and the echoes of a slap. He smiled at the tumult raised by Mordecai and Honey. The Chief jabbed him with a thumb. "Brodsky, put your mind somewhere else. That's private business."

"Isaac, who is that guy? Your mother's boyfriend, or what?"

"I went to high school with him."

"You're kidding me. Isaac, he could be your grandfather, I swear."

"Forget about it. Mordecai doesn't have a Park Avenue dentist to look after his gums."

"Isaac, what's his trade?"

"Mordecai? He's a leftover from World War Two. He minded all the Victory gardens from Chinatown to Corlears Hook, but he didn't save a carrot for himself."

What could Isaac tell his chauffeur? Mordecai squatted down a hundred yards from his high school, Seward Park, and never stirred. Isaac had nothing against fixed perimeters. He was born on West Broadway, in a block owned by London Jews, men and women who had a more powerful vocabulary than their Yankee neighbours. Yet he preferred Essex Street, where his mother kept a junk shop, to the London Jews of West Broadway, or the Riverdale of Brodsky and Kathleen, Isaac's estranged wife.

The chauffeur stopped at the pickle factory on Essex and Broome for a jar of grated horseradish roots, pure and white, without the sweetening effect of red beets. Only dehydrated women and quiffs from the District Attorney's office would buy red horseradish. He put his nose in the jar, sniffed until his eyes went blind, and recovered in time to watch Isaac pass Sophie Sidel's junk shop.

"Isaac, aren't you going to sit with your mother?"

The Chief wouldn't answer. "Brodsky, the First Dep needs his car. Bring it to him."

Isaac was hoping to skirt away from his mother. He had too many unexplainable items in his head. He'd visit her after Paris, not before. He went into Hubert's delicatessen, five doors up from Sophie's. The place seemed in perfect order, with fish balls steaming the counter glass, and the juice of several puddings bubbling down off the stove, but Hubert himself was in disarray. A little man, with pointy shoulders and a lion's shaggy scalp, he had lumps on his brow and pieces of toilet paper covering dark spots along his chin.

"Hubert, what's wrong?" Isaac said, occupying his favorite chair. "Did you shave with one eye this morning?" Isaac couldn't have anticipated any evil. The delicatessen was his roost. Other Deputy Chief Inspectors sat in the chosen clamhouses of Mulberry and Grand, elbows away from Mafia lieutenants and princelings. But Isaac ate alone. At Hubert's he could follow the cracks in the wall without interruptions. Hubert hadn't lost a dime from his cash register in fifteen years. East Side pistols learned to steer south of the delicatessen by habit. If they did come inside Hubert's, to warm their hands over a cup of winter tea, they made sure to leave an elaborate tip.

The Chief wasn't insensitive. When that big lion's head didn't come back at him with a pout, and splash barley soup on the tablecloth with customary verve, Isaac took a different turn.

"Who did it to you? Were they white or black?"

"White as snow," Hubert said.

"How much did they take?"

"Nothing. They didn't touch the register. They broke a few chairs, slapped me, and left."

"Hubert, what did they wear?"

"Army coats, navy coats, who remembers? Their faces were covered up. With ski masks."

"Then how can you be sure they were white?"

"By their hands, Isaac. By their hands. One of them was a girl. I'm no detective, but I can tell the outline of a tit."

"When did it happen?"

"Yesterday. Just before closing."

"How come it takes a whole day for me to hear about it?"

"Isaac, close the inquisition, please. It isn't a police matter. Crazy kids. They could have picked on anybody."

"Absolutely," Isaac said, with a thickened tongue. "They were playing trick-or-treat. Only Halloween doesn't come in February. Your cash was too good for them. So they took their profits on your skull? How many of them were there?"

"There were three." Hubert's mouth was crammed with spit.

"I'll be gone for a week. My man will look into it."

The lumps grew dark on the lion's head. "Isaac, I don't want a bully in my store. Brodsky has wide elbows. He doesn't give a person room to drink his soup."

"I'll send you Coen. He's small. He'll charm your customers to sleep with his blue eyes."

Isaac knocked in the window of the dairy restaurant on Ludlow Street; it was a place he liked to avoid. It was crammed with hungry playwrights and scholars who tried to tangle Isaac into conversations about Spinoza, Israel, police brutality, and the strange brotherhood of Aaron and Moses. The playwrights weren't scornful of him. They recognized Isaac as the patron saint of Ludlow and East Broadway. He kept the bandits off their streets, but his strength was no surprise to them. He'd been suckled on strange milk. His mother was a woman with an obstinate heart. She befriended Arabs and Puerto Ricans over Jews.

They laughed at the reaction of the cashier lady to Isaac's knock. Ida Stutz threw off her uniform and smacked powder on her face. This one was Isaac's fiancée. They knew Isaac had an Irish wife up in Riverdale, but it would have been unwise of them to offend Ida. She furnished the scholars with toothpicks, sneaked them pats of butter and extra rolls, because she had a kindness for undernourished men. Ida was a girl with ample arms and legs. Whatever prettiness she had came from such proportions. She made her own lunch hours at the Ludlow restaurant. She was a dray horse most mornings and afternoons. The owners of the restaurant worked her silly. They could count on Ida's sweat, and Ida's husky back. So they allowed her one oddity. When the Chief knocked, Ida disappeared.

Isaac kept two stunted rooms on Rivington Street. He had to share a toilet with an ancient bachelor who peed wantonly. He washed his body in a kitchen tub that couldn't accommodate all of Isaac until his ears crept between his knees. It was in this undignified position that Ida found the Chief. She saw his suitcase on the bed, burgeoning with starched underwear, notebooks, and unbleached honey.

"Isaac, I know you. Soaping your belly is just a blind. Your brains are already in Paris."

Squirming in the tub, a prisoner to his own knees, Isaac had to smile. His wife Kathleen had been an extraordinary beauty. Even at forty-nine (she was five years older than the Chief), she had bosoms that could make Ida blush. But Isaac had never been a connoisseur of flesh. He gave up his home in Riverdale because Kathleen had grown

independent of him. She was a woman with spectacular real estate.
She had properties in Florida that ate up most of her energy. Isaac
didn't have to crawl to the lower East Side for love. He could have
stayed uptown with handsome widows, starlets who were hungry for
intellectual cops, or bimbos with penthouses and rebuilt behinds. Ida
pleased him more. She had a tongue that could scold him properly,
and a mouth that could suck up all his teeth. It didn't matter to her
how Isaac behaved. Ida wasn't fragile. She could match the Chief in
kisses, bear hugs, and bites. She began to undress.

"This is your last bath in America. Aren't you sorry you don't
have a bigger tub?"

"Ida, there's a tub at Headquarters that could fit you, me, and
five more cops. Should we go?"

"We'll go," she said. "When you're not in a rush." And she
dried him with Florentine talc from Mulberry Street, a powder so fine
that it could cure the most subtle rash. She lay on the bed near Isaac's
sweetened body, without bothering to push the suitcase aside. His
bull neck, evenly talced, couldn't intimidate her. Ida didn't suffer
from delusions about her fiancé. He had torn out the eye of a bandit
from East New York, broken the arms of suspicious characters,
survived gunfights with Puerto Ricans and hardened Jews. But she'd
seen the infant inside the bear. He was a man who loved to be babied.
Under the talcumed skin was a dread that Ida knew how to smother.
The Chief made no pretense of masculinity. He shuddered in Ida's
arms. His passions were the primitive clutch of a drowning man.

The bear was quiet after loving her. Ida wouldn't give in to his
sulkiness while she dripped with Isaac's sperm. So she pulled his
nose. The Chief kicked one leg over the honey jar and a stack of
underpants.

"Where are your troubles coming from, Isaac?"

"Ah," he lied. "I was thinking of a case." He mumbled Hubert's
name. "A gang beat him up. They didn't touch the register. It sounds
flukey to me."

"They're probably rejects from the Jewish Defense League.
Maybe Hubert isn't kosher enough. He serves butter with meat."

"Don't, Ida. That's not the work of Jewish kids. Giving an old
man puffs on his head."

"You think that's special? Look at my arms."

He glanced at the bruises on Ida's flesh, thumbprints turning
brown. The halo surrounding each bruise told him the pressure that
must have been applied.

"Same gang," she said. "They visited me too. They stole blintzes, not money."

"Ida, what else did they do?"

"Little stunts. One of them grabs my arms, while the other sticks a hand in my blouse."

The Chief scattered underwear off his bed.

"Ida, I'll find that hand and chop it off when I get back."

With two fingers Ida straightened the curl in his lip. "Should I tell you the number of times a customer has tried to grab a handful of me?"

"These weren't customers," the Chief said. But Ida had him by the ears. She was massaging the tiny bones at the back of his head. Isaac should have been putting on his tie. He didn't have ten minutes to spare. His face was deep in Ida's chest. The suitcase fell.

Isaac, couldn't wrestle free of old questions. Ida's milky smell brought Marilyn home to him. The Chief wasn't playing incest on his bed. He didn't confuse the girls. But kisses could hurt. He was coveting Ida's milk, when he had a daughter who went from husband to husband, and couldn't confide in him.

TWO

Marilyn survived on lumps of tuna fish. She didn't peek about until Blue Eyes could assure her that Isaac was on the plane for Paris. The First Dep's office had verified the news: Isaac embarked at 7 p.m. She'd been lazing with Coen since noon. She watched him button his pretty neck into the collar of a white shirt. The holster went on last. "Manfred, wait. I'm going with you."

Coen was minding Isaac's car. Blue Eyes hated to drive. There were too many stirrings in doorways, beggars jumping into the street, dogs chasing buses or crawling under his wheels, old women losing their memories in the middle of the road, to thwart a cop's eye.

"You suppose Isaac is going to revise the entire French police?" Marilyn was bored. She couldn't get Coen to jabber. So she enticed him with her father's secrets. "Manfred, you have a tricky boss. He won't be mingling with detectives over there. Isaac went to visit his father."

Lines formed on Coen's chin. Marilyn was ashamed of her crude tactics. Coen's father had killed himself. Ten years ago, while Blue Eyes was stationed in Germany, Papa Coen decided to take gas.

Coen wore his sad face ever since.

"I didn't know Isaac had a father . . . a father that's alive."

"It's an embarrassment to him. Like having a brother in jail."

Coen had learned not to mention Isaac's baby brother Leo, who was entombed in Crosby Street, in a temporary annex to the old Civil Jail, because of alimony trouble. The Police Department shrugged at this indignity to itself. But the First Dep was powerless. Leo refused to step out of jail.

"Marilyn, what's embarrassing about a father?"

"He deserted the family years ago. Isaac had to leave school. Didn't he tell you? His father was once a millionaire. Joel Sidel, the fur-collar prince. He threw it over for a stinking paint brush. He had a long nose, like Gauguin. He thought Paris was the new Tahiti. He wanted to paint the jungles around Sacré Coeur."

Jungles in Paris meant nothing to Coen. "Why did Isaac pick now for a visit?"

"Because he's had intimations of mortality." Coen's starved cheeks made her sorrowful of her rotten vocabulary, fed at Sarah Lawrence and at the dinner tables of her many husbands. "Manfred, he's going on forty-five. That's a dangerous age. Isaac needs his father. Seeing Joel will prove to him that he's got years to go."

Coen dropped her at Crosby Street. He would park in Isaac's slot at the police garage, march into Headquarters, blow dust off Isaac's desk, and answer phone calls in the name of his Chief. He would say, "First Deputy's office, Inspector Sidel," with Marilyn's perfume ripening on him.

It was past official visiting hours at the Crosby Street annex, but Marilyn had no difficulty getting in. None of the guards could recollect the name of her current husband. They knew her as "Miss Sidel." Not even the deputy warden was willing to tamper with Isaac's girl. He brought Leo out to her himself, mumbling little flatteries about Isaac's trip. "He'll teach Paris how to nab their crooks. You can bet on that, Miss Sidel."

Leo was floundering in an oversized prison shirt. It was hard to consider him an uncle. He'd be Isaac's baby brother for life.

Leo was devoid of prison scars. He set his own hours at Crosby Street, ate candy out of a machine, destroyed the guards in pinochle, checkers, and bridge. There were no criminals to mingle with. Just cases like Leo, men who had faulted on their alimony, and were being held in civil contempt. Detectives from the Sheriff's office had swiped Leo out of a congested lobby in the building where he worked, exposing him to the shameful stare of executives, buyers, and girls from the typing pool, and led him away in handcuffs, on a complaint from his former wife. The Sheriff's detectives were as restless as Leo. It made them miserable to be recognized as the men who had collared the brother of Isaac the Just.

Marilyn had a softness for Leo. She hadn't come to him as Isaac's compassionate daughter. She could identify with Leo's plight. Leo was her special kinsman: both of them had endured busted marriages, both of them had been skinned alive.

They could hug and kiss in the prison's reception room without one snarl from the guards. "Marilyn, are you laughing same as me? I can breathe. The word has come down that Isaac is out of the country. I'll grow fat in the next few days. What about you?"

Marilyn extended the hug.

"Uncle Leo, I wish I had three thousand to get you out of here. Would that be enough to satisfy stupid Selma? I'd strangle her for you, if you want. Don't you think Isaac could spring me? Only that would leave you a widower with kids. Have Davey and Michael come to visit you?"

Leo grew somber in the reception room. He broke away from Marilyn. "They stick with their mother," he said. "They send me poison notes. Selma forces them to practice their penmanship on me. I can hear her tongue behind the words. 'Dad, you're killing us.' Marilyn, that woman has the money to choke an elephant. She keeps her bankbooks in an old brassiere."

Marilyn chafed at her inability to help Leo. Her last two husbands had been rich, but she was left a pauper. She had to borrow money from Coen.

"Sophie or Isaac would put up the till. Leo, I could ask."

"Never. Marilyn, don't forget. In October I was forty-two. Can I go begging to my mother, or scrounge from big Isaac? Better they should take me out and shoot me. I don't care how they finish me off. As long as Sophie doesn't know. Marilyn, Isaac didn't tell mama, did he? I call her every morning. I say I'm at a hotel that doesn't have a phone in the room. Funny, she didn't answer today. She must be out buying more junk."

"Isaac fucks over everybody, but he won't snitch. Not because of you. It would make him too uncomfortable. He'd have to explain to your mother why you're sitting in a jail. Leo, don't fidget. I'll convince Sophie for you. I'm going there right now."

The guards groped for banalities on the way out. They were

fishing to stay on Isaac's good side. "We'll watch Leo, Miss Sidel. We've made it like a country club for him."

Marilyn crossed the Bowery into Isaac's territories: the Puerto Rican-Jewish East Side. She had to smile at the old Forsyth Street synagogue, now a "Templo Adventista," with its Star of David still intact in the little circular window near the roof. Later she would shop for underpants on Orchard Street. She had to see Sophie first.

Israel had taken over Essex Street. Apricots from Galilee, Haifa plums, and spaghetti made in Tel Aviv dominated the windows of tiny groceries. She realized what a blight this must be for her grandmother, who championed the Diaspora, homeless Arabs and Jews in a Gentile universe. Sophie didn't have the usual allotment of junk on parade outside her door. Was she feeding soup to hobos? Or feeling up a plump goose at the Christian butcher? The door was ajar.

Marilyn had no knowledge of Haifa plums. She was a girl with an Irish nose, a captive of churches on Marble Hill, with memories of communion gloves and priests who dribbled spit. Hot-blooded, she allowed her cherry to be swiped at twelve and a half. Past fourteen, her fame extended from Riverdale to Washington Heights, with pieces off her underpants rotting in the cellars of Fordham Road. Uptown precociousness couldn't connect a girl to her mysterious grandmother, Sophie the Hoarder. So Marilyn interpreted the lay of things. Sophie wouldn't spite her own wares to give her affections to a hobo. She was more careful than that. Marilyn stepped over the damaged perambulators that Sophie prized. They were hopeless vehicles. None of them could move. But Sophie had trussed their bodies with great lengths of wire.

Marilyn ventured deeper into the shop. Torn lampshades couldn't trouble her. That might have been Sophie's doing. She peeked under a mound of blankets with odd lumps in a corner. She wasn't shocked by Sophie's arm; it rested in a natural position, without a flaw in the beautiful veins. Was this how a grandmother sleeps?

Marilyn tugged at the blankets, following the course of that arm. Sophie's head emerged, lying in blood that had turned to a thick, corrosive jelly. The jelly reached to her ears. She had marks on her forehead that resembled the sink of a belt buckle into skin. Marilyn's screams came in a dry wisp. She shambled towards the telephone. She didn't consider ambulances. In her panic she could only think of dialing for Coen.

THREE

Isaac sat in a damp palace high on the Quai Voltaire. His feet were cold. Surrounded by gunsmiths, retired police inspectors, manufacturers of snooping devices, and a team of specialists from the crime labs of Antwerp and Bruges, he tried to make do with his high-school French. Sentences galloped in his ear. He couldn't decipher all the sputter. Isaac was miserable at heart. His first walk in Paris had broken him.

Armored with New York, he came swollen-eyed, ready to lick his honey jar and scorn this town. Isaac had no instinct for sightseeing. He wasn't the sort of man who could gravitate towards the Eiffel Tower and the Champ de Mars. A few months back, Herbert Pimloe, the Harvard boy, an underchief with the First Deputy's office, and a voracious traveler, had returned home from Paris with a newspaper clipping for Isaac, which advertised a certain Monsieur Sidel, Portraitiste, with permanent headquarters in the lobby of an avenue Kléber hotel, near the Arc de Triomphe. "Chief," Pimloe said, with a finger on the clipping, and proud of himself. "Could that be a relative of yours?" Isaac had a burn in his throat. He hadn't expected his father to play Lazarus after twenty-five years. Joel Sidel was supposed to be among the missing and the dead. Isaac had wanted to forget his father's name. Now he thought of murdering Joel, or confronting him on the avenue Kléber, and bruising his head. Isaac schemed and scratched a little. He invited himself to a conference on crime staged for gunsmiths and provincial detectives. He was in Paris to kill, maim, and collect his due.

On his way to the conference, crossing the Seine, Isaac was prepared to spit at barges in the river, ignore shrill parrots belonging to old women with dust on their clothes, and avoid bookstalls and organ grinders. But he couldn't guard himself properly against the Ile de la Cité. A stone island, a medieval city that rose out of the water, it turned Isaac dumb. He stared at the island's grassy point, a twitch of green in front of gray mansion walls and the tips of Notre Dame. Stone pushing through the blur of a smoking river was insufferable to Isaac. Nothing in New York could swallow up this kind of vision. The chimneys of Welfare Island were piddling things compared to such damp walls. Isaac arrived at the conference with a scowling face.

One of the specialists from Bruges cornered Isaac after a short address on Parisian bank robbers. The Flemish man, who spoke a powerful English, made pessimistic swipes with his head that Isaac failed to comprehend. "Inspector Sidel, what is the position in America? Do you have amateurs committing crimes? Disgusting little apaches who are impossible to trace? Paris is flooded with them. I don't mean the scum of the African quarters. They're no threat to us. But young savages from the government projects around Clignancourt, and the other little holes at the ends of Paris— cockroaches with pistols in their hands. These roaches appear on the Champs-Elysées, stick up a bank, and crawl into their holes. What can one do? No grid, no organized gang, no strict underworld. Nothing but roaches, isolated roaches."

"We have them in the United States, Monsieur, but not so many," Isaac said, preoccupied with the painter Joel, his recreant father at the avenue Kléber hotel.

"Then what advice do you have for our friends in Paris, Inspector Sidel?"

"Go into the projects."

"With an army?"

"No, with spies."

"Ah," the Flemish man said, warming to Isaac. "It's a matter of infiltration. If you can't flush out the roaches, you sleep in their beds. Inspector, stay in Paris. You have a future with the Sûreté."

Isaac abandoned the conference before lunch. He regained his stride on the Quai Voltaire, walking towards the Invalides. He would be fine so long as he could distance himself from the sweating stones of the Cité. New York crept back to him; the Mansard roofs of Commerce Street, the crumbling walls of Cherry Lane, the slaughterhouses at Gansevoort, the incredible steel-shuttered factories of Lafayette and upper Mulberry. He could take Paris in a wink.

The boulevards above the Trocadero were welcome ground to Isaac. He didn't have to deal with crooked streets. He could close his eyes and sniff out Madison Avenue in the little bakeries and jewelry shops off the rue Hamelin. He wasn't astounded by The Iroquois of avenue Kléber: it had to be a hotel for rich Americans. All the tributaries of the Ohio snarled over Isaac's ears from a huge pictograph on the front wall. He had to go around an enormous Eiffel Tower in the center of The Iroquois. Isaac refused to smile.

He had his father at a disadvantage. Joel Sidel was the only painter in the lobby. Isaac couldn't be compassionate to the easel of a seventy-year-old. This was the man who had turned his mother crazy, and made a weakling of his brother. Sophie blundered into a rag shop, Isaac became a *flic,* and Leo drifted from boyhood to marriage to alimony jail.

Isaac couldn't ignore his father's technique. Joel snared Americans off the elevators; with a wag of his finger and artful hunchings of his back he would lure a couple over to his bench. While husband and wife posed with camera, light meter, and guide books, Joel dipped his fat brush into a can and painted their outline and obvious features in under a minute, before they had a chance to protest. He charged twenty francs for his work. Verisimilitude didn't count. The couples would have been offended by too much accuracy. They were in awe of Joel's speed with a brush. Isaac grunted into the lapels of his raincoat. He hadn't come to Paris to play spy.

Joel wasn't asleep. He made a primal recognition: this had to be one of his two boys. "Leo?" he said.

"No, papa. Look again."

Joel slapped his brush into a paint rag; it wobbled like the head of a fish.

"Isaac, you must have inherited your brother's face. I'm not disappointed that it's you. You're my oldest. Half a century goes by, and you can still call me 'papa'."

"Papa, don't exaggerate. I wasn't in this world fifty years ago."

Isaac squinted at his father's unnatural coloring, heightened reds around eyes, cheeks, and nose, and blue on the bumps of the skull. Joel was wearing rouge. He had a scarf on his throat, and a bottle-green painter's smock that would have identified him as a portraitist in any setting. It was Joel's uniform at The Iroquois.

"I was expecting you, Isaac. I'm not surprised. Have you come to murder your papa?"

The forks under Isaac's burly jaw twisted up into his mouth, leaving him with a stingy smile.

"Papa, search me. I'm clean. You can't smuggle guns into Paris."

"Isaac, you could smuggle anything. Don't think I'm ignorant of your career. I may be a piece of shit, but I follow my boys. Marilyn's the name of your daughter. She's an Irish beauty. She carries husbands on her back. Isaac, are you shocked how much I know? A boy from Seventh Avenue who used to work for me, he's in Paris once a year. An international buyer, with millions in his pocket, he sips wine and talks about my family. What's Leo doing?"

"Leo's in jail," Isaac spit through his teeth.

The rouge jumped under Joel's eyes. He retreated into his painter's smock, rising over the easel with his blued skull. He was scanning the elevators for American bait. "I'm neglecting my business, Isaac. I can see I'll have a poor afternoon." He mentioned an address on the rue Vieille-du-Temple. "It's in the Marais, on top of the Rivoli. Just ask for the Jews. You'll find it, Isaac. It will take you a while. You can murder me when you get there."

Isaac left The Iroquois so his father could begin to hustle. On the rue Hamelin he took out a gigantic map of Paris and searched for the proper grid. With his policeman's logic he timed his walk at two hours. Isaac cut east, above the bend in the river, and landed on the Place des Etats-Unis.

Two men in shiny brown coats hovered close to Isaac looking for pigeons to feed. Isaac watched the play of their hands. Their pursuit of birds seemed elaborate to him (Isaac couldn't locate a smear of pigeon shit in the Place des Etats-Unis). The shiny coats belonged to a dip artist and his squire. Isaac appraised this pickpocket team with a cool turn of his mind. They can't be from South America. The Guzmanns (a tribe of pickpockets out of Peru) would never wear shiny coats. These are locals from Algeria, or Sicily. Starving kids with the soft, beautiful fingers of a girl.

The team broke apart to encircle Isaac. The squire, a boy with a scarred nose, bumped Isaac into the dip. The boy heard a terrible scream. The dip's hand was caught inside Isaac's raincoat. Isaac crunched the girlish fingers with a squeeze of his fist. He brought the dip down to his knees.

He didn't forget the other boy. The squire was the vicious one, Isaac could tell. The squire had his blade, a pathetic kitchen knife without a handle. He meant to skewer Isaac with it. But he couldn't draw blood from the Chief. Isaac cracked the boy once, behind the ear, and the squire shot across the Place des Etats-Unis. The Chief was growing fond of Paris.

He made the Tuileries with over an hour to spare. He liked the measurements of a long, dead garden. The tramps who collected at the borders of the Tuileries had an independence Isaac could admire. Dressed in warm coats, none of them shuffled after him, or acknowledged his presence.

Isaac's exhilaration began to fade on the rue de Rivoli. A gorgeous line of mounted police, with plumes down their backs and silver pots on their heads, made him think of his father's uniform. Isaac scowled. His anger increased against Joel. My father's a clown, he muttered to himself. A clown in a snot-green shirt.

The rue de Rivoli became a region of shabby department stores, with windows that had the defiled look of a battlefield, and soon Isaac was in the Marais. Narrow streets with hump-backed buildings spilled over into each other's lap at crazy, undefined angles. Chimney pots cropped out over Isaac's head like warts on a monstrous finger. He passed kosher butcher shops, restaurants that sold "*Boercht Romain*" and "*Salami Hongrois*," signs that spit competing slogans ("*Israël Vaincra!*" and "*Halte à l'Agression Arabe*"), and a synagogue strictly for North Africans. Joel, who cursed the rabbis of New York, had gone religious in his old age.

Isaac regretted his trip; he should have visited London instead, the London of Whitechapel, where Joel's father came from; he'd been a petty merchant, hustling bloomers on Princelet Street, and a "deacon" of the Spitelfield synagogue. Even then the Sidels didn't pray; they were in charge of the synagogue's economic affairs and its soup kitchen for indigent Jews. They were all charitable men.

Isaac discovered Joel's place on the rue Vieille-du-Temple. There seemed to be no court in reach, no passageway for him to use. He stood by the house until an old woman emerged from an opening in the wall. Isaac went inside.

He groveled in the dark, searching for nonexistent bannisters with both his palms; he touched greasy wood and roughage on a low ceiling. He came out in the back somewhere, sliding against a tricky doorsill. He was in a court with ravaged blue ground and a nest of sinking trees. He clumped towards a set of stairs. His father lived on the top floor.

Joel's mistress was Vietnamese (Sophie had never bothered to divorce her wandering husband); a woman with delicate jaws and exquisite bones around her eyes, she worked as a chambermaid at The Iroquois. Joel called her Mauricette. She couldn't have been over thirty, but away from The Iroquois Joel was a much younger man. He abandoned his bottle-green smock and the trappings of a portraitist, and sat in an old velvet shirt that forced Isaac to contend with the handsomeness of his father. Joel wasn't a clown at home. The rouge had been wiped off.

"Isaac, who ripped your coat?"

"It's nothing, papa. I met two pickpockets in the street. They wanted to dance with me. I refused. They won't be so nimble for the next couple of weeks."

Joel shrugged at Isaac's delivery; he couldn't unravel detective stories. He summoned Isaac to the table. The fragrance of perfectly cooked rice caught Isaac by the nose. He softened to his father's circumstance. Joel didn't need more than one room. All his articles were here.

They ate fish with their hands, sucking between the bones. Isaac drank a silky wine that growled in his throat. Joel didn't plague him until the end of the meal.

"A super detective with his kid brother sitting in jail—Isaac, there has to be a moral in it. Did he rape the Police Commissioner's wife?"

"Papa, he isn't inside with criminals, I swear. It's only a civil complaint. I wouldn't let perverts near Leo. I have a brother who thinks it's chivalrous to be deaf, dumb, and blind. He's free with his own guts, that Leo He scratches his ass with a leaky pen and signs his life away. Now he's a slave. His ex-wife owns the teeth in his mouth. Leo runs with his testicles stabbing the floor. He can't catch up on his alimony."

"Isaac, I could raise five hundred dollars. How much does he need?"

"Don't talk money, papa, please. Wouldn't I help that miserable prick? He won't take a nickel. He enjoys his misery."

Isaac walked down the stairs with bandied knees. The wine had put a blush on his neck. He groped against the walls giggling like an idiot boy who'd escaped from his father's house. Wavering in the moist blue earth of his father's court, he grew lenient with Joel. His mother had been crazy long before Joel left. She picked through garbage cans, collecting foul cardboard and ugly pieces of string, while Joel had his millions. Isaac loved her, and had a fondness for her piles of junk, and the Arabs she brought home, beggars, failed musicians, and unemployed cooks, after scavenging on Atlantic Avenue, but why should his father elect to stay with a woman who had permanent whiskers and rust on her fingers that couldn't wash off?

Isaac liked Mauricette. She was no mean stepmother to him, and no simple appendage to his father, no superficial wife. She mingled her spit and blood with Joel's in that one salty room.

Isaac returned to his hotel near the Place Vendôrne. He tried to nap; the metallic click of the telephone tore through his drowsiness. He didn't need the help of overseas operators. He recognized Coen's nasal hello.

"Come home, Isaac. Your mother's been hurt."

FOUR

Headquarters was invaded with shock troops. You couldn't miss them in the corridors, the locker rooms, and the johns. They collected near the marble pillars on the ground floor, sucking bitter lozenges, men in black leather coats, with dirty eyes. They barked at each other and spit at low-grade detectives and ordinary clerks, who called them "crows" and "undertakers" because of the vast amounts of black leather. The "crows" worked out of competing offices. They were rivals, members of elite squads that belonged to the Chief of Detectives, the First Deputy, and the Police Commissioner himself. The PC had spoken with uncommon bluntness: he wanted the scumbags that wounded Sophie Sidel.

Isaac shunned the leather boys. They scattered behind their pillars when they saw the Chief. Isaac had his own squad, boys without leather coats, blue-eyed detectives, marksmen who never sneered. He went to his office, across the hall from "Cowboy" Rosenblatt, the Jewish Chief of Detectives. Isaac had been gone three days, but his great oak desk was cluttered with memorandums and personal notes, letters of condolence from all the Irish chiefs at Headquarters, from the Mayor's office, from Newgate, the FBI man, who played gin rummy with the First Dep, from Barney Rosenblatt and the PC, and an old-fashioned blue card in the fine scrawl of First Deputy O'Roarke. His phone had been ringing continuously for an hour. He held the earpiece over his cheek and growled his name. He wasn't in the mood for Mordecai.

"Isaac, I heard about your mother. The neighborhood is up in arms. We're forming patrols, Isaac. We'll repay slap for slap. How's Sophie?"

"She's still in a coma."

"Sophie's a tough girl. She'll pull through."

Isaac understood the habits of an old friend. Mordecai wouldn't have called him at the office to cluck words about Sophie. He was a delicate man, Mordecai. He had to be angling for someone else.

"Is it Honey?" the Chief said. "She hasn't fled the coop again, has she? I can't grab her this morning. But I can lend you Brodsky, or Coen."

Isaac heard a sound that could have been Mordecai sighing, or an electrical hiss. "Honey's at home . . . it's Philip. Can't you visit him? Isaac, he's in a terrible way."

"Jesus Christ, my mother's lying in Bellevue with tubes sticking out of her, and you pester me with Philip. Has his chess game been deteriorating? Philip doesn't move off his ass. So long, Mordecai."

Mordecai, Philip, and Isaac had been the three big brains of Seward Park High. Stalwarts of the chess club, devotees of Sergei Eisenstein and Dashiell Hammett, they were inseparable in 1943, 1944, and 1945. But Mordecai and Philip remained visionaries, and Isaac joined the police. He screamed for Pimloe, who ran the First Deputy's rat squad whenever Isaac was away. Pimloe arrived with his clipboard and a gold-nubbed fountain pen. He was wearing his Harvard Phi Beta Kappa key. Isaac despised Pimloe's key. He'd had four miserable semesters at Columbia College, living in a monk's closet on Morningside Heights.

"Where's Coen?"

"He's out tracking leads, like everybody else." Pimloe waved the clipboard, which held a detailed map of lower Manhattan, with green boxes for City parks, and a blue star for Headquarters; the map was littered with marks from Pimloe's fountain pen "Isaac, they hit twenty places last week. Six between Essex and the Bowery, six in Chinatown, five in Little Italy, one in SoHo, and two on Hudson Street. Barney calls them the lollipop kids. Some old guinzo in Little Italy swears they came into his store sucking lollipops."

"Herbert, are you cooperating with Barney Rosenblatt?"

"Isaac, you can't shove Cowboy out of this. The PC is backing him up."

"I'll shove when I have to shove. Herbert, there's more than one gang working the streets. Could be your map is a little off, and we've got a whole bunch of lollipops on our hands."

"Isaac, it fits. They punch old people. They wear masks. They won't take money."

"What's your theory, Herbert? Tell me your thoughts."

"Freaks. Definitely freaks. They attack, hide, and attack. A fucking lollipop war."

"Is my mother included in your theory?"

"Isaac, what do you mean? That was strictly random. It could have been any old woman in a store."

"Random, my ass. Somebody's sending me a kite, and I can't figure why. Herbert, what have you got?"

Pimloe led the Chief to his favored niche outside the interrogation room on the second floor. They stared through the one-way mirror at the suspects Pimloe, Barney Rosenblatt, and the "crows" had rounded up for Isaac: retards from an Eighth Avenue hotel. winos fresh from Chinatown, a black whore with scabs on her knees, runaways from a New Jersey mental hospital; and two Puerto Rican cops disguised as pimps, so that Isaac could have a spectacular lineup. He scanned the faces only once, his lip curling high. "Let 'em go."

Isaac went around the corner to Margedonna's Bar and Grille. The barman wouldn't grin. Isaac tried the back room, where the Chief of Detectives was sitting with his "crows," their black leather coats humped against the wall on a line of pegs. Isaac approached Barney Rosenblatt's long table. None of the "crows" stood up for him. They stuffed their cheeks with eggplant and watched.

Barney Rosenblatt was the number-one Jew cop in the City of New York. He hated Isaac more than the Irish chiefs who surrounded him. Isaac undermined Barney's detectives with his squad of rats and personal spies. Both of them were officers in the Hands of Esau, a police fraternity for Jews. They squabbled here as much as they did at Headquarters. The Hands of Esau was in constant jeopardy on account of them.

Barney wore a Colt with his name and rank engraved right over the trigger, and a quick-draw holster with tassels at the bottom, like Buffalo Bill. Sliding out from the table, he gripped the holster's beard to prevent the Colt from stabbing him in the belly. The "crows" had swallowed too many red peppers: their eyes watered at the vision of Barney embracing Isaac. Were these burly men or dancing bears?

There was nothing sanctimonious about Cowboy's embrace. He squeezed Isaac's ribs with devotion. Barney wasn't a piddling warrior; he shared the grief of his enemies.

But Isaac hadn't interrupted Cowboy's lunch for a bear-hug, and the smell of Chianti in a bottle brushed with straw. "Don't try to steal chickens off me, Barney. Stay out of my coop. I can handle this alone."

"Who's a chicken thief?" Cowboy said. He fought back his desire to take Isaac by the ears and throw him under the table.

"If there's a riddle, I'll solve it. The persons who touched my mother will have to deal with me."

"No vendettas, Isaac. This is police business. I can bring the whole Manhattan South down on those freaks, whoever they are."

"Barney, I don't want your boys rushing in and out. It's my caper. Hands off."

"Isaac, who have you got? Blue Eyes? That imbecile couldn't find his dick in the street."

"Barney, don't curse. You're talking about my man."

Cowboy had to let him go. As Chief of Detectives, he stood above the ladders that inspectors had to climb. But the First Deputy was dying of cancer, and the cop that inherited the First Dep's chair controlled the City police. Barney didn't have to guess who O'Roarke's heir would be. Still, he was in a celebrating mood. His oldest daughter, a spinster of thirty-two, would be a bride in eight days. This was Barney's last unmarried child. What had Isaac accomplished? He'd married off the same daughter three times.

Isaac didn't signal upstairs for Brodsky; a chauffeur could distract his mind. He rode in a cab, unwilling to discuss sugar scares, crime, or the weather.

The driver figured Isaac was a pornography czar, or a manager of small-time queens: no one had ever asked him to cruise the all-night movie houses on Forty-second Street. "That's the one," Isaac said, jumping out of the cab. The driver saw him disappear into the foyers of the Tivoli Theatre. He couldn't believe Isaac's gall. "The guy must think he's invisible. He walks through ticket windows."

Isaac foraged in the back rows. He couldn't borrow a flashlight from a Tivoli usher. Wadsworth, the man he wanted, would have hidden from him. He avoided the male prostitutes who were soliciting near the aisles. "Need a finger, baby? It'll cost you. Six dollars an inch." Isaac could have put them away, but he would have lost his man. He had to protect Wadsworth's house.

He heard a low crackle behind him. "*Vas machst du,* Isaac?" The Chief had to laugh. Wadsworth wouldn't recognize the fact that Isaac was an English-American Jew without a Yiddish vocabulary.

"Wadsworth, I'm doing fine."

Wadsworth was an albino, a milky nigger with pink eyes. He couldn't survive in sunlight. Wadsworth needed twenty-four hours of dark. He lived at the Tivoli, rinsing his mouth in the water fountain, doing his underwear in the sink, sneaking out after midnight, and returning to the theatre before the sun had a chance to rise. He existed on buttered popcorn and candy bars from the Tivoli's machines. He could sit through cartoons, features, and coming attractions in one position. Wadsworth claimed he never had to sleep.

"Did you look after my uncles, Isaac? My uncles are important to me."

"I'm trying, Wads. I can't jump over the civil service lists. But there may be room for a typist with the Department of Parks."

"Isaac, my uncles can't type."

The Chief had to groom Wadsworth with favors, little and big. He found temporary jobs for Wadsworth's long family of uncles, cousins and friends. Wadsworth would take no profit for himself. He was the best informant Isaac ever had. A burglar by trade, and a sometime arsonist, he sold watches and shoes to firemen, sanitation workers, and the sons of mafiosi. Connected uptown and downtown with pickpockets, shylocks, and pinkie-breakers, Wadsworth cornered information before it hit the street.

"Isaac, if you're here about your mom, I can't help. Mother-fuckers with masks, busting faces without putting a finger in the till, that sounds like amateur stuff."

"Or a hate job. Wadsworth, do you know anybody who dislikes me so much he'd send a gang of rotten kids to grab my tail?"

"Isaac, you asking me if you got enemies? I can name ten cops who'd love to murder you, including Cowboy Rosenblatt."

"I could name twenty, but this isn't the work of a cop. What about the Guzmanns?"

Gamblers and pickpockets from the Bronx, the Guzmanns were becoming a tribe of pimps. They had entered Isaac's borough to find chicken bait, thirteen-year-olds, all of them white, and Isaac vowed to drive the Guzmanns out of Manhattan. He stationed his men at the bus terminals to frustrate their ability to snatch young girls. "Wadsworth, are the Guzmanns paying me back?"

"Na," Wadsworth said, showing his pale lip. "The Guzmanns have feelings. They wouldn't hit on your mother. They'd come direct to you." The deep red of his pupils burned in the dusty air of the Tivoli; Isaac had to look away from Wadsworth's eyes. Wadsworth said, "Try Amerigo."

"Why would Amerigo come after me?"

"He's been grumbling, Isaac, that's all I know. He thinks you're sleeping with the FBI's."

"Wadsworth, that's office politics. The First Dep has to be polite. We use their labs sometimes. But Newgate's a dummy. Why would I sleep with him?"

"Don't explain it to me, man. Save it for Amerigo."

Isaac blinked in the raw sunlight outside the Tivoli. He was a cop who wasn't used to caves. He scowled at Inspector Pimloe's theories on the lollipop gang. His office had come up with shit, stupid shit. Pimloe brought Isaac a gallery of hobos and talked of random attacks. Isaac had other ideas about these lollipops. They scared Ida, his fiancée, raided his hangout on Essex Street, and beat up his mother in a single night. They wanted Isaac to get the news. Could Amerigo Genussa be their benefactor, the man who fingered Isaac, and supplied the kids with masks and all-day suckers?

Amerigo was president of the Garibaldi social club and the *padrone* of Mulberry Street. Before he went into real estate and bought up a sixth of Little Italy, he'd been a miraculous chef. He had to give up the Caffè da Amerigo to supervise his holdings and safeguard the streets. The Puerto Ricans were making inroads, Chinamen were grabbing vacant buildings north of Canal, but Amerigo had kept out the blacks. His hirelings liked to boast that their mammas and girlfriends couldn't see a black face a half mile around the Garibaldi social club, unless it belonged to a cop, or an FBI man.

The Garibaldis were having a personal war with the FBI, whose scarecrows and paid informers swarmed Amerigo's streets, tapped his telephones, peeked in his window, dug wires into his walls, tried to flirt with the daughters of Mulberry grocers, bakers, and ravioli men.

Isaac took a second cab down to Grand Street. He visited the fruit stand of Murray Baldassare, across from Ferrara's pastry house. Murray had been a marginal stoolpigeon, registered with the First Deputy's office, until Isaac had turned him over to Newgate. Now he was Newgate's decoy, a fink for the FBI. Newgate financed Murray's career as a fruitman, throwing four thousand dollars into the stand. Murray had no time for the fruit. Women from the neighborhood were fleecing him out of his bundles of tangerines. Murray was supposed to spy on Ferrara's; Newgate had the notion that the *dons* of Grand Street conducted their business over Ferrara's coffee mugs and trays of Sicilian pastry. There wasn't a child in Little Italy over the age of six who didn't know that Murray Baldassare was a fink. He stayed alive because he had nothing to feed Newgate. Amerigo himself ate Murray's tangerines.

Murray recoiled at the image of Isaac shining through the tiny window of his stand. He developed hiccups that knocked underneath his lungs. Isaac had to drive a fist into Murray's shoulder before the fruitman could get back his speech. The tangerines had a scarlet flush; their skins bled for Isaac. He swiped one from Murray's window, its skin tearing under the force of Isaac's yellow nail. The nectar inside was frozen to the strings that covered the fruit.

"Chief," Murray said, "why come here? You want to see me dead?"

Isaac licked his fingers. "Relax, Murray. Amerigo knows you were married to me. He won't hurt you."

"It aint Amerigo. It's the FBI's. Newgate'll cripple me. You think he's stupid? He can figure for himself. The reports I'm shoving him are a bunch of crap. He'll say me, you, and Amerigo are dancing on his head."

"Didn't I put you in business, Murray? Don't complain. You're a celebrity now. Nobody ever copped a fruit stand off the FBI's before."

"Isaac, I'm begging you, get me out of this."

Isaac put the injured tangerine back in Murray's window.

"Talk to me, Murray. You watch the street. Has Amerigo been hiring any goons lately?"

Murray's eyes wandered from the ceiling to Isaac's shoes. "I think so."

"How many, Murray, how many has he hired?"

"Three or four."

"Are they lollipops—kids? One of them a young girl? Did he send them to stomp on my mother?"

Quivers rose inside Murray's cheeks that went beyond the possibility of a bluff. "Your mother, Isaac? . . . Newgate never told me. Who could do such a terrible thing?"

Isaac made the corner, with Murray caught behind his glass, tangerines up to his groin, his trunk twisted and inert, and his face turned mechanical: dim leering eyes in a nest of hollows. He was a discard, a spy that Isaac had manufactured, stroked, groomed, and shelved, and then fobbed off on the FBI.

The Chief was remorseful about Murray. But Newgate had hounded the First Dep for one of Isaac's famous spies, and Murray was the spy Isaac could spare. He passed the social clubs of Mulberry Street, their windows shuttered with broad stripes of green paint, with the inevitable "MEMBERS ONLY" scratched into the green.

Isaac entered the Garibaldi club. The members glared at him, but no one threw him out. The Garibaldis endured his policeman's smell, his blunt tie, his calfskin shoes, his orange socks, and the desecration of a pistol in their rooms. Most of them were men over sixty, snug in the thermal underwear exposed at their ankles and their wrists. They were drinking black coffee mixed with anisette, or cappuccinos from the Garibaldi's big machine.

Growls escaped from Isaac's stomach. He was addicted to coffee with steamed milk. He shunned the espresso joints of Bleecker and MacDougal, the Caffè Borgia, where they drowned your coffee in whipped cream, the Verdi, with its bits of chocolate in the foam, and the Reggio, which had a tolerable caffè moka, but little else. Isaac went to Vinnie's luncheonette on Sullivan, where he could enjoy his cappuccinos in a simple glass, or Manganaro's on Ninth Avenue, if he was in the mood to banter with the countermen, who begrudged pulling the handles of their espresso machine.

The aroma of coffee inside the Garibaldi club, thickened by the push of radiators, could drive a cop mad. The Garibaldis had the best cappuccinos in New York. You couldn't attribute this to the wonders of a machine that produced sensational foam and squeezed boiling water through a bed of coffee grounds. It was the devotion of the Garibaldis themselves, who wouldn't consider making cappuccinos for hire.

Amerigo Genussa sat among the Garibaldis in a stunning red shirt that was wide in the sleeves. A man no older than Isaac, with scars around the eyes from fights he'd had in the kitchens of Little Italy, he was concentrating on his game of dominoes.

Isaac resolved not to break the silence at the Garibaldi club. He would outlast dominoes, cappuccino mugs, Amerigo's hatred for him. But the whistling heat off the radiators clung to Isaac, attacking the skin behind his ears. The redness of Amerigo's shirt turned bitter in Isaac's mouth, and he could taste the dry surface of the dominoes. "You want a coffee, Isaac?"

"No."

Amerigo brought two mugs down from the shelves. Slyly, without a crease in his nostrils, Isaac watched the coffee-making. The machine shivered with a sucking noise as Amerigo steamed the milk. He cranked the lever, and coffee poured from two metal fangs.

"It hurts me to have a sullen man in my club. Stay out if you can't smile."

He pushed one of the mugs at Isaac. The Chief stared at the bubbles in the milk. "Bite my fist, landlord, but don't you ever go near my mother again. I'll kill you so slow, your brains will leak into your ear before you have the chance to die."

"Isaac, I fuck you where you breathe. If I wanted your mother, I wouldn't have messed up the job."

The Garibaldis fingered their dominoes while Isaac and

Amerigo grimaced at one another near the cappuccino mugs.

"Tell me you haven't been hiring goons off the street."

"Sure I'm hiring. You think your mother was the only casualty? The little bastards come into my precincts, slap Mrs Pasquino over the head, demolish her bakery, and run home to Jewtown so they can eat their kosher baloney. Isaac, I'll break their feet."

"Amerigo, are you saying it's a gang of rabbinical students? A Jewish karate club? Take a walk for yourself."

"Two of them are Yids, definitely. A boy and a girl. The last one's some kind of nigger. If he's not a spade, then he's a Turk or a Jap. Isaac, it's gotta be."

Isaac dug his jaw into the cappuccino mug. He licked the coffee, his throat purring at the taste of browned milk. "Amerigo, I'll handle these lollipops. Call off your goons."

"Impossible. Isaac, why argue? We're both soldiers. You have your precincts, I have mine. How's your daughter? Did she make a good marriage this time?"

"She's okay," Isaac said, with coffee in his teeth. "She has an architect." Could he tell the landlord that Marilyn was running wild? That she was on the loose with lollipops stalking the streets?

"And your brother Leo, is he out of his troubles yet?"

"Leo's doing fine."

The coffee oozed through Isaac's system, causing the skin on his knees to curl, and whishing into the pockets around his eyes. Isaac would have sold his daughter for a second cappuccino. The Garibaldis had him in their grip.

"Isaac, I hear your boyfriend has his own pillow at Headquarters. Now he doesn't have to snore in the Commissioner's lap."

"Landlord, I can't count all my boyfriends. Identify him for me."

"Newgate."

"Jesus," Isaac said, coming out of his coffee lull. "How can Newgate hurt you? He'd drown in the puddles if the PC didn't hold his hand."

"Isaac, he gives me a bad name. He frightens young Italian mothers with his ugly eyes. The mothers say Newgate's a witch. They could have deformed babies, and I'll get the blame. What's he got against the Italian race? Does he think Sicily was the devil's country? Half my buildings have busted toilets. I'm swimming in shit with my plumber's boots, and that schmuck talks about organized crime?"

"Complain to Cowboy, not me. Cowboy's the one who loves the FBI's." Isaac sucked at the bottom of the mug with the spaces between his teeth. "Amerigo, keep your goons on your side of the Bowery. If I catch them near Essex Street, they won't be in any condition to search for lollipops."

He got up without fantasies of destruction in his head. He wouldn't spit on dominoes, smash the espresso machine, bring the Garibaldis to Headquarters. He had no grudge against Amerigo Genussa. He walked around the tables and landed in the street.

FIVE

Marilyn didn't mourn her penniless state. Shuffling from Bellevue to Coen's to the Crosby Street jail, she narrowed her problems down to the question of logistics: how could she avoid her father on her father's turf? She sat in Bellevue with her Jewish grandmother, surrounded by bottles and tubes that could draw the wastes out of Sophie and drip vital sugars into her body. Sophie's bruises had turned yellowish. The coma she was in wasn't absolute. She would come out of her sleep to frown at the pipes in her nose and signal to Marilyn with her dry tongue. Marilyn couldn't gauge the extent of Sophie's recognition. Was Sophie calling for a nurse or mouthing "Kathleen," the name of Marilyn's mother?

"I'm with you, grandma Sophie. Kathleen's daughter. Your grandchild Marilyn."

She escaped the stare of interns and orderlies on the prowl. Isaac could be behind the door. He had a whole catalogue of spies to trap her with; men in hospital coats, detectives wearing powder and a false moustache, who would point a finger at Isaac's skinny daughter and cluck for the Chief. She saw this type of man scrounging on Crosby Street. She was carrying cookies for uncle Leo that she made with flour from Coen's single pantry shelf. The man had pieces of charcoal around his lips. He tried to mimic the auras of a bum. He blew on his knuckles, tore at the threads of his coat, bit hairs off his wrinkled scarf. Marilyn laughed at the flaws in his disguise. The cop had protected feet: only a police bum would walk around in Florsheim shoes.

A crease near the eyes disturbed Marilyn. "Brian Connell," she said without embarrassment. She knew him from Echo Park, and her junior-high-school days. She'd had several "sweethearts." Brian was one of them.

"Mary?" he said. He couldn't understand how a girlie could pinpoint him under a coat, a hairy scarf, and a blackened face.

"I'm Marilyn. Marilyn Sidel."

The cop blew on his knuckles again. He had gorgeous teeth. Memories of Marilyn ruined his charcoal complexion. His cheeks burned with color as he recollected a bony girl with big tits.

"Marilyn, it's insane I should meet you at the bottom of Manhattan. I'm with the anti-crime boys. I work out of Elizabeth Street. The bosses are sitting on our heads. They'll murder us if we can't produce the mutts that hit your grandmother. That's why I'm in my Bowery clothes."

Marilyn felt silly shaking the paw of an old, old boyfriend, someone who'd licked her flesh eleven years ago. Brian had never been shy with her; now he rocked on his Florsheims, knuckles in his mouth. He's afraid of my father, Marilyn guessed. She showed him the cookies. "I have to deliver them to my uncle. See you around, Brian. Goodbye."

Brian moved his jaw in a cunning way. He wouldn't release Marilyn's hand. He had to bend one knee to hide his erection from her.

"Marilyn, don't be brief. We could divide Marble Hill and the North Bronx between ourselves. We share the same freaky past. Have a beer with me."

Brian contemplated a quick romance. If he could get close to Marilyn, blow on her nipples until she was crazy about him, he would have an opening to Isaac. Brian needed a big Jew. (None of the Irish rabbis at Headquarters had picked him up.) Isaac was the First Deputy's whip and high chief of all the rabbis, white, black, and Puerto Rican. Brian couldn't fail once he had Isaac for a "father-in-law." So he escorted Marilyn to a bar on Spring Street, fondling his visions of a detective's shield.

The barkeep winked at Marilyn and stuck a bottle of gin in Brian's arm. Cradling the bottle, Brian waltzed around the bar stools in his floppy coat. He had to gesture three times with his long neck before Marilyn would follow him into the back room. "I thought we were drinking beer," she said. The door clicked shut behind her.

"Brian, this is a real Bronx reunion. You haven't changed any of your tricks."

"It's damp at the bar. In here we can have some quiet." Brian was in a quandary: should he make her first, or squeeze promises out of her to whisper his name and badge number in Isaac's ear? "Marilyn, tell me about your family."

"What's there to tell? I'm a victim of combat fatigue. I've been through three husbands. Brian, how many wives do you have?"

Mother of Mercy, she's still a fucking tramp, Brian sang to himself. He made no attempt now to hide his erection.

"I'm single, Marilyn, I swear. Which husband did you like best?"

Marilyn had to lie. "I can't remember." She wouldn't tell him about the husband she adored, her first one, Larry, a blond boy with a lisp, whom she brutalized with her affectionate rages and jealousies. Reared by Kathleen, the real estate goddess, and Isaac the Pure, she'd been much too tough for a blond boy. The beautiful Larry ran away. Coen, the blue-eyed orphan, could remind her of him.

Brian sucked on his bottle with an angel's smile. He was thinking of gangbangs in cellars, weightlifting rooms, and the woods of Isham Park, with Marilyn satisfying each and every star of the Inwood Hill Athletic Club, her lean body trembling under the impact of Brian and his friends, who could assuage their dread of purgatory with the knowledge that Marilyn wasn't wholly Irish. The boys interpreted her willingness to undress as a spiteful Jewish streak.

Brian rinsed his tongue in sweet alcohol. His smile turned sullen, giving his teeth a wolfish edge. Marilyn's three husbands enraged him. Whore, bitch, he babbled in his head, she's always going down for bunches of three. He poked a finger into Marilyn's blouse. The finger stood on her collar-bone. Brian didn't know where to explore. His brains were swollen with gin.

Marilyn removed the finger from her chest without cursing Brian. She wasn't mean. She had cookies to deliver. She saw Brian's cheeks explode. The gin was in her face. The blouse came off her shoulders in one hard rip. Brian's knuckles mashed against her cheekbone. She had little mousies under her eye. She wanted to vomit blood. Brian stooped with his thumbs in her hips, and Marilyn's skirt fell under her knees. The cloth around her ankles prevented her from kicking him. She made feeble shoves with her elbows. Brian knocked her to the floor.

He was struggling with Marilyn of Isham Park. He could eclipse husbands, wedding bands, and marriage beds with the mesh pants he took from her and rubbed in his fist. She was Brian's whore child. Isaac didn't exist. The split of her bosoms, the trembling line of her ribs, the rise and fall of her complicated navel, proved to him she was a creature of the cellars, someone with tainted blood and a vague history. He pushed her knees apart and dug with his hand. He tolerated scratching elbows and the mischief of a whore's fingernails. He kept his knuckles in Marilyn's eye. He snapped her head back with a tug of her scalp. He punched her until she grew quiet.

Marilyn tried to think of Larry. But she started to cry. So she thought of Coen. She imagined the shape of his neck, the aroma of talcum powder on Amsterdam Avenue, the feel of Coen's blond knee, and the pressure that knifed down from her bosoms to her shanks eased a bit. Brian figured she had to be crazy when he heard her mumble "Blue Eyes."

His partners caught him reciting Hail Marys behind a pile of beards. They dragged him out of the property closet, glowering at the scratches on his face. These were the anti-crime boys, and they couldn't afford to have their reputation besmirched by a religious freak. The house bulls would laugh at them. Their own sergeant would pass them off as imbeciles. They were sworn to find the lollipop gang, to impress Headquarters with their ability to work undercover and wear a sensational disguise. "Brian, wake up."

He clasped his partners' knees and cried into their trouser cuffs. "Isaac is gonna kill me."

"Brian, what would big Isaac want with you?"

"I fucked his daughter," Brian said.

They smiled and looked at Brian with new respect.

"She's a bimbo who collects wedding rings. I had to beat her up."

His partners were horrified. They shook Brian off their cuffs. Big Isaac could reach into any precinct and squash a cop in bum's clothes. But if Isaac found Brian Connell, he might sink all of them. "Get back into the closet," they said.

Brian crawled on his belly like a snake in a wool stocking. Loose hair from a moustache on the shelf drifted down to him, and Brian had to sneeze. It was nasty in the dark. He promised the Holy Mother two consecutive novenas if She would make Isaac disappear. The closet opened. He could see into his partners' mouths. "It's only Blue Eyes," they said.

They hauled him out again, tickling him under his holster. Brian guffawed. "Isaac's afraid of us. He sends his rat to meet with me. I'll bury Coen. Just watch."

Coen had baffled the anti-crime boys. He came to their precinct
with stubble on his chin. They remembered him in herringbone; Isaac
loved to groom the First Deputy's spies. His squad of manicured
detectives had become a legend in Manhattan stationhouses, where a
cop learned to distrust any sweet-looking boy without a little dirt
under his nails. But Coen was in a lumber jacket and pants that were
as grubby as Brian's. The anti-crime boys hunched near the walls so
that Coen could have a direct path to Brian in their locker room.

"Brian Connell?" he said in his natural voice.

Brian didn't like being greeted by a nasal man. He knew he had
quicker hands than Blue Eyes. He stuck his service revolver in
Coen's jaw. "You think you can shame me in front of my own squad?
Who told you to speak my name? You'd better ask permission, Mr.
Blue Eyes."

Coen didn't blink with a Police Special in his jaw. The gun's
nose was grinding into his back teeth. The boys near the wall
whispered something about coroners and morgues for Coen. Brian
couldn't get Coen to grimace. The corners of his mouth wouldn't
turn. The disintegrating flecks of color in his irises had little to do
with Brian. Coen's eyes whirled independent of the locker room.
Brian put the gun away. He sensed the futility of his bluff. Blue Eyes
was merciless.

Brian sank into the property closet door, his knees dropping out
from under him. He couldn't breathe until he was below the level of
Coen's eyes. Stirring air through his pockets, he considered Isaac's
mysterious ways. The Chief wouldn't enter a locker room. He'd hire
Coen to do his killings. Brian was remorseful now that he bungled his
drinking party with Marilyn. He could have been one of Isaac's
deadly angels.

He was afraid to touch Coen, to embrace a killer's knee. So he
sobbed with his thumbs in his sleeves. "Manfred, never mind what
Isaac says. Me and Marilyn once were going steady. Check it out. I
didn't swipe her off the street . . . Manfred, she knew me from Echo
Park. We had accordion lessons together at the parish . . . some girl.
She was the first Jewish mick I ever saw."

How could Coen pull the ears of a man this close to the ground?
Marilyn had wandered into his apartment an hour ago, naked under
her coat, her cheeks puffed out, and blood in her nose. Coen realized
these markings couldn't be accidental. Her head was mapped too
methodically with swollen ruins. He discovered her skirt, blouse, and
shredded pants among the cookies in her shopping bag. He couldn't

believe this was Isaac's work. If the Chief had been in the mood for corporal punishment, he wouldn't have broken Marilyn's face. He would have gone to Manfred, who was hiding her from him. Coen took advantage of Marilyn's dizziness. He was able to shake Brian Connell's name out of her. He rushed down to Elizabeth Street. Coen didn't have Isaac's agility. He was poor at contriving schemes. He meant to slap Brian, and then what? Should he undress Brian in the stationhouse, have him crawl without his clothes?

Brian's sobs made Coen miserable. The cop's ears were wet. Coen distrusted the anti-crime boys. They were meddlers who liked to play detective in the street. He lost his desire to steal Brian's pants.

"Listen to me, you glom. Wherever Marilyn goes, you walk the opposite way. If you're ever in her neighborhood, you'll wish Manhattan didn't exist."

Brian's partners remained near the walls with their guts sucked in. They didn't have the clout of a blue-eyed detective. They were only glorified patrolmen, cops out of uniform, so they couldn't pounce on Coen. Isaac would have flopped the entire squad, fed them to niggers and man-eating sharks in the Bronx.

From Elizabeth Street Coen went on a tour of youth centers in the lower East Side. He was scouting for ferocious teenagers, boys and girls who might be lollipops. His third stop was a Jewish center at Rivington and Suffolk. He noticed a remarkable absence of skullcaps and religious memorabilia. Where were the Jews of Suffolk Street.

The center proliferated with Chinese boys, Latinos, blacks, and surly whites from Seward Park. Its oblong game room looked as if it had to confront a nightly whirlwind. The walls were plundered dry, the woodwork having disappeared, and holes existing where ornaments and basketball fixtures should have been.

There was a series of huge, snaking genitals on the front wall, signed by "Esther Rose." The artist had been meticulous about pubic hair, stippling it in with eye shadow and different shades of lipstick. "Esther Rose" seemed to have a slanted mind; her clitorises were much taller than her cocks. Coen enjoyed the lipstick art. "Esther Rose" had put little eyeballs and chicletlike teeth around the swads of pubic hair.

Slogans were scrawled in shocking pink under "Esther Rose's" genitals.

"RUPERT SAYS WE'LL ALL DISAPPEAR IF ARABS AND

JEWS DON'T KISS"

"THE GROSS NATIONAL PRODUCT IS THE INVENTION OF BANKERS WITH A LOW SEMEN COUNT"

"RUPERT SAYS GEORGE WASHINGTON WILL BE FORGOTTEN LONG BEFORE WILLIE MAYS"

"SACHS AND GIMBEL'S ARE THE WHORES OF NEW YORK, RUPERT SAYS"

Coen couldn't devote himself to Rupert's sayings. He had to mingle with the center's population, cast about for suspicious objects and faces, fish for a gang of womanbeaters.

Boys in jerseys and brimless hats milled from corner to corner, avoiding Coen and his lumber jacket. Their vocabulary baffled him until he realized that "red mountain," "torro," and "colony" were the names of cheap wines.

The baby winos began to sneer at Coen. They collected around a ping-pong table that consisted of a crooked green net and a series of hills. The local champion, a loud, argumentative boy with wiry hair, challenged the winos to a game if they could come up with fifty cents. The winos were too poor. So the champion enticed Coen with his eyebrows and a suck of his lips. "Hey bro', got some pocket money?" Coen agreed to play.

The winos hooted at him. They smelled another victim of the hilly ping-pong table. Coen acknowledged their noises with a grin. They were reasonable hoodlums. He was hoping to flush them out, find the lollipops through them. The champion had a sponge bat with fresh sheets of rubber glued on. He gave Coen a sandpaper bat worn down to the wood. Coen didn't worry. Ping-pong was his game. He'd perfected his strokes at an uptown club after his wife divorced him.

The champion had an illegal serve. He wouldn't throw up the ball. He held it in his fingers, and slapped at it while turning his wrist. The ball sped across the table with an evil spin. The champion had memorized the peculiar surfaces of this table; he knew every hill, every dull spot, every dip in the net. But Coen wasn't a country player. He minimized the boy's advantages by blocking the ball with his shallow bat. He added a delicate push, and the ball went back over the net with the same exact spin. The champion stared at the ball. No one had ever made him hit his own spins. He grew

demoralized after three short volleys with Coen. He began eating the
rubber off his bat.

The winos refused to cheer. They rolled their eyes with a
menace Coen couldn't ignore. He'd never seen fourteen-year-olds
with such dispassionate faces: they had the glint of hard, old men.
They marched around Coen, berating him in a babble of Spanish and
English.

"Who is this *borinqueña*?"

"*Yo no sé,* man, but I think he came down to fuck with us. Bring
Stanley."

"Stanley'll picadillo him for hustling fifty cents."

Stanley was a Chinese boy with spectacular biceps. He arrived
in a Bruce Lee sweatshirt with ripped-off sleeves. Coen wouldn't pay
court to the boy's muscular twitch. Biceps couldn't frighten him.
Stanley had a beautiful face. That's what disturbed Coen. Muscles
seemed incongruous with soft eyes. The winos' monkeyish glint and
bitter cheeks were missing from the boy.

He had a perfectly tolerant voice. "Mister, what do you want
from us?"

"A little news," Coen said.

The baby winos squeezed their eyebrows together. They were
appraising Coen. A shrimp like him couldn't take them by surprise.
They had a gift for smelling cops. Cops don't play ping-pong, they
decided among themselves.

"Hey sister, you from the Board of Ed? You know what we do
to truant officers? We suck their noses and tickle them to death."

"You gotta be wrong, bro'. . . this *muchacha* is a Treasury man.
He saw you licking on a bottle, and he's trying to collect his whiskey
tax."

"You full of shit. I say he's an uptown fairy. He's here to
redecorate."

Coen unbuttoned his lumber jacket. He was going to scratch
himself. But the spring in his holster had loosened during the
pingpong game, and his gun fell out. The winos fluttered near the
gun. "*Mira, mira,* look what uncle brought. Spread out, man." Coen
was chagrined; he hadn't intended to menace the winos with a gun.
They ran from him. The Chinese boy was the only one who stayed.

"I'll ask him about the lollipop gang," Coen mouthed to himself
trusting Stanley's intelligence. The center cleared out, leaving Coen
an uncomplicated view of rotting walls and broken electrical wire.
Stanley wouldn't move. Coen was about to mention the lollipops

when he felt two enormous claws climb on his chest and throw him over the ping-pong table. He could have sworn Stanley's ankles never left the ground. The boy had kicked air without going into a crouch or tightening his beautiful face, and he crashed into Coen's lungs with his feet. Coen was on the floor with a pain scooping under his heart that rattled his throat and brought his guts into his mouth. He figured he would have to die. But his lungs were blowing in and out. Blood rushed into his head. Coen stood up. He was thinking lollipops again.

SIX

The owners of the Ludlow Street restaurant were angry at Ida Stutz. They could no longer work her twelve hours a day. Ida had grown sullen. She was insisting on her rights to a genuine lunch break. The Chief hadn't knocked on the restaurant's cloudy window since he returned to America, and Ida meant to find him.

She was worried about Isaac. He'd become a skinny inspector if she couldn't fill him with mushrooms and barley soup. It wasn't in her nature to be stingy with men. Isaac needed her flesh to rid himself of anxieties and the strain of being a father, husband, son, and brainy cop. Ida simplified his life. She knew he had a missing daughter, a shrill wife, and a mother in the hospital, poor Sophie, who took Arabs into her bed. Ida was on her way to Rivington Street, and Isaac's rooms. She would freshen the earth in his flower pots, scrub the inside of his refrigerator, wait for him by the fire escape.

The streets had a pernicious look to Ida. The remains of boxes from the pickle factories flew across the gutters, bumping like fingers and limbs off a doll's body. The February wind could eat into the wood, slice through the corners of the low, gutted buildings make the old Jewish beggar on Broome Street sink his head into the middle of his overcoat, blow under the deepest layer of Ida's skirts, and pinch the seams of her powerful bloomers. Ida was praying for snow. The dark *snegu* of her Russian grandmother (the snow that fell near Delancey Street was more blue than white) could cake all the gutters with rich ice, hide the debris, force the pickle factories to conduct their business away from the sidewalks.

Ida didn't bemoan the past. It was no matter to her that the Essex Street market sold wigs instead of farmer cheese, The Cubans had come to Essex Street along with an influx of Israeli grocers. Ida

welcomed them. She battled with the Israelis over her heathen
principles, her distrust of promised lands and Jews with tanks, but she
battled out of love. And the Cubans adored Ida's blintzes, although
they couldn't pronounce the word.

Hands, rude hands, without mittens or gloves, snatched at her
near Isaac's building, pulling her into a hallway. She was surrounded
by a confusion of masks. She shivered at the hot, breathing eyes on
top of her. Ida recognized the lollipop gang. This was the threesome
that had visited her in the restaurant, stealing blintzes, fondling her
breasts, and had gone around the corner to break Sophie's head. Ida
could smell a girl's hair under one of the masks. Growls came out of
the girl. The other two were quieter.

"Isaac's pussy," the girl said, holding Ida by the jaw. The two
boys had to restrain her. "She's harmless," the shorter boy said.
"Take a look."

The girl couldn't be placated so easily. "She goes down for him.
It must rub off. A homely bitch is what I say." And the girl got up on
her toes to grab hunks of Ida's hair. "Tell sweet Isaac regards from
Esther Rose."

"Shut up," the shorter boy said.

The taller boy slouched against a row of bruised mailboxes, his
body turning away from all the banter. As Ida pushed at the fingers
tearing into her scalp, she felt the boy's restless moves. He was
retreating from his friends. The shorter boy, wedged close to Ida and
Esther Rose, brought Ida out of Esther's reach. "Get smart," he said.
"That man's too piggy for you. He has shit in his ears. He made his
name sucking off New York. Now the city's taking revenge."

"Let's fuck her," Esther rasped. "Let's fuck her under her fat
clothes . . . it'll be like throwing harpoons in a whale. I'll bet she's
filled with mush."

She whacked at Ida with the blade of her hand. The taller boy
stumbled along the wall, catching metal pieces off the mailboxes with
a shoulder. Esther nudged the other boy. "Are you with me, Rupe?"

He blunted Esther's chops with an elbow. "We're going . . .
come on."

They pushed Ida deeper into the hall, packing her into the space
behind a door, and ran, their masks struggling towards the street in a
steady wave. Ida didn't whimper. It wasn't strictly fear that kept her
behind the door. She couldn't figure out the three masks. What did
they want with Isaac and her? She wished she could drown herself in
the smoky air of the restaurant. Ida loved to breathe salmon and

baked cottage cheese. She wallowed in her shoes, trying to hurl the wind out of her ankles. It was freezing in the hall.

Isaac was scratching his brain for logical enemies. He'd come to Bummy's chop house on East Broadway to interview Milton Gulavitch, a dispossessed murderer and thief with blood clots in both legs and a grudge against Isaac. Twenty years ago Gulavitch had been the "controller" of Brownsville and East New York. No dry cleaner in that long, muggy corridor between Brooklyn and Queens could survive without a license from Milton, who remained powerful in middle age because he had a legitimate means of protecting his empire: two of his brothers were homicide detectives in lower Manhattan. These younger Gulavitches, Myron and Jay, had their own slender business behind Little Italy; they fleeced Puerto Rican, Chinese, and Jewish grocers, and bloodied noses for the landlords and bondsmen of Baxter Street. Issac, the boy detective, stumbled upon Myron and Jay, and helped send them into retirement and disgrace. Milton grieved for his brothers. He swore to take out Isaac's eyes; blind detectives couldn't squirrel into other men's affairs. He crossed the Williamsburg Bridge and waited for Isaac in Mendel's of Clinton Street, a bar inhabited by Jewish cops and hoods.

Isaac couldn't permit Gulavitch to scare him out of Mendel's bar. He was chubbier then, a boy with skin hanging off his fists. He arrived in a tweed suit, aware of the strength in Milton's thumbs, that ability to pluck eyeballs. Isaac put his blackjack and gun on Mendel's counter. He didn't want customers to think he was here on official business. Gulavitch laughed. He had nothing but thumbs in his pockets. With a deceptive, languid motion, he came off one hip to grab Isaac around the head. Isaac burrowed his eyes into the "controller's" chest, so Gulavitch had nowhere to dig. He hadn't anticipated such tactics from a boy; he left his face exposed. Isaac reached with a chubby hand. Knuckling hard, he split Gulavitch's eyebone. Gulavitch clutched his face. The customers around him opened their mouths in wonder and disgust. Gulavitch became Gula One Eye. He drifted out of circulation, his empire passing into other hands, and reappeared as Bummy Gilman's dishwasher and sweep after a lapse of fifteen years.

Isaac had contempt for Bummy, who fawned over Barney Rosenblatt and Jewish precinct captains, but he didn't come to wreck Bummy's place. "Where's Gula?" he said.

Bummy was nervous with Isaac in his bar. He couldn't get

around the Chief, bribe him with lamb chops and pornographic shows. "Don't touch him, Isaac. He's senile."

"Good. But maybe he has a few grandchildren who run errands for him. I have to know."

"Isaac, he can't remember his name. If you blow on him, he'll fall down."

"Don't worry. I'll catch him before he falls."

Isaac went into Bummy's kitchen. It stank of animal fat and old men's sour pants. Milton Gulavitch was screwing warts out of a potato with his thumb. He held Isaac's attention with the furrows in a thumbnail. "Gula?"

Isaac wasn't paranoid about the old man. Gulavitch often stood outside Headquarters to curse Isaac and cry for his brothers. Lately he'd been threatening to reassemble his empire and smack it over Isaac's head. Barney Rosenblatt offered to drag Gulavitch away. Isaac wouldn't allow it.

"Gula, listen. Do you have nephews and a niece in Brooklyn? Did you encourage them to hate me?"

Gulavitch looked up from the potato. "Die, Isaac. That's what you can do for me."

He wasn't wearing his patch, and Isaac had to stare into a blue socket, his own grizzly work. Spittle began to flow under Gulavitch's tongue. "Isaac, your prick will drop off one day, and then you'll be at my mercy."

Isaac closed the interview. He ignored Bummy's frowns at the bar and walked to Crosby Street. Dissatisfied, without a solution behind his big ears, he was going to see his brother. He could have gotten Leo past any guard or deputy warden, but Leo wouldn't budge. Isaac didn't have to growl Leo's name. The guards brought him into the reception room, shuddering under the eyes of the Chief. Leo was an embarrassment to them; each day he wore a prison shirt, the guards had to scrape their noses on Isaac's shit list. They were very jittery men.

"Leo, are they treating you with respect?" Isaac muttered, while the guards fled the room;

This scattering of the guards made Leo glum. He didn't want to be alone with his brother. "Isaac, you shouldn't have done that. They're good to me."

"Schmuck, they'd slap your brains if you weren't my brother. So how good can they be?"

"I don't care. It's a fact of nature. I'm invulnerable because of you." Leo shivered like a scarecrow in his loose shirt; he wasn't even safe inside a goddamned jail. Isaac could reach into every hole. Manhattan was his honey jar.

"Leo, I saw our dad. He's alive . . . doing portraits. He asked about you."

A sound broke out of Leo that was almost a snarl. "I have no dad."

Isaac was amazed by Leo's churning jaw. "I say he's alive . . . Joel, Joel. I met him twice."

Leo clutched the little pocket on Isaac's vest. "There are no fucking Joels. Isaac, I'm warning you. Don't get me mad."

The pocket ripped. Isaac left his brother's fingers inside the torn seams. The violence to Isaac's pocket seemed to quiet Leo. He took his fingers away so he could cry into his knuckles. "Sophie's in the hospital on account of him. She'd be a saner person if that miserable furrier hadn't disappeared. You think she would have fallen in love with a junk shop? Isaac, you had your handgrips and your chess diagrams and your great chums, Philip and Mordecai. You didn't need a thing. What about me? Brother, I was slow. I couldn't hold a line of pawns, or make improvements in the Sicilian Defense. A father might have helped."

Isaac grew restless under his brother's scrutiny; he hadn't come to argue over the existence of Joel. And why should he have to be ashamed of ancient skills? Isaac lost his prowess in chess twenty-five years ago. He turned policeman in the reception room, beginning to probe his baby brother.

"Where's Marilyn? I know all about her moves. She visits you here. She jumps in and out of mama's hospital room. Leo, tell me who's putting her up? She's too particular to hide in a garbage can. Somebody's been keeping her day and night."

"I can't say."

"Can't, Leo? I don't like that word. Are you shielding her from me? Remember where your privileges come from. I'm not blind. The jailors let you sneak uptown to Bellevue. Call it kindness, Leo, but I'm the one who put the idea into their heads. Not for your sake. It's for mama. You're her special boy. I didn't want her to wake up in a stinking hospital without you around. Now tell me who the bastard is, the fuck who's got my girl? Name him for me."

"Isaac, go to hell."

Isaac could have throttled Leo without wrinkling his career. With the First Dep behind him, the Chief had the right to bluster with

impunity. Leo's devotion to Marilyn gnawed at him. The Chief was a
little jealous. Forty years I fight his battles, Isaac said to himself, and
he picks Marilyn over me. Isaac's love for his brother was mingled
with a kind of criminality; fondness could turn to bile in a matter of
seconds. The Sidels were a bitter crew.

"Leo, you're taking advantage of me. There are tiny pricks and
cunts out there who are looking to murder us. They got to Sophie. It
won't happen again. But don't expect me to pamper you. I want your
ass out of this jail. I'll stroke the Commissioner of Corrections if I
have to. I'll fix it with your wife. Mama shouldn't have to be in a
room with strangers. You stay with her until I find those freaks. Leo,
I give you three days. Then I'm going to tear the jail apart."

Isaac moved across the room with hops of his broad neck. The
guards peeked in. They sidled up to Leo, surrounding him with
sheepish looks. "Pinochle. Leo? We have four hands today. We're
ready to lose."

Leo still had the shivers, but he wouldn't disappoint the guards.
"Gentlemen, I'll deal first." The guards searched for folding chairs.
Leo tucked in the corners of the deck. He was hoping pinochle would
save these men. Melding flushes and marriages might ease down
their terror of the Chief.

The guards shivered as fast as Leo. They fumbled with the deck,
throwing cards away. They couldn't auction off their marriages, or
bid for trumps. Isaac had murdered their afternoon.

SEVEN

The FBI man wouldn't leave Isaac alone. He had his own pillow at
Headquarters, and he carried it in and out of Isaac's office. Newgate
adored the Chief. Jumping from Bethesda, Maryland, into a universe
of Jews, Irishmen, and black detectives, he wanted Isaac to
understand that he wasn't an ordinary Episcopalian. He claimed to be
part Cherokee. Isaac's men sniggered at this bit of exoticism; the
threat of Indian blood couldn't bring Newgate closer to them. He was
made of straw, a Maryland idiot who stole words out of Isaac's
mouth. He couldn't impress them with his talk of "burying" Amerigo
Genussa and "sinking" Mulberry Street. Italians might be out of
fashion in a year, and the FBI would be climbing trees for black
militants and Puerto Rican nationalists.

Newgate squirmed on his pillow after a white nigger arrived in

Isaac's office, a white nigger in a blue suede suit. He had never come across such a weird creature in his life with the FBI. It was Wadsworth, the albino from Forty-second Street, hiding his face from the sun in Isaac's windows. Only Isaac could comprehend Wadsworth's sacrifice: the albino wouldn't have exposed himself to the ruinous effects of daylight unless he had something important to deliver.

Barney Rosenblatt interrupted him. The Chief of Detectives blundered into Isaac's rooms, his suspenders forking with irritation. He wouldn't address a nigger bundled in blue suede. So he pretended Wadsworth was invisible, and he carped at Isaac. "Are you crazy? You bring a clown to Headquarters? Couldn't you negotiate with him someplace else? You'll give the PC a shit fit. Gloms like that leave an odor. Isaac, he'll scare the pants off my men."

"Eat it, Cowboy," Wadsworth said, picking dust off his sleeve.

Barney lunged at Wadsworth without taking his eyes away from Isaac.

"Out," Isaac said. "This man's registered to me. You do him any harm, and I'll collar you so fast your tongue will fall off."

Barney glowered behind his suspenders, at Wadsworth, Isaac, and Newgate. "Isaac, take the cotton out of your ears. This is Barney Rosenblatt, remember? I'm not Manfred Coen. You won't have a piece of wood left in your office, Isaac, if you come down on me."

"Pistols, Barney, is that what you want? Come, we'll have a shoot-out in the hall."

"Isaac, don't be wise." And he trudged out, the pearl handle of his Colt wobbling like a nasty stick in his pocket. Wadsworth didn't smirk; he had no interest in Barney Rosenblatt. He could piss on the walls at Headquarters, dangle his prick in front of any commissioner. Wadsworth was immune from arrest. If the burglary squad caught him napping on a fire escape, or prowling in a shoe store after midnight, they had to let him go. He belonged to Isaac and the First Dep. Wadsworth had once been a practicing arsonist. Now he was semi-retired. Not even the First Dep could rescue him if a baby died in one of his fires. So he abandoned his career as a "torch" under instructions from Isaac. He burned only vacant buildings and parking lots. "I'm sorry to cause you trouble," he said, having to nod at Isaac around Newgate's head.

"You're no trouble to me, Wads. Would you like a cherry coke?"

"Isaac, we don't have time for beverages. I think I found a

lollipop for you."

"Where?" Isaac said, the hump in his neck refusing to rise with Newgate around.

"At a hospital in Corona."

Isaac rubbed his nose. "Corona? Why Corona?"

"Isaac, who knows? My uncle Quentin works in the emergency room. A kid crawls in with broken arms and legs. But there aint a scratch on the rest of his body. My uncle's not a dope. That's the mark of the landlord, Amerigo Genussa."

"What kind of kid? White or black?" Isaac said, trying to throw off the FBI man.

"Isaac, you can see for yourself."

Isaac rounded up his chauffeur Brodsky, Pimloe, his deputy whip, and his angel, Manfred Coen. Newgate began to whine. "Take me, Isaac. I'll drop a portable lab right into the kid's bed. You can tape him, fingerprint him, test his urine and his blood."

Isaac couldn't deny Newgate without creating a stink: the FBI man might blab to Barney Rosenblatt. "Come," Isaac said, "but leave your lab at home." The FBI's could pull fingerprints and semen stains out of the ground with their magic laboratories. But it was never the print you needed, and the semen usually came from cats and dogs.

Brodsky telephoned for the First Dep's sedan. He marched with Isaac, Pimloe, Newgate, and Coen to the ramp in back of Headquarters. They crossed the Manhattan Bridge, Newgate marveling at the enormity of Brooklyn, which, he believed, could swallow the whole of Maryland. Brodsky was happiest with Isaac in the car. Coen annoyed him. The chauffeur despised pretty boys. Coen was the one Isaac lent to the Bureau of Special Services when an ambassador's wife grew restless in New York. Women stuck to Blue Eyes. He was the Department's prime stud. Isaac could populate the city with white niggers, Puerto Rican stoolies, and beautiful wooden-headed boys.

A dumb Maryland Cherokee like Newgate could only come alive by touching Isaac's sleeve. Isaac taught him how to sniff. He would plant evidence in your shoe, blackmail your sister, force Coen to romance your mother or your wife, until you could do nothing but cry out your guilt. This was Isaac the Pure, who didn't waste his scruples on a thief.

They arrived at St. Bartholomew's, a dinky hospital off Corona Avenue. The hospital couldn't accommodate big police cars. Brodsky found a parking spot across the street. Wadsworth had no badge to show the hospital clerks, so he walked behind Isaac, with long, pinched lines developing in the suede. The five of them burrowed into the main ward, past nurses, orderlies, and patients in rumpled gowns. Isaac was looking for a boy in traction, with his arms and legs in the air. The search became futile. They caught an old man pissing behind a screen. The man threw a pill bottle at Isaac; it struck Newgate over the eye. Isaac closed the screen.

Wadsworth led him to a boy with plaster mittens on his hands and feet; none of the mittens extended beyond the ankle or wrist. The boy was Chinese.

Coen didn't have to stare too hard; it was the boy who jumped on his chest at the Jewish youth center. He couldn't decide what to tell Isaac. The Chief didn't need prods from Coen. He examined the identification card attached to the bed: Stanley Chin didn't have an address; his age was listed as sixteen and a half. The evenness of the mittens disturbed Isaac. He couldn't be sure this was Amerigo's work. The landlord's hired goons wouldn't have restricted themselves to cracking fingers and toes. They didn't have that much finesse. The boy should have been bent at the elbows, or suffered a broken knee.

Isaac came up to the bed. His voice wasn't harsh. "Stanley Chin, do you know me?"

The boy said nothing; he watched Coen and the albino in blue.

The Chief brushed against the bed's high, criblike gate. "I'm Isaac Sidel."

The boy pushed air through his nose and wiggled his teeth against his bottom lip. Did I collar the boy's father. Isaac wondered, did I bite his family in some horrible way? He couldn't remember capturing any Chinamen in the last five or ten years.

"Why's Amerigo Genussa after you?" Newgate screamed at the boy. Isaac told him to get back. He promised to kick Newgate past the Rockaways if he interfered again.

"Stanley, tell me where your school is? Brooklyn? Queens? The Bronx?"

Wadsworth whispered to Isaac. "The kid goes to Seward Park. My uncle Quentin got that much out of him." Then he moved behind Coen. Wadsworth was getting jumpy in the hospital. A white glare came off the walls. He couldn't function without the buzzing of a movie screen. He was addicted to technicolor and dust on his face. He'd have to beg Isaac to ship him home pretty soon.

Isaac sensed the slithering motion under the suede. But he

couldn't free Wadsworth until he pressed the Chinese boy.

"Stanley, did you know I went to Seward Park? I graduated in 1946. No lie. I spoke at the school a few months ago. Do you remember that?"

The boy wouldn't respond to Isaac; he rubbed the mittens on his feet while scrutinizing Wadsworth's pink eyes and colorless hair. The albino had bewitched him. Brodsky nudged Isaac on the wrist. "Chief, you'll never make this kid trading school stories. Ask me to step on his fingers, or let Manfred kiss him in the mouth."

Isaac didn't have the chance to scold Brodsky. The head nurse, an enormous black woman with a pound of starch in her midriff and her sleeves, descended upon all five of them. "What the hell do you mean busting in here without my permission?"

Brodsky answered her. "Lady, this is Chief Sidel of the First Deputy's office. He goes where he wants."

"Not in this hospital, fat man." She turned on Wadsworth. "Who the hell are you?"

The starch bristled in Wadsworth's eye, confounding him. He squeezed between Brodsky and the FBI Man. Newgate fished for some identification. "Madam, I'm with the FBI."

"Jesus God," she said. "How did you lunatics get inside the door?"

Newgate's Cherokee blood bleached his nose red. "Nurse, you can check me out. I'm Amos Newgate of the Manhattan bureau."

"Sure," the woman said. "And I'm Mother Goose." She hovered over Newgate, her midriff buckling against her breast pocket. "That boy's hurt. He don't need crap from you."

Isaac would have liked to borrow this nurse; she might hold Barney Rosenblatt away from his door. Pimloe was strangely quiet. The deputy whip usually fronted for Isaac, shagging different pests off Isaac's back. Pimloe had to be in love, so Isaac mollified the nurse. "Mrs. Garden," he said, reading the name tag on her starched chest. "You're right to worry about Stanley Chin. He's your patient, and we're intruders in your ward. But we believe he's been beating up old women and destroying grocery stores. I'm leaving two of my officers here. They won't touch Stanley, I promise."

He herded Wadsworth, Newgate, and the First Deputy men out of the ward. He stationed Brodsky in the hall. "Whoever visits the kid gets a tap from you. I don't care if it's an army of midgets. Find out who they are."

"Isaac, should I stay with him?" Coen said, his cheeks

slackening with drowsy lines.

"No, I want Pimloe . . . Herbert, find the resident on this floor. Tell him to keep his bitches out of our hair."

Newgate elected to remain at the hospital. Pimloe seemed morose. "Isaac, who's gonna drive you out of Brooklyn? Wadsworth can't take the wheel."

"Coen will drive."

Brodsky's lips sank with contempt. "Chief, he doesn't know north from south. He'll lead you into the ocean. You'll drown with Coen."

"Wadsworth will save me," Isaac said, anxious to disappear from the hospital. The Chief had an errand to do. He sat with Wadsworth and Coen on the First Dep's wide front seat. Coen was hunched against the upholstery. Wadsworth kept his hands under his thighs until he had a crisp view of Manhattan. Brooklyn was a meager island in Wadsworth's head. It didn't have the proportions of a solid world. In Brooklyn the ground could sink.

Coen dropped Issac at the Essex Street houses. Wadsworth tried to jump out of the car. Isaac was reluctant to grab some suede. He blocked Wadsworth with a knee. "You'll offend my man if you don't sit."

Wadsworth seemed afraid to sit alone with Blue Eyes. Deep colors made him crazy. The albino convinced himself that a blue-eyed Jew could only be a witch.

Isaac was in the mood for old boyfriends. Stanley Chin had thrown him back to Seward Park. The Chief scrambled for Mordecai and Philip, recollecting conversations on the roofs, fistfights over Trotsky and Stalin, chess tournaments that ruined Mordecai's appetite and made Isaac cockeyed for a week, as Philip dazzled them first with a strange opening and clubbed them over the head with his bishops and his rooks. Isaac had been fond of Mordecai, nothing more. Philip was his rival. He couldn't touch Philip in chess, or harm his defense of Trotsky's beautiful face. Isaac had always been a creaking Stalinist.

It was aggravation over Philip that caused him to abandon chess. Isaac studied the masters, absorbed the fierce play of his three gods, Morphy, Steinitz, and Alekhine, but Philip overshot all of Isaac's theories with his rough knowledge of the board; Philip moved with a crazy, internal music that contradicted Isaac's chess books. And Isaac fell to brooding. His three gods had befouled themselves. Morphy, an

American boy, once the shrewdest player in the world, drifted into voyeurism during the last years of his life; he would peep out of a closet dressed in women's clothes. Steinitz, a Jewish midget from Prague, a man with spindly knees who revolutionized chess by discovering the patterns of opening play, died unloved in a beggar's grave on Ward's Island. Alekhine, the Russian genius, fled his country to play master chess throughout Europe and South America in a state of constant drunkenness, pissing on the trousers of an opponent, retching over chess clocks, and becoming the champion and sainted fool of Nazi Germany.

Philip himself went "blind" at twenty-four, lost his feel of the pieces, neglected to safeguard his king, grew restless at the board, and dropped out of tournaments. Philip became a businessman, selling lightbulbs and toilet articles to East Side stores, a husband, a father, and a recluse. His family life wasn't so different from Isaac's; both of them had stray children. Philip's boy was a stubborn genius of fifteen who could clobber his father at chess since the age of nine. Isaac decided to chat with Philip and interview the boy; he was hungry for news of Seward Park. Maybe the boy could enlighten him about Stanley's gang, and Isaac could also cry to Philip about his missing daughter, Marilyn the Wild.

One of the housing cops recognized Isaac in front of Philip's building. The cop was slightly lame, and the pieces of his uniform didn't seem to fit his body. "Chief Isaac," he shouted, "if you're shopping around for the lollipop freaks, try a new project. I control this house. Those bandits wouldn't mess with me."

"It's a social call," Isaac muttered. "I'm visiting Philip Weil."

He rode up to Philip's door. The buzzer wouldn't work, and he had to keep knocking until his fist went dead. "Philip, it's me . . . Isaac." The door opened for him. He couldn't get in without hunching himself around Philip's back. "Mordecai says you've been asking for me . . . Philip, what's the matter?"

Isaac could pull Mordecai by the nose, pluck Mordecai's daughter out of a pimp's garbage can, but he couldn't get near Philip. Philip didn't have stubble on his cheek, or the symptoms of a decayed chess master. He wore an impeccable shirt with buttons made of elephant bone and a collar strengthened with metal clips. Isaac couldn't begrudge the crease in Philip's trousers, or the neat fall of his cuffs. Philip was a stay-at-home who dressed to kill.

He'd kept his boyishness. He hadn't succumbed to Mordecai's slow fattening, or Isaac's accumulation of hard flesh. His persistent

love of Trotsky and his old mania for chess must have protected him
from the most common ravages. Philip lived in a closed box.

He made coffee for Isaac and himself that nearly burned Isaac's
tongue. Isaac couldn't believe a man would drink such bitter stuff. He
dreamed of cappuccinos at the Garibaldi social club. "What's your
problem, Philip? I should have come before . . . three little bastards
hurt my mother, and they've been on my mind."

Philip had a disturbance in his collar, a slight, nagging twitch
that may have spread from a bone behind his ears. "We got lucky,"
Isaac said, his eyes on the turbulent collar. "I think we caught one of
them. A Chinese boy. Philip, imagine this. He goes to Seward Park."

"I know. It's Stanley Chin."

Philip held the collar down with his thumb. Isaac was looking
mean. "Who told you that? Philip, did you fly in from Corona this
morning? Are you a patron of St. Bartholomew's? Have you been
blowing through the wards?"

"No. Rupert's with the gang. He's their leader."

A shudder ripped from Isaac's jaw, putting dark creases in his
neck. Philip's boy was a lollipop. Isaac grabbed for the buttons on
Philip's shirt. "You fucking shit, is that why you've been sending
kites to me from Mordecai?" The buttons sprang from Philip, and
Isaac squeezed elephant bone in his fist. "Philip, if my mother dies,
I'll give you a permanent earache. Crippling isn't good enough.
They'll bury you with pawns in your eyes. You'll have all the time in
the world for chess."

Philip didn't shiver with Isaac breathing over him. "Isaac, I
couldn't tell you direct. . . . I was paralyzed. I hoped you'd come to
me. I thought it was a local craziness, something he'd get over quick.
Raiding stores in the neighborhood. For what purpose? When I heard
what he did to your mother, I saw it was too late. Isaac, nobody
escapes you for very long. I've been waiting for you to kill me,
Isaac."

Isaac threw the buttons on the floor.

"What the fuck are you talking about? Philip, I'm not going to
be your avenging angel. You'll suffer on your own. Give me facts. I
don't want your lousy opinions. Why does Rupert hate me?"

"Isaac, I've never said a bad word about you to him."

"Maybe that's the problem. Philip, who's the cunt? The girl who
runs with Stanley and Rupert."

"That's Esther Rose."

"Where does she live?"

"Isaac, she lives in the streets. Esther doesn't have a home. She used to belong to the Jewish Defense League. They kicked her out, I'm pretty sure. She was too crazy for them."

"A JDL girl? Rupert must keep a photograph of the little cunt. Where's his room?"

Philip took him into a room cluttered with pamphlets, cigar boxes, chess boards with broken spines, ping-pong bats with scars in their rubber flesh, posters advertising nudist colonies, back-gammon, and guerrilla warfare, all sitting on a mound of books that hid Rupert's dresser, Rupert's closet, Rupert's lamp, and Rupert's bed. Isaac searched through the mess, up to his knees in books. He juggled a ping-pong bat, muttering hard. "Rupert ought to play with my man Coen. Coen's a whizz. Coen could seduce a polar bear with his strokes." He found a stash of photographs in one of the cigar boxes. "Is that her?" he said, pointing to a girl with frizzy hair, full bosoms, and big brown eyes.

"Yes, that's Esther."

Isaac stuffed the photograph into his pocket. Then he stole Rupert's junior-high-school graduation picture (the genius was frowning under a mortarboard hat) from a hook on the wall. The glass in the frame began to splinter as Isaac extracted the photograph.

"Where's Rupert now?"

"Isaac, he hasn't been home in a couple of weeks. He's with Esther, that much I know."

"Philip, if you catch him, don't let him out of your sight. He's offended the biggest social club on Mulberry Street with his tactics. The Garibaldis are eager to break his shins. Philip, bring him to me."

"They won't hurt him at the stationhouse, will they, Isaac? . . . he's a baby, fifteen."

"Philip, I'd push him out a window, that boy wonder of yours, but I need him to sing. None of my men will lay a hand on him."

Isaac called St. Bartholomew's from a phone booth in the street. "Inspector Pimloe," he growled to the hospital receptionist. "Gimme Inspector Pimloe." The receptionist growled back. There weren't any Pimloes registered at the hospital. "Lady, don't cause trouble. He should be roaming in the halls. Page him for me . . . tell him Isaac says he better get his ass on the wire."

Isaac heard a sigh, and the clunking of shoes. Brodsky took the call. "Boss, it's me."

"Brodsky, jump on somebody else's wire. I asked for Pimloe, not you."

"Pimloe disappeared. Maybe he's cooping in the basement. Who knows? . . . boss, we're up shit's creek."

"Why?" Isaac said, glaring with his teeth. "Has Stanley Chin bought wings for himself? Did he tie up that nigger nurse with his bandages and flap right out of the ward?"

"Isaac, Cowboy's here."

Isaac hissed into the phone. "You dummy, how did he find you?"

"Isaac, he took me by surprise. His leather boys climbed all over me. He brought an army to the hospital. Shotguns and everything. Newgate must have snitched. Go trust the FBI!"

"Forget about Newgate. Pimloe's the man."

"Isaac, are you crazy? Pimloe works for you."

"But he's also taking care of himself. He thinks Barney Rosenblatt's armpit is the hottest place in New York City. Brodsky, use your head. It's Pimloe. It couldn't have been anybody else. Now what's Cowboy up to?"

"He's shoving us out of the picture, Isaac. You know Cowboy. He's a hog. The Chinaman is immobilized, right? So Barney kidnaps two assistant DAs, brings his camera, takes Polaroid shots of the kid, fingerprints him with his own fingerprint board, and makes a bedside arrest."

"Is Barney flaking kids these days? What the fuck does he have on Stanley Chin? Did he stick a ski mask under Stanley's pillow, or what?"

"Isaac, you can't worry him. Barney says he can produce a horde of Chinese grocers who'll swear on their lives that Stanley ripped them off. A judge is coming down tomorrow to arraign the kid."

"Tell me one thing. How did he get around the nigger nurse?"

"He didn't have to. His leather boys stuffed a shotgun in her blouse and barricaded her behind her desk."

It was idiotic to hound Brodsky for Cowboy's attack on St. Bartholomew's. Isaac hung up. He couldn't outgun the Chief of Detectives. Cowboy would yap to the Chief Inspector, the Chief Inspector would mumble to the PC, the PC would invite the First Dep into his private elevator, and the First Dep, who couldn't divorce himself from the Irish Mafia at Headquarters, would get back to Isaac. Isaac was cooked. He'd have to cooperate with Cowboy's investigation. He couldn't even hide his photographs of Rupert and Esther Rose. The credit would go to Cowboy. He's set up a command post inside the hospital, with "crows" on every floor.

The Chief had one alternative. He could steal the boy out of St. Batholomew's with the help of Brodsky and Coen, and keep him in a cellar. Then Cowboy would fall from grace. But Isaac risked internecine warfare at Headquarters. He'd have to match his "angels" against Barney's "crows." The First Dep had a cancer in his throat. How long could he stay with Isaac? The Irish chiefs preferred Barney Rosenblatt. Cowboy wouldn't break ranks. He was willing to destroy any detective the PC disliked. Isaac had too much rapport with the cops in the street. He trafficked with Puerto Ricans and milk-white spades. His stoolpigeons were loyal to nobody but him. Isaac endangered the calm at Headquarters. The Irish chiefs were suspicious of him.

He waited for a Checker cab. Isaac was particular how he rode uptown. He wanted to sulk in a fat leather seat. He went to Coen. Coen would soften his misery with hot tea and a game of checkers. Isaac wouldn't play chess with Blue Eyes. Chess brought out the Chief's ferociousness, his yen for bullying weak bishops and a ragged line of pawns, and Isaac preferred not to reveal this to Coen. He had less of an appetite for checkers. He could execute double and triple jumps without relishing his victories. And Coen didn't seem to care who would win or lose.

Isaac kept away from the fire escape. He didn't have enough gusto today to climb in Coen's window. He was fond of visiting Blue Eyes at all hours. He tried Coen's doorbell. The Chief had trained ears; he heard swishing feet behind the door. "Manfred, let me in." No bolts moved. So he picked Coen's lock. "Manfred, what's doing?" He found Marilyn in Coen's foyer. She was glinting at him out of merciless eyes, with puffs on her face that had turned solid green.

Isaac backed away. He couldn't remember the last time he had trembles in his arms and knees. "I should have figured you'd be with Coen. That boy has a good heart. He'll take in anybody. Who marked up your cheeks? It wasn't Manfred."

Marilyn realized what her father might do to that old boyfriend of hers from Inwood Park. Isaac was liable to make a corpse out of Brian Connell, or destroy him in a more subtle way: he could pull Brian out of his stationhouse in the name of the First Dep and bounce him through all five boroughs until the boy lost his mind from dizziness and fatigue. Marilyn swore she'd been mugged. She knew about her father's passion for details, his eye for inconsistencies. She had to invent a full scenario for him.

"Where did it happen?"

"Midtown," she said.

"East or west?"

"Isaac, will you stop bothering me, for Christ's sake. I suppose you keep a file on every mugger in Manhattan."

She had her mother's Irish temper, that crisp, beautiful frown of Kathleen's.

"Can't you call me dad?"

"Oh God," she said. "Are we going to start that all over again? Everybody calls you Isaac. Why should I be different?"

Isaac felt his strength coming back. His fingers began to claw.

"Pack your bags. You're moving in with me."

"Bullshit."

He could have dragged her to his flat on Rivington Street, made the bumps in her face go from green to pure violet, but he didn't. He would take her from Blue Eyes by persuasion alone, and he would find her no more architects to marry. The girl was miserable in a married state. She scattered husbands around her, fell from man to man. Isaac would tolerate the itch in her thighs. But she couldn't have Coen. He didn't want her craziness with Blue Eyes to follow him into Headquarters. Coen belonged to him.

"Marilyn, if you stay, I'm staying too. Manfred can fix us hot chocolate . . . he can lull us to sleep in separate rooms. We'll keep a chart on the wall about who bathes first. Manfred must be good at scrubbing backs. You understand me, Marilyn? I'm not going without you."

"Isaac, how did you ever get to be such a son-of-a-bitch?"

"It took learning," he said. "Now pack up."

She didn't prepare to leave. She watched the pinched line under Isaac's nose, pitying her father's enemies and friends; nobody could ride over Isaac.

"Marilyn, if he sees us together, he'll be the one to suffer, not you . . . don't make me bury Coen. I can turn him into a glorified clerk. Would you like him to file cards in a commissioner's basement for the rest of his life? Then cooperate with me."

"You wouldn't," she said. "You can't get by without Coen."

"I'll teach myself. Marilyn, don't misjudge your old father. Affection means nothing in my business. I'd cripple Manfred if it would take me where I have to go."

"Daddy Isaac," she said, with her nostrils smoking, "you don't have to tell me that." And she located her underwear, those mesh panties of hers, in yellow, red, and blue, and stuffed them into her suitcase. She flung a sweater at Isaac. "Fold it, for Christ's sake. How many hands do I have?"

"Should I leave a note for Manfred?"

"No. He'll figure out the plot. Who else would bother to kidnap me?"

Suddenly Isaac turned shy. He couldn't adjust to victories over his daughter. "Marilyn, you can still invite him down to my place . . . I didn't say you have to avoid him altogether."

"Isaac, drop dead."

She bit her lip to keep from crying. Isaac saw the blood. He was too timid to swipe at the blood with his handkerchief. He could thank Kathleen's bloody Jesus he didn't have another child. Two Marilyns would have wrecked him. He'd rather duel with Barney Rosenblatt outside the PC's office than contemplate his skinny daughter. Isaac was a wretched man. He couldn't tuck away his love for Marilyn. She was part of his own thick flesh. Her shoulders came together, and she began to cry with little blubbering noises that tore into Isaac's throat. He touched her hair with a finger. She didn't move. He held her in a bearish grip. "Baby, it'll be all right."

They went down Coen's stairs, with Isaac managing the suitcase, and clutching Marilyn with one hand. He would have killed for the right to hold his daughter. Rupert, Stanley, and St. Bartholomew's tumbled out of his head.

PART TWO

EIGHT

"Mr. Weil, Mr. Philip Weil."

The reporter crouched under Philip's doorknob, his eye against the keyhole, waiting for the darkness to subside. He was a clever young man, fresh out of journalism school, with a flair for identifying the peccadilloes of his own generation. He'd received encouragement from a fistful of magazines: nothing firm, nothing really bankable, but if he could interview the father of Rupert Weil, the monster with baby fat on his chin, no magazine could deny him for long. His thighs burned. He wasn't used to crouching so much. And the blackness in the keyhole had smogged his eye.

"I've got fifty dollars for you, Mr. Weil . . . conversation money." he said, with a torn dollar bill and two subway tokens in his pocket.' He would lure the monster's father out, this recluse, this failed chess player, this Essex Street clown who had once been the friend of the great Isaac Sidel, or bluff his way into the apartment. "You're not talking to a sharp, Mr. Weil. I would never degrade your boy. This is Tony Brill, the journalist. I have connections, Mr. Weil. . . . I can cream the police and make Rupert come out like a hero . . . it's up to you."

Philip was hiding in the kitchen, immune to the imprecations of Tony Brill. He wouldn't sell Rupert's story, no matter what figure the journalist could name. He'd been besieged with phone calls, telegrams, knocks on his door. The newspapers had Rupert's face smeared in their centerfolds, with captions about derangement and banditry. The Lollipop Gang and the Urban Blitz. Rupert Weil, Teenage Ghoul. Esther Rose, Temptress, Evil Saint, Dropout from the JDL, and Mama to the Lollipops. And Stanley Chin, Hong Kong Bully Boy. A fat detective, Cowboy Rosenblatt, haunted Philip's television screen. Cowboy spit warnings to potential lollipops from Stanley's hospital bed, which had been turned into a compact prison, and he hogged every channel with profiles of Rupert and Esther

Rose, self-congratulations, and anecdotes about his police career. Philip couldn't find Isaac in any of the programs and news reports featuring Cowboy Rosenblatt; none of the detectives who badgered him over the phone came from Isaac's office.

When soft-spoken men from the District Attorney's office tried to scare information out of him, Philip would bray into telephone, "I'll talk to Isaac and nobody else." But Isaac wouldn't come. The Chief had disappeared from Philip's life after a single visit. And Philip was left alone to slink in his kitchen and contemplate the madnesses of his boy.

Philip closed his eyes; he wanted to shake off the briny calculations in his skull. Thinking could ruin him, rub his nose into the painted squares of a chessboard. He wasn't able to kill the barking outside his door. The moment he surrendered to these noises and slumped against the wall, the barking had a definite appeal: it drew him out of the kitchen. The yelps were growing familiar. He pressed his ear to the door.

"Papa, let me in."

"Rupert?" he said, struggling with the chain guard. Even if Tony Brill were some kind of sound magician, how could he have known the exact tremors of Rupert's voice? Philip put his hand out the door, clutched a jacket, and hauled Rupert inside. The fat cheeks were gone. Rupert looked emaciated. He wore the jacket of a housing cop. This was his only disguise. With a hard pull, the jacket could have reached to his ankles. Bound in dark, billowing cloth, Rupert had no fists, no throat, no chest. Philip unraveled him. Except for old, disheveled sneakers and pants, he was naked under the jacket, the first manly hairs, almost blond, sprouting over his nipples. A squeal escaped from Philip's throat; his mad love for the boy turned to an incredible rage. He had Rupert's ear in his fingers. He would have gone for a nose. Rupert knocked him down. Philip sat with his knees in his chest. A simple push had stunned him, not a wicked blow.

"Papa, don't touch my ear again. I'm too old for that."

Rupert didn't sneer; he hugged Philip under the arms and straightened Philip's knees. He was delicate with his father, picking him up. Then he walked into the kitchen. Philip had to stare at his back; half of Rupert was inside the refrigerator. He tore into the flesh of a tomato, marking the refrigerator walls with red spit. He swallowed sour pickles. He crammed his face into a container of cottage cheese. Philip was appalled by his son's appetite. He'd never encountered a boy with such greedy jaws. Rupert was all tongue and teeth. Philip had lost his way with him. How could he confront this child of his, who was trying to shove the universe into his mouth?

"Rupert, did you notice a journalist in the hall, a man named Brill?"

Rupert emerged from the refrigerator, cottage cheese falling from his eyebrows. "The fatass in the trench coat? He saluted me."

"But he saw you standing by the door."

"So what? What can he do, papa? Let him blab to Isaac. Who gives a shit."

"Isaac was here," Philip declared with a pull of his shoulder, as Rupert dove into the cottage cheese again. "I said Isaac was here."

Rupert mumbled with his lips inside the container. "I heard you, papa." He came up for air, flicking cheese off his nose. "Why did you supply him with pictures of Esther and me?"

"Rupert, he would have torn out the walls. Isaac doesn't give you much room to breathe. But he wants to help . . . Rupert, has he done bad things to you?"

"Papa, you're a woodenhead. Isaac's been fucking you blind. You and Mordecai can't stop paying homage to him. He's your king. At least Mordecai gets some satisfaction. He brags about Isaac. He talks about the Jewish god who presides over New York City, the kosher detective who can solve any crime. And you, papa? You eat your liver without saying a word. Where's your terrain? Isaac's left you his droppings. He's made you prince of the Essex Street project. You walk around in your three good shirts wishing you were Isaac."

"That's crazy," Philip said. "I don't envy his success."

Rupert sucked with wolfish teeth. "Success, papa? That's it. Success to do what? Blow people away? To prance in front of Puerto Ricans and poor Jews. Isaac shits in peace because he has his worshipers and his props. He can enter any church or playground on both sides of the Bowery and be guaranteed a smile. Even the horseradish man bows to Isaac. Papa, if you could learn to despise him, he'd run uptown with a handkerchief over his ears. He'd disintegrate. He'd cry in Riverdale."

Rupert scooped up his jacket off the floor and began stuffing the pockets with food. After scavenging his father's refrigerator, he climbed into the jacket and waddled to the door. The pockets hung below his knees.

"I'll hide you," Philip said. "You can stay here."

"What happens when Isaac sweeps under the bed?"

"He'll find twenty years of dust, and a few missing pawns."

"Thanks, papa, but I have to go." Rupert pulled up his sleeves so he could hug his father. Then he rushed into the hall, jars smacking in his pockets. Tony Brill appeared from behind a fire door. "That's him, Mr. Weil, isn't it? Rupert himself. I can spot a fugitive by his walk."

Tony Brill didn't go after Rupert. He lunged at Philip's door. Philip locked him out. "I can save him, Mr. Weil . . . trust me."

Philip returned to the kitchen, ignoring the babble. He was interested in weather reports. Did the television predict snow? Rupert would catch pneumonia in his sneakers. Philip shouldn't have let him out of the house without a proper undershirt. The boy had no mind for cold weather. His thumbs would have to freeze before the idea of frostbite entered his head. How could Philip signal to him? Should he fly scarves from his fire escape? He laughed bitterly at his own incompetence. He had just enough energy in him to become a father. His wife, a Russian girl with handsome bosoms and a flat behind, stared him in the eye for eleven years and ran away before Rupert was six. Sonia, the Stalinist, must have found other causes than a man who would die for Trotsky and chess and a boy who looked more like her husband than herself. She was supposed to be in Oregon, living with a band of apple pickers, a gray-haired Russian lady.

Philip berated himself. A father should have the right to make a prisoner of his son, if only for a little while. He meant to jab the boy with questions, brutal questions, not a dialectical checklist that would give Rupert the chance to invent a shabby scheme, a rationale for frightening old grocers and sending Isaac's mother to Bellevue. But Philip was powerless; his own questions would glance off Rupert and bite Philip behind the ears. If Rupert had a dybbuk in him, a demon sucking at his intestines, who put it there? Such a dybbuk could only be passed from father to son. The violence Philip had done to his body, the gnawing of his own limbs, the self-lacerations that came a nibble at a time, the rot of living indoors, the poison of chess formulas, degrees of slaughter acted out on a board, the insane fondling of wooden men, pawns, bishops, and kings, must have created a horrible, scratchy weasel that crept under Rupert's skin, grabbed his testicles, tightened his guts, and caused conniptions in his brain. The dybbuk was Philip. No one else.

Rupert was on the run. He had to fight the weight in his pockets, the shifting, sliding bottles and jars, the wind that slapped the enormous collars of the jacket he stole out of a grubby bungalow that belonged to the housing cops. His belly gurgled from the pickles he swallowed in his father's apartment. He couldn't dash across a housing project with burgeoning pockets and also digest pickles and cottage cheese. Hiccoughs broke his miserable stride. He avoided the shoppers huddling out of the bialy factory on Grand Street with their bags of onion bread. They might have recognized him, in spite of his jacket. They would scream, splinter bialys in his face, and call for the big Jewish Chief, Isaac Sidel, or the nearest housing cop. He didn't have the patience to dodge bialys and pick onions out of his eyes. He was going to Esther Rose.

Rupert couldn't grasp all of Esther's fervors. She'd come out of a Yeshiva in Brownsville that would only accept the daughters of the Sephardim of Brooklyn. Stuck in a neighborhood of Puerto Ricans, blacks, and rough Polish Jews, it had gates on every side. The Yeshiva was impregnable. None of the Polish Jews could gain access to its prayer rooms and library. The girls were rushed in through a door in the back. They had little opportunity to examine what existed outside the Yeshiva's front wall. They understood the hypnotic candlepower of a 25-watt bulb. They could feel bannisters in the dark. They had a gift for reciting Ladino, the gibber of medieval Spanish and Hebrew that was used exclusively at this Yeshiva. The Sephardic priests who ran the school took it upon themselves to push every girl towards hysteria. The girls had to consider what worthless creatures they were. They became despondent over the largeness of their nipples, the untoward shape of their breasts, the sign of pubic hair, the bloody spots in their underpants. Nothing on this earth except the lowly female was cursed with a menstrual flow, their teachers advised them. Husbands had already been selected for the girls by a system of bartering inside their families. Only a girl with the resources of her family behind her could command a proper husband, usually twice her age.

Esther was taught the rituals of marriage at the Brownsville school for Sephardic girls, the veils she would wear, the menstrual charts she would keep to warn her husband of the exact days of her impurity. Esther had seven years of this, muttering prayers whenever she touched her nipple or her crotch by accident, dreaming of her life as a workhorse for her future husband and his family, trading pubic hairs with a sinful schoolmate, feeling razors in her womb at the onset of her periods, despising bowel movements, sweat, and the color of her urine. A month before she was scheduled to marry a merchant with hair in his nose, Esther ran away. She drifted through Brooklyn, working for the telephone company. Then she joined the JDL. Her parents, who lived in an enclave of Spagnuolos (Sephardic Jews) between Coney Island and Gravesend, included Esther in their prayers for the dead. They couldn't tolerate the existence of a daughter who would shun a marriage contract to embrace the Jewish Defense League. Zionism meant nothing to Esther's people. Israel was a place for Germans, Russians, and Poles, barbarians to most of the Sephardim, who remembered the kindness of the Moors to Spanish Jews. The ancestors of Esther Rose, mathematicians, prophets, and moneylenders, had flourished under Arabic rule; it was difficult for the south Brooklyn Sephardim to hold a legitimate grudge against Egypt and Saudi Arabia, or the Syrians and Lebanese of Atlantic Avenue.

Rupert first bumped into Esther Rose outside the Russian embassy in Manhattan half a year ago. She was carrying a placard denouncing Soviet intransigence towards the State of Israel. She harassed policemen and the citizens of Fifth Avenue, wearing an old, smelly blouse and a wraparound skirt that exposed her unwashed ankles and knees; she flew at her adversaries with uncombed hair and fingernails that had all the corrugations of a saw. Rupert couldn't take his eyes off Esther Rose. He had never known a girl who lived at such a raw edge. Esther noticed the chubby boy staring at her. She didn't bite his eyebrows. She looked beyond the pedestrian nature of fat cheeks. This wasn't a boy she could frighten with placards or a rough fingernail.

She had coffee egg creams with him at a dump on Third Avenue. He blurted his age: fifteen. She'd picked up a child (Esther was two years away from being twenty). The fat cheeks had an erudition that could touch a Yeshiva girl under her brassiere. This baby talked of Sophocles, Rabbi Akiba, St. Augustine, the Baal Shem, Robespierre, Nikolai Gogol, Hieronymus Bosch, Huey P. Newton, Prince Kropotkin, and Nicodemus of Jerusalem. He had the delirious, twitching eyes of a Sephardic priest, the sour fingers of a virgin boy. She would have climbed under the table with Rupert, licked him with coffee syrup on her tongue. The egg cream must have made him reticent. He was suspicious of lying down in a field of cockroaches and candy wrappers, under the gaze of countermen.

Esther relied on ingenuity. She picked Atlantic Avenue, where she knew of a mattress they could rent by the hour. Rupert wouldn't go. It violated his sense of purity. He brought her to an abandoned building on Norfolk Street. They undressed in the rubble, Esther's knees sinking through the floorboards. The boy was passionate with her. He fondled Esther with a sly conviction, and soon they were eating dust off one another's body. Esther was a Brooklyn girl. Norfolk Street remained a mystery to her. But she could love a building with missing staircases, rotting walls, and windows blocked with tin. She gave up the question of Palestine for Rupert's sake. She two-timed the JDL, staying near Norfolk Street to become Rupert's permanent "mama."

Rupert slinked away from his father's house, crippled by jars in his pockets. He was trying to shake that journalist, Tony Brill. He stumbled in and out of street corners, his ankles beginning to swell from the pressure of jars sliding off his hips. Esther had to jump from building to building, protecting herself from nosy people and cops of the Puerto Rican and Jewish East Side. Rupert found her on Suffolk Street. She was a choosy girl, hiding in a tenement with gargoyles near the roof, rain spouts with broken noses. He entered through a window on the ground floor, grabbing his pockets and heaving them over the sill. He could follow Esther's ascent in the building by the drawings over each set of stairs. She'd crayoned faces next to the landings, faces with swollen foreheads and frothy mouths: men and women drugged with the burden of their own heavy brains. The drawings stopped abruptly at the fourth floor. Rupert didn't have to peek any higher. "Esther," he called. "It's me."

She sat on her haunches in deep concentration, wearing a blanket, like a Brooklyn squaw (Esther despised street clothes). She was cooking something in a pot, with the Sterno can Rupert had given her. The stink coming off the pot settled under Rupert's tongue; he walked around the room biting his jacket to keep from swallowing his own poisoned spit. "What the hell are you making?" he shouted with Esther's fumes in his eyes.

"Food," she said. "Food for Isaac."

"Isaac's not a schmuck. He won't drink mud out of a pot."

"Then I'll feed it to him. I can stuff Isaac anytime."

"How?" Rupert asked. "Are you going to mail him some

doctored horseradish?"

"No. I'll sneak it into his lousy Headquarters."

"Esther, Isaac's got a fortress on Centre Street. You know how many guns there are on every floor? Detectives sleep in the woodwork. You can't pee without an escort."

"So what?" she said. "I'm not going to hold Isaac's prick."

"Esther, listen to me. You haven't eaten in four days." He smacked the bulges in his pockets. "I have my father's sour pickles. I have stuffed cabbage. I have grape leaves."

"I'm not hungry."

Esther had been cold to Rupert over the past week; she blamed him for losing Stanley Chin. They'd all gone out to Corona because Manhattan was flooded with cops and gorillas from Mulberry Street. They were shrewd enough to outrun the gorillas, who seemed stranded outside Little Italy, and couldn't tell the difference between a ski mask (Esther's contribution to the gang), a wool helmet, and a winter scarf; these gorillas must have come from a warmer climate, where a sane person wouldn't think of putting a rag on his head. But the lollipops weren't so sure of the police; cops came smart and dumb, and even a dumb cop could signal Isaac with a portable radio.

Corona was Rupert's idea; he intended to plague Isaac from a fresh neighborhood. The lollipops would attack grocery stores, spit Isaac's name at their victims. But a gang of baby Chinamen had followed them out on the Queensboro line, old compatriots of Stanley Chin's from his days as a strong-arm boy for merchants and Republican politicians on Pell Street. The gang was seeking revenge; Stanley had insulted his former employers, the Pell Street Republican Club, with his raids on Chinatown as a member of the lollipops. These baby Chinamen, called the Snapping Dragons by their enemies, had no interest in Rupert and Esther Rose; they weren't out to punish a pair of round-eyed Jews. They jumped on Stanley's back outside the subway stop in Corona, wrestled him to the ground, broke every single one of his fingers and toes, while Esther screamed and dove into their ranks, and two unoccupied Dragons held Rupert by his arms. Esther forbid explanations from Rupert. With her head burrowing in the groin of a Snap Dragon, she'd heard the pop of Stanley's fingers. Rupert had come out of Corona unmarked.

She stared at his unwieldy jacket. "Take that thing off," she said. "It makes you look like a traffic cop."

Rupert obeyed her. He stood with goose bumps sprouting on his

chest. He couldn't get her away from that concoction she was
brewing for Isaac. His motives were simple: he wanted Esther to
fuck. Rupert had a perfect right to be lascivious with her. He
worshipped Esther's body, loving the damp skin of a Yeshiva girl,
the exquisite bends in her shoulder, her arching wings, the salt he
licked out of her navel, the swampy aromas from the underside of her
knee, the scissoring of her thighs. He had touched one
junior-high-school girl before Esther, felt the exaggerated pimple on
this girl's chest, dry, odorless skin, and the random hairs that grew
out of the hems in her underpants. But he couldn't have conceived
the delicate, moist machinery of a female's parts without Esther.
Rupert would have murdered the whole of Essex Street for the
privilege of putting his face between Esther's legs, or fucking her
until her neck throbbed with the power of her orgasm.

She would give him nothing today. Rupert understood that.
Esther was punishing him for Stanley's fall. Should he break his own
thumbs to please her? The denial of her body terrified him. He would
have groveled on the dirty floor to suck Esther's kneecaps if he knew
this might arouse her, or at least catch Esther off her guard. He stuck
his hands in his armpits to keep them warm. He shivered and sulked,
the goose bumps snaking up and down his spine.

Esther whipped one elbow and cast her blanket out at Rupert,
drawing him into her reach. They stood belly to belly in the cold;
then Esther relocated the blanket, and they descended together, with a
rub of their hips, while Rupert's pants came down. They rolled on the
blanket, Rupert amazed by his sudden change of luck. No matter how
many times their bodies clapped, he would never fathom Esther's
needs. But he didn't question the grace of sleeping with Esther. She'd
grounded him in a blanket, and he was stuck with bits of wool over
his ears, Esther underneath. He crept into her, loosening her thighs
with a fist that hadn't quite lost its baby fat. Esther had her frenzy
with Rupert's hair in her mouth. Now she lay still, watching the
agitation build in his nose. Esther knew what it means when a man
begins to blow air. She brought Rupert out of her with a great
squeeze of her abdominal muscles before Rupert had the chance to
snort in her face (Yeshiva girls didn't believe in condoms,
diaphragms, or coils). Rupert dribbled on her chest. He wasn't surly.
He tried to paint her bosoms with his come, draw on Esther with a
sticky finger, but she wouldn't let him. She snatched up her blanket
and returned to the pot.

"I need some ammonia for the soup," she said.

Rupert put on his pants. "Why ammonia?"

"Just get some for me."

"Esther, I can't trade in pickles for cash. Who's going to give me free ammonia?"

"Steal it," she hissed into his ear. "Don't come back without my goods."

Rupert fled the building with the same bottles and jars (he'd forgotten to empty his jacket). He stumbled out into the narrow gutters of Suffolk Street, his sneakers sliding over raw stone. He hitched up his pockets and tried to remember if the Cuban grocery stores carried ammonia. He couldn't determine the nature of Esther's stew; whatever she was feeding Isaac, would it come hot or cold? A fat man in a vague, military coat cornered him on Norfolk Street. It was Tony Brill. Rupert sneered.

"Follow me, man, and I'll torture your balls. You know what I do to people. I'm Rupert Weil."

Tony Brill ran after Rupert. Soon both of them were huffing insanely for air. The journalist managed to claw three words out of his throat. "Talk to me."

They rested on opposite sides of a lamppost. Rupert extended his palm. "Cash, you fuck. Gimme all your money."

Tony Brill urged a torn dollar into Rupert's palm. "That's it. Now will you talk?"

Rupert made a fist, the dollar showing through his fingers. He had his ammonia money; he was too exhausted to steal from a grocery.

"Rupert, you can be a famous man. Tell me, do you suffer when they call you an urban bandit? What's the significance of your refusal to touch cash? Is it blood you want, not money? Will you and Esther raid stores without Stanley Chin? Are you a different kind of Robin Hood?"

"No," Rupert said. "I'm my father's boy." He pushed Tony Brill off the sidewalk and ran towards a section of grocery stores.

Esther was tired of churning soup in a scummy pot; she could hear the suck of bubbles underneath the scum. Nothing but ammonia would ever quiet such a noise. She'd make Isaac swallow her soup with his ears. There was more than one way to poison a big Jewish cop. Isaac would piss blood by tomorrow. Rupert was too soft. He couldn't punish the Chief without Esther Rose.

Yeshiva girls aren't blind; she'd seen the fat on Rupert disappear. Who was gouging Rupert's cheeks? Isaac the Pure. All of Rupert's dread came from the big Jew. She'd told him. "Rupert, you love your father too much. Is it your fault he's under Isaac's thumb? Why didn't he pack years ago and move out of Essex Street? Isaac's killing your father. Don't let him kill you."

He'd get angry with her. "How the hell do you know so much? Did your rabbis teach you the philosophy of Philip Weil? My father's scared to move. You expect him to crawl over the Brooklyn Bridge? He'd die in a strange place. Ask the scientists. You can lose your head if you stray from where you were born."

"We'll find him another one. When your guts shrivel, it's too late."

"Stop talking about my father. Leave his guts alone."

It didn't offend her. She could only love an obstinate boy. The sweat would pour from his eyebrows. The hollows in his cheeks would curl. He was handsomer to her than Isaac's baby, Mr. Blue Eyes. She wouldn't take down her underpants for the prettiest cop in the world. She was particular about the men she laid. Truck drivers, grocers, JDL boys, but no blond detective could get on her list.

The soup in Esther's pot smelled worse then the semen of a Williamsburg cat. The vapors were attacking her sinuses. Esther had to get out. She grabbed for her pea coat. Her fist burrowed into her sleeve like the skull of a groundhog, but she wouldn't button up. The blanket dropped below her calves. Esther didn't believe in skirts. You couldn't feel the wind on you if your legs were muggered in cloth. She had a ski mask balled in her pocket. She could bring terror to the neighborhood by pulling that mask over her head. Merchants would scream, "Lollipop, lollipop," and rush to the deepest corner of their shops. Seeing a merchant quake couldn't satisfy her any more. The merchants had a king with curly sideburns. Isaac the Jew. Esther swore to unhinge him.

The first time Rupert brought her into the East Side, to Norfolk Street, Essex, Delancey, Grand, Esther had realized the conditions of this territory. "Who's the big tit here? Tell me the name of your rabbi."

The boy couldn't answer her. "Esther, what do you mean?"

"Somebody's been squeezing these blocks for a long time. It's too quiet. There isn't a drop of anarchy on East Broadway. Where's the chief?"

Rupert thought for a moment. Then he mumbled, "At Police Headquarters." And he told her about Isaac, and Isaac's grip over hoodlums, policy men, shopkeepers, Seward Park High School, Ida Stutz, Mordecai, Philip, and Rupert himself. "He stinks," Rupert said. "But nobody's willing to say it."

Esther understood. Isaac was the Moses of Clinton and Delancey. Hadn't the idiot priests at her school shoved stories into her face about the sanctity of patriarchs? The Jews had more fathers than Esther could bear. An army of fathers with a single word under their tongues: Obey. When she married, said the priests, wouldn't her husband be like a father to her? A father who could enjoy Esther's parts. She'd have to cleave to her father-husband, make herself bald for him (hair on the female scalp was a sign of degradation and lust), feed him, fuck for him, mend his shirts, rub the pee stains out of his skivvies, stuff her womb with male heirs.

A wife was little better than any beast of the field. She was instructed to close her eyes and grunt when her husband climbed on top (intercourse in all other varieties, or positions, was immodest and perverse). He, the lord of the house, had to fuck with the Torah in his head, while his wife suffered the stab of her master's knees and prayed for a male child. Thank God for menstruation, Esther figured. A wife with blood in her drawers was unclean property. Her lord couldn't drink from her cup, or graze her with a forefinger after the first trickle. Then she had her nights and days to herself. She couldn't become pure again until she removed the wax from her ears and dipped her pink scalp into a pool of slimy water. These were the joys of a Yeshiva wife.

Esther had a solution. She could become Isaac's bride. It would be no marriage of convenience, arranged by rich uncles, with fat dowries and long trousseaus. Esther would bite away the traditional Ladino blessings. She'd construe a marriage without bridal veils and jeweled canopies as old as the Moorish occupation of Seville. There would be nothing between Esther and Isaac other than pride, venom, and a goatish itch. Bride and groom would ravage one another on their wedding night, fornicating with the energy of absolute hate. She'd tear off Isaac's nose with an early orgasm. He'd pound her kidneys with every smack of his hard, policeman's belly, and scald her groin with his steamy come. She'd suck up all the delicate glue in his eyes. Isaac would rage with his fingers over the shells of his face,

ruined by the powerful flicks of Esther's tongue. The butchery would
continue into the morning, when the remains of Esther and Isaac
would be found in the crush of lavender wedding sheets: two
well-peserved shinbones and a purple knot of blood.

Esther carried her visions into the street. Several laborers who
were digging holes in the sidewalk happened to see a girl with tits
peeking out of her coat. They abandoned their shovels to howl at
Esther. "Sweetheart, honey, baby dear, you'll catch cold without an
undershirt. Ask us, we'll block the wind for you." She stepped around
the holes, refusing to change the course of her buttons. Delivery boys
and retired men from Grand Street gaped into the open pea coat and
felt a knock between their eyes: it was painful to stare at a nipple
moving in winter light. "*Cuño*," the boys said. The old men gave
embarrassed shrugs and consoled themselves with thoughts of a bialy
and piss-colored tea.

Rupert was ten feet away. He heard none of the commotion
surrounding Esther. There were deep bumps in his forehead. Esther
didn't nudge him, or cry hello. She had too much respect for Rupert's
brainstorms. He was hugging Esther's ammonia under his arm. He
walked past her, oblivious to the howling of laborers and delivery
boys. Esther adored him chubby or thin, but she was frightened of his
skeletal look. Rupe, she wanted to say. Forget about them Chinese
Dragons. Stanley won't die in Corona. It's not your fault you never
learned kung-fu. I'm not mad any more. But the sharp line of his ears
startled her, and Esther didn't say a thing.

She developed a hunger strolling on Ludlow Street. Shutting her
pea coat to confound the Puerto Rican clerks, she entered a tiny
supermercado. A second girl came into the market while Esther
shoved a mushy tangerine under her coat. The girl's Irish nose and
kinky Jewish hair got to Esther. *I know that cunt.* Isaac's skinny
daughter. It had to be. The cunt was living with Isaac now. Rupert
and Esther had noticed her sitting on Isaac's fire escape. Marilyn
liked to bathe in cold air. They watched her from the roofs, Esther
wishing she could break off Marilyn's kneecaps. She was less
ferocious in the supermarket, having only one small urge to take out
her mask and spook Marilyn the Wild. The moist touch of tangerine
skin on her breasts calmed Esther Rose. She went about her business
of swiping more fruit.

The clerks grew wise to Esther. How many *muchachas* ranged
through their market in a pregnant pea coat? They yanked the bottom

of her coat, yelling thief, thief. Tangerines, avocado pears, and overripe green peppers plopped to the floor of the market with an agonizing squish. Esther struck at the clerks with a whirling elbow. "You want a slap in the balls maybe?"

"Call the cops, man," the head clerk screamed. Then he recognized Marilyn, who was trying to get between Esther and the clerks. "Your father should come, Señorita Marilyn. This muchacha needs the handcuffs and a pistola in the mouth."

"I'll pay," Marilyn screamed into the clerk's bobbing hairline. She saw the foam build on Esther's lip. It was dumb to make an arrest over avocados and green peppers. The girl was either crazy, or starving for fruit. Marilyn grabbed a dollar from her pocketbook. The clerks refused her money. "No, no, Señorita Marilyn." They released Esther's coat. She stuck her teeth near Marilyn's chin.

"Who asked you for your fucking charity?"

"Loco," the clerks whispered to themselves. Little crooks like Esther were a common nuisance in their trade. Roaches, ants, dogs, mice, and other predators could destroy your inventory.

Marilyn didn't remain with the clerks; she followed the track of Esther's pea coat. The two girls bumped across Grand Street. "What's your name?" Marilyn asked.

Esther smiled. "Me? I'm Rupertina. I live in the projects. I have eleven brothers, Miss, so help me God. My mother's dead. My father doesn't have a tooth. He licks the gutters for a living. Tell me, is your daddy alive?"

The girl's dire history caused Marilyn to brood. But there was a curious edge to this Rupertina's voice. "Do you know my father? He's a police inspector. Isaac Sidel."

Esther had to hold back her pity for Marilyn the Wild. The cunt will be an orphan in twenty hours. "Miss, I never heard of any Isaac."

Esther jumped onto the sidewalk and scampered away. She wished she had a lollipop embedded in her ski mask. She could bite through the wrapper and get some colored juice on her tongue. The growls in her belly pushed her towards Suffolk Street and Rupert's sour pickles. The dudes from the Seward Park handball courts wouldn't stop pestering her. They were boys with scarves, blue sneakers, and silver posts hanging from their left ears. They had canes with points sharp enough to stab a girl's pockets. "Come on down to the playground with us, little mama. We gonna feast on you."

Esther growled at the dudes, slapping their canes off her sides. "Don't you know who I am?" she said, ready to grab a silver post and pull on a dude's ear. "I'm Isaac's daughter."

The boys retrieved their canes. "Honky Isaac?" they said. "The Papa Jew?"

"That's him"

They were suspicious. "What's the big honky's daughter doing in the street without no pants and skirt?"

"I'm coming from a rendezvous."

"What's that?" the boys demanded of her.

"A religious meeting. With a rabbi. You hold it in a swimming pool. Every month. It washes all your germs."

The dudes spread apart from Esther; she could contaminate them with her talk of rabbis, germs, and swimming pools.

Esther arrived on Suffolk Street. Rupert was waiting on the fourth floor of Esther's tenement with a bottle of ammonia. They went into the room where Esther kept her pot. She relit the Sterno can and poured some ammonia into her soup without thanking the boy. "Pickles," she said. "Bring me a pickle."

Rupert brought over his father's jars. While Esther stirred the pot, he fed her sour pickles, grape leaves, and bits of cabbage. She stepped out of her coat, and Rupert had to squint at the wall to keep his mind off the thrust of her ass and the beautiful pull of her ribs. Esther had a frightening concentration. She'd scream at him if he tried to fuck her in the middle of mixing the soup. Rupert saw his limits. He was only the nominal head of the lollipops. The gang's spirit came from Esther. She's the one who planned their forages into the East Side. They would chop up the giant a finger at a time, attack Isaac at the peripheries, nestle in his armpits, slap his appendages down.

Rupert's eyes were burrowing into the wall when he felt a hand inside his coat. Esther had started to undress him. He didn't resist. He took her favors however they happened to come. "I still think Isaac isn't going to drink your soup so fast."

"Shut up," she said. His heart beat against the bumps in her palm. Soon they were lying in Esther's coat. This was a fragile boy, with the heartbeat of a captured bird. According to the Sephardic priests, it was sinful to fornicate with Esther on top. Fuck the priests. Esther would invent her own religion. She was in love with a boy who had watched his father nibble at himself for fifteen years.

Piecemeal deaths were the ugliest. Rupert caught his father's disease. He couldn't creep out from under Isaac.

Her tongue crowded into Rupert's teeth. She heard the boy snort. She'd have to fatten up his face. It was impossible with Isaac around. Esther meant to win, even if she had to become Isaac's bride. She didn't fret over it. The marriage would be very lean.

PART THREE

NINE

Isaac arrived at the Neptune Manor on Ocean Parkway in ordinary clothes; he wouldn't retrieve any of his five velvet jackets (champagne yellow, cucumber green, orange, red, and mole gray) from his wife's apartment, up in Riverdale, for the wedding of an old maid. Marilyn refused to come with him, so he had to bring Coen. The "crows" from Barney Rosenblatt's office, who sacrificed their leather pockets for Cowboy and came in sharkskin and rich gabardine, tittered at Isaac's "date." Coen was in the doghouse, all of them knew; he'd committed the primary sin of romancing Marilyn Sidel.

Isaac and Coen had been put in a corner, far from the wedding table, where Cowboy sat with his oldest daughter, his new son-in-law (a haberdasher with rotten teeth), First Deputy Commissioner O'Roarke, the Chief Inspector, and the PC, together with their wives, and two young deputy mayors, honorable men with side-burns and advanced college degrees, who felt smug in a room filled with cops. Anita Rosenblatt wore a veil that obscured a crooked nose and the long, burrowing chin of her father. The bride was thirty-two. She suffered from falling hair, the result of a nervous condition that left her with a poisoned scalp. Even Isaac, who hated Cowboy, couldn't deny the appeal Anita had in her wedding gown. She survived bald spots and imperfections in her face. Staring at the haberdasher, she had a flush that could swallow any veil, or pinch the sourness off the cheeks of an Irish commissioner.

Anita presided over the smorgasbord. The assistant district attorneys of Manhattan, Brooklyn, and Queens, standing opposite the bride, devoured enormous boats of pickled cabbage. A fountain governed by the figure of Neptune climbing out of the sea (done in silver and gold), spit lemon punch into a basin near Neptune's toes with enough force to drown a baby, or a small dog.

Isaac discovered Herbert Pimloe behind a tray of midget

salamis. Only respect for Commissioner O'Roarke, the First Dep, prevented Isaac from shoving a salami down Pimloe's throat. O'Roarke was a sick man. He didn't need to be shamed by his own inspectors at a catered affair. Isaac wedged Pimloe into the salamis without a hint of malice. "Herbert, they tell me Cowboy has a new steerer."

Pimloe tried to slip outside the smorgasbord. Isaac held him in place with two fingers. Pimloe was reluctant to move. "Isaac, you can't believe everything you hear."

"Herbert, did Cowboy give you a wedding ring? Or is it an informal engagement?"

Pimloe accommodated Isaac with a toothless smile. The veins in his ears showed red. "Chief, you shouldn't listen to the FBI."

"Herbert, how much did Cowboy promise? Half the city? Is that what it took to turn you around? Is he giving you Brooklyn, or the Bronx? Herbert, I want to know."

"Isaac, I didn't screw you, I swear."

"Pimloe, you told Cowboy where to find Stanley Chin. And don't hand me shit about Newgate. Newgate wouldn't suck Cowboy's nipples. He's got too much pride. It takes a Harvard boy."

Isaac left Pimloe to brood against the moist skins of the salamis. His anger was mostly counterfeit. The Chief couldn't blame a quiff for trying to improve himself. Herbert played the percentages. He had to figure Cowboy was a better rabbi than O'Roarke. Why should Pimloe attach his badge and his pants to a dying commissioner?

Isaac marched to the wedding table. He might bang shoulders with Barney, but he wouldn't insult the bride. He kissed Anita under the veil, wishing her a long and happy marriage in spite of the feuds at Headquarters. The veil rubbed Isaac's nose. He could feel the stiff corseting of her gown. He prayed Anita wouldn't lose her haberdasher-husband. He knew all about daughters who had a talent for wiggling away from their men. Thinking of Marilyn brought Isaac back to Coen. He'd rather have her single than see her with Blue Eyes. Coen made a perfect cop. Without brains, or ambition, he was utterly reliable. What could he offer Marilyn except those damn blue eyes?

Under the cold, rabbity gaze of the Police Commissioner and his wife, who shoveled potato salad into their mouths as they scrutinized each wedding guest, Isaac was obliged to shake Cowboy's fist. "Luck," Isaac said, smiling into the ruffles of a sleeve. Cowboy

welcomed Isaac with the scorn and panoply of a master pimp. He
wore a midnight-blue ensemble, with a silk cravat, a cummerbund,
and trousers wider than a skirt; his rank, "Chief of Detectives," was
filigreed on cufflinks made of speckled pearl. Cowboy had dropped
thirteen thousand dollars to capture a hall big enough to launch his
balding daughter, and he'd hang himself with the magnificent drapes
in the PC's office (installed by Teddy Roosevelt seventy years ago),
before he allowed Isaac to muck up his one day of glory. He'd made
certain that Isaac and his boyfriend were exiled to a table practically
inside the kitchen, so that the reek of chicken fat could remind them
of their low station. Blue Eyes disgusted him even more than Isaac
did. It was pretty boys like Coen who had toyed with Barney's girl,
disappointing Anita again and again until Cowboy had to act. He
produced a bridegroom for Anita, a fifty-eight-year-old merchant
without any merchandise, a bachelor with incredible dental bills, an
orphan hungry for a father-in-law who could bully detectives in all
five boroughs. Barney found a niche for him on Schermerhorn Street,
a crack in the wall two pushcarts deep, and turned this orphan into a
haberdasher. The Chief of Detectives couldn't have his oldest
daughter in bed with a propertyless man.

"Isaac, you shouldn't worry. Stanley Chin won't die of hospital
food. My men have been feeding him chocolate bars."

Cowboy deserved to gloat; he'd secured Anita for life (the
haberdasher would have had to orphan his skull if he disappeared
from Schermerhorn Street), he'd grabbed a lollipop away from Isaac
in Corona, and he'd already whispered to the PC how Blue Eyes had
been caught with cunty Marilyn. But Isaac stepped around him,
muttering awkward hellos to the PC and his wife, and steered south
along the wedding table until he reached the First Dep. Isaac hadn't
come to discuss police business with his boss. He didn't tell
O'Roarke about the nest of car thieves his "angels" had uncovered in
the Third Division, cops supplying North Jersey gamblers with Fords
and Buicks. Isaac had the details in his head; he would only burden
O'Roarke after he was ready to pounce on the cops and rip their nest
apart. Isaac leaned into the side of the table. "Can I get you and Mrs.
O'Roarke something from the buffet, Commissioner Ned?"

The First Dep watched Isaac with crisp green eyes that could
withstand the corrosion of drugs, and the radium he had to swallow:
before the tumor in his throat began to eat away areas of his
concentration, O'Roarke had been the most feared cop in New York.

The Police Commissioner was strictly the Mayor's bride; enmeshed in city politics, a PC would vanish within a few seasons. The First Dep had remained in office thirty years. He broke in each new Commissioner, and had to sweep up the junk of the old PC. O'Roarke was the nearest thing to permanence a cop would ever know. And now the Deputy Commissioner was dying in his chair.

Gentle with Isaac, the First Dep asked for Coen. "Why is Manfred so far away? Is he catching fly balls? I can't see him from this end of the table."

"It's nothing, Commissioner Ned. Cowboy doesn't want him near the bride."

"That's fine for Cowboy. What about us? I always cheat on my indigestion when Manfred smiles."

"I can bring him, but he'll get into trouble down here. He's much better off in Cowboy's woods."

Isaac sent for Blue Eyes. Coen passed the tables reserved for detective sergeants, minor relatives, and lowly precinct captains who sneered at the angel boy behind their napkins because they couldn't afford to alienate Isaac in the open. Isaac disappeared. He'd suffered through the smorgasbord, showing his eyeteeth to commissioners, deputy mayors, and choice Rosenblatts, and he crept out of the hall on ripple soles to avoid a sit-down dinner, where he would have had to swallow turkey breasts, string beans, Neptune cabbage, and shreds of fruit cocktail with Barney's "crows" and a hierarchy of fat cops. Blue Eyes could double for him. Isaac tapped Coen's chin on his way out. "Watch the First Dep. If he spits blood, or anything, you call me."

Coen had to shift for himself. He couldn't abscond, like his Chief. He was resigned to a dead Sunday. The First Dep found a chair for him. Blue Eyes was squeezed into the wedding table. Cowboy gobbled grapefruit sections with dark spit on his tongue. He couldn't overrule Commissioner Ned. Coen would have to stay. The smorgasbord was wheeled out, pushing towards the kitchen like an exhausted mountain, delicacies tottering in their trays. A three-piece band appeared during the first course, a saxophone, an accordion, and a bass fiddle. The band set itself up in what had earlier been the inner ring of the smorgasbord. Wedding guests were encouraged to dance between courses, so the kitchen crew would have the chance to clear every table; the assistant chefs had to decorate five hundred platters with minced potato balls for the second course.

The hard scream of the saxophone cluttered the hall with a whiff of metal. The fiddler had thickened fingers. The accordionist could barely tease a cop out onto the floor. With pistols stuck in their belts, most cops were reluctant to dance. Their wives didn't brood over this; they wanted to dance with Coen. Blue Eyes had to leave the table. The "crows" were giving him murderous looks. One by one the wives embraced him. The accordionist had prepared a spicy Hebrew song for the Hands of Esau and Irish jigs for the Holy Rood of Catholic cops. The wives interrupted his melodies. They demanded something slow. Coen went from fox-trot to fox-trot. He couldn't tire the wives. They forced him to change partners in the middle of a dip. The constant scrub of skin gave Coen an unfortunate erection. The wives seized upon such vulnerabilities to dance up close to Blue Eyes. The husbands grew exceedingly grim. They were taking mental target practice at the Neptune Manor, popping Coen's pretty ears and pretty mouth. Blue Eyes was intolerable to them. These men trudged through their tours of duty worrying about the spies the First Deputy had planted in their stationhouses; they didn't have to see Isaac's angel bumping with their wives.

The haberdasher's bride must have sensed Coen's desperation. She got up, holding pieces of gown with a fist, to cut in on the wives and lure them away from Coen. But she hadn't reckoned on the delicacy of Coen's lines, the touch of a fingernail in her palm, the feel of an embarrassed prick. Her face began to erupt, blotches glowing under her veil. She sucked her own spit to distract herself. The haberdasher was mortified. His Anita danced two feet from him with her wrists unfurled. The creases in her back were unmistakable. Anita was bending to Coen. The haberdasher sought his father-in-law with narrowed cheeks. Cowboy didn't idle at the wedding table; he'd been plotting Coen's downfall from the beginning of the fox-trot. Barney knew a grocer in Bath Beach, a kind Italian boy, who might be willing to shut Coen's eyes for a hundred dollars. The grocer came with a guarantee; he wouldn't accept a penny if he should happen to fail.

But the wedding hall was brushed by a miracle; Coen's prick went down. Anita bent away from him. She kept a few inches between Blue Eyes and herself. Her fierce complexion dwindled under the veil. Soon she could have her native coloring again. Coen escorted her to the table, the commissioners clapping feebly for the bride. The haberdasher was having evil thoughts about his wedding night. Blue Eyes sat with his nose in the silverware, determined not to peek at Anita's veil. Barney could politick with wedding guests now that sweetheart Coen had his dancing shoes under the table. The waiters were coming; little feathers of steam rose off the turkey breasts, which had their own potato balls and a gulley of peas.

Isaac enjoyed Sunday afternoons at Centre Street when the commissioner's rooms weren't swollen with detectives and boyish cops who served as runners and secretaries. He could poke through half-deserted halls without confronting dignitaries, or FBI men, and visiting inspectors from the London murder squad and the French Sûreté; just Sunday cops, like Isaac himself, who were married to their notebooks and their shields, and who loved the smell of dark woodwork, and the comforts of a sinking building: Headquarters was falling into the ground at the rate of two inches every five years. Stanchions had been put around the building to shore it up, and the city engineers claimed they could retard the sinkage by almost an inch.

Isaac ducked under the stanchions, which clung to Headquarters like an enormous iron skirt, passed through a tight front door (Headquarters had to screen its enemies and its friends), and paused at the security booth; the guard, who worked in Brooklyn the rest of the week, sat behind a bulletproof cage. This Sunday man had a shrewdness for picking girls off the street. He would babble to them as they stood outside the cage, their tits against the green bulletproof glass. Phinney, the Sunday man, was too discreet to invite them into the booth. There was a girl with him now. Isaac could only see one side of her face. Her legs were bare under her pea coat. The stretch of her calves appealed to Isaac, but he couldn't understand how any girl could go without socks in the middle of February. He saluted the guard. Phinney said, "Good afternoon, Chief," with a cowlike smile. Isaac could afford to be lax with him. The Irish Mafia would rush to communion after Barney's wedding: Headquarters was free of commissioners.

Isaac went upstairs. The duty sergeant who belonged to Commissioner O'Roarke was sleeping on a bench. Isaac wouldn't disturb him. He closed his office door with a soft pull of the knob. He was going to play back several tapes a stoolie of his had prepared of cops shaking down a supermarket. He sat behind his desk searching for spools. He stabbed his fingers in a drawer, but Isaac wouldn't howl out his pain. He could swear his desk had begun to shiver. A loud crump, like the pop of paper bags in his skull, catapulted Isaac off his chair. The window was shitting glass. Isaac had his cheek in the wall. Shock waves came up through the floor, thick patterns of congested air that shoved smoke into Isaac's mouth. He crawled out of the room, spitting up phlegm and crumbled plaster. Splits had developed in the ceiling. The walls had turned to bark.

The duty sergeant was under his bench. His head emerged to glower at Isaac, whose scalp was mostly white (the Chief hadn't shaken off the plaster). "Mercy, Isaac, it's happened. The building's caved in. Will they get to us, Chief? Will they be able to tunnel us out?"

The sergeant's delirium made Isaac smile. "Relax, Malone. It will be an easy rescue. We couldn't have sunk more than a thousand feet." The sergeant drew his head all the way in. Isaac felt ashamed. "Malone? I'm sorry . . . it was a small bomb. It must have gone off in the bathroom under my office."

Malone didn't move his head. "Isaac, could it be those crazy Puerto Ricans, or the Black Liberation boys? Were they trying to bury a few cops alive?"

"No, no, that kiss was meant for me."

Isaac ran down to the next floor. He walked into the bathroom with a handkerchief over his face. A pea coat had been dropped under the sink. Isaac called himself a dummy and a toad; he should have stared harder at that girl without her stockings. Phinney couldn't have brought her into Headquarters. The girl was using him. He had a better view of her face. It was bitten with glass and burnt powder. He couldn't find her underwear. She'd come to Isaac in a pea coat, moccasins, and skin. Three cracked mayonnaise jars were near the body. It took Isaac time to sniff the jars before he noticed that one of the girl's arms had been ripped off in the blast.

Two men charged into the bathroom wearing helmets, hard aprons, asbestos jump suits, and gigantic terry cloth gloves. They were members of the bomb squad stationed at the Police Academy. Isaac stepped in front of them. "You can go home," he said. "The case is closed. You'll hear about it in my report."

Both helmets muttered "Fuck you" at Isaac. This was their turf. No one could tell them they were intruders at a bombing. They had to sift through the debris.

Isaac mentioned his name and then shouted into the asbestos

hats. "I have the First Dep's warranty. If you touch a piece of glass, if you disturb anything, I'll have your tongues burned."

The men shrugged behind their aprons. They couldn't wrestle Isaac the Pure with terry cloth gloves. They peeked at the dead girl's crotch and walked out, uninterested in a dismembered arm. Phinney, the Sunday man, was crouching by the stairs, his face gone sallow. He called into the bathroom, frightened to step inside. "Isaac, who is that stupid girl?"

"A lollipop, Esther Rose."

"She said she had to go pee . . . I didn't . . . Isaac, how should I know she was smuggling hot ones under her coat?"

"Phinney, you fucked yourself. Headquarters isn't a public piss pot. Nobody's supposed to get up those stairs. They'll wire you to the ceiling and bleed your pension out of your ears."

Phinney chewed on a knuckle. "What should I tell them, Isaac? Gimme a story, please."

"It takes a clever man to lie, Phinney. You tell the truth. Now shut up and get back to your post. Cowboy's only a river away. There'll be a hundred cops on our heads any minute."

TEN

Marilyn had difficulties sustaining her new bachelorhood. There was more than one woman in her father's house. Isaac had brought his "fiancée" to Rivington Street. He couldn't have Ida Stutz prowling in her own flat when Rupert Weil could attack a fire escape. So the three of them had to blow air in two small rooms. The girls couldn't get along. Marilyn tried. But Ida was fidgety around an educated girl. She grew ashamed of her sweat, and the bits of cheese that always fell into her hair while she was making blintzes at the restaurant. Her body seemed like a miserable article next to Marilyn's fine elbows and goyisher ribs. Ida sniffled into the cheese; she wanted to throw her head in a tub of barley soup and drown.

Marilyn could only relax after Isaac and his "fiancée" went to work. Then she had Rivington Street to herself. She would bathe in the afternoon, scratch her fingernails, consider the veins in her hand. She missed Blue Eyes. But if she connived behind her father's back and rushed uptown to Coen, she'd ruin his chances with Isaac and the First Dep. Marilyn sensed her father's vindictiveness. Isaac was jealous of Coen.

As Isaac's bachelor daughter, she shared the toilet with an old man across the hall. This old man hogged the facilities. A bachelor himself, he despised any woman who peed sitting down. Marilyn had to flush the toilet after him; he was much too squeamish to touch the plunger attached to the water box. She might have avoided the bachelor altogether if he had bothered to close the toilet door. He would sit with his pants bunched around a nail over his head, bang his raw knees with a fist, and sing outrageous songs through the door, courtship songs, Marilyn imagined, because of the bachelor's feverish intonation. She had no other clue. The songs wouldn't cohere into a language Marilyn understood; he seemed to chirp scraps of English, Yiddish, and Hungarian. Marilyn had little desire to tease out their intent.

This morning, desperate to pee, she stumbled into the toilet. She swerved to miss colliding with the bachelor's knees. Her bosoms struck the wall. "Christ," she said. He sat clicking his teeth, with an incredible red prick that rose out of his belly to serenade an Irish-Jewish girl. Marilyn wanted Coen.

Not even the PC could get Isaac away from his desk. His subordinates were baffled by Isaac's foul mood. A lollipop who sabotaged herself couldn't hurt him. Isaac was a hero. Hadn't he survived Esther's homemade bombs, concoctions in mayonnaise jars? What did the Chief have to mourn?

Isaac sat for hours without a sign of slackness in his heavy cheeks. He wouldn't humor his men. They were part of the rubber-gun squad, former "angels" of Isaac's who had suffered the ultimate humiliation: they had their .45s snatched from them by the PC because of overzealousness in the street. The medical bureau accused them of being trigger crazy. They'd shot off too many noses, it seems. Now they clerked for Isaac. They were sensitive to each little shift in Isaac's character, to his porcupine scalp, those rigid patches behind his ears that betrayed his anxiousness. What could the Chief be waiting for?

The phone rang around three in the afternoon. The rubber-gun squad watched Isaac's scalp unbridle; these men had grown psychic about the noises a telephone could make. Isaac put his tongue near the mouthpiece. "Hello?"

"Is this Isaac the Pure?"

The air blew out of Isaac's cheeks, leaving them soft.

"I'm calling about Esther Rose. You killed her, you pimp. She brought you soup, and you had to throw her on top of a shithill."

"Some soup," Isaac said. "It came in a funny jar. Rupert, where are you?"

"Wouldn't you like to know? Isaac, did she cry when you tortured her? Or did she spit in your policeman's face?"

"Rupert, we have to talk. I'll meet you anywhere you say."

The rubber-gun boys were scrambling to monitor Rupert's call. The Chief warned them away from the sound equipment with a wag of his jaw. They couldn't believe Isaac would cow to a lollipop.

"Was it the pretty blond detective who took care of Esther's arm? I'll fix him too."

"Blue Eyes? He never saw Esther Rose. Rupert, stay off the street. Some grim Italian boys are looking for you."

"Isaac, you trying to hold me while your technicians trace me to a telephone booth? Forget about it. I'm signing off."

"You're overrating us, Rupert. The FBI untangles wires, not us. We're primitive men."

"You'll be primitive sooner than you think. I'll play with your jawbone. I'll soak your teeth in pickled water. I'll send your guts to Headquarters, C.O.D. You'll be remembered, Isaac. You'll wish to God you hadn't fucked with Esther. Goodbye."

Isaac held a cold telephone in his lap. The rubber-gun squad shied away from him. The Chief was in the middle of a brainstorm. The medical examiner and the fingerprint boys who dusted the mayonnaise jars had given him nothing beyond the fact of Esther's immolation. Isaac had to scratch with his thumbs. Careless girls don't leave their coats under a sink. Esther's nakedness cut into the easy theory of an accidental death. Did she love to finger bombs without her clothes? Who'd believe a girl would want to die with Isaac? He hoped Rupert would reveal Esther to him. The boy's instructions were slow. Rupert turned Isaac into a murderer.

He'd sent Coen deep into Brooklyn to interview Esther's family. Coen barely got out alive. The Spagnuolos cursed him and attacked him with their fingernails. They disclaimed any knowledge of Esther. Isaac wasn't satisfied. He'd dealt with stranger Jews than these. Hadn't he made the tzaddik of Williamsburg smile? He'd danced with Hasidim in a synagogue that was bigger than a soccer field. So Isaac went searching for Esther. He took Brodsky along. Isaac wouldn't have sought company in Manhattan or the Bronx, where he could determine any street with his nose. But Brooklyn was a second Arabia, uncrossable for Isaac without a limousine, a desert of contradicting neighborhoods, murderous, soft, with pockets of air that could drive chills through a cop's sturdy drawers. Isaac found Esther's people in a block of private houses near Gravesend and Coney Island Creek. He wasn't invited inside. A man in a skullcap who could have been Esther's father, uncle, or older brother (his twitching eyebrows and pendulous ears made his age impossible to tell) came out to greet Isaac with a butcher knife. Isaac backed off the sidewalk, disenchanted with Sephardic Jews. He signaled to Brodsky, wiggling at Manhattan with a fist.

Now he was calling for Brodsky again. Isaac wanted the morgue at Bellevue. The rubber-gun squad crammed his raincoat with a fresh supply of pencils (the Chief liked to scribble on his rides with Brodsky). The chauffeur had a glum look. He preferred to keep away from hospitals and morgues. Isaac wasn't trying to push Brodsky towards a ghoulish medical examiner. The Chief was after Esther's body. The Spagnuolos had left her in a city icebox, unclaimed. If the Hands of Esau refused to bury a Jewish lollipop on society grounds (Barney Rosenblatt had the power to stall Isaac's request), he would fish for a grave out of his own pocket, a grave with a legitimate marker.

The morgue attendant was coy with Isaac. He swore on his life that Esther had disappeared. "Isaac, you have the authority. Tear down the walls. The coroner's afraid of the First Dep. But you won't find shit. The girl was picked up."

"Did they row her out to Ward's Island on the paupers' run?"

The thought of Esther being dumped in a potter's field maddened Isaac. It was gruesome to him. A grave would be turned out every ten or twenty years to accommodate a different crop of bones.

The attendant smiled. "Isaac, it wasn't Ward's Island. Somebody signed for her."

"Show me the release, you scumbag."

The attendant returned with a long card.

"Was it a relative?" Isaac muttered.

"No, it says 'admirer.'"

"What's the admirer's name? . . . could it be Rupert?"

The attendant squinted at the card. "Isaac, it aint so clear. One word. It begins with a Z."

"Zorro," Brodsky said, with sudden illumination, his chin in the attendant's shoulder.

The attendant curled his eyes. "Isaac, you can't trick the morgue. Who's Zorro?"

"One of the Guzmann boys." The cemetery was in Bronxville, where the Guzmanns had a family plot. Checking with another attendant, Isaac discovered that Zorro Guzmann had snatched Esther's body only two hours ago. He rushed out of the morgue.

Brodsky fumbled behind the Chief. "Isaac, it makes no sense. What could the Guzmanns do with a lollipop? Are they planning to revive her? Will they sell her in the street?"

A tribe of Marranos from Peru, pickpockets, thieves, and pimps, the Guzmanns had settled in the Bronx, becoming the policy bankers of Boston Road; they thrived amid Latinos, poor Irishers, blacks, and ancient Jews. Isaac hadn't concerned himself with their penny plays. But the tribe was beginning to infest Manhattan. The Guzmanns would kidnap young girls from the Port Authority and auction them to local whorehouses. Isaac meant to squeeze the tribe out of his borough. The lollipops were slowing him down. He could no longer concentrate on grubby pimps.

The chauffeur took him to Bronxville. The Guzmann burial ground was a hummock of frozen grass. Three old men stood shivering over a fresh scar in the hummock. They were expert mourners. The Guzmanns had hired them to wail for Esther. They wore the caftans of a chief rabbi, only each of them came with a pectoral cross. Zorro was with them, in a checkered overcoat. Brodsky nudged the Chief with a loud cackle. "Isaac, should I throw him down the hill? Let these old men mourn for Zorro while they're here. One tap on the head, and you can close the Guzmann case. Zorro won't have a brain left."

Isaac pointed to a man on the other side of the hummock, a man without Zorro's penchant for clothes; he had earmuffs from a Bronx variety store, a scarf as mottled as a hankie, a thickness of sweaters, overalls that ballooned in the seat and stopped just below the calf, galoshes that wouldn't buckle. His nostrils were flat, and he had a forehead that was uncommonly wide.

"Do me a favor, Brodsky. Whisper your threats from now on. That's Jorge over there. Zorro's big brother. Bullets can't touch him. He had elephant skin. He'll shovel dirt in our eyes if we move on

Zorro. So be nice."

Isaac walked up to Zorro Guzmann (César was his baptismal name) without a hand in his pocket, so Jorge wouldn't misinterpret Isaac's peaceful signs and come galloping down the hummock with squeaky galoshes and his earmuffs askew. Zorro had mud on his pigskin shoes. His coat of many colors turned orange in the afternoon. Isaac tried not to stare at Zorro's dainty feet.

"Zorro, since when does Papa interest himself in the affairs of a Yeshiva girl? Brooklyn isn't your borough."

"Isaac, you calling my father illiterate? He reads the *Daily News*. The girl's a Ladina, isn't she? You think my father's going to allow her to sleep in an unholy grave? Not when she's a Spanish Jew. You see those criers on the hill? The holy men. They've been cursing Esther's mother and father since two o'clock."

"That's a touching story, but are you sure Papa isn't sanctifying Esther because she tried to murder me?"

"Isaac, don't blaspheme in a graveyard. My father's a religious man. He doesn't care if you live or die."

"Good for him. Zorro, I respect your family. I never interfered with Guzmann business on Boston Road. So take the wax out of your ear. Manhattan's not for you. The cockroaches have a nasty sting."

"Isaac, I can't even spell Manhattan. Why would I go there to live?"

Isaac was finished with obligatory advice. He had plans to shred Zorro's spectacular coat. He would push the Guzmanns into a sewer once he caught those fish in Manhattan.

"César, aren't you going to ask me about Blue Eyes?"

Zorro dug the earth with the pigskin on his feet. "Don't say blue. Blue is a filthy color in my religion. Isaac, teach yourself some history. All the magistrates used to wear blue cloaks in Portugal and Spain six hundred years ago. Can't you figure? A dark color could prevent the stink of a Jew from poisoning their armpits."

"Did your father tell you that?"

"No, I learnt it from my brothers."

Zorro's four brothers, Alejandro, Topal, Jorge, and Jerónimo, were Bronx wisemen who couldn't read the letters off a street sign, or manage the intricacies of a revolving door. Jerónimo, the oldest, slept in a crib.

"César, you still haven't asked me about Coen?"

"There's nothing to ask. Manfred flew from Papa's candy store.

He made his nest with you."

Coen had been raised on Boston Road, where Papa Guzmann maintained his empire under the cover of egg creams and soft candy. It was Papa who shoved Coen's parents towards suicide, controlling them with little gifts of money until the miserable egg store they had came into Papa's hands.

Zorro edged away from Isaac. He was in Bronxville at his father's bidding, to put an unwanted Ladina under frozen grass, with three Christian rabbis in attendance, hovering over the Guzmanns' sacred mound. "Isaac, this is a funeral. I can't talk no more."

Isaac trudged with Brodsky down from the cemetery. The chauffeur spied at Jorge Guzmann from the corner of his sleeve; he was baffled that a moron with open galoshes could frighten the Chief.

"Please, Isaac, lemme pop this Jorge once behind the ear. We'll see what flows out, water, piss, or blood."

The Chief closed Brodsky's face with a horrible scowl. He wasn't looking for company. He sat at the back of the car. He could have taken off Brodsky's lip with the heat spilling from both his eyes. "Esther," he muttered. He was sick of a world of lollipops.

ELEVEN

A girl could go crazy smelling pot cheese in her father's refrigerator. Stuck between Isaac and his "fiancée," Marilyn fell to brooding over the conditions of her past and present life: Sarah Lawrence, three husbands, pot cheese, and Rivington Street in seven years. She had to get free of blintzes and Ida Stutz. Marilyn needed Blue Eyes, but her father had stolen him away. She put on her winter coat, locked Isaac's door, and went into the street. There was no escaping Isaac. They nodded to her at the matzoh factory, at the appetizing store with prunes in the window, at the Hungarian bakery with its crusts of dark bread that could cure widows and divorcées of constipation, boils, or the gout.

"Hello, Miss Sidel. Tell me, how's the Chief today? Honey, don't be bashful. Take a piece of strudel for your father and yourself. Please. Why shove a pocketbook in my face? It's too early in the morning to cash a ten-dollar bill."

The whole fucking East Side was her father's house. She had to shop in Little Italy if she wanted to stay alive. In her father's territories no one would allow her to pay for her goods. A block from Rivington Street she was loaded down with packages. She had strudel, whole wheat matzohs, salt sticks, and pumpkin seeds. She walked to Bummy's on East Broadway, where she could get some relief from Isaac's worshipers. At Bummy's her father was despised.

Marilyn ordered a whiskey sour with two stabs of lemon and a lick of salt. She knew about the old crook that worked in Bummy's kitchen, one-eyed Gulavitch, maimed by her father. Isaac had poked his knuckles in Gula's eye. She wondered if the old crook might revenge himself on her. But she couldn't see into the kitchen.

Bummy Gilman came over to her stool. He was perturbed about having a skinny girl with tits in his bar. A cunt like Marilyn could bring trouble to him. Isaac was capable of wrecking any bar.

"Bummy, don't frown," she said. "I'm not Isaac's messenger. I didn't come with greetings from him."

"Marilyn, who's calling you a stoolpigeon? Not me." He shouted to the barman. "George, this lady needs more ice in her glass."

The barman arrived with a cylinder of ice. Then he withdrew to his station, fingering the buttons on his red jacket. Bummy left Marilyn to whisper in the barman's ear. "George, keep her busy. If she asks for apple pie, give it to her."

The barman licked his teeth. "God, would I love to get into that."

"Forget it, George. She's poison. Her father has terrific hands. He could pull your nose off with half a finger. She's a dragon lady. I wouldn't lie."

Bummy strolled into his kitchen, searching for Gula One Eye. Gula was crouching over the potato bin. He could flick warts off a potato faster than a Marrano pickpocket from the Bronx could reach inside your pants. "Gula," Bummy said with a cackle. "Would you like to get laid?"

"Bummy, you shouldn't joke," Gulavitch said, climbing off the bin.

"Sweetheart, you know who's sitting out there with her legs crossed? Isaac's daughter. She's itching for you."

"Let her itch."

"At least make her a present. You lost an eye. Get it back from her."

"That's no good," Gulavitch said. "What's she done? I'll pay

Isaac, not the girl."

Bummy couldn't argue with a feeble-minded crook. He returned to George. His head was boiling with images of Isaac. The Chief owned East Broadway. Bummy had to dance with the big Jewish bear at Headquarters, curtsy to Isaac, or move his bar to Brooklyn. He was sick of it. "George, you got the green light. The dragon lady's all yours. Take her. I don't care. But watch yourself. She bruises. If Isaac ever catches your thumb marks on her skin, you're a dead man."

George stroked one of his red cuffs. "Bummy, leave it to me."

Bummy sat down near his register, fingering yesterday's receipts, as he watched the barman sweet-talk Marilyn the Wild. He had to marvel at George's abilities. The barman waltzed with his thumbs on Marilyn's ass before Bummy could finish the receipts. There was a little arena behind the bar where Bummy staged dog fights for special customers, or an occasional burlesque show (the girls who took off their clothes at Bummy's place were borrowed from Zorro Guzmann). The arena became a dance floor whenever Bummy was short of bulldogs and Zorro's girls.

Marilyn went into the arena with George. She couldn't get by on whiskey sours and salt under her lip. She needed some sweat and male companionship to ease her off Rivington Street and the color of Coen's eyes. She wasn't solemn about a cock in the furls of her groin. She knew what it meant to dance with George. She didn't intercept the track of his wrist. George liked to cuddle with a finger in her underpants, and Sinatra on Bummy's phonograph machine. "Baby," he said, "come home with me."

Silences couldn't discourage him. George was a patient barman. He ran for Bummy's keys. "Bummy, it's open house. I can tell." His hands were trembling. "I swear, she's three yards wide."

Bummy gave him the keys to the bedroom he maintained over the bar. It was a retreat for his customers, who could romance one of Zorro's burlesque queens without having to abandon East Broadway. George led Marilyn through the kitchen, where she could peek at Gula and his potato bin (the bin had deep sides, and was very, very dark), and marched her up Bummy's private staircase. He undressed her, with the keys in the door, piling her skirt and blouse on a chair. He was much more fastidious about his own red jacket, which he refused to stick on a hanger in Bummy's closet until both shoulders were aligned. He wore garters around his knees, and a truss to keep his hernia in place. George had no pubic hair. Marilyn saw a lump, shaped like a pea, at the top of George's thigh, when the truss came off. He kissed her with his garters on. His plucked crotch had an itchy feel. He pushed her down into Bummy's queen-sized bed, the hernia traveling along the wedges in his thigh.

Marilyn wasn't spooked by a pea sliding under some skin. A man with a hernia might have made her into a passionate girl, only George was too gruff. He climbed on Marilyn, with his garters scratching her legs, and forced his way in. She didn't complain. She hadn't come to Bummy's for a tea party. She had whiskey in her lungs. She endured the rub of garters, and George's mean little plunges. She couldn't even hold him by the ears to catch a piece of his rhythm. He wouldn't lower his head. His orgasm was like a snarl. He climbed off Marilyn, hitched up the belts of his truss, and brought his jacket out of the closet. "I'm in a rush," he said. "Bummy needs me . . . he gets lonely when I'm away from the bar."

Marilyn stayed in bed. She didn't want to creep downstairs too soon and suck on a maraschino cherry. Whiskey sours would turn her against Coen. She fought her bitterness by grabbing Bummy's lavender sheets. Jesus, Joseph, and Mary, if Blue Eyes wouldn't come inside her, she could always look for George.

She got dressed finally, retrieving her stuff from the chair. She couldn't find a washcloth in Bummy's room, so she walked out with milk on her thigh. "Being a spinster isn't so bad. I'll survive without Manfred Coen." She wasn't nervous about the kitchen. Gulavitch could have her neck to play with. She'd help him drive his thumbs into her windpipe. Gula called her over to the bin. "Missy, I got a potato face for you."

He'd carved a warty potato with his nails. The face had nostrils, ears, lips, and a pair of warts for eyes. Gula made a sloping chin. and the depressions of a widow's peak, giving the potato the twisted features of a penitent. Marilyn wasn't put off by somber details. The potato was a kindness to her. She had a fit of blubbering, ravaged by the markings on a lopsided face. The gift had an urgency no husband could bring. Gula must have seen the mad streak in her when she crossed the kitchen with George. Was he telling her with the potato, Missy, you aint alone? She could have screamed, "Blue balls and father shit," into Gula's chest without feeling ashamed. He drew a rag out of his sleeve for Marilyn. She wiped her eyes with it.

"Don't sit at the bar. Bummy's a cocksucker. Nobody loves you here. Tell your father Gula One Eye fucks him in the nose."

"I will, Mr. Gulavitch. I promise."

And she sailed out of the kitchen with the rag in her fist, passing Bummy, who mocked the ratty glide of her skirt, and George, who cursed her for inflaming the lump in his groin. Marilyn didn't care. She grabbed her packages off the stool, the matzohs and the pumpkin seeds, and left East Broadway.

TWELVE

Rupert clawed Esther's furniture and artifacts, a broken chair, a pincushion used by Spagnuolo seamstresses, ribbons from her Yeshiva days, tampons in a candy box, pieces of colored chalk, assorted chemicals, and a crusted pot, all the worldly goods she had brought with her to the tenement on Suffolk Street, Esther's last address. Rupert was hungry to curse her. His fingers mauled the pincushion. The ribbons disintegrated after a few pulls. The chalk bled green and yellow against his palms. He couldn't say the word "bitch."

Why had he been so dumb about the ingredients in Esther's pot? She must have stolen a recipe from *The Anarchist Cookbook*. Stinky Rupert forgot how to smell a bomb. Did Esther invent a woolly fuse? Ignite her jars with Tampax? Or did Isaac nab her at the door, bite her tits, throw her in a room, and supply the match? Such sequences weren't Rupert's concern. However Esther died, he would pinch Isaac soon as he could.

It was the Chinese New Year, the Year of the Swan, and Rupert had a prior commitment. He intended to free Stanley Chin. With Esther thick in his skull, a hard, bitter longing that nudged him with mad ideas (was it kosher to fuck a dead girl?), shaking him with impressions of her, mind and body, that could unhinge him any minute, he planned his attack on St. Bartholomew's. He would tear out the throats of detectives and nurses who got in his way. He would take the prisoner on a piggyback ride, ferry him to Chinatown (Rupert could wink across a river), so Stanley could celebrate the New Year in a Chinese café.

Rupert first met him at Seward Park, where they were freshmen together. Stanley was a muscle boy, a bill collector for Chinese merchants and landlords, and a bodyguard belonging to the Pell

Street Republican Club. It was the futility of Republicans in Chinatown that impressed Rupert: Stanley Chin always picked the losing side. He was a boy from Hong Kong, in love with barbells, American cigarettes, and Bruce Lee. He could crumble bricks with his teeth, kick through a wall, smash the legs of a table, until the Snapping Dragons of Pell Street, Stanley's old gang, sent him to St. Bartholomew's with crippled fingers and toes. Rupert felt responsible; he had drawn Stanley out of Chinatown, recruited him to his own brittle cause, the dismantling of Issac, and introduced him to Esther Rose.

Gorillas from Mulberry Street were cruising Rupert's neighborhood with firm instructions in their heads. Amerigo Genussa of the Garibaldi social club had warned them not to return to Little Italy without some token off the body of Rupert Weil; an ear, a fingernail, a Jewish bellybutton, anything that would leave him incapacitated for the next ten years. Rupert could see them in their long gray coats, huddling on Suffolk Street while they blew between their knuckles to soften a chill that was murderously close. A rotten wind off the Bowery must have pushed them onto Rupert's heels. He had no respect for gorillas. The idea of bullying for profit was loathsome to him. He would have hurled Esther's chair off the fire escape, watched it float down on top of their brains, if he hadn't been in such a rush.

He climbed out of a cellar window at the back of the house. The gorillas could blow air for the rest of their lives; the snot would have to freeze in their noses before they could find Rupert Weil. He ran to the pickle factory on Broome. The merchants had lit a small fire on the premises to keep their pickles warm. The brine coming off the barrels stuck to Rupert's heart. He would have liked to soak his ears in a barrel. A fat man snorted at him with obvious disgruntlement. It was Tony Brill. The journalist had been waiting near the pickles for an hour.

"Gimme," Rupert said.

"First talk. What did it feel like beating on Isaac's mother?"

Rupert glowered at the journalist. "It didn't feel. We had to smoke out Isaac. That was the necessary thing."

"Did you enjoy it?"

"You a creep?" Rupert said.

"But you almost killed her."

"Na. She fell. She hit her head. That wasn't us . . . listen, it's not so hard to kill when you got Isaac for a teacher."

The journalist removed a collection of dollar bills from his pocket, twenty singles that he'd borrowed from his landlady and his current employer, an underground newspaper called *The Toad*. "Now tell me your story," he said, his tongue twisting in his mouth. "All of it. You, Esther, and Stanley Chin."

Rupert said, "Tomorrow."

Spit leaked off the journalist's face. "Are you crazy? Are you insane? It could snow tomorrow. I could die of the flu. Money talks. I'll take the story, or the twenty bills go back to me."

Rupert was halfway to Ludlow Street. "You'll get it," he shouted, the dollars squeezed inside his fist.

The journalist was trying to keep up with him. "Rupert, do you ever dream about Isaac's mother?"

"Only when my stomach is empty."

"How often is that?"

"Every other night."

Stanley Chin couldn't have lunch or dinner without two detectives at his side. These gentlemen ate his stewed prunes. Stanley ignored the nurses' harping about the state of his bowels. He was their favorite prisoner; the nurses of St. Bartholomew's could adore a delinquent with a beautiful face. But his bowels shrank after detectives Murray and John told him Sunday's news: the Jew girl, Esther Rose, had eaten powerful mayonnaise at Headquarters; the medical examiners had tweezed her eyebrows off the wall. The detectives poked behind their ears. They worked for Big Jew Rosenblatt, but they wouldn't cry for Esther Rose. They'd handcuff this China boy to the bed if they had to. They were expecting Blue Eyes. Isaac had to send his "angels" down to kidnap Stanley Chin. The Chief was losing face.

Stanley was beholden to detectives Murray and John; he couldn't reach very far with fingers stuck in plaster mittens. So Murray, John, or a nurses had to put the water glass against his lip, change his pajamas, turn the radio on and off, take itchy mattress hairs off his leg. The detectives noticed Stanley was in a rotten mood. He hadn't asked them to scratch his back once during their last three shifts. His biceps were growing haggard. The ropes of muscle in his neck had gone to sleep. He had Esther in his guts.

It was no puppy love, the passion of a Hong Kong boy for a girl with white skin, an Anglo from Brooklyn, an ordinary "round eyes." It had nothing to do with pale colors. Esther was darker than him. She had sweat in her armpits, a generous damp run from her shoulders to her elbows that made Stanley sneeze a lot. She couldn't have enticed him with her frizzy hair. And it wasn't her religious training (he'd never heard of Yeshivas before Esther Rose). It was a clutter of things; the throaty rasp of her voice, the way she rolled her sleeves, her ability to argue ancient and medieval philosophies (Esther knew the lore of five or six Arab priests), the grab of her nipples under her one dark shirt, the shape of her toes, the sores she had on her arms and knees from painting ceilings with chalk, the chalkings themselves, lashes of color that exemplified bitter mouths, long tongues, and hard, swollen genitals that grew and twitched without relief. The horrors Esther manufactured on a ceiling or a wall comforted Stanley; they were shriekings he felt inside his own head.

He'd been dreaming of Esther with a pill the nurses had stuck in his mouth, a yellow thing that he would soon squash under his tongue, when he saw a wizard come into the room, a wizard with bony ears, in a St. Bartholomew orderly's coat a size too small, pushing a wheelchair with his sleeves. The wizard steered around the detectives' triple-tone shoes. "Pardon me," he said. Detective Murray didn't care for the orderly's tight cheeks, but he wouldn't contradict hospital rules.

The wizard smiled. "Therapy room. Help me get him off the mattress."

Detective John raised the slats of Stanley's hospital bed, and the two detectives sat him down in the wheelchair with a soft push. John growled at the orderly. "You be careful with Stan. We want him back alive." Then his natural suspicion came out. "Hey sonny, what floor's this therapy room on?"

The wizard started to pull the chair. "It's on the roof. By the solarium."

Stanley was giggling before they arrived at the door. "Rupert, where'd you get the outfit, man?"

"Quiet," Rupert said, wheeling him into the corridor. "I stole it from a laundry closet."

"What about the chair?" Stanley said, shaking the armrests.

"That I got from the nurses' station."

"Out of sight . . . Rupe, the detectives in there, they would've shot your face off if they figured you was Rupert the lollipop. They got no brains. But they were nice to me."

They found a ramp that took them to the main floor. Rupert ordered nurses and hospital men about. His official gruffness seemed to cut through the illogic of a boy leaving St. Bartholomew's in a wheelchair, with plaster on his fingers and toes, and pajamas. Rupert spilt him into a taxi cab by angling the wheelchair against the door. The cabby wanted to fold the wheelchair for the boys. "Leave it," Rupert muttered. They bumped across the flatlands of Corona. The exhilaration was gone. Thinking of Esther, the boys grew morose.

The cab was alive with static that rubbed off Stanley's knees; he couldn't snuggle into the upholstery without suffering little electrical shocks. Rupert seemed strange to him with sunken jaws. Up to a month ago he'd been Stanley's pudgy messiah. It was torture for Stanley to read a book (the English alphabet made him gag), but Rupert could pull meanings out of any text. He chased off instructors at Seward Park with his deliberations on Coleridge, Karl Marx, and Shakespeare's corpse. The world was suicidal for Rupert. He got Stanley to sense the polarities between Manhattan and Hong Kong. The rich climb higher, Rupert said, and the poor shake like roaches at the bottom of the can. They squeeze one another and die. Stanley tried to resist Rupert's attitude. "How you know Hong Kong?" he said. "You been there, Rupe?" The messiah sucked on his cheeks, which were fatter at the time.

"Schmuck, I want Hong Kong I look at you."

Stanley could have broken Rupert's ear. He could have taken off a nose with one hooked finger. He could have severed Rupert from his scalp, Indian-style, by pushing at the temples until this messiah felt the burn in his skull. He respected bookishness too much. He kept his fingers out of Rupert's face.

The messiah didn't fail. He discovered a locus for his cause: Isaac Sidel. The Chief had come back to Seward Park on Career Day to give the key address. Rupert pointed to the stitching on the great man's sleeve (Isaac wore his Riverdale coat). "There's the cunt who rules us all." Isaac sang about opportunity, about the openness of his Headquarters to fresh ideas, about the job of a detective in New York; he brought the pretty boy with him. He paraded Coen. The girls ogled in their seats. Blue Eyes was asked to show his gun. Rupert and Stanley shrank down inside their row. The venom passed from boy to boy; their tongues were raw.

The cab couldn't make it to Chinatown. Mott Street was clogged with celebrants. So they had to disembark on Canal. Rupert lent his body as a crutch. Stanley could only take short hops on his mittened toes. They approached Mott from Bayard Street. Firecrackers roared around their ears, puffing their faces with smoke and impossible noise. Rupert shivered with the deafness that invaded his head. Street dancers, wearing dragon masks with molded eyes and horns that reached the fire escapes, slithered behind the boys forcing them into johnny pumps and the windows of fruit and vegetable shops. They laughed at the banners of the Pell Street Republican Club, honoring the New Year with slogans that had been shot through with cherry bombs.

With Rupert crouching low, they picked their way across the gutter and landed at the New Territories tea parlor, a hangout for gentlemen from Hong Kong. Rupert had to shove a bit. He seated Stanley at a counter decked with oranges and tangerines. No one smiled at the boys. Rupert began taking dollar bills out of his pocket. "Here," he said crushing the singles into Stanley's pajamas. "I got to split. We can't be ten blocks from Isaac's office. I don't need detectives sitting on my tail."

Stanley scowled at the mittens on his fingers. "I wish I could help you, Rupe . . . give Isaac an earache that wouldn't go 'way."

"Ah, forget about it. Isaac's my baby."

Stanley felt a touch on his shoulder, and Rupert was gone. He shook off images of Esther by ordering shrimp balls and bean curd soup in strict Cantonese. Watching the Hong Kong bachelors with their rice bowls next to their chins, he realized the futility of his situation. He couldn't hold a fork (chopsticks would have crashed into his lap). The shrimp balls arrived. Stanley wouldn't grovel with his face on the counter, licking under the dough for pieces of mashed shrimp. He couldn't even drop the shrimp balls into his soup. Gesturing ferociously with his mouth, he was able to steal a cigarette. He smoked, leaning into the counter, trapped on his stool. He couldn't have gotten to the door by himself.

A line of faces peered at him from the window. One by one the faces registered a grin. Stanley thought of whiskered cats. These boys had short hairs stuck on their chins. They were the Snapping Dragons. Joey, Sam, Sol, and Mary could have been the names of Yeshiva boys. That's how Stanley figured. With a stiff-legged walk, their bodies knifed into the New Territories café. The air turned thick with the fragrance of oranges and Hong Kong soap. The bachelors drew their knees together to accommodate the Snapping Dragons of Pell Street, who overturned napkin holders and mustard pots with a swish of their winter jerseys. The Dragons surrounded Stanley Chin.

"Aint this a trip. The man himself."

"How's it going, Big Stan? Do you still love all the 'round eyes'?"

"He looks sad without his lollipop."

Marv was the quiet one. He took a fork from the counter and scraped it against Stanley's thigh. The other three Dragons scrambled for silverware. Sam tried to force a shrimp ball down Stanley's throat. Joey fed soup inside the neck of Stanley's pajamas. They grabbed the dollar bills. Stanley had his weapons. He could whip at them with an elbow. He could rupture a Dragon with his teeth. But he couldn't maintain his balance. He fell off the stool going for Marvin's nose. The boys began to trample him. He had a heel in his kidneys. He was swallowing blood. Four Dragons stood on top of him. They they got off. He heard them say "Mother." The winter jerseys floated out of his reach. Somebody had frightened them away.

Stanley couldn't find who his savior was. He saw strings of oranges. He peeked right and left. The café floor nudged the bones in his skull. The bachelors were sloppy with their rice. His mittens were dirty. His mouth hurt. Soon he was muddled in overcoats. Three men had picked him up. They could only be cops. Even with blood in his nose he recognized Isaac's blue-eyed detective, Manfred Coen. This cop had a way of creeping into Stanley's life. Blue Eyes, Stanley wanted to say. Bubbles came out. Rupert hates you, Mr. Coen. Manfred wiped the blood with an embroidered handkerchief. Stanley bit down on the handkerchief to release the pressure in his nose. He didn't want to sneeze blood on a camel's hair coat. Blue Eyes had tender pinkies. He could massage a boy's skin under a bloody handkerchief.

THIRTEEN

Brodsky had been glowering at transvestites for the better part of an hour. He couldn't direct his rage at the Chief. Isaac scrounged on Times Square when he was due at Headquarters for a press conference to celebrate the recapture of Stanley Chin. Talk about sleuths. Isaac was the only cop at Headquarters who had the brains to guess where Stanley would run. A Chinese boy goes to Chinatown, Isaac announced, while Cowboy Rosenblatt had his tongue in his ass, shoving detectives through Brooklyn and Queens. Ten minutes after the dispatcher gave Isaac the news of Stanley's flight from St. Bartholomew's, a squad of "angels" led by Manfred Coen walked from Centre Street to Mott, scooped the lollipop out of a Chinese cafeteria, and delivered him to the prisoners' ward at Bellevue. And now Isaac the Just was sleepwalking on Eighth Avenue.

"Downtown, Isaac, that's where we belong. Why are you pussying up here?"

The Chief ignored him. He was looking for a girl. Honey Schapiro had fled the coop again, disappeared from Essex Street to rejoin her pimp. Isaac wasn't on an errand for her father now. Mordecai could play his own shepherd. Isaac wanted information from the girl. The Chief couldn't squeeze Esther out of his mind. Living with Ida and Marilyn in two congested rooms, he imagined Esther Rose sitting naked on a floor with her finger in a mayonnaise jar.

"Isaac, there she goes."

They trapped Honey Schapiro between two Cadillacs. She had eyelashes on with thick corrugations that couldn't have been contained in a fist. You could see the imprint of her crotch through the flimsy material of her skirt. "Screw," Honey said, seething at Isaac. "My father's man."

Five pimps, "players" in floppy hats and suede coats that brushed against their ankles, came down the block to rescue Honey. Ralph, her old protector, was one of them.

"Brother," he said, "why you annoying an innocent girl?" With four other "players" backing him up, Ralph could afford a touch of arrogance.

Brodsky interposed himself between Isaac and the "players." "This isn't a pinch. It's a friendly conversation between my Chief and Honey Schapiro. So walk away, or you'll lose your pimping hats."

Isaac snatched Honey up from the bumpers of the Cadillacs and deposited her on the sidewalk. "Tell me about Esther and Rupert Weil."

"Fuck you."

The "players" chortled under the protection of their hats.

"Honey, have you ever been to the Bronx juvenile house? The

lady wardens have ticklish thumbs. They turn girls into zombies. You'll wake up with a baldie head. The wardens like to explore with pliers. Do you know what it means to have a bleeding nipple?"

Honey was petrified. Her shoulders wagged.

"Give me Esther's pedigree . . . You must have grown up with Rupert. What's he like?"

Honey scratched around her eye. "What do you want from me? I never saw them get it down together. Rupe, he came out of the crib pretty weird. With a chessboard tattooed on his belly. Call that normal? It takes Rupert to pick a mama who's a bigger fruit than him."

"Did Esther say anything to you?"

"Yeah, she said I should save my cunt for the proletariat. Shit like that. Who asked her advice?"

The five pimps figured Isaac was a crazy man; why else would he interrogate a bimbo in the street? Brodsky had his own suspicions. Isaac was stuck on a dead girl, a lollipop who would have been happy to kill him. "Chief, it's getting late. Those crime reporters have no loyalty. They'll interview Cowboy if you aint there to satisfy them."

The First Dep's sedan remained on Times Square. Brodsky had to go inside the Tivoli Theatre to scratch around for Wadsworth, Isaac's milky nigger. The chauffeur came out alone. He popped his head through Isaac's window. "Wadsworth says he don't sit in police cars. He'll meet you in the lobby. That's as far as he goes."

Isaac sent the chauffeur into the Tivoli again. "Brodsky, tell him I'm hurting today. I'm too nervous to breathe the air in a movie house."

Wadsworth sneaked into the sedan; he sat up front with Isaac, while Brodsky dawdled under the marquee, staring at the bosoms on a signboard near the ticket booth. Wadsworth kept hunching into his seat. He had the pink eyes of a captured flounder. He wouldn't greet Isaac in Yiddish, or English. Isaac had to speak.

"Wads, I wouldn't pull on your shirt without a reason. You know that. I need. The Guzmanns stole a corpse away from me. They're meddling in my affairs. I don't want their dice cribs, Wads. Let them gamble in peace. Just tell me where the local whore market is, the place where the Guzmanns can trade in all the little girls they snatch from the bus terminal."

Wadsworth wouldn't shift from his corner. He showed Isaac a crumpled palm. "Put a razor in my hand, why don't you,

Commissioner? So I can slit my throat before the Guzmanns get the chance."

"Don't be foolish, Wads. I'm not looking for a bust. I'll lean on the whore merchants, that's all. The Guzmanns will never know who my source is. How could they? And why curse me with the title of 'Commissioner'? I'm just a lousy chief."

"Isaac, Zorro doesn't sleep with his ears in the ground. You tap his marketplace, and he'll know."

"Wads, the Guzmanns are creepy pimps. If they touch you, I'll stick their balls in a medical jar." Wadsworth didn't smile. "You have a big family, Wads. A boy with uncles and cousins living in city dormitories shouldn't be so particular. Get what I mean? You can float out of my house, Wads, that's your privilege. But if Cowboy finds out you're no longer registered to me, he'll take away your seat at the movies."

"Isaac, the Guzmanns are angels next to you."

"I agree. The Guzmanns wrap their money in prayer shawls, but can they keep you out of the Tombs? I'm your friend, not Zorro. Remember that. Now give. What's the name of that whore market?"

"Zuckerdorff. It's an outlet for diseased merchandise. Seconds and thirds. Zorro rents the showroom every week."

"A dummy corporation, is that it?"

"No. You can get a blouse for one of your girlfriends from Zuckerdorff. Isaac, be careful with the old man. He's Zorro's great-uncle."

Brodsky drove the Chief to "Zuckerdorff's of Sixth Avenue," which was in the basement of a pajama factory on Fortieth Street, between Tenth and Eleventh. Zuckerdorff had no secretaries or shipping clerks. He was a man with handsome eyebrows and prominent bones in his skull. He must have been eighty years old. Isaac had to extricate him from a wall of haberdashery boxes. Zuckerdorff didn't take kindly to this intrusion. "Gentlemen, do you have a piece of paper from a judge? Otherwise leave me alone."

The Chief wouldn't go for his inspector's badge, so Brodsky had to pull out his own gold shield. Zuckerdorff laughed in the chauffeur's face. "Mister, I seen plenty of those. They're good for scaring the cucarachas."

"Isaac, should I bend his mouth?"

The Chief stepped around Brodsky to catch Zorro's great-uncle at a sharper angle. Plaguing an old man with bluish skin on his temples made Isaac bitter with himself. But he couldn't allow a tribe of Bronx pimps to laugh him out of his borough. "Zuckerdorff, if you're counting on Zorro, forget it. I eat Guzmanns in the morning. They're tastier than frogs' legs. So consider what I have to say. Either you shut Zorro out of your company, and forbid him to walk his whores through these premises, or you'll have to stack your boxes in the street. I can turn you into a sidewalk corporation faster than Zorro can pedicure his father's toenails."

Zuckerdorff hopped to the telephone. He dialed without looking back at Isaac. His conversation was quite brief. "Zelmo, this is Tomás . . . I have two faigels in my office . . . funny boys . . . cops with bright ideas . . . they like to threaten people."

Zuckerdorff tittered with a finger on his lip. The bones shook in his skull. "My friends, you'd better vacate the building. Because your badges are going to be in my toilet bowl in another minute. If you decide to wait, I can fix you some beautiful red tea."

Isaac wondered if the Marranos poured jam or blood in their teacups. He was more curious about this than the identity of Zuckerdorff's benefactor.

A man clumped into the basement. He must have thick soles, Isaac assumed. "What precinct are you from?" the man growled, without seeing Isaac. "Are you grabbing for the nearest pocket? I'll break your knuckles off."

Isaac recognized Zelmo Beard, a disheveled detective from the safe and loft squad. Zelmo stared into Isaac's eyes. His chin collapsed. His ears seemed to crawl into his neck. He waltzed in his baggy overcoat, toppling the wall of haberdashery boxes. Zuckerdorff had all the omens a seller of damaged blouses could need. He blinked at Isaac. This cop had a capacity for pure evil. How else could Zuckerdorff explain the explosion of blush marks on Zelmo Beard?

Zelmo began to genuflect near Isaac's thighs. "Chief, I didn't know the First Dep was interested in Zuckerdorff . . . he takes in pennies, I swear. Garbage deals. He's a glorified junkman."

"Zelmo, I thought you had more sense. Why are you out muscling for a family that's been a nuisance to my life?"

"Isaac, I couldn't give a shit about Zorro."

"Prove it. I don't want him finding any more outlets for his little girls. Wherever Zorro turns, you chase him, Zelmo, understand? You can start with Zuckerdorff. Hit him with summonses, sprinkler violations, the works. That way Zorro will know I'm sending him my regards. Brodsky, come on."

The chauffeur basked on Tenth Avenue. His boss had to be the greatest detective in the world; better than Maigret, better than the Thin Man, better than Cowboy Rosenblatt. Isaac the Just could destroy the Guzmanns and all their Manhattan links without raising his thumb. He carried honey and acid inside his mouth. He could bite your face, or purr you to sleep. "Isaac, the reporters, Isaac. You'll snow them out of their pants. Should I signal Headquarters?"

"Brodsky, we're going to Bellevue."

The sedan pushed east, Brodsky sulking behind the wheel. He hated hospitals with fat chimneys and raw brick. Isaac went up to his mother's room. He found his nephews in the hall, Davey and Michael. The boys wore their hunting clothes: Edwardian suits cut to the measurements of a child, stiff collars, and identical flame red ties. "Uncle Isaac, uncle Isaac," they screamed, lunging at him. Isaac had to bribe his nephews with fifty-cent pieces before they would give up their hold on his knees. The hallway would soon be a battle-field. The boys were waiting to pounce on their father. Where was Leo's ex-wife? Davey and Michael couldn't have plunked themselves outside their grandmother's door.

"My father's a killer man," Michael said.

"Who's he been killing?"

"My mother and me."

Isaac couldn't argue with a seven-year-old. He abandoned his nephews for a peek at his mother. Sophie had her vigilers: Marilyn, Leo, and Alfred Abdullah, her suitor from Pacific Street. Abdullah greeted Isaac with a sorrowful smile. An American Arab out of Lebanon, he could grieve over Sophie's wounds as hard as any son. Isaac nodded to the chairs around the bed. His mother lay in her pillows with blue salt on her lips, fluids leaking in and out of a nest of pipes. Marilyn barked a husky hello. Isaac felt uncomfortable with his daughter in the room. He saw the strain, the nervous flutter of her eyelids. She was miserable without Coen. And Isaac had contributed to this. Blue Eyes was only two flights away, in the prisoners' ward, minding Stanley Chin. Marilyn couldn't get through; the prisoners' ward didn't entertain the guests of jailors, nurses, or cops.

Leo could feel the chill between father and daughter. He edged closer to Marilyn's chair. Marilyn was his buffer zone. He remembered Isaac's promise to tear off a lung if he refused to give up his hiding place in civil jail. Leo hadn't made preparations to leave

Crosby Street. The climate suited him. He could smoke, play cards, sneak out to visit his mother. Sitting next to Marilyn, he waited for Isaac's wrath to fall. He'd misinterpreted the Chief. Isaac was too occupied with Rupert, Esther, and the Guzmanns to worry about one of his own simple threats. Leo's tenure at Crosby Street didn't concern him now. Abstracted, with leaking pipes in his eye, he spoke to Alfred Abdullah. "How's Pacific Street?"

Abdullah stared past Isaac in alarm: Sophie's head came off the pillows. "The baby," she said. "Bring me the baby." Sleeping, she had the look of a woman whose skin was on fire, her face deepening with blue salt and the passage of blood. Coming out of a coma, her complexion changed. She was pale, with a mouses's color, during her periods of lucidity. The glass pipes swayed over her arm, impeding the flow from gooseneck to gooseneck. "Bring me the baby," she said.

Isaac stood with both fists in his chest. Abdullah made little grabs at his throat. Leo covered his eyes. Only Marilyn had the sense to clutch the pipes and narrow their sway. "Jesus Christ," she said. "Can't you see? Mama's calling for Leo."

Leo sprang out of his chair. His shoulder landed in the bed. Sophie began to caress his bald spot. Leo was crying with his mother's fingers in his scalp. "Shhh," she said. "Where's the philistine?"

Abdullah crouched behind Leo. Sophie rejected him. "Not you," she said. "Where's the philistine? . . . "

"Mama," Isaac said, his ankles sinking under him. "I'm right here."

"Did you meet the cock-a-doodle?"

Isaac shrugged, rendered incomplete by his mother.

"The cock-a-doodle," Sophie insisted. "In Paris, France."

Isaac was caught with pimples on his tongue. Leo must have snitched; mama couldn't have known about his rendezvous with Joel in the Jewish slums of Paris, unless the fluids dripping into her also fed her intuition.

Sophie was through with bald spots. She reached for Abdullah's hand. Leo wouldn't move; he kept his ear against Sophie's hospital shirt. Sophie smiled.

"Alfred, are you making a living?"

Abdullah answered yes.

"Good. Because I aint putting out for paupers."

Devoted to her, Abdullah didn't reveal his embarrassment. Leo drew his ear away from the bed. "Mama's getting delirious," he whispered into Marilyn's shoulder.

"Isaac, are you fucking lately?"

"Mama, who has the time."

Leo twisted Isaac's sleeve. "Don't answer her . . . Isaac, her brain is swelling up. Do you know what it means to be without a husband thirty years?"

Sophie dropped into the pillows. Her mouth twitched once. Her eyes registered a certain confusion. She tasted the salt on her lip. She belched. She tumbled into a profound sleep, holding Abdullah's hand. Leo crept out of the room.

Trapped between Abdullah and Marilyn, Isaac grew shy. He couldn't belittle Sophie's quest for boyfriends, in and out of her comas. No sugar leak could kill his mother's sexuality. Her skin was turning deep again. Isaac was left with his daughter. He heard bitter screams from the hall.

Leo was wrestling with his ex-wife. The elusive Selma lay under his knees, breathing sporadically, with Davey and Michael climbing up their father's back. "Let me finish her once and for all," Leo choked out, his voice edged with a violence Isaac had never encountered in his brother. Leo wouldn't acknowledge Michael's clawing fingernails. Davey was sitting on his neck. Leo had his knuckles in Selma's windpipe. "Do I have to suffer on account of you?" Isaac had to pluck Davey and Michael by the seat of their Edwardian pants before he could get to Leo.

"Go back to your jail Leo, the guards will miss their pinochle without you."

Leo stumbled towards the exit, nurses, patients, and visitors popping out of doors to stare at him with loathing in their eyes. Davey and Michael blinked scowls at their father. Selma began to writhe on the floor. Spit collected under her nose. "He ruined my insides . . . oh, my God . . . oh, oh." Selma grimaced and squeezed her ribs. "Help me, nurse, nurse." The boys leaned over their mother, battle-weary, but terrified of the snaking motions of her body. Isaac understood Selma's scam. Her sputum was clear; he couldn't find a fleck of blood. Her cries had too much rhythm. He bent down, curling over Selma, so the boys couldn't hear him. "On your feet, sister-in-law. This place doesn't carry collision insurance. If you're thinking of hospitalizing yourself, here's my opinion. Some of the wards have handcuffs hanging from the beds. Sister, I'll lock you in. This is Bellevue, remember? People have been known to wander for years in the crazy ward."

"Fuckface," Selma mouthed into Isaac's chest as she fixed her stockings. The boys witnessed Selma's miraculous rise. They hugged her, pushing Isaac off with mean little blows.

Marilyn smiled from her grandmother's doorway. Isaac was plagued by a swarm of relatives, like any Jewish patriarch. He supplied the family glue. The Sidels would have crumbled long ago without the ministrations of Isaac. He soothed, he slapped, he mended broken wires, Marilyn's incredible daddy.

The crime reporters wanted their conference in the Police Commissioner's rooms, where they could peek at the furnishings of an old commissioner, Teddy Roosevelt; draperies, a gigantic desk, portraits of Teddy on the wall. Isaac wouldn't allow it. He herded the reporters into his own office, which had no marble fireplace, no chandeliers, no maroon on the windows, no desk with historic chinks and scars and a spacious hole carpentered for the knees of a future president of the United States, and could only remind such men and women of their ancient, cluttered "news shack" on Baxter Street. Isaac wouldn't provide sandwiches, or a police captain in a handsome tunic to coddle the reporters; Brodsky became his press secretary. The chauffeur clucked behind Isaac with envelopes belonging to the lollipop case.

The Chief talked of Rupert and Stanley's Chinatown escapade in primitive style, without embellishments, winks, and anecdotes, or the mannerisms of Barney Rosenblatt (Cowboy loved to rattle his cufflinks at reporters). Brodsky didn't hear the scratch of a single fountain pen. Cradling their notebooks, the reporters stood with slanted heads. The *Times* man was the first to jump on Isaac. Could the Chief enlighten him? What did the First Deputy's office make of isolated rat packs such as the lollipops preying on old men and women without real cause, devoting themselves to senseless destruction?

"It's a worldwide phenomenon," Isaac said, cuddling his chin. "The same thing is true in Paris. The French police can pull any master criminal out of a chart, but it's teenage bandits—lollipops— who are taking over the Champs-Elysées. Babies robbing banks. Without a name or a face. Some Billy the Kid with a cheap kerchief on his nose."

"Or Robin Hood," said Tony Brill, the fat man with credentials from *The Toad;* neither Brodsky nor Isaac had ever noticed him at Headquarters.

Isaac frowned at this *Toad* man, ignoring Robin Hood. "Eight-year-old muggers and rapists in New York," he said. "Killers at nine and ten. Are we supposed to keep infants in our confidential files?"

The stringer from *Newsweek* had a passion for intelligence tests. He led Isaac away from abstract causes, and asked him to fish through the envelopes in Brodsky's hand. "Chief, you must have a sorry bunch of detectives doing research for you. Where's your fact sheet on Rupert Weil?"

Brodsky grew miserable fumbling inside the sleeves of different envelopes. The stringer was already smug. "What's the kid's I.Q.?"

"Two hundred and seven," Isaac said, making Brodsky close all the sleeves.

The *Daily News* man began to titter. "The kid must be a genius. I hear Mozart only came in at a hundred and ninety-nine."

"Two hundred and seven," Isaac said.

The stringer was obstinate. "What about Esther?"

"She went to parochial school," Isaac said. "Her teachers are Spagnuolos, suspicious people. They refused to supply us with any records. But I don't have much faith in intelligence quotients. They tell you very little. Rupert was a chess player once. He could have been a grandmaster, who knows? He gave it up at twelve. Was it 'intelligence' that told him where to place a knight? Look at Bobby Fischer. He has an I.Q. of a hundred and eight or nine. So give me a theory about geniuses? I'm not begrudging Rupert's terrific score. But his genius comes from willfulness, from a maddening obstinancy, not a talent for checking the right box. Take my word. Your geniuses come narrow these days. They have the power to stare at an object, a piece of fruit, a man's heart, and block out everything else in this stinking world."

The reporters hadn't anticipated philosophical notions from a police inspector. The two nice ladies from the Brooklyn *Squire,* who were partial to Cowboy Rosenblatt, considered it an odd turn of events that Stanley Chin and Sophie Sidel should land in the same hospital. Was Isaac slinging mud in Cowboy's eye? Had the caper at St. Bartholomew's been staged for the benefit of newspapers and magazines? Was Rupert Weil working for the First Deputy's office? Did he steal the Chin boy at Isaac's request?

"Pure coincidence," Isaac muttered. "Stanley has nothing to do with my mother now. And it's a crazy idea to think that Rupert works for me."

"Not so crazy," said Tony Brill.

"What do you mean?"

"Nothing . . . " Tony Brill had to retreat from Isaac's terrible glare. *The Toad* couldn't insure him against potholes and loose bannisters at Police Headquarters. "Chief Sidel, weren't you friends with Rupert's dad? Maybe the kid was trying to find a subtle way to cooperate with you."

"Bullshit," Brodsky said. The members of Isaac's rubber-gun squad peeked into the room. Because they didn't have pistols at their hips, the reporters mistook them for civilians, and figured they could be rude to ordinary clerks. The rubber-gun boys were waving frantically at Isaac, without a bit of color in their cheeks. Brodsky mingled with them. His pants began to slide under his belly. He had to grab his pockets to save himself. "Conference dismissed," he croaked with a tight mouth.

The reporters piled out of Isaac's office, dissatisfied with the surreptitious moves of First Deputy men. Isaac remained with Brodsky and the rubber-gun boys. "What's wrong?"

"Isaac, a package came to you . . . from Rupert Weil. We called the bomb squad. They're bringing over a special dog to sniff it out. It could be a booby trap."

"Dummies," Isaac said. "I don't need a lousy dog."

It was wrapped in butcher paper, with heavy string on the outside, the kind of string a bialy maker might use to secure a bag of rolls. It was a tremendous package, over two feet high. Isaac couldn't bite through the string; the fibers were too coarse. Brodsky ran for a pair of scissors. Isaac snapped at the knots. He tore under the butcher paper. The rubber-gun boys could see the rounded edges of a hatbox, a hatbox with a name on it: Philip Weil. Isaac opened the box. Brodsky put his hands over his ears. Isaac's other men slinked to one side. They saw a hand rustling in crumpled newspaper.

"Isaac, what the fuck is it?"

He held a chesspiece, a black bishop made of wood, with the points of a miter sitting on top, an inexpensive piece out of Rupert's own collection. The rubber-gun boys were bewildered. The package confirmed Rupert's craziness for them. Isaac wouldn't offer his opinion. He chased out all his men. "Brodsky, close the door."

Isaac fingered the chesspiece, all the undulations in the wood (Rupert's bishop had a swollen belly), the weak black paint that was beginning to bald, the strip of velvet at the bottom, the rough spots along the miter. Rupert's telling me something, Isaac muttered in his head. The present of a bishop couldn't have been a caprice. Was the boy challenging Isaac to a game of postal chess? Should Isaac counter with a bishop of the opposite color? No. Rupert wasn't into that. This chess piece had to go back to his father's game. Philip was a master with a pair of cooperating bishops. He always drew black against Isaac, giving him a clean advantage. Isaac had the opening move. Philip wouldn't sit on his pieces. He eschewed the normal lines of defense. Philip had to slap at you. He didn't gobble up your pawns, or badger your king into slow strangulation. While you attacked with an armada of knights and rooks, your pieces sailing on some grandiose mission, Philip crept around them and used his bishops to tear out the throat of your queen.

"He's after one of my ladies," Isaac spit into the hatbox. How many queens could a cop possess? Three or four? Rupert's going to slap me like his father did. Isaac couldn't believe the boy would touch Sophie again. But the Chief had a cautious heart. He'd put another "angel" outside Sophie's door in case he slipped over Rupert's logic. Was it Isaac's wife, the baroness Kathleen? Rupert would have to dig her out of the Florida swamps, Kathleen's new dominion. Ida Stutz? What could Rupert want with Isaac's fiancée? "Marilyn," Isaac said with a definitive nasalness. It had to be.

The dog arrived from Twentieth Street, where the bomb squad had its own kennels on the roof of the Police Academy. Isaac was expecting a German shepherd with brilliant ears and a very long nose. This one was a mouse, a snip of a dog, a cocker spaniel with stunted legs and a body that hugged the ground. Isaac could pity such a creature. He wouldn't send it home to Twentieth Street without a sniff inside the hatbox.

The prisoners' ward at Bellevue had a ping-pong table, old-fashioned sandpaper rackets, and a bag of dusty balls, perfect for Manfred Coen. He could pass the time slapping balls into the table. There were only three patients in the ward today: a black Muslim with a wound in his thigh, a deranged Puerto Rican car thief who tried to hang himself in a police station, and Stanley Chin. None of them was in proper condition to play Coen. But the little pecking noises coming off the sandpaper were beginning to make them twitch. Stanley had to shout from his bed to halt Coen's slaps. "Blue Eyes, you wanna play?"

Coen laughed. "You'll hurt your fingers, Stanley. You can't grip a bat."

"I don't need no bat." He waved a mitten in the air. "I play with this."

"With your cast?" Coen said. "The doctors would skin me alive."

"How they gonna know? Blue Eyes, don't be afraid."

Coen found a wheelchair. He pushed Stanley from the bed to the ping-pong table, setting him up so his chin would be near the table's center mark. Coen picked up the racket. He wouldn't angle it. He didn't want to confuse the boy with side spin off the sandpaper. He stroked the ball over the net. Stanley punched it back with his left mitten. Coen lunged with his knees wide apart. He missed the ball. He frowned at the sandpaper and took another ball out of the bag. He blew on it, testing the seams by mashing it into the table with his palm. He listened for the dull pock that would have told him there was a crack in the ball. The pock didn't come. He served again. Stanley punched the ball with his other mitten. Coen knocked his knees together. The cop was astonished. His racket kissed nothing but air. Stanley had developed top spin with the plaster on his knuckles.

"That's kung-fu, man."

Stanley put a mitten in his mouth. He couldn't stop giggling. He hadn't meant to tease Coen, but the cop's disgust with the racket in his hand could make a boy piss with his eyes. "It's called the iron fist. It takes concentration, man. You aim for one spot. Sometimes it screws up, Mr. Coen. But when you hit the ball, it stays hit."

An orderly motioned Blue Eyes over to the telephone. Manfred was still confused. How could a boy in a wheelchair with mittens on destroy his game? Coen wished he'd brought his sponge bat, his Mark V, to the prisoners' ward. Then he'd discover what an iron fist could do against a few millimeters of sponge. Brodsky was screaming at him.

"Coen, you deaf, or what?"

Manfred wiggled the receiver. "Brodsky, I can understand every word."

"Then move your ass over to Headquarters."

"What about Stanley Chin?"

"Forget the little Chinaman. Coen, bring your piece. If you drop a bullet on the floor the First Dep will murder you. It's Rupert Weil. I think Isaac wants you to blow him away."

PART FOUR

FOURTEEN

Marilyn could hear the wind in the struts of her daddy's fire escape. The radio promised a blizzard. She shuddered at the prospect of blinding snow. Marilyn was a Riverdale girl. Snowstorms could make her crazy. She remembered the blizzards out of her childhood, when Riverdale was blocked off from the rest of the world, and she couldn't go to school. She had to live on peas and sesame sticks in her mother's cupboard. She would see puff balls on the Hudson, the wind rolling loose masses of snow. Her mother was in Baltimore, or Miami, and her father was caught downtown. Isaac couldn't telephone. The snow had strangled the wires. Crackles came out of the telephone box, a disgusting electric snore. And Marilyn would suck on her braids, exhausted, the peas growling in her belly, too frightened to cry.

She couldn't even laugh at her ancient hysteria, anxieties that were fifteen years old. She was in her daddy's house. After three husbands, she hadn't outgrown her fear of rotten weather. She could call her mother in Florida, beg Kathleen to soothe her with tales of soft Miami, winters without a peep of snow. Marilyn was ashamed to dial for Florida. Kathleen would pull her outside weather reports, and Marilyn would have to pick through all her marriages, provide Kathleen with details of husbands two and three. Somebody was knocking on her father's door. Marilyn opened up.

A snowman had come for her, Manfred Coen with white eyebrows and blood-red ears. Marilyn could adapt to such a snowman. She didn't ask him impertinent questions. She shook the icicles off his camel's hair coat. She set his trousers on the radiator cover. She gathered up the ends of her skirt so she could rub his eyebrows with warm material. She put a turban made of washcloths over his ears. The snowman didn't have the sense to wear galoshes. She got him out of his shoes. She wrapped his feet in Isaac's towels. The snowman gave a sneeze.

"It's a witch's tit outside, a whore of a day."

"Chauvinist," Marilyn laughed. "Can't you think up a few male items? . . . like scummy snow, or a witch's balls. How did you get past Isaac?"

"I didn't have to." The snowman blinked. "Isaac sent me over."

Marilyn's chin rose off the snowman's knees. "Then this wasn't your idea? You arrived because of Isaac?"

"Marilyn, that Rupert kid's been reaching out. Isaac says he's after your throat. You need a bodyguard, and Isaac figured . . ."

"Get out of here."

Marilyn threw her hairbrush at the snowman. She ripped the turban off his ears. Coen hopped on Isaac's linoleum.

"Fucking Blue Eyes, don't tell me what Isaac figured. Isaac figures shit. Don't you ever do your own bidding? Errand boy. Damn him, first he keeps us apart, and now he pimps you over to me. What's he going to come up with next? Does he want me to put out for the whole Police Department? Tell him a girl can get awful choosy about her dates. I'll try a new pimp if he doesn't watch out."

"Marilyn, maybe it wasn't so evil. Isaac knows how much you'd hate having a cop around . . . he thought he could make it more bearable if the cop was me."

"Coen, take your pants off the radiator and put them on. I don't fraternize with bodyguards."

Coen went for his trousers. He got one leg in before Marilyn wrestled him down onto Isaac's daybed. He could feel the tremors in her fist, the squash of her thigh, the frenzied weight of her attacking body. She was all over him, elbows, breasts, and knees. Coen wouldn't defend himself. Marilyn spent her energy beating up a snowman. Her old hysteria had come back. She was stuck in Riverdale again, with blizzards in her head, implacable snow walls between Manfred and her. She didn't recognize the cop; pure blue eyes couldn't bring her out. Marilyn was immune to hypnotic specks of color. She felt a hollow in the snowman's chest; she crawled inside.

Marilyn awoke with a blink that worked itself into the roots of her nose. She could smell a man's flesh. She wasn't naked, no, but she was out of her skirt. Blue Eyes had turned her into a papoose. She was tucked to the bed in a woolly blanket. She could barely move her arms. "How long did I nod off?" she said.

"Maybe an hour," Coen answered from the radiator. He had a fat lip, scratches on both sides of his face.

"Was I awful to you?"

"Not so bad." The scratches wiggled out when Coen smiled. "But I had to tie you down. You were thrashing pretty hard."

He loosened the blanket for her. "I'm sorry," she said, fighting back the urge to touch Coen's lip. "I always freak out before a big snow. . . . Manfred, sit with me."

Coen sat across from her, mindful of the storms she could conceive with her elbows and a swiping finger. "Marilyn, I would have come without a push from Isaac. I was trying to sneak away. He had me running into corners. He bounced me to the end of the borough. I couldn't eat a meal sitting down. I followed the moon skipping for Isaac. Then he locks me inside with Stanley Chin. I was sleeping with ping-pong balls."

"Shh," she said. "You don't have to explain." She crawled up to Coen's knees. She must have become a witch in her father's bed. The scratches on Coen's face were arousing her. She wanted to lick the wounds she'd made. It wasn't out of gruesomeness. Marilyn didn't have the instincts of a torturer. She was raw to Coen. She'd murder her father if it would save Blue Eyes. Crazy thing, she couldn't have exposed her feelings for him without marking up his cheeks. Coen was still babbling.

"Marilyn, I should have stalked Rivington Street, snatched you coming off the stairs, pulled you uptown. Kidnaping is my specialty . . . only it had to be outside. He's my boss. I couldn't invade Isaac's premises."

She would have pounced on him with the affection of a woman who'd outgrown three husbands, but she knew this would scare him off. Coen was suspicious of her. She had to move slow. She reached around him with her neck and kissed the swelling on his lip. It wouldn't have been a proper strategy to take off his clothes. Marilyn pecked outside his undershirt. She sucked on an ear. How do you wake a snowman?

Coen was coming alive. He blew spit into the spaces under her cheekbones. He nibbled the shells of her eyes. He wouldn't grind at her with his trousers on. The cop had gentle ways. But she could feel his prick through the gabardine. His tongue began to snake into the corner of her mouth. The wetness chilled her teeth. Her armpits bled a powerful water that was like no ordinary perspiration. Coen had sweetened her with his tongue in her face. Marilyn wasn't used to such slow kissing. "I could love you, Manfred." She had nothing more to say.

Headquarters was besieged with copies of *The Toad*. Someone, presumably Tony Brill, had piled them on the front steps, indifferent to snowballs and the mud on a cop's shoe. Cowboy's men must have been the first to gather up these wet copies. Twitching with thoughts of revenge, they distributed bunches of *The Toad* to every floor. Brodsky sat outside Isaac's office with a muddy newspaper on his hips. The chauffeur was incensed. That fat worm Tony Brill cluttered the second page with photographs of Rupert Weil, and an exclusive report on the three lollipops. Rupert was snarling at the camera, in the overstuffed uniform of a housing cop.

Brodsky couldn't read without moving his lips. *The Toad* offended him. A rag, Brodsky concluded, a goddamn hippie rag for pinkos and society whores. He had never seen such a mishmash of swearwords and bleeding type. Tony Brill talked of children's crusades, lollipop wars, and the martyrdom of Esther Rose. He accused Isaac of "fucking the brains of all New York." To amuse his readership he'd scratched a primitive cartoon of Isaac pissing on Delancey Street. Pictures that mocked his Chief (Isaac had flabby testicles in the cartoon) couldn't make Brodsky laugh. Brill was a maniac. He swore Isaac had ruined, or was about to ruin, Philip Weil, Mordecai Schapiro, Seward Park High School, Honey Schapiro, Cowboy Rosenblatt, Stanley Chin, Esther Rose, the Puerto Rican people, the Spagnuolos of Brooklyn, the citizens of Chinatown, and Manfred Coen (Brodsky chortled at the mention of Coen. Only Rupert had escaped him, and Rupert was making war. Who else but a lollipop, said Tony Brill, would have dared represent the grievances of his borough?

Brodsky knocked on Isaac's door. The Chief summoned him inside with a dreamy hullo. Isaac had to be hatching a plot, or gruff noises would have come down on Brodsky's shoulders. The Chief was sitting with *The Toad*. Brodsky seemed reluctant to interfere with the traffic in Isaac's head.

"Isaac, should I attend to Tony Brill? It's a ripe time. People can drown in snow."

"Leave him alone," Isaac muttered. "He can't hurt us." Then Isaac came out of his gloom. "The kid'll make me notorious. They'll tremble when I across the street. Didn't you know? Crime disappears wherever I walk."

The chauffeur had trouble with Isaac's twisting speech. He felt obliged to titter. "At least let me do something. Isn't *The Toad* on La Guardia Place? Isaac, I could sabotage their press. It's easy. They'll have to print with crayons and rubber bands."

The Chief was putting on his slipover. He didn't liven to Brodsky's plan for wasting *The Toad*. Isaac was superstitious about journalists. You couldn't kill their stories. If you took their print from them, they'd write on the bark of a tree. Cut off their fingers, and they'll spell with a nose.

"Isaac, don't you want your limousine?"

"Never mind. I'll walk."

"Eighteen inches, Isaac, that's what they predict. The car has snowshoes. Why should you wet your feet?"

Isaac met a few "crows" on the stairs. They leaned into the bannisters to give the Chief some clearance. None of them would whisper "Tony Brill" in his face. Even a "crow" might not survive one of Isaac's bearhugs. They needn't have worried. The Chief was into his own head. He stepped on a "crow's" foot without excusing himself. The problem was Marilyn. With Rupert sending bishops through the mail, Isaac had no cheap solution. Should he strap her to his shoulder, take her everywhere with him? Or find a cubicle for her in the women's house of detention? He had to rely on Coen. Marilyn would have bitten off the tongue of any cop or matron Isaac could provide. Now he'd have to move into Ida's place. His own detectives would laugh at him; they'd say Coen had dispossessed him, bumped him into the street.

Brodsky was wrong about the snow. Eighteen inches? Isaac felt a thin powder under his shoes. He noticed a man on the sidewalk through the haze of falling snow. Isaac thought he could recognize the grim shoulders of Jorge Guzmann. He wasn't in the mood for a heavy embrace. Isaac looked again. It was Gula One Eye, his old nemesis.

"Gula, you'll catch cold. They're predicting a hurricane."

Gulavitch couldn't talk without eating some snow. "Isaac, you should have blinded me twice. It wasn't smart. I'm your enemy. Why did you leave me with a good eye in my head?"

Isaac didn't have to slap Gulavitch's pockets: the old man wouldn't carry a weapon other than his extraordinary thumbs. Still, Isaac had to get him out of here. If the "crows" spotted him, they'd squeal to Cowboy Rosenblatt, and Cowboy would arrest Gulavitch for blocking the sidewalk. They'd take him down to the cellar, make him pose without his eye patch, call him Isaac's idiot.

"Gula, don't you have to peel potatoes for Bummy? Go to East Broadway. Bummy needs you."

The old man licked snow off the top of his lip. "Isaac, I got plenty to peel. Your nose, your eyes, your mouth."

Isaac hailed a patrol car coming from the garage on Mulberry Street. The driver squinted through his window. He couldn't understand why a big Jewish Chief would be hanging around a retard with snow on his face. But he didn't question Isaac.

"This is Milton Gulavitch. He's a friend of mine. Take him to Bummy Gilman's on East Broadway. It better go smooth. Milton doesn't like bumpy rides."

Isaac walked to the Garibaldi social club. He didn't bother peeking over the green stripe in the window. He went inside. This was a poor hour to annoy Amerigo Genussa. The landlord was making pasta for the Garibaldis. He had his own witchery. Amerigo could transform the club into a trattoria with a few mixing bowls, crumbled sausage, anchovies, green and white spaghetti, walnuts, Parmesan cheese, and a pepper mill, bunched around the club's espresso machine. The landlord had niggardly counter space. He was obliged to hop from bowl to bowl, with a wire beater in his chest.

Isaac didn't wait for overtures from Genussa. "Landlord, I told you once. I don't want your stinking goons near Essex Street."

Amerigo continued to hop. The beater would fly into a bowl with little turns of the landlord's wrist. He dealt with Isaac only after the froth began to rise. "Did I invite you to dinner? You've been copping too long. I mean it. Your manners are in your ass. I don't hire degenerates. All my men have families. It looks funny to me, Isaac. You have the best detectives in the world, and you can't catch a Jew baby. So it's up to us."

"He's my property, Amerigo. You won't enjoy your spinach noodles if your friends cross the Bowery one more time."

Isaac heard the wicked suck of the espresso machine. Cappuccinos couldn't tempt him now. The landlord sprinkled walnuts into a bowl.

"Go scratch yourself," he said, walnuts dropping out of his fist. "Isaac, don't tell me how you're going to torture us with the FBI's. Newgate's a prick, just like you."

Isaac shoved a helping of walnuts and anchovies into the nearest bowl. His hand came out stiffened with egg white. The Garibaldis glowered from their tables. The landlord smiled.

"Play, Isaac. You can be the new macaroni man. No cock-sucker's going to provoke me into a fight. The City pays you to kill. Wait . . . be careful at the corners, Inspector. You could get run over by a bicycle thief."

Isaac couldn't blame Amerigo too much. The landlord had to avenge the old people of Little Italy for the trespasses of Rupert Weil. But Isaac wouldn't tolerate baboons peering into the windows of Puerto Rican and Jewish grocers. The snow was thickening on Mulberry Street. An enormous Chrysler cruised behind Isaac. The Chief scowled at the car.

"Brodsky, who told you to hang a tail on me?"

The chauffeur stuck his head outside the Chrysler to gape at Isaac, and spit a few words into the snow. "Chief, the dispatcher's been paging you for fifteen minutes. Wadsworth bought it in the neck."

"With a slug?" Isaac said, getting into the limousine.

"Isaac, there aint a hole in the nigger's body. It must have been a crowbar."

The Chrysler hugged the ground with the help of Brodsky's miracle "snowshoes," tires that could climb walls and stick to any ceiling. They weaved around ordinary sluggish automobiles and arrived at the Tivoli Theatre in under ten minutes. The theatre had already been roped off. Patrolmen in high galoshes and yellow raincoats kept civilians outside the rope and planted "crime scene" placards behind the ticket booth. Brodsky had to hold his belly while he ducked under the rope. The lobby was swollen with homicide boys and "crows" from the Chief of Detectives' office. Isaac paddled between them. He didn't have to fish for the corpse. Isaac's milky nigger was huddled over a chair in the middle of the orchestra, surrounded by a small band of detectives. He had a blue hump where his neck was broken. His eyes stared out of his skull. His tongue was in his shoulder. "Jesus," Brodsky said, with the taste of puke in his nose. He put his hand over his mouth and ran for a drink of water, his trousers falling to his knees. The chauffeur had flowered underpants. The skin of his thighs was pale white. One of the detectives turned to Isaac.

"Any ideas, Chief?"

"No," Isaac said.

"I thought the little nigger belonged to you."

"So what," Isaac growled. "Get him into a goddamn body bag. I don't want him lying around like that."

"Isaac, have a heart. We can't interrupt the investigation. We'll bag him soon as we can."

The police photographer was on his knees snapping pictures of Wadsworth from different angles. Two "latent" experts dusted the chairs in Wadsworth's row. The man from "forensic" was busy chalking the outline of Wadsworth's body, the exact fall of his arms and legs. Isaac had scant respect for these laboratory freaks. Chalk marks made pretty clues, but they couldn't sniff out a murderer for you. Brodsky came back from the water fountain. He whispered in Isaac's ear. "It was a crowbar. I'm telling you. You can't twist a human being like that without a piece of iron. Look, they gave him a hunchback."

Isaac couldn't see the bite of any metal; Wadsworth had no scrapes on his neck. The "crowbar" was Jorge Guzmann's elbow. He walked out of the Tivoli, Brodsky chasing after him. "Isaac, don't leave me behind."

"Why not? I don't need you until tomorrow."

The chauffeur shuffled on the sidewalk. "Isaac, what should I do?"

"Talk to yourself. Sit in the car. Read a porno book."

Isaac trudged to Tenth Avenue in search of Zorro's great-uncle Tomás, the haberdasher who dealt in seconds and thirds. The snow had begun to penetrate Isaac's shoes; their tongues were growing wet. The haberdasher had a tight cellar door. Isaac wouldn't fiddle with locks today. He toppled the door with a heave of his shoulder. Zuckerdorff wasn't alone. A Puerto Rican gunsel sat with him, a killer from Boston Road. Isaac raised the gunsel by the tufts of his sideburns, carried him around the cellar until a rusty pistol and a roll of quarters in a handkerchief spilled out of the gunsel's shirt. Then he placed him gingerly at Zuckerdorff's feet. The gunsel was in agony. He had a torn scalp from this loco policía. "You pull on my brain, man? You crazy motherfucker." Isaac booted him behind Zuckerdorff's chair.

The haberdasher put his head in his lap, leaving Isaac to stare at blue veins on a chiseled skull. He's older than my father, Isaac realized. The Chief hid his compassion from Zuckerdorff. "Uncle Tomás, your grandnephews have committed atrocities in my borough. They murder innocent men. If Zorro wanted a neck to crack, he should have come to me."

Isaac couldn't vent his fury on blue veins. He attacked Zuckerdorff's haberdashery boxes, kicking them with his snowy shoes. The boxes crumpled around Isaac; he buried the gunsel under a pile of smashed lids. Zuckerdorff didn't move. Isaac stubbed his toes. He found no murderers inside a box. Isaac was the guilty one. He fed Wadsworth to the Guzmanns. He allowed his own feud with Zorro to compromise his stoolie. He'd forced Wadsworth to reveal a piece of information that could only point back to him. Like a schmuck, a police animal, he'd turned Wadsworth into expendable merchandise. The Chief was through with boxes. He kicked his way out of Zuckerdorff's cellar showroom.

Ida wasn't fickle with her best customers. She put paprika in their cottage cheese. But her mind wasn't on blintzes and petty cash. She forgot to shave the celery stalks. The spinach bled into the egg salad tray. The dollar bills sitting in the register turned orange from paprika thumbs. The dairy restaurant wasn't used to such shabby tricks. What could Ida's bosses do? They were helpless without this horsey girl.

Ida Stutz was seeing snow, not pishy water, a mean Manhattan trickle, but dark Russian snow, the kind that could swallow lampposts and suffocate a pack of wild dogs. The Ludlow Street professors had to blow into their split-pea soup. None of them could get Ida out of the window. The girl had her nose in the glass. Let her dream, the professors advised. She'll get pains in her calves. And then we'll have our Ida. They smiled when Ida shook, tearing at the flesh on her hips. They figured she was coming back to them. It wasn't so. Ida saw a face on the other side of the glass, the face of an uptown savage, with harsh lips and rubber cheeks, a chin that dandled in and out of a bullish neck, piggling eyes, and a pumpkin's ingrown ears. Ida ran out of the restaurant.

"Isaac, did you lose something uptown? Maybe your life?"

She didn't think a man could sweat with snow in the air. The Chief was burning up. Ida scrutinized him. Poor inspector, he has engines that work overtime. "Where are you going, Isaac? That isn't the way to Rivington Street."

Do powerful engines make you dumb? The Chief kept marching towards Broome Street. "Your place," he mumbled with his big teeth.

"Isaac, how come?"

"Marilyn has a guest."

Ida fell in behind him. She wasn't frail. She had her own combustion machine. "God bless that Marilyn of yours, is she keeping company again? A fourth husband?"

"No. I put him there. One of my detectives. Coen."

Ida didn't enjoy his abbreviated talk. Does a simple "Coen" solve everything? She knew about this handsome cop. Why was he throwing Blue Eyes at his daughter? She couldn't pluck more words out of him. The Chief had sinking shoulders. She tried to take him by the hand. He slapped at her fingers, Isaac the snarling bear. "I can walk," he said. She'd have to feed him honey at home.

Ida lived on the sixth floor. The Chief was hugging bannisters. He could be exhausted by a flight of stairs. Ida pushed. The Chief arrived on her doorstep. She poked her key in the lock. Ida didn't bother with herself. She fixed a tub for Isaac, with perfumed bubble water from a town in Roumania. It said so on the box. She undressed him, got him out of his slipover, sharkskin trousers, and holster straps. She tested the bath with a whirling finger under the bubbles. She sat him down in the tub. She combed his sideburns. She brushed his teeth with the clear toothpaste that came as a sample in yesterday's mail. She couldn't find Isaac's scrotum. The Chief was shriveled up. He blinked at her with a hooded eye.

"Take off your sweater, Ida. It's warm in here."

She brought him brown honey in a tablespoon. Isaac took the honey in one lick. He rose out of the tub, refreshed. Was the bear ready to dance? Sweet Isaac, he had foam on his pectorals. Ida blotted him with the inside of her sweater. The Chief was playing with her clothes. Buttons snapped under the pressure of a thick hand. Isaac was into her cups; he could nurse a nipple as well as any other man. The brassiere dangled at her side. Isaac was on his knees. He had her navel in his mouth. The suction on her belly produced an incredible shiver. Ida couldn't hold on to her legs. She crashed into him. He fell back with Ida, but he wouldn't come out from her belly. Ida thought she would have to pee. Her thighs contracted with the force of a mule. She couldn't throw the Chief.

"Don't stop, Isaac. Please don't stop." But she could feel his mouth begin to drift. Her belly was no longer occupied. He wouldn't graze her with his tongue, nuzzle the walls of her chest. It was Isaac's turn to shiver. The bear had blood between his toes. Uptown bruises?

She should have explored him better in the tub. Ida wasn't alarmed.
She would rub off the anxious spots. She stroked the bumps of skin
behind his ears.

FIFTEEN

The prisoners' ward at Bellevue suffered a whiteout. Its windows
were going blind. Snow packed into the spaces between the grilles,
and froze to wood and glass. Stanley Chin was tripping out on the
hard blinks of snow in the windows. Rupert Weil was full of shit.
Only a tilted brain would compare Hong Kong with New York. There
were no white storms in Kowloon. None of the orderlies would lend
him a cigarette. They were asking fifty cents a smoke. Stanley
wouldn't trade with robber barons. He had a quarter in his pajama
pocket. He wished Blue Eyes would come back.

The ping-pong table was growing bald without Detective Coen.
The net had droops in its bottom line. The balls were getting yellow.
A shrill song from the edge of the ward drove Stanley into the slats of
his hospital crib. The noise was spooking him. He hadn't heard a
telephone ring since yesterday night. Bellevue was supposed to be
snowbound. "Hey Chico," he said to the orderly on call inside the
prisoners' room. "You told me nobody could get through. What's
happening?"

"I dunno," the orderly snapped. His eyes were red from staring
into blind windows too long. "Maybe it's the Holy Spirit."

The orderly picked up the phone. "Yeah, yeah . . . speak louder,
huh?" He plucked a portable wheelchair from the wall, opened it,
climbed in, and wheeled himself to Stanley's crib. "The ding-a-ling,
it's for you."

"Who is it?"

The orderly laughed. "Your favorite boy. Blue Eyes. You got
luck with that cop. You must be a special customer."

The orderly lowered the slats, but he wouldn't give the
wheelchair over to Stanley. "Let him wait. You don't want him to
think you're an easy lay."

"Chico, I got a quarter in my pocket. Take it, and push me to the
telephone."

The orderly reached into Stanley's pajamas, stroked the quarter,
flushed it out, and made Stanley climb into his lap. He paddled them

both around the ward at a reckless clip, bumping off bedposts, shaving walls, heckling the other prisoners, who were groggy with snow, then slid out of the wheelchair, and left Stanley with the phone in his elbow. Stanley had to dig with the side of his face to clutch the ear-piece. "Mr. Coen?"

He heard a horrible buzz, scratching that had a murderous resonance against his jaw. Then a giggle came through the wire. "It's me."

"Rupe?" Stanley was befuddled, but he turned away from the orderly to shield the voice of this crazy giggler. "Chico said it was Blue Eyes."

"Schmuck, how could I give my real name? Would they let Rupert Weil call Bellevue? Blue Eyes gets you anywhere."

The static began to suck at Stanley's cheek. "Rupe, the hospital's closed to the world. They can't find milk for the babies. The nurses go 'round asking prisoners for blood. How'd you make the call?"

"With my middle finger. You know another way to dial?"

"Don't sound on me, Rupe. I got warts in my ear from the telephone."

"Ah, I'll pull you out of that dump. Not today. I'm running errands for my father."

"Who does errands in a storm?"

"I'm going to fuck Lady Marilyn."

Stanley burrowed his head into the earpiece. "Rupe, what'd you say?"

"I'm going to fuck Isaac's daughter . . . in the face."

The phone spilled out of Stanley's elbow and knocked into the wall. "Chico, could you bed down for a guy?"

The orderly scooped up the phone. "Hey man, send Blue Eyes a kiss and say goodbye."

Stanley grabbed with his cheek; the static could burn holes in a boy's mouth. He dropped the telephone. Rupert wasn't there. The orderly dumped him into the crib. "Chico, write a message for me . . . please. It's important."

"Write it yourself. We got a union, man. I aint your slave."

Stanley wagged his plaster mittens. "Would I bother you if I could write? . . . I'll give you a dollar."

"I touched your pocket, man. You aint got no green."

"I'll owe it you. Don't be scared. Blue Eyes will pay."

The orderly leered at him. "Is Coen into sponsoring rats?" He
unclipped his ballpoint pen, twirled it in his mouth for a second, and
started doodling on the back of a hospital menu. "What's the
message?"

Stanley was reluctant to recite his dread to the orderly, but he
had no choice; he couldn't buy wheels to Manfred Coen. He hadn't
been asleep at St. Bartholomew's. The detectives who guarded him
reviled Coen. They also hated Isaac and his daughter, whom they
called a skinny cunt. Stanley learned from them that Blue Eyes was in
love with Marilyn. He wouldn't snitch on Rupert, but he didn't want
Coen's girl-friend to die, So he dictated to the orderly: "Dear
Detective Coen, please watch out for Marilyn the Wild. She'll be in
big trouble if she opens her door tonight. Sincerely, Stanley Chin."

The orderly scratched out an I.O.U. Clamping the pen to
Stanley's mitten, he forced him to sign his name. The signature was a
series of bumps. "It goes to Police Headquarters," Stanley said. "Blue
Eyes will pay you more than a dollar."

The orderly smiled. Leaving Stanley, he shoved the message
through a slot in the prisoners' iron door, placed his tongue in the
peephole, and whispered to the guard on the other side of the door.
"Freddy, you see that paper. Stuff it in the toilet, fast. It's a
poison-pen note from the lollipop gang."

The orderly had a horselaugh behind his fist. He wasn't worried
about the I.O.U. Stanley would have to pay up with a little skin,
blood, or Bellevue chocolate pudding.

Rupert was stuck inside a telephone booth at the corner of Essex
and Grand. A quartet of goons from Little Italy, fellows in long coats
who had been stalking Rupert for a good two weeks, drifting in and
out of grocery stores, restaurants, and horseradish stalls, eating bialys
and kosher pickles, were standing on a snowbank in front of the
booth. They rubbed shoulders to stay warm. All four of them carried
odd bits of Amerigo Genussa's plumbing tools: lead pipes to pin back
Rupert's ears, a metal snake to twist out his eyes, wrenches and
screwdrivers to play with nostrils and lips. Rupert cursed his rotten
luck. He'd have to huddle in the booth until the goons picked another
snowbank. Rupert had no shirt on under the coat he had stolen from
the housing police; his nipples were about to freeze to the lining.

He dialed Headquarters to badger Isaac before the goons
disappeared; he got a recorded voice that whispered husky things to

him. Rupert couldn't understand a word. He had weapons in his pocket: a fork, a spoon, a blunted can opener. They were sharp enough to go under the skin of a woman's neck. He would undaughter Isaac with the push of a spoon.

"Mister, once in your life you'll know what it means to lose."

Rupert held no grudge against Lady Marilyn. Being Isaac's daughter was a question of circumstance; her one misfortune was Isaac himself. And Marilyn would have to pay for that. Rupert was no ordinary butcher; Philip's boy wouldn't have been able to bleed a duck, or a cow. But he had to take something from Isaac that was more valuable to him than his own police inspector's skin. Rupert wasn't unmerciful. He would bleed Marilyn faster than Isaac had bled Philip and Mordecai, and the whole East Side.

Rupert had all the cunning of an Essex Street coyote. From the stairwells and soft walls of abandoned buildings he learned how to live on the fly. He always kept a source of nourishment somewhere on his body. Ruffling his coat, he pulled a yellow lollipop out of the sleeve. Esther had been addicted to lollipops, and he caught his sweet tooth from her. He watched the gorillas on the snowbank and manufactured some yellow spit. The lollipop disabled him; yellow spit could only suck up images of Esther. Enclosed in a booth, with a candy brick in his cheek, he flashed on Esther's bosoms. He was smelling Esther Rose, feeling the stripes of fuzz on her back. He had to crumble the lollipop, or go silly in the head.

He jumped out of the booth. The shivering of the door must have reached the snowbank. The gorillas turned their heads. They were much too cold to make a significant leap. Girding themselves, they began to plod after a hopping overcoat.

Mordecai Schapiro faced snowstorms with cucumber slices, schnapps, and a lick of salt. These were the limits of his appetite. He was grieving over his daughter Honey, who couldn't stop running away from him. Would she catch pneumonia in such a thick porridge of snow, with her short shirts and flimsy stockings? Why should he kid himself? His daughter was a whore. She walked the streets in all kinds of weather. A strict professional, she even had a manager, a pimp with a silk handkerchief, Mordecai supposed, and a card saying she was free of the crabs. The schnapps mingled with the salt on his tongue, and the cucumber eased his bitterness, the pain of a father who felt mislaid.

Mordecai had a guest. Only a moron would visit you in the middle of a squall. He opened his door to a phantom in Cordovan shoes. A Manhattan snowdrift couldn't influence Philip Weil's queer sense of fashion. Philip came in his church clothes, Scotch plaids and tight gloves. Always the dapper hermit, in Mordecai's estimation. Their friendship had soured over the last twenty years. Without Isaac to cement them with his bearish charm, they slipped apart.

"I didn't expect you, Philip. I would have prepared. But it's hard to shop in a storm. I hear the A & P is out of goods. People hoard, you know. They want to safeguard their deliverance. You can't blame them. If you're old, you remember the hard times. And if you're young, you have a brutal imagination."

"Don't be alarmed, Mordecai. I didn't come to steal your salt herring. Tell me about Honey. Has Isaac found her yet?"

"Isaac's a big man. Why should he help me twice in the same month? He drinks tea with commissioners. He rides in limousines. He knows the best opera stars."

"So he isn't perfect," Philip said. "He can still find Honey for you."

"Sure, stick up for him. He could have saved Rupert, but he didn't. I begged him. 'Isaac, go to Philip. Philip needs you.' Does a Chief listen? He has special wax in his ears to make him deaf to old friends."

"That's how a policeman survives. He shuts out certain noises. Do you expect him to redeem every wandering boy in New York?"

Mordecai glowered at the fineries of Scottish wool. "And how do you survive? Philip, it interests me. You sit home morning and afternoon. You can get pimples on your ass from so many daydreams. It's no picnic sorting mail in a post office, but it keeps me occupied."

"I don't daydream, Mordecai. I watch soap operas, I browse in Rupert's library, I play handicap chess against myself, I polish my shoes. My mornings aren't dull to me."

Mordecai despised talk of handicap chess. He couldn't tolerate Philip's eccentricities today. But he smiled at the joke in his head. "We're dunces," he tittered out. "We could have put together a small family of Schapiros and Weils. What's wrong with arranged marriages? Rupert and Honey. They wouldn't have crept so far."

"Why curse fifteen-year-olds with marriage?"

"Hypocrite, your boy wasn't sleeping with that Yeshiva girl?

Everybody knows the Sephardim are a little crazy. They're more Arab than Jew. Did you want *that* in your family?"

Mordecai was ranting to an empty room. Philip had gone back into the storm. "Fuck him," Mordecai said. "He's too much of an aristocrat to fight with me." But Mordecai couldn't find much solace in his schnapps. The cucumber was pulpy in his mouth. He wouldn't get through the winter without his girl. Let her be a whore, he reasoned flatly, staring at the buttons missing from his robe. Whores can manage a needle and thread, whores can sew. Mordecai was exuberant. If enough pimps died in the storm, Honey would have to come home.

Cowboy Rosenblatt couldn't withdraw to the Rockaways, where he was keeping house with a Polish widow who owned a chain of hardware stores. There were no exits out of Manhattan that Cowboy could use. Rows of abandoned cars blocked every bridge, and the subway lines into Brooklyn couldn't unsnarl themselves; no train got beyond Flatbush Avenue.

The Chief of Detectives had made provisions for the storm: he wore his thermal underwear. But it couldn't exempt him from the wind that howled through his suite of offices, rattled his many drawers and his great supply of lamps, hurled pencils off his cabinets, toppled wastepaper baskets, and bit into his secret files. The lamps began to twinkle around 8 P.M., and Cowboy's office went dark. He groaned his way to the outermost room, calling for some lieutenant with a flashlight, or a match. "Where is everybody?" he shouted. "Son-of-a-bitch."

He strolled out on the landing, clutching the bannister rail. Dark stairs couldn't intimidate him, a man with two guns, a superchief, three thousand detectives under him. He was dreaming of his Polish lady, and the empire of bolts and nuts he would soon share with her, Rosenblatt the hardware king. He felt a shiver in the rail. Cowboy was no mystic; wood didn't shiver on its own. Another policeman had to be moving up or down the stairs. A match sputtered near Cowboy's thighs. He saw a pair of cheeks in the shadows, a burrowing forehead, the broad nose of Isaac the Just. Cowboy fondled the pearl on his Colt. He could have shot out Isaac's eyes.

"Isaac, you shouldn't walk these steps without an escort. God forbid, you could fall on your face. Where's Coen?"

Isaac let the match go out. Cowboy leaned into the bannisters.

"Push me, Barney. I'd love the ride. But remember I have a gun next to your ribs. It sits at a funny angle. If you shake me hard enough, it could explode in your groin."

"You're an animal, Isaac, that's what you are. My family comes from a line of cantors, all holy men. The Rosenblatts raised three synagogues in Brooklyn alone. You, Isaac, you suck garbage in the street."

Isaac brushed past him without uttering another word. Cowboy kept to the rail. Where could he go? Should he run to the cellar and kibbitz with the fingerprint boys, or throw himself into the storm and tunnel a path to the property clerk on Broome Street? He decided to stand still. Tinkering with Isaac brought him to the subject of daughters, Isaac's and his own. The Chief of Detectives was crawling with lecherous ideas. He had an insane urge to make Marilyn the Wild, get inside her clothes, chew her nipples, scratch her armpits, drop sperm between her eyes. He'd avenge his daughter's ugliness on Marilyn's body. Cowboy had to grub through Brooklyn locating a husband for his Anita, nab a struggling bachelor older than himself, wed his last daughter to a man with rotten teeth and a swollen prostate, while cunty Marilyn flew from her husbands, and had an affair with Manfred Coen. The world wasn't right. Cowboy had been passed over by whichever angel distributed charity to fathers in the boroughs of New York.

A hand swished against his jacket. Cowboy jumped. A flashlight snapped on. It was one of his "crows."

"Boss, what are you doing here?"

"Idiot," Cowboy said, "I'm airing my pockets," and he took the flashlight away.

Rupert plunged from snowbank to snowbank. His progress was minimal. It took him half an hour to go from Essex to Orchard Street, two skinny blocks. He couldn't see the end of his thigh. He would sink down to his hip pockets with every forward push. He had to wiggle with all his might to rise out of the snow. Rupert was disappointed in the Mulberry Street gorillas. They couldn't keep up with a growing boy. He shook them without having to disguise the stab of his sneakers. He left tracks in the snow that an elephant could follow.

Not all of Rupert's plunges were successful. He landed in a snowslide that carried him off his feet. He couldn't get out of the drift. At ten miles an hour he could carve a path with his ears. Coming into a patch of firmer snow, Rupert held on, and found himself overlooking the signboard of Melamed's Grand Street department store. Rupert was amazed at the fury of moving snow; he must have flown twelve feet off the ground. The signboard couldn't be any lower than that.

The wonders of a snowslide began to wear off. Rupert became depressed. Melamed's reminded him of his former struggles, when he and Esther had been put at the mercy of a store detective, maybe a month ago. They were shopping for clothes in Melamed's underwear department. Rupert made a little belly for himself, stuffing boxer shorts under his shirt. Esther was the brazen one. She squeezed an entire load of lollipop pants through the neck of her blouse, and toured Melamed's with a hump on her back. A short rabbi with curling sideburns and a black religious coat, who had been sifting through the barrels of underwear together with Rupert, came behind Esther Rose, mumbling "Pardon me," and clapped a handcuff on her wrist. Rupert gawked at him. The rabbi tugged, his politeness gone. "Girlie, shake a leg, before I tear your arm off."

The rabbi dragged her up three flights to Melamed's detention cell, a cage about four feet high, designed to humiliate shoplifters, forcing them to live with their shoulders bent, while the assistant manager called the police. Rupert stalked the cage, testing the thickness of its wire mesh. The rabbi plucked off his sideburns and shed his religious coat, coming into the natural grubbiness of a store detective with tobacco between his knuckles and spit on his tie. Rupert couldn't pierce the mesh. Esther screamed, with her forehead under the detective's ribs. "Daddy, I have to pee."

"Pee as much as you like," he said, muggering at her. "You aint coming out."

Shippers began to collect around the cage. Esther dipped her thighs and peed. The shoppers backed off, their mouths widening with disgust as Esther's urine streamed towards them. The detective couldn't be swayed. The urine traveled under his leg in two long fingers. "You'll wipe it up, sister. With your tongue."

Esther unbuttoned her blouse. The shoppers crept back to the cage, standing in pee to gape at a shoplifter's nipple. The detective skipped in front of Esther, screening her with his arms; even a touch of nudity in the cage might cost him his job. He unlocked the cage door and prepared to handcuff Esther again. He shouldn't have turned his back on Rupert. As Esther moved into the door, her blotchy, pissed-over skirt clinging to her thighs, and her neckline plunging below her bosoms, Rupert dug his teeth into that portion of the detective's heel resting outside the hump of his shoe. The detective howled, losing the handcuffs, grabbing at his wounded foot. He was still in Esther's way. She had to tweak his testicles before she could slip between him and the cage. The shoppers had never met such a vicious girl. They pinched their bodies in to avoid fouling themselves with Esther. She shoved Rupert towards Melamed's escalators, helping him bounce off the metal tips of the stairs. Esther wasn't finished with Melamed's. She had more lollipop pants and a huge, impractical girdle when they arrived at the main door. Esther hadn't gotten off totally free. It took a week for her shoulders to unbend.

Rupert crawled to a different snowbank. It was easier to launch himself with his fists. Having no gloves, he stretched the sleeves of his coat. Rupert enjoyed the heights; the snow was mushier near the ground. He could see into living rooms, touch the fire escapes, eat a crisp hunk of snow. Crossings didn't matter to him; traffic lights blinked their colors. Rupert snuffed at the warning signals. He was perfectly safe on Grand Street. Cars and buses couldn't ride over a mound.

Crawling with abandon, snow in his eyes, he bumped into the window of a live poultry market. Rupert was a vegetarian. He despised the smell of roasted flesh. The idea of meat darkening in a stove made his gums twitch. The only flesh Rupert would have nibbled on was Isaac's. No lie. He'd have gone cannibal for Isaac the Pure.

He saw young roosters, hens, and rabbits in the window. The roosters were the lords of the market. They lived two in a cage, while the hens were piled four and five deep, sitting on each other's back, some of them picking at their own necks until bald areas emerged above the wings. These chickens disgusted him. He watched the pink-eyed rabbits, white and gray chewing lettuce, sniffing for their water trough near the edge of the cage. Their coats seemed incredibly soft. Rupert wanted to stick his thumbs in the fur, stroke their pink eyes to sleep. Who the hell would eat a rabbit? he argued to himself. The transom over the window wasn't snug. Rupert could squeeze a knuckle inside. He began clawing at the space between the transom and the window bar. His knuckles were growing raw. He rubbed them in freezing spit. The transom couldn't worry him. He was three fingers into the market.

Squirming, wedging with a shoulder, he raised the transom high enough to slip through the glass. The chickens squawked. The roosters wagged their fleshy combs with a sad pull of the head. Who had castrated these birds, fattened them, groomed their combs for marketing? The bunnies blinked their noses in terror of Rupert. It was dark in there, the snowbank ending just below the transom, allowing a meager peck of light. Rupert had to deal with so many eyes. He walked on his toes to calm the hens. He funneled bits of corn into the roosters' mouths, getting scratches on his hand. He felt the pulse in a white rabbit's pink wet nose. He wished for Esther. She would have loved a live rabbit under the blanket, nudging against her skin. What would the bunny do when Rupert and Esther went down together on the blanket? Rupert stopped. He could hurt himself with blanket dreams. Tasting Esther put smoke in his skull, made him recollect how much Isaac had stolen from him. Rupert preferred a bunny with a drier nose.

Brian Connell shouldn't have budged from the stationhouse. No one would have blamed him for sleeping in the locker room during a hard snow. But he had to redeem himself. He undressed the big Jew's daughter, fed her whiskey in a bar, fucked her, and sent her home to Blue Eyes. The cunt had snitched on him. She cried rape, rape, and now the First Dep's killer squads were gunning for Brian Connell. How do you duck an "angel" with a sharpshooter's ribbon? Brian had one means of escape: catch little Rupert before Isaac takes his revenge.

He'd been stalking Rupert's grounds, from Clinton to West Broadway, in Bowery clothes that were beginning to rot. He had a few appendages today; a silk scarf that he wore on his face, and hunter's boots from Abercrombie's to protect his delicate ankles from snowbite. The wind imposed hallucinations on him. Rabbits were crossing Grand Street. It had to be devil's work, or a mirage caused by the particular slant of falling snow. He kept a medallion in his pocket from the Holy Name society. But rubbing a piece of cold metal couldn't scare the rabbits away. They would come and go between the nod of an eyelash. Brian was terrified. He'd have to surrender his body to a Catholic nursing home, or move out of the state. Run to Delaware and join his cousins on a skunk farm.

He couldn't ignore the squabbling in the snow. There was a

rooster near his legs. This was no pale beast, fickled over by a storm. The rooster had wattles and a red hat. Brian chased after the stupid bird; it rushed between his Abercrombie boots. He flopped in the snow, unable to keep up with a chicken. He noticed a man skulking on the opposite side of Grand Street. Brian drew his gun. The man was trying to stuff the rabbits in a shopping bag. Brian called to him. "Sonny boy, stay where you are."

The man hurled the shopping bag; a rabbit flew out. Brian fired over the man's ears to prove that you couldn't throw shopping bags at a city cop. A hill collapsed behind the thief. "Come out with your hands in the sky."

He heard a loud slapping noise. His own hill of snow was disintegrating under his boots. The thief had a gun in his hand. Brian dove into the tires of an abandoned truck. He squinted around the tires to shoot at the rabbit thief. He could feel dull, trembling pocks in the snow. The guy had to be holding a cannon on him, or a Detective Special. Nothing else could make holes like that. The man was waving a yellowy object. Brian shuddered when he recognized the indentations of a gold shield. "Prick," the man said, coming out of the snow. "I'm from the Second Division. Who the hell are you?"

Brian was too weary to sniffle. The sergeant would slap his eyes with paper work. Brian would be typing forms in triplicate until his fingers dropped off, explaining why he had the urge to blow skin off a detective's ears. They'd flop him for sure. And Isaac had all the authority in the world to kidnap Brian, feed him to the rat squad, who would nibble on his ears, suck his lifeblood away, sneak him out of the borough, and deliver him to Ward's Island in a box, before the snow disappeared. The property clerk would claim his Smith & Wesson. Brian could look forward to a wet grave, and the anonymity of a policeman buried without his gun.

"Are you nuts?" the rabbit thief said, shaking Brian out of his gloomy visions. "You shoot at a man for finding pets in the street? Bunnies are dumb. They could die in Manhattan. I was bringing them out to Islip, for my kids."

Brian shrugged. "Dangerous," he said. "Lollipops . . . I'm looking for Rupert Weil."

All things returned to Isaac. Isaac was the freezing river, the rock, the snow. Isaac was the sewer under Grand Street, the snot in Philip's handkerchief, the dust on the wings of Mordecai's nose.

Isaac was the holy warrior who swept Philip and Mordecai under with his good deeds and gutted Esther Rose, who sleeps in the vulva of his daughter and gets his nourishment from the pubic hair of a fat blintze queen . . .

Two men were following Rupert while he speculated in the snow. These weren't the Mulberry goons. They didn't have long overcoats. They were dressed like foreigners, it seemed to Rupert, in softer clothes: sweaters, earmuffs, and wool hats. It was hard to appraise their look in a storm, but Rupert could swear they were brothers. Their faces had a cunning that didn't respond to the snowbound shops of Grand Street. The brothers might be slow in commercial matters, in geography and arithmetic; they walked with a mental twitch, as if they were moving into strange territories. They couldn't be connected to Isaac; they were much too awkward for a team of cops.

Rupert didn't bother trying to shake them; he'd ride under their fists, if he had to. He'd wrap the earmuffs around their eyes. He'd bite the wool on their heads. They couldn't grab Rupert off the snow. He cut into Allen Street, but the wind drove him back. He had to burrow with his knees, dig his way around the corner. The trip exhausted him. He winked at the sweater boys, whose tits were covered with snow. Woolly heads were no match for Rupert Weil. He had a spoon in his pocket, a spoon that could gouge a path to Lady Marilyn, or splinter the cheeks of an enemy. He revived, watching the earmuffs labor. The brothers were stuck. They couldn't make Allen Street. Rupert dismissed them as Brooklyn refugees. He was clear to move at a pace that was convenient for him. He had ice on his toes, and his nipples had turned blue. He put a hundred yards of crawling between himself and the refugees. He fell over a hand. "What is this shit?" A foot wiggled out of the snow. Rupert pulled. An old man emerged, hugging bits of snow to his body. He'd been buried alive, without galoshes or a scarf. Rupert rubbed the old man against his coat. "Who are you? Where do you live?"

The old man pointed to a building. "I was going for a knish," he said. "A kasha knish. It's foggy out. I can't see."

"Do you have a wife?" Rupert asked.

"I live with my daughter. The knish was for her."

"This aint knish weather, if you ask me. All the delicatessens are closed. Come on."

The storm had tailored the old man's building, cutting it off from its own ground floor with a snowbank that was humped up like an elephant's back. Rupert charged into the hump, searching for an entrance to the building. He slapped out a crooked furrow with his hands and feet, and brought the old man inside. The building was chillier than the snowbank "That's a greedy girl," Rupert said, huffing for warm air. "I'd kasha her nose for her, but I'm in a hurry."

Coming out of the furrow he'd made, he was snatched up by four long overcoats. His enemies, the gorillas of Mulberry Street, had been waiting for him. They spotted Rupert as he stalled to unbury the old man. They banged his arms with their lead pipes, menaced his eyes with their plumber's snake. "Go quiet, little pest, or we'll divide you into twenty packages. You have an appointment with Amerigo Genussa."

Rupert struggled in the snow, unable to reach his can opener, fork, or spoon. The plumber's snake ripped into his eyebrow. He was sneezing blood. He had pipes in his shoulder-blades. The refugees arrived, the sweater boys, the brothers wrapped in earmuffs and childish hats. Was it snow, or blood, that was beguiling Rupert? How could four gorillas be off their feet? Only one brother battled with them. Pipes bounced off the head of this refugee. He could tear a whirling metal snake with his fingers. Take two gorillas into his chest with a single arm. Hug the color out of a man's face. Rupert heard the crunch of bone under the long coats. The four gorillas had rubbery knees. They twitched and groaned near the second brother, who said, "Jorge, that's enough."

He attended to Rupert's eye with spit on a paper napkin. "I'm César Guzmann. Some people call me Zorro. That's my brother Jorge. Don't blink. You'll get snow in your eye."

"Why are you following me?" Rupert said, growing surly.

Zorro pecked at the blood. "Be polite. I don't care for myself. But you'll offend my brother. The good fairy sent us to watch out for you."

"I fight with my own elbows, Mr. Zorro, thank you. I'm Rupert Weil."

"We know that," Zorro said, finishing with the napkin. "We buried you lady, Esther Rose. My father hired two cantors to sing at her funeral. The best songs you can find in Latin and Portuguese."

Rupert peered out of his bloody eye. "What was Esther to you?"

"A Ladina without a decent grave. Nothing more. We had a friend in common. Big Isaac. He should be in the ground, not your lady."

The gorillas slithered away from Rupert and the Guzmann boys,
with lumps in their overcoats.

"See," Zorro said. "It pays to keep you healthy. Could you
torture Isaac if they took your elbows off?"

The Guzmanns were delicate people. Zorro wouldn't have
introduced himself without bearing trinkets from his family; he stuck
a hand through the neck of his bottommost sweater, his fingers
moving like giant pimples under the wool, and dragged up an ice pick
and a tiny handgun in a square of dirty cheesecloth. "My father wants
you to have a choice. You can dig into Isaac, or blow his tongue
away. Don't worry about the pistola. It can't be traced. It bites hard
for a .22. Drop it near Isaac's feet and run."

Rupert shrugged at the offerings. "I have my tools, Mr. Zorro."
Were the Guzmanns out of their minds? He couldn't keep from
staring at the refugees, who walked into a storm bundled up like
chubby snow gods to rescue him from a pack of goons. "Are you a
Brooklyn boy, Mr. Zorro?"

"Never," Zorro said, making grim pulls with his chin. "We come
from Peru. Remember, you have a place to hide. My father can get
you into Mexico City, Bogota, Lima, or the ten Little Havanas in the
East Bronx. Just ride the train to Boston Road and ask for me."

He signaled to Jorge. The brothers fixed their earmuffs and went
into the snow with shuffling knees.

Coen had feathers in his mouth from Isaac's mushy pillow.
Marilyn wouldn't let him out of bed. He was unbridled now, minus
his holster and his socks. The blizzard had simplified their lives; no
interruptions from Isaac for thirty-six hours. Rattling fire escapes
couldn't frighten her with Blue Eyes in the house. She licked him
clean, until he lost the nervous shivers of a cop. She wasn't a dreamy
girl. She understood Coen's obligations, his loyalty to her father, his
somber ways. She hadn't slept with too many orphans before Coen.
She wouldn't have believed a man could hold his dead father and
mother in the furrows of his chin. He had a deathly feel. His
lovemaking was profoundly beautiful and slow. He didn't spit. He
didn't nibble on her ear with an obscene patter, like her second
husband, and her early beaus. He moved in her with the rhythms of a
somnambulist, a drugged devotion that pinned her to the walls of
Isaac's flimsy mattress and made her squeal.

She felt like Isaac, who could taste paradise every night by putting his nose in a honey jar. That's how greedy she got with Coen. She wanted him to nuzzle her until her orgasms traveled to her fingers and her eyes. "Mother God," she said, thrown back to her church days when she had to confess the crime of liking to touch her own bosoms. "Make me come, Manfred, make me come."

At rare intervals she'd climb off the mattress to fix a meal for Blue Eyes and herself; she clawed into the heart of her father's lettuce, dropping chunks onto a plate, with cucumbers and a dip of garlic, onions, and cottage cheese. Marilyn was worried about the blandness of this feast. She couldn't vary the menu in a blizzard. It was cottage cheese, or starve, because the refrigerator had been stocked by Ida Stutz. But there was a little red wine in a goosenecked bottle, and they sipped at it judiciously, conserving the bottle in case they had a visitor. Isaac might come through the window; he had a passion for fire escapes, and he hated climbing stairs. Let her father fly in! Marilyn wouldn't blush. She was old enough to be caught naked with a man. Isaac must have seen her tits once or twice during the short tenures she'd had with her three husbands. He didn't complain. Marilyn wasn't her father's deputy. She'd sit him on the window if he badgered husband Coen.

She decided not to skimp with the bottle. She poured wine over Blue Eyes, into the trenches of his body, collarbone, elbows, kneecaps, the line of blond hairs that split his chest, the grooves around his balls. She was planning to devour Coen, drink the wine off her new husband, catch him with her tongue. She fell into his shoulder, caressing him with her forehead and her jaw, while Coen shut his eyes, grunting like a dead man, wind coming from his lungs in low, even squalls, and Marilyn cursing all the wedding rings she had worn, the bridal veils, the embroidered sheets of honeymoon hotels.

Rupert's bad eye was beginning to close. He had to sight unnaturally, with his cheek jutting into the storm, or bang out a path with his knees. He bumped along, enduring the windburn on his lips, trying to figure Isaac's doom. He wasn't so resolute near Delancey. The traffic was dead. He had a whole boulevard to himself. He could have hopped across on the roofs of abandoned cars if that had been his wish. He wasn't in the mood to make a crooked metal bridge.

The window of a men's slack shop on the north side of Delancey had been smashed in the storm. He saw looters, men and boys in grubby coats, sacking the store; they carried great bundles of pants through the jagged teeth in the window. One of the looters, a *portorriqueño* with scars on his lip, swerved into Rupert, glaring at the uniform of a housing cop, he came up close to inspect the sneakers, the damaged eyebrow, Rupert's hairless face, and he smiled. "*Yo no sé*, man. There's plenty for everybody. Dig in."

Rupert wasn't interested in slacks, but the looters wouldn't let him go. His uniform was too valuable, he became their lookout. Rupert stood outside the window with a glum demeanor. He disapproved of anarchy done for profit. These slacks wouldn't cover the gang's own legs; they'd be sold at a thieves' market, or hawked uptown, with the looters turning their arms into clothes trees to display the wares. The leader of the gang was a gringo, like Rupert. He wore a stocking cap and an old Eisenhower. He noticed the condemnation in Rupert's narrow cheeks. "What's eating you, bro'?"

"Nothing." Rupert said.

"Then why you looking at me with unkindness?"

"Because I'd like it better if you stole what you need and went home."

Boys were coming out of the window who had to be runts, midgets, or creatures under ten. They bobbled under Rupert's neck, carrying their load of slacks in a line that ended with a blur of snow. This same line could have reached for blocks, Rupert understood. The runts might be marching straight to the Chrysler building. The leader took one of the loads off a runt and pitched it at Rupert. "You must be a rich man's kid," he said. "A mama's baby. You don't know shit about stealing."

Rupert ran for his life. He couldn't have fought an army of runts. The snow was pitted with obstacles and dangerous traps. He walked on crushed glass, smacked into the domes of submerged johnny pumps, skidded off the carcass of a frozen dog. He arrived in Rivington Street with a raw nose. Could he murder Isaac's daughter now? He was fortified by the lay of snow in the street. The storm had worked for him. There was a snowbank near the fire escape he had to reach. He could grip the bottom rung of the ladder without performing acrobatics under Isaac's window.

Rupert, Esther, and Stanley Chin had wasted whole afternoons spying on the window from a neighboring roof. They had seen Isaac slash like a bloated sea animal on top of Ida Stutz, his policeman's ass rolling in deep, tortuous waves. Such turbulence seemed comical to them. Rupert had to wonder how his own buttocks behaved while he was down with Esther. Did they slap in the air, waver high and low? Rupert wasn't a sea elephant. His thrusts had to be sweeter than those of Isaac the Pure. Before Esther died, he saw another woman in Isaac's window. It was Lady Marilyn. He'd come here alone to watch her shamble across the living room, or go into Little Italy with a shopping bag. She was a skinny girl. She didn't have her father's thick neck, or the complexion of a blintze queen.

Rupert walked up the hump of the snowbank. He was on the ladder, hands and feet. He climbed with his elbows in his chest. The going wasn't easy. He had to measure the distance between every rung, or slip down the ladder. The wind could be devilish at this altitude; it beat against Rupert's nose, lashed him into the rungs, the higher he got. He reached Isaac's fire escape with snow on his chin, his fingers swollen with ice. The fire escape shook as Rupert crouched onto the landing. The bedroom window was dug through with frost. Rupert had to blow on it and rub the wet, murky glass with the cloth over his wrist. The window began to clear: Rupert caught a naked woman through a patch of glass. Lady Marilyn. She was lying on a rumpled bed, with half her body out of the blanket. He had never seen a human creature in such repose. Isaac's little girl, without a dent on her face. Only the size of her breasts and the roundness of her nipples could have warned you she was fully grown. A crease appeared on her forehead. Marilyn scratched her nose, and the crease was gone.

Rupert was in misery. Those bosoms reminded him of Esther. She had the same spill on her chest, a soft swell under her arms. Rupert was no connoisseur of a woman's fleshy parts. Esther had been his only girlfriend, first and last. But Marilyn's tits made him cry. They could turn a boy gentle if he didn't have an irrevocable mission, and bile in his heart from Essex Street. He would have to murder her with his eyes closed.

Marilyn had been dreaming, not of Blue Eyes, not of Isaac, not of her mother Kathleen, but of Larry, her first husband, the one Isaac hadn't picked. He wasn't respectable enough for the daughter of a police chief; Larry had no permanent occupation. He fingered his guitar for a macrobiotic restaurant, sold scarves in the street. Isaac didn't chase Larry out of Manhattan; it was Marilyn's own gruffness, inherited from Isaac and Kathleen, the hysteria of an Irish-Jewish child, that got him to pack the guitar and leave. She was too wild for her men. Her devotion came with claws. She'd wanted to scratch the air around Larry to protect him from her father. But Larry disappeared. She didn't have to scratch for Coen's sake. Blue Eyes had a holster and a gun.

She heard a squeak from the window. Something pushed against the glass. The window chains were rattling. Marilyn could see a line of snow. There was a face in her window, a face with a bloody eye and a sinister nose. She didn't scream for Coen. She watched the hunching boy, one leg on the fire escape, the other leg in her father's room. He wore sneakers in a storm, and a crazy police coat. "Don't be shy, Mr. Snow Pants, come on in," Marilyn said, with the blanket still in her lap. She wasn't going to curtain herself for a boy in the window.

Blue Eyes came out of the bathtub after Marilyn's call (he'd been soaking off the wine Marilyn had poured on him). Blood in an eye couldn't throw him off: he recognized Philip's boy from the circulars Isaac's men had prepared. But he couldn't understand what Rupert was doing with a spoon in his fist. Coen was undressed. He could feel a chill on his balls. Rupert climbed out the window. Coen grabbed for his pants and shirt. He didn't have time to lace his shoes. Marilyn pulled on his shirttails. "Manfred, what the fuck is going on?"

Blue Eyes left his gun in the bathroom; he wasn't going to duel with a fifteen-year-old bandit. He had to shove Marilyn's hand off his back. "It's your father's war," he said. He was out on the fire escape before Marilyn could find another hold on his body. The wind blasted under his shirt. "Jesus," Coen said. The fire escape was dipping like a boat. He felt certain it would break from the wall and crash into the street. He followed Rupert up the ladder. It wasn't recklessness in Coen. Nothing could chase him off the fire escape. He had to take little Rupert.

"Blue Eyes," Rupert muttered on the ladder. He should have figured Isaac's sweetheart would spoil it for him. He grew careless about the rungs, leaping crookedly with a squeeze of his hands and a rapid kick. He was aiming for the roof. His foot got caught in the ladder, his sloppy left sneaker wedging under the side bar, between two rungs. "Goddamn," he said, trying to work his heel out of the sneaker.

The ladder rocked under the weight of Coen and the boy. Blue

Eyes had to hug the ladder with both arms to keep his balance. He went up with the crawling motions of a baby. He pushed snow off his eyebrows, so he could watch Rupert's struggles with the ladder. "Rupert, wait for me." The snow smothered his voice.

Rupert's heel came free. He abandoned the trapped sneaker and started to climb again. He couldn't grip a ladder with a naked foot. It slipped off. Clutching with his hand, he missed the rung over his head. He had air and snow in his fingers. He fell. He didn't shape screams with his lips. No phantasmagoria pursued him as his body whirled. He didn't have flashes of Esther, Marilyn, or Isaac. He remembered nothing but his father's face. The squeezed-up skin with forty years of hurt. His mouth puffed open. He was trying to say dad.

Blue Eyes couldn't break Rupert's fall. The boy plunged in widening arcs outside Coen's reach. It was a dangerous wish: Coen didn't have steel pinchers to fetch a diving boy. Rupert's body would have ripped him off the ladder. Coen felt that smack into the snowbank with the hollows of his eyes. The shivers came down to his jaw. Was he crazy? Or had the boy begun to move? A hand pushed out from under a pile of snow. Rupert wasn't dead.

SIXTEEN

The woman with the suitcase was muttering in the hall. Doctors and nurses jumped out of her way. "Blue Eyes," she said; Marilyn had invaded Bellevue. She climbed up to the prisoners' ward and screamed at the metal door. "Manfred, come on out." The watchman thought she was insane.

"That's police business, young lady. You can't go in there."

"I am the police," Marilyn said.

The watchman grumbled to himself about the retards who were running loose on his floor. His name was Fred. "Yeah, you're a cop, I'm a cop, and the junkies in this ward wear badges on their pajamas."

"My father's a commissioner," she said. "Now open up."

"Lady, do me a favor. Disappear. You know how we get rid of pests? We stuff them in the laundry chute."

"Scumbag," Marilyn said, in her father's voice. "Did you ever meet Isaac the Pure?"

The watchman began to doubt himself. "What about Isaac?"

"I'm the only daughter he has. You understand? Bring me Blue Eyes."

"Blue Eyes? Why didn't you say you wanted him?" The watchman paged Manfred on the house telephone. Marilyn heard the click of an electric lock, and Blue Eyes came through the door. The watchman stared at the two of them; they had the same miserable look: runny noses and raw, scratchy eyes. Lovebirds, the watchman suspected. Goddamn lovebirds.

Coen picked up Marilyn's suitcase and spoke to the watchman. "Mind the store, Freddy. I'll be right back." Then he took Marilyn over to a closet behind the elevator shafts. He didn't say a word about the suitcase.

"They'll strangle me if anybody catches you up here."

"How are they going to manage that? You're the man with the gun . . . Manfred, come with me."

"I'm supposed to be guarding Stanley Chin. Isaac rings every half hour. He still thinks Cowboy intends to swipe the kid."

"Manfred, are you deaf? I'm splitting, and I want you to come."

"Marilyn, I'm a city boy," Coen said, groping with his tongue. "I wouldn't dig weekends in New Rochelle."

"Jesus," she said, "don't play stupid with me. Rupert is lying downstairs with a broken back. He nearly got himself killed on account of Isaac."

"What was he doing in your window? You don't climb fire escapes in a blizzard without an excuse. He was reaching for you."

"Sure he was reaching. With a spoon."

"Marilyn, he didn't come over to crack hard-boiled eggs. Not him. You can rip a person's throat off with less than a spoon." Coen touched the metal corners of the suitcase. "Where you going?"

"As far as I can get. Seattle maybe. Vancouver. Manfred, do I have to beg? He'll make you kill somebody, that father of mine. Or get you killed. It's all the same to him."

Coen shrugged. He had a dent in his cheek. "I aint so hot at running away. What could I do in Seattle? I'd miss the cockroaches. I'd go woolly without the street."

She could have grabbed him by the nose and led him out of Bellevue, but she sensed the futility of that. He couldn't abandon her father's fort. He was the blue-eyed "angel" of Isaac's squad. She stood on her toes to kiss him, caressing the blond hairs on his neck with her tongue flicking in his mouth. She didn't give him the chance to return the kiss, or squeeze her into the closet. She pulled the suitcase away from him and ran down the hall. She wasn't a girl who could tolerate slow goodbyes.

Coen listened for the clump of her shoes. He was afraid to watch. A bouncing suitcase would have fucked him in the head. He loved that skinny girl. But the blizzard had stopped, and they couldn't hide in Isaac's blanket, or crawl to Seattle. How could he walk away from Isaac with Isaac's girl in his fist? The Chief had communed with his spies: two petty gamblers from Ninety-second Street swore on their mothers' holy graves that Zorro Guzmann would be coming down to the Port Authority terminal to collect a load of runaway girls arriving on a bus from Memphis. Isaac was suspicious of gamblers who took to swearing on a grave, but he couldn't snub the opportunity of catching Zorro with twelve-and thirteen-year-old bait. So he crouched on a platform over the big clock with four faces, where he could pick out Bronx pimps and Tennessee girls sneaking along the main concourse of the terminal.

He kept his chin behind an early edition of *The New York Times,* with a police radio tucked under his belt. The radio allowed Isaac to confer with his "angels," who skulked through different parts of the terminal, some of them in women's clothes.

"Isaac, we'll grab the Guzmanns with their pants down, you'll see," said Newgate, the FBI man. He had come along with Isaac as a neutral observer, trying to steal the First Deputy men's techniques. He wore wraparound sunglasses in late February, with a piece of Isaac's newspaper against his mouth. He had the grubby feel of a white slaver.

The radio ticked in Isaac's belt. One of his "angels" was summoning him from the Greyhound baggage room near the Ninth Avenue exit. "Isaac, it's going down. The two gloms are here. Zorro and his brother."

"Not so loud," Isaac muttered into his belt.

"Chief, should we piss on their earmuffs?"

"No. Stay where you are."

Zorro and Jorge Guzmann strolled onto the main concourse in wool sweaters and balding earmuffs, tracked by Isaac's "angels." Zorro came without his checkered coat, or his pigskin shoes. Earmuffs must have been his uniform in Manhattan. Newgate tittered at the Chief. "Remember, Isaac, if they touch one little girl coming off a bus, they belong to me."

Jorge stood under the big clock while his brother went into a telephone booth. Newgate sucked his fingers. Zorro came out, and the Guzmanns continued their stroll. They didn't look at the platform over their heads. They ignored the "angels" on the escalators, and the weird women with walkie-talkies in their shopping bags. They didn't smile, or tinker with an earmuff. They left the terminal without a boodle of Tennessee girls.

Newgate sulked. "Isaac, how did they make us? Who gave them the word?"

Isaac rushed down to the telephones east of the clock. He found a slip of paper in Zorro's booth. It read, "Eat me, Isaac." He sent his "angels" back to Headquarters. He had to duck the FBI man now. "Newgate, I'm going to see my mother. So long."

He rode crosstown in a taxi, stopping the cab a block from Bellevue, near the old medical college. He paid the driver, got out, and lunged at a girl. Her suitcase spilled open. Marilyn began picking underpants off the street. Isaac wouldn't help.

"You don't have to worry, papa. I'm not going to bother Manfred any more. He's yours. God, you get loyalty from your slaves. He had the choice. Blue Eyes wouldn't budge. Isaac, you must be the greatest lay in New York."

Marilyn crept over the underpants. Isaac had to lift her off the ground. Holding her, he could feel his shame. He had manipulated Marilyn and Coen, tricked them into coming together with Rupert on the prowl. Still, her jabber didn't make sense. He pulled Coen once Rupert dove under Marilyn's window, but that didn't qualify him as a "great lay," or anything else. Isaac wasn't pimping for Manfred Coen. He slapped at the suitcase, with garter belts and shirt sleeves dangling from the bottom. "Where the hell are you taking that?"

"To Far Rockaway," she said.

"Don't get cute with your father. I'll march you right home. I'll strap you to Rivington Street."

"I know," she said. "You'll roll blintzes for me and Ida."

She ran towards the medical college, hugging the suitcase with one arm. Isaac couldn't smile at the feeble pumping of her knees. His own skinny daughter was trying to escape from him, running to a college for protection. He had to yank her by the hair before her knees would slow down. "Crazy bitch, you think you'll get asylum in there? You'll ask mercy from a bunch of imbeciles who've been looking at corpses all day. They'll wheel you to the morgue with a lump of sugar in your mouth, those ghouls."

Her eyes were bulging from the knuckles in her scalp, and Isaac let her go. She had that mad concentrated scowl of her mother; Kathleen was the single person in this world who could frighten him. Mother and daughter, they knew how to squeeze the flesh under a man's heart. "Baby," he said, "what's wrong?"

His purring had no effect. She was shaking under her coat. Burrs appeared in her forehead, long burrs that could split a girl's brain. Isaac launched her with a soft shove. "You're free," he said. She didn't move. With two fingers he quieted the burrs in her head. She trudged towards Second Avenue, losing a sock on the way. Isaac recognized the queerness of that sock. Magenta wasn't Marilyn's color. The sock belonged to Coen.

Isaac crossed over to the hospital. He walked under the hump of a glass canopy that was shedding layers of ice. He entered Bellevue with two wet ears. Isaac couldn't afford to bully the girl at the main desk. Police chiefs weren't allowed near Rupert's bed without a pass. Rupert was in the custody of Manhattan children's court; Isaac had to keep his fingers off a fifteen-year-old boy. He mumbled "Rupert Weil" to the girl at the desk.

The girl said, "Sorry. You can't go up. His pass box is empty. He has visitors in his room."

Isaac drew out his badge. "Miss, I'm a friend of his father. A personal friend. Deputy Chief Inspector Sidel. Would I harm the boy? Ask your supervisors. I'm at Bellevue twice a week."

The girl stared at the blue and gold leaves on Isaac's badge. She scribbled a pass for him. "Fifteen minutes," she said.

"That's all you're buying from me."

Isaac crouched upstairs. He showed his pass to a measly sheriff from the children's court who was guarding Rupert. Any quiff could have gotten past this sheriff. it was lucky for the children's court that Isaac had Stanley Chin, or the hospital would have lost Rupert and the sheriff's pants.

Isaac could see Rupert from the door. The bastards had mummified him; he was taped to a board, with a pulley near his feet. Only a piece of him remained unbandaged, a crooked oval from his eyebrows to the cleft under his lip, including most of his ears. His cheeks had turned a hospital yellow.

There was nothing sickly about Rupert's eyes; they were bearing into Isaac with the hunger of a boy who couldn't be trapped on an inclined board. Isaac had to look away; you could catch brain fever gaping at a boy who never blinked. His body caught in traction, unable to move, he would have finished Isaac with the hooking power in his eye. The Chief respected such intransigence. But he wasn't getting into a staring war with Rupert Weil. Isaac couldn't win.

He was hit with a maddening smell by the door; he noticed boxes of caramels, black halvah, lollipops with sharpened sticks sunk into them, colored sugar water in little wax bottles that you had to break with your teeth, swollen marshmallows, and white chocolate sitting on a chair. These items must have been transported from the Bronx, where the Guzmanns owned a candy store. Isaac howled at the sheriff, who was asleep.

"The visitors Rupert had, did they come with earmuffs on their stupid heads?"

The sheriff made a timid "yes" with a shake of his jaw. Isaac sprang into the corridor with a closed fist. Zorro had been in and out of the hospital before Isaac could scratch his nose. Jorge brought the lollipops and the Russian halvah. Isaac came with empty pockets. The Guzmanns were too primitive to destroy with the rough, grinding hours of orthodox police work. They could slip between spies and two-way radios, and make themselves invisible to undercover men in padded brassieres.

Muddling over the Guzmanns, Isaac crossed shoulders with Mordecai and Philip, and the three Jewish musketeers of Seward Park were reunited after a lapse of twenty-seven years. They were awkward with each other. Mordecai molded his cap between his knuckles. Philip pulled the webbing under his hand-painted tie. Isaac brushed the radio in his belt with a fingernail. Mordecai, who was always in the middle, a trifle less severe than the two geniuses, spoke first.

"Isaac, a detective should know something about the human body. The doctors tell us stories about a severed nerve. Do you think Rupert will ever talk again?"

"Mordecai," Philip said, "is Isaac a magician? How can he predict?"

"Philip, don't cheapen his talents. Isaac is a master at predictions. Didn't he predict where my daughter was? He took Honey out of the gutter . . . only that was a month ago. And he gave your son back to you. What does it matter that Rupert will have to walk with three canes? He's alive."

"Mordecai," Philip said, "that's enough."

Isaac's puckered belly itched inside his slipover. Could he play the Chief with old friends? "Philip, I'm sorry. It was a crazy accident. I swear to you, my detective didn't throw him off the fire escape."

Mordecai sniggered in Isaac's face. "Coen? That guy couldn't push a baby into a puddle. Isaac, your hand was behind the whole thing. You gave the push from your lousy Headquarters."

Philip said, "Shut up."

"Why? Didn't he have Rupert's face on his posters? They would have shot him in the street like a dog. Isaac, I don't forgive what Rupert did to Sophie and the other people. But there's a difference between a demented boy and a cop with dirt in his ears."

Philip dragged Mordecai by his arm. "Isaac, we have to go." They shuffled down the corridor, closing in on the sheriff and Rupert's ward, Mordecai struggling against Philip. Isaac had to shout. "Philip, I'll call you . . . tomorrow."

Isaac's shoes dug into Bellevue linoleum. He could march downstairs to his mother, or up one flight to Coen. The cuff of his trouser leg swished into the wall as Isaac selected Blue Eyes and the prisoners' ward. He'd sit with Sophie in the afternoon. He needed Coen's smile.

The watchman upstairs saluted Isaac. Freddy was in awe of the Chief. "Isaac, do you have a daughter with light brown hair? She was shouting high and low, but I couldn't let her in. That's the rules."

Even on a day shattered by the Guzmanns and Mordecai, Isaac had enough pluck to soothe a watchman. "Fred, you did right."

Freddy clicked the lock for him, and Isaac went inside. The prisoners' room was bombed out. Isaac had stepped into a war zone. The beds were scattered in a wretched design that made no sense. A junkie lay under one of them, huddling with a child's top that was much too feeble to spin for very long. The walls had large seams in them, and fresh bites; Isaac could have gone into the plaster with his elbow. Coen was with Stanley Chin.

They didn't have any greetings for Isaac. They stared at him from Stanley's hospital crib, adrift in their own shallow sleep. Isaac had the urge to blow dust out of their eyes. "Manfred, what's happening?"

Finally Coen smiled. Isaac expected more. Manfred's cheeks were too tight. Isaac understood the source of it: the boy had Marilyn on his mind.

"Isaac, should I send out for cupcakes and tea?"

"No cupcakes," Isaac said. "Where's the checkerboard?"

"We only got chess players in here," Stanley hissed at the Chief.

Isaac frowned. Pushing pawns with Coen could remind him of fire escapes and a certain black bishop. He noticed the warped ping-pong table, and the yellow balls. He wanted to challenge Blue Eyes in front of Stanley Chin, take Coen at Coen's game. But the two sleepy faces near the crib unsettled him. Isaac grew timid. He didn't reach for the yellow balls.

The Chief had a gift waiting for him at Centre Street: a special edition of *The Toad*. Isaac's mug was on the cover, with the word "ASSASSIN" in boldface and the by-line of Tony Brill. Brodsky and the rubber-gun squad couldn't hide the covers from Isaac. Barney's men swarmed through Headquarters, from the basement to the giant cupola over the PC's rooms, stuffing *The Toad* into every available corner.

"Garbage," Brodsky announced, after reading Tony Brill. *The Toad* accused Isaac, in wavering margins and blotchy ink, of mounting a "death campaign" against Rupert Weil and the children of New York. "Who's next?" Tony Brill screamed from the second page. "How many of us will have to give up our sons and daughters to the Behemoth at Police Headquarters? Will we all land inside the Blue Whale?"

"Pure shit," Brodsky told the Chief. "Isaac, should I break his feet?" The chauffeur realized the absurdity of his threat. Tony Brill was unapproachable now. The rumor at Headquarters was that Brill had jumped from *The Toad* to *Time* magazine.

"Brodsky," Isaac said, "go scratch yourself. I'm busy." He made Brodsky close the door. The Chief had something to do. If he concentrated on the Guzmanns, he wouldn't have to think about Marilyn the Wild. So he planned his next assault. The Guzmanns were immune to First Deputy snares. Jorge had forks in his earmuffs that could sniff a handgun out of girdles and brassieres. Isaac wouldn't use ordinary spies. He'd have to place a cop in deep, deep undercover. Who would go into the Bronx to poison the Guzmanns' black halvah? Brodsky? Coen? Cowboy Rosenblatt? Isaac was in a fix. He had nobody to send. Marilyn crept into that country between Isaac's walls. He couldn't fish her out of the room.

The rubber-gun squad stood with their chins near Isaac's door. They were cursing Tony Brill and tearing Isaac's picture off the covers of *The Toad*. "Shhh," Brodsky said. "You want to disturb the boss? He's thinking in there."

Marilyn the Wild had gone to Port Authority. She sat by herself on the uppermost deck of the terminal, hunched against her suitcase. She had hours to kill before the next crosscountry bus. She roosted a quarter of a mile from the escalators, in an isolated spot. The prospect of company, male or female, could make her nauseous. She'd spill her guts on the wall if she had to explain her flight from three husbands, blintzes, and her father. She didn't want to say "Isaac."

A dude in vinyl buckskin spotted Marilyn on his fourth stroll through the terminal. This dude went by the name of Henry. The sweep of Marilyn's stockings couldn't turn him on. Henry was interested in her suitcase. He'd swiped a Polaroid in the morning, and a silk umbrella; with Marilyn's stuff, he could visit his Jew on Thirty-seventh Street and collect a twenty. He'd fallen in love with a hat in Ohrbach's window.

"Hiya, sweet potato," he said, sitting down next to the suitcase. Marilyn's scowls couldn't pull him away. Henry wondered if the girl was a "pros." Who else would rest on a balcony with one foot off the ground? Only a whore. She had adorable knees, a strong Irish face, with bumps under her coat where her tits ought to be. Somebody owns this broad. Suppose it was Zorro, the Bronx spic, who had pimping rights at every bus station in New York. Henry could get his ears chopped off. The Guzmanns weren't human. They came from a forest in Peru. If you tampered with their women, they would bite your nose and leave parts of you in a paper bag. It was a risk Henry had to take.

First he'd explore a little. "Are you a friend of Zorro, sweetheart?" The whore wouldn't answer him. "Are you Guzmann merchandise?" Henry felt safer now. He snatched the suitcase, shouting, "See you, baby," and ran for the stairs, because the fucking escalators were too far away.

Marilyn stayed on the bench without crying "Thief." She wasn't so attached to a pile of underpants. She'd get another pair when the bus stopped in Chicago. Unencumbered, she could travel with a toothbrush in her pocket. She began to doze.

Dreaming, she saw a buckskin suit, a thief with dangling legs.

She didn't have to touch her cheeks. The suitcase was near her toes.
A man was lugging Henry by the nape of his fake buckskin collar.
Blue Eyes. She could have strangled him with affection if that thief
hadn't been around. She was dying to lick behind his ears.

Coen was sheepish with her. "Marilyn, I snuck out of Bellevue. I
have forty minutes. Stanley is covering for me. I figured you'd be
here. But I wouldn't have gotten to you without this glom. I noticed
what he was carrying."

"Manfred, there's a million suitcases like mine?"

"That's true. But how many of them have purple underpants
sticking out of the side?"

They laughed, while Henry had a crick in his neck. He assumed
Coen was a gorilla who worked for Zorro. He stuck his fingers in his
chest and prayed. He'd heard that in spite of Peru the Guzmanns were
religious people. Would they send a priest for him before they peeled
his face?

"Marilyn, should I let him go? He led me to you, didn't he? And
if I pinch him, we won't have any time for ourselves."

Marilyn wasn't greedy. She kissed Henry on the forehead and
thanked him for bringing Coen. Henry creased his lips into a quarter
smile. Then he galloped towards the escalators. After Coen he
couldn't trust the stairs.

Marilyn fumbled with Blue Eyes, her arms inside his camel's
hair coat, her teeth knocking into his jaw. The cop didn't resist. He
had most of her blouse in his hand. Marilyn kicked off her shoes and
wiggled out of her skirt. She would have pulled Coen down on the
bench with her, but the cop became suspicious. "Marilyn, there are
Port Authority detectives running around. They could snitch on us to
Isaac."

"Who cares about snitchers?"

Coen spied an alcove about twenty feet behind Marilyn. It was
the entrance to an abandoned toilet. He picked up skirt, blouse, and
suitcase. Marilyn carried her shoes. The alcove was narrow, and they
had nowhere to lie down. Marilyn leaned into a dirty wall. Coen's
pants dropped to his knees. Their bellies met under the coats. "Blue
Eyes," she said. Soon her mumbling was indistinct.

Taped to a moveable bedboard, a hospital boat with wheels,
Rupert stared up at his father and Mordecai, the two shabby princes
of Essex Street. He couldn't say papa, or mouth welcomes to

Mordecai. Falling off Isaac's fire escape, he'd landed on his neck and
lost the power of speech. He wasn't dumb to his father's words. Only
Mordecai kept interrupting Philip.

"Rupert, listen to us. No cocksucker cop can get into your room
again. There's a guard outside with a gun. If that's not enough, me
and your father will sit with you. We'll stop Isaac next time. Rupert
you want some orange juice? Just wiggle your chin."

Rupert's chin was encased in thick swads of gauze. A nurse had
shaved his skull, and wrapped him in a hundred feet of bandage. He
didn't have one free toe.

"Moron," Philip said. "How can he signal for juice?"

The princes began to bicker. A team of nurses drove them out of
the room. Mordecai scratched his knee. Rupert watched the hunched
lines of his father's back. Candy stripes on a twenty-dollar shirt
couldn't hide the bumps under Philip's shoulder blade. Rupert
screamed inside his head. So long, papa. So long, Mordecai. He'd
have to mother these two men. They had gray tufts behind the ears:
neither of them was a grandfather yet. Mordecai walked with bent
knees. Philip had a crooked neck from the years he'd given to
crouching on Essex Street. Rupert would take his father out of Isaac's
territories. They'd ride the currents on Third Avenue in Rupert's
hospital boat. They'd settle in a different part of the borough (Philip
would die without a few yards of Manhattan). They'd send for
Mordecai. The three of them would make war on the pimps who were
holding Honey. Then Rupert would bounce upstairs on his bedboard
and pluck Stanley Chin out of the prisoners' ward. The cops would
scream for the big Jew. Rupert wouldn't care. Isaac didn't exist
above Delancey Street.

Rupert's bliss began to fail. How could he pull Esther out of the
ground? Clay in her ears wouldn't bring her alive. His groin was
shrewder than miles of bandage. Bellevue, Isaac, and the mummy's
bag they'd wrapped him in couldn't stop his erection from pushing
through the gauze. He was crying without a pinch of water in his
eyes. These weren't a mourner's brittle tears. His hunger for Esther
Rose couldn't be quieted with a doctor's needle, or sugar in his veins.

From time to time an intern would appear and marvel at the
broken boy and his erection. The boy's nurses could see the swelling
in the gauze. They giggled among themselves. "Practically
unconscious and he gets it up." Rupert would growl at them behind
immobile cheeks. Where's Mordecai? Where's my dad? And when

they flipped him over, spanked his thighs to lessen the possibility of bed sores, Rupert would hiss through his nose. Ladies, you can't kill a lollipop.

The door opened. He expected orderlies in filthy green coats to change the tubes and pans under his. bed. He saw mittens in a wheelchair and a sad-faced cop. It was Blue Eyes and Stanley Chin. Rupert smiled without untightening his lips. The cop was reticent. He wouldn't approach the bedboard. "Tell him," Stanley pleaded. "Can't you tell him?"

Coen dangled an arm behind the wheelchair. "Didn't mean to chase you in the storm . . . you shouldn't have climbed for the roof . . . the Chief's got a tricky fire escape. Rupert, I'm sorry."

The cop was silent again. Rupert didn't have to look very hard. The storm wasn't over for Blue Eyes; flecks of color exploded around Coen's enormous pupils. Where's Lady Marilyn? Coen was as sad as Mordecai. Mummified, stuck to a bedboard, he was glad he hadn't spooned blood out of Marilyn's neck. Coen could use her kisses.

"Rupe," Stanley said, grazing the mummy with plaster on his fist. "The bulls can't keep us apart. Shit, Mr. Coen snuck me down here. I'm not supposed to have visiting rights."

Rupert laughed underneath the canals of his nose. He could no longer feel the distant points of his body. He existed without fingers, elbows, or the blades of his knees. He had eyes, ears, and a sensitive prick. He couldn't laugh with his kneecaps, or get his belly to shake. His tongue lay dead. But he was grateful to Blue Eyes for bringing Stanley. He'd roll tongues in the back of his head. Clap out a dozen words. Stanley, we'll mend together. We'll grow new hands. We'll flood Bellevue with Isaac's songs.

The boys couldn't scrape their bandages in private. Nurses charged into the room. They had swollen red skin. "What do you mean, Detective Coen? Rupert Weil can't have any guests. Take your prisoner upstairs."

He heard the rattle of handlebars, the grunt of wheels, and he was in a world without Blue Eyes and Stanley Chin. The nurses grabbed his bedboard. They rotated him between their elbows, so Rupert couldn't fall. His erection was gone. His cheeks wobbled against the gauze. He was beginning to feel his knees again. The nurses put him back. "Rest," they said, as they hustled away from him. They screamed at the guard who had been assigned to Rupert by the children's court. "No one gets through this door. Not even the Chief of Police."

Rupert dreamed with an eye on the wall. There were shouts and sputters in the corridor. He saw patches of Philip and Mordecai. The two princes from Essex Street were arguing with nurses, doctors, orderlies, and Rupert's guard. "Are you crazy?" Mordecai said. "This is the boy's father. We want some satisfaction, please. We'll crush your lungs if we can't get in." A hole formed in the wedges of nurses' uniforms. The princes slipped through. They arrived at the bedboard. Rupert didn't have the capacity to wink at them. Papa, he said. Papa and Mordecai.

THE EDUCATION OF
PATRICK SILVER

PART ONE

ONE

Patrick Silver left the baby in the lobby of the Plaza Hotel. The baby, who was forty-four, sat in an upholstered chair, with his knuckles in his lap. His name was Jerónimo. A boy with gray around his ears, a Guzmann of Boston Road, his education had stopped at the first grade. He lived most of his life in a candy store, under the eye of his father and his many brothers. But the Guzmanns were feuding with the police. They couldn't protect the baby on their own. They had to put Jerónimo in Patrick Silver's care. Patrick was his temporary keeper.

Jerónimo had blackberries in his head. With a carpet under his feet, and candelabra around his chair, he was thinking of the Guzmann farm in Loch Sheldrake. It was the blackberry season, and Jerónimo wanted to stick his fingers in the briars and drink blackberry juice. But he was a hundred miles from Loch Sheldrake, waiting for Patrick Silver in a hotel with rust-colored wool on the floor.

Patrick Silver rode the Plaza elevators in a filthy soccer shirt. The elevator boy was uncomfortable with a giant who stank of Dublin beer. Silver had a ruddy look. He came to the Plaza without his shoes. He was six-foot-three in simple black socks.

Patrick began roaming the corridors of the third floor. Chambermaids pushed their linen carts out of his way; a shoeless man was anathema to the maids, who glanced at Patrick's socks with their noses hidden in the carts. They returned to their business once Patrick knocked on a door. He muttered three words. "Zorro sent me."

He walked into a room that seemed uncommonly small for a hotel that had elevators with gold walls and carpeting that could hide a man's feet. A girl stood behind the door in a sweater that once belonged to Jerónimo; it swam around her shoulders, but it couldn't tamper with the shape of her breasts. Patrick didn't have divided loyalties. He was paid to protect the Guzmanns and all their interests.

Still, he wasn't a man who could ignore the impression of nipples inside an old sweater.

The girl smiled at Patrick's socks. She'd heard of this crazy bodyguard who lived in the basement of a synagogue and wore soccer shirts and a holster without a gun. She liked the scratchiness of his face, the white hairs on his knuckles, and his imperfect nose. She was Odile Leonhardy, the teenage porno queen, and she admired men with enormous beaks. She had moved uptown, taken a room at the Plaza, to break into legitimate films.

"Where's your yarmulke, Patrick Silver?"

"In my pocket," he said.

"Why don't you put it on?"

"I wear it when I'm praying, miss. Or when I have the shivers."

"What happened to the baby?"

"He's downstairs."

"Is it safe to leave him alone?"

"Miss, no cop would ever lift him from the Plaza Hotel. I ought to know. I was a detective for thirteen years."

"Don't call me *miss*. I'm Odile. Didn't Zorro tell you to bring Jerónimo to me?"

The girl was confusing him. "No. Zorro went to Atlantic City. He asked me to visit you and say he'd be gone for a while."

"What's he doing in Atlantic City? Zorro hates the ocean. Did you ever see him take off his shirt?"

"He didn't go there for a swim. He has some business in New Jersey."

"Good for him. Now do your job, Patrick Silver, and show me Jerónimo."

Did she intend to play clap-hands with the baby? It wasn't Patrick's affair. He ducked around the chambermaids' carts and pulled Jerónimo out of the lobby. What kind of power did Zorro have over the girl? She unbuckled Jerónimo's belt and growled at Silver. "Wait outside."

Patrick was becoming a middleman in his old age (he'd be fifty in another eight years). The Guzmanns had made him into an Irish pimp: he was the one who steered Jerónimo to Odile's bed.

Patrick had to listen to a whore's music; he couldn't stray from the door. Odile mumbled "Jerónimo, Jerónimo," and the baby began to groan. He didn't cry out of displeasure, Patrick understood.

The groans stopped coming through the wall. Jerónimo couldn't have been inside more than three minutes. His belt was buckled when Odile brought him out. She had the same rumples in her sweater. "Tell Zorro Odile wishes him luck in Atlantic City."

"I'll do that, miss."

Patrick took the baby's hand and held it on their stroll through the corridors. Jerónimo had a wet palm. He walked with great swipes of his head, his shoulders dropping on the downswing and his chest whistling as he dragged Silver to the elevator cars.

Jerónimo exhausted his Irish keeper. Patrick had to fight for air. The two ancient boys stepped into the elevator. Passengers stared at them. Patrick and Jerónimo had huge tufts of gray-white hair; their thick clothes had a winter smell; the giant with the soccer shirt didn't believe in shoes.

They walked out of the elevator holding hands again; the baby had Patrick by the thumb. He led his keeper beyond the edges of the Plaza awning and into a damp July.

There were quiffs at the terminal, quiffs and spies, with the imprint of shotguns under their dashikis, police aerials climbing up their backs, newspaper stuffed in a brassiere; behind the bushy wigs they were blond "angels" from the First Deputy's office. They belonged to Isaac Sidel. Their Chief had lost his war with the Guzmann family, a tribe of Bronx pimps and policy rats, Marranos from Boston Road. Papa Guzmann and his five sons, Alejandro, Topal, Jorge, César, and Jerónimo, had irritated the Chief by crossing the Third Avenue Bridge to run a whore market in the middle of Manhattan. Isaac the Brave couldn't trap César, who was called Zorro in the Bronx, with his gang of baby prostitutes. So the Chief had himself pushed out of the First Deputy's office, disappeared into the Bronx, and emerged as a factotum to Papa Guzmann, on Boston Road. But his nearness to the Guzmanns brought him few advantages. He came out of the Bronx with a tapeworm, a black tongue, and no arrests.

The blond "angels" were going to avenge their Chief's disgrace. They scoured Port Authority for hints of Zorro and his brothers. They would have broken Alejandro's neck, drowned Topal's brains in a toilet bowl, shoved nickels and quarters in Zorro's eyes.

They didn't catch a thing. Zorro stepped around the dashikis in silk underpants. His face was smeared with the wax of a melted brown crayon, and he carried a straw suitcase like the Chicanos who were smuggled into New Jersey every summer to farm for sweet potatoes. His brother Jorge had come with him. The melted crayon left tiny bits of rubble under Jorge's ears.

The brothers climbed aboard a coach with ancient rattan seats. Zorro had a Bronx banana for his brother and a suitcase full of apples from his father's orchard. The apples were slightly bruised. The Guzmanns had picked them just before Isaac's friends in the FBI sneaked onto the property with an acetylene torch and put an end to Papa's farm.

The boys endured rattan spears in their buttocks for Papa's sake. They were going to visit a bagman named Isidoro, who was one of Papa's distant cousins.

The bagman owed his existence to Papa. He was starving in a shanty outside Bogotá when Papa rescued Isidoro and delivered him to a candy store in the Bronx. This candy store had a multiplicity of lives: it was the Guzmanns' headquarters, hospital, bedroom, and numbers bank. Isidoro would have been content eating bitter chocolate and growing bald in the candy store if Isaac hadn't come along. Unable to corrupt any of Papa's five boys, the Chief whispered in Isidoro's ear. He frightened the poor *bogotano*, advising him what the Manhattan police did to bagmen. "They'll drill holes in your tongue unless I help you, Isidore. You have no future here."

He turned Isidoro around with this and other blandishments. The bagman became a spy for Isaac. His revelations were small; he would only sell the Chief isolated scraps of information. After Isaac shucked off the candy store, the bagman skipped to Atlantic City. The disappearance of Isidoro and Isaac made Papa scratch his head. He began to guess the cozy relationship between his cousin and Isaac the Shit.

The brothers arrived at the old terminal on Arctic Avenue. Jorge was having hunger pains. He clutched his belly and made pathetic squeals, searching for candy vendors who didn't exist. Zorro had no more bananas in his pocket. But he had to quiet Jorge; squeals from a man with a twenty-inch neck would call attention to them, place the Guzmanns in Atlantic City. "Jorge, don't cry. You'll get candy on the beach."

They took the Arkansas Avenue route to the boardwalk, stopping at a Hadassah thrift shop to buy Jorge a hat that would keep the sun out of his eyes. They passed a row of forlorn hotels crouching near Pacific Avenue, with little beaten porches and stoops, and old men behind the screens. The great mildewed cupola of the Claridge blinked at them from South Indiana. The smell of suntan oil oppressed the brothers soon as they struck the beach. Without the shelter of Arkansas Avenue, they had to suck hot wind.

The curve of the boardwalk made Zorro grumpy. He couldn't go very far on wood that bent away from his feet. He led Jorge to a fudge shop. Jorge smiled at the conveyor belt that carried roasted peanuts from the window to an oven deep in the shop. A puppet with lively hands was mixing fudge in a copper bowl behind the peanuts. The puppet's bushy hair reminded Jorge of his older brother. "Jerónimo," he grunted, forgetting his belly for a minute. He didn't want fudge—black, white, green, or yellow. Zorro had to buy him red-hot dollars, candy fish, and almond macaroons.

They crept over the hump in the boardwalk, avoiding the linked trolley cars that were swollen with passengers in banjo hats who licked on miniature bottles of rum and laughed at Zorro's coloring. "Follow us, Crayola Face." Jorge would have bumped the trolleys, spilling every banjo hat under the boardwalk, if Zorro hadn't restrained him with a thumb in his pants. "Papa warned you not to feud with idiots. We'll lose track of Isidoro. Brother, remember what Isaac did to us. He tried to kill Jerónimo. He took our country home."

Jorge hurled pieces of macaroon at the trolley cars. He grunted curses that only the Marranos could have understood. He spoke in muddled Portuguese. But he didn't knock fenders off the cars. He fell in behind his brother. People stared at them from the sun decks of monstrous stone hotels that pushed into the edge of the boardwalk. The rust on the hotels' copper roofs had turned a slimy green. The stone walls of the sun decks were splintering under the surface. Jorge followed the lumps in the nearest wall.

The impurities in the stone shimmered under the soft bill of his cap. Jorge would have dawdled with a hand on the wall, but Zorro steered him away from the sun porches. A tug of his pants brought him inside a gypsy booth that was nothing more than an ugly gash in the wall. The word "Phrenologist" was painted over the booth in a pretty yellow. It frightened Jorge, who couldn't read thick words, although he was smarter than Jerónimo. Jorge could iron a necktie, utter whole sentences, and pee with fortitude into the heart of a toilet bowl. Like all his brothers he had no specific birthday (his father was superstitious about such events), but he was a summer child, born in January, during the dry Peruvian season, just under forty years ago.

Jorge felt a breeze on his neck in the gypsy cave. A pregnant woman sat near the entrance of the booth in a man's undershirt. She welcomed the brothers into her cave with a powerful yawn, wrinkling her undershirt and sending fissures through her belly. Zorro didn't interest her. She liked small ears on a big head. Jorge had to stoop for the gypsy. The woman breathed into his scalp. Without fingering Jorge she could interpret the design of his earlobes and the magnitude of bumps on his skull. "This boy covets women," she said. "Be careful with him. His knees aren't strong. He's going to fall."

"Fine," Zorro said. "Terrific. I'll watch my brother's knees." He dropped five dollars into the gypsy's undershirt. "Madame Sonia, save your forecasts. Our religion doesn't allow us any future. We're Catholics in a prehistoric way. We love Jesus but we don't have much use for his mother. So don't expect pity from us. My father's getting lonely for his cousin. Where's Isidoro? You're supposed to be his landlady now."

The *bogotano* was short on brains. Half of Papa's runners and pickup men vacationed on the boardwalk between Texas Avenue and Steeplechase Pier, because Miami was too far away. The runners had seen Isidoro with the pregnant witch.

"Sonia, don't be mean. You counted the ridges in my brother's hair. He's getting homesick. Can't you tell? He has gas pains whenever he leaves the Bronx. Where's Isidoro?"

A boy sprang out from behind the witch's chair. He put a small revolver against Jorge's head. He had crooked teeth, Zorro noticed, and the revolver's taped barrel shivered in Jorge's ear. "That's my son," the pregnant gypsy said. "He listens to me. He'll blow your brother's face off, I swear. Get out of Atlantic City."

Jorge didn't turn glum. A gun in his ear couldn't make him freeze. He swallowed a candy fish and stuck two fingers around the cylinder of the boy's gun. The flight of Jorge's hand puzzled the witch; it seemed idiotic to caress a gun with two lazy fingers.

Zorro rubbed his cheek. The Marranos despised firearms (guns were for city bandits and cops like Isaac the Toad), but Zorro understood the tenacity of his brother's grip. He dug a fingernail into the witch's belly. "Bring me Isidoro."

The boy hissed at Zorro and tried to curl the trigger; he couldn't get the cylinder to spin. Jorge's two fingers had smothered the action of the gun. The witch rolled in her chair. The Guzmanns had to be less than human, creatures with stinking souls; who else would eat lead bullets with the pounce of a thumb? "Misters, don't hurt my boy."

The gun disappeared into Jorge's sleeve. The gypsy wagged her head. Only men who drank the boiling piss of Christian-Jewish saints could be such strong magicians. Sonia had heard of the Marranos, who could call upon Moses of Sinai, Jesus, Jacob, and the kings of Babylon to protect them. She led the brothers out of the cave and into the dense grass of her private lot, a wedge of ground behind Pennsylvania Avenue. There were no boardwalk trolleys in the witch's grass, just the signboard of an old restaurant, The Merman's Roost, pieces of tin meant to look like a gondola, or another long ship, rusting on the ground, the gondola with its edges bitten off and enormous pocks in its middle.

Jorge was confused by a gondola in the grass. He could shred his pants crossing a boat that had teeth in its two gigantic ears. Zorro had to walk his brother over the signboard, knee by knee. The rust disfigured Jorge's shoes.

The gypsy brought them to a bungalow at the end of the lot. The brothers couldn't find a serviceable door. They had to crawl through a hole in the porch screen to get into the gypsy's house. The bagman didn't give them any trouble. He yelled to Zorro from the kitchen. "César, what can I make you? I miss your father's tea. I don't have the patience to say prayers over the kettle. Not like Papa."

"Isidoro, my tongue isn't dry today. I'll live without your tea."

The bagman shuffled through the kitchen in his pajamas. Zorro's spite was gone: he shouldn't have been harsh with his father's cousin. The Guzmanns drank deep red tea with Isidoro. Jorge burnt his fingers on the glass. Isidoro allowed himself a timid smile. The crypto-Jews of Spain, Portugal, Holland, Brazil, Peru, and the Bronx could only enjoy scalding tea; the fire in their gullets told them they were still alive.

With red tea inside him, Zorro's anger slowed. He had finances to discuss. "Isidoro, Papa owes you a hundred and seventy dollars. I saw it in his ledger. How should it be paid? To the gypsy and her son?"

"Half," the bagman said. "Half to Madame Sonia, and half to the orphans' home on Stebbins Avenue."

"Isidoro, you know the fools who administer that place. Your charity will go into some rich doctor's pocket." The bagman's puffy eyes clipped Zorro's arguments. He penciled in a figure on his shirt cuff, where the Guzmanns did most of their arithmetic. "Eighty-five dollars to the orphans of Stebbins Avenue," Zorro announced. Then he and Jorge hugged Isidoro; the three of them swayed near the gypsy's stove. The brothers hadn't lost their affection for the *bogotano*.

They held their embrace while Jorge sniffled and the bagman inquired about Jerónimo. "The baby's in good hands. Papa hired a bodyguard for him. An Irish baboon." Zorro began to smell Isaac on the bagman's pajamas. He finished the embrace.

"Isidoro, you shouldn't have taken Isaac the Shit for a sweetheart. Why didn't you sing to a different cop? . . ."

Jorge clapped his elbow under the bagman's mouth. Isidoro didn't writhe against Jorge's chest. His eyeballs didn't have a bloody expression. The veins didn't rise on Isidoro's cheeks in slow, horrible clusters of blue. The bones cracked once behind his ears, and the bagman was dead.

A truck would arrive late in the afternoon. The Guzmanns weren't sacrilegious people. Provision had been made for Papa's cousin. He wouldn't have to lie under Jersey soil. The truck would transport him to the Guzmann cemetery in Bronxville, where a company of mourners would rip their clothes in Isidoro's behalf and wail until the sky got black.

The brothers left the bungalow through the same hole in the screen, crossed the rusty gondola, and came out of the gypsy's cave. They locked themselves in a toilet on Stepplechase Pier. Zorro spilled articles out of his suitcase. Apples, two bandannas, skirts, a blouse, high-heeled shoes. Jorge left the pier with the two bandannas on his head and apples in his blouse. This was the way Zorro would sneak him back to their father's candy store. Isaac the Shit had cops everywhere on Boston Road. Only niggers, children, and girls in bandannas were safe.

Jorge grew somber under the scarves, blouse, and skirts. He pushed the apples down to his waist. He hobbled on the boardwalk. Zorro couldn't get to Arkansas Avenue without buying more candy fish for his brother.

TWO

"The dark bottles, Sammy, if you please. In the usual tub. I've a thirst on me could destroy a hippopotamus."

Patrick Silver drank his Guinness warm. It came from Dublin in tiny bottles that were packed religiously behind the counter. The Kings of Munster couldn't fail its principal client. An Irish bar on Horatio Street, it was never out of Guinness.

Silver needed his twenty nips. He would stumble into the Kings of Munster exhausted from his tribulations at the synagogue. The barman had a pitcher waiting for him after evening prayer. It was Patrick's lot to raise a minyan (a quorum of ten upright Jews) for his shul. He had a curious affinity for capturing Jews. He would roost on the steps of the synagogue and chirp at passers-by, whether infant, man, or boy. "Are you Jewish, sir?" If you hesitated for a moment you were lost. Patrick would swipe at you from the stairs, clutch an arm, and haul you in. He could carry two men or three boys in a single trip. Having Jerónimo made it easier for him. He would stick a prayer shawl over the baby's head and include him in the minyan. Jerónimo's mewls didn't upset the minyan's droning music. If he was short one Jew, Patrick had his prayer book. He would wrap it in the fringes of his shawl, pronounce a blessing, and the prayer book became Patrick's tenth man.

But the strain of so many minyans was beginning to tell on Patrick, who had to mind the synagogue and the baby. So he sat in the Kings of Munster on the stool he preferred, away from the window and the dog shit on Horatio Street that traveled so fast in July; it was dangerous for an Irishman to be out of doors. "God bless," he said to barman Sam before drinking from the pitcher.

Silver nursed his bottles. He didn't grow a Guinness mustache until the fifth bottle had been poured. The Kings of Munster wasn't a bar for guzzlers. Patrick nibbled on the beer, scooping in the bitter foam with his tongue. He loathed American beer, pissy blond water that could have been brewed in a bubble-pipe. Silver was a Guinness child, born with a black bottle in his mouth. His da, who made pencils in Limerick until a mad priest chased out all the Jews, took him to the Kings of Munster when he was a month old and sat him on the bar. Patrick learned to crawl this way, on a bumpy sheet of iron that was galvanized with whiskey and Dublin beer. He didn't have to sneak his nose into a gentleman's pitcher. He drank his Guinness right off the bar, warmed over with a slight taste of zinc.

By the twelfth bottle Patrick had mustaches on three sides of his face. He began to croon his father's songs about the witches, giants, toads of Limerick, and the burning of Wolfe Tone Street. Pissed in the head, with Guinness blowing out of his ears, he saw a wicked Chrysler pass the Kings' window three times. Patrick spit into his hand to scare off any avenging angel who might be hovering near Horatio Street. He knew the owner of the car, and its principal passenger. He said goodbye to Sammy, picked up his britches, and hobbled out of the bar.

It was treacherous to go around the bend of Abingdon Square in stockings alone. But Patrick couldn't wear shoes. Leather bands on his feet gave him ungodly blisters. As a cop he'd been at the mercy of his superiors: the PC wouldn't allow unshod detectives near his office. Patrick had to stuff cotton balls through the neck of every shoe in his closet. He walked on cotton for thirteen years, howling at the number of blisters he endured. The medics at Bellevue had never heard of a cop with such sensitive feet. Patrick avoided the chiropodists and their talk of miraculous foot powders. He would hop about in agony when he had to chase a thief.

Now he was watching for dog shit. He curtsied up close to the benches of Abingdon Square park, suspicious of the gray areas between lampposts. He was a bit nearsighted in the evening. He didn't notice the baldish head inside the park until it hissed at him. "Silver, come here."

Patrick groaned. "I could tell that was you in the First Deputy's car. Why the fuck are you following me?"

The man on the bench was Isaac, Isaac the Brave, who'd left his ruddy cheeks in the Bronx. And most of his handsomeness. He had splits in his forehead that wouldn't go away in the dark. His jaw sat crookedly on the spindles of his neck. A Guzmann must have slapped back Isaac's teeth.

"Patrick, it isn't fair for you to ignore us. Commissioner Ned was a mother to you. He raised you at Headquarters. You ought to visit him once before he dies."

"If I ever went near Headquarters, you'd put me in chains and clip off my toes."

"Your head could stand some clipping . . . where's Jerónimo?"

Patrick began to falter in his black socks. He knew all the First Deputy tricks. Isaac hadn't waylaid him in the park just for a chat. These were clever people. Isaac's "children" had to be poking about, angelic boy detectives who wouldn't have been ashamed to sack an old shul. Patrick had to run home before the angels kidnapped

Jerónimo. But the Guinness had clubbed him behind the ears. He couldn't march with two tangled legs.

"I asked you where Jerónimo was."

"Isaac, me darling," Patrick said, putting on his best Irish, a brogue that had been nurtured in a Bethune Street synagogue, around a dwindling band of "Hebes" who hadn't seen Ireland in sixty-nine years. "The lad's asleep. We had a feast today. Chocolate pie from his father's candy store. He likes to nap after a big meal."

"Is there any blood on his fingers?"

"Why?"

"Because he's been playing on the roofs."

A young boy had been found on the roofs above Charles Street with a ripped neck. Someone had crayoned his eyes, ears, and lips in dark red. Homicide squads from Manhattan South were scouring the district for possible child murderers.

"Isaac, you're full of barley. The lad never goes higher than the ground floor. He can't function near windows and fire escapes. Wouldn't I know? We've been stuck together for a month. I'm with him every minute."

Isaac came out of the shadows. There wasn't a single curl on his face. He had rough patches where his sideburns used to be. He seemed bereft without his tufts of hair. But he could still hiss at a man.

"No wonder Jerónimo lives with you. That's a perfect couple, you and the baby. Patrick, you're the dumbest detective in human history. The First Dep was your survival kit. You would have drowned years ago without his devotion. If you can account for Jerónimo minute by minute, where is he now?"

Black fumes bubbled out of Patrick's nose: he was snorting air and Guinness at Father Isaac. "Didn't I say the lad was asleep?"

He managed to push off, get himself beyond the park and Abingdon Square. His legs were carrying him. His knees held. He could ignore Isaac's whistles. "Get a pair of shoes, you son-of-a-bitch." He was over the gutters, onto the curb of Bethune Street. "If you don't deliver Jerónimo to me, I'll put rat poison in your beer. Your lungs will smoke. Silver, stay off my streets." He didn't have to position the fall of his toes. An Irishman always landed well. Patrick couldn't miss. He banged into the shul, striking one of the awning rods with his skull. "Jesus," he muttered, with a lump on his head. He went under the stoop, fumbling for his latchkey. Pissed blind, he couldn't contend with a keyhole.

"God of Esau," he said, "come to me." He cursed Jacob and Rebekah, who had swindled Esau out of his birthright. Esau was a hairy man, like Patrick Silver and Jerónimo. But Patrick had no birthright to lose. His father left him a prayer shawl with plucked tassels and the obligation to preserve a synagogue for Irish waifs.

The key turned in Patrick's hand, and the synagogue unlocked itself. He stumbled towards his room, afraid to peek for Jerónimo. He heard snores behind the wall. He thanked the God of Esau for preserving hairy men. He opened the door. Jerónimo was in Patrick's bed, under a summer blanket. The blanket rose with the thrust of his snores. The baby drooled in his sleep; a piece of the blanket was wet. Patrick didn't care. He'd slept in the baby's spittle before.

THREE

Isaac the Brave drank his slug of castor oil and went into the craphouse. It was part of his Wednesday morning routine. The craphouse belonged to Presbyterian hospital. Isaac had to donate specimens to the tropical disease lab. Technicians examined his stool once a week. The Chief had a worm in his gut, spiteful and intelligent, eight feet long, with hooks and many suckers.

Isaac's worm was the prize of tropical diseases. Doctors and technicians couldn't remember another worm that thrived so spectacularly in a man. They would shoot dyes into Isaac to fluoroscope the worm.

"Inspector Sidel, are you sure you haven't been to South America? This isn't 1905. Nobody picks up a pork tapeworm in Manhattan any more."

The Chief began to dread his walks to the craphouse. He left the hospital weakened by castor oil. But he didn't have to crawl to Headquarters like a wounded bear. His chauffeur would bring him downtown.

Detective-sergeant Brodsky was waiting outside the hospital in Isaac's enormous Chrysler. He couldn't warm to the Chief's new look. Isaac had gone into the Bronx with curly sideburns. He came out with ashes in his nose, his Moroccan suspenders ruined: the supports were crusted with layers of white chocolate. His teeth were brown. His hair had the disordered feel of plucked chicken feathers.

The Chief was all gray. Six Guzmanns in a candy store had sucked on his marrow. It couldn't have been a small winter for Isaac. Papa Guzmann didn't allow hibernations on Boston Road.

The Chief stumbled over to the Chrysler. "Brodsky, a little boy was killed on Charles Street. They brought him down from the roof. He had red shit on his face. Isn't that familiar to you?"

Brodsky was trying to draw the shivers out of his neck. Isaac had startled him. Brodsky could live with grunts, but he hadn't expected whole sentences from the grizzly bear.

"Isaac, it can't be the lipstick freak. Didn't Cowboy put him away? The guy is in the Tombs. A Puerto Rican dressmaker."

"Cuban," the Chief said. "And he never made dresses. They were dolls."

The bear grew silent again. Brodsky maneuvered the Chrysler with a thumb. He felt some wind behind his ears.

"Are you going to take Cowboy's word that our freak is still in jail?"

Chief of Detectives in the City of New York and president of the Hands of Esau (a brotherhood of Jewish cops), "Cowboy" Barney Rosenblatt was Isaac's great rival at Headquarters. Cowboy could have squashed an ordinary police inspector, but Isaac worked for the most powerful cop in North America, First Deputy Commissioner Ned O'Roarke. The First Dep had a tumor in his throat. He wasn't supposed to be alive. Cowboy couldn't depend on the ravages of any disease. While Commissioner Ned sat in the First Deputy's chair, the Chief of Detectives had to curtsy to Isaac the Brave.

"Isaac, why should Cowboy lie to us?"

"Because he's a prick."

The chauffeur was stuck. Who could question the logic of a bear? "A prick," he muttered. "Definitely." And he drove into the First Dep's private ramp.

Isaac had to shuffle around an army of clerks. Headquarters was picking itself out of Centre Street. The City had built a huge red brick fortress for the Police Department near City Hall. The cops would have their own plaza and a building that was impregnable to thieves, revolutionists, and crumbling rock. Even with the Guzmanns pulling on his brain, Isaac was disheartened by the move. He didn't want air-conditioned chambers and a memory bank that could give you the size of a criminal's smelly blue sock. No data system could trap Papa Guzmann, or explain why Jerónimo wore earmuffs in June, July, and August.

Isaac had one of his "angels" call the Tombs. This angel reported back to the Chief. "Isaac, they lost their records on Ernesto, the lipstick freak. They don't know where he is."

"Then let them dig. If they can't locate the cubano in five hours, I'll have to bite the warden's ass. You tell them that."

This wasn't the first prisoner who'd disappeared from the Tombs. A Corrections officer would arrive in a few days with evidence that a crocodile had swallowed the lipstick freak. There would be drawings of Ernesto inside the crocodile's mouth, and a pocket saved from the freak's chewed-up pants. Isaac went in to see Commissioner Ned.

Four sergeants patrolled the First Dep's anteroom. Isaac had put them there. They discouraged crime reporters, nosy clerks, and police captains who thought they could improve their lot with genuflections to a dying Irish commissioner.

The First Dep sat in the corner, with a blanket over his knees. His green eyes were licked with dull yellow spots. Cobalt treatments had burnt his vocal cords and left him with a hoarse whisper. His yellowish eyes were a poor clue. O'Roarke's mind didn't drift, no matter how much of him had been eaten away. He ran Headquarters from his little chair, supervising the slow exodus from Centre Street.

His eyebrows didn't bunch for Isaac. His wrists crept under the blanket. "Where's Patrick Silver?"

Patrick had once been the darling of Ned O'Roarke. They were Limerick men, worshipers of the river Shannon. Patrick's touch of Judaism couldn't disturb Commissioner Ned. Irish Jews had lumps of Catholic tissue under their foreskins. Only Silver had crazied himself drinking Guinness and Irish coffee. He's shot too many chickenshit thieves. He'd gone into pimps' lairs waving his .45, with Guinness coming out of his eyeballs. The PC had to take his gun away. Silver was made into a clerk, a member of the rubber-gun squad. He jumped the First Deputy's office, leaving his pension behind.

"Patrick's in his synagogue, Commissioner Ned. Asleep. I've sent a few kites down to him. With regards from you and me. They landed in Silver's park. My detectives have more kites to deliver. They'll revive the sleeping beauty."

Isaac left O'Roarke's private room with a twitch in his gut. It could have been the worm. Or an outbreak of jealousy. Those Irishers liked to cuddle one another around the ears.

There were hyenas in the hall. Herbert Pimloe skulked with Cowboy Rosenblatt outside the First Dep's office. Pimloe worked under Isaac. He was O'Roarke's deputy whip. But he'd attached himself to Cowboy. The moment Commissioner Ned faltered in his chair, they would push down on Isaac's scalp and tear the skin off his face.

"Cowboy, what happened on Charles Street? Tell me about the mutilated boy."

Cowboy played with the studs on his holster and ignored the Chief. Isaac crept in front of Pimloe. "Wasn't there lipstick on the little boy's cheek? It sounds like an old story."

"Herbert," Cowboy said, leaning into Isaac to nudge Pimloe's arm. "It's the Rasties, aint that right? They're into cult murders this time of the year."

Headquarters was frightened to death of the Rastafarians, a community of black Jamaicans who worshiped King Haile Selassie and wore their hair twisted into long "dreadlocks" to resemble a lion's mane. The Rastafarians had settled in Brooklyn and the Bronx, and were busy making war on these boroughs and murdering themselves.

"Cowboy, this is a different cult. The Rasties wouldn't take a nine-year-old onto the roof. It's the lipstick freak, or one of his brothers."

"Yeah," Cowboy said. "Jerónimo. Maybe I ought to send the homicide squad down on Papa's baby. Who knows? All the Guzmanns could be lipstick freaks."

"Don't laugh. You wouldn't have any dead boys if the Guzmanns stayed in Peru."

"Isaac, I'm sick of your theories about Jerónimo. That boy's a white-haired dummy. Just because you hate the Guzmanns, it don't mean they produced the freak. The freak is in the Tombs, and I put him there."

"Cowboy, guess again. Ernesto is missing. Somebody walked the dollmaker out of the Tombs."

Isaac didn't send for his chauffeur. He crossed the Bowery with his own feet. No one waved to him from the barber colleges and the candy stores. Once Isaac had been the only bishop of the Puerto Rican-Jewish East Side. Merchants would rush out of their stores to kiss the bishop's hand. A nod from Isaac meant prosperity. The old *dueñas* of Eldridge Street could walk with their purses dangling from their thumbs. They had big Isaac to retrieve any articles stolen from them. But Isaac had fallen out of touch with the landladies, grocers, and pensioners of his bishopric. The Guzmanns had pecked under his sideburns and devoured the white meat in his head. Isaac stumbled through the East Side like an unbrained bear.

He stopped at a dairy restaurant to guzzle five bowls of split-pea soup. Isaac had to feed his worm. The countermen weren't impressed with Isaac's devotion to split peas. They waited for the bear to climb off his stool. Isaac could corrupt a place with the sweat clinging to his nose.

The Chief had more than split peas on his mind. He was looking for his girlfriend Ida, who was head cashier of the Ludlow Street café. He couldn't find her around the cash box, the butter tub, the vegetarian salamis, or the stove, where Ida loved to roll square pancakes for the blini and blinchiki that were a special feature of the house. Isaac made inquiries from his stool. The countermen shrugged at him. "Isaac, honest to God, she vanished one day. Don't think she wasn't loyal. She stared out the window month after month."

"Myron," Isaac said, with a finger inside the counterman's shirt. "You'd be bankrupt without that girl. The blintzes would crack if she ran too far. So tell me where Ida is?"

"Home," the counterman said. "She's fixing her trousseau."

"What trousseau?" Isaac said, with his lip stuck out.

"She has a suitor . . . he's here. In the restaurant."

Myron pointed to a man with plastic on his sleeves who sat eating mushrooms off the edge of his thumb.

"That's Luxenberg . . . our accountant."

Isaac went across the street and knocked on Ida's door. She swallowed hard after she recognized the Chief. Ida wasn't malicious. She offered tea and sponge cake to the cop who had deserted her. She wouldn't spoil the occasion with shrill cries. How often does a man come back from the dead?

"Isaac, believe me, what's nine months between friends? But couldn't you have sent me a postcard from the Bronx?"

"Police business," Isaac said, with sponge cake in his mouth. "My own daughter didn't know. Ida, I was caught in a freeze. The Guzmanns dipped me in cold chocolate. They put spiders in my hair. They gave me a worm."

"Isaac, who are the Guzmanns that they should do such disgusting things?" Ida watched him lick some honey off the side of his spoon. The Guzmanns, whoever they were, hadn't robbed him of his old habits. The Chief loved to sniff for honey. "Isaac, I'm engaged."

"They told me at the restaurant. Luxenberg. An accountant with plastic cuffs. Ida, does he wear plastic when he pees?"

Ida walked into the kitchen. The Chief followed her. He began taking off her clothes. He didn't rip Ida's blouse. He was diligent with all her buttons. He had Ida's skirts and summer bloomers on the kitchen table without scratching her legs. He didn't need a blanket under him. He could grovel on Ida's linoleum. She coughed when Isaac licked the gulley in the middle of her chest. She felt the bear's hot nose in her belly. Ida understood. He was sniffing for his honey jar. He stirred, pushed his head away. The Chief forgot to undress himself. His pants came down. He crept into Ida.

The bear was miserable. He copulated with his skull against the wall. Only a retard could be blind to Ida's motives. She was afraid of the Chief. The girl had deep grooves in her mouth. She went walleyed under Isaac: her pupils shrank inside her head.

Isaac bit his tongue. The doctors had told him about the vague discomforts a worm could bring to a man. Isaac cursed the doctors and their fluoroscopes. The worm was eating him alive. Its armored head pinched and scraped his gut. He swore to Jesus he could feel the cocksucker twist around. The worm was conspiring with Ida to agonize the Chief. He slid out of her, clutching his pants. He knew a cashier's tricks. The girl suffered Isaac on top of her to deflect him from her suitor's plastic sleeves. Ida gave her own honey to the bear, so he wouldn't go back to Ludlow Street and rage against Luxenberg and the dairy restaurant.

Isaac stole out of the kitchen. His knees were stamped with the print of Ida's linoleum. He fled across the Bowery with sludge in his heart. The Chief had lost his old avenues of comfort. The bishopric was gone.

Herbert Pimloe was a cop with a Phi Beta Kappa key. He'd dreamt of Oliver Cromwell and Thomas Hobbes years ago in Harvard Yard, under a wet coat and a miserable wool hat. Pimloe rejected the mundane boundaries of a Harvard degree. He had contempt for lawyers and other government boys who longed to smell an ambassador's breath and die for the diplomatic corps. Pimloe became a cop in New York City.

He married a girl from Chappaqua. He moved to Brighton Beach. He had three boys, who inherited Pimloe's gruffness and Pimloe's brains, and grew obsessed with the shape and gold color of a Phi Beta Kappa key. Pimloe patrolled the streets of Brooklyn in a blue bag. He didn't mouth idle bits of knowledge at his precinct. But he couldn't escape from Harvard Yard. A young inspector in the First Dep's office picked him out of Brooklyn. The inspector was Isaac Sidel. Isaac wanted a patrician on the First Deputy's lists, a boy with a gold key.

Pimloe carried fingerprint cards up from the basement. He brought sandwiches to the Irish commissioners. "Find my shoelaces for me, Harvard. Get me some ink for my pen. Harvard, where the fuck are you?"

He became the deputy whip, sweeping up after Isaac, coming down on cops whose ears had begun to corrode. Whole precincts were afraid of Isaac. No one could figure where he would pounce. A deputy whip lacked this option of surprise. Familiar at the station-houses, much more visible than the Chief, Pimloe was the man you hated.

He survived on swift elbows and memories of Thomas Hobbes. He annexed himself to Isaac's rival, Cowboy Rosenblatt. With Cowboy's help he would crawl around Isaac and sit in the First Deputy's chair.

Isaac was a tainted man. Feuding with the Guzmanns, he'd crippled himself. He could no longer inherit O'Roarke's chair. The Irish commissioners would never trust a cop who jumped into the Bronx for a tribe of Marrano pimps and penny bankers.

Pimloe stood under a designated tree in Central Park (close to South Pond), and dreamt of the First Deputy's chair. He had a sour time. There were twenty inspectors at Centre Street who could outrank a deputy whip. Cowboy would have to push him over their heads.

Meanwhile Pimloe kept to his tree. He had an appointment with Odile Leonhardy, the retired porno queen. Odile wouldn't take him up to her room at the Plaza Hotel. She claimed that a cop could scare off film producers. She was dying to break into the movies. So she picked a spot that couldn't endanger her; it was a tree with a split trunk that gave Pimloe an uncompromising view of the Plaza. She wanted the cop to eat his heart out.

The grayish walls of the Plaza turned light pink at the end of

July. It was a color that reminded Pimloe of frozen entrails in a fish store, and blooded-out meat. The whip was growing somber. Pimloe was jealous of all the producers who mixed with Odile. He imagined men without their clothes, making Odile into another Merle Oberon, while she sat on someone's hairy knee.

"Herbert."

Pimloe saw a lump of sky through sunny leaves, and a heel broader than the back of any yellow duck in South Pond. The heel dangled right above Pimloe's nose. Odile was inside the fork of a powerful branch. Pimloe didn't have to peek around the hump of her platform shoe. The girl wore a dress that was totally transparent.

"Couldn't we sneak into the Plaza?" Pimloe begged from under the limbs of the tree. He had a horrible lust for Odile. "How much would a few minutes cost?"

The whip could have frightened her; he had titles to throw at Odile. Herbert Pimloe would be the new First Deputy the minute O'Roarke fell off his chair.

"I'll buy you a dress at Bloomingdale's," Pimloe shouted into the tree. "Come down."

"No."

"Then tell me what you want."

"Pommes frites."

Pimloe began to shake; Odile would lure him into the Café Argenteuil on Fifty-second Street, where she would gobble French fried potatoes that cost two dollars a sliver. Pimloe would have raided Bloomingdale's to glut Odile with clothes. Material draped on her body gave pleasure to the whip. But he wasn't going to make a pauper of himself for *pommes frites!*

"Odile, cafés are out. It's too early to eat French fries. What about some whiskey? I brought my flask along."

He offered Odile a drink. Whiskey fumes crept up the tree. Odile wouldn't surrender to a puny silver bottle that was going black from the grease on a policeman's thumb.

The whip's knees came together in one bitter knock. His shoulders drooped. He spilled whiskey on his pants. "Okay," he said. "Pommes frites."

The tree shivered once. A pair of veiled buttocks slid off the branch. Pimloe heard hissing in the leaves. Odile was on the ground. She stood higher than the whip in her platform shoes.

She was the miraculous lady of Central Park, a leggy creature without a hint of underwear; all the hermits and banditos from around the pond left their hiding posts to gaze at Odile. The swing of her legs out of glorious hip sockets caused each of them to choke on his tongue. She had the stride of an ostrich. She covered merciless territory with the flick of her knees.

Pimloe could taste the ligatures of Odile's spine. The dents in the small of her back gave off a salty perfume. He'd have to slip away from Brighton Beach to marry Odile. Pimloe could fight off the wrath of those Irish superchiefs. He'd wait until they crowned him. Then they'd have to kneel to Commissioner Pimloe. The First Dep could have any number of wives.

FOUR

The cab driver had two ninnies in the back: a gray-haired infant and a huge Irishman in stinky socks. He'd picked them up at Abingdon Square because it was a slow day and he couldn't afford to select his passengers. He shuddered when he heard the giant mention Boston Road. "Excuse me, I couldn't find Boston Road in a hundred years."

"We'll teach you how to find it," Patrick Silver muttered, with a knuckle in his toes.

A piece of scratched leather stuck out of Patrick's soccer shirt, but the driver couldn't see the bulge of any gun. What kind of mick wears an empty holster? A crook from Boston Road? Or a cop with a fascination for leather? The driver knew all the precincts from Chinatown to High Bridge, but he hadn't met scruffy cops like these: gray-haired boys in charity suits. The small one kept shoving caramels into his mouth. The driver humped down into his seat to absorb the shock of exploding caramels.

Patrick chose the Willis Avenue Bridge. The driver began to sulk. The black water under his cab swelled up like overcooked blood. The Harlem could never be a genuine river in his estimation; a toilet for the Bronx, it ran on hot piss, carrying blood and garbage into the sea. A boiling piss-hole and two imbeciles with gray tufts behind the ears had cut him off from Manhattan.

They passed over the skeleton yards of a freight terminal on the Bronx side of the bridge. They were in Mott Haven, on the lip of an old industrial region, cluttered with warehouses and an uncertain railroad that seemed to exhaust itself near the water, with pieces of track about to spill off the end of the borough. The warehouses leaned into the bridge like huge, prehistoric teeth.

The driver felt much safer moving across the bones of Southern Boulevard, with street after street of rubble. The whole Bronx could vanish in front of his eyes. Why should he care?

Little bodegas with tin walls began to crop up around Boston Road. The driver saw a flood of green cars. He smiled as he recognized the outline of institutional green: only a cop sitting under a blanket would ride in a big green boat. Could the imbeciles in his cab be part of the same team?

"Jesus, tell me, who are you guys staking out? Dope fiends, niggers, voodoo men?"

The mick made him stop in front of a miserable candy store. It was a matchbox of dying tin and wood, wedged into the wall of a tenement with disconnected fire escapes; struts were missing from every ladder.

An old man came out of the candy store wearing the traditional smock of a petty entrepreneur. His thick body was completely uncombed. His eyebrows grew wild on his head. A furrier would have envied the hair on his knuckles and his wrists. The driver couldn't believe that this old man had created the fuss of cop cars on Boston Road.

"Shove off," the mick said, slapping a twenty-dollar bill into the driver's pocket. The driver wagged his head. He was in a nothing borough, outside a candy store that sat in the ruins, surrounded by a squatters' army of cops in green boats. He waved to the infant, Jerónimo, anxious to get out of firing range. "Thanks," he crooned to Patrick Silver. "Thanks."

Papa Guzmann waited for the cab to leave before he hugged Jerónimo. He'd been itching to touch the boy, to fondle the ears of his oldest child, but he wouldn't hop towards Jerónimo in the presence of strangers. The Guzmanns were a sensitive race. Papa could tolerate the big *irlandés*. Silver worked for him. And Silver didn't have a devious smell. Papa judged you with his nose. He could pick out a lying, sinful creature with his very first snuff.

He brought Jerónimo into the candy store, away from the smog of Boston Road. Jerónimo began to mewl for his brothers. Two of them, Topal and Alejandro, arrived in their pajamas from the back room, which had bunk beds and a crib (for Jerónimo) and served as a dormitory and a way station for cousins from Peru and pickpockets from Ecuador and Miami who came under Papa's largesse. The two pajama boys disappeared inside Jerónimo's embrace, but they couldn't stop his mewling. Jerónimo licked their foreheads with a creamy tongue while his face grew wet from prodigious, penny-round tears. The baby could have raised his grandfathers out of hell with the energy he provided. César and Jorge were missing. Jerónimo called for his youngest brother. "Zor-r-r-o."

Papa couldn't help his child. Zorro had been exiled from the candy store by Papa himself. It was Isaac's fault. The Chief had produced a moronic twelve-year-old girl who swore in front of three assistant district attorneys, and a Manhattan judge that César Guzmann, alias Zorro, alias the Fox of Boston Road, had captured her off a Port Authority bus, sodomized her, and sold her into prostitution. Papa realized the falsity of this claim. No Marrano would ever sodomize a cow, a girl, or a horse. Papers were prepared for Zorro's arrest. Now Isaac's killer squadrons sat on Boston Road with bench warrants in their pockets. Zorro would lose his scalp if he came near the candy store.

Jerónimo bent behind Papa's malted machines, looking for César and Jorge. He put his fist through comic book racks stuffed with school supplies, Valentine boxes, and pornographic displays. Papa had dioramas that told the story of abductions in Egypt, wife-swapping among the Eskimos, concubines in Sardinia, brothels in Peru. Jerónimo didn't enjoy cardboard women poking out of a corrugated landscape. He bruised their heads with a fist.

"Zor-r-r-o."

Papa offered him a chocolate egg, pink licorice, some runny marzipan. Jerónimo scorned such food. It was only after he scraped the walls of Papa's dormitory, with his nose under the beds, to prove Zorro wasn't available to him, that he settled down to eat. He had a brick of halvah, white chocolate that couldn't be broken without a hammer, a pound of Turkish delight, and an egg cream Papa made with a pint of syrup and two quarts of milk.

Nothing he ate or drank could put the baby to sleep. He was restless in the candy store. Papa had given him away. He lived in the basement of a synagogue now with Patrick Silver. He shuffled through the dormitory with his belly in his hands, but he couldn't get familiar with his old crib. He took his naps in Silver's bed.

The baby's nervous walk saddened Papa. He muttered words with Silver to take his mind off Jerónimo's estrangement from the candy store.

"Do the cops haunt your synagoga, Irish?"

"Not at all. Moses, Jerónimo is safe with me."

Papa dug a finger into his smock. "Isaac has his spies. Couldn't he plant one inside the congregation?"

"Moses, not to worry. We haven't had a new face at the shul in forty years. Anyhow, you can't hide too many pistols under a prayer shawl."

"Irish, take him home," Papa said, squinting at the baby. "He's outgrown the people here. None of my other boys has ever been to a Jewish church."

"Should I bring him next week?"

"No," Papa said. "Isaac's children are getting too close. We'll have green sedans on my counter in a few days."

Silver understood Papa's bitterness about the green sedans. Until Isaac's "children" arrived on Boston Road, Papa's candy store had been the premier numbers bank in the east Bronx. But Boston Road was dead. Papa's runners had to eat their own policy slips. The green cars followed them everywhere. They couldn't accept a nickel play from the hog butcher on Charlotte Street without interference from the cars. Detectives hissed at them and banged on the hog butcher's window. The runners came to Papa with a twitch in their eyes. Papa had to let them go. "Chepe, here's a fifty. Don't be bashful. You have an aunt in New Jersey, no? Visit her for a while. I'll tell you when to come back."

Father Isaac had turned the candy store into a tomb for Guzmanns. Jorge was the only one who crept in and out. Papa would pin a grocery list to his shirt (Jorge couldn't remember the names of different breakfast cereals), and send him to the bodega on the opposite side of the street. The cops were frightened of Jorge. He was a boy who could pull a detective out of a car and shake the clothes off his body. Jorge had the squeeze of a python. It wasn't fair. Isaac's "children" had a complete armory in their cars. Blackjacks and clubs would have disintegrated on Jorge's skull. Shotguns were inadequate. A detective had his limits. You couldn't blow a man's head off in the middle of Boston Road.

Papa launched the baby with a fresh supply of caramels. "Jerónimo, listen to the Irish. He's your father now. Don't forget to wash your mouth. If you misbehave, the Jews will clip your hair." The baby kissed his brothers and left with Patrick Silver.

Patrick wasn't a jittery person. The cop cars that bumped around his feet couldn't make him scramble for the sidewalks. A detective sergeant taunted Patrick and the baby from the lead car. "Silver, stop wiping Papa's ass. Give us the dummy, and you won't have to slave for the Guzmanns any more. I can promise you your gun and your shield."

Patrick slapped the sergeant's fender. "You can have him, but not alone. The lad goes with me." He opened the door and got in with Jerónimo, pushing the sergeant to the edge of his seat. The sergeant broke his discomfort with a smile.

"Silver, I could drive you straight to Headquarters with the siren on. Isaac will know what to do with the dummy."

"Me and Isaac have the same rabbi. His name is O'Roarke. The First Dep watches over me. He's a clansman of mine. Our people are from the kingdom of Limerick. O'Roarke will smash your fingers if you whistle in my face. We'll go to Bethune Street, thank you. Hurry up. I'll be late for evening prayer." Papa wasn't blind. He saw the baby sitting in a police car. It didn't worry him. Silver's nearness to the police was beneficial to Papa. An ordinary goon couldn't have preserved Jerónimo's life. Papa had no choice. It was the synagogue or the candy store, and Papa didn't trust himself. He had swallowed llama shit in Peru, drank the blood of a mountain goat to fight starvation, but Jerónimo couldn't survive on Boston Road. Isaac would have seized him from the candy store. Papa couldn't keep that son-of-a-bitch out of the baby's crib, no matter how many cops the Guzmanns happened to kill.

Isaac had been born into this world to plague Guzmanns. That's what Papa believed. Every man has a personal devil, according to Marrano law. Isaac was Papa's devil. What other explanation could there be for a cop who tossed his badge out the window so he could come to the candy store with tales of banishment from the Manhattan police and dig into the flesh under Papa's heart. Moses could have turned him away. But he followed the instincts of his forebears, the crypto-Jews of Portugal, chamberlains and monks who wouldn't have let a devil out of their sight. It was better to hug Isaac and sniff the color of his urine, a pale yellow and blue.

Papa should have whispered in Jorge's ear; Jorge knew how to clog a devil's windpipe. Only Papa was wary of cops. He'd killed another policeman years ago and had to flee Peru. He wanted Isaac to suffer a more natural death. The Guzmanns had been sophisticated poisoners for a century and a half. But Papa didn't have to cultivate toxins for Isaac. He sat Isaac at his table, fed him pork, tripe, and black pudding. No devil could survive Guzmann food. Papa and his boys had enough acid in them to purify a field of wormy pudding (the family lived out of a garbage pail during Papa's first years in the United States).

Isaac's skin began to turn. His sweat was dark green. His ears had ugly secretions in the morning. The Chief was dying bit by bit. A fingernail would come off. His bushy sideburns, the envy of Manhattan, thinned to lusterless shreds of hair. He tramped Boston Road in a constant state of dizziness. But Papa couldn't get him to fall down. He escaped the Guzmanns by walking out of the candy store and returning to Manhattan.

And Papa suffered ever since. He lost his hegemony in the Bronx. It did him little good to bribe the cops of his borough. The green sedans didn't come from there. Isaac held all the ganglions at Headquarters like puppet strings. He could tug at the Guzmanns from Centre Street. Papa shut the candy store in May and retired to Loch Sheldrake, where he had a small farm with orchards and a country well. But those ganglions could shake a blackberry bush. Isaac reached into Loch Sheldrake. He got the FBI to burn Papa's farm. The fuckers would have kidnapped Jerónimo if Papa hadn't hid the baby in his well.

He relied on Patrick Silver now. Papa had no one else. If Patrick failed him, devil Isaac would hurl the baby into the sinking lime under Headquarters. Maranos couldn't sleep in an unholy grave. That's why Papa kept a cemetery in Bronxville. The baby would scream for a thousand years without Marrano earth in both his eyes. Could a father ignore such screams? Papa would haunt Manhattan borough like a golem, slaying policemen until Isaac disinterred his boy. He shuddered to think of the consequences. Manhattan would swim in cops' blood. On the death of his sons Papa had no mercy.

A broadnecked bandanna girl hobbled into the candy store with a blind man clutching her arm. The blind man had yellow cheeks, brittle glasses on his nose, and a white cane that was longer and thinner than a fisherman's rod. The bandanna girl unraveled her clothes. Jorge emerged. Papa hugged his middle child. He threw Jorge's bandannas, skirts, blouse, shoes, and apples (meant for tits) into a barrel under the soda fountain. He scowled at the blind man.

"Zorro, you know how much Isaac admires you. Why did you

come here?"

Zorro snapped the eyeglasses off his nose and got rid of his white cane. "I wanted to sit with my brothers." He had candy fish for Topal and Alejandro, and purple fudge from Atlantic City.

Papa couldn't control his youngest child. The Fox of Boston Road had to spite those green cars and peek into his father's candy store.

"You missed Jerónimo," Papa said. "By two minutes."

"I saw him," Zorro said. "Did you expect me to stand in front of Isaac's car and bow to Jerónimo? How's Patrick Silver?"

"Why don't you visit his church on Bethune Street? You can ask him yourself."

Zorro mashed his teeth. "I don't trust that Irish prick. He came out of Isaac's belly. Just like Coen."

"Coen never harmed us. And where would we put Jerónimo if we didn't have the Irish?"

"Jerónimo could stay with me."

"Wonderful," Papa said. "He'll sleep in a telephone booth with his brother. He'll live on whores' snot. You'll wash his handkerchiefs in the rain. Pretty. Very pretty."

The malteds Zorro drank as a child must have shrunk his ears. He still had a grudge against Manfred Coen. Coen was dead. They grew up in the candy store, Manfred and Zorro. They were schoolmates. They did their lessons with ice cream in their cheeks. They fed pigeons on Boston Road. They picked bugs out of Jerónimo's hair. But Coen went to work for Isaac, became a blue-eyed cop, and lost his life in a crazy accident. He caught a bullet in the throat at the end of a Ping-Pong game. Patrick Silver used to chase bandits with Coen. He was one of Coen's many partners until the Police Commissioner took Patrick's gun away.

"Zorro, the Irish loves Jerónimo. Don't abuse him. Where's cousin Isidore?"

"He's safe, Papa. Our friends carried Isidore out of Atlantic City."

"Did you get mourners for him? I don't want my cousin to remain unblessed."

Zorro was a blind man again. He put on his brittle eyeglasses and found the thin white cane. "Papa, would I spit on cousin Isidore? I gave him more blessings than he deserves. It cost me a hundred bills to find a cantor who would pray for him."

The Fox kissed Jorge, Alejandro, and Topal, muttered a goodbye, and started to leave the candy store, tapping with his cane.

"Zorro, be careful," Papa said. "The dark glasses don't mean shit. Police cars run over blind men too."

Zorro didn't wave. Hunching his shoulders, he sniffed the air, and stepped into the gutters of Boston Road.

FIVE

The Congregation Limerick sits on Bethune Street between a Chinese laundry and a hospital for cats and dogs. No one can remember its proper name. In the delicatessens and bars around Abingdon Square it is known as the Irish synagogue, or Patrick Silver's shul. A crumbling brownstone, its stained-glass windows are shuttered with pieces of cardboard, and its awning, extravagant in 1930, is now an ugly stretch of cloth.

This is a suffering shul. It exists without a president and a governing board (the elders of the synagogue, a disabled troop of bachelors and widowers, do not have the energy to govern). It is attached to no other congregation in the world. It doesn't commune with the chief rabbi of Dublin, or the old synagogues of Cork. No rabbinical council in the United States can claim any ties with the Irish synagogue of Bethune Street. It has no sisterhood to perform charities in Greenwich Village and search for odd bits of stained glass that are missing from the windows. It cannot afford a cantor's fee; no one comes here to lead the chant for the dead.

Bethune Street has a rabbi, Hughie Prince, a tight-lipped man who was never ordained. Ask him where he studied. Hughie didn't come out of a rabbinical college. The elders chose him because he was the single person among them who understood a word of the Mishna and the Gemara. Hughie brought *talmud* to the Irish synagogue, limiting his pronouncements to five or six sentences a week about the laws of dispersion as they applied to Limerick Jews. He cuts glass for a living, and you can only find him at the synagogue mornings and evenings. Most of the time Hughie is out repairing windows; you have to go up and down Hudson Street screaming "Rabbi Hughie Prince," if you expect any religion from him.

Patrick Silver runs the shul. He's the unpaid "beadle." He won't allow besotted Irishmen to piss in the study hall. He feeds the poor (gentile and Jewish beggars can always get a sandwich from Patrick in the shul's tiny kitchen). He settles arguments between parishioners by thwacking both parties on the left ear. He goes into the streets to collect bodies for Rabbi Prince (without Patrick's minyans the shul would forget to pray). He travels through the synagogue with a shillelagh of a broom, slapping mosquitoes off the wall, clubbing rats out of the damp holes in the cellar, lopping off the head of any evil nail in the pews that might scratch the pants of unsuspecting widowers, poking for weak spots in the chapel's crooked ceiling to prevent the synagogue from falling on Hughie and the sacred scrolls, banging dirt from the underside of the awning, scaring off burglars and bill collectors, and occasionally sweeping the floors.

Even when he had his gun, Patrick lived at the shul. He would shuffle from Bethune Street to the First Deputy's office, with bottles of Guinness in his shirt. Most of his salary went into the shul. Congregation Limerick was a firetrap. Inspectors and City marshals received their monthly "tithes" from the shul and ignored the rumblings in the walls.

Then Patrick lost his gun. A few days after he quit the police, building inspectors arrived with flashlights, complaining about mud in the cellar and rats nesting in the pipes. Patrick needed a fresh supply of cash. He had nothing but muscles to sell. No white man would hire him. The gangster families of Atlantic Avenue and Mulberry Street were suspicious of Patrick Silver. They couldn't understand the pedigree of an Irish Jew. They figured a big commissioner still kept him on a string.

Patrick had to go into Harlem and become the bodyguard of a black policy bank. This nigger bank liked the idea of a giant with a yarmulke in his pocket. Patrick's soccer shirt was soon a familiar item on St. Nicholas Avenue. The bankers grew fond of him. They introduced him to an Abyssinian shul near Mt. Morris Park. Every congregant at this shul was considered a rabbi. Patrick read *torah* with the black rabbis of Mt. Morris Park and discussed the laws of Moses with them. The rabbis had their own Book of Genesis. Jacob was white, the rabbis said. But Moses and Esau were Abyssinian. "Rabbi Silver, you're as black as any of us." Patrick couldn't agree or disagree. Didn't some of the Irish say that St. Munchin, the first bishop of Limerick, had come out of Africa with a colony of leprous Jews?

Patrick's seat in Harlem didn't last. The nigger bank had to let him go. The cops downtown were flying kites over Seventh Avenue. Policy runners were being nudged off the street. "Shit," the bankers said to Patrick. "Somebody's got it mean for you. Irish, we can't afford you any more." The bankers didn't leave Patrick stranded without a job. They tossed him to the Guzmanns.

That's how Patrick inherited Jerónimo. But the boy came with a dowry of sores. The morning after Patrick returned from Boston Road, a squad of Isaac's "children" descended upon the shul. Nine blue-eyed cops broke into Patrick's room and caught him sleeping with the baby (the cellar room couldn't hold more than one bed). Patrick reached for his shillelagh with his prick out. He wouldn't wear pajamas at the synagogue. Jerónimo remained under Patrick's summer blanket, his face wet from the energy of a fourteen-hour sleep (he'd been dreaming about his brother Zorro). All the blue-eyed cops had Detective Specials in their hands. They stayed clear of Patrick's enormous broom. Their spokesman, a detective-lieutenant with a blond mustache began to bray.

"St. Patrick, we haven't come to harm you. Praise the Lord, we're on a peaceful mission. The First Dep is in the hospital. He had a hemorrhage in the middle of the night. I didn't see him but I hear the blood poured out of his neck. There's a priest with him now. The Father's laying holy oil on old Ned while they're pumping new blood into him. Isaac doesn't want him to die without a peek at your face. So don't cause trouble for us, St. Patrick. We're taking you to the hospital one way or another."

Patrick kept his chin on the broom. "Isaac must be shaky if he had to send nine dogs like you."

"He's conservative," said the mustache (Lieutenant Scanlan), with an eye on Jerónimo. "He knows how ferocious a Jewish saint can get. Isaac has faith in numbers. He thought nine of us would be enough to discourage you. St. Patrick, do we have to wreck your little church?"

"Put your guns away. They stink of metal. And close your eyes. Me and Jerónimo have to dress."

Isaac's "children" wouldn't slap their guns into their holsters, or shut their eyes; they watched Jerónimo's balls as he wiggled out of bed. The baby climbed into underpants that came down to his knees. He wore sweaters rather than a shirt, and his trousers had a shrunken seat. He pulled earmuffs out of his pocket, winding the tin band around his elbow. Patrick had to lace his shoes.

The cops giggled at the two gray-heads and prepared to march them out of the synagogue. "Not so fast," Patrick grumbled. "This aint an amusement park. Scanlan, you'll have to lend me a few of your pretty boys. They'll be darling Jews for half an hour. Isaac won't object. I'm not leaving until I find ten live customers."

He pushed through the detectives and stationed himself at the doorway. Six old men stood in the corridors. Stalwarts of the congregation, they hung out on Bethune Street and were the hub of Patrick's minyans. They carried their prayer shawls in soft velvet bags, these friends of Patrick's dead father. Patrick shouted into the corridors.

"Where's Hughie?"

The old men shrugged at him. "Hughie's shitting somewhere, or chopping glass."

But Hughie appeared. He had a warped back from bending over glass so long, and his fingers were nicked from all his cutting tools. He wouldn't wear the traditional fur hat (with pigtails) that identified the rabbis and wise men of Eastern Europe. And he didn't have a yarmulke done in gold to set him apart from ordinary men. He came in a simple cap, threadbare at the rims, with a crown that was permanently collapsed; it had goggles sitting on the bill that kept glass splinters out of his eyes. Hughie wouldn't remove his goggles inside the shul. He saw no contradictions between *torah* and his trade. You couldn't be a good rabbi and a bad glazier, according to Hughie. He cut glass with the fingers of Benjamin, Jacob, and Elijah on his wrist.

Hughie stared at the detectives and their arsenal of guns. "Patrick, chase them out. They don't belong in a synagogue."

"Not to worry, Rabbi. I invited a couple of the lads to pray with you."

Three detectives were left behind. They hiked upstairs with Hughie and the six old men of the shul. They had to pass the kitchen, the study hall, the toilets, and the winter room (open to beggars from November to March), before they got to the chapel. The detectives snickered at the circumstances of these Limerick sheenies, who prayed in a dunghill. It was the most abominable church they had ever stumbled upon. The pews were shoved into the corner like a line of bishops in ragged clothes; the carpets running from the pews had trails in them that could have swallowed a yarmulke, or a mouse. The women's gallery, two gnarled porches over the cops' heads, had been stripped of all its benches, since women no longer came to the synagogue.

The chapel itself was in ruins. The furniture made no sense: silk rags on a broken closet, a platform with feeble bannisters, a chair nailed to the wall. They asked Hughie about the odd dip of that chair.

"Rabbi, do you drop your sinners out of the bucket?"

"That's Elijah's chair. It faces north, to Jerusalem, Baghdad, and the Irish Sea. That's the path Elijah takes when he zooms over the world. Next time he comes down from heaven, he'll sit with us."

Isaac's three "children" couldn't believe the gullibility of Irish Jews, Donkeys out of Limerick. (Scanlan, their boss, was descended from Donegal Bay.) Limerick had always been the idiot's house of Ireland.

The sheenies began distributing prayer shawls, and each detective was obliged to bury his head in a huge linen shawl with broad stripes and primitive tassels that were no more than knotted strands of cloth. The detectives were called to the praying box (that miserable platform at the center of the shul), with Hughie and the six old men. They stood on the bottom step, trapped in Patrick's minyan. They heard sounds that froze to the linen on their heads. The minyan bellowed and moaned like a company of sick cows. The detectives would rather have prayed among Rastafarians, or another lunatic cult, than fall into the maw of a prayer shawl.

The Irish synagogue was only three blocks from St. Vincent's hospital, but the lieutenant had to take his fleet of cars. He couldn't walk Silver and the dummy Jerónimo across Abingdon Square with guns in their backs. Silver was practically a saint on Bethune Street. Idiots would pour out of the bars to retrieve him from Scanlan, who would be charged by some civilian board with kidnapping church officials. So Scanlan kept them off the streets.

He was sick of Guzmanns. He'd been exiled to the Bronx since June, riding up and down Boston Road like a Mississippi pilot. You could ground yourself in a pothole, disappear into the crumbling gutters. A Bronx detail couldn't guarantee your life. He would have been happy to get rid of Jerónimo, make one less Guzmann in New York, but he couldn't move on the baby with Patrick Silver in the car.

"St. Patrick, should we stop for a lick of ice cream? Jerónimo won't survive the morning without his chocolate mush."

Silver wouldn't talk. He sat with his knees against the door, thinking of Commissioner Ned. He wasn't a total ignoramus. He could have gone to Headquarters from the synagogue, or the Kings of Munster, and visited with O'Roarke. He didn't forget the route. Only his legs wouldn't carry him there. The First Dep had half a floor to himself. Patrick dreaded those rooms. They'd nurtured him for over ten years.

Patrick was the mad cop of Centre Street, a Limerick lad with a yarmulke, the only kike who belonged to the Shillelagh Society (a brotherhood of Irish detectives). He brawled with the Shillelaghs, whored with them, met them at weddings, wakes, and society dinners, but Patrick didn't go to Mass with his brothers, or follow them on retreats. He pissed into a bottle at Headquarters. He napped with a yarmulke over his eyes. He broke away from an assignment to nab victims for morning and evening prayers. No one but Patrick had a key to the shul. Field commanders couldn't punish him for his lapses. Commissioners were forced to smile at him. Patrick Silver had the biggest rabbi in the universe: First Deputy O'Roarke.

O'Roarke was a distant cousin of the priest who had thrown all the Jews out of Limerick in 1906. He didn't share his dead cousin's belief in sheenie devils. He had a primitive love of Irishmen that could tolerate any church. He knew the family names of Patrick's congregation. He had dialogues with Hughie Prince at the Irish synagogue, or Hughie's shop, on the question of messiahs, golems, and antichrists. He'd been to chapel with the Limerick Jews. He had a skullcap in his desk. He adored Patrick Silver and kept him out of harm.

Only Patrick was a rotten diplomat. The shul exhausted him, making him blind to the little wars at Headquarters, the schemes of rival commissioners. A healthy, vigorous O'Roarke enabled Patrick to step around the different Irish chiefs without any bother. Once the First Dep began to die in his chair, the chiefs weren't so bashful with the yarmulke boy. They bumped him in the halls. They hid his peeing bottle. Patrick paid no mind to them. He gathered his minyans and watched the shul.

It was Guinness that brought him down. He got abominably pissed one afternoon at the Kings of Munster. He challenged four Innisfree lads to a fight after they insulted the river Shannon. Patrick forgot to hand his gun to the barman. The Innisfree lads stripped him of his holster and shot away the fixtures at the Kings of Munster. The shooting couldn't be hushed. Patrick was called to the firearms board at Headquarters. The chiefs who sat on the board accused him of being a drunken sod who couldn't hold on to his gun. They gave him the choice of resigning, or becoming a clerk.

Lieutenant Scanlan nudged Patrick out of his reverie. "St. Patrick, we've arrived. You'd better grab Jerónimo's hand. They don't let infants into a hospital without a father."

Patrick got out of the car, with Jerónimo clinging to his soccer shirt. The baby had never been to a hospital, and he was mortified. His fist lay deep in Patrick's shirt. The weather had changed. It was drizzling now. Jerónimo went up the steps of St. Vincent's, his gray head under Patrick's arm, so that the six detectives pushing behind them figured they were in the company of middle-aged twins.

Another detective was standing at the top of the stairs. Fatter and uglier than the rest of Isaac's blue-eyed squad, he'd come out of the hospital to greet Patrick Silver. "Go home, you miserable prick."

"Be nice," Patrick said to Brodsky, Isaac's chauffeur and errand boy. "You'll corrupt the lad. He isn't used to cops who swear. He sleeps in a synagogue. He prays with me."

"Then teach him how to pray for your life."

"Brodsky, your wires are crossed. Isaac sent for us. I'm supposed to see Commissioner Ned."

"Silver, that's a shame. Your timing was always lousy. The great O'Roarke died half an hour ago."

Patrick shambled on the stairs, his stockings at the edge. The baby nearly toppled. He hung on to Patrick with both hands, his ears growing wet.

"Died a half hour ago?" Patrick muttered through his teeth. "Then I'll pay my respects to the corpse."

"Not a chance," Brodsky said. "Isaac doesn't need you any more. He told me to lock the doors in your face."

"Brodsky, I can punch out all your doors. Don't rile me. I'm going in to Commissioner Ned."

Brodsky grinned from his superior position on the stairs. "Silver, your protector is in another world. So walk away from here. You won't have your feet for long without old Ned."

Patrick charged up the stairs. He might have bowled into Brodsky, and gotten through the hospital door, but having to lug Jerónimo hindered his attack. The six detectives caught him by the pants and threw him off the stairs. Patrick rolled onto the curb, with Jerónimo across his chest. Scanlan hovered over him. "St. Patrick, don't sit in the rain."

A growl escaped from Patrick. He wouldn't move. Gradually Jerónimo slipped off his chest. The baby was no fool. He could tell wet from dry. He put his earmuffs on. Patrick's growls grew familiar. "Suck Isaac's eggs." Then he rose up with Jerónimo and hobbled towards the shul.

SIX

Headquarters was in a powerful slumber during the five days it took to bury Commissioner Ned. All activities ceased. Deputy inspectors wore black ribbons on their coats. The Irish chiefs went uptown to sit with old Ned's coffin. The PC stayed behind his door and wouldn't deliver any mandates. Nothing could happen while O'Roarke was above ground.

Pimloe had a difficult time. He couldn't ascend to O'Roarke's chair before the burial was over. Old Ned began to roll in his box. The corpse pointed a finger at Cowboy Rosenblatt, Pimloe's greatest ally. The First Deputy's office was the one corner of Headquarters that didn't fall asleep; O'Roarke's undercover units had gathered information that Cowboy was accepting bribes from a chain of Brooklyn restaurants. Somebody leaked the news. The PC had to act. He suspended his Chief of Detectives.

Cowboy screamed in his rooms. "Isaac fucked me. He's the guy. I swear to God, I never stole a dime." His rage brought him little bits of nothing. He no longer had three thousand detectives under his command. The Irish chiefs shunned Cowboy's office. They recited Hail Marys around his door. They couldn't think of old Ned without crossing themselves. They were having chills in the first week of August. Their mouths turned gray. They were convinced that Commissioner Ned had the Holy Ghost on his side. How else could a dead man indict a Chief of Detectives?

There was no investiture for Herbert Pimloe. The commissioners couldn't anoint a cop who had been promoted by a thief like Cowboy Rosenblatt. Pimloe seemed loathsome to them now. But the commissioners were beginning to panic. Headquarters couldn't function without a First Dep. They scratched for a candidate. Isaac's was the only face they saw. He was still a tainted man, reckless, obsessed, cursed with a tapeworm and marks on his forehead, so they anointed him halfway. His title was never solemnized. They could drop him in a second. He was made Acting First Deputy Commissioner.

This slight to his integrity didn't bother Isaac the Brave. He had Guzmanns on his mind. But he couldn't chase every celebrant out of his new office. Big and little cops were coming to shake the hand of First Deputy Sidel. The Irish chiefs wished him a long, long tenure (they could be damaged by a First Dep). Newgate, the FBI man, who worshipped Isaac, envisioned an age of cooperation between his bureau and the high commissioners. It was the FBI man who had huddled with state troopers and agents from Middle-town to help Isaac flush the Guzmanns out of Loch Sheldrake. Newgate himself had led the raid on Papa's farm, nearly capturing Jerónimo. Isaac was indebted to him. He allowed the FBI man to move his pillow next to the First Deputy's chair.

Pimloe was the last person to call on Isaac. He'd become a disheveled cop since yesterday, sleeping in his pants. He approached the First Deputy's chair with a miserable face. "Isaac, don't worry. I'm getting out."

Isaac wouldn't let him go. He liked having a Harvard boy scramble for him. "Herbert, I'm making you my number-one whip."

Isaac didn't covet O'Roarke's chair. He had no intention of rampaging through Headquarters. He'd delegate Pimloe to spy on stationhouses and turn marginal thieves into stool pigeons. Isaac was sick of police affairs. The Bronx had cured him of conventional ambition. He agreed to wear a badge with the gold points of a commissioner because it was an excellent blind. The First Deputy could eat up Papa's candy store. Isaac couldn't laugh, couldn't shit without castor oil, couldn't embrace a woman, until the Guzmanns capitulated to him.

A captain of Corrections arrived bringing felicitations from the Inspector General's office. His name was Brummel. He had a small-caliber gun strapped to his chest.

"What happened to Ernesto Parra, the lipstick freak?"

Captain Brummel produced a gigantic loose-leaf book. He went through the pages with a lick of his finger, and brought out a section of the book that was fat as a loaf of bread.

"Brummel, I didn't ask you for a prison encyclopedia. Where's the freak?"

"He hanged himself four months ago," Captain Brummel said,

twiddling with the rings of his book.

"And you hide it in a yard of paper."

"Isaac, it was a slip, that's all. A clerk misplaced the file."

"Sure. Brummel, give my regards to the Inspector General and get the fuck out of here."

Isaac wasn't displeased. Ernesto's death supported his case against Jerónimo. The whole of Headquarters could scream at him: Isaac, you're persecuting the baby. Headquarters was wrong. Isaac knew in his bones that Jerónimo was the freak. Little boys died on roofs wherever Papa's baby happened to be. Poor Ernesto was a victim of Cowboy Rosenblatt's lust for solving mysterious crimes. The dollmaker could barely speak a word of English. A team of homicide boys exhorted a confession from him with a series of nods and blinks. Cowboy went on all the local channels with Ernesto's tools, a dollmaker's kit of scarred Exacto knives. These are the murder weapons, Cowboy said. He showed how an Exacto could be used to slice a little boy. Isaac was on Boston Road at the time, working for the Guzmanns, and he couldn't shove himself between Cowboy and the dollmaker. Ernesto died in the Tombs.

The Acting First Dep broke away from all his admirers. He walked out of Headquarters with no escorts on his tail. Two battered Chevrolets were waiting for him behind Cortlandt Alley. These weren't ordinary sedans out of a police garage. They belonged to the First Dep's private fleet. They were cars that floated through the City, staying an ugly green all year. Summer or winter, they never got the chance to be indoors.

Isaac was going into the Bronx. He didn't take his chauffeur along. Brodsky had become like an old wife. His presence reminded Isaac of his days as the scourge of Manhattan. The Guzmanns had butchered Isaac's memory. He could only dream of candy stores and white chocolate and Jerónimo's curly head.

A young detective-lieutenant with a blond mustache sat in the front Chevrolet. He had a merciless eye for detail, this Lieutenant Scanlan. He could remember the routes Jorge Guzmann took crossing Boston Road, or what Alejandro wore last Friday, and tell the color of an ice-cream soda from a hundred feet. He was driving for Isaac today.

"Scanlan, roll up your windows. I don't want people getting curious about us."

The Chevrolet was filthy enough to hide Isaac's face. The air turned sour with the windows up. The weather inside the car made Scanlan's eyes swim. The Chevrolet baked to a hundred and twenty degrees. Stuck in a blinding hot storm, Scanlan drove on intuition. "Mother of God," he intoned to himself. Isaac didn't mind a sweating car. He'd always been partial to steam baths.

The two Chevrolets arrived on Boston Road. They didn't tie up with the rest of Isaac's fleet. The First Dep pulled his other sedans off the road. He wouldn't let Scanlan near the candy store. The Chevrolets kept out of sight. Isaac napped with scowls in his head.

He knew Jorge would have to come out of the candy store. Boston Road had once been Papa's exclusive territory. Now his empire shrank to the perimeters of a candy store. He had to send Jorge out twice a day to prove that the Guzmanns were still alive. Jorge couldn't be bullied by detectives in a car. He was Papa's middle child. His fingers behaved like the prongs of a nutcracker when Jorge had you in his grip. He could tear the jaw off a man's head. But Jorge was a sweet Goliath. He wouldn't frighten shopkeepers, babies, and old women. He tickled cats in the Spanish grocery, even if they clawed him. Until you threatened his father's territories, Jorge would never harm you.

Scanlan was too intimidated to poke the First Deputy Commissioner of New York. He leaned over his seat to mutter a few words. "Papa's animal,' he said. "Jorge is on the loose." Isaac's scowl disappeared. He woke with a little smile. Isaac had spent six months inside the candy store, smelling Guzmanns while his hair dropped out and a worm grew in his belly. Was it worth giving up his sideburns to see Papa's boys in their underpants? Isaac ate Guzmann chocolate until his face began to rot, but he learned to distinguish among the boys, tell their weaknesses and their peculiar habits. Alejandro played with his prick in bed. Jerónimo could gobble great quantities of white chocolate, but one dark brick would put him in a daze. Topal's thumbs were soft and girlish. Jorge had skinny legs.

The Chevrolets began to move along Boston Road. They followed Jorge for half a block. Papa's boy had a marker in his head. He would drift from lamppost to lamppost, without straying from the curb. Isaac couldn't catch a Guzmann who hugged lampposts. He glowered at Scanlan. "It looks like Jorge's staying on his side of the road."

"He'll cross," Scanlan said, hunched into his seat. "It takes him six lampposts."

Isaac wouldn't reduce Jorge's drifting walk to coordinates of lampposts. He was staring at the bend in Jorge's knees. He'd have to cripple Papa's boy, or the Guzmanns would rat away in their store, living on chocolate. Isaac wasn't taking revenge on Jorge's legs. He had to deal in vulnerabilities. Jorge was impenetrable above the waist. His Guzmann chest could defy any number of Chevrolets.

Papa and Zorro were Isaac's enemies, not the boy. He'd played with Jorge in the candy store, building shadows on Papa's wall with a finger, a stocking, and a spool of thread. Jorge could have smashed Isaac's skull, only Jorge was gentle with Isaac, stroking him like a big doll, or a half-brother. Isaac would have preferred to attack Alejandro and Topal, useless boys. But Jorge was the one who could lead him to Papa.

Jorge kept to the line of the curb. Scanlan was beginning to doubt himself. Should he ask Isaac's permission to climb the sidewalks and run after Jorge? Isaac would have said no. While Scanlan despaired of catching Jorge in the gutters, Jorge stepped off the curb. Scanlan signaled to the second Chevrolet, which cut in front of Jorge. They had him in a sandwich now.

Jorge's mind was closed to fenders and green cars. He thought of the change in his pocket, milky nickels and dimes. He had to buy turnips for his brothers. Papa would fume at Jorge if the bodega man robbed him of a nickel.

Scanlan was on top of the boy. He didn't have time to exult. If he crashed into the other car without Jorge on his bumpers, Isaac would ride him out of Headquarters and drop him into a cow barn for surplus cops. The Chevrolet was choking him. He couldn't breathe in rotten weather. Scanlan had maimed a dog once with this car, never a man. He tried not to look at Jorge's rounded back. He aimed for the rear license plate of the second Chevrolet. Closed windows couldn't protect him from the sound of crumpled bone. It was a terrible noise, much worse than the squeal of metal. Where was Jorge? The two Chevrolets unclapped themselves and crept out of the borough.

Zorro Guzmann, the Fox of Boston Road, stood in a phone booth on Eighth Avenue. He wasn't making telephone calls. This booth was his Manhattan office. Whore merchants would leave notes for him under the telephone box, with descriptions of the girls they wanted: blonde or brunette, with or without beauty marks, with bosoms or lean chests, thirteen or under. The telephone box was free of notes. The whore merchants were going elsewhere for their goods. Zorro had been squeezed out of Port Authority. He couldn't grab runaway girls any more. His talent was still there. He would stroll in a parrot-green shirt and smile into the windows of a bus, with a packet of flowers in his hand. But the terminals were crawling with Isaac's men. Zorro couldn't get near a bus without melting a brown crayon over his cheeks. And no girl would look at a pimp who waxed his face.

It wasn't the death of his business that slapped Zorro under the heart. He stumbled outside the booth. Pedestrians figured a catatonic man was stalking Times Square. Zorro bit his shirt to keep from howling. The attack wouldn't go away. Something had happened to one of his brothers. Nothing smaller than that could have made his chest knock with this sharp a rhythm. The Guzmanns had umbilical cords that could cover the girth of Manhattan island.

The Fox felt paralyzed. His brothers were in two places: the candy store and Silver's shul. Not even the Fox of Boston Road could dash uptown and downtown in a single furious leap. Zorro had to choose. Silver wouldn't let Isaac the Shit hurt Jerónimo, he decided in midstep. So the Fox went north with easterly swipes, bouncing in and out of gypsy cabs. Isaac's blue-eyed detectives had been cautioning Manhattan cabbies about the Fox; he was wanted for sodomizing young girls.

Meddling cabdrivers couldn't alarm Zorro. He would change cabs in the height of traffic, without giving his route away. "Hombre, go straight ahead. I'll show you where to turn." He was the only Guzmann who had graduated from elementary school. But he couldn't go far into the seventh grade. At Herman Ridder Junior High School, on Boston Road, all his teachers pestered him. They filled his brain with irrelevant geography, contradicting his notions of the world, which he got from the candy store.

Zorro knew more about Columbus (Cristóbal Colón) than any of his classmates. Cristóbal was born into a family of Marrano usurers, pickpockets, and thieves. The family fled Spain and went into hiding in Genoa. Around the age of ten Cristóbal became a pimp, then a convict, a murderer, and a religious fanatic. He had a mad conversion in the Genoa prison, believing himself to be the messiah who would lead Marranos, convicts, and the scattered tribes of Israel out of a corrupted Europe. Frightened of Cristóbal Colón's messianic talk, his jailors released him and banned him from Genoa for life.

Cristóbal went to the king of Portugal. The king wasn't interested in convicts and apostate Jews. The monarchs of Spain were more sympathetic to Cristóbal's schemes. He promised them remarkable wealth. He could find the east by sailing due west and award Ferdinand and Isabella with the jewels of India and the island of Cipango (Japan). Seeing a profitable way of getting rid of Jews, they financed Columbus' trip.

Cristóbal was a fraud in Papa's eyes. No Marrano could ever have thought the world was anything but flat. Falsifying his charts, Columbus sailed east and landed in the Bahamas with his three boats and a crew of convicts and Marrano pimps.

Zorro recited this story to his class at Herman Ridder. The boys and girls tittered behind their desks. "Flat," Zorro insisted. "There aint a bend in Boston Road."

He was called an imbecile, a depraved boy, a hoodlum from a candy store. The brightest girls laughed the hardest at him. "Zorro Guzmann, planets come in spheres." He was gawked at and told to sit down. He stopped going to school.

Zorro had one friend in his class, Manfred Coen, a blue-eyed Boston Road Jew, just Zorro's age. Coen didn't laugh. A flat world was perfectly tolerable to him. Rounded things like balloons and eggs (Coen's dad had a tiny egg store) held no delight for him. Coen and his family spent their summers at Papa's farm. Then Coen decided to draw pictures and attend the High School of Music and Art. He drifted away from Zorro. He became a cop, worked for Isaac the Shit, who tried to exploit the boy's old relationship with the Guzmanns. Trapped between Headquarters and the candy store, Coen died in a crazy duel with one of Zorro's pistols. Zorro couldn't mourn for him. Coen had been fucked by his boss. The big Chief threw Zorro's pistol at Manfred Coen. Isaac was the killer man.

The Fox crayoned his face after sneaking out of the ninth taxicab. He had used up all his brown. His cheeks were Crayola blue. But Zorro didn't have to paint himself for Isaac's fleet of cars. No one was on Boston Road. The Fox stumbled into the candy store, his heart growling at the omen of desolate streets.

The front of the store was deserted. A cop or any other thief could have walked off with Papa's malted machines. Brats could have fingered Papa's jellies and stolen bricks of halvah. The Fox let out a groan. He went into his father's dormitory with his ears dripping blue from crayon sweat. Alejandro and Topal were hiding in their bunk beds under an array of towels, blankets, and sheets, like humps on a mountain. Papa leaned against the wall. He wouldn't give Zorro a recognizable wink, or mutter with his head. Jorge lay on Papa's linoleum floor with bloody pillows over his legs. A team of Marrano witch doctors were with him, men from Uruguay with amulets hanging from their necks, garlic cloves and the fists of dead monkeys.

"Papa, was it Isaac, or the FBI?"

Papa kept to the wall; the ridges along his back told you he was crying, only Papa didn't make a noise. Zorro wouldn't question the witch doctors. He approached his brothers' bunk beds, discovering Alejandro under a sheet.

"Brother, what happened?"

Zorro had listened to Alejandro's muddled talk for thirty-eight years (the Fox would be thirty-nine in October). He didn't falter now. He pulled clusters of words from Alejandro's babble. Devil Isaac. Bumpers. Green cars. The Fox sank down next to Jorge and peeked under the bloody pillows. "Jesus and Moses," he said. He chased the witch doctors out of the candy store.

Zorro, Topal, Alejandro, Jorge, and Jerónimo were *hermanos de padre,* boys without mothers. Papa didn't have any use for a permanent wife. He was an itinerant pimp and pickpocket in Lima, Peru. His boys came from five different wombs. These "aunties," mestizos and marketplace whores, would rear a child for six months and leave. Zorro was the youngest. His "auntie" must have had more brains than the others. He inherited a certain curiosity from her, whoever she was, and the ability to speak in coherent sentences. He was the one child who got restless in the candy store. Even in a flattened world, the Fox had to crawl beyond the limits of Boston Road. And he knew that garlic on a string couldn't heal his brother. Jorge would die unless he was bandaged and given blood.

But Zorro had to shake his father into mobility, and bring Topal and Alejandro out of bed. The Fox didn't hesitate. He wasn't a person who liked to brood over a problem while scratching his balls. He threw the towels off his brothers. "Topal, grab two pillowcases. Pack our winter stuff. We aint coming back. Alejandro, go to the taxi company on Southern Boulevard. Knock on the window, but don't let the hombres drag you inside. They'll steal your shoes. You understand? Knock on the window and make a fist. They'll know we want a limousine. Brother, don't stop for a charlotte russe. We'll be dead before you come home."

The Guzmanns had a chauffeur once, by the name of Boris, but Isaac scared him off the road. Now they had to rely on a portorriqueño limousine service for most of their travel. The Fox and his brothers were city people; none of them could have solved the touch of a steering wheel.

Zorro stroked his father's ear. "Papa, if you don't help me move Jorge, Isaac will finish him and the rest of us. Papa, we can't stay. Isaac murdered the store."

Papa was conscious of the fingers in his ear. Zorro didn't escape him; he knew each of his sons. He was thinking of the Bronx and North America. The Jews here were wild men. Devils like Isaac didn't exist in Peru. Ten months ago Papa had been a citizen of the Bronx, a creature of many properties, with a farm and orchards in Loch Sheldrake, a Westchester graveyard for Marranos only, a numbers bank, and a candy store. He gave money and food to the orphans' asylum, to the Sisters of Charity, to the priests from the Spanish church, to the widows of dead firemen, to gypsies, retarded children, and the poor of Boston Road. The captains of Bronx precincts had drunk malteds with Jerónimo. Detective squads came to Boston Road for Papa's ice cream. The climate changed after Isaac descended upon the candy store, begging for mercy and a job. Detectives wouldn't touch the ice cream. Papa's runners were moody with Isaac in the house. Papa despised his own Peruvian arrogance. He was going to devour Isaac in slow shifts, cannibalize him in the candy store. Isaac was the better cannibal. While Papa ate off small chunks of him, Isaac had started to swallow the candy store, the farm, and Papa's boys.

The fingers were going deeper into Papa's ear.

"Papa, wake up. Jorge's dying in our lap."

Papa left the wall. With a violent energy he stripped all the beds, pieced towels and blankets together with incredible Christian-Jewish knots, and made a stretcher for Jorge. It was an act of desperation and love. The Marranos had spent their lives packing and unpacking, running from home to home. Papa sinned against his children, seeking permanence in the Bronx. America had befuddled him, turned him into a landed baron. Maybe he was wrong about Isaac. Suppose that whore of a cop had been sent by the Lord Adonai to punish Marranos who fattened themselves in America. No matter.

Papa could walk away from his fixtures and his malted machines.

It took three Guzmanns to get Jorge into Papa's stretcher of towels, blankets, and rags. They carried him out of the candy store on bended knees. Papa didn't bother locking the store; the vultures would come soon as the Guzmanns disappeared. Grandfathers, pregnant women, and little boys would crawl through the window like a colony of enormous ants and gut the candy store, brutalizing beds, walls, and woodwork; the store would lose its history in half an hour. Bums would sleep in the ravaged dormitory, with newspaper on their heads. Rats would jump out of empty sockets and sniff for crumbs of halvah. The shopkeepers of Boston Road would shrug and say, "Those Guzmann pimps, they ran to Buenos Aires with their millions."

The limousine was waiting for Jorge. Alejandro sat near the driver, licking a charlotte russe. Zorro didn't begrudge the whipped cream on Alejandro's tongue. How could he reprimand a brother whose memory died every fifteen minutes? The Guzmanns put Jorge on the rear seat. Then Zorro snarled at Miguel, the driver. "Hombre, my brother had a belt, a watch, and cuff links when he came to you. You shouldn't have undressed him without asking permission."

Miguel smiled. "Zorro, you must have left your army somewheres, because all I can see is blood and a pile of shit."

The Fox grabbed Miguel by the wings of his collar. "Hombre, I can buy Mass cards for your funeral without an army."

Miguel opened the glove compartment and fished for Alejandro's goods. "Zorro, I was teasing the boy. Would I steal from a Guzmann? Let the Holy Mother break off my nose if I'm telling a lie. Zorro, where am I taking you?"

"To the orphans' asylum."

"Por Dios, are you committing the whole family? Zorro, they don't accept children over twelve."

The Fox held on to Miguel. "Stop searching. It's not your business to tell me about orphans."

Miguel drove the Guzmanns to Stebbins Avenue. They entered the orphans' asylum through the back, with Jorge on the stretcher. The Fox paid off Miguel. "Hombre, if anybody finds us here, you'll sit with your taxi company at the bottom of the Harlem River. That's for a start. I'll throw your mother, your father, your wife, and your wife's mother out the window. And don't think they'll rest in a grave. I'll tear the bodies out of the ground and hire dogs to piss on them.

Hombre, I'll shame you for the next two hundred years."

Miguel walked out with twitching eyes, grateful that he wouldn't have to chauffeur Marranos again. The Guzmanns were having trouble in the asylum. The matrons were furious that a boy was allowed to bleed in their halls. Calvarados, the chief doctor, stepped between his matrons and the Fox. Zorro pinched the doctor's sleeve. "Calvarados, I think we should have a talk."

They went into the doctor's office. Closeted behind a door, without matrons and his brothers, the Fox began to glower. "Calvarados, the Guzmanns have paid your orphans' bills. My father was generous with you. We know a lot about orphans, understand? My family couldn't afford a mother. So we deserve your charity. My brother Jorge will bleed to death if you refuse us."

"Señor, we're not a hospital, we're a children's home."

"I agree. But you're a doctor, and you have a small dispensary, enough to provide for my brother's wounds."

"I beg you, take him to Jacobi, or Bronx-Lebanon. We don't have a blood bank here."

"Calvarados, if I wanted Bronx-Lebanon, would I come to a dump on Stebbins Avenue? Hospitals are cozy with the police, and it's the police who fucked my brother. Don't I have a family outside this door? We'll give you all the blood you need."

"That's impossible," the doctor said. "I can't close off part of the home to accommodate you Guzmanns. The children will get suspicious."

"Calvarados, you aint listening to me. You're the only doctor we can trust. It's a simple thing. My brother's in your hands. So you can't disappoint us. We're terrible mourners. We chew heads in our grief. We start fires. We wouldn't harm an orphan, not me, not my father. But I can't be sure about your staff. Alejandro likes to broil fat ladies. Topal sucks on fingers a lot. Thank God Jerónimo isn't here. He's good for an eyeball and some teeth."

Calvarados surrendered to the Fox.

"Hide us for three days," Zorro said. "Then you're rid of the Guzmanns. Doctor, I swear on Jorge's life, I have a place we can go."

Patrick Silver was in the sanctuary with Jerónimo, Rabbi Hughie, and the elders of the synagogue, saying kaddish for First Deputy O'Roarke. He'd gone to Ned's wake, bringing Jerónimo along, but the Irish undertakers were mean to Jerónimo and wouldn't let Patrick buy indulgences for Ned, or kneel in front of the coffin. Patrick's former brothers, the detectives of the Shillelagh Society, ignored him at the wake, and sneaked off to the nearest Irish bar without inviting him.

So Patrick brought his black ale into the shul and sang the mourner's kaddish, while Jerónimo sulked under his prayer shawl. The baby had grown quiet since the middle of the week. He no longer mewled. He wouldn't eat dark or light caramels. Patrick would have rushed him to the candy store to see his brothers, only Papa had forbidden Jerónimo to walk on Boston Road.

The baby started mewling towards the end of the kaddish. He wouldn't close his mouth. The prayer shawl whipped around his head. Was he calling Patrick to the window? Silver peeked through a crack in the glass. "God bless," he muttered, seeing a rickety ambulance outside the shul.

Silver removed himself from the prayer box. "Excuse, please." He kissed the tassels on his shawl and went downstairs. The ambulance must have come from a Bronx orphanage. The words STEBB NS AV NUE ORPHAN were painted on its side panel. It drove away, leaving five Guzmanns and a portable hospital bed on the steps of Congregation Limerick. Jorge was under the sheets, with a bluish-white face. When he smiled at Patrick Silver, his cheeks became thin as tissue paper. He had flecks of dried blood in his mouth. His hair was pasted to his skull.

"Irish, are you going to stare at us?" Zorro said. "Jorge had an accident. He ran into Isaac. You get what I mean? Can your church hold a few boarders besides Jerónimo? Irish, they don't like us at the uptown hotels."

Patrick could never get a straight line out of Zorro. The Fox moved and talked in zigzags. "Come in, for Christ's sake. You can have the winter room."

Zorro and his brothers carried the hospital bed over the humps in the outer stairs. Patrick neglected to tell the Fox that the winter room was the unofficial almshouse of Congregation Limerick, a place where beggars could come for a meal and a pillow. But it was the fifteenth of August, and there were no beggars around (they preferred to sleep in doorways until December).

Papa was the last one to enter the shul. The loss of his territories had begun to squeeze him behind the ears. He was wallowing in America. The synagogue frightened him. Papa had never been inside a shul. For five hundred years the Guzmanns of Portugal, Spain, Holland, Lima, and the Bronx avoided God's house, spilling their secret lives into corners and damp rooms. They prayed at home or at the back of the local church, to confuse the *católicos* and humble themselves to the Lord Adonai. Not even a dead Inquisition could push them into a shul. They didn't know how to pray among Jews. They recited the paternoster and asked forgiveness from Adonai.

Jerónimo had gone from the chapel to the winter rooms to find his father and his brothers. He blinked at Jorge on the hospital bed and began to howl. Patrick, Topal, Alejandro, and Papa couldn't console him. He humped down near the bed and mourned Jorge's blue-white face. Only the Fox could teach him not to cry so loud. "Jerónimo, Jorge will be fine. You and the Irish will feed him soup. But he's not too strong. If you cry, his hair will fall out."

Jerónimo returned to his ordinary mewl. Zorro hugged his father and his brothers and left the winter room.

"Where's he going?" Patrick said.

"Irish, detectives are looking for me. They could come into your church with their warrants. Why should I give them a second chance at Jorge? It's not smart to have so many Guzmanns under one roof. Irish, watch all my brothers. Adios."

And the Fox ran down the stairs.

PART TWO

SEVEN

Odile Leonhardy sat in the Edwardian Room of the Plaza Hotel reading the breakfast menu in a crepe suit without pockets or sleeves. She shared a prestigious balcony table with the film producer Wiatt Stone. The menu wiped her out. The Plaza wouldn't poach an egg for under two dollars. Odile was becoming parsimonious in time for her twentieth birthday. She ate nuts in her room, or depended on Herbert Pimloe to satisfy her lust for French fries.

She'd lived at the Plaza three months, waiting to be discovered by legitimate movie people. She must have picked the wrong hotel. Wiatt was the only producer Odile ever met in the lobby. And the productions he had in mind didn't seem far removed from her old career as Odette the child porno queen. Wiatt fondled her leg under the balcony table and offered her the role of Abishag, King David's infant nurse, in an epic he was planning on Jerusalem, the City of God. Odile would have to spend the film stroking the loins of a dying king. "I'm too old for that part," she said, using her napkin to pluck Wiatt's hand off her knee.

Wiatt wasn't perturbed. He had Odile wedged in the corner. He could badger her with grapefruits, croissants, and either of his thumbs. "Baby, it's a natural. I want you for *The City of God*. Abishag doesn't stay twelve forever. She ends the film a distinguished lady in King Solomon's bed."

Odile stared at the beamed ceilings of the Edwardian Room, the chandeliers, the pink wallpaper, the exquisite teacups, poached eggs, and the patterns in the chairs, and she made excuses to Wiatt. 'Sorry, I have to pee."

She got out of the corner muttering damn! At least with porno moguls like her uncle Vander a girl knew where she stood. Vander didn't snow you with three-dollar grapefruits. He'd squint at a nipple under your crepe de chine and say yes or no. There wouldn't be any talk about Abishag and religious epics. Odile, he'd tell her, I want you to go down on an old king.

She was off the balcony, past a giant strawberry bowl near the reservation table, and out of the Edwardian Room. Men and women in the lobby gulped at her crepe suit. The elevator boy rubbed close to her. Odile had to remind him who she was with a bang of her hip. "Sonny, I'm not your private tree. Lean on somebody else's tit for a change."

She was downstairs with her bags packed before Wiatt had his second cup of tea. She saw Pimloe come into the hotel. He nearly missed her in her breakfast clothes. She had to wiggle some crepe in front of his eyes. "Herbert, did you just get out of a funeral?"

"Big Isaac put nails in my head. Odile, we'll have to skip the pommes frites for a little while. My stomach's out of commission. Can we meet in the park?"

"Not today. Do me a favor, Herbert. Go into the breakfast room. Ask for Wiatt the film producer. Tell him Abishag's going home."

Odile hadn't stripped herself bare for the Plaza's sake. She kept an apartment on Jane Street. It was a doll's place, a room and a half where she could entertain all sorts of men, cops like Pimloe and customers that Zorro found for her. She was Zorro's girl, but who could rely on the Fox? He would space his visits according to the calendar in his head, sleeping with her on different Mondays of the year. She couldn't understand his preference for Mondays, or the way he could open and close his passion like a fist.

But she wasn't worried about Zorro. The Fox would track her to Jane Street some Monday when his need was great enough. The Guzmanns had their virtues. With Zorro as her protector, Odile was clear of burglars and thieves. Every rat in Manhattan and the Bronx was leery of Zorro and his brothers. If you pimped in their territories, or molested one of their girls, you could lose your neck to brother Jorge.

Odile got to Jane Street in a Checker cab. Being short of cash, she signed her name and the sum of two seventy-five on a slip of paper and gave it to the driver with a hug. He wouldn't carry her luggage up the stairs. So Odile had to make three trips, cursing the incivilities of New York.

The state of her apartment baffled her. There was a saucer on the rug with crumbs in it and banana peels in the sink. Her mirrors were covered with towels. She walked into her tiny bedroom. Zorro was asleep.

"Fox," Odile said, batting the towels off her mirrors. "Fox." She tore at the lavender bedclothes around his feet. He wouldn't wake up. "You crawl into a girl's apartment the second she moves uptown. Guzmann, you're taking advantage of me."

A toe moved. His head turtled out of the sheets. He wouldn't look at Odile. The unclothed mirrors made him gloomy. He muttered something about evil eyes, Peru, and the properties of glass.

Odile was merciful to him. She clothed all her mirrors. "Guzmann, you'd better get out of here. That cop Pimloe likes to follow me. You remember Herbert. Isaac's apprentice. He could be downstairs."

She thought the Fox would jump out of bed. He picked his toenails. "I aint moving for Pimloe. I'll shove him at Isaac with a berry in his mouth."

He told her what happened to Jorge, Papa, and the candy store.

"Zorro, where'd you put your family?"

"In church, with the big Irish."

"You left them with Patrick Silver? God, that dummy came to the Plaza without his shoes."

Zorro was finished yapping with Odile. He caught her by her crepe pants and threw her into the sheets. He shook off her breakfast clothes as if they were leprous articles. The Fox despised the feel of crepe. Pants on a girl always drove him crazy. He wouldn't allow Odile to hide in any of her decorative husks. He was on his knees licking her body with the salty tongue of the Marranos.

Odile wasn't embarrassed without her clothes. She enjoyed the liberties Zorro took. He wasn't Wiatt Stone with his pinkies under the table. She wouldn't have to be Zorro's Abishag. She'd rather have the Fox in her bed than lie with any old king.

Two days of Zorro, and Odile had wool in her brains. She wasn't a girl who could survive very long without peeking into a mirror. She couldn't wear clothes around the Fox. No panties or ankle bracelets. He wouldn't eat legitimate meals. She had to chew bananas and stay in bed.

The Fox seemed to have a slow recovery. He licked her once and wouldn't go near her again. The Guzmanns behaved like little rabbis. They crept into a girl, writhed, and fell asleep with a pious look on their faces. Odile had gotten down with all six of them at different times of the year. She liked the sound of their orgasms; it was the same melancholy moan. Her other boy friends didn't come like that: loud or soft, their cries couldn't wrench Odile. Only one other boy, a cop named Manfred Coen, had made Odile's teeth chatter against her pillows. And Coen was dead.

She had to get away from the Fox for a little while and breathe air that wasn't perfumed with bananas. She'd find a mirror in the street, have a good search for wrinkles and moles. It wasn't vanity in Odile; it was the business sense of a girl who was going to sell her face to the movies and had to be aware of every mole.

Odile sneaked out while Zorro was having a snore. She didn't have the patience for underwear. She put on a wraparound skirt and went downstairs. She could have had all the mirrors in the world if she was willing to spy into antique shops on Hudson Street. But Odile was a discouraged girl. She loved Merle Oberon, Mary Astor, and Alice Faye, women of real quality, with generous foreheads and sorrowful eyes, but everybody wanted her to be Odette the porno queen, a spindle with perfect tits.

Going down Jane Street to Abingdon Square she saw Jerónimo and the big Irish standing in the park. The baby mewled at her. "Leohoody." (He liked to call her by her family name.) The Irish wasn't so talkative. He had beautiful gray-white hair. Small black bottles were sticking out of his pants. She adored his great Irish beak. Silver was handsome away from the Plaza.

"What's that in your pockets?" she said.

"Stout."

"Stout?" she said. "What's stout?"

Silver clicked his teeth. He handed her a bottle of Guinness to taste.

"Is it sweet?" she said.

"No. It's black ale."

"Thanks," she said, returning the bottle to Silver's pants. "I don't like bitter drinks."

Silver began to sway in his soccer shirt. "That's a pity," he said. "Because we'll never get on, the two of us. Your not liking Guinness and all. It's got more vitamins than milk."

"Why do you wear that rag of a shirt?"

"Not a rag," he said. "It used to be black and red." He showed her the faded skull and crossbones on the midriff of his shirt. "It's the colors of University College, Cork."

Odile kept frowning at the obscure edges of the crossbones. "Patrick Silver, you're too old for college."

"You didn't get my meaning, miss. It could have been my school, you see, if certain people hadn't chased my father out of Ireland."

She couldn't follow his crazy stories. How do you get from Ireland to Abingdon Square? But she would have liked to discover what was under Patrick's shirt. Did the Irish have gray-white hairs on his chest? She thought of bringing him home to Jane Street, only the Fox was sleeping in her bed. She couldn't undress Patrick at his synagogue. The Guzmanns had overrun the place.

"How's Papa?" she said.

"Alive. He's learning to pray with us."

"Tell him Odile is living on Jane Street again. He can visit whenever he's in the mood. With his boys, or alone. It's all the same to me."

"Any more messages now?"

"Yes. I think there's a cop watching us from both ends of the park."

"I know. The lads belong to Isaac. Not to worry. They eat Baby Ruths and stare a lot. They won't harm you."

Odile kissed Jerónimo and waved to the Irish. If Zorro woke without finding her, he'd bite the walls and swear Odile had abandoned him to the evil eye in her mirrors. She rushed past the blond detective at the top of the park. He smiled at the flimsy opening of her dress, with his cheeks full of candy. "Baby Odile," he said. "Uncle Isaac will give you a whole bunch of presents if you lead him to that stupid Fox."

God, Isaac had his jaws on every block. A dog couldn't piss on a lamppost without some commissioner hearing about it. She ran to Jane Street to warn Zorro about the blond detectives and their Baby Ruths. She came home to an empty bed. The Fox was gone. Maybe he went shopping for bananas. She said shit, shit shit! She could have sunned herself on Abingdon Square and flirted with Jerónimo's Irish keeper.

EIGHT

Isaac's "children" moved from Boston Road to Bethune Street. Green Chevrolets were patrolling the Irish synagogue two days after the Guzmanns arrived. Jerónimo could see their wide fins from the

different cracks in the chapel windows. Isaac brought his infantry to
the steps of the shul. You could find detectives on foot from
Washington Street to Abingdon Square. The new First Dep had
Silver and all his people in a shoebox. Isaac could suffocate them, or
allow them a few inches of peace.

Patrick wouldn't surrender to blue boys and a fleet of Chevrolets
He didn't have to charge into the gutters for random Jews. He could
build his minyans inside the shul. Patrick had four new heads to play
with: Topal's, Alejandro's, Papa's, and Jorge's. But he wasn't crude.
He lured three Guzmanns into the sanctuary, but he wouldn't invade
Jorge's bed. He found a yarmulke for Papa's middle child and placed
it on the prayer stand after Rabbi Hughie pronounced that a sick
person who was already inside the shul didn't have to appear bodily
at religious services; he could be represented in spirit and substance
by a skullcap or another article of faith, according to the *torah* behind
Hughie's ears.

Papa was uneasy in the chapel. Afraid that the Lord Adonai
might be offended if an apostate muttered prayers in Hebrew, Papa
sang under his breath in Portuguese. He covered himself with a huge
linen shawl, just like the elders of the shul. He encouraged Topal not
to swing his shoulders until the Torah was removed from the closet
near the wall, and he wouldn't let Alejandro crumble halvah on the
stairs around the prayer box. But cautioning his sons couldn't relieve
Papa's sorrows. How could he forget the Chevrolets? Hearing them
gun their motors in the street, he would pull the shawl over his face
entirely and withdraw into the only ark a Marrano could make for
himself: the dead air in front of his nose.

Seeing Papa in a shroud, Patrick would console him with
whispers at the end of a prayer. "Moses, be all right. I don't care a fig
if Isaac is king of the sidewalks. He can't climb through windows
with a Chevrolet. Be all right."

But he couldn't hold Papa's hand throughout the morning
service. Patrick was the guardian of the scrolls. The elders had
empowered him to dress and undress the Torah. This, the most sacred
office of the synagogue, was given to Patrick in memory of his father.

There would have been no Congregation Limerick without
Murray Silver, the dead vicar of Bethune Street. The wobbly closet
that held the scrolls of the synagogue was Murray's ark. It once stood
in the King's Island shul of County Limerick. Carved in Baghdad
(Patrick learned from his father), the closet went from Iraq to Turkey,

from Turkey to Spain, from Spain to Ireland, in the course of seven hundred years. No one dared question the pedigree of the Baghdad closet. It was the holiest vessel in Ireland for the Jews of Wolfe Tone Street. When the mad people of Limerick chased out every Jew, Murray wouldn't permit the ark to rot on King's Island. He carried it to Dublin in a wagon, rowed it across the Irish Sea, and sat with it on a freighter from Liverpool to New York.

Weakened at the corners from its many rides, the closet landed in America with one leg gone. Murray wasn't disturbed. He walked the hobbled ark past immigration officers and moved it into a boardinghouse with the help of a society for penniless Jews. He met a handful of his former congregants at the society, took them to the boardinghouse, where they rejoiced over the survival of the Baghdad closet and made plans for a synagogue that could house Murray's ark.

It was this ancient closet with a tattered Irish curtain over the door (designed by the Jewish weavers of Limerick, the curtain was shedding its hair) that so appalled the Guzmanns. Papa and his boys were convinced that the Lord Adonai lived in the Baghdad closet. They looked for smoke whenever Patrick reached under the curtain. They would shudder as the big Irish brought his Torah to them. The Torah had to be kissed. They would peck at its velvet mantle with crinkled lips. The velvet burnt their mouths. They closed their eyes when Patrick undressed the Torah. They couldn't bear to peek at a raw scroll. The bloodred tongue of Adonai might slap at them from the skein of Hebrew letters.

Except for his periods in the chapel, Papa wouldn't come out of the winter room. He sat with Jorge, winding pieces of string in a mad game of cat's cradle that he would play with himself. Patterns snapped in and out of his fingers at a dizzying rate. Papa had no other occupations.

From time to time Zorro would send doctors into the shul. They were always oldish young men in hospital coats, interns, male nurses, and paramedics that Zorro had bribed away from emergency wards in one of the Little Havanas of the Bronx. Only Zorro's doctors could get Papa off cat's cradle. They would huddle around Jorge, snipping at his bandages with filthy hospital shears, and then have their consultations in a corner of the winter room. This jabber didn't make sense to Papa. They talked of silver kneecaps, spinal fluids, stolen pints of blood. They were eager to turn the main floor of the synagogue into a surgical unit. Masks and little knives began to accumulate near Jorge's bed.

It took Papa a few weeks to discover that these men were poseurs, idiots in hospital coats. They were capable of murdering Jorge with their little knives. He didn't want silver kneecaps on his boy. He threw Zorro's doctors out of the synagogue. They hissed the Fox's name at him from the bottom of the stairs. "The Fox won't like this. The Fox paid us to watch over his brother. Old man, what do you know about medicine?"

Papa wouldn't hold a dialogue with imbeciles. "Tell my youngest that I'm not giving Jorge's knees to you."

Papa called in his Marrano witch doctors. They had much softer faces than the oldish young men. They knew how to cry for a crippled boy. And they were able practitioners. They hovered over the bed, breathing their cloves of garlic into Jorge's wounds. Papa had no difficulty with the cures they mentioned in their chants. They promised manifold resurrections: snow in Jerusalem, restored ankles and knees, hospital beds that could rise up a wall, and the return of all Marranos to Arabic Spain. Papa wept at the news. He was beginning to recover from the stupefaction of a thirty-year roost in the Bronx. America was no country for him. The Marranos couldn't survive around Christians and Jews. But the Spain they were seeking died eight hundred years ago, when the Moors got out of Seville.

Patrick had to feed the Guzmanns and their witch doctors, who were finicky people. Marranos eat with their hands, they announced, scorning Patrick's spoons. They wouldn't touch his sandwiches or his soups. Patrick had to run to a Cuban-Chinese restaurant near the Chelsea Hotel for quantities of pork and black beans.

Attending to the Guzmanns could wear a man out. Patrick escaped to the Kings of Munster whenever there was a lull at the shul. He would snort his Guinness and come back to the winter room utterly smashed, singing bawdy songs (about the witch of Limerick and the traffic under Ballsbridge) that no one understood.

Papa couldn't keep the geography of Ireland in his head. He had his troubles remembering both ends of Bethune Street. Even Boston Road was beginning to disappear. He could forsake a generation of blackberries, malteds, and halvah with the bat of an eye. The chapel was still a frightening place. It had a chair for Elijah and a closet for Adonai. So Papa made his cosmos in the winter room. He could bump into walls with a certain tranquility. He could pester the witch doctors for clearer prophecies. He could wash Jorge's face with a dishtowel. He could observe Patrick's restlessness and hear the groans of his boys. Papa wasn't blind: Topal had a brick in his pocket. What can you do for a boy who stays erect sixteen hours in a row? Papa begged Patrick to bring a prostitute into the house.

"Irish, help me. He's splitting through his pants . . . Topal's in danger. His prick could break."

"Moses, I'm sorry for the lad, but you can't have whores in a shul."

"What about Zorro's wife?" Papa said, with a burr in his throat.

"Who's that?"

"The little goya. Odile."

"She can come if she likes," Patrick said. "But not to fornicate. That's the law."

Papa was gritting now. "Didn't know we were visiting in a monastery, Irish. My boys got pricks, thank God. Take them to the little goya, one at a time. Irish, I'm depending on you. Don't lead them into Isaac's fenders. I have one boy without legs. It's enough."

"Moses, not to worry. These are narrow blocks. I can dodge a Chevrolet."

Patrick ran his shuttle from the synagogue to Jane Street. Topal had the greatest need. So he was the first to go with Patrick. "Hold his hand," Papa shouted from the stairs. "Irish, don't let him stumble. He could lose his knees."

They went out of the shul with their hands clapped together. Detectives crowed at them from the green cars. "Patrick, why don't you give this baby to us? We're sweet on Guzmanns. We'll lick his eyes."

"Be gone," Patrick muttered, "before I shit on your windshield," and he dragged Topal away from the cars. He couldn't get into Odile's house. He had to buzz her from the street. "Open up, Miss Leonhardy. I brought a lad for you. Topal Guzmann And greetings from Papa."

Odile was waiting for him at the door in a party robe. Patrick stood in his black socks The little goya had patches of skin that could wobble an Irishman's brains. He was becoming a bloody go-between, chauffeuring Guzmann boys to Odile.

"Should I stay in the hall until you've finished with him?"

"No," she said. "Come inside."

He'd been to whores' apartments, but none of them had tea cozies, and waffle irons on the wall. Her bed was tiny. Patrick would have had to cut off his ankles to make himself fit. Papa's little goya was a strange sort of tart. She undressed Topal with affectionate tugs. Was she really married to the Fox? Or did the Guzmanns have a lien on her? Patrick couldn't understand the expansions and contractions of Moses' empire. He was the family strong man, that's all, and caretaker of three of Papa's boys. Topal had a curly chest. His cock flared over his belly, but his scrotum was hard to find. The Guzmanns were precious about their balls. They tucked them away, where no enemy, male or female, could ever dig.

Patrick felt his gums shrink into his head when Odile's robe came off. He couldn't believe the grip her buttocks had on the stems of her thighs. God preserve us, the little goya didn't have a wink of loose flesh. And she wasn't shy around Patrick Silver. She moistened Topal's cock with gobs of spit and climbed on the boy. Patrick withdrew into the kitchen.

He heard a noise like the grunt of a distempered dog. Then nothing. The silence bothered him more than the grunt. A religious man, nearly a vicar at his father's shul, Patrick was no peep. But what could Odile be doing with the boy? He looked out of the kitchen. Topal was sleeping on a pillow (he'd had his pleasure for the month). Odile couldn't have swindled him; there was a deep angelic flush on his face. The little goya sat on the bed without disturbing Topal's sleep. She was in her robe again.

The silk on her legs made Patrick melancholy. He was an Irishman who carried the Torah in his arms. Could he approach the little goya? Offer her some money? She'd say he was included in the Guzmann bill. Hypocrite, he'd lectured to Papa on the sins of fornicating in a shul. He would have hidden Odile in his father's sacred closet and stuck himself to her after prayers. He'd have flung Hughie out the chapel window if the rabbi challenged his rights to the girl. And he'd bite off the face of any elder who interfered with him. Patrick would have his concubine, or he'd close the shul.

The madness of his lust began to frighten him. "Jesus," he said, "I'm going home."

Odile walked into the kitchen. She didn't flirt. She didn't unwind her robe. She didn't put her hand in Silver's pocket. He was dour with her, St. Patrick of the Bethune Street Shul.

"Tell us how you got to be the Fox's bride?"

"Who says I'm a bride?"

"Papa says. Is it a Guzmann fairy tale?"

"No. But it was a rotten wedding. I had to marry six people. Papa and the five boys. It was Zorro's idea."

"That's a good Fox. Was he going to parcel you out like Jerónimo's chocolate? Every Guzmann gets a slice. It's a pity they didn't spread you seven ways, so I could have had my share."

"Don't be crazy," she said. "The Guzmanns weren't interested in a wife. Zorro was collecting marriage certificates. The preacher was a dingbat. He didn't have a church. He had to marry us in the chapel of a Puerto Rican funeral parlor. Zorro figured they couldn't throw Guzmanns out of the country if the whole family married an American girl. I signed the certificates with different names. The preacher didn't care."

"Mrs. Guzmann," Patrick said. "Congratulations."

She pouted at him as she loosened the bindings on her robe. "Don't call me that. A girl can't have six husbands. It's illegal in New York. Besides, I'm under-age. I was seventeen when the Guzmanns married me."

Patrick couldn't fight the logic of her arguments, or get to the door. She trapped him in the wings of her robe. The weight of her bosoms on his soccer shirt hit him below the knees. He sank into Odile, numb from the neck down. He wanted nothing more than to hug the little goya, have her nipples in his chest, stand on rubbery stalks, for the rest of his miserable life.

NINE

There was a history of bachelorhood in Patrick's line. Over the past hundred and fifty years no Silver in Ireland or America had married under the age of forty-five. Murray Silver brought his closet out of Ireland in 1906, as a boy of twenty-two. He labored for his synagogue twenty-five years before he could choose a wife. He was the vicar of Bethune Street, and he despised miserly shuls. Congregation Limerick had to have a proper awning, red and blue glass, and a winter room for the unfortunates who lived around Abingdon Square.

He married Enid Rose, an eighteen-year-old orphan who delivered bread to the shul, in 1931. She was a quietly sensual girl, with hips that broadened out of her many skirts (the vicar met Enid in the winter), and a tongue that could receive a vicar's kiss. Murray was nearing fifty. He had a permanent stoop from climbing up and down the synagogue's ladder to scrub ceilings and replace pieces of stained glass. His Irish brethren thought a young bride would murder him. They advised Murray to take her slow. The vicar said pish! to their advice. He drank black ale and spent himself on Enid.

The elders of the shul were frightened by the signatures of Murray's passion. The girl was pregnant very soon. These old men prayed to God she wouldn't have to carry an orphan in her womb. The elders were wrong about Murray. He survived the birth of Patrick Silver. But Enid caught a cold. It spread to her lungs. She was buried before Patrick could be circumcised.

The boy grew up on the steps of the synagogue. His pabulum came in a dark bottle. He sucked Guinness at the Kings of Munster with his da. While Murray scrubbed ceilings, Patrick slept in the pews with a skullcap over his face. He had his soup in the winter room along with the beggars of Abingdon Square. He lived in the basement with Murray, who gave up his furniture and his apartment after Enid caught her cold. The synagogue was Patrick's new mum. The elders became aunts and uncles to him. And he had the Kings of Munster for a nursery.

Murray began to lose his vigor. He could no longer maintain the synagogue by himself. He would stand on the ladder dreaming of his bride. Patrick had to sweep the shul. He learned to remove splinters from a window, foraging in the cracked glass without cutting his fingers. He prepared a thick soup for surly beggars who considered it a blow to their dignity that a nine-year-old should feed them. Raised on Guinness, Patrick had the strength to overcome their mean looks. "Kind sirs, it's piss or barley soup," he would say. "Have your pick."

In a few years it didn't matter how often the beggars outnumbered him. At twelve Patrick was a good six feet. He wore a black and red soccer shirt (Murray had swiped the colors of Cork College on his way out of Ireland). The beggars came to respect the skull on Patrick's shirt. If they rioted in the winter room, blowing soup into a neighbor's ear, the boy would pack them in bundles of two and three, roll them down the stairs, and leave them on the sidewalk. He would also protect his father from basement drafts, keeping the vicar in sweaters and double pairs of socks. Murray took to his bed, mumbling Enid, Enid Rose, and falling back into the days of 1931, when he undressed Enid and the Torah with a madman's piety. He lingered for another ten years, dying in 1954, a vicar of seventy.

Now it was Patrick's turn to clutch for a wife. A boy of forty-two, he decided to come out of his bachelor-hood sooner than his father did. But his courtship ran into the ground. The girl he wanted to marry was already a bride.

He couldn't go against his employers, the Guzmanns of Manhattan, Lima, and the Bronx, who had their names affixed to Odile's wedding papers. But since he was expected to deliver Jerónimo, Topal, and Alejandro to Jane Street, he had his opportunities with the little goya. He would bring her a yellow rose with disgusting prickles, scarfs from Orchard Street, a charlotte russe, doilies that should have arrived on St. Valentine's Day, chocolates filled with a medicinal sap that Jerónimo himself couldn't swallow.

The Irishman had to be crazy. Odile had never come upon such an assortment of gifts. Although she chided Patrick, stuffing the doilies into his soccer shirt, giving his charlotte russe away, the little goya was pleased. No one else had thought of wooing her in an old-fashioned way. She liked to get down with Patrick Silver on the kitchen floor while one of Papa's babies slept in her bed.

This morning it was Jerónimo. Lying next to Patrick, with her fan puttering in the window, she could hear Jerónimo breathe through his nose. She'd scattered some bedding on the linoleum so Patrick wouldn't scratch his knees. The bedding grew damp in August weather. The gorgeous white hairs on Patrick's chest had the slippery feel of seaweed.

"Irish," she said. "You fuck like Manfred Coen."

Patrick wouldn't talk about a dead cop (Coen had been Isaac's sweetheart, his angel boy). He knew Isaac loved to fish with Coen on the hook, sending his angel into forbidden territories, but Patrick couldn't figure why Coen had to land in Odile's bed. It didn't make him suspicious of Odile. He understood all her avocations, her career with Zorro and other pimps. He intended to marry the whore child. He'd buy her from the Fox if he had to. Patrick wasn't a bloody reformer. He wanted to take Odile off the street. That was it. There was nothing untoward about the little goya's age. Nineteen? She could grow up in the basement of a synagogue, whoring for one man, Patrick Silver.

His devotion began to frighten her. She'd cling to his chest, satisfy any of his Irish whims, bathe in Guinness if he liked, but she couldn't bear his mumbling about synagogues and brides. The

Guzmanns had soured her on the subject of marriage. Patrick
wouldn't give up his bride songs. To cool him out, she told him her
escapades with Herbert Pimloe, Wiatt Stone (Odile had to lie a little),
Zorro, her uncle Vander, and Coen.

Patrick couldn't listen. A series of whimpers came from the
bedroom. Jerónimo was waking up. His noises didn't seem like
hunger pains. Patrick climbed into his pants. He assumed the baby
was lonesome for the synagogue. He peeked in: Jerónimo lay on
Odile's bed with his knees in his face. Patrick couldn't understand
this tortured position. Jerónimo was shrieking now. Odile called from
her swampy bedding. "Did he swallow his fist?"

The baby had his own repertoire of noises. Patrick knew most of
it. He could tell when Jerónimo was starving, sick, or sleepy. But the
shrieks baffled him until he discovered their melody. Jerónimo was
imitating the sound of a fire truck. He had incredible ears. He could
isolate a noise from ten blocks away, sing to a fire truck on Houston
Street. Patrick only moved when he heard the same shrieks outside
the window. He put on his socks faster than Jerónimo could blink his
eyes. He didn't kiss Odile, or stick a finger in Jerónimo's scalp.
Patrick had no time for minor affections. He muttered, "Esau, stay
with me," and ran down the stairs.

The shul was on fire. Smoke spilled from the roofs. The walls
crackled. Splits appeared in the stained glass. Patrick shoved into the
crowd that collected on Bethune Street to watch a synagogue burn.
"Coming through lads." The two fire trucks parked on Patrick's block
were in a comatose state. A single fireman swung close to the shul on
an aerial ladder and stabbed at the windows of the sanctuary with a
long metal pick. Other firemen kept unwinding enormous bands of
hose. The bands went nowhere. They snaked between the firemen's
legs and rubbed against the gutters. One of the firemen said
something about the water pressure in July.

"The bastard doesn't know what month he's in," Patrick
muttered to himself. He couldn't locate a fire chief, but he found the
Guzmanns and Rabbi Prince behind the second truck. Jorge was in
his hospital bed.

"What happened, for God's sake?"

Papa had a filthy nose. "Irish, who can tell? The fire didn't come
from our room. It started in the basement. Another few minutes and
Jorge would have had smoke coming out of his ass. Where's the
baby?"

"Safe, Moses. He's playing with Odile."

Patrick turned to Rabbi Prince. "Hughie, what did you bring out?"

"Nothing but Jorge Guzmann. And we had a heavy time accomplishing that."

"My father's closet," Patrick said, his eyes getting grim. "Did you leave it in the shul?"

"I've got one pair of shoulders on me, Patrick Silver, and a crooked pair it is. There wasn't enough room on my back for Jorge and the closet."

Why was he behind a fire truck quizzing Moses and Hughie when the closet was inside the shul? Hughie was able to interpret the mad thoughts under Patrick's beetling eyebrows. "Jesus Christ, I'm a rabbi now and then. Wouldn't I have saved the ark if I could?"

But Murray had a stubborn boy. He grabbed an asbestos coat off the back of a fireman. Other firemen yelled at him. "Hey motherfucker, you can't go in." Patrick lifted them out of the way. Wearing the coat over his head like a prayer shawl with skirts and sleeves, he rushed into the shul, closing the door behind him. The heat smacked his nose and made him stagger. Patrick couldn't see a bloody thing. Smoke bellied through the synagogue, hiding the stairs. It ate into Patrick's lungs until his saliva turned a nasty color and he felt a squeeze in his ears. The baking floorboards attacked his dark socks. He had to ride on the nub of his toes. His chest ripped with every swing of his body. He hadn't gone a foot from the door.

Then, flapping the asbestos skirts around his arms, he walked through smoke. Patrick could swear he was losing his skin to the fire. He smelled his own cooked flesh. He'd gotten to the stairs. The bannisters were burning hard. He had to climb with low, hunkering moves, or ignite himself.

Patrick couldn't be far from the sanctuary. He heard the popping of glass. He had to be in the winter room. He sank into mattresses on the floor, his feet snarled in Guzmann blankets and pillowcases. Patrick kicked them off with swipes of his stockings. The saliva became a crust on his lips while he groped for the chapel door. He was in another room. Hughie's study? The shul's brittle toilet? Patrick had his bearings: his knees touched a pew. If he went to the top of the pews and took fifteen paces north, he would miss the prayer box and bang into the closet.

But his calculations failed. He must have run athwart of the closet. He was grounded in the sanctuary, scraping woodwork. The smoke had robbed him of his senses. He searched for his father's leaded windows, that thicket of glass in the north wall. His fireman's coat had begun to crack. The sleeves were ruined. The asbestos near his skull gave off a mean roar. A foul, swollen gas was swimming in the dead air. It flooded Patrick's eyes, nose, and lungs, and the lining of his coat. Bits of his hair were catching fire. He stumbled backwards and forwards, slapping his own head. He saw a tiny flame lick the ends of a gold rag. It was the Irish curtain that hung over the doors of the ark. Hopping like a madman, with his scalp on fire, Patrick found the Baghdad closet.

Outside the shul Rabbi Prince was saying kaddish for Patrick Silver. He hadn't met any flameproof Irishmen in America. There had to be a crazy angel squatting on the chapel wall, in Elijah's chair, an angel who loved to burn down churches and shuls. Which of the angels in the Mishna and the Gemara was a firebug? That one had murdered Patrick Silver.

The Guzmanns stood next to Hughie, mumbling their own prayers. They knew how to mourn for an employee. The Irish was Moses' hired man. He had guarded Jerónimo, befriended Papa's other boys, leading them straight to the little goya, and hid all the Guzmanns (except the Fox) in his shul. Even if Isaac should grab him off the street, Papa would smuggle candles into the Tombs and light them for Patrick. No jail could keep the Guzmanns from paying their respects. They would sing to their fellow prisoners (in English, Spanish, and Portuguese) how Patrick had fared in the war with Isaac the Shit. Papa wouldn't enter the prison mess without screaming Patrick's name. That way the Irish would never be forgotten.

There was a disturbance at the mouth of the shul. The door had swung open. Smoke escaped. The firemen didn't cherish apparitions who danced out of a synagogue. "Crap," they said. "That's a miserable guy." A spook tumbled onto the sidewalk with a closet on his back. He was nothing but a pair of eyes set in a blackened face. He wore a shredded jersey. His stockings were shriveled up. Smoke was coming from his forehead.

The firemen were appalled. They tried to cover him with their asbestos coats. The spook didn't want to be smothered by firemen. His lips parted. He had coaly teeth. His tongue was a disgusting yellow. "Get out of here," he said. "I've got another chore to do."

Five detectives burst into Isaac's sanctuary. Their neckties flew away from their collars. They had buttons off their shirts. Their holsters were awry.

"Mad Patrick is here . . . "

"He's dressed like a nigger, sir. In black rags."

"We thought he was a Rastafarian. He charges past Security. I almost shot the fuck."

"What's he want from us? He bit Morris on the ass."

"Should we escort mad Patrick to the basement, sir? We could chain him to a filing cabinet and finish him off."

Isaac stared at his five detectives, who made their own little fury in his office. "Be gentle with St. Patrick. I invited him to tea."

There were shivers coming from Isaac's door. You could hear the scratching of knees. Patrick hobbled into the office with two more detectives riding his ankles and his ribs. His famous soccer shirt had lost its sleeves. The crack of his buttocks showed through the top of his pants. His toes curled out of his stockings. He had blood and dark shit on his face, like soot from a fire storm.

"Isaac," he said, with somebody's arm in his mouth. "Are these lads part of your fire patrol? Did they recite a prayer over the kerosine? You shouldn't have touched my shul. If I can get past your fireflies, I'll show you how things were done in Limerick. I'll tear your pizzle off and slap it over your head."

Isaac emerged from the wooden enclaves of his commissioner's desk. "You tin Irishman. The only Limerick you ever saw was your father's pubic hair. You can't fool a tit with your smelly Irish shirt. You were born near Hudson Street, like the rest of us. Only your father diapered you with leftover yarmulkes."

Patrick struggled against the detective who was sitting on his ribs. "Mention my father again, and you'll be living with the worms, Mr. Sidel."

"Let him up," Isaac said. "I'm sick of his blabber. Silver, I'm waiting for you. Push your legs and come to me."

The detectives riding Patrick loosened their hold. He sprang up and seized Isaac by the throat. The two of them started to whirl in the middle of the room. The cops in Isaac's office couldn't believe a common man like Patrick Silver, a refugee from the rubber-gun squad and the janitor of a shul, would dare wrestle with the Acting First Dep. They rushed Patrick Silver, pommeled him, and made grabs at his shirt; pieces of charred cotton came off Patrick Silver and stuck to their fingers. The First Dep shouted at them. "Lay off. Patrick's all mine. I'll fix any mother who interferes with me and him."

So they had to desist. They put their fingers in policeman's handkerchiefs and watched Patrick and the First Dep roll on the floor. They were mystified. They no longer knew how to protect their Chief. They had leather points on their shoes that could penetrate the skull of any Irish giant. But Isaac wouldn't give them the word. All they could do was shut the door and confine the wrestling match to a single room, or the whole of Headquarters would be privy to the news. The story of Isaac grovelling with wisps of feathery material in his face would spread to the other offices, arrive at the main hall, and every cop in Manhattan would know that Isaac had wrestled with a janitor.

Isaac wasn't concerned about issues of protocol; he had a thumb in his Adam's apple. He didn't panic, he didn't squeal for help; he was used to ferocious men. He survived six months of standing next to Jorge Guzmann, hadn't he? Isaac had his share of scars; dents in his forehead from a gang of hammer-throwing junkies, a button of flesh on his jaw that was given to him by a crazed thief with a pair of pliers in his hand. Isaac had fought the bandits of all five boroughs and come out alive. He wouldn't succumb to an Irish giant who wore an empty holster like a fucking codpiece.

The detectives couldn't decide what to make of the blood in Isaac's mouth. Was the commissioner choking to death? They were satisfied when they saw Isaac spit out small chunks of enamel. A commissioner couldn't die of a broken tooth. Then Isaac's lot improved. With his sledgehammer elbows he snapped Patrick's chin around and forced the thumb away from his Adam's apple. "Had enough, you stupid son-of-a-bitch?" he said, climbing on top of Patrick.

"I'll stuff turds in your ears before I'm through," the Irishman remarked as he hurled Commissioner Isaac off his chest. It grew into a seesaw affair, with much crossing of elbows and bumping of skulls. Such ambiguous scrabbling gave the detectives fits of insecurity. Nobody would win or lose.

Finally Patrick and Isaac came apart. Both of them lay huffing on the floor. Their faces were grim, their knuckles rubbed blue. Patrick's shirt had disintegrated. He plucked white hairs off his body. Isaac inspected the damage to his mouth. "Bring us some tea," he growled. His staff began to function again. Detectives ran for the commissioner's tea pot, for his favorite honey biscuits, for sugar, spoons, and delicate china. "Now get the fuck out of here."

Alone, without a clutch of nervous hens, Patrick and Isaac drank tea and cognac from blue-veined cups. They didn't speak. They grunted once or twice. Isaac's men stood outside the door and wondered at the periods of silence in the commissioner's room.

The tea had gone to Patrick's head. "Mr. Deputy," he muttered, with cognac blowing off his tongue. "What is it you've got against those Guzmanns? That's a poor clan. You've been skunking Zorro for a year." He slapped the commissioner's desk with the heel of his stocking. "You'd better pick on a different family."

"They murdered Manfred Coen," Isaac said, sniffing the cognac in his teacup.

"Everybody talks about Coen," Patrick said, sucking up more tea while he remembered Odile and that blue-eyed cop of Isaac's. Sad, sweet Manfred was supposed to have been irresistible to the female population of the City. According to the snitches at Headquarters, women couldn't hold up their pants around Blue Eyes for very long. The Bureau of Special Services loved to steal him from Isaac once or twice a week: Coen was in great demand as a bodyguard for starlets, lady politicians, and the wives of foreign diplomats.

Patrick hugged his knees. There were rumors in Manhattan and the Bronx that Isaac tossed Blue Eyes to the Guzmanns because his daughter, Marilyn the Wild, had gone crazy for Coen. The commissioner had a girl who ran away from all her husbands (she'd been married eight times, Patrick heard) and went to sit on Coen's lap. Patrick used to see her at Headquarters, a daughter that any cop would have been glad to chase if she wasn't so close to their Chief. A skinny, green-eyed girl with tits she was. And an Irish mother (Isaac's estranged wife Kathleen, the real estate goddess, lived in Florida most of the year). The First Dep had no luck with women. His wife, his girlfriends, and his only daughter abandoned him. Marilyn the Wild was in Seattle gathering a new crop of husbands and hiding from her dad.

"Isaac, speak the truth now? Did you sacrifice poor Manfred on account of the lady Marilyn?"

Isaac took a honey biscuit and chewed on it. He'd wrestle Patrick a second time unless the big donkey shut his mouth. "If you're so interested in Coen, why don't you help us trap the Guzmanns?"

"Isaac, that's a pitiful request. What difference can it make to you if the Guzmanns live or die?"

"They put a worm in my gut. I ate their shit for half a year."

"Did you expect Papa to kiss you on both eyebrows? He knew about your masquerade. Isaac, the fallen Chief. The lad who gave up Manhattan to lie down in a candy store. I was a lousy detective then, the low man on the First Deputy's pole, and even I couldn't believe that Isaac the Pure could ever bring himself to take a bribe from gamblers. You were always so big on logic, making your lovely little charts on the criminal mind like it was a glass ocean you could skate across with your leather shoes."

Patrick's tongue was growing heavy with the froth of his own words, but he wouldn't let Isaac go. "Your logic stinks. You could have had a vacation in the Bronx without your elephant stories. But why did you want to sleep with the Guzmanns in the first place? Is it Papa's hairy legs that turned you on?"

"No," Isaac said, the cognac burning into the hole in his cheek that Silver had made for him. Isaac was mourning his lost tooth. He nearly rose off the carpets from the rawness in his gums.

"Not Papa," he said. "Not Jorge, not Zorro. It's Jerónimo."

Patrick shuddered into his tea. "God damn you, Isaac. Don't revive that ancient story. I'll scream, I'll piss on your walls, if you mention the lipstick freak."

"Jerónimo's a faigel."

"Some faigel," Patrick said. "He does fine with Zorro's wife. Should I tell you how often he's crawled into her bed?"

"You mean the great Odile? I thought she was married to Herbert Pimloe. That girl goes down for an army every night. Name me one man who hasn't fucked Odile."

Patrick didn't give a fig about the commissioner's china. He would have bitten the teacup and presented Isaac with the shards, but he wanted to drive him off the subject of Odile. "Weren't we talking about the baby?"

"Absolutely," Isaac said. "A faigel, I promise you. He likes to mutilate little boys. What can you expect from a family of pimps?"

"You're wrong. Moses didn't raise his boys to attack infants on a roof. I'm the baby's keeper, am I not? Wise to all his habits. I'd know if he went freaking on the roofs."

"He's been stuck at home lately. Ever since the Guzmanns moved in with you. The baby's shy with his father around. But it won't last. The craziness is in his blood. He'll sit on his hands for a while, then he'll have to jump. How long can you live on white chocolate? I give him another week, and he'll be out hunting for boys."

Patrick was tired of cognac in a teacup. He grabbed a corner of Isaac's desk and pulled himself up from the carpets.

"What are you going to do, Isaac? Place a dwarf on every roof?"

"We won't have to. Are you blind? I have enough men on Hudson Street to pick needles off the ground. We'll catch him in the act."

"Isaac, who stuck a fiddle up your ass? Why don't you push uptown with your lads and burn a few more shuls, you miserable fat shit."

Patrick fled the room, walking on shifty ankles. He was bloated with tea. He passed a maze of offices packed with First Deputy boys. They had malicious smiles for him. "Mad Patrick." These were Isaac's snakes. Patrick could ignore them. He was brooding over more important things. The Chief had called him a tin Irishman, a lad from Bethune Street. I'm as Irish as the toads of Killinane, Patrick should have said. He'd got his Ireland from the neck of a Guinness bottle, studying history and magic at the Kings of Munster, on Murray Silver's knee.

Isaac's men heard him groan to himself. He had an odd look in his eye, this St. Patrick of the Synagogues. His lips were going at an incredible rate. Isaaaac, he said, I knowww about wizards, saints, and kings. Brian Boru, the first king of Munster, he threw the Danes out of Limerick, slapping their heads with a dried bull's pizzle until they dropped their knives and ran down to Skibbereen. St. Bridget, abbess of Kildare, she fornicated with the wild fishermen of Dungarvan to keep them from ravaging her community of nuns. The witch of Limerick, a frightful bag, she lived a hundred and ninety years, laying curses on her town, and died of a sneeze that tore her chest. St. Munchin, the hermaphrodite, he brought the lepers into Ireland and suckled them on his own milk. Murray once told him there might have been some Jews among the lepers. How many Silvers drank from Munchin's tit? God knows. Patrick's thirst for black ale had come from the saints.

Detectives in the halls were squinting at the shreds of clothing on his back. Here's a man that goes in and out of Isaac's den! Who gave him the mumbling lips? They marveled at the powers of their Chief, convincing themselves that the First Dep had turned St. Patrick into a spy. They hadn't noticed Patrick's blue eyes before. "Mother," they said. Isaac had a new "angel," another Manfred Coen.

TEN

He could have finished the afternoon in his office, had a flunky shave him and pick the remains of Patrick's shirt off his body. The First Dep wasn't a fastidious creature. He could survive with burnt cotton on his face. He had enough tangerines and honey biscuits to outlast the clerks camped around his door. Issac would sign no documents today. He kept a small apartment on the other side of the Bowery. He could step into his private elevator, walk out of Headquarters, and go to Rivington Street for a bath and a fresh linen suit. But Isaac had lost his bishopric. He wasn't loved on Essex and Delancey any more. He dialed the police garage. "Warm up the Chrysler, will you? And fetch my man. He's probably in the toilet with his comic books."

Now that he was the First Dep, Isaac could avoid the main stairway at Headquarters and bypass other commissioners and other cops. He rode his elevator down to the garage, got into his Chrysler, and shut the door. The air conditioner sucked under his clothes. His thighs were still wet from his match with Patrick Silver. He knocked on the glass partition that isolated him from the driver. "Palisade Avenue," he said. "It's at the end of the Bronx."

Isaac was going to his old apartment up in Riverdale. It belonged to his wife. Kathleen was in Florida converting swamps into condominiums; Isaac could have the apartment to himself. He would find a suit in one of the closets, a silk shirt with brocaded pockets, a hand-painted tie, sets of underwear.

The First Dep ruled over a kingdom of fat and skinny cops; he could turn chief inspectors into patrolmen, flop a whole division, take a man's gun away, groom his own squad of "angels," destroy the Guzmanns one by one, but he was still a slave to Centre Street. He was on call twenty-four hours, like the grubbiest intern at Bellevue. He had an automatic pager on his belt that could summon him back to Headquarters, or put him in touch with the PC. When he got to Riverdale, he would throw the gadget under a pillow and climb into

Kathleen's tub.

He didn't feel sorry for the big Irish. St. Patrick shouldn't have dragged the Guzmanns into the shul. Isaac wasn't running a hobby shop at Police Headquarters. He'd smoke the Guzmanns out of all their nests in Manhattan. The First Dep couldn't be accused of starting any fires. Isaac simply told a spy of his (Martin Finch belonged to a gang of pyromaniacs from Cobble Hill) that he knew of a synagogue that was a perfect firetrap. "Martin, it's ready to fall. A match in the cellar, a whiff of kerosine, and goodbye. But be careful. The janitor's an Irish giant. You'll recognize him by his white hair and his smelly feet. Wait until he goes out for a walk. There's a family of idiots inside. You can burn their noses, but I don't want a funeral pyre. No cremations, you hear? Just get their asses out on the street."

The doormen on Palisade Avenue saluted the First Dep. Isaac had become the celebrity of the house. They'd read articles about him in the *New York Post,* articles that declared Isaac was the brainiest First Dep the City ever had: he lectures at John Jay College, he squeezes criminals, he plays chess.

He found a brassiere and an open pocketbook on Kathleen's parquet floor. Was there a burglar in the house, a crazy guy who liked to sniff brassieres while he went through your belongings? Isaac had a pistol near his gut. But he wasn't going to wag it at a pathetic boy in a duplex apartment. Or search the closets on two floors. He began switching on the lights. A pair of checkered trousers was draped over Kathleen's favorite settee. The boy had a peculiar trademark: he worked in his underpants.

"Come out, you fucker, wherever you are. I'm a cop. Don't make me pull you by your ears."

The burglar jumped out of Kathleen's bedroom, hugging his shirt, tie, sock, and shoes. He was a man of sixty, or sixty-five, with deep gray sideburns and a little belly. Isaac recognized him. He was Miles Falloon, one of Kathleen's many partners. He plucked his trousers off the settee before Isaac could say hello.

"'S all right, Miles. Only came for a bath and a change of clothes. Go on back in."

But Falloon had disappeared. Isaac shrugged and started to unbutton his summer jacket. Kathleen watched him from the bedroom door. The real estate goddess was almost fifty-two. The Florida swamps hadn't wrecked her Irish beauty. She was voluptuous in a purple robe. None of the bimbos Isaac knew, girls twenty years younger than his wife, had Kathleen's cleavage. It was like a wound under her throat, a vulnerable patch of skin between her breasts, that could drive Isaac insane after twenty-seven years of marriage.

Isaac was a groom at nineteen, a father at twenty. He'd met the Irish beauty at a real estate office near Echo Park while he was a college student looking for a cheap flat in Washington Heights. Kathleen took her college baby on a real estate tour, making love to him in one empty apartment after the other. Isaac figured he was an amusement for Kathleen, a pastime with a bullish neck, an anonymous boy she kept around during office hours. But she wouldn't let him rent a flat. The college baby had to move in with her. He married Kathleen in a church on Marble Hill, Isaac the skeptical Jew, a Stalinist in 1948, a boy who believed in the forces of history and the erotic truths of his twenty-four-year-old wife.

"Where's your darling?" she said, remaining inside the door.

Would he have to tell her how Ida Stutz threw him over for an accountant with plastic sleeves? Only Kathleen couldn't have heard about Ida in the swamps. The Chief became shrewd with his wife. "I have a lot of darlings," he said. "Which one do you mean?"

"Manfred Coen."

"Blue Eyes? He's dead."

"Then why aren't you wearing a mourner's cloak?"

Isaac began to fumble. "I didn't kill him. It was a stinking family . . . the Guzmanns. They had a pistol, Chino Reyes. Manfred slapped him once. The pistol got even. He blew on Manfred with a stolen gun."

"Where were you when it happened, Prince Isaac? You're the holiest cop around. Couldn't you save Manfred Coen?"

"Kathleen, it was an accident. I was only two minutes away."

Kathleen stepped out of the door to scrutinize Isaac. "Turd," she said. "I know your rotten vocabulary. You're always *two minutes away* when you need a good excuse. Now what the hell are you doing here? I didn't call for a chaperone. Who asked you to scare off my friends?"

Isaac gulped the word *Florida*. "I thought you were in the Everglades." He told Kathleen about his desire to crawl into her tub. "I got messed up at work. This crazy Irish Jew tackled me in my office. He would have run home with my neck in his hands if I didn't fight back."

"Look at you," she said. "God bless the Irish Jew. I'd like to thank him for shoving coal dust in your face."

"It's not coal dust," Isaac said, turning glum. "They're flakes off Patrick Silver's shirt. That lunatic walked out of a fire to wrestle with me."

He could feel some fingers inside his jacket. Kathleen was stripping him. "Get undressed," she growled. "What are you waiting for? Don't you want your bath?"

They went down one flight to Kathleen's master tub, Isaac carrying his gun and soiled clothes. Kathleen stuffed the clothes into her hamper. Isaac climbed over the great wall of the tub. Kathleen had no use for a husband, but she could still admire the firm hold of Isaac's buttocks, the flesh that stood like pliable armor in the middle of his back. She'd stuck with the Jewish bear until her daughter left for college. Then she ran to Florida, and with a realty corporation of nine senior partners (the other eight were all men), she chopped into the Everglades and built a slew of retirement colonies over the swamps. The clerks at her headquarters in Miami were in awe of Kathleen. They had contempt for her partners, whom they considered inferior people. "The lady's got a pair of balls on her," they would murmur to themselves. According to their own calculations, Kathleen was worth a million and a half.

Isaac sat in a puddle of water. Kathleen threw bath oil at his knees. Her breasts looped under the robe. Isaac beckoned her into the tub. "Not a chance," she said. "Prick, I have to be at the airport in an hour. I'm not taking a bath with you."

The bear was getting hungry. His cock rose out of Kathleen's bubblebath. She threw more oil at him. Kathleen wasn't going to fornicate in a sunken bathtub with her own burly husband when she had five millionaires chasing her, Florida men without scars on their body from a murderous hammer, knife, or gun butt.

"Marilyn split with her new man," she said, hurling information at Isaac. His cock fell under the water. His eyes were grim.

"Who told you that?"

"She called me in Miami. I begged her to come down for a visit. I wired her the fare. But she never showed."

"Why didn't she call her father?"

"She's afraid of you. Four husbands in six years. That must be some kind of record. Anyway, it's your fault. She loved Coen. And you kept him from her."

"Coen," Isaac said, splashing with a paw. "I didn't take Blue Eyes out of her bed. But she has a craziness for marriages, that girl. Coen worked for me, remember? I didn't want a son-in-law sitting on my shoulder. Manfred was beautiful, but he had trouble spelling his name. He was an orphan. Orphans don't last. He would have died one way or another."

"But he didn't need a push from you, Prince Isaac."

The Chief couldn't argue with Kathleen. He had a claw in his belly: the worm was migrating again. It grabbed his bowels with a short, hooking rhythm. Isaac had to scream. "Oh, my God, Jesus motherfucker shit." The real estate goddess blinked at him.

"Isaac, did you swallow your thumb? What's wrong?"

He slapped around in the water, his knees over his head. He gobbled sounds to Kathleen, who thought her husband was having a fit. He grew pale. His pectorals began to wag. "Worm," he said. "Strangle me. Have to feed the worm."

She didn't laugh at his talk of worms. The bear was whimpering. Then he whistled through his teeth. "Yogurt. Gimme yogurt."

"Isaac, there's no food in the house. I'm only in New York one day a month."

Seeing Isaac grimace, she ran upstairs to her pantry. The shelves were vacant except for a box of tea and an old honey jar. She brought the jar down to Isaac and fed him globs of honey with a spoon. Isaac shivered. The spoon couldn't revive him quick enough. He snatched the jar and ate honey with his tongue. The paleness was gone. Isaac the Brave had sticky cheeks.

"Should I ring the doorman for a chicken bone? I could boil your shoelaces in a cup of tea?"

"It isn't funny," Isaac said. "I caught a tapeworm from the Guzmanns."

"Is it contagious, Isaac? Like the clap? You shouldn't have been so intimate with that family."

"Intimate? Those cocksuckers poisoned me."

Isaac hunkered down in the tub until his lips touched water. Even the most powerful cop in the City had to soak his balls. The Chief was coming apart. His people had fallen away from him. His father deserted the Sidels when Isaac was eighteen. His mother had been beaten up by a gang of teenage lunatics. She lay in a coma for seven months and died in her sleep while Isaac was in the Bronx with Papa Guzmann. His daughter was in Seattle. Marilyn the Wild ran around the country collecting husbands and discarding them. His angel Manfred was dead because of him. Isaac dropped Coen into his war with the Guzmanns and couldn't get him out in time to preserve the angel's neck. His benefactor, Ned O'Roarke, sat in the First Deputy's chair with a tumor in his throat, and presided over his own death for six years. And his wife Kathleen preferred her share of Florida to Isaac's company.

The tapeworm interested Kathleen. She liked the idea of a tiny animal tugging at Isaac's gut. His suffering began to excite her. He was less of a holy cop with his mouth twisting into a scream. She took off her robe and stepped into the tub with Isaac. The Chief made a powerful snort. It was the old days for Isaac: the college boy waiting to suckle his Irish beauty. He couldn't outgrow his early lusts. He would have been willing to die with his face in Kathleen's chest.

Both of them hopped in the water as they heard a row of disgustingly loud bleats. Kathleen tried to shake the noise out of her ears. "I'm deaf, by God," she squealed. Isaac had to climb around her legs and root for his clothes. He found the automatic pager under a towel on Kathleen's commode. He clicked off the screaming, idiotic thing and apologized to his wife. "Sorry. Can't be helped. That's how my men keep in touch with me." He dialed his office from the phone in Kathleen's dressing room. Pimloe took the call. "Isaac, the Guzmanns are off the street again."

"Are they living in a gutted synagogue?"

"No."

"Herbert, don't get elliptical with me. Where's Papa and his boys?"

"They moved into a bar."

"What bar?"

"The Kings of Munster. On Horatio Street."

"Herbert, how do you think they got there?"

"I dunno. Is Papa fond of Irish whiskey?"

"Schmuck, St. Patrick sneaked them in. That's his bar. He grew up on Horatio Street. He'll feed Papa Guinness for a while."

"Should we burn them out?"

"Herbert, shut your face. I'll attend to Papa."

"Isaac, don't worry. I have a boy on every roof that connects with the Munster bar. The baby can't walk an inch without our knowing it. Jerónimo's in trouble if we catch him near a roof."

"That's good, Herbert. Goodbye."

Pimloe had become Isaac's dedicated whip. Without Cowboy Rosenblatt, he lost his own ambitions and trapped mosquitoes, gnats, and Guzmanns for Isaac. The Chief went into the bathroom with a smile. He wanted Kathleen and his tub. But the real estate goddess was at her vanity table in a blouse and skirt. "Airport," she said. "I'm going now."

Isaac grabbed up his clothes and left Kathleen with Blue Eyes, Marilyn and Jerónimo bubbling in his fat commissioner's skull.

PART THREE

ELEVEN

Rabbi Hughie Prince, who read the Talmud with a glazier's strict eye, had declared that any body of land with a roof and four walls could qualify as a synagogue, so long as it housed the holy ark. And Patrick Silver had planted his father's closet in the storage room at the Kings of Munster. Sammy Doyle, the Kings' publican, was shrewd enough to allow the old Jews of Congregation Limerick to pray in his storage room. If Patrick Silver carried his shul into another neighborhood, the Kings of Munster would have to close. Patrick was half of Sammy's trade. The Irish of Abingdon Square showed up at Doyle's bar to drink with the Limerick giant.

Sammy had his problems. The Guzmanns caused him grief. He'd never heard of a shul with five permanent boarders. His customers would talk about the gypsies who lived with him. They blocked traffic into the Kings of Munster. The bar had to accommodate a steady flow of witch doctors (Papa brought them in to change Jorge's bandages and chant over the boy's shattered legs). A stink came out of the sanctuary that clung to the bar for days. Papa was roasting chickens in the storage room. The witch doctors had demanded this offering of chicken flesh to appease the ancient god Baal, protector of the cities, who could heal a crippled boy or wash him into the gutters, depending on his mood.

The publican had to tolerate the stink. He couldn't bother Patrick about it. Silver was in love with the little goya from Jane Street. Sammy had to comfort him when he stumbled into the bar asking for bottles of Guinness. The publican remembered him as a boy. Everybody thought he'd be bigger than the old Munster giant, Cruathair O'Carevaun, who destroyed the harbor at Cork in a fit of rage after he was ordered out of a sailor's brothel somewhere in 1709 (the girls were frightened of what lay under Cruathair's pants). But the Limerick giant stopped growing at twelve. Patrick would stay six-foot-three for the rest of his natural life.

Saying "God bless" with Guinness on his cheek, he moped

through the Kings of Munster, which was now a synagogue, a saloon, and a boardinghouse. He left the Kings in his own fit of rage. He was trying to shorten Odile's list of suitors. He would park himself on Jane Street with one of Sammy's brooms (he lost his shillelagh in the fire) and scare away the men who arrived with flowers and little gifts for Odile. Patrick stood chest to cheek with Pimloe (Herbert was a lot shorter than the Limerick giant) twice a day. Pimloe would dance under Patrick's nose and swear, "I'll crush you, St. Patrick. Do you know who I am? I'm Isaac's new whip. The First Dep can't blink without Herbert Pimloe."

"Then run home to Isaac. Because I'll spank you in the street, Herbert, so help me God."

Patrick was in a fix. He couldn't patrol Jane Street the entire afternoon. He had an appointment uptown. So he left the broom on Odile's steps to remind every caller that his presence was in the house. He plunged east, to the tall hotels and fashionable dormitories of lower Fifth Avenue. He walked up Fifth in his ruined soccer shirt, swabs of cloth trailing from his back like dirty fingers. People crept away from him, children pointing to the man in the shredded shirt who was too poor to wear shoes.

St. Patrick had more than the little goya in his head. His meeting with Isaac puzzled him. A First Dep didn't have to bang shoulders with a retired member of the rubber-gun squad. Did Isaac roll on the ground with him to spit words in Patrick's ear, words about Jerónimo? Passing Thirty-fourth Street, he paused to shout into the window of a men's boutique. "That lad's no faigel. God strike me dead if Jerónimo's the lipstick freak!"

Boys came out of the boutique to stare at the big dummy in rotten clothes. St. Patrick departed from them. He climbed to Fiftieth Street, frowning at the beautiful wallets in a leather store. He preferred simpler goods, wallets that could live with a scratch, shirts that could deteriorate on your body. He was going to visit Odile's uncle, the Broadway angel Vander Child, and discuss Odile's future with him. All his proper clothes, shirts and suits from his detective days, had been destroyed with the Bethune Street shul. He wouldn't borrow a jacket from Hughie. He was Patrick of the Synagogues, apostle of the rough.

Vander's doorman smirked at him. Patrick removed a bottle of Guinness from his pants and nudged the cap off with his teeth. He finished the bottle in one long gulp. "You can tell the squire that his nephew Patrick is coming up."

The doorman rang Vander and told him about the giant in the hall. "A mean one, sir. Claims he's a nephew of yours. He swallowed black piss and left his bottle on the floor." Vander met St. Patrick near the elevator car, shook his hand, and guided him into the apartment.

Patrick drew his shoulders in. He saw room after room of bone-white furniture, highboys that reached over his forehead, lowboys that were broader than three of him. He turned to uncle Vander and made his plea. But the black ale, the walk uptown, and distress over Jerónimo had impaired his speech. Sentences collected under his tongue and broke from him in great mealy blusters. ." . . marriage certificate . . . Zorro . . . false wedding . . . wife . . . "

Vander smiled. He'd heard about St. Patrick from his niece. The big dope was plaguing her. He stood outside Odile's building and chased off customers and friends with a broom. No one could get near Odile except Papa Guzmann's idiot boys and St. Patrick himself. His devotion was ruining Odile. She couldn't entertain in her apartment, or undress for a man. She'd become a pauper on account of him.

"Odile doesn't want you on Jane Street, Mr. Silver. You're interfering too much. She's fond of you, I think, but she isn't looking for a grandfather. So keep away."

Patrick got his tongue back. He seized Vander by his lapels, lifted him up so he could be eyeball to eyeball with him, and said, "I'm nobody's grandpa, Mr. Child. I'm a lad of forty-two. My father was a vicar, my mother delivered bread, and I'm going to marry your niece."

He returned to the Kings of Munster, stood the bar to a round of Guinness, blew his nose, and announced his engagement to the little goya. Her many husbands, Papa, Jorge, Alejandro, Topal, and Jerónimo, welcomed Patrick's news. "Irish, I can't speak for Zorro," Papa said. "But you can have my share of her. The goya is yours."

To celebrate, Sammy shoved frozen hamburgers into his automatic oven. "Everybody eats, by God." Papa stared at this sweating box with absolute scorn. He switched the oven off and threw all the hamburgers away. Then he whispered a shopping list into Topal's ear. Topal brought some crayons out of the back room, colored his cheeks to disguise himself, and went to the sausage factory on Hudson Street with his father's list.

While the Irishmen at the bar had another round of Guinness, Papa made a casserole of sausages and beans. The aroma of spiced pork baking in a dish nearly crippled the Irishmen, who had chewed nothing but flimsy sandwiches and potato chips at the Kings of Munster.

As keeper of the house Sammy had the right to walk ahead of his customers and dig into the casserole with a large spoon. His sampling of the sausages and beans convinced him that the Kings of Munster shouldn't let its boarders go. The Irishmen found napkins and plates in the narrow pantry behind the bar and helped themselves to Papa's casserole. They sat near the Limerick giant sucking up sausages and beans.

Patrick wouldn't touch the casserole. He sat on a stool watching Jerónimo play with the Guzmann crayon box. Jerónimo was in the sanctuary. Crouched under the doors of the Babylon closet, he softened crayons with the heat of his thumb. Then he took the crayons over to Jorge's bed. The baby began to paint his brother's lips. Jorge smiled with wax on his mouth. The baby was much more deliberate. His face grew taut as he applied the wax. He had a keen artistry, Papa's oldest boy. He moved from Jorge's lips to his earlobes and his eyes. There was nothing circumstantial about his work. He could account for the irregularities of a cheekbone or an eyebrow. He drew perfect halos.

Patrick turned away from spying on the two brothers. He had an ugly revelation: Jerónimo was the lipstick freak. He painted little boys and murdered them. Patrick had always been a lousy detective. Isaac was the wizard, not Patrick Silver of the rubber-gun squad. The Chief could examine any crime scene and weave a history from a book of matches, blood on a corpse's shoe, movie stubs, phlegm in a handkerchief. But Patrick saw the halos around Jorge's eyes. He could piece together a history from the flight of a crayon in Jerónimo's steady fist. The baby's lines were strong. His elbow never dipped. He judged you with his crayons. He marked you up and took your life away. Jerónimo was the freak.

Did it start with a game? Jerónimo required a docile creature to exercise his art. One of his brothers, or a dollfaced boy. Up to the roofs, hand in hand. The boy must have liked the wax at first. Then he wouldn't sit still. Is that what angered Jerónimo? Made him carve the crayoned boy?

Patrick searched for the weapon Jerónimo used. He found only blunt instruments among the family treasure: ice-cream scoops, plastic whistles, shoelaces made of bone. Where was Jerónimo's knife? Patrick had to crawl into the sanctuary while the Guzmanns were occupied, and Jorge was asleep. He probed every possible hiding place. He wedged his knuckles into the cracks behind the ark and had a miserable time getting them free. He came up with wads of dust and a dead mouse.

Patrick stopped marching to Odile's. He stayed inside the Kings of Munster. He supped black ale with his eyes on Jerónimo and attended to the business of the shul. Rabbi Hughie had placed a collection box on the bar to help the shul entice a cantor for the high holidays. With St. Patrick around, the Irishmen had to reach into their trousers and stuff Hughie's box with dollar bills. Hughie despaired, even with a fat collection box: what cantor would sing the Kol Nidre at the back of a saloon? The shul would have to hire a renegade, a hazan who had been barred from the synagogues of New York.

Patrick couldn't hold the subject of cantors in his head. He was waiting for Jerónimo to jump into the street. The baby wouldn't move. He had his crayon box, his brothers, white chocolate, halvah, and his father's casseroles. Stuck in an Irish bar with nothing to do, Papa took up Sammy's invitation to become the Kings' principal cook. The bar fell heir to a glut of food. Papa didn't limit himself to sausages in a black-bean grave. He had his witch doctors bring Marrano powders and spices to Horatio Street. He prepared dishes that no Irishman had ever dreamed of. Hacked chicken and squid in mounds of yellow rice, garnished with pimentos, olives, and sea cucumber; scallops sliced so thin, they shriveled against your tongue; sauces that could make you sneeze; strips of abalone that curled in your mouth like baby fish; and ten varieties of pork.

Papa's dishes began to pull in Irishmen from other bars. You couldn't find an empty stool at the Kings of Munster from four P.M. to midnight, which were Papa's serving hours. Patrick had to forage through the bar with both elbows out to get his bearings, or the baby would have been lost in the haze of Irishmen. When the crowds became intolerable, he would seek out the crayon box, knowing that Jerónimo couldn't disappear without his crayons. While the Irishmen gobbled abalone and squid, he would catch the baby staring at him, Jerónimo with a crayon in his mouth, his eyes growing enormous, his ears swelling in the heat, and Patrick having to squint or look down at his stockings.

One afternoon Patrick was waylaid by a dozen Irishmen who obliged him to Indian-wrestle with them all. Patrick took these Irishmen four at a time. With the last of them leaning against his elbow, he happened to twist his face towards the sanctuary. He blinked at the Guzmann territories in the back room, beds, bundles, and floor space. The crayon box wasn't there. "Mercy," Patrick said, flinging Irishmen off his arm. The baby had sneaked out under Patrick's long Irish nose. "Whhere's thaaat childdd?" Sammy's customers flew to the ends of the bar when they heard St. Patrick roar.

Patrick shoved Guinness bottles into his rotting pants, snapped his thighs, and landed on the street. Where would a baby prowl? The old horse barns and factories of Greenwich Street couldn't do Jerónimo any good. The baby would go down to Perry or Charles, Patrick reasoned. Abingdon Square was too crammed with people and cars to pluck a boy off the sidewalk. Patrick went to the top of Charles Street. There wasn't a boy around. Perry Street was filled with touring parties of gay lads who scoffed at a ragged, shoeless, white-haired giant.

Patrick hiked to Bethune Street. Half a block from the scorched shul, he saw Jerónimo walking with a little runt of a boy. The giant followed them on shaky knees. He could find nothing untoward about their walk (Jerónimo didn't paw the runt, grab at the little boy's clothes). He prayed to hairy Esau, unfortunate son of Isaac and Rebekah, to uncloud an Irishman's brain. The runt bothered him. He wore a cap in the summer, a pile coat, and one of his ankles was fatter than the other. Patrick had lived around "fat ankles" for fifteen years; they were a common sight at Police Headquarters. Either the runt suffered from elephantiasis, or he had a holster near his shoe.

Patrick cursed his own gullibility. The runt was a decoy, sent by Isaac to trap Jerónimo and tease him onto the roofs. Patrick had been hasty to judge Jerónimo. Why couldn't Papa's boy walk on Bethune Street? Was it wrong to visit a dead shul? The runt had been put there to seduce Jerónimo. They'd go up to a roof that Isaac had selected in advance. The runt would suck Jerónimo's cheek, according to a special plan. Then the cops would pounce on the baby, handcuff him, and yell freak, freak!

But it couldn't happen if St. Patrick fucked over Isaac the Brave. He tried to warn Jerónimo. Cupping his hands, he shouted into the street. "Jerónimo-o-o-o!" Jerónimo wasn't headed for the roofs. The runt went into the shul with him. "Jesus," Patrick said.

He ran for the shul, the Guinness bottles clinking in his pants. Woozy with beer, the giant had to hold his knees to prevent himself from crashing into the ground. City marshals had thrown up boards around the entrance of the shul. Jerónimo and the runt must have crept under these boards. Patrick couldn't get in. He ripped his fingers clutching wood. He stepped on long carpenter's nails, the rust eating into his heel. He invoked the Munster giant, Cruathair O'Carevaun, to give him strength over the boards. Finally he made a hole big enough to crawl through.

The shul was black as a potato bin. Patrick couldn't see his nose. He kept to a single spot until his eyes grew accustomed to the dark. There were no stairs to climb. The shul stood like a shaved box. The walls still smelled of fire. St. Patrick trudged through pieces of rubble. "Jerónim-o-o-o!" The rubble began to slide. Somebody said "fuck" and "shit." It sounded like a girl. Patrick trudged some more. Flicks of coaly brown light came through the leading in the wall where the stained glass used to be. Jerónimo and the runt were rolling next to Patrick's feet. The runt was a tiny policewoman with cropped hair.

"Miserable spy," Patrick said. He picked her off Jerónimo. She struggled in Patrick's arms, screaming at him with shul dust on her jaw while Jerónimo escaped. She must have lost her handgun in the fracas, because her ankle holster was free.

"You big son-of-a-bitch," she said. "Obstructing a police officer. You'll sit in Riker's Island for that."

Patrick dropped her into the rubble. "A lovely bit of entrapment. Kissing a mad boy in my shul. Pray I don't report you to Isaac."

The lady cop sneered at him. "He tried to kill me, you Irish ape."

"With what? His crayons? Or the pebble in his pants?"

"With this," she said, thrusting a shiny thing into Patrick's hand. It was warm against his skin. Patrick squinted in the potato-bin light and recognized the handle of an ice-cream scoop. The giant pricked himself. The toy was sharp at both ends. Jerónimo must have rubbed it against the pipes in Papa's candy store. Patrick felt a crayon between his toes. He retrieved the crayon box and hobbled out of the shul.

TWELVE

A squad of blue-eyed detectives burst into the Kings of Munster with shotguns and a warrant for Jerónimo's arrest (the runt must have told every commissioner at Headquarters how she wrestled with the lipstick freak in St. Patrick's synagogue). The detectives shoved Irishmen aside, stuck their fingers in Papa's casserole, searched behind the bar, leered at Jorge Guzmann, peeked into the Babylon closet, bowed to St. Patrick, and left.

Papa wouldn't serve food that had been touched by Isaac's "angels." He dumped all his abalone and squid into Sammy's garbage pail and started to prepare another casserole. He stirred saffron into a pot of rice and seethed at Patrick Silver.

"You're my man, aint you, Irish? Why did you let them piss on us?"

"Moses, it wasn't the shotguns that bothered me. I know plenty of incantations that would cure a buckshot wound. But you can't fight a judge's signature."

"True, but you can swallow the paper it's written on."

"Moses, what's the good? They'd only come again. Where's Jerónimo?"

"God knows. He's running from you and the cops. Did you have to scare him, Irish? He trusted you."

"Faith, I pulled a runty female off his back. What more could I do?"

"You could have taken his hand and brought him to his father. Zorro had you figured right. He said you and Isaac could snarl for ten years and you'd still end up with your thumb in his ass. Isaac owns your guts. Irish, you're a cop without a badge."

"Zorro's full of crap," St. Patrick said. He dropped Jerónimo's "knife" on the bar. "Moses, there's a toy could scratch anybody's face. Not the sort of plaything you'd expect from a forty-four-year-old lad."

Papa eyed the sharpened stump of metal on Sammy's counter. "Irish, is that your only evidence? Your uncle at Headquarters steals a fucking ice-cream scoop from Boston Road, breaks it in half, and plants a piece of it on Jerónimo, so a prick like you can buy his story. Didn't you catch a lady cop with Jerónimo? Isaac trains a little whore to dress like a boy. Jerónimo can read her disguise. She wiggles her ass at him, and they go into the shul that Isaac burned down. Does that make Jerónimo the lipstick freak?"

"I'm not a Yankee lawyer. I can't argue the delicacies of right and wrong. But if Isaac's wonderboys grab the baby's cuffs, he'll be limping for a long time. Isaac knows how to smile at a judge. They'll build a hole for the baby, and you'll never find him."

Papa touched his lip.

"Moses, I can help you if I get to the baby first. Is he in Manhattan, or the Bronx? Tell me."

Papa shrugged and went to his casserole.

Patrick drifted into the street. The Guinness had begun to boil in his pants. He opened a bottle with his thumb and drank the hot black ale. He got to Abingdon Square with the sun in his eyes. A patrolman in a summer blouse mistook him for a hobo, and dug a billy club into his left wing. "Go on, you scag. Move your shit to the Bowery. Respectable people live around here."

Patrick didn't complain; he allowed the energy in a cop's stick to push him uptown. He'd have to scrape two boroughs for Jerónimo's hideaway. The giant was lost. Should he cover the playground on Little West Twelfth Street? Drudge towards Ninth Avenue? Infiltrate the brownstones of Chelsea? His crooked hops carried him to Twenty-third Street. He had no more bottles in his pants. He'd have to duck into an Irish bar and reload himself with Guinness. Should he get off the streets and follow the baby from roof to roof? While he maundered in the gutters, a dusty cab nearly chopped off his knees. The rear door opened. A familiar grunt beckoned to him from the dark interiors of the cab. "Irish, move your ass."

Patrick ruffled the shaggy ends of his sleeves and plunged into the cushions. The cab shot away from the cluttered sidewalks of Twenty-third Street. The giant was sitting with Zorro Guzmann, the Fox of Boston Road.

"Congratulations, Irish."

"Zorro, the Guzmanns don't congratulate without a touch of malice. Where did I offend you now?

"Irish I promise you, it's heartfelt. Papa says you're in love with Odile."

"Papa says a lot of things."

"Take the goya, Irish. Don't cry. Zorro is giving her to you."

"Maybe the goya's not yours to give."

"Why throw insults?" Zorro said, lounging on the cushions. "I own forty per cent of her, at least. But who's stingy? Irish, you took care of my brother. That's worth forty percent of any goya."

"Your father thinks I sold the baby to Isaac."

"Don't misjudge him, Irish. He'd murder half the Bronx for Jerónimo." Zorro took the baby's metal toy out of his pocket. "You shouldn't have showed this to Papa. You hurt his feelings."

"Pity," St. Patrick said. "Papa swears it's Isaac's tool, a sinker to drown the baby."

"No," Zorro said. "It belongs to Jerónimo. It stays in his shirt most of the time."

The giant leaned closer to Papa's youngest boy. "Then your father ought to admit who it was that's been tearing up infants on the roofs."

"Irish, you work for us. Remember that. Your job is to protect Jerónimo, not to handcuff him."

"Jesus," Patrick muttered. "What am I supposed to do about the dead little boys? Did you want me to find new bait for Jerónimo? Should I escort him up to the roofs, Señor Zorro?"

"Irish, we aren't like the norteamericanos. You have Zorro's word. My brother won't go near the roofs again."

"I'm grateful for that," St. Patrick said, watching the swollen, heavy streets from his window. Like his forebear, O'Carevaun the giant, he was in the mood to destroy certain property. If Cruathair could dismantle the harbor at Cork, Patrick would chew up Manhattan, block by block, digesting people, lampposts, dogs, and bricks. He had an ungodly rawness in his throat. Patrick's thirst was killing him. "I'm parched," he said, rising out of the cushions. "I'll vomit blood in half a minute. Stop the car."

Zorro had to restrain the giant. "Irish, don't move. We're getting out."

The cab dropped them on Columbus Avenue, in the West Eighties. Zorro tapped the window, and the cab flew downtown. Patrick couldn't remember seeing the driver's face. Could the Fox run a whole fleet of cabs with the twitch of his hand? They went into a Cuban bar on Eighty-ninth Street. Zorro must have known the men in the bar. He rubbed up against these cubanos, saying "hombre, hombre." The cubanos smiled at him with their gold teeth. But they were suspicious of a giant with a holster in his pants. Patrick could feel this angry mugger of eyes surrounding him. He plopped onto a stool, figuring he would have to drink pale beer with the cubanos.

"Cerveza de perro," Zorro croaked to the barman.

Patrick's forehead crumpled at the sight of Guinness on the counter. "Mercy," he said. The barman had produced two lovely bottles of black ale. St. Patrick took the miracle without a complaint. "God bless." The bottles were chilled. He warmed them over with his fist (the "fevered" bottles would restore the bitterness that Patrick loved). Then he drank with the Fox.

"Zorro, who turned these lads onto Guinness?"

The Fox had brown foam on his lip. "Irish, you're a pathetic man. Living in a synagogue makes you stupid. How can you see the world with a shawl over your head? There was Guinness in Cuba before an hombre like you could get himself born. The habaneros call it dog's beer. Fathers give it to their young boys. It puts fur on your chest. Irish, let's go. I have to find my brother."

Patrick plagued him with questions once they arrived on the street.

"Is Jerónimo in the neighborhood? Are the cubanos hiding him?"

"Irish, shut up. Coen had an uncle named Sheb. He used to play with Jerónimo. They pissed in the toilet together, they sucked hardboiled eggs, they took sunbaths outside my father's candy store. Sheb's in an old-age home near Riverside park. That's where we have to look. When my brother gets tired of walking, he'll run to Sheb."

"Coen doesn't die so easy," Patrick said. "Blue Eyes is the tit that everybody uses. Me, you, Isaac, Odile, Papa, Jerónimo, and this crazy uncle, all of us fed off Coen's milk and blood. Now he won't disappear. You can't pick your feet without finding pieces of Manfred between your toes."

"Hombre, we have work to do. So don't shit in my ear. Isaac isn't an ignorant. He knows my brother's moves. I'll bet he has five cops sitting with Sheb Coen. I can't warn Jerónimo. Isaac's scumbags would kick me into the ground. But you can grab my brother before he gets to the old-age home. Isaac's afraid of your yarmulke and your black socks. He won't mess with a synagogue boy."

A lamppost away from the Cuban bar, and Patrick was hungry for dog's beer again. Mentions of Isaac went straight to his throat. He couldn't even go an Irish mile without lapping on a bottle. Zorro tried to skirt across Broadway. He was worried about the undercover cops who mingled in the crowd of pimps, whores, beggars, cripples, transvestites, widowers, retards, skagheads, snow cone vendors, runaways, pickpockets, and street musicians, and who might recognize the Fox. But the giant squeezed Zorro's shirt and pulled him into an Irish bar, the Claremorris, on Broadway Patrick was remembered at the Claremorris; he haunted this bar when he was a lad with the First Dep. He could come uptown and drink his Guinness warm, with or without an egg.

"Irish, are you crazy? This is a detectives' bar. You can't walk two inches without breathing on a cop."

"Not to worry," Patrick said. "You're safe with me."

"What about Jerónimo?"

"We'll get to the baby. In a minute. I need some fur on my chest."

Patrick saw a few of his old brothers from the Shillelagh Society. First-grade detectives, they snubbed a cop who had fallen into the life of a janitor and went around in stinky clothes. They assumed Zorro was a rat that Silver had dragged out of his burning shul. Who else would have yellow wax on his cheeks? Patrick didn't give a fig about the frozen attitude of his brothers. He was staring at the holy rump of a girl who danced with four sailors at the back of the Claremorris. Her thighs worked like long, winnowy roots as she plunged from sailor to sailor. Jesus, she had a familiar shape under her narrow skirt. She didn't have to turn her head and wink. That rump belonged to Marilyn the Wild.

What was Isaac's skinny daughter doing in the Claremorris? He couldn't be wrong. He'd spied her often enough as she strolled the corridors at Headquarters on the arm of her husband, who would change from year to year. Patrick disapproved of these husbands. They always had slick leather boots and a tweezed mustache. Every clerk in Isaac's office knew that the girl was in love with Manfred Coen. She would deposit the mustache with her father and hang around Coen's desk. Her father's cops would feast on Marilyn. A blind man couldn't have missed her bosoms, and the draw of her Irish bum. Everybody looked until Isaac came out to glare at Blue Eyes and recall Marilyn the Wild. St. Patrick of the Synagogues, the deacon-detective of Bethune Street, had the stiffest prick in New York City on the days that Marilyn showed.

Patrick would have left her to grind with her sailors, only something was amiss. Marilyn seemed to tire of their company. She had a suitcase under a chair, and the sailors wouldn't allow her to reach for it. The four of them had her in a jumble of arms, legs, and middy blouses. She couldn't break out of the sailors' net. Hands crept up her skirt. The gentlemen at the bar seemed to glorify this multiple courtship of Lady Marilyn. There was much clapping and whistling inside the Claremorris. Such encouragement livened the sailors. Marilyn bounced between their shoulders, her head twisted back, her eyes fixed on the ceiling as four sailors nuzzled her at the same time.

St. Patrick began to pull gentlemen out of his way. "Watch it, lads, coming through."

Zorro hammered on his neck. "Hombre, don't meddle. They love sailors in here. What's that skinny broad to you?"

"She's a friend of mine" Patrick said.

"That's something else. You take their arms, Irish, and I'll go for their balls. But make it fast . . . what's her name?"

"Marilyn the Wild."

The Fox revealed his teeth. "Hombre, Isaac is out there trying to finish my brother, and you expect me to save his girl? I ought to waltz with those sailors, give them my congratulations."

"Fine," Patrick said. "Then I'll have to bust your face too. Zorro, don't blame Marilyn for her daddy's shit."

Patrick held two sailors by the nap of their long, square collars and flung them off Lady Marilyn. Zorro grounded a third sailor, biting him just below the knee. The fourth sailor looked up at mad Patrick and rushed out of the bar. The patrons of the Claremorris were furious at Silver and his little toad. They considered it immoral to bite a sailor's knee. The detectives of the Shillelagh Society had tiny blackjacks in their pockets that could cuff the ears of janitors and their friends.

Zorro went into a crouch. He appealed to three of his saints, Moses, Jude, and Simon of the Desert. "Hombre," he whispered. "don't fight with your elbows. We'll never win. Stick your fingers in their eyes."

The Shillelaghs advanced towards Patrick. They liked the idea of a Donnybrook in the late afternoon. They were crooning now. They began to leer at Marilyn.

"St. Patrick, do we have permission to dance with your sweetheart?"

"Are you engaged to the bimbo, Pat?"

"Be a good boy. Show us how to bless her quim?"

"Hold your tongues," Patrick said. "That's the First Dep's baby.

She's Isaac's child."

A stink ran through the Claremorris. The Shillelaghs were smelling their own doom. They'd insulted Father Isaac, said filthy things to Marilyn the Wild. They pitied the loss of their livelihoods. "Lady Marilyn," they said, dusting off her suitcase. "Lady Marilyn."

Patrick took the suitcase from his brothers and walked Lady Marilyn out of the Claremorris. She hadn't forgotten the sullen Irish giant who shared a desk with Manfred Coen. Her father's cops had dubbed him St. Patrick of the Synagogues because they'd never heard of an Irishman who was so devoted to a shut. Blue Eyes had been fond of the giant. The two of them would sit at their desk eating from a single cup of cottage cheese. Marilyn smiled at St. Patrick. Her ribs were sore from the crush of sailors. She'd stopped at the Claremorris to have a whiskey sour. She felt sorry for one of the sailors and agreed to dance with him (she'd just come home from a sailor's town, Seattle, where lonely boys drifted through the streets dressed in a white that was so absolute, it wouldn't grow dirty in the rain). Marilyn didn't expect dry humps on Broadway; she had to dance with eight knees in her crotch.

"Patrick," she said, "you won't tell my father I'm in Manhattan, will you?"

"Me and your dad aren't much for speaking to one another. Do you need a rooming house? You're welcome to stay with us, if you don't mind sleeping near a whiskey barrel."

"Thanks," she said. "I'll find a place. And I'll visit Isaac when I'm ready for him."

She clutched the suitcase, got on her toes to kiss St. Patrick, then stood level to kiss the Fox, and walked into the thick of Broadway, while the snow cone vendors and other hombres commented on this chica with the fine tits, ass, and legs. The giant would have battled every hombre in the neighborhood to protect Lady Marilyn (he admired her rump in a more quiet way), but Zorro tugged on his holster.

"Irish, this aint the time. Jerónimo's on the loose."

They had to squeeze between Broadway mamas to get down to Riverside Drive. A green gas boiled up from the sewers. Patrick craved the calm, beery mist inside the Kings of Munster.

Zorro stationed him a block from the Manhattan View Rest Home, where Manfred's uncle lived. Then he disappeared, flicking his tail behind the humped backs of cars parked along Riverside

Drive. The giant grew restless waiting for Jerónimo. Images of boys with wounds in their necks entered his skull. The baby had hoodwinked Patrick with those afternoon naps in the old shul. Jerónimo sneaked out of the cellar while Patrick yawned over bottles of ale. With his guardian tucked away at the Kings, Jerónimo could prowl. Patrick rubbed his fists. Mercy, the Guzmanns had used him to shadow the baby's tracks. All the lucre he'd gotten from them, money that kept a shul alive, was smeared with children's guts.

His eyes stayed open. Patrick had sworn himself to Papa Guzmann. He wouldn't betray the clan. He was a lively lookout, standing in his socks; the edges of his shirt twitched in the hot breeze coming off the park. The giant was turning to lead. He didn't want to flag Jerónimo.

How many hours passed? Five? Two? One? It might have snowed in August. Patrick wouldn't move. His white hair had begun to crispen. The rest of him was gray. A stopped boy turned the corner, onto Riverside Drive. His hair was Patrick's color: white with a shiver of blue. He hugged the walls of apartment buildings, which burnt to a furious orange in the evening sky. The boy galloped through this orange haze. Nothing could interfere with the stab of his knees.

Patrick called to Jerónimo. His forehead thumped with grim reminders of the baby's art: crayons, lips, raw handles, and eyes. God help us all, he couldn't condemn the baby. An Irishman had enough flint in him to set a planet on fire, but he couldn't squeeze affection out of his heart. He put away the monster stories. He was Jerónimo's keeper again. He would steer him off the roofs, hide his crayons and his piece of metal. "Jerónimo."

The baby looked up from the orange bricks. His mouth wriggled open. The skin tightened around his eyes. His stoop deepened. He crept backwards, rocking on his heels, then plunged into Riverside Drive.

"Jerónimo, don't run away from me."

The baby dashed into the gutters. He never got across the street. A car stopped for him. It was Zorro's dusty cab. Patrick could see the Fox through a wormy window. He heard the squeak of a door. The baby's legs were in the air. His belly slid along the cushions; most of him was inside the car.

The giant could have recaptured Jerónimo. He only had to borrow the powers of Cruathair O'Carevaun, hold on to Zorro's bumpers, and hurl the cab into Riverside Park. Patrick watched the Fox drive off with Jerónimo. "Brother to brother," he said. "God bless."

He went up to Broadway. He could still have his dog's beer in an Irish bar. He was the savior of Marilyn the Wild. The Shillelagh Society could announce his many sins: Patrick Silver, the Guzmann slave who lost his gun and fell in love with a Jane Street tart. No matter. He could walk into the Claremorris with his holster sitting like a lame prick on his thigh. None of his old brothers would ever throw him out.

THIRTEEN

The Fox hugged Jerónimo during the ride. It was a greedy embrace. He wanted to feel the knit of his brother's bones, the earmuffs in his pocket, the mothballs every Guzmann crinkled into the cuffs of his shirts (these mothballs could fight the devil's stinky perfume). Zorro wasn't afraid of losing him. Jerónimo wouldn't jump out of the car. The baby looked into Zorro's eyes. He didn't whimper. He didn't flail with his arms. He sat cuddled in Zorro's chest.

The Fox was talking to himself. His eyes were black. He cursed Isaac and Isaac's control over the streets of Manhattan and the Bronx. He knew his father's plans. Moses was leaving America. Zorro could have dodged Isaac's blond angels for the rest of his life, sleeping in telephone booths, eating falafel sandwiches in doorways, pissing into a bottle, waxing his jaws a different color every day of the week, but he couldn't desert his family. Zorro was an American baby. He could thrive in Peru, Mexico, or Isaac's Manhattan. He'd pick your pockets, sell you a girl, take your nickels for a lottery that didn't exist. The Fox enjoyed his nakedness. He could cover himself with wax, mud, newspapers, green stamps. But his father had gathered heavy plumage in the Bronx. And Isaac had plucked him dry. Lost without his farm and his candy store, Moses was sick of the New World.

Zorro could taste his brother's heartbeat. It was strong as Papa's Boston Road curry, spiced with powders that arrived from Uruguay. That was the aroma of the crypto-Jews, hot and sour, the crazy Marranos whose dread and love had the same powerful smell. The Fox's shirt was wet. Was Jerónimo teething against Zorro's stomach? The baby peeked out at the fire escapes on Ninth Avenue. He brooded over ideograms in the windows of fish and poultry stores, smiling when he recognized the snout of a swordfish, chicken feathers, the webbed feet of a duck.

Zorro's taxi probed the truckers' slips behind the markets of Gansevoort Street. The chauffeur, Miguel, was a native of Boston Road. Zorro hired him because the limousine companies of Manhattan were filled with Isaac's spies. Miguel drove for landlords, pimps, and petty thieves like Zorro and Papa Guzmann. He was paid to keep his eyes on the road. A chauffeur who got curious about his job might return to the Bronx without any ears. But this skinny borough confused Miguel. He couldn't understand how West Fourth Street could bend far enough to collide with West Thirteenth. Zorro knocked on the glass. Miguel drove into the yard of an old warehouse on Washington Street. He saw a man in the yard: Moses Guzmann.

Miguel tried not to stare. The Guzmanns were touchy people. If your nose wasn't pointed at the ground, Papa thought you were giving him the evil eye. But they had no more instructions for him. The Fox and the baby got out of the car. Miguel hunched into the steering wheel to narrow his line of sight and avoid the Guzmann's terrible eyebrows, necks, and chins.

Papa wore his cooking smock from the Kings of Munster. He'd escaped from the bar between casseroles and trudged around the corner to Washington Street. Customers would be calling for his squid in half an hour. Papa had little time. He'd left Jorge with Topal and Alejandro. If Isaac's blue-eyed gorillas raided the bar again, Moses would have three missing boys. He manufactured his own weather under the smock. His ribs were cold. He had trembles in his back when he touched the baby.

Zorro whispered in Papa's ear. "We can hide him on the boat."

"Never," Papa said.

"I could go away with him. To Florida. We could live with the cubanos."

"Half the cubanos work for the FBI. They'd sit him in Isaac's lap in two weeks."

"Then let me strangle Isaac, Papa, and we'll have a little rest."

"Another Isaac would come."

Papa watched his youngest boy go slack in the shoulders. The Fox's cheeks were pale under the yellow wax. But his jaws remained grim. Papa had no grand ideas about his family. Four of his boys were idiotas, He'd slept with syphilitic women in the market-places of Peru, fornicated like a mongrel dog. None of his wives had a tooth in her head. Zorro was an accident, the only Guzmann whose brains weren't soft. Papa thanked the Lord Adonai every hour of his life for giving him a child who didn't have to count with his thumbs. At an early age Zorro solved the intricate geography of Papa's candy store, and became the Fox of Boston Road. He extended Papa's empire into Manhattan with his natural guile. But he didn't forget his brothers. He adored Topal, Alejandro, Jorge, and Jerónimo, and he looked after them. He showed the boys how to zip their flies. He made an abacus of their fingers, getting them to add and subtract with a furious concentration. He would stall traffic on Boston Road to herd his brothers across the street. Breathing saffron in an Irish bar had clogged Papa's vents: couldn't Moses understand how maddening it was for Zorro to give up one of his brothers? His instinct was to clutch Jerónimo and shit on the world, hold out against Isaac and his Manhattan army.

"César, don't be an ignorant. He won't last a day in the Tombs. The convicts are more vicious than the police. You know the names they'll call him. *Rooster. Queen Jerónimo.* I don't want their ugly hands on his throat."

Papa removed a brick from his cooking shirt; it was the only weapon he'd carried out of the Bronx. He had himself to blame. He'd seen the mud on Jerónimo's boots. Did it rain in Papa's candy store? The baby fell asleep with wet hair. Papa closed his eyes to the fact that Jerónimo loved to prowl. The baby crawled out the little back window while his brothers were snoring and Papa was fixing ice-cream sodas or deciphering the hieroglyphics of his numbers bank.

Papa's fingers clawed into the brick. He wouldn't let Isaac shove Jerónimo into the Tombs. The baby would never see a jury. The prisioneros at the detention house had their own punishment for molesters and murderers of children. They would choke him to death for playing with the testicles of young boys.

Jerónimo didn't scowl at the brick. He turned his face to Papa. He rubbed Zorro's shoulder with his Guzmann neck. He was thinking of all his brothers. The baby didn't have the word goodbye in his vocabulary. His nostrils sniffed for air. His tongue lay curled on his lip.

The chauffeur, Miguel, prayed to Santa Maria for the courage to hold his chest on the steering wheel and blind himself to the

Guzmanns. Miguel was weak. His head peeled over the bottom of the window in time to watch Papa's brick. He would swear on el día de los Inocentes that Papa skulled Jerónimo with a kiss. Either Miguel was crazy, or Papa's elbow didn't move more than an inch. Moses touched Jerónimo between the eyes. The baby crashed into Zorro's arms with a puckered forehead. Miguel slid down into his seat. He would have stayed there for a month unless the Guzmanns commanded him to rise. The door opened. Miguel heard the scuffle of several bodies. Señora, they had turned his taxi into a hearse!

Someone tapped him on the ear. Miguel wouldn't forget a signal from the Fox. He drove out of the yard. There were two Guzmanns in his mirror. Zorro and the dead baby. Papa wasn't in the car. Jerónimo's brains were mostly blue. He had a swollen head. He sat in Zorro's shoulder, like a live boy. Miguel screamed under his tongue. He was afraid to utter a sound. The Guzmanns could murder you before you had the opportunity to blink.

"Miguel," Zorro said. He wasn't unkind to his chauffeur. He didn't growl. His voice was gentle and low. "Take us uptown."

The chauffeur felt a pinch in his spine. Was the Fox going to caress a dead baby from Fourteenth Street into the Bronx? Miguel was aware that the Guzmanns could provoke a miracle. Any Marrano could make himself into a male witch. Would the Fox breathe into Jerónimo's nose and set the baby to yawn and smile before they got across the Harlem? Would they hold conversations in Miguel's back seat? He squinted into the mirror for obvious signs. He waited for the swelling to go down. If the Fox caressed the baby long enough, the pinkness would return. Jerónimo wouldn't be stuck with blue brains. The Fox was beginning to murmur. Were these the incantations of a Marrano witch, or love songs to a brother? Miguel didn't care. He wanted a resurrection in his car. Who would believe him when he told his compadres that he'd watched a middle-aged boy die and get reborn in under half an hour.

Papa had to cook, or the bar would have grown suspicious. Was there a rat among the Irishmen? Papa couldn't be sure. The brick was under his shirt, hidden from Sammy's customers. The gallants at the Kings of Munster couldn't have noticed Papa's distress. He shredded chunks of abalone with perfect control. His other boys were sleeping in the sanctuary. They would moo for Jerónimo after their heads came off the pillows. What excuse could Papa make? Jorge would

bawl with a finger in his eye. Topal and Alejandro would hug behind
Silver's holy closet. The bar wouldn't understand their wails.

Moses was sick of breathing Dublin ale. He meant to pack after
he prepared his last bowl of squid. The Guzmanns were going to
Europe. Now that Spain had a king, young Juan Carlos, the Marranos
could return to their original home. Moses would keep out of Madrid.
The madrileños were a light-skinned race. Papa would try the north.
He would settle in Bardjaluna, a city the Arabs helped build. He
would live in the old Chinese district, near the oily port, in virtual
retirement. He would set up a stall of birdcages on the Ramblas and
pick the pockets of Swedish and German tourists. He would take his
boys to see Charlie Chaplin films. Zorro wouldn't be content. He
would go above the Ramblas, into the boulevards, and drink coffee
with pretty girls. He would wear soft scarves and shun Papa's birds.
But he wouldn't neglect Jorge and the other two. The Fox adored his
brothers.

Silver came into the bar. He looked forlorn. He wouldn't chat
with Sammy's customers. He had Guinness in a corner, without a
taste of Papa's squid. The giant didn't bother peeking for Jerónimo.
He was the only Irishman at the Kings of Munster who understood
where the baby was.

The giant wasn't Papa's chattel any more. But he couldn't get
free of the Guzmanns. He was tied to that miserable family. He
realized the choices Papa had. Once the baby was arrested, even the
Marrano saints couldn't have kept him alive. Papa had to hide him, or
put him to sleep.

Moses and the Irish were watching one another. They could
grieve without opening their mouths. They didn't embrace. Nothing
passed between them except the sad energy in the coloring of their
eyes. Patrick sucked on a bottle without leaving his corner. Papa
attended to the squid.

PART FOUR

FOURTEEN

Each Thursday morning in September a blue limousine would park outside the John Jay College of Criminal Justice to deliver Father Isaac. The Chief had to make his eleven o'clock class. He was lecturing on the sociology of crime. His students were a privileged lot. Patrolmen, firemen, and sanitation boys, they had never sat in a class with the First Deputy Police Commissioner of New York. They were crazy for Isaac. He would talk to them about Aeschylus, with a gun sticking out of his pants. They would go dizzy from his insights, his remembrance of poets, hangmen, crooks, politicians, and carnival freaks.

The First Dep had one liability: his automatic pager would force him in and out of class. The bleeps coming from the region of his tie could curl the ears off any student. Patrolmen and firemen wagged their heads until Isaac turned off his gadget and got to the telephone in the hall.

On this Thursday morning Isaac was morose. Headquarters switched him to a gravedigger's shack in Bronxville, New York. He grumbled to Herbert Pimloe, who picked up the phone. "I'm lecturing Herbert. What's so important?"

"We found the baby," Pimloe said.

Isaac felt a crack in his mouth. "Where, Herbert?"

"In the Guzmann yard. Isaac, you were right. The fucks buried him in the family plot. I swear to God. It took an hour to dig him up. Isaac, you couldn't believe the bones in that yard. Papa must be an orderly guy. He sank all his enemies in the same place. You remember that creepy runner of his, little Isidoro? I think he's down there, sleeping with Jerónimo. We sent for the morgue wagon. Isaac, should we wait for you?"

"No," Isaac said, his mind drifting to the vultures at the morgue who would hover over Jerónimo, pathologists from Bellevue with their dissecting kits, tubes, laboratory handguns, airtight jars for liver and kidney samples.

"Herbert, call Bellevue. Tell them to cancel the truck."

Pimloe stood in the gravedigger's shack with the phone stuck in his cheek, waiting for the First Dep to clarify himself. Father Isaac didn't mutter a word. "Why should I stop the truck?" Pimloe finally said.

"Because we're leaving the baby in the ground."

The Chief was deranged. The PC would come down on them all if he discovered that Jerónimo hadn't been exhumed. Pimloe had to supervise a team of gravediggers to get at Jerónimo. They'd been pushing bones around since a quarter to seven.

"Isaac, the baby has a dent in his skull. That's Guzmann work, if you ask me. What about Isidoro? Isaac, look how many corpses we could pin on the tribe. The Fox can't squeeze out of this."

"Herbert, button up the mess you made and go home to your wife."

Father Isaac returned to his section of firemen and cops. There was a wormy boy in his head. He didn't feel like jabbering about Aeschylus, blood, and crime. His pager began to scream again. Isaac dismissed the class.

He didn't have to argue with Herbert Pimloe. Headquarters switched him to another location. He had his old chauffeur on the wire, Sergeant Brodsky, calling from a West Street diner. Brodsky was jubilant. "Isaac, the Guzmanns belong to us. They're booked on a Spanish freighter. Barcelona's the last stop. Isaac, imagine. They used your name. They registered as the four Sidels. What fucking nerve they have. They're on board this minute. They carried Jorge in a mattress. Isaac, I didn't see Jerónimo."

"Jerónimo's on top of the Bronx," Isaac said.

Brodsky scratched his nose. "What d'you mean?"

"The baby isn't going to Barcelona."

"Isaac, have a heart. Is the moron with you, or Pimloe? You want me to raid the boat? We got sledge-hammers. I could chop that pier to shit and pull Zorro off his Spanish freighter."

"Brodsky, the Guzmanns can do whatever they please. Zorro doesn't exist for us. Let Papa have his ocean voyage. The Atlantic will be good for Jorge's legs."

"God, Isaac, can't I collar one of them? Just one? Alejandro, or Topal. I don't care."

"Brodsky, goodbye."

Isaac got to Horatio Street in his blue limousine. He dismissed his driver with a polite nod and entered the Kings of Munster. Irishmen fled from the bar. The lone dog in the place, an ancient terrier who loved to lick empty Guinness bottles, scampered under a table. Sammy wouldn't say hello. Isaac ground his teeth and walked into the sanctuary. Patrick had his minyan. He didn't need Father Isaac. He was standing with Rabbi Hughie and the elders of the shul, and three bearded gentlemen in soft white prayer shawls. "Cover your head," Patrick growled. "You're in a holy room."

Isaac put a handkerchief over his ears.

"Silver, I didn't mean for the baby to die."

"Isaac, don't bring your rotten business into my father's house. This is a synagogue. We pray here. We don't mention the police."

The three bearded men began to wail in their soft white shawls. The shawls obscured parts of their anatomy. Either they had humps on their backs, or they were leaning too hard. They collected near the Babylon closet without a prayer book among them.

Isaac whispered now. "Who are they? Greenwich Avenue mystics?"

Patrick glowered at Father Isaac.

"Papa sent them to us. They're cantors from Peru. Isaac, close your mouth. The cantors are singing Kol Nidre for the shul."

Isaac had to whisper again. "Forgive me, Silver. I'm not a rabbi. I'm a cop. But who sings Kol Nidre ten days before Yom Kippur?"

"The cantors have a different calendar, Isaac. Leave them alone. They celebrate Yom Kippur whenever they can."

Isaac listened to the Peruvian cantors. Their singing made no sense. Was it a muddle of Spagnuolo and Portuguese? Only the Marranos could recite the Kol Nidre in a variety of tongues. It didn't matter to Isaac. The rhythm these cantors could produce, the warbling sounds that seemed to shatter inside their throats, appealed to Isaac's worm. His belly turned smooth. The flesh under his heart didn't have any claws. But the handkerchief was quiet on his skull. The First Dep wouldn't sway to the cantors' melody. They screamed with enormous tears in their eyes. Isaac hardened himself. He knew about the reputation of Marrano cantors and priests. The best of them had the power to stir the dead. Isaac didn't want to hear Jerónimo chirp at him from a Westchester grave. He left the Kings of Munster.

People saw a man with a hankie over his ears. Isaac couldn't outrun the cantors' wails. Their Kol Nidre stuck to his body like a cloak of thick, wet fur that was making him stink. He couldn't go back to Headquarters. He'd have to watch the furniture men dismantle his desk and move all the drawers to Chatham Square. Isaac was the last commissioner to remain on Centre Street. The Irish chieftains were already installed in their brick fortress next to Chinatown. After this month Isaac would be chewing green tea with his fellow commissioners in the mandarin restaurants of Bayard Street.

He crossed the Bowery with crooked eyebrows. The worm was beginning to crawl. He couldn't take a step without squeezing his belly. Someone barked at him from the window of a Ludlow Street restaurant. It was his old "fiancée," Ida Stutz. She came out of the restaurant to gape at Isaac.

"You expecting a sun shower?" Ida said. "Or is it a cap for your brains?"

Isaac remembered the handkerchief. He took it off.

"Where's your husband?" he said, with a canker in his voice.

Ida blanched. "Who could get married with blintzes on the fire? . . . what husband?"

"Your accountant, Luxenberg. The one with plastic on his sleeves."

"That embezzler? Isaac, did you ever see such a man? He hides behind my shoulder so he can monkey with the restaurant's books. Luxenberg wiped us out."

"Why didn't you tell me? I could have ripped the plastic off his arms."

"You were busy with the Guzmanns," Ida said. "Who could talk to a commissioner like you?"

Isaac looked sad without the handkerchief. He was no longer bishop of the lower East Side. Ida began to take on the musk of an old "fiancée." She could have fallen on Isaac in the street, hugged him under his commissioner's jacket.

"Isaac, should I meet you at your place, or mine?"

"Mine," Isaac said.

"Mister, give me twenty minutes. I have a potato pie in the oven."

Isaac went to his flat on Rivington Street. He had two small rooms, where he could shuck off his clothes and get clear of his obligations at Headquarters. At home he was a boy with garters on his legs, not the Acting First Deputy Commissioner of New York. Isaac didn't have to turn his key. The door was unlocked. He wondered if Papa had left a few "cantors" for him, gentlemen from Peru with mallets in their sleeves that could erase Isaac's memory, knock the stuffing off his scalp. Isaac would greet Papa's "cantors" with gruff hellos. He didn't hesitate. He walked inside without fingering his gun.

A naked woman sat in his kitchen tub, smoking a cigarette. How could Isaac mistake the tits of Marilyn the Wild? It wasn't every father who could peek at his daughter's chest. He heard a whistling in his ears. Would the Irish-Jewish fairies who guarded Patrick's shul burn out his eyes for squinting at Lady Marilyn? Isaac must have had a prissy worm in his gut. It grabbed his colon with a spiteful energy that drove his knees together and sent him crashing into the side of the tub.

"Christ," he said, "can't you put something on?"

He gave her a shirt to wear. Marilyn got out of the tub with a sinuous move that startled Isaac. He wouldn't stare at the wall while Marilyn pushed her body into his shirt. The shirt came down to the soft furrows at the front of her knees. A clothed Marilyn couldn't help Isaac the Brave. The proximity of his girl—the bittersweet aroma rising off her hair, the curve of her neck against one of his own collars, the penguinlike awkwardness of her kneecaps—unedged the Chief. He wished he could arrive at his fiftieth birthday without a daughter. He couldn't exist in a single room with Marilyn the Wild.

"I won't bother you for long," she said. "I didn't want to live in a crummy hotel until I found an apartment. I'll be out of here in a week."

"Fuck an apartment," Isaac said. "You can stay with me. It's not as stupid as you think. Marilyn, I'm never here."

"You wouldn't like the friends I brought upstairs."

"Bring whoever you want."

"What about Blue Eyes?" she said.

Isaac cursed all his fathers who had given him a daughter that could bite. His tongue was trapped in his mouth. The Chief had to sputter. "Marilyn, not my fault. I got enemies. Manfred happened to grow up with them. It was a shitty piece of work. I had to bounce him at the Guzmanns . . . I had no choice."

"Balls," she said. "Manfred would be alive today if he went with me to Seattle. I tried to steal him from the police. He wouldn't budge. He was devoted to a prick like you."

"Seattle," Isaac said, his cheeks a horrible color. "Blue Eyes couldn't have made it in Seattle. It's too wet. The rain would have warped his Ping-Pong balls. He'd have had to come back to us."

"Papa, why is it that everybody around you dies, and you walk away without a scratch on your ass."

"Not true," Isaac said. "I have plenty of scratches if you care to look."

The Chief stumbled in his own room, searching for his honey jar. Marilyn had depleted him. Isaac had to have his lick of honey, or die. Marilyn caught him with his finger in a jar. Isaac, the sorry bear.

"Papa, should I run down for a dozen eggs?"

The bear was whimpering with honey on his nose. Daughter, I've got a worm that's more precious to me than all my battle scars. Didn't I catch it in the field? It's with me when I shit, when I snore, when I go to John Jay. It can spell "Blue Eyes" with the hooks in its mouth. A goddamn educated worm.

The mad, Peruvian Kol Nidre wailed in Isaac's head. He was surrounded by priests. Whose design was it? Big fat cop, Isaac the Brave, murdered Blue Eyes, murdered Jerónimo, how many more had he managed to kill? He didn't need a gun. He snuffed you out with logistics. Isaac was lord of Manhattan and the Bronx. He worked you into a corner, and let someone else supply the instruments. You couldn't shove your pinkie into his face. Isaac was always clean. He loved that blue-eyed bitch. Hadn't he nourished Coen for ten years? Marilyn should have picked up a high commissioner for her man, not a cop who played checkers with Isaac. He didn't want Coen to fuck his daughter. It rankled Isaac. Blue Eyes was a piece of him. Should he have spent his life imagining his own "angel" rutting with Marilyn the Wild?

There was a knock on Isaac's door. The Chief recalled his date with the blintze queen. Now he'd have a surplus of women in his room. Marilyn and Ida would stalk one another and growl at Father Isaac. "Baby," he said, touching Marilyn on her long, long sleeve. "It's only a friend. Ida Stutz."

FIFTEEN

St. Patrick of the Synagogues courted the little goya with Jerónimo in his brain. He stood outside her building with his new shillelagh, discouraging suitors, girlfriends, and pimps. There was a bit of pishogue in his snarl, a touch of Irish sadness in the handle of his broom. Silver had helped destroy the baby. He'd allowed Jerónimo to drift into the war zones that Isaac had manufactured as a kind of plaything, a dollhouse for the Guzmanns and himself. Damn their rotten armies. Patrick was the baby's keeper, and he'd let him slip away.

His pants weighed down with Guinness, his shirt corroding on his chest, Patrick kept to Jane Street, singing about witches and dead Irish kings. It was a freakish serenade. Odile's windows were in the back. All she could hear was a wretched yodeling and a blather of words. She would come downstairs in a gauzy nightgown to collect St. Patrick. Neighbors spied her buttocks under the gauze, lovely moons of flesh, as she got the Irishman and his bottles into her tiny flat. He built up a passion off the street. Odile had shallow bruises on her neck from St. Patrick's grizzled chin. He made love to her in a serious way. The little goya could scarcely breathe, with a giant living on her bed. His climaxes caused the walls to shake. His whole body rumbled during one of his spectacular comes.

After the lovemaking he would suck on his bottles and devour a loaf of bread. Then he lay back, belched, broke wind (his farts had a timbre that could have healed a sick dog), and sang to Odile, mumbled songs that terrified her.

> There was a lad named Jerónimo
> Who caught a disease, a disease
> In his father's candy store.
> He saw Moses giving little boys
> Licorice and ice cream
> Licorice and ice cream
> And he wanted to color their lips
> Color their lips
> With his father's crayons.

"Jesus," Patrick said, "were they going to cure him with a dose of halvah? Why didn't they put the lad in a hospital? Couldn't Papa discourage little boys from visiting the candy store? Who's going to pray for the infants who died on the roofs?"

St. Patrick would weep with bread in his mouth and gorge his throat with Guinness. He discovered a circular on Odile's dressing table, an advertisement for the Nude Miss America Follies.

"What's this?"

"Nothing," she said, and she snatched the circular from out of his hands. "They slipped it under the door. Crazy people. Can't stop inventing new contests."

"Is that an entry blank at the bottom of the page?"

"Didn't notice," she said, stuffing the circular into her nightgown. She would shriek if she heard another song about Jerónimo. The goya missed that weird family. The Guzmanns had provided for her, given her customers and pocket money. She'd gotten one postcard from Zorro. He scratched out thirteen words to Odile. "Love it here. You can smell the shit under the streets. Love. César."

Odile was approaching twenty. She'd retired from porno films eleven months ago. Living at the Plaza had thrown her into obscurity. Producers couldn't keep their noses out of her tits. The men she knew wouldn't honor the emotions of a nineteen-year-old. They wanted a mechanical baby, a doll with nipples that could go hard and soft. But Patrick was in the way. That idiot Irishman talked marriage in her ear. He'd make Odile into a washerwoman yet. She'd have to scrub the drawers of every rabbi at the Kings of Munster.

Odile had to break off with the Irishman. She couldn't earn a penny with St. Patrick guarding the house. She packed a suitcase of cosmetics and underpants and ran from Jane Street the next time Patrick attended morning prayers. She picked a good hideout, where she would be safe from any man. It was a lesbian bar on Thirteenth Street called The Dwarf. She could play parcheesi in the back room, eat cucumber salads while she sandpapered her bunions for the Nude Miss America Follies. It wasn't vanity that compelled Odile. She didn't need two thousand men to admire the geometry of her pubic hair. It was business, nothing but business. If she won the Follies, she could revive her stage name, Odette, and become a porno queen again.

The bouncers at The Dwarf were broadshouldered cousins, Sweeney and Janice. The cousins could sniff out transvestites, FBI agents, and undercover cops for miles around The Dwarf. Both of them were in love with Odile. They hadn't seen the little bitch in over a year. Janice wasn't utterly pleased with Odile's invasion of the premises. That girl created havoc at The Dwarf. Bartendresses wouldn't mix drinks. Customers quarreled. Everybody wanted to dance with Odile.

Janice came up to her table. The bitch was wearing a mint julep face masque, light green mud that was supposed to purify her skin.

"Honey, there's a man outside. I think he belongs to you."

The mud splintered close to Odile's eyes. "Shit," she said. "How did that Irishman find this place?" She walked over to the window. She smiled through the mud. It was only Herbert Pimloe. He arrived at The Dwarf in a wilted cotton suit. Isaac's whip forgot his handkerchief. He wiped his forehead with the ends of his tie. The mudpack made him sulky. He was frightened of a girl with green jaws.

"Odile, what the fuck?"

She wouldn't stand on the sidewalk with Pimloe. "Herbert, I'm in training. Go away."

Pimloe had a cowish look. "I want to live with you."

"Herbert, your wife wouldn't appreciate that."

"So what? I'm never home more than twice a week. I swear. Isaac keeps me in Manhattan."

"Are you the big Jew's baby?"

Pimloe jumped in his cotton suit. "Who says?"

"Patrick Silver."

Pimloe began to sneer. "That quiff. He got burned out of his own synagogue. Odile, Isaac can't sign his name without me. I'm a chief inspector now. Silver's a cunt who wears a naked holster on his belly."

"Don't curse," she said. "I might decide to marry him."

Odile retreated into The Dwarf and left Pimloe flat. He intended to hop over the doorsill and chase Odile, but the image of Sweeney and Janice in their tailored suits soured him. The whip returned to Headquarters. He would raid the bar tomorrow with a squad of blue-eyed cops and drag those fat cousins into the street so he could be alone with Odile. Pimloe was a Harvard man. He would convince the girl to stay with him, bribe her with promises of champagne, chocolate, and pommes frites.

The little goya didn't have time to dawdle over Herbert the cop. She had to peel mud off her face. Sweeney lent her a small valise to hold her nightgown in. Janice wouldn't wish her luck at the Follies, or say goodbye. Sweeney pushed her out the door with a soft kiss. "You don't have to undress for those pig men. You can stick to parcheesi with Janice and me. I'll be at the show. If the pigs try to handle you, I'll tear up the floors."

Odile hiked to the Greenwich Avenue Art Theatre with
Sweeney's valise. Posters of nubile ladies and girls had been slapped
to the theatre walls. The creatures on the walls existed without a
blemish; the girls had amazing white teeth and no brown spots on
their nipples. Odile wondered how many photographers had been
paid to brush beauty marks off the posters (even the porno queen had
a few baby moles on her ass). She went in to register herself.

The manager of the Follies, Martin Light, ogled Odile. He sat in
his undershirt distributing pink cards to all the Follies girls. It was
sweltering inside the Greenwich. Martin couldn't get the thermostat
to dip below ninety degrees. He held onto Odile's wrist for half a
minute. "Baby, it's a lousy crop this year. You'll walk away with
everything. I can tell." He winked and sent her into the bullpen that
had been set up behind the stage for the convenience of the Follies
girls.

Odile was grossly uncomfortable around such girls. They
giggled, chewed gum, and had scowls under their eyes that betokened
a mad determination to walk on stage without their clothes. It
saddened Odile. None of them could compete against the perfect
ripple of her bosoms, and the cool outline of her back and legs.

Odile got into her nightgown and stood away from the girls, who
prowled in their kimonos, pajamas, and little robes, or rubbed against
the walls in bikini underpants. The air grew thick in the bullpen. The
ceiling began to cloud with the girls' hot breath. Pajamas came off.
Panties were flung across the room. The Follies girls had a passion
for getting undressed.

They had a visit from Martin Light. The manager plowed
through a bullpen of sweating nipples. He stopped at Odile. This one
was in her nightgown. The sight of gauzy material in the midst of so
many yards of flesh unsettled Martin. He laid a finger on her hip.
"Girlie, you can't lose. Meet me after the show."

Odile did stretches and pliés in her nightgown to prevent her
arms and legs from falling asleep. The Follies girls watched this
litheness of Odile with swollen faces. They began to despise their
own raw bodies. They had lumps on their behinds that couldn't be
smoothed away with all the stretching in the world. They might have
finished Odile, ripped the gauze off her shoulders, devoured her
fingernails, if the manager hadn't come for his girls.

He herded them out of the bullpen, keeping the girls in a
scraggly line. They bumped knees wherever they went. You could

hear shouts and muttering through the walls of the bullpen. The auditorium was alive. The girls didn't see a thing. Stumbling in the dark, between paper walls, they couldn't determine chairs, aisles, or the shape of individual men.

Martin led the girls into a pit under the stage that was inhabited by a clutch of fiddlers and trumpet players. Amplifiers and trumpet cases were packed near the girls' feet. No one could bend without striking an amplifier. The girls had to lick each other's hair, or learn to breathe in a new way. Martin took his undershirt off. Grinning murderously, he powdered his neck, his bald spot, and his eyes, and slipped a dinner jacket over his bare chest. There were scars in the velvet sleeves. A cuff was missing. Martin held his grin. He squeezed around the girls, fumbling into elbows, hairdos, and pieces of crotch, and climbed out of the pit on tiny, wicked stairs. You could say goodbye to the nudie show if you lost your footing. You would have tumbled into the fiddlers and broken your head.

Martin pranced on stage with his traveling microphone, while Odile brooded in the pit. The fiddlers scraped on their instruments. Spit from the trumpets flew into Odile's eye. The little goya began to sob. She was stuck with the Follies girls, pinned to their bellies and their crinkled behinds. She couldn't run home to The Dwarf.

The girls mounted the Greenwich stairs, smiling, one by one. None of them fell. Martin shouted their names to the audience. "Here she is, lovely Monica, the pride of Kips Bay. A hundred and three pounds in the flesh. Good people, what do you say to Monica?"

Odile had to guess the audience's mind from her station in the pit. She heard a lot of booing for Laura of Washington Heights, Tina of Hudson Street, Monica of Kips Bay. Monica never returned to the pit. Did Martin hide a girl after the boos and the stamping of feet that could swallow the noise of his fiddlers? The girls in the pit were moaning now. Ushers had to hoist them up the stairs when their names were called (the audience was surly in the lull between the presentation of girls).

"Odile of Jane Street," Martin said. No usher had to drag her out. She grew dizzy on the stairs. She saw the fiddlers' brains. She stepped out of her nightgown and continued to climb. The stage lights turned her body raisin blue. "Also known as Odette," Martin cried into the microphone, his powdered neck deep inside the dinner jacket. No one hissed at him. The audience mooed for Odile. She didn't have to jiggle her parts. The natural sway of her bosoms in the raisin-colored light could stun an auditorium.

There was whimpering in the front row. Handkerchiefs sailed off the balconies. "Oh my God, oh my God, oh my God."

Martin crouched behind Odile. He had her by the ankles. "Girlie, don't leave. The theatre's in love with you."

Odile prayed for her deliverance. It would take a whole contingent of girlfriends from The Dwarf to get her out of the Greenwich Art Theatre. Sweeney didn't come. Odile stayed frozen in the light, with Martin on her ankles. Only Zorro could have saved her. The Fox would have gone from seat to seat slitting men's throats until the auditorium emptied out. But Zorro wasn't in the United States.

The little goya heard a bellowing over the chorus of moos. There had to be a rhinoceros in the house. "Put on your clothes." She saw a hand grab Martin Light and bowl him across the stage. The hand belonged to Patrick Silver. Men were clinging to his back. The giant shook them off with a twirl of his neck. He had blood in his ears. "Jesus," he said. St. Patrick didn't want to fight an army of lovesick men. He was grieving for Jerónimo.

The giant would recite the mourner's prayers on a little bench at the Kings of Munster. But he couldn't say kaddish all day long. He was lonely for Odile. He prowled the streets with Guinness bottles in his pants. Then he read the marquee at the Greenwich. Nude Miss. His head wasn't right. American Follies. His brains were pissed over with Irish beer. He stumbled into the theatre without buying a ticket. Ushers whacked him with their flashlights while Patrick squinted at the stage. He saw precious ugly women shake their hips under a wrinkle of blue-black light. "It must be market day at Kilkenny." People told him to get quiet.

He crossed his elbows and leaned against the wall, weary of so much shivering flesh, until Martin Light announced Odile. St. Patrick cleared the aisle. He dumped men and boys over the backs of chairs. A rabbit bit him on the ass. Patrick howled. "Jesus, I'm through." Fingernails scraped his nose. His ear was on fire. He reached the pit with entire bodies clamped to his leg. He had to slap down two heads to raise his thigh. He tore into the fiddlers, climbed the treacherous stairs, dispatched Martin Light, and tunneled into the curtains with Odile.

The auditorium rose up against St. Patrick. Men from the orchestra and the lower balconies jumped onto the stage. They would have murdered the giant to hold on to Odile. They didn't have sturdy weapons. They had to slap him with buckles, fists, and shoes. The shirt came off St. Patrick's back. His trousers fell below his hips and stood clinging to his buttocks. Fists and shoes made squeaky noises on Patrick's skull. The buckles stamped red dents into his shoulder blade. The giant was growing angry.

"Esau," he muttered, "where's your daddy now?"

Cradling Odile in one of his armpits, he began to fight. He pummeled noses and eyes, struck at Greenwich Avenue gentlemen with his elbows, chin, and knees. They were caught in a September whirlwind that none of them could describe. You couldn't get close to Patrick Silver. The storm around him could fling a man over the lip of the stage. Patrick didn't have to grovel in the memory of Brian Boru. The witch of Limerick was only a frizzled hag with all her hundred and ninety years. Patrick could have destroyed the Greenwich Art Theatre with the wind he produced on stage. He couldn't restore Jerónimo, protect the Guzmanns in Barcelona, sing to Manfred Coen, but he could break out of Martin's bullpen with the little goya.

Living in a heated armpit, with Patrick's blood pounding in her face, Odile had gotten used to the giant. She wouldn't let go of his chest.

Patrick shouted into her ear. "Jesus, will you marry me?"

The little goya thought she would die. The whistling in her head attacked the insides of her cheek. But the deafness was only temporary. The whistling went away. She laughed and nibbled his armpit.

SIXTEEN

Moses was a tradesman again. He acquired fourteen parrots. Sleepy
birds with bald shoulders and hairlines in their beaks, they were
without a particular pedigree. Papa couldn't have told you whether he
had macaws, Amazon birds, or cockatoos. The parrots seemed
reluctant to move their heavy brains. But Papa could cure them of
their sluggishness for a price. If the turistas dropped a few Barcelona
pennies on the counter of his stall, Moses would whisper to the birds,
prod their bellies with a piece of wire, grin at them, until they showed
a bit of liveliness. They would break walnuts with their stunted bills,
scoop berries out of Papa's fist, do somersaults inside their cages,
sing raucous one-word songs.

These were English birds. They could scream "Piss" at you, or
mention Isaac the Brave. The parrots' exotic coats had been given to
them by Moses, who painted their feathers every other week. He
allowed the birds to dry in the outhouse that belonged to the
Guzmann flat on the Calle Reina Amalia, in the Barrio Chino. Topal
and Alejandro had to squat down with parrots over their ears.

Zorro snickered at Papa's outhouse. He wasn't going to drop his
pants in the vicinity of birds that told you when to piss. The Fox
couldn't get Manhattan plumbing out of his head. He would relieve
himself in the mirrored toilet at the Hotel Presidente, throwing ten
pesetas to the concierge. He always wore an orange suit inside the
Presidente; he wouldn't buy any of his furnishings at a men's shop on
the Paseo de Gracia. Zorro's handkerchiefs, cuff links, shoelaces,
socks, and ties came from Boston Road.

The Fox had his morning chore. He would bring Jorge to Moses'
stall on the Ramblas, while his father and brothers carried the birds.
Moses and the boys would sit on their bench dreaming of Jerónimo.
Absorbed in themselves, they forgot to swipe pocketbooks from the
German tourists. They would have starved without Zorro's thumbs.
Even the parrots were at his mercy.

It was childish work for the Fox. With an American
handkerchief covering half his chest, he walked up and down the
Ramblas, brushing against turistas who crowded the stalls. He
avoided the pillbox hats of the guardia civil as he moved away from
the stalls with a wallet under his handkerchief. Sometimes he took a
parrot along. The bird would nest on his shoulder, with its claws in
Zorro's summer wool, its beak inside his hair.

Zorro didn't endure birdshit on his clothes for the sake of companionship. The parrot helped him steal. The turistas would marvel at the plumage on a sleepy bird, while Zorro went in and out of their pockets. He could earn nine hundred pesetas in an hour.

The bird dug into his shoulder today. Zorro could smell the paint on its wing. He stopped at the Calle del Hospital for a café tinto and mocha ice cream. The bird woke long enough to peck at Zorro's mocha. "Cocksucker," Zorro said.

The bird sprayed ice cream on the Fox. Zorro would have banged its head into the stones of the Barrio Chino, or slapped its damaged bill, but he had stolen goods in his pocket and he didn't want to bring attention to himself.

The Barcelinos mistook him for a pimp. You couldn't have found another orange suit in all of Catalan (it had been put together by a Polish tailor in the Bronx). Zorro gave up pimping when his brother died. He was barely a thief. He wouldn't have plagued the turistas if his father and the birds were able to feed themselves. He would have strolled under the statue of Columbus in the harbor, lunched on fisherman's soup near the Calle del Paradis. He would have posed for Germans, Italians, and Swedish tourists, with the parrot on his shoulder, and wheedled pesetas out of them. Then he could pee at the Presidente or the Ritz, go to Barcelonita, and sit on the Muelle de Pescadores, at the edge of the city, and throw one of his shoelaces in the Mediterranean. The scum would buoy it up. A shoelace never drowns in Barcelonita.

"Jerónimo."

Zorro turned his cheek. The parrot was nibbling on his brains. He stared into its left eye. The eye was smudged with yellow paint.

"Don't you mention my brother," Zorro said. "I'll tear your neck off, you bald piece of shit."

The Barcelinos stared at man and bird.

Zorro finished his café tinto. The parrot nudged Zorro's ear. He fed it the last of his ice cream. The mocha began to fill the splinters in its beak. Zorro swabbed the bird with his handkerchief. They left the Calle del Hospital and continued down to the sea.

SECRET ISAAC

PART ONE

ONE

Who's that lad that barks at us and bites our cheeks? Tiger John, Tiger John. They sang that in the hall when he wasn't around, those Irishers from the Commissioner's office. They laughed at him and feared him too. You couldn't tell where his rage would fall. He was a crisp little man with gray hair that had lost its shine and turned a bitter yellow, it was like straw, that crop of dead yellow hair, but it didn't ruin his looks. He was sixty-one years old, and he had the energies and the eager face of a slightly dumb boy.

The Irishers couldn't remember if he'd been a captain in the Bronx, or a shoofly for the Chief Inspector. You didn't talk about his past. John had lived in deep winter a long, long time. He was attached to a little Irish club on First Avenue for decrepit and alcoholic cops until he came out of retirement with the Honorable Sammy Dunne. They were brothers of a sort, the Mayor and his Commissioner of Police.

The PC would closet himself for an hour and comb his dead yellow hair. At the old Headquarters John had a fireplace and a private balcony and his own elevator car. He could ride up and down as often as he liked. No one but his First Deputy could use that car. Now he didn't even have a First Deputy to comfort him. His First Dep was gone. Disappeared into the dust. The famous Isaac Sidel. This Isaac was always on some idiotic mission.

John had a sudden thirst for tea. He didn't have to yell for his chauffeur. Chinatown was across the street. He chose a small dirty cafe, the China Pot, where he wouldn't be recognized as the "Commish." Policemen didn't come here. It was a hole in the wall on Baxter Street.

You couldn't see Tiger John from the window. He sat at a table that was obscured by the counter, a crooked shelf, and the coffee urn, and he drank green tea. He had chicken buns and a cookie made of almond paste. John felt a sudden wind in the care. He looked up from his tea and buns. "Jesus, is that Jamey O'Toole?" he said to the man at the next table. The man was six feet seven, and his legs took up half the China Pot. It wasn't his impossible size that disturbed Tiger John. He could live with such prodigious things. But *two* Irishmen in the same cafe, that was a bad idea.

Jamey flipped a bankbook into the Commissioner's lap. "A present for you . . . from the king." John cupped the little book in his hands and opened it under the table. The amount was six thousand dollars and twenty-three cents. The name was *Nosey Flynn*.

"Boyo," he said in a whisper, "how am I going to create the signature of Mr. Nosey Flynn?"

Jamey told him to use his left fist.

John had a pile of these bankbooks. He held them together with a rubber band. They arrived from O'Toole with different names in them. The names were always Irish. *Simon Dedalus. Paddy Dignam. Gertrude MacDowell. Molly and/or Leopold Bloom . . .*

Who the hell was this king of Jamey's? An Irish thug with an Ivy League education. He removed himself to Dublin, because the freeze was on. The Special State Prosecutor, Dennis Mangen, had begun to ride herd over the City. It was Mangen who made life so miserable for Tiger John. Mangen ate up Police Commissioners.

"Jamey, don't come down here anymore."

"Why not?"

"Because I don't want Mangen to catch your ass in Chinatown. He'll wonder why you've been traveling so far."

Jamey smiled. "What's new with the great god Dennis?"

"Shut your mouth," John said. Mangen had a squad of shooflies, and the shooflies went into every crack. They could have been hiding in the China Pot. "You belong uptown . . . go on."

O'Toole got up from the table. He had to walk with a slanted step. There was no room for his shoulders in the cafe. He stopped near the door and called back to the Commissioner. "How's your First Dep?"

"I haven't seen a hair of him."

"I have," Jamey said. "He mucks around Forty-seventh Street in filthy clothes."

"That's Sheeny Isaac . . . the brains of the Department. He's a bit of a psychopath, if you ask me. Mooning over a dead boy. You remember Manfred Coen?"

"Blue Eyes," Jamey said with a sneer.

"That's the baby. Isaac's daughter put a jinx on Coen."

She was a hungry girl, Marilyn the Wild. The daughter put out
for anything in pants. She was the marrying kind. She'd have herself
a husband, and shed him in a week. The poor girl went bats in the
head. She fell for Isaac's "angel," Blue Eyes Coen. But Isaac wasn't
giving Coen away. He tossed him to a family of Bronx pimps, and
Blue Eyes got killed. Now Isaac walks around in rags, chasing pimps
and lamenting Coen.

"Give him my love, Jamey, if you catch that stinky man on the
street."

Both of them hated Sheeny Isaac. O'Toole had been thrown out
of the Department, robbed of pension and shielded by Isaac the
Brave. He had to grovel for the king. He delivered bankbooks to John
in a dirty cafe.

John dialed his chauffeur from the China Pot after O'Toole went
out the door. "Christie, I'm on Baxter Street . . ." He wouldn't have
an Irish chauffeur carry him around. An Irish chauffeur would have
sung to him from the driver's seat. John didn't want that much
familiarity in his car. Christianson was a Swede, and the Swedes
were quiet.

"Cheerio," he said to the Chinese countermen. "So long, boys."
His black Mercury was outside the China Pot. He climbed over the
curb, and he was gone from Baxter Street, Chinatown, and Police
Headquarters. The cushions inside the Mercury were his chief
comfort. No one could pester John, or attack him as the PC, when he
sat on those high cushions.

A blinking light on the radiotelephone box destroyed his good
cheer. It was the Mayor's light. John picked up the phone. He had to
make sure it was Sammy on the line, and not one of those
dunderheads from the Mayor's office.

"Your Honor . . . is that you?"

"Himself," the Mayor said.

Sammy had turned remote. He was up for re-election, and he
didn't need the Tiger hanging on his tails. *Isaac* was the Mayor's
hero. *Isaac* was the grand boy. The newspapers reviled Tiger John.
They called him the "Know-Nothing Commish." Isaac could dance in
his own shit, and the Police reporters would sniff for gold. They
loved whatever sloppy music the First Dep made. It didn't matter to
them that Sheeny Isaac had removed himself and gone into the
Manhattan wilderness. He was their favorite child.

"I'll be having my bath tonight . . . tell the lads to give it a good scrub. How are you, Johnny?"

"In the pink."

He'd become a buffoon for Mayor Sam, a Commissioner who could be trundled in and out of the closet, depending upon the political climate. These were John's closet days. You never found him at the little parties Sam liked to give. John was keeper of the bath. His club had installed a sauna room for Mayor Sam, so "Hizzoner" would have somewhere to hide. It was John's function to regulate the sauna's heated rocks by spilling cups of water over them. Such were the duties of a Police Commissioner.

The Mayor's light went off. John put the receiver back on the cradle and muttered to himself. *Now that he's in trouble he wants his bath.*

"Take me to the Dingle," John barked.

Tiger John Rathgar was a Dingle Bay boy The Dingle was *his* club. It began as a kind of temperance league for drunken Irish cops. The Sons of Dingle had the right cure. They would pound that terrible love of "the whiskey" out of any man. John had an added moral obligation. He could visit with the wives, and seduce them if he could. The Dingles had more than temperance on their minds. They were bully boys in the County of Manhattan. They collected bills for local merchants and delivered votes for Democrats who could afford the price. But they'd grown a little obsolete. They couldn't whack men and women outside a polling booth, even with Tiger John as "Commish."

He arrived at a battered storefront on First Avenue: the Dingle Bay. It made no pretense of being a gentleman's club. It was for the hairy Irish. Crossbones were painted on the window, crossbones and a harp. Its sills were crumbling, and its metal awning was eaten with rust. Yet no other society of Hibernian cops could boast a sauna bath.

John sent the Mercury home to Chinatown and made three long knocks on the club's iron door. It was a signal to his mates.

He had to knock again. "It's me . . . John."

The door opened enough to let him through. Jesus, it was dark in there. Those lads didn't believe in sunlight. They had a fetish about covering their freckled pates. Summer and winter, indoors and out, they would wear eight-piece caps of pure Donegal wool. The caps left a deep mark on their foreheads. They were proud of the "Donegal" mark. Others wore black derbies. They were lads from the retired Sergeants Association who would visit the Dingle from time to time.

John shucked off his suit jacket. He didn't have to play Commissioner at the Dingle. He could go about in his shirtsleeves and not feel compromised.

"Kiddos, the Mayor's coming tonight."

The old men chuckled to themselves. They built a sauna for Mayor Sammy Dunne, but they weren't so fond of Sam.

"Christ, we haven't cleared out the piss from the last time he was here . . . we won't disappoint His Grace. We'll mop up the putrid thing . . . how goes it at the Headquarters, John?"

"The usual shit," he said. "I can't complain."

His Chief Inspector was retiring in another few months. McNeill had a castle in the Old Country. He'd live in it like a duke and fish for salmon in his waters. What would happen to John? He was already shy a First Dep. He'd have to whistle for Isaac.

The old men were in a singing mood. They had their bottles of root beer and Tiger John. It was a temperance society, and they wouldn't keep liquor in the house. They would run next door to sneak Irish whiskey into the root beer.

We're the sons of Dingle Bay
The wild geese who left our home
Who left our home
Who left our home
For Americky . . .

It's true, true, Johnny said. *Wild geese. Gone from home.* The Dingles were lucky. They didn't have to preside over Police Headquarters. They could visit the Mother Country, like Coote McNeill and old Tim Snell, and those other lads from the Retired Sergeants Association. Live in Wexford or Dublin half the year. Bring back neckerchiefs, derbies, and a fresh box of Donegal hats.

We're the Sons of Dingle Bay . . .

The song rid him of Sheeny Isaac. John didn't have to think of Isaac, Chief Inspector McNeill, or the Mayor's bath. He brushed his tongue over a bottle of root beer and began to sing:

Who left our home

Who left our home
For Americky . . .

TWO

There was once an old man who had a worm in his gut. The worm
liked to wiggle. The old man would clutch at himself, as if to tear out
the insides of his body. He lived at a disgusting hotel on West
Forty-seventh Street. The hotel didn't even have a name. It was just
off Whores' Row. The pimps stayed clear of him. They kept suites at
this hotel for all the "brides" they owned, or managed. The "brides"
were black girls under nineteen. At least one of them was pregnant.
They enjoyed the old man. He wouldn't snarl at them, or look under
their summer shirts. A whore's sweaty nipples could surprise him.

So they talked to the old bum, shared orange drinks, confided in
him. These "brides" had their own corners. No one could intrude on
their rights. If it rained, they worked out of little storefront parlors. It
was a rotten year. Five dollars could get you half the world. There
was nothing, nothing they wouldn't do for a man. The "brides" were
on the street twenty hours a day. The old man could see the rawness
in their necks, the hysteria when they would grab at a john and say,
"Honey, goin' out?" The seduction was very thin. The black girls
were faithful to their pimps. Most of the white whores, who worked
the same strrets, hated any man who touched them. They were dykes
and religious freaks. They'd grown suspicious of the old bum. They
wouldn't kiss their girlfriends in front of him. They tried to get their
"players" to run him off the street.

The old man had an odd immunity. It had something to do with
the worm. He'd been at war with a retarded family of South
American pickpockets and thieves. This family had given him the
worm. The old man killed one of them, maimed another, and threw
the rest of them into some foreign hell. They were groveling in
Barcelona, selling parrots with split beaks. And this old man had their
worm in his belly, a hookworm that was eating him inch by inch.

Certain men would step out of shiny Buicks and whisper to the
old bum. They were much too regal to be members of any vice squad,
and they didn't wear the wide trousers of homicide boys. The pimps
would wonder to themselves: who is this geek? Their friends at the
nearest precinct grew mum when you mentioned the old man with

the worm.

He developed a lousy odor. He didn't think much about
changing his pants. He wouldn't shave more than once a week. He
fed his worm at a Greek dive on Eighth Avenue and Forty-fifth. He
would eat salads and whole wheat bread. Then he'd give in to his
appetite and crawl to Ninth Avenue for a cappuccino. It was a
weakness he had. Strong coffee and steamed milk.

The coffee was bad for his worm. Its thousand little hooks
grabbed at the old man's intestines, and he would stumble through
the street, saying "Fuck, God, shit," or whatever madness came into
his head. He would avoid the coffee for five or six days. Then he
couldn't help himself.

It was after one of these cappuccino fits, when the worm was
twisting him half to death, that he saw her on Forty-third Street. It
wasn't a good corner for a prostitute. There was always a heavy load
of cops that guarded the trucking lanes around the *New York Times*
building. The Mayor was scared of the *New York Times*. He had his
Police Commissioner, Tiger John, flood Forty-third Street with cops
in and out of uniform. So who had stationed this girlie over here?
Some forlorn "player," a beginner's pimp who hadn't learned the
truths of Times Square? She was no mulatto queen. The old bum
watched her in profile. A white whore who didn't have that hard glint
of a manhater. She was beautiful. She should have been a rich man's
escort, not a bimbo in the street.

The old bum wasn't filled with lecheries. He wouldn't have
brought this beauty to his hotel. He had a daughter with the same
skinny ankles. The daughter was a sucker for men. She couldn't keep
from getting married and divorced. She was on her seventh husband,
and she was only twenty-nine. He decided to play the father to this
beauty, chase her from Forty-third Street before the Chief Inspector's
men picked her up. But he was trembling at the fineness of her nose.
Why didn't some Cadillac whisk her off to White Plains? She was a
girl to marry, not whore with. Then the old man saw the other side of
her face.

It was scarred, wickedly scarred. She had the imprint of what
seemed to be a knuckle, as if she'd been gouged with a metal fist. He
took a closer look. The letter "D" had been scratched into her face.
Christ. A scarlet letter on Forty-third Street.

"Miss, you can't stay here. The cops are fond of this corner.
You'd better shove up to Forty-fifth."

"I can't." She smiled, and that gruesome letter wriggled on her cheek. "I don't have a union card. The other girls would bite my ass."

"Who's looking after you?"

"Martin McBride." The smile ended, and the "D" corrected itself.

"Well, this Martin is an idiot. Is he the one who put you in the street?"

The scarred beauty turned agitated.

"Mister, take me somewhere, or go away. Martin doesn't like me talking to strangers."

She didn't have a bimbo's voice, and it confused the old bum. He had no plans to undress her. "What's your name?"

"Annie."

"Annie what?"

"Isn't Annie enough for you?" she said. "It's Annie Powell."

He smuggled her into a French restaurant on Forty-eighth Street, Au Tunnel. The headwaiter was frightened to throw him out. The old bum had twenties in his pocket and a Diners Club card.

Annie Powell laughed. "God, you're crazy."

"Who's Martin McBride?"

"Somebody's uncle," she said. "That's all."

The old man pointed to the scar. "Did he do that?"

"No."

They drank a muscatel, had scallops, green beans, trout, and a chocolate mousse.

"Mister, how are you going to make me earn this meal? I might not be kinky enough for you." He hadn't told her his name.

The bum gave her forty dollars. "Do me a favor, Annie Powell. Stay off the street for the rest of the night."

The old man was irritated. He'd gone to his hotel room, but he couldn't sleep. He had visions of Annie being pawed by bull-dykes in some detention cell. "Shit," he said. He put on his clothes, and walked downtown to Centre Street. It was the site of the old, neglected Police Headquarters. Its rooms were abandoned now. The Police had moved to a giant red monolith in Chinatown. Only a few extraneous cops watched the floors of Centre Street, for rats and other vermin. Most of the files were removed. Even the photo unit in the basement was gone. There was a guard at the main desk, but the old man had no trouble getting into the building. He didn't have to flash any identification card. He went up to the third floor, walked through a clutch of rooms, and entered an office with an oak door. The office had a telephone. It was the only phone in the building that worked. He dialed the new Headquarters and shouted into the phone. "I told you," he said. "A cunt named Annie Powell. If she's taken off the street, if she's bothered, if she's touched, I'll flop the whole pussy patrol. And find out who this Martin McBride is. Does he have a nephew with a name that begins with a big D? . . . yes, a *D* . . . like dumb . . . or dim . . . or dead."

He hung up the phone, and managed to fall asleep. He didn't have much of a rest. A boy from the Mayor's office rang him up. His Honor had fled the coop again, walked out of Gracie Mansion in his pajamas on a midnight stroll.

The old bum took a cab uptown. He had the cabbie rake the streets around Carl Schurz Park. Then he got off. His Honor, Mayor Sam, had gone down to Cherokee Place. He didn't seem deprived in striped pajamas and a red silk robe. When he saw the old bum he began to weep. He was sixty-nine, and he'd turned senile on the Democratic Party over the past two years.

"Laddie, what happened to you?"

"It's nothing, Your Honor," the old bum said. "Just the clothes I'm wearing."

"You gave me a fright," the Mayor said. "We have to fatten you up."

His own aides accused him of being a decrepit fool. He belongs in a nursery, they said. Ancient Sam. But he had no difficulty recognizing the old bum. The Mayor was as lucid as a man in pajamas could ever be. It wasn't a drifting head that brought him out of his mansion. It was a fit of anxiety. All his politics was shrinking around him. Most of his deputies had abandoned Sammy Dunne. He was a Mayor without a Party. He'd become a ghost in the City of New York. You didn't speak of Mayor Sam.

He still wept for the old bum.

"Isaac, I know the enemies you have. They'll eat you alive after I'm gone."

"Let them eat, Your Honor. I've got plenty of hide for them."

"Laddie, what are you talking about? You're skin and bones."

The old bum was thinking of Annie Powell. That scar of hers stuck to him. Annie's "D." He walked the Mayor home to Gracie Mansion and went to his hotel without a name.

THREE

Why should a whore have turned his head, a bimbo with damaged goods? She couldn't have fared very well with that gash on her face. The worm was biting at him. "Cunt," he told the worm, "are you in love with her too?" He would stroll down to Forty-third to be sure no one molested her. His shuffling with his hands in his pockets didn't please Annie Powell. She couldn't have too many clients with an old bum hanging around. "We're having lunch," he would say. "Come on." It sounded like a threat to her, not an invitation. And she had to leave her corner.

This time he took her to the Cafe de Sports. A bum and a girl in a whore's midriff eating liver pâté. "Annie," he said, "there's going to be a raid at two o'clock. The Commissioner has decided to grab single women off the streets. So you'd better have a long, long lunch."

They had three bottles of wine. "What's your name?" she said, with a drunken growl, "and what the hell do you want from me?"

"Just say I'm Father Isaac."

"A priest," she said, mimicking him, "a priest without a collar . . . is it your hotel or mine, Father Isaac? . . . I perform better in strange hotels."

"Don't bluff me, Annie Powell. You haven't done too many tricks . . . I want to know who put you on the street?"

"Mister," she said, "that's none of your business."

The old bum had to let her go. The worm dug into his bowels when he thought of her going into doorways with other men, getting down on her knees for them. He had to find this Martin McBride and break his Irish toes. But Father Isaac had an appointment today. He washed the dirt off his neck. He shaved the hairs under his nose that might have been construed as a crooked mustache. He bought a half-hour's time of the hotel's single bathtub. You wouldn't have recognized him when he stepped out of the tub. The old bum had shed twenty years. He had a pair of argyle socks in his room. He unwrapped the only suit in his closet. A silk shirt materialized from his drawer. A tie from Bloomingdale's. Underpants that were soft enough for a woman's skin. The ensemble pulled together. A younger man, fifty, fifty-one, emerged from the hotel. He had a sort of handsomeness. The worm had helped redefine the contours of his face. It gave him character and fine hollows in his cheeks.

A cab brought him to a lounge at the New School for Social Research. People shook his hand. He was more despised than worshipped here, but everybody knew him. Isaac Sidel, First Deputy Police Commissioner of New York and mystery cop. He was fond of disappearing, of putting on one disguise after the other. He wouldn't sit at his offices on the thirteenth floor of Police Headquarters. Isaac called the new brick monolith a "coffin house." He did all his paperwork at the old, abandoned Headquarters. You had to search him out at Centre Street, or in some hobo's alley. Isaac was unavailable most of the time. His deputies were loyal to him. They ran his offices without a piece of discord. Isaac could always get a message inside.

The PC, Handsome Johnny Rathgar, couldn't scold him. Isaac was becoming a hero with all the news services. He would walk into a den of crazed Rastafarians and come out with a cache of machine guns. He settled disputes with rival teenaged gangs in the Bronx, parcelling out territories to one, taking away bits from the other. Arsonists and child molesters would only surrender themselves to First Deputy Sidel. Isaac had no fear in him. He danced with any lunatic who came up close. You could throw bricks at him off the roofs. Isaac wouldn't duck his head. The First Dep was in great demand. Most organizations in the City wanted to hear him speak. Synagogues, churches, political clubs. Either to heckle him or clap. The Democrats had to live with him for now, because he was close to Sammy Dunne, and it was a little too early to drive "Hizzoner" out of Gracie Mansion. But the Mayor was about to turn seventy, and he couldn't hold a squabbling Party together. The Democrats would lash at Isaac when Sammy vacated City Hall. Republicans were frightened of Isaac's popularity, and the Liberals hated his guts. He was only a cop to them. Isaac despised them all, hacks and politicians who would grab the coat of any winner, and sneer at a Mayor's loss of power. He liked the old Mayor, who was being jettisoned by his Party. The Mayor didn't have a chance in the primaries. He was too dumb, too weak, too old. The *Daily News* had already spoken. New York would have its first Lady Mayor, the honorable Rebecca Karp, who'd come to politics via the beauty line. She was Miss Far Rockaway of 1947. She grabbed votes for Democrats with her bosoms, her bear hugs, and her smiles. She'd been a district leader in

Greenwich Village. Now she was Party boss of Manhattan and the
Bronx. Rebecca needed *two* boroughs to fight the pols of Brooklyn
and save New York from the bumbling political machine of Samuel
Dunne.

Isaac was here, at the New School, in liberal territories, to act as
the Mayor's dog in a debate with Melvin Pears, sachem of the Civil
Liberties Union, and a defender of Rebecca Karp. Isaac could have
told Rebecca to shit in her hat, but Mayor Sam was in trouble. He
hardly went downtown to visit City Hall. His margins were being
eaten away. Isaac was the only voice of strength he had.

Pears was seated with the First Dep at a table near the end of the
lounge. The Mayor swore that Melvin was romancing Becky Karp,
but Isaac didn't always believe Mayor Sam. Melvin came from an
aristocratic family, and he had a pretty wife. He was a man of
thirty-five, with a fondness for rough clothes: he had workingman's
boots at the New School and a cowboy shirt with a button open on his
paunch. The boy likes to eat, Isaac observed, thinking of the worm he
himself had to nourish. The wife sat next to Melvin. She had
unbelievable gray-green eyes that sucked out Isaac with great
contempt. He wondered where her shirts came from. The wife wasn't
wearing Western clothes. Isaac felt uncomfortable sitting near those
boots of Mel's. He shouldn't have arrived in argyle socks. His bum's
pants would have held him better in this lounge.

Pears called Isaac a lackey of the Mayor, an instrument of
repressive law. Isaac, he said, who drives prostitutes off the street at
the Mayor's convenience, without considering the plight of these
girls, or their histories. "I'll defend every prostitute you haul in,"
Pears said. "His Honor always sweeps out before the primaries.
You're Sammy's broom."

Isaac growled inside his head. Sammy had enough trouble
getting in and out of his pajamas. Isaac couldn't figure what was
going on in the street. He had his spies. It wasn't the Civil Liberties
Union that was keeping the girls hard at work. You couldn't hold
them in a cage for more than half an hour. They had a league of
bondsmen holding hands with their "players." The whores multiplied
with or without the Police. Inspectors at Isaac's office claimed to
know every dude in town. They talked of a mysterious nigger gang
that was organizing pimps into some kind of union. Black Mafia,
they said. The "blues" of Sugar Hill. Only you couldn't find any of
them. Where were the "blues" of Sugar Hill? It made no sense.

Isaac's spies had nothing to sell. They shrugged their shoulders and swore some "heavy shit" was landing in the gutters. That's why Isaac had to go underground, become the old man of Forty-seventh Street. Isaac only trusted what he himself could sniff. And this Melvin Pears was babbling about whores' rights. Every bimbo in Manhattan had more rights and privileges than Rebecca Karp or Pears' green-eyed wife.

Pears had a bald spot, bigger than Isaac's. He was still chopping at the First Dep. "All the glory comes to you," Pears said. "You solve the big murder, the big hit, and anonymous old men and women are afraid to go out at night."

Isaac interrupted him. "Would you like us to keep every fourteen-year-old boy in the bullpen after six o'clock?"

Pears leapt on Isaac. "That's the smug answer you can always get from a cop. Arrest *everybody* and crime will go away."

Isaac didn't have Melvin's courtroom wit. He shut his mouth and let the boy talk. His head drifted to Annie Powell. That "D" on her could sting a man's eyes. That girl's no goddamn hooker. She was being punished for something she did. Annie's sin.

Pears had stopped talking. What was Isaac supposed to do? Defend Mayor Sam? List Police accomplishments? Talk about the new Headquarters and that idiot, Tiger John? Promise an end to sodomy in the women's house of detention? Isaac talked about Oswald Spengler. Pears scratched his head. Rebecca Karp's admirers must have considered him a little cracked. "It's ungovernable," Isaac said. ." . . this terrain. Psychosis is everywhere . . . in your armpit . . . under your shoe. You can smell it in the sweat in this room . . . we're all baby killers, repressed or not . . . how do you measure a man's rage? Either we behave like robots, or we kill. Why do you expect your Police Force to be any less crazy than you?"

There was laughter in the room, some hissing.

Pears shouted at him. "Sidel, you haven't gotten to the point at all. What do I care about your philosophies? Silly contrivances. Glib remarks. We do have a City, and it has to be governed. And the Mayor, *your friend,* is doing an invisible job."

The debate was over. People were congratulating Melvin Pears. He's gotten around the ignorant carp of a half-educated cop. Isaac only had one semester at Columbia College. He couldn't have told you about the theories of John Locke. He had bits of Nietzsche in him, Spengler, Hegel, and Marx. His readings were savagely curtailed.

Crowds formed close to the lawyer Pears. One old lady came up to Isaac. She was muttering something he couldn't understand. All Isaac could make out was the green in Mrs. Pears' eyes.

One of his own inspectors, Marvin Winch, was waiting for him on the curb. Isaac promised himself that he would manufacture several little talks before he entered another lounge. Pears had cut out Isaac's throat. The First Dep had only a skimpy sense of logic. His ideas came from the worm in his gut. He wasn't a civilized man.

"Well?" Isaac said to Inspector Winch. "Who's Martin McBride?"

"A low life. He runs with the nigger pimps."

"Does he have a nephew?"

"Yes, a carload of them. Our Martin's got nephews everywhere."

"How many of them have that big *D* I told you about?"

"Only one. Dermott."

"Dermott McBride?"

"No. He took the Irish out of his name. He shortened it to Bride."

"Bring that cocksucker to me. I'd like to have a chat with Dermott Bride. We have a girlfriend in common."

"Isaac, I can't. Nobody knows where Dermott is."

"Then plug into your computer and find him for me."

Oh, they could laugh and call him Sammy's dunce, but Tiger John Rathgar had eyes and ears, like any man, and a mouth to bark with and eat cigarette paper when he was in the mood. A year ago "Hizzoner" had said, "Johnny, the pimps have to live like the rest of us. What's the point of chasing nigger girls off the street? They'll be strolling again in twenty-four hours." So John throttled his pussy patrol, yanked out most of its teeth, and then the bankbooks began coming in. With the Irish names inside. Simon Dedalus, Molly Bloom, and all. John didn't perform one crooked act to earn his *Molly Blooms*. He promised nothing to the pimps of Whores' Row. Could he help it if Jamey O'Toole tossed bankbooks in his lap?

Now it was an election year, and "Hizzoner" wanted the Black Marias out, wagons to hold nigger prostitutes. John had to activate the pussy patrol. But the Mayor warned him. "No white girls. We can't afford a mistake. If your lads pick up a housewife, the papers will crucify us. I'm depending on you, Johnny boy."

John went along with the pussy patrol. His chauffeur, Christianson, put him in front of the Black Marias, which were ancient green wagons with dented roofs. John decided what whores would go into the wagons. He picked the fattest girls, girls with low midriffs and pockmarks on their thighs. The wagons filled up in less than an hour. The girls sat in them and bitched. They couldn't get away from the heat of their own bodies. They tore at their midriffs to cool themselves, and they took long bites of air. John signaled to his chauffeur. "Christie, I've had enough. Come on."

"Where are we going, boss?"

"To the Mayor's house."

Christianson flipped his sirens on and shot across town, ahead of ambulances and fire trucks, and brought the "Commish" to Carl Schurz Park. The policeman came out of his sentry box to salute Tiger John and open the gate for him. John walked under the blue canopy at the side of the house. He loved to visit Gracie Mansion. It was a grand old house with black shutters on the windows and white porch rails. Sam had three bedrooms for himself. He was the first bachelor Mayor to occupy the house.

Through the front door Johnny went, under the fanlight, with Sammy's live-in maid to smile at him and ask about his health. "Thank you, Sarah, I'm tiptop."

"That's good, Commissioner John."

"And how is the Man today?"

"He's bristling," she said. "It's them straw ballots. Everybody's picking Rebecca to win."

"It's meaningless stuff," John said. "He'll pull through."

He walked up the winding stairs on the Mayor's green carpet. It was almost three o'clock, but the Mayor hadn't risen yet. John stood outside the master bedroom and knocked on the door.

"Come in, for God's sake."

Sam was in his underwear. He put pajamas on for his Police Commissioner and returned to bed. He lay under the covers until Sarah arrived with a pot of coffee and sweet rolls for the two bachelor men. He winked at John when Sarah left. An enormous black accounting book poked out of the covers. It was the Mayor's budget for the coming fiscal year. Sam kicked at the book with both his feet. "Becky Karp says I can't add or subtract. But it doesn't take more than ten fingers to know that the City is sinking in shit. Some wizard in the Comptroller's office is always finding a million here and there . . . then he loses it the next day . . . did you run the girlies into the precinct, John?"

"I did."

Sam fell silent and munched on a sweet roll.

Christ, how do you talk to a Mayor? John finished his coffee, taking care not to break the cup. "Ah," he said, "you'll murder Rebecca at the polls."

But the Mayor wasn't listening to him. His jaws churned while he stared into the great mirror alongside his bed. Poor old man. *Hizzoner can't sustain a conversation. His memory is on the blink.*

John walked out of the master bedroom as quietly as he could. He said goodbye to Sarah and thanked her for the coffee and the sweet rolls. Christie was parked near the gate. He had an envelope for Tiger John.

"Who gave you this?"

Christianson held out his hands to indicate the overwhelming breadth of the giant. "It was that rogue cop, O'Toole."

"O'Toole? How could he tell I was coming to the Mayor's house?"

Christianson shrugged and pursed his lips.

The PC glared at him, "The Special Prosecutor is on our heels, and you monkey with that whoreboy outside Gracie Mansion? . . . come on. Take me to the Dingle."

He opened the envelope, and a bankbook spilled out. John didn't bother with the sums in the book. Five or six thousand, it was the same to him. They were getting cheeky with the "Commish," these messenger boys. The giant had followed him to Sammy's gate! He shielded the bankbook in his palm, so he could peek at that mother of a name. *Anna Livia Plurabelle.* Go figure out O'Toole and that king of his in Dublin town. John got his bankbooks if he went after whores or not. What in hell were they paying him for? Would the bankbooks come faster and faster, the more Black Marias he sent out? *Anna Livia and Molly Bloom.*

"The Dingle," John said, "when do we get to the Dingle?" Then he noticed that the car had stopped.

"Boss, we've been sitting here for five minutes."

"Oh," John said. He got out of the car, knocked three times, muttered his name, and crept inside with the Dingle Bay boys.

FOUR

He was that bum again, but he didn't have a dirty neck, or so much stubble on his face. His cheeks were lean, and he had the suffering look of a suitor. Annie Powell didn't like it at all. The bum was wearing cologne, an after-shave lotion it was. He would scare anybody away with the dark hollows in his eyes. "Jesus," she said, laughing at him. "How am I going to earn my keep? Buy me for half an hour, but don't feed me another lunch. I can't work on a full stomach."

Isaac stole her from Forty-third Street before she could complain. He had the grip of a large monkey. She couldn't free her hand. The pimps and the young black whores laughed at the image of Annie and Isaac trundling along. You would have thought the bum had himself a wife. They went to the Vinaigrette. Isaac bought her little bottles of champagne. His tactics seemed more aggressive today. Annie preferred white wine and green beans. But those little bottles didn't soften the bum. "I can take you off that corner," he said. "I can make it so you won't have a foot of space to prowl on."

"God, you really are a priest . . . if you'd like to buy a share of me, you'll have to ask Martin McBride."

"Fuck McBride," Isaac said. "I want you to live with me."

She didn't laugh at his proposal. Her eyes began to sink into her skull.

"I have a place downtown. On Rivington Street. Don't worry. You can have your men. I won't interfere. I'll mix drinks for them. Go out for bottles of wine. But I don't want you on the damn streets."

"Mister," she said. "I don't need an uncle, thanks. I already have a pimp."

Could he tell Annie Powell she was torturing him and his rotten worm? That he'd bump any john who went near her corner? He was jealous, stupidly jealous, of a girl he hadn't even slept with. That scar had gotten him crazy.

"Who's Dermott?" he said.

She ate a mouthful of fish.

"I asked you about Dermott Bride."

She got up from the table, put her napkin down, and walked out of the restaurant. Isaac was left with three corks and his little bottles of champagne. He phoned his office. A limousine was outside the Vinaigrette in seven minutes. The waiters at the restaurant saw the bum get into that big car. They were wise men. They understood that strange things existed in this world. The very rich often preferred to dress like *cloches*. They wouldn't forget this bum with the scarred beauty, the limousine, and the splits of champagne.

Isaac's deputies had located Martin McBride, who lived with a fat wife in eight rooms near Marble Hill. Martin had emphysema. But he had to suffer August in New York. He collected money from the pimps of Manhattan and heard their complaints. He was known in mid-town as "Bagman Martin." He'd been a petty crook for over half his life. Poor Martin didn't have much of a record: arrested as a vagrant two or three times. Short spills in the Tombs. But that was twenty years ago. He'd prospered in his old age.

Isaac's men kidnapped him out of his apartment in a three hundred dollar suit. The old bagman was bewildered. Centre Street was completely black. Why was he being shoveled through the halls? He didn't believe Isaac's deputies were cops. But this was the old Police Headquarters. They deposited him in a back room on the third floor. The room was dark except for the lamp in his face. Who in Jesus was behind that desk?

"Scumbag, is Annie Powell yours, or not?"

"Sir," the old bagman said, "I don't know who that sweetheart is."

"But she happens to know a lot about you . . . How's Dermott these days?"

"Who, sir?"

Isaac reached over his desk to twist McBride's two ears.

"Ah, the nephew. He's doing fine."

"Could it be that you're working for him, Martin McBride? . . . that the nickels you collect from every whore's purse goes to little Dermott?"

"That's impossible, sir. Dermott's a Yale man, swear to Christ Helped put him through that college. He was training for the bar . . . but he never got to be a lawyer, sir. The nephew tired of his studies."

"Where is he now?"

"I haven't a clue."

Isaac was tired of twisting ears. He was readying to bang Martin's head against the wall. But Martin suddenly had a coughing fit. It wasn't contrived. Isaac could see the awful blue and yellow of emphysema on him. He had his deputies send Martin home. He learned nothing from the old bagman. He didn't get one bit closer to Dermott Bride.

FIVE

The pimps wouldn't talk to him. The black whores couldn't even pronounce Dermott's name. Annie would run from him soon as Isaac appeared. She'd have no more lunches or dinners with the old bum. He walked into a pornography shop managed by a friendly Russian Jew. The Jew was smart enough to read under Isaac's disguise. He knew about the legendary First Deputy of New York.

"Sidel, don't play the schmuck with me. Ask me a question, and I'll answer it, but only if I can."

His name was Lazar. And he carried a pistol under his counter, wrapped in a handkerchief.

"The girl with the scar on her face, who is she? She wasn't here a month ago."

"The gorgeous one?" Lazar said, making perfect breasts with his hands. "The knockout? Sidel, lay off of her. She's Dermott's bride."

And he began to titter. Isaac wouldn't smile.

"Who's Dermott?"

"Dermott? Dermott's the king."

He was mum after that. Lazar had to attend to his shop. Isaac was sharp enough not to pull at him. Lazar had told him as much as Lazar cared to tell. Dermott's the king. Now Isaac was beginning to understand why there was peace on Whores' Row. This Dermott had to be the overlord of all the pimping traffic. Uncle Martin was his bagman, the old boy who settled Dermott's accounts. But why didn't some gang of mavericks slit Martin's throat? Was Dermott that much of a king? And how could he hold his little empire together if you couldn't catch sight of him? It all didn't fit. Isaac Sidel shouldn't have been ignorant of the emperor of Times Square.

He had no more time to ruminate in a pornography shop. He was expected at John Jay. Isaac gave lectures twice a week at the School of Criminal Justice. He walked to his hotel, shaved, put on a pair of fresh dungarees. That was Isaac's teaching clothes.

The worm itched when he arrived at John Jay. It was a bad sign for Isaac. The worm was hardly ever wrong. He had a new pupil in his class. Melvin Pears' green-eyed wife. She sat at the back of the

room with a notebook in her hands. That notebook inhibited Isaac.
He forgot to prance round the classroom. He stood near the window
and talked about the futility of criminal justice. "The Bronx is dying,"
he said to the young firemen and cops in his class. "Street by street.
We can't send in artillery. The kids would only burn all our tanks.
Soon the edges of Manhattan will go . . . then you'll have towers on
the East Side with machine-gunners in the lobby . . . you'll need
armed guards to get you in and out of the supermarkets."

One of the firemen raised his hand. "First Deputy Sidel, what
can we do about it?"

"Go into the Bronx," Isaac said. "Build over all the rubble. Why
can't we have shopping plazas in Crotona Park?"

The cops giggled to themselves. The areas around Crotona Park
looked as if they'd been napalmed. There were more arsonists in the
Bronx than grocers. These cops would have figured Isaac for a
bolshevik if he wasn't the First Dep. They enjoyed jeremiads from a
deputy police commissioner. You could light up in class. Isaac didn't
care what kind of junk you smoked. But that green-eyed lady worried
him. Was she going to use Isaac's words against old Sam in Becky
Karp's bid for Mayor? He could watch her scribbling between her
legs. That's no place to keep a notebook.

She was there, in the same seat, at his next class. The worm
nearly hobbled him. He had to lean against the wall. "Sure," he
muttered to himself. "It's not too hard to recognize a traitor.
Especially when she has green eyes." But he wouldn't coddle her,
sweeten his own talk. He mentioned Stalinist solutions. "Mobilize.
The cops can't do it themselves. Have a goddamn citizens' army.
Fight the shits who won't cooperate. Bring back Joe DiMaggio. Get
Willie Mays to build a new Polo Grounds . . . behind the Grand
Concourse. Where's Durocher now? Take ten percent off
everybody's salary . . . a tithe for the Bronx . . . no, make it twenty
percent."

The cops laughed, but the green-eyed wife of Pears clutched her
notebook. Isaac grew sad. I'm burying Mayor Sam. He ended the
class twenty minutes before the bell. He tried to skirt away from Mrs.
Pears. She trapped him at the exit. He would have had to crawl under
her bubs to get around her. She put a slip of paper in his hand. The
specks in her eyes were incredible. They flashed shiny gray dust like
small planets about to break apart. He was jealous of Melvin Pears.
Isaac also had a wife. Kathleen. A tough Irish lady who had married

him before he was twenty. The wife was in real estate. She developed swamps in Florida, had ten suitors and a million in the bank, and she didn't need a cop who liked to go around in bum's pants. He saw her once or twice a year. They made love if Kathleen was in the mood. It was more of a friendly hug than anything else. Now he had to deal with Mrs. Pears.

"I didn't mean to blunder into your class . . . I'm sorry . . . it's just that I was interested in what you had to say . . . can you come to dinner tomorrow night?"

"Your husband's too tough for me, Mrs. Pears."

"I'm Jennifer," she said. "Jenny . . . Mel likes you . . . don't mind his scowls . . . he has to practice making faces to satisfy all the juries . . . he's much nicer at home."

SIX

He expected Rebecca Karp to come out of the closet and eat off his neck with the hors d'oeuvres. It was only a party of three: Pears, his wife, and Isaac Sidel. Jennifer hadn't been wrong. Melvin wasn't the lawyer at home. He offered Isaac sucks from his hash pipe. The First Dep smoked with Mr. and Mrs. Pears. Why not? He was fifty-one. He ought to have a taste of hashish before he died. It didn't offend the worm, and it warmed Isaac's head. But he couldn't let go of the cop in him. "Mel, did you ever hear of an ex-law student named Dermott Bride? . . . went to Yale."

"I don't think so," Pears said, and they all took sucks from the pipe. "I couldn't scribble a brief without some hash in me," he said. "I always work better when I'm stoned."

Isaac didn't see a nudge of affection between husband and wife. Their bodies seemed to exist in some kind of neutral sphere. It's the hash, Isaac figured. They probably fuck three times a day. Mel had the grace not to mention Rebecca Karp. And Isaac didn't talk about the Mayor. A little sleepy boy came out of one of the rooms. He wore fireman's pajamas. He ran to his father. "Alex, say hello to Isaac."

He shook hands with Alexander Pears, who had his father's mouth and his mother's green eyes.

"Isaac's a policeman . . . smarter than Dick Tracy."

Alexander was four and a half. He kissed his father and went to bed. He couldn't stop looking at Isaac. Jennifer was in the kitchen putting whipped cream on a pie.Thank God there had been no politics tonight. Pears didn't say a word about why the Police Commissioner ran prostitutes off the street. Isaac was the one who started to talk about hookers. He was dreaming of Annie Powell. "There are certain pimps. They get their fingers on a girl. And she's owned for life . . . or until she gets ugly and has to be shipped to Nova Scotia, where anything that walks will pass as a woman."

He noticed Jennifer standing over him. "Sorry if that sounds cruel. But it's a fact. You know, if a girl's too beautiful, and her pimp is afraid of losing her, sometimes he'll scar her face. It's a fantasy he has . . . he thinks the scar devalues her in the eyes of other men. But it doesn't always turn out that way. The scar can make her even more desirable. And the pimp will lose her anyway."

They had cognac and chunks of pecan pie. Melvin slumped into his chair and fell asleep. Isaac whispered with some embarrassment to Mrs. Pears. Melvin was snoring hard. Jennifer didn't apologize. She accompanied Isaac to the door. The worm was rising in his gut. The cognac caused his bald spot to twitch. The hash must have been like a love potion to Isaac. He had Mrs. Pears against the door. That's how he found himself. A stumbling man. His tongue was deep in her mouth while he swallowed half her face. He could still hear Melvin snore. That fucking kiss, there was no end to it. The worm didn't keep Isaac's clock. He could have been gnawing at her for an hour. What if the gentleman wakes up? Or the little boy in the red pajamas marches out of his room and sees mama with Dick Tracy's tongue in her mouth? It was Isaac's nervousness that got them apart. He told her about his hotel. "It's too decrepit to have a name. You don't have to meet me there . . . "

He was downstairs, on Madison and Seventy-ninth, outside Melvin's place. What the fuck was it all about? Was it some game plan in Melvin's head to bring him over to Rebecca Karp? Feed the boy some hash, get the wife to kiss him, and he'll fly from Mayor Sam? His tongue was raw as shit. Did Jennifer entertain every guest in a similar way? He was so busy kissing her, he hadn't even felt her tits. God, he was dumb about women. His wife Kathleen was right to head for Florida. You couldn't get much companionship from a cop who was married to his own love of mystery and technique. He'd slept with a hundred women, whores and businessmen's wives, and while he probed, stroked, and sucked, his head would grind away at some caper that had been bothering him. The First Dep solved a quarter of his mysteries in bed. Fucking seemed to drive the trivia out of him, to hold his concentration for detail. But that was before the Guzmann family gave him his worm. The worm had idled Isaac's need for sex. That's why this tonguing business with Jennifer was crazy to him. It's the hash, Isaac said. The hash roused a part of him that the worm had laid to rest. He was convinced he wouldn't see Mrs. Pears again. She'd avoid his classes. She'd never come to a shithouse hotel.

Isaac hobbled to West Forty-seventh Street. He changed into his bum's clothes. He had this urge to prowl. Annie wasn't at her corner. So what? Was she sucking off a tie manufacturer from Hoboken? Isaac would murder the son of a bitch. He'd hold every whore in detention. White or black, to ruin Annie's trade. Let no man finger that scar. The First Dep was going mad. He wanted to kiss that "D" Dermott Bride had put on her. To feel the ridges in it with his mouth. He'd keep his tongue in his own face. The tongue was for Mrs. Pears.

She must have given him a bit of luck, Melvin's green-eyed wife. Isaac saw Martin McBride outside Lazar's pornography shop. The bagman wasn't alone. He had Jamey O'Toole with him. Tiny Jim. O'Toole was a renegade cop. Isaac's own investigators, the First Dep's "rat squad," had brought evidence against Tiny Jim. He'd been taking bribes without mercy, "black rent," breaking the heads of local businessmen to further the cause of protection agencies in Brooklyn and the Bronx. Isaac put him out on his ass. O'Toole lost his pension money, but you couldn't hurt a lad who was six feet seven and had a pair of fists on him that could give shorter men a permanent headache. O'Toole was still in business. He'd lent himself out to Dermott and Martin McBride. He was the old bagman's walking shotgun. There weren't too many gangs in New York that would meddle with Jamey O'Toole. You'd need a hatchet to get at him. A bullet would only leave a little nipple in his chest.

But Isaac had a worm to hearten him. He wanted to devil this O'Toole. "Jamey," he said, "I hear your old shield is lying in the property clerk's drawer."

O'Toole had a warm smile for Isaac. "How are you, Chief? It's hard to remember all the different uniforms you own. Isaac, I don't have a grudge, I swear . . . but keep out of the alleys, will you? You could fall and lose one of your eyes on the ground. Have you met my employer, Martin McBride . . . Martin, don't be fooled by the man's stink. It's Isaac himself, the First Deputy of New York."

McBride's fist was soft and wet in Isaac's hand.

"We're already old friends," Isaac said. "Martin visited me . . . at Centre Street."

McBride's fist shot out of Isaac's hand.

"O'Toole take a message to Dermott, will you, please? Tell him I'm fond of his Annie . . . and I'd like to dig my own initial into his royal Irish face."

Martin scampered behind O'Toole.

Jamey didn't harden to the First Dep. "You'll have to forgive me, Chief. I don't think I'll relay that message. It's a declaration of war, you see. And I might be caught in the middle. You'll have to sing to Dermott yourself."

"I would, if you'd tell me where he is?"

"That's your problem, Chief. Dermott, he doesn't like the notoriety. He's in a bit of retirement now. But you might send him a postcard. If you could get the proper stamps."

O'Toole walked off, taking Martin by the hand.

SEVEN

Isaac went to brood in his hotel. You needed some Celtic harp to unwind an Irishman's words. Fucking O'Toole. Proper stamps? Retirement? Dermott had to be out of the country. And Martin was doing his trade for him, with O'Toole serving as the muscle. The Italian lads wouldn't soil their fingers with black whores in the street. But not even O'Toole could fight off every nigger gang; there were plenty of "blues" that would have been willing to strangle pimps for nickels and dimes. They were all getting pieces of the pot. That was Dermott's magic. Then why was he in such a shroud?

The bum didn't come out of his room. Knocks on the door couldn't get him off his unmade bed. The worm itched at him and forced him to recognize a face. He had a visitor. Jenny Pears. She wasn't sure it was Isaac until he put on another shirt. He began arranging pillows. She laughed at his pathetic urge to clean up four weeks of filth. She liked Isaac's room.

He tried to explain. "Have to live this way . . . on a heavy case."

"Why are you so skinny?" she said.

"Jennifer, I was a fat man until a year ago. Had the thickest neck in Manhattan. But I was trying to hook a gang of thieves. The

Guzmanns. I lived with them six months. Had to make them think I'd broken with the cops. But that was a smart family. I did their chores and they put a worm in my belly. And the worm's been feeding off me ever since."

"Isaac, there are hospitals, you know. Laboratories that can shrink your worm, dissolve it, kill it, prevent it from growing new tails."

"I've had my fill of hospitals. Used to run up to Presbyterian like a religious man. They flouroscoped me, gave me pills to eat. Nothing happened. And I've been growing fond of my worm."

Isaac begged her to let him wash up. Jennifer refused. Her body gave him the chills. She didn't have a flaw on her back. Her thighs had a strange burnish in Isaac's room. He loved the circles her nipples made, pinkish mounds. What was Melvin's wife doing in his room? Why wasn't Pears with her, his head resting in her groin? Her low, mother's breasts didn't bother him at all. It was amazing to Isaac. He moved in her with a gentleness, a slow, soft rhythm that he'd never had in his possession before. Was the worm bridling him, holding him back? Was it that creature who was making Jennifer Pears, not him? With its own smooth motion, its worm's rocking parts? Do worms have pricks and tongues? Isaac wanted her out of his room.

"Late," he said. "An appointment with the Mayor. Christ, we have to be at this synagogue by six." It was no lie. The little Irish Mayor had to crawl to the Hebrews for votes, run to obscure shuls in the far boroughs. He'd already lost the Irish vote. The Irish loved Rebecca. She was a former beauty queen, and she had a loud voice, wit, humor, and pishogue. She was five feet eight and could tell a good story. His Honor was nearly a dwarf. Five feet one without his shoes. He was a Party loyalist, a bureaucrat who could barely put two sentences together. He'd had his great rise three and a half years ago. He was chairman of the Potholes Complaint Board, a member of the Landmarks Commission, and an unpaid governor of the Manhattan Shelter for Women. Sam had never finished high school. He seemed perfect for the Mayor's job. The pols liked his mumness, his devotion to their cause. The other candidates, six growling men, were chewing at each other's throats. The dems turned to Sam. They rewarded him for fifty years of labor. He'd carried milk pails for Party bosses, lit the fires in Democratic clubrooms, slept on his knees in City Hall. But he arrived at Gracie Mansion in the wrong year. "Hizzoner" had a corpse in his arms. The City died on Sammy Dunne. It was fighting bankruptcy and a terrible loss of jobs.

"Hizzoner" wouldn't step out in his own car. He was afraid people would jeer at him. So Isaac sent a limousine to collect the Mayor at Gracie Mansion. Jennifer watched the First Dep get into his synagogue clothes. She had more affection for Isaac the bum. She kissed him goodbye and left him to struggle with his cuffs. The limousine was waiting for Isaac outside the hotel. Mayor Sam was hiding in the back seat. He didn't question Isaac's choice of hotels. He might bully Handsome John Rathgar, the Police Commissioner, but he had absolute faith in Sheeny Isaac.

The car took them to Hollis, Queens. Sam and Isaac had to engage a shul full of retirees, pensioners and their wives who were worried about their own shrinking revenues, crime in their housing projects, and the worth of a Mayor who wouldn't come out of his mansion. They were for Rebecca of the Rockaways. They were indulging Isaac and Sam out of boredom, anger, and frustration. The Mayor had nothing to say. His tongue lolled in his mouth while he whispered to Isaac on the podium. "Jesus God, will you save us now?" Isaac saw the bitterness of their plight. An Irish Mayor and an apostate in a house full of Jews. Isaac had never prayed in a synagogue. But he and Sam had to wear skullcaps over their brains. Isaac became the good policeman for Mayor Sam, but question after question was beginning to break his hump. He had pity for these old men and women. They were stroked at election time, and then forgotten. That was the law of politics. Functionaries ran the City, men and women in gray buildings, who didn't even know there was a synagogue in Hollis, and wouldn't have cared. Rebecca would scream about more golden age clubs, but the same functionaries would rule whether she got in or not. Still, Isaac had to lapse into petty lies. He invented master plans for Mayor Sam Dunne: more cops to walk old women to the bank, patrols to discourage baby thieves, police sergeants to talk about better burglar alarms. The worm was biting him fierce. It had little tolerance for Isaac's shit.

Then the auditorium mellowed. It had no idea of Isaac's apostasy. The synagogue figured it was talking Jew to Jew. One old woman mentioned *their* Nobel laureate. What did Isaac think of Moses Herzog and Saul Bellow? All Isaac could remember about cuckold Moses was that he liked to fornicate belly to belly, face to face. Thoughts of Jennifer Pears crept in to him. He had a sudden

desire to ravage every inch of her, to lose that gentleness the worm
had thrust on him, and eat her out like a crazy Chinaman. His Honor,
who was incapable of reading any book, nudged Isaac. "We have
them now. Tell them about Herzog's Bellow."

Isaac mouthed some blather about Herzog and the modern Jew,
and he and Sam were permitted to go. The worm dug at Isaac in a
miserable fashion. He had to keep wrenching from side to side in the
limousine. But Sam was happy. "You got them," he said, "you got
them with Herzog's Bellow."

Something was drilling in Isaac's skull. "Your Honor, you must
know every Irish society in New York . . . does any of them carry a
member named Dermott Bride? A rich man, a man who might make
contributions here and there?"

Sam wasn't listening. He kept singing, "Herzog's Bellow,
Herzog's Bellow," and Isaac thought, he'll lose the primary
mumbling that song. And Molly would probably get a kiss from Mr.
Bellow and throw Isaac to the dogs.

EIGHT

He wasn't wrong about Jenny. She didn't come to his hotel again.
Ah, she's found another primitive guy. Jesus, with a body like that?
And those green eyes. He looked at her at John Jay College. There
was no green-eyed lady taking down his words. His lectures fell to
shit. He stopped caring if the Mayor won or lost. He had only
Dermott Bride to consider. His deputies rang him at the hotel. They
had no news of Dermott, but Melvin Pears had invited him to a party,
a party for Rebecca, at her campaign headquarters in an abandoned
Dodge showroom on West Fifty-third. Isaac thought, pish on Becky
Karp. He wasn't going to lend himself as a whipping boy to her
campaign, appear as the curiosity cop, so Rebecca and her people
could get at Mayor Sam through him. But Jennifer might be at the
party. Jenny of the flawless back. Isaac arrived at the Dodge
showroom in dungarees.

The showroom was packed. All the movie stars had come out
for Ms. Rebecca. Streisand; Dustin Hoffman and his wife. The First
Dep went unrecognized until Rebecca grabbed him by the shoulders
and pulled on him. "Isaac," she said, "Isaac." Even the worm could
feel one of Becky's shoulder grips. Isaac was squeezed into her like a

bunny rabbit. It was a calculated move on Rebecca's part. She wanted him near enough so she could whisper into his throat. "Cocksucker," she said. This was the Rebecca Isaac enjoyed. "I'll stick your balls in a jar of honey and give them to the rats for a lick . . . Fuckface, why did you marry yourself to a sinking man? You're not supposed to be a fool."

Isaac wiggled out of Rebecca's bear hug and kissed her on the mouth. "Senile he is. There are days when Sam can't remember his name . . . "

"Then come over to us," she said.

Isaac smiled, but his lips were narrow, and Rebecca realized she'd just been given a Judas kiss.

"Cunt, he's a better Mayor than you'll ever be."

He would have gone out, tunneled under Streisand's kinky hair on his way to the door, but he discovered Jennifer standing with one of Rebecca's aides, a boy with red eyebrows. They were smiling, talking under their breath. What hotel did *he* live at? Did the boy have red hair on his chest? Would he like to borrow Isaac's worm? Would she fuck him in a doorway? Isaac bullied through a crowd of campaigners, and snatched Jennifer away from the boy. "My savior," she said. "With the iron grip . . . what synagogue do you have on your agenda today? . . . Isaac, my husband's about three feet behind us. *Mel.* Do you remember him?"

"He won't notice," Isaac said. The First Dep was in a burly mood. "He's fixing strategies for Rebecca."

So they walked down to Isaac's hotel. He was into her body before she could get her panties off. It was a kind of friendly rape. He licked her armpits, filled her navel with spit, and sucked between her legs with a brutal energy. He left marks on her thighs, souvenirs for Melvin to look at.

"Isaac, why are you so angry at me?"

"Who knows?"

Was he getting even with the worm, showing it the authentic Isaac, who could take any woman into his bed. He began to eat her nipples like a goddamn baby. She stroked his head, held it there, and the worm had screwed him again. The lust was gone. "Stay with me," he said. "Tonight."

"Isaac, how can I? . . . I have a four-year-old at home . . . and Mel."

"Telephone the kid. Tell him Dick Tracy will play with him

tomorrow if he goes to sleep. Mel can take care of himself."

Her green eyes were throwing off that beautiful gray dust again. He put her in a cab. She kissed him thickly, with her fingers in his ears. It wasn't a joke. He was losing his guts to Jennifer Pears. He'd better find himself a bimbo fast, a girl who would let him concentrate on Dermott while he rolled her over and fucked her from behind. He blackened his face with charcoal and got into his bum's clothes. The First Dep was dying for a fight. He'd roam the streets like a crazed animal, slapping pimps, cops, or tourists. You'd have a hard time arresting Isaac, no matter what outfit he wore. The worm could tear at him. Isaac wasn't going to be ruled by a little snake in his belly.

He had the customer he wanted. A man was chatting with Annie Powell, a timid john from the look of him. Was she settling on a price? Isaac could rip the scalp off her ears, give him a beauty treatment he wouldn't forget. But Annie didn't go with the john. Something had scared him off. It wasn't Isaac. His mania couldn't have been obvious from a block away. It was someone else. A horse of a man. Tiny Jim O'Toole. Jamey was bending over her now. Isaac drew close. That horse wasn't making her smile. He had his huge knuckles in the waistband of her whore's shirt.

"O'Toole," Isaac said. "Jamey. You ought to be nicer to King Dermott's bride. If you don't put your hand away, I'll have to chew it off."

It was a ridiculous bluff. O'Toole could have sat Isaac on top of the lamppost and left him there for the fire trucks to bring him down on a ladder. But he took his knuckles out of Annie's shirt.

"Isaac, be kind to the Irish. Don't meddle. Annie, she belongs to another man. Ask her yourself."

Jamey whistled with his knuckles in his pockets, winked at Annie, and stepped into the gutter. Cars stopped for him. No one could be sure how his bumpers would fare against a lad who was six feet seven.

Annie was growling at Isaac. "Who are you . . . Jesus, can't you play on the next block? And why do you have that black shit on your face? You're comical, you know that . . . with your questions and your little bottles of champagne."

She was sobbing now. "Don't I have enough without a pest like you? . . . you're trouble to me . . ."

"Annie, I could help . . . if you'd tell me what it was O'Toole wants."

"Wants? . . . he has regards to me from somebody I know."

"Dermott?"

But she wouldn't talk to him. And Isaac had to gather up his bum's pants at the waist (he was growing skinnier by the hour), and skunk off to his hotel.

NINE

Was it a code name? *Dermott Bride*. Was Dermott the secret hero of Londonderry? Using his whores' profits to collect money for the "rebels" of Northern Ireland, with Annie the deposed queen of the Provisional IRA? Isaac had his men infiltrate the tough Irish bars around Marble Hill. There was no Dermott Bride or Annie Powell attached to the Irish Republican Army. But Isaac was a stubborn man. He had his agents burrow everywhere. They went into the First Dep's own files. They came up with a memorandum from Ned O'Roarke, the old First Deputy Commissioner, whose death had put Isaac into office. It took them a week to ferret out that pink slip with one sentence written on it eighteen years ago. "*Get Isaac to help little Dermott.*" Isaac was horrified. He couldn't mistake the scrawling hand of Ned O'Roarke. O'Roarke had been Isaac's rabbi. He'd sponsored him, brought him into the First Dep's territories, built him up. What did Ned have to do with "little Dermott"? The worm was erasing Isaac's memory, that's it.

He dialed Kathleen in Florida. It was four A.M. The wife had to be in bed with one of her suitors. "Kate," he mumbled, "did *we* ever know a boy named Dermott?"

He had to ask her again. She yawned into the phone. "Isaac, go fuck yourself."

So he was left with a Dermott he might have known, but didn't know now. Ned O'Roarke wouldn't have launched Dermott as a pimp. It couldn't have been Ned who made a "king" of Dermott Bride.

Isaac had Jennifer to console him three days a week. She was the only woman who could drive Dermott out of him. The worm never pinched Isaac when he was with Jennifer Pears.

But he had other pulls on him. "Hizzoner" was growing desperate. The *Daily News* vouched Sam would only get one vote in ten. He was told to remove himself from the primary lists.

"Hizzoner" refused. He went on more excursions with Isaac. Then he had a heart attack in Gracie Mansion. He was carried to the hospital across the street. Rebecca sent a full page of condolences to the *New York Times*. People were already calling her Mayor Karp.

Isaac felt sorry for old Sam, but he was glad he didn't have to parrot little lies in churches, shuls, and social clubs. He did more strolling as Isaac the bum. Annie seemed to have fled from her corner. Lazar came out of his pornography shop to chat with Isaac. "Sidel, stop dreaming about that woman . . . I can get you a beauty with poems written on her chest."

"Lazar, you didn't leave your shop to become my pimp . . . what happened to Annie Powell?"

"She's in hospital . . . Roosevelt. They found her unconscious last night . . . somebody stepped on her face."

Isaac hailed a patrol car. "Get me to Roosevelt Hospital, quick." The cops were ready to laugh at the bum who was giving orders. "Call my office on your radio. I'm First Deputy Sidel."

They ran up to Roosevelt with their sirens on. He found Annie in some rear beggar's ward. The nurses couldn't understand what this bum was doing with two cops. The cops took their eyes off Annie Powell. Her face was one huge, distorted puff. The lips were split apart. The "D" on her cheek had lost its continuity. Its pith was broken and submerged. Dermott had erased himself from Annie. "Get her out of this fucking hole," Isaac shouted to the resident in charge of the ward. "Put her in a private room."

"Hey," the resident said, trying not to look at Isaac's baggy pants.

"Prick, it's Police business . . . and stop blinking at me. I'll pay for the room."

The patrol car brought him up to Marble Hill. Isaac burst into Martin McBride's eight-room flat. The old bagman was having dinner with a covey of nephews, nieces, and his wife. Isaac lifted him off the floor in front of everybody. The nephews weren't much good. They shrank from the mad bum who was shaking their uncle up and down.

"Martin, you tell me where Dermott is, or I'll squash you into a piece of shit."

"Dublin," Martin said, riding against Isaac's shirt. "The nephew's in Dublin town."

"What's his address?"

"The Shelbourne. St. Stephen's Green."

"Wasn't one scar enough for him? Did he order O'Toole to smash both sides of her face?"

"I don't know, sir. I swear to Christ. Dermott never talks to me . . ."

Isaac didn't return to the hotel. He went down to his monk's corner at Centre Street. He sat in the dark, his fingers rubbing under his nose. The king's in Dublin. Isaac had to murder him. It didn't matter that there was no logic to it. The creature was purring in his belly. That's all the encouragement a man could need. Isaac still had a cop's head. What did Annie Powell mean to him? There were other scarred whores in the world, plenty of them. He hadn't slept with this Annie, hadn't touched her. And she'd mocked his offerings of champagne. But he was already smitten by that letter on her face, Dermott's mark. He could have had his own inspectors swipe O'Toole off the street. Five or ten of Isaac's deputies for each of Jamey's arms. They would have unwired him. But Isaac would fix Jamey himself, when he got back from Dublin. Jamey was only a vassal to that king. It was Dermott Bride who had stepped on Annie's face. He was the lad Isaac wanted. He'd already booked a flight with Aer Lingus, crazy as it was. Isaac was leaving tomorrow.

He wasn't going to Dublin as the great Isaac Sidel. A trusted deputy might have doctored a passport for him. Isaac could have flown under any name. But he didn't want to involve his office. He used a crooked engraver, Duckworth, a thief that Isaac had kept out of jail. He had him smuggled into Centre Street with his bag of tools. The engraver was nervous. He liked thirty-six hours to "make" a passport. And he preferred his own darkroom off Canal Street, where he could exercise his artistry without any pressure from the First Dep.

"Isaac, are you sure there's a camera downstairs?"

"Duckie, why do I have to repeat myself? You've been here before. The photo unit was always in the basement."

"But how do we know what equipment the bastards left behind?"

"That's what we're going to find out."

Isaac grabbed a flashlight and they marched down three flights. Rats scurried around their legs. The smell of rat shit was enough to destroy a man. Isaac kept the engraver on his feet. Duckworth had his camera. The photo unit was intact.

The engraver took half a dozen passports out of his pocket. They were samples of his own work, names he'd invented. All he needed was a photograph of Isaac to go with any one of them. He would legitimize the photograph, fix it to the passport with the State Department seal he carried in his bag. Duckworth rummaged through the passports. "I can give you Larry Fagin O'Neill, Marvin Worth, Ira Goldberg . . . Isaac, they're practically real people. We're just gonna throw one of them your face."

"Keep them for your other clients. Duckie. I have a name. Moses Herzog."

The engraver was heartsore. "Why Moses Herzog? That will triple my work. I'll have to start from scratch. Fagin O'Neill isn't good enough?"

But Isaac was without mercy. Moses Herzog. That's what it would have to be.

PART TWO

TEN

The Irish stewardesses were gentle with this businessman, philosopher, poet from the City of New York. They fed him coffee and chocolate mints. The worm adored the taste of mint. Moses was asleep when they arrived at Shannon. Passengers disembarked. Then the plane took off for Dublin town.

His baggage was light. He figured on two or three days to dispose of his business with Dermott Bride. They wouldn't miss him at his office. Isaac had disappeared for much longer periods than that.

The cab ride to the Shelbourne cost him nearly three pounds in Irish money. It was a hotel with white pillars, a blue marquee, statuettes holding lanterns over their heads, tall windows, and a white roof. The Shelbourne sat opposite a long, handsome park. St. Stephen's Green. Isaac couldn't see the park from his window. But it still cost him twenty pounds a night. He'd have to kill Dermott and get out of here, or borrow from his pension money to stay alive.

He had no idea what Dermott looked like. Would the king materialize on the staircase and present himself, like a fucking Druid? You couldn't tell what magic Dermott owned in Dublin. But Moses had the rottenest luck. A man latched on to him in the lobby. It was Marshall Berkowitz, the dean of freshmen at Columbia College and vice-president of the James Joyce Society. Marshall had been Isaac's English prof during his one semester at college. He made a pilgrimage to Dublin every year to walk the streets of Leopold Bloom. How was Isaac supposed to know that Marshall always stopped at the Shelbourne? He had a new, young wife. She had bangs over her eyes, this Sylvia Berkowitz, powerful calves, and a thin, rabbity smile. Something wasn't right with her. Had she taken a graduate course with Marsh, fallen in love with him while they plowed through *Finnegans Wake*? It must have been a devastating courtship. Marshall could capture any man or woman with that purity he had for Joyce. He'd converted Isaac after the first day of class. That was thirty years ago. Isaac had wept at the opening of *A Portrait*

of the Artist as a Young Man. Moocows coming down the road.
Molly Byrnes and her lemon platt. He was a barbarian from
Manhattan and the Bronx. He hadn't known such language could
exist. He followed Marshall everywhere, begged him to explain the
meaning of this page or that. Isaac walked the campus with a fever in
his eye. It couldn't last. Isaac's father deserted his family during
Christmas, stole off to Paris in middle age to teach himself how to
paint, a fur manufacturer with a craze in his head to become the new
Matisse, Isaac had to leave school and help support the family.

He didn't read Joyce after that. He married an Irish woman who
worked in real estate, four years older than himself. He became a cop.
It was Kathleen who introduced him to First Deputy Commissioner
O'Roarke, Kathleen who connected him to all the Irish rabbis who
ran the Police Department of New York. It was her Irishness that
made him a big cop. Now he had Marshall and Marshall's wife, both
of whom had unmasked him on his first day in Dublin.

"Isaac," the dean said. "For God's sake. What's a commissioner
like you doing here?"

Isaac had an "agreement" with Marshall Berkowitz. From time
to time he would recommend young boys for Columbia College, lads
who were the sons or nephews of some cop. Isaac would interview
them, and pass on his feelings to Marsh. He had an instinct for who
would survive at Columbia and who would not. Marsh always went
by Isaac's word.

"Isaac, how the hell are you?"

The First Dep had to shut him up in the Shelbourne lounge.
"Marsh, I'm on a caper, please . . . you'll have to call me Moses."

The dean's wife began to laugh. She took those bangs away
from her eyes. There were blackish lines around them. Sylvia
Berkowitz couldn't have slept a lot.

"Goddamn," Marshall said. "Moses, come with us. You'll do
your cop stuff later."

"Where are we going?"

Berkowitz smiled. "To Number Seven Eccles Street."

Thirty years couldn't wipe away *Ulysses.* Isaac knew that book.
Number 7 Eccles Street was where Joyce had dropped Leopold
Bloom.

"Moses, the Irish are a miserable people. A landmark, a literary
property that's impossible to duplicate, and they molest the place. It's
a shell of a house . . . but it still exists."

So Isaac borrowed a sweater from the dean, and they went about the city. Moses had his jet lag. He couldn't remember buildings, monuments, and stores except a MacDonald's hamburger joint. Trinity College was only an old wall that bent around a street. They crossed the Liffey at O'Connell Bridge. Joyce could have his river and his quays. The currents seemed pissy to Isaac. Then it was O'Connell Street and the Gresham Hotel. "The Gresham's gone down," Marshall said. "They frisked us the last time we went for tea."

These mutterings made no sense to Isaac. His ears were freezing, but he wasn't going to buy a hat in August. It was a turn to the left and up another street, narrower, with a row of gray houses. Then a turn to the right, a high street again with broken signboards and pubs with blue walls that had begun to chip and peel. A jump to the left and they were on Eccles Street, in what had to be a bitten part of town, a much lesser Dublin than Stephen's Green. Marshall led him by the hand to Bloom's house. The roof had been lopped off. The windows were boarded. Weeds showed through the cracks in the wood. The front door was torn out and replaced with ribbons of tin. The cellar was overgrown with harsh, bending flowers that were beginning to stink. The steps had mostly turned to rubble. Marshall swayed in front of Bloom's ravaged house. He was a heavy man, with a thickness behind his ears. The dean was about to blubber. Isaac heard a dry, hacking sound.

"Poldy," he said, "Poldy Bloom . . . God save us from the Irish and ourselves. We don't deserve James Joyce."

The Irish could destroy Dublin for all Isaac cared, long as they held Dermott Bride. Eccles Street was like portions of the Bronx. Bombed-out territories and a few pubs. Marshall recovered himself. He wanted to drag Moses to a second landmark. A chemist's shop important to Bloom. Sylvia rescued Isaac. "Marsh, why don't you go? I'll take Isaac back to the hotel."

Marshall shrugged and kissed his wife, and he was gone from Eccles Street. Sylvia began to curse her husband. "Did you ever see such a big fat wobbly ass? . . . he was putting on a show for you."

"His crying in front of Bloom's house?"

"That's not it. He *always* cries."

Isaac looked at Mrs. Berkowitz. He was getting used to her sleepless eyes. Moses Herzog muttered to himself. He promised the worm he wouldn't cuckold Dean Berkowitz. Swear on Dermott's life.

Sylvia took him on another route. They didn't pass O'Connell Street. They were in a goddamn alley. Isaac couldn't have told you whether they'd crossed the Liffey or not. Sylvia's skirt was up. He had her against the roughened wall of some poorman's lane. He thought they'd get arrested on account of her screams. Sylvia could move against a wall like no other woman. She was wet, wet, wet, but Moses had no feeling in his prick. Was it the worm's doing? He'd have an operation, magical surgery that could cut that bastard out of him. Isaac had a revelation at the wall. He wasn't fucking Sylvia. Her hunger had nothing to do with him. Isaac had a terrible, crazy, killing need for Jennifer Pears. He hadn't even said goodbye to her. Just got on a plane. To avenge a whore with Dermott's mark on her. Bouncing into Sylvia cursed him with visions of Jennifer's body. Was it a kind of punishment? Moses' hell? Why couldn't he keep away from other men's wives?

Marsh was at the Shelbourne, drinking cider with lemon peel, when Sylvia brought him in. The dean should have been in a darker mood. Isaac had Sylvia's smell all over his pants. A school of Dublin orphans could have sensed they'd been out fucking in the streets. But the dean had come back from his landmark, and he wouldn't chastise his wife. "Moses, guess who's living here at the Shelbourne with us?"

"Who?"

"Dermott McBride."

Isaac was prepared to kill. A dean of freshman had more avenues to King Dermott than the First Deputy of New York.

"Marsh, how did you get to know little Dermott?"

"Are you crazy? You're the one who introduced him to me."

"I led you to Dermott?" Isaac said.

"He couldn't have gotten into Columbia without your vote."

"I thought Dermott went to Yale."

"He did. He left us after one semester . . . like you."

Isaac scratched his ear. "I interviewed so many lads for Columbia. I can't remember them all."

"Dermott had a miserable record . . . but you were so fierce about him. And you were right . . . never met a boy who could plunge into *Ulysses* like that. Dermott had the gift. But he's Irish, of course. And now he's a millionaire. Has a whole wing at the hotel, a wing for himself."

"And six bodyguards," Sylvia Berkowitz said.

"Where's that wing of his?" Isaac asked.

"East of the elevator. On the fifth floor."

Isaac excused himself. He strolled up to the fifth floor. The Shelbourne had royal banisters and rugs, with gold leaning posts on the rails. Fuck the costs. He would park at no other hotel in Dublin town. The fifth floor was full of little wings. Isaac couldn't tell east from west. He recognized a man standing behind a closed fire door. It was a retired cop, Timothy Snell, who had once been a sergeant with the Chief Inspector's office. He went up to the old sergeant. Snell didn't open that fire door for Isaac. The First Dep had to mumble through the glass.

"Tim, do me a favor. Tell the king I'd like a word with him."

Old Timothy was playing deaf. "Isaac, what king is that? All the kings I know are dead."

Isaac spoke Dermott's name into the fire door.

"Dermott isn't expecting any guests. But if he wants you, we'll knock on your door."

"Timmy, who told him I was staying here?"

"Nobody. We bribed a porter. And we figured Mr. Moses Herzog of New York City had to be Isaac Sidel . . . "

"He knew I was coming, didn't he?"

"Not at all."

Isaac skulked down to his room. He did have a knock on his door. Close to midnight. It was Sylvia Berkowitz, wearing a raincoat with nothing underneath.

"Where's Marsh?"

"Asleep," she said.

"What if he wakes up? He won't think you're with Dermott. He'll come to my room. I don't know how Marsh will take to having three in a bed."

"He'd never notice. And he won't wake up. He likes his dreams too much . . ."

"Does he dream of Number Seven Eccles Street?"

"No," she said. "He dreams of fucking his wife."

The Berkowitzes were too profound for him. It was much easier to lie on his bed with Sylvia. She left her raincoat on. She nibbled Isaac a bit and then climbed on top of him. She writhed with a fury, and Isaac felt like some wooden soldier with a great toy prick that could be sucked on and used as a hilt. She wasn't oblivious to him.

She fondled his bald spot, kissed him with devotion, but he couldn't keep up with that hunger she had. He was thinking of his daughter, her many marriages, her wildness for men. And Jennifer Pears? Was her good husband going down on her this minute? Or was Dublin time confusing him? Sylvia's writhing stopped. She fell asleep on Isaac's shoulder. Women, crazy women, were soaking his head. He dreamt of Annie's scar. The scar had moved to her belly in Isaac's dream. She had an "S" on her, for Sidel. The "S" began to wiggle. Isaac woke up, his legs kicking out in some kind of panic. Sylvia wasn't there.

ELEVEN

He had breakfast with the Berkowitzes in the Shelbourne's Saddle Room. The Dean had kippers, bacon, haddock, eggs, one of Isaac's sausages, most of Sylvia's ham. Sylvia bumped Isaac under the table with both her knees. Isaac had to beg the waiters for toasted whole wheat bread. They weren't impolite. "Sorry, sir, brown bread doesn't toast easily." He was beginning to wonder if the king took his breakfast in his rooms. Then, at half nine, while Marshall was stealing scraps from Sylvia's plate, Dermott came down to eat with his bodyguards. They occupied four tables. You couldn't mistake the king. It was Dermott and six retired New York cops. The calm on Whores' Row began to make sense for Isaac. Dermott had his own rabbis in the Department. He couldn't have kept the nigger gangs from warring with each other over all that revenue unless Dermott had some fat cop in his sleeve.

His vassals ate like pigs around him. Dermott had coffee and white toast. He was a dark and handsome man. He couldn't have been over thirty-five. He had a stronger chin than Isaac. And no bald spot. His hair was black as Moses. It had a lovely sheen in the Saddle Room. But it wasn't marks of physical beauty that bit at Isaac. Dermott was a thinking man. You could see the grooves and gutters in his brow. His eyes had more clarity than those six vassals who ate with him. That was Dermott's power to attract. And he didn't have a worm to give him shunken cheeks.

The First Dep could feel some pressure on his arm.

"Moses, can I have that sausage if you're not going to finish it?"

"Absolutely," Isaac said. "And I'm not Moses anymore. Half of Dublin knows I'm here."

Dermott got up from the table. His vassals had to leave their kippers because of him. He nodded once to Marshall and his wife, but he had nothing for his old sponsor, Isaac Sidel. The First Dep was grateful that the Berkowitzes were going on a trip to the outskirts of Dublin for the morning at least. Howth Castle and Sandycove. Isaac begged to God that Marsh and his wife would lose themselves somewhere. The First Dep needed time to stalk, to fix Dermott's hours in his head, find a schedule, so that he would know when to leap, and he couldn't do anything with Sylvia pulling on his pants.

But he had a hard time looking for weak spots in Dermott. The king kept to his rooms. The vassals had a porter bring up his lunch. About four in the afternoon he went down to eat his tea. The king's party occupied a little nest of chairs in a corner of the lounge that was furthest from the windows. Was someone other than Isaac after the king? At five he went out for a walk in St. Stephen's Green. It wasn't much of a stroll. He kept to the gazebo on the near side of the pond. He was back at the hotel by five-fifteen. At eight he went out again. It was to a little Chinese restaurant on Merrion Row, the Red Ruby, a block and a half from his hotel. He was up in his wing at the Shelbourne before nine. An Irish Cinderella. Did his vassals tuck him in?

Isaac had his first bit of luck. The Berkowitzes were stranded in Sandycove. He could follow Dermott unmolested for a second day. The king's schedule didn't vary very much. Breakfast at the Saddle Room. Lunch upstairs. Tea. A stroll near the pond. Dinner at the Red Ruby. And good night.

How could Isaac get to him, and where? He couldn't make it out of Dublin in less than a week. The Berkowitzes came back. Sylvia would have drifted into Isaac's room without her underpants if the First Dep hadn't taken to the streets on that third day. The girls weren't pretty. They had freckles everywhere and their waists weren't high enough to please him. He was crazy about long-legged girls. The men seemed to have a dumb look around the eyes and a grimness in their cheeks. A nation of halfwits. Isaac wasn't fair. He had mingled with too many American Irish. He couldn't get along with them. His marriage to Kathleen had been twenty years of strife. The Irish were crazy, in Dublin and New York.

He rumbled back to the Shelbourne and sat in the lounge, where he saw an Irish beauty. She must have been a blueblooded wench. She didn't have much of a brogue. Was she one of the Anglo-Irish who had ruled Dublin for centuries? She was with a perfectly tailored man about Isaac's age. They drank white coffee and muttered things that escaped the First Dep. They could talk without moving their lips, these Anglo-Irish. The woman had a long face and hot green eyes. She never looked at Isaac. The First Dep felt shabby in his clothes. He had no miracle tailor. And it wouldn't have mattered. The best of coats would have wrinkled on his body. The worm was quiet. Isaac trudged upstairs.

He couldn't sleep. He was going to get through that fire door hours before breakfast and squeeze Dermott Bride. Six vassals? Isaac would take them one by one. His only weapon was a hairbrush with a powerful handle and a hard black spine. If he smacked you between the eyes with it, Isaac could put you to sleep. He hid from the porters going up and coming down the stairs. He got to Dermott's floor. He could tell east from west tonight. He didn't see any vassals behind the fire door fronting Dermott's wing. He smuggled his way in. Six hands must have grabbed at him from different rooms. Isaac was sitting on his ass. Old Tim Snell wasn't laughing at him. "Laddie, it's an odd vacation for you . . . did you come with blessings from Mayor Sam? We hear that dunce is in the hospital. Is it money you want from Dermott? We ain't poor, but tell us why we should give a penny to you?"

"Dermott can keep his whores' gelt. There are enough fingers in the pie. I'd like to ask him about Annie Powell."

Old Tim crouched next to Isaac. "Oh, you're the world in New York City, Isaac, me dear, but you couldn't sell a fart in Dublin. If you ever say 'Annie' to Dermott, you'll have yourself the grandest Irish funeral. We'll give you something to remember for a long time."

"Thanks, Timmy, but I'm curious why Dermott leaves his signature on a girl's face and then hires a thug to wipe it off."

All six hands grabbed at Isaac and pitched him through the fire door. "Isaac, it would be a pity if we had to throw you out of a window . . . we're respected in this hotel. Have your vacation, and don't you bother us."

Sylvia was under Isaac's covers when he returned to his room. He didn't fight her off. Those six hands on Isaac must have livened him. His passion surprised the girl. Isaac licked all her parts. But it was Jennifer's nipples he was feeling in his mouth. The king must have put a spell on him, else the worm was doing its work. Fifty-one years old, and the schmuck was falling in love. Sylvia took his passion, but she wasn't Isaac's fool.

"You're worse than Marsh, do you know that? I come here to punish myself. It's just like a whipping. I'd walk out on that dope, but he'd wear the same underpants for a month if I didn't strip them off his ass. So I have to keep myself happy with the likes of you. Isaac, you're the shittiest lay I've ever had. You know what your cock feels like inside me? . . . a little boy's finger with some jelly on it . . . why are you in Dublin?"

He wasn't going to trifle with her after such appraisals. "I'm here to kill Dermott Bride."

"Moses, you really are a little nuts." But she had softened to him. "Why's it so important to you that Marshall's little scholar be dead?"

"Because the prick happened to torture a woman I like."

"My God," Sylvia said, "you are a human being." And she didn't seem so dark around the eyes. "Moses, who was she . . . this woman of yours?"

"A hooker on Forty-third Street. King Dermott put her there . . ."

Sylvia jumped on top of Isaac. "I'll help you kill the bastard, I swear . . . we won't tell Marsh . . . Marsh's a chickenshit . . . I'll go up to Dermott in my raincoat . . . get him to visit me in your room . . . we'll club him with a pair of lamps . . . hide him under the bed . . . how will we get rid of the body?"

Murder drew her close to Isaac. She was caressing him with wild strokes of her hand. Sylvia discovered a cock on him. The First Dep didn't have a little boy's finger poking out of his groin. Off the wall, Isaac figured to himself, but her comradeship, her willingness to take on Dermott, touched him, and he was much more tender to Marshall's wife.

TWELVE

Sylvia Berkowitz had become the nightwalker of the Shelbourne Hotel. She traveled abroad, in and out of her husband's room, whenever she pleased. The porters had gotten use to her. She was an American lady. The professor's wife. They would nod to her, taking in the bare knees under her raincoat. *Did you look at the pins on her?*

Lovely piece, that. But they weren't disrespectful of Sylvia. "Good night, madam," they would say, each time she passed them in the halls. They knew she was going to her husband from Mr. Moses Herzog's bed. *A ladykiller he is. The man in 411. Mr. Herzog of New York.*

Sylvia was born a Mandel, one of *the* Mandels of Yonkers, Miami and Hurricane Beach, men's clothiers for thirty-seven years. The Mandels could have found a dentist for Sylvia, a Jewish heart and lung man, a widowed accountant, or the scion of another clothing chain. They had the clout to buy any husband that appealed to them. They wanted something more exotic than a lung specialist. They had to have a scholar in the family, a secular rabbi, a man of words. They grabbed onto Marshall Berkowitz. They didn't worry about his field of interest. James Joyce? A blind Irishman who wrote filthy books. They could forgive such aberrations in a scholar. Even two earlier wives.

The family would assume Marshall's debts, and alimony payments if only Sylvia agreed to marry him. They expected trouble from her. Sylvia had an independent streak. Her full, brazen calves spelled lasciviousness to the Mandels. She'd pick an Arab tuba player to spite them, and they'd have to support a cove of tiny Ishmaels. They were wrong. Sylvia didn't have to be coaxed. Marshall wooed her with maps of Dublin, quotes from a cosmology that he stored in his head. Dublin was a fogtown that sprang out of James Joyce. This man-god could create rivers and streets. The Liffey and Fumbally Lane. Sylvia believed in him.

They were married under a canopy in the chapel of a Yonkers catering hall. A cantor sang the wedding prayers. Marshall wore the *kittel,* a white marriage shroud. Sylvia drank under her veil. She had to walk around the groom seven times to show that he was the center of her universe. The rabbi read the articles of their devotion. Sylvia took off the veil. Marshall broke a wine glass under his foot. They kissed. The family pelted them with bits of wheat and straw. They were ushered into a private room. Sylvia had her period. They weren't allowed to make love.

That was her history with Marsh. Menstrual blood and Leopold Bloom. She'd had four years of it. Excursions to Dublin that were holy pilgrimages. Marsh had little energy outside his books. He could raise up a passion for Molly Bloom. But he copulated like a baby boy. Bubbles appeared in his mouth. He would snort after a minute, suck in his belly, and go to sleep.

She couldn't sing to the Mandels. Hadn't she walked around Marsh seven times? They wouldn't listen to the complaints of a wife. God, was she supposed to say, Marshall, Marshall, why won't you chew my tits? She had to take scraps of love wherever she could find them. From Marshall's colleagues. A lonely sculptor at a Beethoven festival. The man from the stationery store. And Isaac.

She was committed to none of them, sculptor, stationery man, or cop. But she did have a feeling for this Moses. Something had eaten the fat out of him. Moses had more character than her other men. There were pieces of chivalry in Isaac Sidel. He didn't peek at women's garters, like Leopold Bloom. Or parade in Nighttown, near the Liffey, with his pants unfurled. He was the kind of man who could kill Dermott Bride for having mistreated a hooker in New York. He wouldn't bawl over a dead house on Eccles Street and shake his big fat ass. Moses had work to do. He was no better than Marsh when it came to chewing her tits. His orgasms seemed to rumble out of him like a bit of dry puke. But she forgave his pathetic courtship. Moses didn't get his Nighttown out of any book. He was in love with a Forty-second Street whore.

So she voyaged through the Shelbourne with a raincoat around her shoulders. Porters were carrying up trays of white coffee and toast. The Irish preferred to rise at six. "Would the madam like her breakfast in bed?"

"Thank you, no."

She might wake the dean, spreading marmalade on her toast. She crept back to Marsh's room, dropped the raincoat on the floor. Marsh was clutching the blanket with his fists. This was the man who wore a shroud at her wedding, who broke a glass under his foot. She opened one fist with gentle pulls on his fingers, got under the covers, closed his fist again, and hugged him around the waist, her Poldy, her Leopold, her Bloohoohoom.

THIRTEEN

Isaac maundered in Dublin. He had nothing to do. He couldn't isolate Dermott from his vassals. Killing the king had become pure whim. Little Dermott was safe in Dublin town. But Isaac wouldn't go home. His students at John Jay would have to suffer without his lectures for a while. He began to follow Dermott's narrow routes, in order to put himself inside the king's head. So he ate at the Red Ruby on Merrion Row, an hour before Dermott was scheduled to arrive. Isaac had his lo mein, a spring roll, and Chinese chicken soup. He imagined Dermott at the table, with chopsticks and hot mustard, his vassals eating with forks. Wasn't there another restaurant in Dublin that would have the boy? Did Dermott need that lo mein a block from the hotel? He had peculiar territories for a king.

Isaac would duplicate Dermott's walk in St. Stephen's park, inhabit Dermott step by step. What did the king look at from his gazebo? The slow, meticulous paddling of the ducks? The way they poked their mouths into the water? Did he notice the scum, leaves, and bottles at the northern end of the pond? The thick green bowls of the trees? And did he stare up at the roofs of the Shelbourne from the park? The iron grilles, the great television aerial, the nude flagpole, dormer windows, the fine white molding, the four weather vanes? A few hundred yards in front of the Shelbourne. Is that where Dublin ended for Dermott Bride?

Isaac had his room changed. The porters moved him to the front of the hotel. *I want to see what Dermott sees.* He would stare out his window at St. Stephen's, at the houses near his corner of the park, with their pitched roofs, the traffic, the hills outside Dublin, and then go to the lounge. Funny people were sitting there. Rowdies with broken noses. They drank jars of Guinness and wore helmets that looked like housepainters' hats, only these helmets came with chin straps. Isaac couldn't understand why the porters didn't throw them out. But the lounge seemed to be in awe of them. Men and women came over from the other tables to shake their hands. Isaac was dumbfounded until a porter told him that tomorrow was All-Ireland hurling day. These were the champions. Hurlers from Cork. What the fuck was hurling about? A game with sticks called hurleys and a leather puck. Ireland's national sport. Sixty thousand would rush to the hills of Croke Park for the final game between Wexford and Cork. Rougher than football, the porter said. Break your mouth with one of those hurling sticks. Isaac wished he had a hurley in his hand to come at Dermott's vassals. He'd win for Ireland and the United States. Use Dermott's scalp for a puck. Roll that head in the grass. He'd be the master hurler, "man of the match." All the Irish bishops would be at Croke Park. Isaac might get canonized. They'd give him the Rock of Cashel to take home with him to America . . .

The First Dep was out of his skull. These men in their painters'
hats wouldn't have served on any team with him. Isaac gave the
lounge to them, the champions from Cork. He decided to walk the
Liffey. He didn't need *Ulysses* as a primary text. He could have his
Dublin without Mr. Joyce. Marshall was the haunted one. Not him.
He wasn't going to court the river goddess, Anna Livia. He'd leave
that to the Irish. But the river seemed fiercer today, much less of a
pissy stream. The sun burnt down on the water, colored it red, like a
king's beard.

He'd entered a section of warehouses on the quays. A poorer
Dublin again. Dog carts and little grocery stores. Children lunged at
his pants. They had dirty faces and torn sleeves. Isaac didn't know
what they expected from him. They were trained beggars from some
gypsy camp north of Dublin. He gave them all his Irish pennies. They
still lunged at him. An old man had to chase them away with a stick,
or they would have followed Isaac inside his pants. He was at Sir
John Rogerson's Quay. Lime Street and Misery Hill. A huge black
sedan was just behind him, trundling at Isaac's pace. Isaac stopped
and started again. He wasn't going to give the car an easy time of it.
Let the bitches stall on Sir John's Quay. The dog carts could drive
them back to O'Connell Street. The car rumbled up close. A door
opened for him. The First Dep was hauled in like a stinking fish out
of the Liffey. He was sitting on Timothy Snell's lap. "Dumb fuck."
There's only two choices, Isaac figured; they'll take me to Dermott,
or kill me in an alley off the quays. The car moved into a blind, dead
street. Moses the apostate had no prayers to mutter. Would they push
him down on his knees? Isaac should have stuck to the Shelbourne,
like the king.

He was still a puppet on Timothy's lap. Couldn't they give a
man a little more room? Old Tim slapped him on the head. "Dermott
is offering twenty thousand . . . he won't go any higher than that.
You're a nuisance, but he can always dig around you."

Twenty thousand? What were they talking about? Timothy
slapped him again. "Isaac, the lad has made you an offer."

Isaac's head was whistling. He didn't mind the slaps, but they
must have scared the worm. His gut squeezed horribly tight. He could
have fallen off Tim's lap, the way the worm grabbed at him.

"Eat your twenty thousand," Isaac said, swearing his belly
would explode and drop his entrails on Timothy's shoe. "Tell the
king my trip was all about Annie."

Old Tim pushed him off his lap. Isaac huddled near the door. He realized now that Dermott didn't care to have him dead. They drove him back to the Shelbourne, and picked him out of the car. The doorman smiled at Tim.

"He's a bit soused," Timothy said. "One jar too many."

The doorman helped Isaac into the hotel.

PART THREE

FOURTEEN

Tiger John Rathgar became the forgotten man at his club. There were peculiar goings-on inside the Dingle. Irishmen appeared and disappeared without so much as a whisper to the PC. Some of them were lads from the Retired Sergeants Association who had sworn themselves to Chief Inspector McNeill. They wore derbies instead of eight-piece caps. McNeill had swallowed them up. John couldn't get a word out of the boyos. They wouldn't sing in his presence. Those wild geese, retired sergeants and Sons of Dingle Bay, had old boarding passes in their vest pockets. They shuttled between Ireland and Americky without telling John.

He was reduced to a ceremonial piece, with his handsome profile and straw hair. He would arrive at the funeral of a slain cop, hug the widow, give his hellos to the padre. He would hang ribbons on female detectives who had fired their guns at some nigger thief. He would shake his jaw and pronounce statistics of doom at the closing of a precinct.

Otherwise he was at his club, sitting in a corner with bankbooks in his pocket. He knew the names by heart. *Gertrude MacDowell. Nosey Flynn. Molly and/or Leopold Bloom* . . . Where was Jamey O'Toole that would show up at the Mayor's house with a bankbook for John? Should he cry to Dennis Mangen, the Special State Pros? *Dennis, find me this O'Toole. I'm lonely for the names in a little book.* Why were his brothers at the Dingle so secretive? Were they frightened of the great god Dennis? Couldn't they come to John? He was their headman, the *first* Son, and the Commissioner of Police.

FIFTEEN

Moses Herzog arrived at Kennedy. He tore his passport to bits. A king and a worm had broken the First Dep. He got out of Dublin with his tail in his ass.

Isaac hid out at his hotel. Phone calls were coming in from his office. Isaac went down to Centre Street, where he could sit in the dark, listen to the scurry of the rats. The cops on duty at the old Headquarters were genuflecting to him. Why? They'd never missed him before. They had a certain terror in their eyes, an awe of him. A miracle passed while Isaac was in Dublin doing futile work. Mayor Sam had won the primary from his hospital bed. He'd smacked Rebecca between the eyes. The Irish came out for Becky Karp, but the "blues" and the Yids went for Mayor Sam Isaac was lord of the primaries. He'd gathered in the votes for Sam with his talks in the synagogues, his lectures in the clubs. The Dublin idiot, Isaac Sidel, owned New York City.

"Hizzoner" was recuperating inside Gracie Mansion. He'd been asking for Isaac. "Where's the lad?" The First Dep had to rush uptown. It was a madhouse near the old Mayor. The deputies who had deserted Sam months ago crowded the master bedroom. They would have gotten into bed with Sam, under the big chandelier. "Hizzoner" had to drive them away. He was much less senile after the primaries. "Isaac, they laugh at us in Chicago. We deserve a better Commissioner of Police. I'm making you the new PC."

A year ago you couldn't have separated Tiger John and Sam. "Hizzoner" wanted a PC that he could wrap around his-thumb. But John had become a hindrance to him. John was an unpopular "Commish." John might lose City Hall for Mayor Sam.

"Your Honor, I won't sit at Headquarters like a loyal mole. Thank you, I'll stay where I am."

"Isaac, you're not a baby anymore. You can't keep wandering around in old suits."

Isaac would avoid Gracie Mansion until winter came. "Hizzoner" had a habit of forgetfulness. The First Dep would creep out of Sam's head in a day or two. Let those rebels who had gone over to Becky find a new Commissioner for Mayor Sam.

Isaac was coming out of his Dublin sloth. He went to Roosevelt Hospital to see Annie Powell. Annie wasn't on the hospital's lists. "What the hell do you mean?" Isaac growled. "She was here two weeks ago with a broken face." The residents, the nurses, and the guards couldn't keep Isaac from going through the hospital. Annie wasn't in the wards. She wasn't in a private bed. "Christ, do sick girls vanish from these fucking rooms?"

A doctor located her discharge slip. "Annie Powell walked out of here."

"When?"

"Last week . . . she got her skirt from the closet and disappeared."

"I suppose that happens all the time," Isaac said. "Losing a girl like that. You didn't have anybody to stop her?"

"We don't run a prison, Commissioner Sidel . . . we can't lock people to their beds."

She was at her whore's station on Forty-third Street, mad-eyed, bruised, with Dermott's mark annihilated from her, that "D" covered over with crisscrossing welts and blue lines. She didn't recognize Isaac without his bum's pants. "Mister, what are you staring at? . . . if you don't like the goods, you can crawl up or down a few more blocks."

"Annie," he said, "I'm Father Isaac."

Those mad eyes whirled in her head. "Keep away from me . . . I don't know any Father Isaac."

"Annie . . ."

Her shoulders began to heave with a terrifying rhythm. Isaac had set her off. She was leering at him with froth in her mouth. "The champagne boy . . . wanna buy some pussy?" She pulled her skirt up to her belly. Annie had forgotten her underpants. Tourists and dudes were blinking at her. A plainclothesman ran over from an Irish bar. Isaac kept him from Annie. "Go back to your whiskey house . . . I'm Isaac Sidel. I'll handle the girl."

Annie lowered her skirt the minute Isaac walked away. She muttered to herself. Anybody could have heard the clacking of her teeth. God knows where she would find any johns. Isaac phoned his office from a booth on Ninth Avenue. "Annie Powell," he said. "She's doing the shimmy on Forty-third. I want two kids to watch her day and night . . . hold her hand if they have to . . . she could hurt herself."

He couldn't put on his stinking pants. He wasn't in the mood to be Isaac the bum, with black shit on his face. Would Annie show her crotch to the universe every time he came near her corner? Isaac went looking for the king's muscleman, Jamey O'Toole.

O'Toole had stepped on Annie, and somebody had to pay. It wasn't Dublin, where Isaac had to sneak around with a hairbrush as his only weapon. He brought six detectives with him to Jamey's apartment house. O'Toole lived in Chelsea with a thick metal plate on his door to discourage burglars, thieves, and cops like Isaac. It was two in the morning. Isaac hadn't come unprepared. His men had shotguns, crowbars, and a sledgehammer.

He didn't knock on Jamey's door. The crowbars bit under the metal plate. The sledgehammer demolished every hinge. The door gave with a scream that nearly sounded human. Isaac wouldn't murder Jamey in his own house, God forbid. But if O'Toole was dumb enough to throw himself at six detectives, Isaac couldn't swear what would happen. A shotgun might go off. And Isaac would have a lot of paperwork. He'd build a good story. Rogue cop, Jamey O'Toole, dies resisting arrest.

Isaac didn't crouch in back of his men. He was the first to climb over Jamey's door.

"O'Toole, come on out . . . it's only Isaac."

Someone was crying in there. It wasn't O'Toole. Isaac and his men trampled into all the rooms. The sobbing didn't go away. They searched the closets next. Isaac found only an old woman sitting behind a pile of brooms. They began to mock her, Isaac's men. "Look at that. Jamey's hiding one of his aunts."

"Shut up," Isaac said.

The men who'd watched that fucking house for Isaac didn't even know Jamey had a mother. Isaac brought her out of the closet. He sat her in the kitchen with a glass of water. He let her drink before he questioned her. He cursed himself for the shotguns and the big hammer. All he'd accomplished was to frighten an old woman. "Mrs. O'Toole, could you help us, please? Where's that son of yours?"

She couldn't say. "He told me the cops was after him."

"Which cops?"

Mrs. O'Toole shrugged at Isaac.

"How long's he been gone?"

She counted on her fingers. "Thirteen days."

What cops could be after Jamey? Isaac's own men hadn't been chasing the big dunce. O'Toole ran from home while Isaac was in Dublin with the king. Why? Irishmen didn't abandon their mothers.

What kind of trouble was the lad in? It's hard to scare a donkey who's six feet seven.

Isaac left the kitchen. His men got in place behind him. They began to sicken Isaac. O'Toole's neighbors peeked out of cracks of light in their doors. The detectives looked ridiculous lugging shotguns and crowbars in shopping bags. But they had their badges pinned to their chests. "Police," they muttered, "police," and the neighbors closed their doors. It was Isaac who should have calmed the neighbors, if only to cover himself. But those shopping bags tore at Isaac's guts. The creature was stirring again. Isaac's personal "angel," Manfred Coen, used to carry his shotgun inside a shopping bag. He was a blue-eyed detective from the Bronx. Isaac appreciated a sad, beautiful, inarticulate boy around him. Blue Eyes. He was loyal to Isaac, and Isaac got him killed. The First Dep pushed Coen into his war with the Guzmanns. Coen didn't have the cleverness to stay alive. Isaac destroyed the Guzmanns, but his trophies were pretty irregular: a live, live worm and a dead Coen.

SIXTEEN

His mind must have gone to rot. He didn't understand the street anymore. He lived among pimps and dudes, but couldn't get a word out of them. The "players" had been organizing in the past two years. They weren't so vulnerable to the pussy patrol that Tiger John sent down on them. None of the "brides" would inform on her man. But the "players" were careful not to beat up on a girl. They'd come under the tutelage of Arthur Greer. Sweet Arthur didn't belong to the brotherhood of pimps. He had no need for a wide-brimmed hat. He acted as a kind of magistrate for most Manhattan dudes. If a quarrel developed between pimps, they took it to Arthur. Arthur decided who was right and who was wrong. He was better than a bail bondsman. He always gave you walking money for any "bride" who got into trouble.

What was his real profession? He owned boutiques, nightclubs, massage parlors, grocery stores, and a cab company. Arthur could afford to snub the Taxi Commission. He gave out his own "medallions" to all his gypsy cabs. They had meters and windows in their roofs. The "players" wouldn't ride in any other cab.

The cops knew all about Sweet Arthur. They decided to leave

him alone. Arthur held tight to his various enterprises and policed them by himself. He was something of a loanshark, but he wouldn't touch any shit. No one bought dope in Arthur's cabs. He warned the pimps to clean their stables of contaminated girls. Junkie whores were cast out of Arthur's zones. They had to operate in the pigsties of Brooklyn.

Arthur had a few comrades under him. It was a family of sorts, a loose confederacy. Killers, bondsmen, pornographers, loansharks, and head pimps. Such were the "blues" of Sugar Hill. But there wasn't much of a Sugar Hill anymore. It was only a name, a manner of describing a certain sweetness among rich black thieves. They lived in co-ops throughout Manhattan and Queens. Arthur had a penthouse near Lincoln Center, whose windows took in half the cliffs of Jersey. Assemblymen showed up for dinner. Judges talked to Arthur at his penthouse. Actresses walked into his boutiques. So it wasn't much of an honor when the First Deputy came to his door.

Isaac had no one else. Whatever black Mafia there was began with Arthur Greer. The pimps hadn't given any of their secrets to Isaac the bum. Black and white hookers shuttled in and out of jail. Money was collected. The king sat in his Dublin hotel. Isaac couldn't put a dent into the traffic on Whores' Row.

Who were the lords of New York City? It was hard to tell. Sam won his primary. But mayors went cheap this year. His own clerks copied his signature behind the Mayor's back. Tiger John Rathgar, Commissioner of Police, prowled the fourteenth floor at Headquarters and bullied cops who got in his way. He could demote you, give you some graveyard for a beat. He terrorized the whole Department, Tiger John. But he couldn't have told you where any of his squads were placed. He didn't have a cop's sense of New York. Arthur Greer probably had more information about Tiger's squads than Tiger did.

"How's my man?" he said to Isaac. Sweet Arthur had a sensitive face. He'd come out of the Bronx, the leader of a notorious gang, the Clay Avenue Devils. You could see the scars along his lips. Who knows how many times he fought with a knife? But he wouldn't take on Isaac, scowl for scowl.

"I hear you've been on the stroll, Mr. Isaac. Wearing funny pants and living at a pimp's hotel. Why'd you wait so long to come to me? I can give you clues about the business. Would you like your own stable of girls? Then you can tell your class at the Police

Academy all about the grubby life of a pimp."

"Arthur, your spies are sleeping on you. I teach at John Jay."

"One school's good as another," Arthur said, and he smiled.

"What happened to Jamey O'Toole? His mother says he's hiding from the cops. But I can't figure that one. Jamey doesn't have the smarts to hide from me."

"You can't always believe what a mother says, Mr. Isaac. Maybe he got disgusted swiping pennies from whores and pimps, and he disappeared with a money bag under his arm."

"Not Jamey. He's a loyal son of a bitch."

"Maybe he eloped with Annie Powell."

A rage was gathering in Isaac. He wanted to send Arthur out into the Jersey cliffs.

"What's Annie to you?"

"Nothing. She's out there with all the other dogs. Don't look so sad. I'm tickling you, baby. Everybody knows you're sweet on that girl."

"We were talking about O'Toole."

"That's it, Mr. Isaac. Jamey's sweet on her too."

"Then why did he bang her in the face?"

Arthur laughed. "You ever meet an Irishman who wasn't a little crazy."

"And Dermott? Would you call Dermott crazy?"

"Man, he's the craziest of them all."

"Is the king a friend of yours?"

Arthur shook his head in disgust. "No wonder you got stuck in that pig hotel. You must be on the slide. Me and Dermott ran together. We were in the same gang."

Once upon a time Isaac was familiar with every boys' gang in the Bronx. He was the cop who kept the peace. He didn't have to work with the youth patrol. Isaac would walk into any cellar to settle a dispute. The Devils of Clay Avenue owned huge chunks of the Bronx. Their territories took them from Castle Hill to Claremont Park. They were successful because they wouldn't fight along racial lines. Sweet Arthur welcomed Negroes, Italians, Irishers, and Jews into his gang.

"Shit," Isaac said. "You mean Dermott was one of yours?"

"The best I had. My minister of war."

"Then why can't I remember him?"

"Dermott, he didn't like to stick out. He was smart, man. I got

most of the glory and the cuts in my cheek. Dermott moved away
from us. He went to college without a mark on him."

"Who made Dermott such a king?"

"I did."

"But you said he didn't fight. Dermott doesn't have the
scars . . ."

"But he talks like a king. You ever listen to Dermott? He could
swipe your beard with five words."

"I don't have a beard," Isaac said.

"So what. He'd make you believe you had one, and then he'd
cop it from you. That's why he was minister of war. We battled it out
with those other gangs right at the table. They didn't have any
crooners on their side. We had Dermott. The king would trade them
blind. Maybe I'd back him up with my knife . . . and maybe not. It
depended on how much Dermott could steal with his tongue."

"Strange," Isaac said. "I saw the king in Dublin. He didn't open
his mouth once. Arthur, what's he doing at the Shelbourne Hotel?"

"Living with his ancestors. The king's got Irish blood."

"What happened between Annie and him?"

"They had a love spat," Arthur said. He couldn't stop smiling at
Isaac. The First Dep was forlorn. He'd lost his strength somewhere,
dropped it in the street the day he'd met Annie Powell. He'd never
shake loose of that girl. He went to kill a man for Annie. He would
have done the same to Arthur Greer.

"That mark on her came from a knife, didn't it?"

Isaac was muttering now.

"He put a perfect *D* on her. Dermott loved to croon, you said. A
talking man. How did he get to be so handy with a knife?"

"Ask the king. Maybe he did some practicing at college." The
smile on Arthur had already turned brittle. ". . . Isaac, I'm getting
busy. You'll have to go."

A white maid had come in to dust all the pillows. A boy left
with a grocery wagon. Isaac saw a plumber walking on his knees in
one of the toilets. Arthur had a functioning army to serve him, but he
didn't offer Isaac one small piece of cake.

Isaac had a touch of amnesia. He couldn't remember what his
next appointment was. Then his intuition caught hold: he had no
more appointments today. He'd grown invisible hiding in that
nameless hotel, and it was hard to get his coloring back. He'd thrown
himself into too many capers. Now he couldn't solve the riddle of his

own existence. Had Annie become Isaac's sphinx? Who was she? Why should Annie's mark have maimed him so?

He went up to Morningside Heights and visited that old school of his, Columbia College. Isaac didn't really have an Alma Mater. Only four months under Marshall Berkowitz. The school year was about to begin. Trunks were being carried into the dormitories. It gave Isaac a scare, reminded him of his own meager education. He shouldn't have stopped reading *Ulysses*.

He didn't wait on line with the other freshmen in the corridors of Hamilton Hall. Isaac crashed into Marshall's office. The dean of freshmen was annoyed with him.

"Isaac, I have a mob of kids outside. Couldn't you telephone?"

"No," Isaac said.

Marshall's desk was littered with folders pierced in every corner with a silver pin. The pins must have represented a kind of system to Marsh. He seemed much skinnier in New York. What had happened to that Dublin rump of his? His ass was gone. Was he still crying over Bloom's dismantled house? Isaac was a pragmatist. He couldn't mourn Number 7 Eccles Street. He had the living to contend with. Specific scars and the king.

"I want that recommendation I wrote for little Dermott."

Marshall trembled over the silver pins. "You see the condition of this place. I couldn't find it in a thousand years."

"Marsh, I'll help you look."

They stood over Marshall's filing cabinets and searched the drawers. Sheets of paper crumbled in Isaac's hand. Folders ripped at the edges. Students were knocking on the door. Marshall wouldn't open up. It took an hour to dig out Isaac's ancient memorandum. It was typed on Police stationery. Isaac had to glimpse at his own language before he could believe a word.

. . . Marshall, I know you're going to think this one is a sweet-faced hood. He wears saddlestitched pants. He has sideburns and a duck's ass. He's "Bronx" up to his eyebrows. I could identify the streets he walked on, the rocks he must have thrown into windows. But he has a head on him. The boy can think. It's saved him from those death-traps of Souhern Boulevard and Boston Road. Forget the shitty grades. High school must have been a bore from beginning to end. I don't know if *Silas Marner* put him to sleep. But talk to him about *Hamlet*. Dermott can tell you about hysteria, idiocy, and revenge. Don't let the kid get away. It would be a shame for Columbia to lose him.

"Isaac, I can Xerox that for you," Marshall said. The search through his files had gentled him.

"Thanks, Marsh, but that's okay. I won't forget it now . . ."

Marshall returned to his desk. He was staring at the walls, surrounded by folders and pins. Isaac came out of his reverie to notice Marsh's fish eyes, that dead abstracted look.

"What's wrong?"

"Sylvia's left me . . ."

Isaac didn't have to hear why Sylvia Berkowitz fled from *Ulysses* and *Finnegans Wake*. How long can you coexist with James Joyce under the blanket with you? But he couldn't utterly abandon Marsh. "How did it happen?"

"I don't know. She didn't take a thing with her . . . no panties. Not even her books."

It wasn't a hopeless case. Isaac had the resources to track a dean's missing wife. He could descend on 1 Police Plaza, the official home of the First Dep, and organize a search party. Isaac was famous for his ability to climb into the roots of any borough and come up with a handful of runaways.

"Marsh, I'll see what I can do."

The freshmen outside Marshall's office looked surly. Isaac couldn't blame them. They probably had to skip lunch on account of him. Isaac also remembered waiting for Marsh. The freshman with the bull neck. Isaac Sidel. He should have been champion of the wrestling team. Isaac was a devil at a hundred and forty-eight pounds. He'd gone out for wrestling because it was the one sport at college that suited his temperament. Football was for the grubs. You needed stamina, psychology, and strong, slippery arms to wrestle. And Isaac's neck. No one could pin Isaac when his neck was bridged on the mat. He would suck oranges before a match, stare at his opponent, and do warm-ups in his beautiful Columbia leggings. He traveled to Yale with the freshman team. The Yalie he wrestled was disqualified for gouging. It was the first and last Columbia win. He stopped going to practice. He didn't have the time. James Joyce had already bitten Isaac in the ass.

He couldn't get out from under Marshall's influence. He idolized the dean. Wrestling was nothing compared to the music of words. The team dropped Isaac Sidel. He had to give those beautiful leggings back to the college. Language was all. He was jealous of oher boys who occupied Marsh. He would catch the dean going in and out of his office. There was always some question to ask. "Why does Joyce say that an Irishman's home is his coffin?"

Had little Dermott behaved like that? Did he follow Marsh around, beg audiences with the dean? Goggle at him over cups of coffee? The romance was shortlived for both of them. Dermott went off to Yale, and Isaac disappeared from college. Were they still votaries of Marsh? Was Dermott writing songs about the Liffey from his hotel room? Is that all his exile meant? A crook returning to scholarship in his middle years? Isaac was the fool of fools. It was business, business, business that was holding the king. And Isaac was a man without a clue. He should have stayed an ordinary Police inspector. He didn't have much resiliency as the First Dep. When a cop falls, he isn't supposed to lie flat.

Marshall must have followed him across South Campus. He ran after Isaac with his tie trailing down the back of his neck. They were like two gaunt, hurt creatures chasing one another. "Isaac," the dean said. "Sylvia told me about you and her . . . she has a habit of confessing her love affairs. But she didn't have to tell. It makes sense. You were her Dublin beau."

"I'm sorry, Marsh . . . it happened. We were going downhill from Eccles Street. We landed in a deserted lane and . . ."

"Stop that. She would have gone after Dermott if you hadn't arrived . . . Isaac, please find her for me."

SEVENTEEN

Isaac thought and thought of Sylvia, and came to Jennifer Pears. He had his men shop for two women at a time. He wouldn't go near that ugly red fortress at 1 Police Plaza. He took a ride to Center Street and sat in his old rooms. He shouldn't have fucked his mentor's wife. Now he owed Marsh. His deputies were going gray in the head. Who were these two cunts that belonged to Isaac? Sylvia Berkowitz was on the loose. They didn't mind scrambling for her. But why did they have to shadow this Jennifer lady? Isaac demanded all her moves. The First Dep was reluctant to get Mrs. Pears on the phone. She might hang up on a prick like him. Isaac was a terrible suitor. He would snake in and out of a woman's life. No one could stand him for very long. He was an uncivilized boy, fifty-one years old.

His deputies had no "buys" on Sylvia Berkowitz. She must have shrunk into the ground, like that big Irish ape, O'Toole. Not the green-eyed one. Jennifer Pears was a piece of cake. Soon as she said goodbye to her doormen, Isaac's deputies had her under control. These weren't dummy cops. They knew how to fatten a page for Isaac. *Takes her boy to the Little Red Schoolhouse.* (They posed as fire chiefs to follow Jennifer inside.) *Plays with him up on the roof with his kindergarten class. She usually stays an hour. Then she goes to Fourth Avenue. The lady likes to buy old books. . .*

Isaac was religious about reading the reports. It gave him a feeling of power over Jenny. He had her moments at his command. He could intrude upon them whenever he liked. Bookstalls weren't for him. He went to the Little Red Schoolhouse on Christopher Street. He didn't have a fire chief's hat. He had to bluff his way past the bulldog lady who stared at him from a cubicle inside the door. Was she the school's concierge? Isaac had so many bumps in his forehead. He might have been a freak about to paw an innocent child. The concierge would have summoned the janitors to get rid of Isaac. But then he smiled, and the bumps went away.

"I'm Moses," he said. "Moses Herzog Pears. My grandnephew is in your kindergarten. Alexander Pears. I'm supposed to meet his mother on the roof. That's Jennifer, my niece . . . "

Isaac climbed up to the roof. It was a playpen fenced around with wire. It had enough material to confuse an army: wagons, sandboxes, tunnels, houses and bridges made of cardboard walls and cinder blocks. He couldn't locate Alex in the muddle of kids. Jennifer stood near the fence. Her green eyes could have sucked in every wagon, tunnel, and bridge. The creep was in love with her. He had crazy knots in his legs. The worm didn't give him any flak. It curled up in Isaac's belly, satisfied with itself.

Jennifer wasn't coy with him. She wouldn't crouch behind a tunnel because the schmuck had disappointed her, gone to Dublin to kill a man without any notice.

"You don't look happy," she said.

He wished her eyes had a more neutral color. Then he could have walked away from that roof without Jennifer Pears. He grunted the word *cappuccino.* Jenny understood. She couldn't leave at Isaac's first grunt. She had responsibilities to the kindergarten. But she met him downstairs in the Cafe Borgia.

Isaac's vocabulary was coming back. "Dublin . . . had to go . . . how's your husband Mel?"

"Isaac, what the fuck do you want from me?"

Sitting next to her terrified him. He licked the coffee with his head between his shoulders, like a snail.

"More sessions at your hotel, is that what you're after? . . . or are you on a culture kick? Isaac, should we take in the Cézanne show at the Modern? . . . do you want to feel me up inside a movie house? What's your pleasure today?"

Couldn't he borrow Dermott's magic tongue? The king would have known how to woo Jennifer Pears.

"I'm pregnant."

The worm beat against the lining of Isaac's gut with its many hooks. His face landed in the cappuccino mug. He came up with milk on his nose, a ridiculous man.

"You're a godsend, Isaac. We've been trying to have another baby for years. A brother or sister for Alex. You know, all that shit about an only child. Nothing happened until you came along . . . would you like a share of the baby? We could form a limited partnership. Put your request in. Would you prefer a girl or a boy? I'm banking on a girl. Should we allow her to pick her own dad? . . . Isaac, do me a favor. Don't visit me at my son's school. It isn't nice."

And she was gone from the Cafe Borgia before Isaac could wipe his nose with a paper napkin. Funny thing, he didn't feel like a patriarch. He had an itch in his testicles. His knees were dead. A worm tore his gut like shavings on a pipe. Was he going to be a daddy every twenty-nine years? He had a daughter who was crazy for men. Marilyn the Wild. She could twist Isaac harder than any worm the Guzmanns had stuck him with. What would Marilyn think of a new half-sister or brother?

Isaac ran out of the cafe. He could have had his men steal Jennifer from the bookstalls of Fourth Avenue, carry her to his hotel, wrapped in a body bag or an old blanket from the horse patrol. He wouldn't have undressed her, no, no, no. I'll take that partnership, he'd say. Half your belly is mine. Whatever lunacy he was into, he still had the eyes of a cop. A man was following him from the next corner. A man with scruffy white hair. Isaac had to laugh. It was a retired captain from precincts in the Bronx. Morton Schapiro. Who would put such a joker on the First Deputy's tail? Isaac led Morton down to Wooster Street and trapped him against the window of a deserted shoe factory. Morton had a Detective Special in his pants. Isaac stole the gun away and tossed it through the crack in the window.

"Morton, who's been hiring you to play Billy the Kid?"

"Nobody."

"Come on. Did Dermott holler in your ear all the way from Dublin?"

"Who's Dermott?" Morton said.

Isaac could have taken him into the factory and pulled on Morton's skull until the old captain lost his beautiful white hair. He'd scalped people before. But he didn't want blood on his fingernails. He was going to be a father again. He grabbed Morton by the collar and jerked his neck. The captain swayed like a large rotting pumpkin. It couldn't have been very serious if Isaac's enemies were hoping to glue Schapiro to him. The captain was no threat. He couldn't hold down a precinct while he was on the Force. The Chief Inspector would ship him from house to house. Schapiro was a "flying" captain, who would take over a precinct for a month and then push on. His lieutenants laughed in his face. The homicide squad wouldn't say hello to him in the hall. There were no parties for Captain Mort when the PC asked him to retire. Whatever job he had now was nothing but charity. Isaac could have choked him to death. But it would have been a bother to round up the guests for Morton's Jewish wake.

"Schapiro, talk to me. What pimp are you working for?"

"Arthur Greer."

"That's insane. Why would Arthur send you after me?"

"Dunno . . . he said stick to Isaac. That's all."

"Did he give you a message for me?"

It was a stupid question. Schapiro himself was the message. A fat kite. Isaac wasn't supposed to ask about Dermott anymore. Why? How often could the First Dep trot to Stephen's Green? Dublin wasn't behind the Jersey cliffs. You couldn't reach the Shelbourne by rowboat. The king was jittery about having Isaac in New York.

"Morton, be a good boy. Give Arthur a hug for me. Tell him Isaac doesn't like mysteries. The king can have his exile. But I intend to open him up."

He shoved the captain uptown. He would have liked to pitch him over the roofs of Houston Street, up to Lincoln Center and Arthur

Greer. That would have been a sensational kite. No matter. The captain would be in disgrace. He couldn't hold on to Isaac the Pure. Captain Mort should have been out looking for catfish in Eastchester Bay. What was he doing with a gun in his pants? Was there a society of old captains for sale? It didn't make sense. Who was organizing the other Captain Morts? Not Arthur Greer. Arthur didn't have the claws to dig that deep into the Department. Isaac would have known. He had his spies in the Commissioner's office. The First Dep could have broken up any ring of ex-captains that was lending itself out to pimps and crooks. Isaac wasn't asleep. He began to dial his office from a telephone booth. He'd put a fix on Morton Schapiro, find out what the old captain's been doing in the last year or so.

Isaac could have sworn he was in Dublin again. A drunken man and woman were having a mean little fight outside his telephone booth. Their slaps seemed pathetic to Isaac. They maintained a slow dance of arms and legs. Then the man got vicious. He had the woman by her hair. He shook her and shook her as Isaac came out of the booth. It was one of those freak encounters. He recognized the woman beneath the roots of her hair. The drunk was assaulting Marshall's wife. Had Sylvia found a second husband in the streets? Isaac tore the man's fingers out of her hair, dragged him into the booth, and closed the door on him.

"You have terrific friends, Mrs. Berkowitz."

Isaac was pissed at himself. Where was his squad of "angels" that was supposed to prowl for Sylvia? Why should *he* have stumbled upon her after leading Morton Schapiro on a little chase through Soho? Was some miserable tinkering god giving out gifts to Isaac? Or maybe a worm can navigate with its hooks. That punk in his belly had steered him to Sylvia.

He took her into an artists' saloon, treated her to black coffee and cigarettes. The artists at the tables seemed to feel a kinship with Isaac. They must have taken his sunken cheeks as a sign of poverty and powerful, suffering thought. The First Dep had traveled far from Center Street in his days and nights as a bum. He'd moved beyond some kind of maddening pale. Isaac was less and less a cop.

"Your husband's been bawling for you," he said.

Doses of coffee and cigarettes had revived Sylvia Berkowitz. "Isaac, don't be his mama. Marsh will pick up a new survival kit . . . a Barnard student to scrub his underwear."

"Got any cash on you?"

"No, but I'll sing carols outside a restaurant."

"Sylvia, you're in the wrong season. It isn't Christmas yet. You'll starve. Who was that clown you were with?"

"Nobody special. I met him in a candy store two hours ago."

"Do you have a place . . . a home?"

She didn't have to answer him. Marshall's wife was living among the garbage cans. If she had that much of a need to break away from Marsh, Isaac wasn't going to twist her head around. "Come with me."

The First Dep had a small apartment on Rivington Street. That's where he kept most of his suits. He gave the apartment to Sylvia.

"Isaac, will you stay with me?"

He could remove her filthy blouse, wash her back, and bring her over to his mattress. Who would be the worse for it? Not Sylvia. Not him. And like some magical rabbi, Isaac might be able to soothe her so she'd want to come back to Marsh. But that child he was making in Jennifer Pears got in the way. The old bum was turning chaste. He left her food money and a number where he could be reached. He was down the stairs before Sylvia had the chance to thank him or crawl into his sleeve. She wouldn't have minded raping Isaac the Pure.

EIGHTEEN

Sometimes he doubted whether he had an office or not. What was going on at the thirteenth floor of 1 Police Plaza? He demanded independence, a footlooseness, the right to range about the City in dirty pants. And then he wondered why his "angels" should function so well without him. His rat squad would probe underground and surface with a bundle of crooked cops. Isaac had put the squad into motion. He'd trained his men to go for blood.

He had other "angels," other squads that were putting out for him. They couldn't deliver the king's Irish donkey, O'Toole, but they did dredge up morsels on the king himself. They'd gone into New Haven, sought out Dermott's career at Yale. They had his transcripts, his dormitory rooms, and notes from the master of his college, from professors, from New Haven's former Chief of Police. It seems the lad had been thrown out of school in a gentlemanly way. The Yale Corporation invited him never to come back. The reasons weren't clear to Isaac's men. Cops had been on campus looking for Dermott

Bride. He was operating a sort of smuggler's ring inside the college. Dermott secured stolen radios, television sets, cameras, fishing rods, and other tripe for Yalies and college groundsmen, dishwashers and cooks. He'd get his supplies from some nigger gang. But no one could tell who that nigger gang was. Isaac smiled to himself: that kid went into business with Arthur Greer. He didn't break with the Devils at all. Arthur's old gang swiped the radios, and brought the merchandise up to Yale.

Isaac looked through the transcripts: it was at Yale that the kid had shortened his name, became Dermott Bride. Isaac could swear that the king never left Arthur's gang. The Clay Avenue Devils were running Whores' Row.

But Isaac's men couldn't pick up on Dermott after he got out of Yale. What happened to those sixteen years between New Haven and the Shelbourne Hotel? How did Dermott groom himself with so much mystery and finesse? Isaac's mind was knocking. He decided to rest. He used the morning to invade the Little Red Schoolhouse. Jennifer wouldn't have a cappuccino with him. He had to propose to her from the doorway that led to the playground on the roof.

"You'll divorce that schmuck," he said.

Her eyes burned a green that was so fierce, Isaac had to grab the wall. "What schmuck are you talking about?"

"Your husband. You'll divorce Mel and marry me."

Isaac already had a wife, Kathleen, who was becoming the empress of Florida with all the condominiums she had built in the swamps around Miami. Kathleen couldn't stand Isaac, but she liked being Mrs. Sidel. She didn't need a penny from the boy, and he'd have to strangle Kathleen to get a divorce out of her. Isaac wasn't thinking of practicalities. He'd fight the laws of Miami and New York, grow into a bigamist, if Jennifer would allow him to be the father of her child.

"Isaac, you must be sick. Eight or nine meetings in a hotel room don't make a marriage. I was fond of you before you ran away to Ireland . . . that worm of yours appealed to me. I liked your crazy room . . . your filthy pants . . . the way you talked. But that doesn't mean I'd ever leave Mel."

"Try me," Isaac said. "I'm as good a father as that schmuck."

"Isaac, if you come here again to annoy me, to talk of marriage proposals, I'll scream downstairs for the cops. I don't give a damn what kind of commissioner you are. I'll have somebody arrest your ass."

Isaac disappeared from the Little Red Schoolhouse. All those infants in their classrooms began to disturb him. He thought of their moms and dads. So many mothers and fathers lived settled lives. Isaac had stations where he could come and go, an office, a room, an apartment to store his clothes, but he was like an animal who existed on the streets. The patriarch was longing for a proper home.

He cruised uptown, ignoring traffic signals. Colors blinked at him. Isaac didn't care. Nothing could break his stride. Cars and trucks had better watch out. You'd have to pay a stiff fine if you ran over the First Deputy of New York.

Annie wasn't at her corner, and Isaac despaired. She was *his* family, even if she revealed her crotch at the sight of him to drive Isaac away. And Dermott? Dermott was family too, though Isaac couldn't explain the connection there. He'd bound himself to the king and his "bride." He'd become lonely at fifty-one, the self-sufficient Isaac, the *brain* of the City Police, who was used to shoving men around like waxed pieces on a board. Chess was too complicated for his dead "angel," Manfred Coen. Isaac loved to play checkers with Blue Eyes. But the First Dep was weary of games. He'd squash the secret rumblings on Whores' Row, the complicated, mysterious shit, and then demand a leave of absence. Sam was snug in the Mayor's house. "Hizzoner" could survive without Isaac Sidel.

He saw Annie totter out of an Irish bar near his hotel. Her face was beginning to heal. But she still had the shadow of a "D" on her. Property of Dermott Bride. She didn't snarl at Isaac, or raise her skirt. She'd passed the morning drinking stout, and she was looking for an early customer, a john who'd pay for her necessities' tampax, lipstick, and beer. That was the only diet Annie could remember. She had enough stout in her not to feel hostile to a nosy, digging cop. "Father Isaac."

"Annie, I . . ."

"If you say anything, one word about a French restaurant, I'll squat right here and piss on the sidewalk. Can't you take a girl to a human place . . . without waiters in black coats who bow at you and want to kiss you on the back?"

She lured him into a Greek dive where Isaac himself liked to go when he was wearing his bum's pants. The restaurant had its own rationale. The waiters weren't Greek. They were Syrian, gruff, sloppy, and lecherous. They uncorked bottles of retsina with their powerful tongues. Annie loved resin-flavored wine. She drank with Father Isaac. He didn't question her about the king. She would flee from the table, and Isaac would have to drink retsina alone.

"Annie, I have a daughter who's a lot like you."

"Mister, keep your daughters to yourself . . . if you give me twenty bucks, I'll wiggle my ass . . ."

That whorish mumble pained the First Dep. She was a madwoman who went down for men in the street. No pimp had taught her to smile. Arthur Greer might have exploited Annie's invisible mark. Disheveled, bitten, she was still the greatest beauty on Whores' Row. It didn't help her much. Even if there had been a school for prostitutes, Annie couldn't matriculate. She'd scream, stick out her tongue, tear off her bra at the wrong moment. If Isaac hadn't put two of his "angels" on her, she wouldn't be alive. They were so expert at their jobs, Isaac had his troubles spotting them: two blondish lads at a far table. They must have arrived at the First Deputy's office after he'd gone to live in his bum's hotel. He couldn't recollect their names.

Isaac wasn't concerned about the sense of diaspora in his own platoons. His "angels" could disperse wherever they liked, so long as they were loyal to him. He had Annie to consider, and the girl confounded Isaac. She was a hooker who didn't know how to bait a man. Her clumsy whore's life belonged to some ritual that was outside Isaac's ken. What weird dream was she acting out? Annie taking vengeance on herself? The retsina came to Isaac's help. It was better than splits of champagne. All that resin in the wine must have loosened the girl. She sang to Isaac.

Who's the Rose of Connemara?
The Queen of Cashel Hill?
Derm had a lady
And the lady ain't no more

She couldn't carry a tune. The lines slurred out of her. Isaac wished she'd go on singing for him.

"Castledermott," she said.

"What?"

"You need a license to fish, you dope."

He'd play to her, tell her what she expected to hear, and then he'd stitch his own tune out of what she said.

"Where can I get this license?"

"From the Fisherman . . . he'll break your balls if you steal trout from his pond. Poachers can get killed. It's happened before. But it's Dermott's castle. He fries the bread."

Isaac didn't have the faculties to compose a tune. Castles? Fisherman? Trout? "Annie, how do you find Castledermott?"

"Put your hand under my skirt . . . that's where it is. You'll reach the right fish."

He'd have to ignore the gibberish about her genital parts. "Was that castle inside a hotel?"

"Prick," she said, "who's the Rose of Connemara? Me or you?"

He felt ugly gorging her with wine. But he couldn't break her riddles unless she drank some more.

"Did the Fisherman try to hurt you?" he said.

"You crazy? An old gent like that. Father Isaac, you ask funny things."

A waiter sneaked up to them with two of those long retsina bottles. "Get out of here," Isaac muttered. He didn't need a waiter's tongue to open his wine. Isaac bit into the cork and pulled.

"Mister, see my boots?"

Isaac looked. Annie was wearing sandals today.

"I only buy boots at Switzer's. None of your shitty stores. My man won't let me touch Irish paper money. It's got germs. Bulges in your pocket. It's indecent for a lady to carry so much cash. But how can you pay for an ice cream cone with a banker's check? Unless you bring the donkey."

"Is that O'Toole? Was Jamey your protector? Then why did he turn on you?"

"The donkey doesn't turn. He's too big."

"Annie, did you live in that hotel with the king? Were you up in the Shelbourne? Was Jamey there too?"

He was beginning to grow frantic in his need for clarity. Why didn't he pursue smaller things, go for the nibble, like that Fisherman, whoever he was.

"I don't like yellow drapes," she told him. "And they always say, *madam* this, and *madam* that. Why do I have to eat with seven forks? A fork for salmon. A fork for lettuce. A fork for soup. It's only silverware. You think he was happy being like that? I know Derm. He likes to stick his finger in the fish. He didn't care if I had my period . . ."

Could he talk about the scar now, the magical *D*?

"Annie, who . . ."

"Show me a barman who can pull a good pint, and I'll give you some of my kish . . . my man is particular. Don't you ruin the cream line on his Irish coffee. The donkey will have to drink a bad glass."

She got up from the table. But she made Isaac sit where he was. "Annie, I could walk you home . . ."

"Mister, don't think of following me. I'm wise to what you're after. The fish stays in my pants. So forget it . . ."

The girl had fish on the brain. Was it some lovetalk between Annie and the king? She hobbled out of the restaurant, the Syrians peeking at the folds in her ass, drawing Annie in with faces hard as fish hooks. His "angels" didn't move from the chairs they were in. They wouldn't even acknowledge Isaac. He had to introduce himself to his own fucking men.

"I'm Isaac," he said, feeling like an idiot. They didn't jump, those blond lads of his. "You're supposed to stick with her."

He didn't like the harsh neutrality under their eyes. His "angels" should have been more passionate about Annie Powell.

"Isaac, it takes her half an hour to cross the street. We have plenty of time."

"That's not the point," he said. "You're supposed to make sure she gets across the street."

They were slow in getting off their rumps. He asked them about Jamey O'Toole.

"Isaac, that quiff couldn't be in Manhattan. We would have spotted him ages ago."

They left with toothpicks in their mouths and napkins on the table. He'd have to call his office and push them off the case. He wanted livelier boys on Annie Powell, lads he could trust. But he never called. Annie's obsession with fish had taken hold of Isaac. Was there a trout pond in St. Stephen's Green? Could Dermott fish from a window? The king would have had to concentrate all his magic and all his luck. Isaac was demoralized. His primitiveness had failed him here. Once he was a man who could sense the pedigree of any situation. Isaac had the gift. But he'd crawled into the Guzmann family and come out with a worm. The worm had blunted him.

PART FOUR

NINETEEN

Rose, Rose of Connemara, Miss Annie Powell. She had to take an awful leak. Enough wine and beer in her to drown a Dublin pony. Father Isaac. She loved to torture that bum who came to her in clean and dirty pants. She wasn't going to be anybody's daughter. Not his. She was selling pussy. Nothing less. She didn't have to eat French dinners with a guy who wouldn't pull off her clothes. She'd had a thousand dinners with her man. He took her to places a bum couldn't afford to go. Steak tartare. She could read all the menus in the world. He let her swipe towels and doilies from the biggest hotels. She could powder her tits with pure Irish lace. Nobody owned her anymore.

The uncle was waiting for her under a lamppost. Mr. Martin McBride. He didn't look very grand. He's got a disease, they say. His lungs are turning to paper. The uncle was scared of something. He'd threatened Annie, then he'd offer cash. It was a disgrace for Dermott to have his lady working in the streets. She wouldn't accept money from this old knish.

"Jesus," he said, "you'll get us all killed. Woman, can't you see? Everywhere you go there's a cop. It means nothing to pay them off. They're after blood. How many times do they have to kick you in the face?"

"I've been kicked before. By uglier people." She ran a finger over that invisible scar. "How's the man?"

"Are you crazy? Dermott won't talk to me. You can't reach the lad. It takes a month to get a call into Ireland. And Dermott never picks up the phone. I have to talk to one of those bulls he keeps around him. 'Sorry, Mr. McBride. But the king isn't here.' Sending a telegram's no good. How do I know who's going to read it? We're in the dark, woman. I take instructions from that nigger, Artie Greer."

"What does he say about Derm?"

The uncle wrinkled his nose. "Merciful God, how can you trust a nigger gombeen man? He swears Dermott's playing golf in his rooms. Woman, do us a favor, please. Walk out of here. I'll get you an apartment in Forest Hills. You can have your own beagle. Six cats if you like. Move, I'm telling you. Shuffle off. We'll all die if you stay too long."

"Dermott knows where I am. Let him come for me."

"Jesus, don't you learn? The nephew's a dead man if he lays a foot in Manhattan. That's the lousy deal they made."

"I didn't put my name on that pact, Martin McBride, so stop bossing me around."

"But you're *his*. You're Dermott's. That's the way they'll look at it. And they'll reach out for you again and again and again."

Annie smiled for uncle Martin. "Not to worry your head about it. I have me a benefactor. A real live beauty. Tough as they come."

"Who?"

"What's the difference? He buys me champagne. In baby bottles."

"Tell me who it is?"

"That high commissioner, Father Isaac."

A grayness overtook uncle Martin, and he rocked on his heels. "That bandit . . . he's the worst of the lot. Woman, he kidnapped me, swear to God. Brought me to a phony precinct, Isaac. He makes his own police stations. He has killers under him . . ."

"So what? He wants to marry me."

Uncle Martin developed a hacking cough; he hugged the lamppost and tried to catch his breath. Annie had to console him.

"I'm not fooling. He's too big a fox to marry. Me with a husband and all. Though I hear Irish weddings aren't too legal in America."

"Woman, eat your tongue. This Isaac, he's got ears in every window."

He trundled away from Annie, bumping into lampposts to regain his strength. Annie went upstairs. She lived in a rooming house that attracted outcasts like herself: rummies, army deserters, whores unbridled by any pimp. It was cheaper, lower, more slovenly than Isaac's hotel. But at least it had a name. Lord Byron's Rooms. Most cops wouldn't invade the premises. The stairs might collapse under their feet. They could lose their holsters in a darkened hallway, or their whistles and their memorandum books. Annie felt secure. She was safe from unwanted company.

She wouldn't think of locking her door. The rummies would only have swiped her doorknob together with the lock. They liked openness at the Lord Byron. But they didn't poke in Annie's room for a bottle of milk. A man with tremendous hands and feet was resting on her mattress. Jamey O'Toole. He could have been Robinson Crusoe. He'd stopped shaving at the end of August. Now he had a crooked beard. He wore the same thing: pants, shirt, and socks that clung to him like pieces of bark. Jamey sweated under his clothes. He was afraid to come out from Annie's room. She'd hidden this Irish donkey, stuffed him away at the Lord Byron. It was strange to watch such a big man shiver. She couldn't desert Jamey O'Toole. The donkey had been good to her. He'd mothered Annie in Ireland, kept her out of harm, saved her from a tribe of gypsy thieves.

No drunkenness could ruin Annie Powell. Dermott's "bride" had been slippery and shrewd at that Greek restaurant. She shoveled bread and cheese under her skirts while she ate with Isaac. Now Jamey had a meal for himself. He ripped the bread with long fingers and gobbled lumps of cheese. Poor man, he couldn't take a bite without Annie. Bread would drop out of his fists. Most of the cheese landed on her mattress. She wasn't too proud to stoop for the donkey. She had to feed Jamey O'Toole. She was grateful for the teeth in his mouth. He still remembered how to chew.

"Jamey, I've got thirty dollars in my pocket. You could jump on a bus, you know."

"They're watching the buses," he said, with cheese stuck on his tongue.

"I could walk with you. I'll scream if they come around."

"Never mind, Annie girl. We'll sit. They're dumb. You can bless the saints for that. They couldn't figure I'd be in your room."

"Why do they want you so bad?"

"Ah, it's a pitiful story. We had the leverage on them. Then Dermott made the peace. He told himself he could spread the waters and hop over the Irish Sea. I begged him not to go. He's nothing but a prisoner over there, Dermott is. They 'yes' him, they bow to the king. But let him try to disappear."

"Is the Fisherman holding Dermott?"

"Yeah, the Fisherman. And other guys."

"Isaac, is he one of them?"

"Who the fuck knows? You can't trust the commissioners or the cops. Isaac has his blue-eyed boys. They'd shoot my ears off if they could. But it's the other cops that worry me . . . old ladies with white hair they are. Retired sergeants. They work for the big McNeill."

She sat with him on her mattress, a loving girl, putting crumbs in Jamey's mouth. What else could she do? When she brought a john into her room, Jamey had to stand in the hall. Customers were suspicious of Robinson Crusoe. They clutched their wallets before and after they made love to Annie Powell. She didn't care. Business was slow. She'd rather fish for crumbs than go out looking for a john.

Miss Annie was a native of Queens. Monday to Friday she took the BMT. She worked in a jewelry store on Fifty-seventh Street. A display girl she was. She didn't handle the expensive goods. She had a lovely figure, you see, and the manager, a Mr. Giles stationed her near the window. She was meant to draw the customers in. That's how she met the king.

He had a passion for books, old books, first editions, things like that. Faulkner and Mr. James Joyce. It was an odd habit for a crook. But he hadn't forgotten Columbia College, and he could afford any book he liked. He had several dealers in town. The best of them, Eichenborn, was next door to Annie's window. He was coming out of Eichenborn's with a copy of *Ulysses*, Paris, 1922, when he saw Miss Annie Powell. Giles had told her to blush if a man looked in. But she didn't blush at Dermott. She noticed the sockets of his eyes. He was coatless in February. And he had the blackest hair. He didn't seem like a man who would trifle in a jewelry store and let himself be used by Mr. Giles. Oh, but she had the wish: not in terms of silver and gold. She wasn't Giles' mercenary. If only that dark man would come in and talk to her and forget about the jewels. Giles could scream. No. He would have been timid around such a man.

Dermott didn't knock on the window. He never smiled. But he did visit Annie on his next book-buying trip. He marched out of Eichenborn's scowling hard. The lad had paid a stupendous price for a set of galley sheets that must have been living with the worms. The sheets were from *Soldier's Pay*, Faulkner's second book. They were in miserable condition: streaked, with ratty edges and cigarette burns. But Eichenborn knew his man. Dermott had a madness to collect. The dealer had been saving these galleys for months. When the bug bites, the lad will buy. Dermott had to have his *Soldier's Pay*. He could have hired a gimp to murder Eichenborn and get back most of his money. But he didn't mind being swindled by a man who loved books. He stood outside Annie's window with a twisted yellow rose. That was as much courtship as Annie could bear. She was sick of baiting men for Giles. She put on her coat to meet with Dermott. "I'm quitting," she told Giles, who couldn't understand why a single rose should propel Annie out of his store.

She had no idea what to do about Dermott. Say hello or goodbye? He didn't rush her into anything. He had a quietness that Annie liked. They sat in a bistro. He talked of books. She wasn't a complete idiot. Ezra Pound meant something to her. It was a name, wasn't it? And William Faulkner's reputation had come to Queens. He showed her the galley sheets. My luck, she said. I had to fall for a professor with dark hair. There was no monkey business. He brought her home in a taxi cab. He didn't leave her stranded at the door. He had doughnuts with her mother and her two young sisters. Her mother felt a strangeness in the house. "How'd you get out of work so early?"

"Ma," Annie said when she had a minute alone with her mother. "He's Irish, I swear. And a professional man. Dermott Bride. He teaches books." Her mother refused to believe that a dark-haired Irishman could exist. "Anybody can call himself Dermott Bride. He has a Puerto Rican nose. Can't you tell?"

Annie wouldn't look for another job or lose her faith that Dermott was descended from the Irish. "Mama, we all broke out of the same potato. Me, Dermott, and you."

She was ashamed to take money from him, but she did. Mothers and sisters have to eat. And Annie's father was long dead. But it was a slow kind of loving they had. He didn't make a mistress out of Annie Powell. They went to the Rockaways. Walked in freezing sand. They had three-hour lunches in Little Italy. She rolled pasta on a fork. She burped into her napkin and said, "Excuse me." She was always home by six o'clock.

What kind of work did her professor do? Available seven days a week he was. Must be a landlord on the side. Dermott had apartments all over the City. After a month he took off her clothes. They were in a flat on Murray Hill. How many maids did Dermott keep? You couldn't find dust under the chairs. Oh, she'd had other boyfriends. But no one had licked her armpits before. He didn't mutter filth in her ears. Or make idiotic marriage proposals. He could touch a woman's body without coming in his pants. He wasn't like her Canarsie beaus, who went in and out of you so fast, you couldn't tell if you had a man inside, a rabbit, or a rush of wind. He had a delicate body that wasn't brittle or soft. It fit into hers like the cardboard teeth of a Chinese puzzle. And she thought, what does it mean to take your pants off in somebody's car? I've been going out with monkey boys. Dermott had magic everywhere, in all his parts. He could make her come with his finger and his mouth. She would twist around and grab pieces of that black hair. She'd never be able to sleep with a Canarsie boy again.

He loved to swipe her underpants, stuff them in his pocket, and sniff them from time to time. It didn't matter where the panties came from, how cheap they were, how flimsy, how many holes they had. She would have carried his underpants too, but her sisters might have gone through her things, spied on Annie, and snitched to her mother. She could imagine how mama would react. "I've raised a whore in my house. Annie, what are you doing with a man's jockey shorts?"

Then Dermott announced to her in a quiet voice, "I'm going to Ireland. Will you come?"

She spoke up like a good Irish girl. "Dermott, my mother would kill me."

"I'll handle that," he said. And it hurt her a little. Because he had to barter with mama, as if Annie were a cow. Mama cursed every misfortune the saints had thrust upon her and accepted Dermott's five thousand dollars. Annie was embittered. Mama should have cried harder and clutched less. It poisoned Annie's lovemaking for a week. But she figured to herself: I'm nobody's cow, That five thousand has nothing to do with me.

Oh, it was a merry life for a girl with a dead father, living in Dublin on a rat's honeymoon. Because wherever Dermott went, that donkey went too. *They* were the married pair, Dermott and Jamey O'Toole. Like brothers they were. Big and Little. And Annie couldn't snuggle between them to locate her man. But she learned to appreciate O'Toole. He would poke drunken men out of her way, choose a nice path for Dermott and Annie. She was a bit unclear about her own Irishness. Mama had never been to the Old Country. Some granddad of Annie's had arrived starving in America after one of those long potato blights. It could have been a thousand years ago. The girl had no sense of history. Irish she was, but she didn't look like any of the freckles she saw on Grafton Street. God, it was a land of freckle-faced people. Her own complexion was kinder than that. Not lumpy, gray, and red. It scared her. She didn't want to become a boiled potato.

You could see row after row of gray heads on the bus to Dalkey. The buildings were gray, or a bloodless brown. But she adored the street signs that were in Gaelic. It was like a fairy's tongue. FAICHE STIABHNA. Stephen's Green. SRAIDIN MUIRE. Little Mary Street. LANA NUTLEY. Nutley Lane.

The town seemed populated with elves. She ran into a soldier four feet high, with a cap and boots and a green, green shirt. The soldier dipped his cap and said, "What do you think?"

Annie struggled for an answer. "Not very much."

"Same as us all," the soldier said, and he was gone from Annie Powell.

And the damn money they had in this Republic. A ten-pound note was big as a napkin, and it had a goblin's face in the back. She didn't know how to spend such things. Dermott gave her banker's checks to use, with her name and his printed on the bottom. ANNIE POWELL OR DERMOTT BRIDE. It was like having a company together. You couldn't cash them at Woolworth's. You had to take Dermott's checks into the prouder stores. She bought everything at Switzer's and Brown Thomas: underwear, peanuts, pajama tops. Cashiers would hold up the checks with their fingers, smile, and shout "Grand!" at Annie. She didn't need identification, no little card with a signature on it. Dermott's checks were finer than gold. That's some man I have, mother dear. The Bank of Ireland sits on his shoulders.

Where was the money flowing from? Dermott took Jamey and her to dinner and lunch. It was a strange kind of eating, more often than not. Dermott might rent out a whole restaurant. He'd reserve twelve tables from seven to nine. O'Toole would be stationed at the door. Busboys and master waiters would hover over them, while Annie stared at empty tablecoths. "Everything to your satisfaction, madam?"

She chugged her head. A sauceboat would arrive on a flaming tray. "Just a dash for you, madam?"

Dermott wore a velvet suit. But she was too miserable to gloat on his handsomeness. Who buys out every chair at a restaurant?

The waiter was a genius. He could slice smoked salmon in front of your eyes. Her man knew all the fancy waiter talk. "Madam would

like a bit of toast." It was like having pet camels in your room to
fetch whatever you want. The busboys sidled up to Annie with ten
racks of toast. Mercy on the miserable and the poor. Annie could
have fed off those racks of toast for a year. But she still couldn't tease
out her man's line of work.

"Derm, are we ever going home?"

She must have hit on something, because his sockets turned
dark.

"We're gypsies now," he said. "But I'll take you to Connemara
in a week."

"Where's that?"

"Near Galway. In the west."

You couldn't talk directions to Annie Powell. West was
nowhere to her. West of Dublin? West of what? Ireland was a
mystery. An Irish cab took them to Dublin airport, and they got on a
plane to Shannon. It was no ordinary rent-a-car that waited for them.
Her man had reserved a huge limousine. Jamey did the driving. He
sang songs about the Rose of this and the Rose of that. "Yes, she's
the Rose of Castlebar . . ."

It was a straight road to Galway, a town with one little square,
like a pinch on your behind next to Stephen's Green. The lads didn't
stop in Galway. But that square confused them. They couldn't decide
which turn to make. Dermott growled under his teeth. "The road to
Salthill, you dummy."

Jamey wouldn't bend. "It's Clifden we want. And Oughterard."

"Who's car is this?" Dermott asked.

"You're the king and I'm the driver."

They didn't take the road to Oughterard. They were near the
ocean in a minute, in some kind of bay. Geese flew over their heads,
wild birds with long skinny bodies and delicate wings. Annie
couldn't understand their powers of locomotion. How could such tiny
wings carry a bird? She was a city girl. Pigeons are what entered her
head, not geese that could caw over the knock of an engine.

They hugged a narrow seawall, and Annie was sure the three of
them would drop into the bay. The donkey started teasing her. "Look,
Annie girl, you can see Manhattan behind them rocks."

"I'm from Sunnyside," she said, and she wouldn't talk to Jamey.
He must have been growing delirious. Because he muttered weird
stories that went beyond the girl. He used a rough English tongue, as
if he weren't enough of a giant without such a voice. "You hear me,

laddies. *Neither O nor Mac shall strut nor swagger through the streets of Galway.* This is British land. *From the ferocious O'Tooles, good Lord, deliver us."*

Dermott laughed. "Jamey, I didn't know your people were from Galway."

"Ah, it's nothing, man. I learned it all from a catechism book. God pity the Irish, at home and abroad. I'm Jamey O'Toole. My people rose out of some pile of shit an Englishman made in Kildare. Show me an Irishman who can trace his ancestry, and you'll find that same pile of shit."

"Agreed," Dermott said.

But Annie took it as an insult. "My granddad dug potatoes. He was a good working man . . . from Omagh, I think. Or Ballyshannon. So speak for yourselves."

"Yes, they'd all love to have one father," Jamey said. "Finn MacCool. Not potatoes, Annie girl. There's a king in all of us. That's why our bones crack so easy."

There was no use arguing with a donkey like him. Her man didn't say a word to defend the Irish. Who was Jamey to talk of people rising out of shit? Annie couldn't find a tree out here. Miles and miles of stone. Rock walls twisted over hills that turned into low, harsh mountains. Yellow flowers grew between the rocks. You saw cows in the hills, bands of sheep, and haystacks with rags on top. The sheep looked odd to Annie when they came up close with their curled horns and black feet and blue markings on their rumps, as if an idiot had gone about stamping sheep's asses with color. Jamey honked at the beasts. "Get on. Climb on somebody else's back."

But they had to sit until different gangs of sheep passed along both sides of the car. Jamey was perturbed. He drove too fast around a bend in the road and struck a cow. It was an awful sight for Annie. The cow lay dead, its hooves in the air, blood running from a shoulder. "Jesus," the donkey muttered. "I thought a rock hit us." He didn't have any mercy for the cow.

"Who's going to move that fucking thing?"

A farmer and his boy appeared in front of the seawall and approached the car.

"An accident," Jamey said. "I swear to Christ . . . I wouldn't bash a cow on purpose. It just stood there, man, and looked me in the eye . . . I couldn't turn . . ."

The farmer and his boy dragged the cow off the road. The boy was crying. Jamey removed a wad of that Irish paper money from his wallet. "We're not villains," he said. "Two hundred quid for a dead cow."

The farmer wouldn't take the money. Jamey bundled it in his fist and tried to give it to the boy. But the boy only stared at him out of freckled cheeks. Jamey threw the money on the ground. Then he drove ahead of the farmer and the cow. He was in a fury. "Did you see the fender that animal put on us? It's lucky we can crawl."

Annie was waiting for her man to slap the donkey on his ear. To murder a cow and then offer money, and not a word of real regret. But Dermott never scolded the donkey.

"Let me out," she said.

"What's that, Annie girl?"

"You heard me, Mr. O'Toole. Stop the car. I'm not riding with cow-killers."

O'Toole banged on the dashboard with a knuckle; the cushions under Annie trembled from the blow.

"Jesus, it's a fine day when your own family is against you. Dermott, you think she'll rat on us? . . . Annie, didn't I lay two hundred on that old gizzard for his cow? It was a worthless animal. Dull in the head. A cow that stands in the middle of the road and hogs your lane! . . . Dermott, ask her to forgive us now. We'll order up a Requiem for that animal at the next church. We'll pay for chanters and all . . . I wouldn't disappoint Annie Powell."

Annie hardened against the donkey and her man. "Have your jokes," she said. "Blaspheme a poor cow that doesn't have a soul and can't defend itself against its murderers. But I won't ride with you."

Jamey pummeled the dashboard again. Dermott wasn't amused. "Let her out," he said. They left Annie on the road to Screeb and Maam Cross. She had her suitcase. She'd strut back to Galway and sleep in that little square, she would. She'd show that donkey and the king. Annie Powell could get along without her man. She had some Irish silver in her bag, coins with a bull on one side and a harp on the other. She'd spend them in Galway, live on coffee and scones, and the lemony biscuits she liked. Maybe she *would* buy a mass for that cow. She'd ask the fathers of Galway if such a thing were possible...

Annie brooded and brooded, but she hadn't gone a step. She already missed the king. Why did her man throw her out of the car? She should have listened to her mama and stayed in Sunnyside. Sure,

she could close her eyes and whisper that her man was in real estate.
But how many realtors would pay five thousand for the right to bring
a girl to Dublin? Dermott Bride was a crook. His men liked to murder
cows. Here she was, a gangster's lady.

It could have been an hour before the dust shivered up off the
road. She saw spots of brown fur and a glue made of blood inside the
big hollow on Jamey's fender. She was glad the cow had marked the
limousine with its own dying. But she didn't say that to her man. She
climbed on Dermott's lap when the door opened. She curled into his
neck. She would never have gotten to Galway by herself.

"Wake up, Annie. Be a good girl now."

It was Jamey's hand on her shoulder. She had a blanket under
her legs. Her man wasn't in the cushions with her, and her ankles
were cold. "Where are we, Jamey O'Toole?"

"Are you blind?" he said. "Look around you, Annie. It's
Castledermott."

She poked her head out of the car. Mother Mary, you wouldn't
believe this world! They were parked in front of an old gray castle on
a yellow lake. It was just the right castle for Dermott and his man.
Part of its stones were chewed up. The turrets were going to rubble.
Castledermott had an ambiguous roof. It could have rained debris on
your head during windy times. The walls had great lapses in them,
thick pockets where Annie would have loved to hide. Some of the
windows were humped with cardboard. But it did have a sturdy door.
Oak, Annie figured, though she couldn't tell you much about wood. It
wasn't the kind of door that Jamey could have heaved up on his
shoulder, famous as he was for uprooting doors, springing them from
their hinges, or smashing their center panels with a fist. She would
have bet her last Irish coins that O'Toole couldn't hurl this door into
the yellow lake.

"Where did Dermott go?"

"He's inside," Jamey said. "With the Fisherman."

She took her suitcase out of the car, and Jamey went to knock on
that big oak door. "It's me, O'Toole . . . and the girl." The door
swung open without the cry of a hinge. An old man with a shotgun let
them through. The house was full of old men. They were on the
stairs, in the kitchen, coming in and out of the dining rooms. They
carried shotguns or pistols in a holster, and they cursed at one another
with cigarettes and cigars in their mouths. Strange folks for an Irish

castle on a yellow lake. They were as American as Annie Powell.
They didn't seem to care for Jamey, these old men. They spit into
their palms when he shuffled between them. "The king's
washing-boy," they said. Jamey had a temper. Why didn't he bounce
them into the walls? They sneered at Annie. They would move close
and sniff her with malice in their eyes. "Does the king get a piece of
that?"

But Jamey wouldn't have them belittle her. "I'll get a piece of
your skull if you don't watch out."

The old men converged on him with their shotguns. The donkey
wouldn't back off. Another old man came out of the parlor. He wore
funny boots that went up to his crotch. The boots were like jelly.
They wobbled with each step he took. "Will you cut it out, for the
love of God. Timothy Snell, curb those hounds of yours. We have
guests. Be kind to Jamey."

This was the Fisherman, and these old men were his people. He
walked into the parlor with those jelly boots. She had ears on her.
Dermott was in the parlor with the old Fisherman. She heard them
mutter back and forth. O'Toole could sing and froth on the road, but
her man did the talking in Castledermott.

"Coote." There were tremors in his sweet voice. "Jamey sticks
with me."

"Not a chance," the old Fisherman said. "The lad goes. He's
needed in New York."

"Coote, I can get you bigger brains and better muscle."

"Granted, but he looks the part. That's what counts. We can't
have an army bursting into the streets to hit at merchants and fools.
I've me own hand to protect."

"You know his history. He grows violent when I'm not around."

"We'll soothe the lad. Don't you fret."

Her man said, "Find another boy. Jamey's not for sale."

"Who's been your daddy these eighteen years? Coote McNeill."

"Then it might be time to change dads . . ."

One of the old gunmen shooed Annie away from the parlor. She
was led up to her room. She walked on stairs that had a wine-colored
finish in the wood. Did those gunmen wax the floors? Why did
O'Toole say "Castledermott." The Fisherman owned this house. They
put her on the third story. A wind pushed through the halls. She could
see out onto the yellow lake from her room. She had glass in her
window. Not scummy cardboard. But the room had a narrow bed.

Dermott didn't come to her at night. The Fisherman's people mumbled in the hall. They fed her and made rude noises with their tongues, as if such silly old men could devour her body. She would have thrown them down the stairs, shotguns and all, if they tried to touch Annie Powell. She ate bananas and cream and listened to their chatter. It made no sense.

—A yellow lake means salmon, you twit. A blue lake's for trout.

—If you're so smart, why do salmon crave yellow water?

—Because they're a strange fish. Your salmon's very haughty. Why else would the McNeill bother with them? They won't lay their eggs in an ordinary lake. It's got to be yellow.

—Shit, I didn't come to Ireland to live in a fisherman's retreat.

—He'll turn a pretty penny, Coote will. Making this old box into a proper hotel. An angler's nook, you understand. A sort of paradise. You can't fish here without paying a fee to Coote.

—Is Dermott going to fish with us?

—Shut your mouth. The walls have ears, you idiot.

And the muttering would stop. Coote, Coote the Fisherman and his salmon lake. She thought she'd go crazy in the dark. She couldn't sleep on a narrow bed, without her man. She twisted under the blanket, her toes on fire. What a foolish thing it was to have a body. It turned hot and cold. There was a breeze on that yellow lake. She thought of the salmon swimming under there, putting silver streaks in the water with the drive of their fins. It was beautiful at Castledermott. But she'd rather die than be without her man.

He didn't come to her in the morning to say he was sorry. They let her out of the room. God, someone must have seized the castle. The whole place shook. The Fisherman's people had turned to carpenters overnight. They were hammering and sawing on the stairs. Annie knew what a carpenter was. Coote had picked funny guys to build a hotel. The saws buckled on these old men. Nails went in crooked. It wasn't going to be much of a fisherman's paradise.

They fed her in the kitchen. It was bananas and cream again. Maybe her man had disappeared on her. But she was still a guest. Annie had her own feelings about what she ought to eat. The Fisherman couldn't run a hotel on bananas and cream. She'd have to tell him that. If he didn't vary his menu, the hotel would sink.

The old men had gone back to their carpentering, and Annie was in the kitchen alone. She was humming to herself. She sang idle songs about salmon in the water. She began to cry under the breath of her songs. Mama, she dreamt of Dermott's face in the kitchen window. She wouldn't open her eyes for fear the dream would slip away from her and she'd be left without the face she loved. Black his hair. Purple lips. She didn't need to sing about salmon runs in yellow water. Thank God she had the gift to imagine Dermott's cheeks. She invented a smile on Dermott. Then the window opened, and her man was whispering to her. "Annie darling, get off your lovely ass."

Who would say such things? Was it magic blowing off the lake? Some salmon god Annie had neglected to mention in her songs? "Girl, are you coming or not?"

He had hands to help her out the window. She gathered her skirts in one fist and climbed. She felt a little clumsy with her stomach on the windowsill. He was laughing now, and she was angry and confused. He raised her buttocks off the window and carried her like a fish. Then he put her down.

"Derm, why did you have to play the ghost with me? Wasn't I scared enough? Jesus, you never said good night."

"I couldn't. Not in this house. I didn't want those lads thinking of us under the same blanket."

"Well, why didn't you put Jamey outside my door?"

"I'd be jeopardizing him. The boy has to sleep."

"Are they your enemies, Coote and his old guys?"

"Don't you ever call him Coote. He's the Fisherman, and he's a partner of mine."

"Coote, Coote, everybody calls him Coote."

"That's a dumb habit we have. But you might say 'Coote' to the wrong party, and it would do hurt to the old man. He's been good to me."

"Dermott, I'll call him the Fisherman forever and ever, if that's what you like, but why haven't you kissed me yet?"

"It's too close to the house. Come on."

"Where are we going?"

"On a picnic, you dope."

He pointed to the hamper near his legs. A basket it was, for a fisherman's lunch. He picked it up, and he ran with her around the lake. She must have been giggling too hard.

"Shhh," he said. "There's an echo off that fucking water."

"It's not a crime to have an echo."

"Yeah, but we don't have to advertise. If the Fisherman knows about our picnic, he might try to come along."

"I'll stuff his head in the basket if he dares to come."

But she wouldn't disobey her man. Annie didn't giggle anymore. They walked and walked in a kind of brown scrub, her skirts tangling in the midst of low, barren blackberry bushes. It wasn't the season for berries, you know, Annie muttered to herself. She couldn't wait to see what was in the hamper. "Love, is this a picnic or a hike?" she said.

"Both. Come on."

She wished now that Jamey had driven them in the car. But could you drive across rocks and fields? Cows blinked at them. And Annie remembered the dead cow in the road. A bull glared at Dermott. The animal had balls that hung below its knees. Dermott wouldn't curtsy to a bull. He didn't let go of the hamper. "Come on."

He must have dragged her for miles. They reached a wire fence, and Dermott separated the wires for her, so Annie could squeeze through. He gave the hamper to her for half a minute and hopped over the fence. They were at the bottom of a mountain. Annie was convinced of that. She could see the crisp, bottle-green waters of a tiny bay. "Are we still on the Fisherman's land?" she said.

"No. Come on. We'll have our picnic on Cashel Hill."

You couldn't tell how many ridges a mountain had. They'd reach one, then find they weren't any closer to the top. There was always another ridge. It was like a magical game for them. The elves were taking over. But you had to watch your feet. Cashel Hill was crusted with goat droppings. Those hard little pellets were on every single rock. A million sheep, or billy goats, must have shit on Cashel Hill.

Oh, God, the skirts on Annie had begun to rip. But she wouldn't let her man climb without her. And always, always she was tricked into believing the next ridge would be the last, the final one. She had a pair of lungs inherited from her mama. She could breathe in and out, and move into Dermott's tracks. She was the Rose of Connemara, the Queen of Cashel Hill, escaping from the Fisherman's house with her man. He hadn't done more than grab her by the hand. But you couldn't lie down in goat shit.

Her thighs were growing sore. She didn't care how many faces a cliff had. It was better than chewing bananas and cream. She'd crawl behind her man if she had to. The air got thick on the mountain, thick and purple-gray, and she'd lose parts of Dermott's back and shoulders for a second, and she wouldn't have any trail to follow.

"What's that?" she said, growling into the purple stuff, thick enough to eat.

"It's fog," Dermott said. "Don't think about it, Anne. You can outrun any fog if you hurry."

Annie appealed to her favorite saint to bring them out of the fog. Jude it was, the protector of travelers, idiots, unmarried girls, and desperate people. What a man Jude had given her! King Dermott, of Dublin and the Bronx. They did climb over the fog, with Jude's help. The mountain didn't have any more faces to mock them with. The elves could jeer. The king had dragged her to the top of Cashel Hill. She didn't think of the cliffs that went down to the sea, or the winding stone walls, the fields, the dots of water that could have been a salmon lake. Her belly was making pitiful grumbling sounds. "Will you give a girl some food, for Christ's sake?"

Dermott crouched on a rock that was relatively free of goat shit and unbuckled the hamper's leather straps. The king understood her hunger. They had a soft red cheese and brown bread and coffee in a great mug. He'd brought milk in a tonic water bottle. Thank God he forgot to bring a banana, or she might have puked. They had oranges, a misshapen yellow pear, biscuits in a wrapper, and Irish fruit cake. Annie looked for napkins and forks from Castledermott. The hamper was empty of that. Dermott packed food like any man. He only brought what came into his head. "How can we spread the cheese, love?"

Dermott reached into his pocket. He had a push-button knife with marvelous ruts in the handle. The blade opened with a noise that could have been the: gentle smack of two lips. He cut the humpbacked pear and spread the cheese, and then he honed the blade on the edge of the hamper.

"You have to exercise a knife," he said. "It can decay like a tooth and fall apart in your hand. I've seen that happen."

"Who gave the knife to you?"

"Nobody. I took it from a hobby shop on Tremont Avenue. Ah, it was a long time ago."

He fisted the knife with a loving hold that made Annie nervous. "How come you never showed it to me?"

"Because it likes to stay in my pocket," he said, his mouth suddenly full of teeth.

She burped, but the king didn't mind. His head was in her blouse. He had her unbuttoned to the waist, and he sucked on her nipples. Her man was like no other man in the world. Soon he was under her skirts, and Annie thought she would die. Her panties were wet from the king. She'd have picnics every day of her life, climb in tattered skirts, gobble a pear with warts on it and a swollen back, nibble cheese off a knife, if that's what her man desired.

They fell asleep on the mountain, among the goat droppings, with most of Annie crooked under Dermott's shoulder. Then she opened her eyes, "Jesus, how did it get dark so fast?"

You couldn't see your fingernails. It was the worst blackness she'd ever known. The elves must have put a roof on Cashel Hill. Mercy on her that she could still hear her man breathe, and grope for his chest. The fingers under his shirt had woken him.

"Dermott, this hill has a witch. We must have slept for twenty hours."

"We didn't sleep much at all. The fog crept up on us. And the fucker won't burn off. We'll have to sit and wait."

"Wait for what?" she said.

"Until somebody finds us."

"Who's going to find us on Cashel Hill?"

"Farmers," Dermott said. "They have to be out looking for their herds. They'll stumble into us."

"Not when you murder their cows," Annie said. "They'll leave us here to rot. That way all the farmers will get even with you."

He laughed in the fog, and it terrified Annie. Because there wasn't a mouth or lips to go along with it. "Annie, how did you dream such a farmers' plot? Stop worrying. The Fisherman won't let it happen. I'm too important to him."

That didn't satisfy Annie Powell. She prayed for Jude to intervene, to pull this fog down off Cashel Hill. The king heard her mumble. "What's that noise?"

"I'm praying," she said.

"I thought it was a dead cow mooing at us."

She began to cry. Her saint wouldn't come. Dermott made fun of the dead. Their bodies would shrivel and sink into the mountain. No more Dermott. No more Anne. The sky must have turned upside down. She saw a dozen moons float in the distance, under her feet. Dermott saw them too. He wasn't surprised. "That's our rescue party."

The moons seemed to draw closer and then retreat. They turned into glowing sticks. They're only lanterns, Annie assured herself. No moon could stretch itself into a fiery stick. It's Coote and his old men, with a pack of lanterns. Now she prayed that the Fisherman wouldn't bump into Cashel Hill. She'd rather stay lost with Dermott and die in peace.

The lanterns broke into packs of four. It took half an hour for one pack to edge up close. A voice came up off the fog. "Derrrrmott Bride."

"Ah," Dermott said. "They've also learned to moo." He called back into the fog. "Hello, boys. It's Annie and me."

Then a lantern was in her face. It blinded her until she blinked over the light. She recognized one of the Fisherman's people. Other lanterns approached in a pattern of sways.

Four lanterns looked down on them. "There he is . . . the king and his whore."

A pistol with a fat nose appeared in the haze off the lanterns. "Oh, we'd love to kill you, my dears."

She heard that soft, familiar smack. Dermott had opened his knife. He pushed Annie behind him. "Come for me, pretty boys that you are." He lunged, and the pistol fell.

"God, he cut me . . . he cut me . . ."

The Fisherman arrived out of the fog. He didn't have his jelly boots. "What's this shit?"

The old men grumbled around him. "Coote, Coote, we come to rescue this bastard, and he shoves his blade at us. He cut up poor Johnny Boyle."

"Bitches, cunts," he said. "I heard you threaten him. Get out of here, or I'll send you back to First Avenue where you belong. You can sit in the Dingle with Tiger John." He came up to Annie and kissed her on the cheek. "Are you all right?"

"Yes," she said. "Thank you." She stood near Dermott and the Fisherman and started to climb down Cashel Hill.

Dermott had to remain at the Fisherman's house. Annie went to Dublin with O'Toole. "You're both so smart," she said. "You and my man. That's Coote's house. Castlecoote. So why did you call it Castledermott?"

The donkey was tightmouthed with her. Then he snarled, but the snarl wasn't for Annie. "It's the Fisherman's castle, all right. But he bought it and fixed it up with Dermott's money. Those salmon in the lake didn't jump out of the Fisherman's pants."

What was she supposed to do in Dublin without her man? Wade the River Liffey and grab whatever salmon she could find? It was a dirty stream. Fish couldn't breathe in there.

"When's Derm coming back?"

"Who knows? Him and the Fisherman are playing cards over my body."

"What does that mean?"

"They're deciding what to do with little James. Keep the lad here, or throw him back to Americky."

"Dermott wouldn't give you away."

"Business is business," he said.

She wasn't going to listen to a donkey all her life. So she shopped on Grafton Street, bought colored undies and other useless things with those banker's checks, and walked on O'Connell Bridge. She couldn't keep away from the child beggars who cut a territory for themselves along that bridge. She wanted to take a cloth with her and wash their faces. The beggars stood below her knees. She couldn't believe children could exist so small. She fed them candy from Switzer's to improve their shrunken state. The beggars got used to Annie Powell. "There's the lovely," they would say, with the practiced smiles of bitter old men. "There's the girl." They had shriveled skin for five-year-olds.

Annie would devote an afternoon to watching them beg. The children never harmed her. But there was something sinister in the methods they used. They would attack tourists on the bridge, feel around in your pockets, a slew of beggars that wouldn't let you go. They would grab at gentlemen's trousers and ladies' skirts, paw you with fists that were impossible to shake free, like an army of educated rats, and you'd be pulling them to the south side of the bridge and onto Lower O'Connell Street before you were finished with them. They'd have a few of your coins and maybe your pocketbook. These children labored at all hours.

Annie found them sleeping in plastic bags, huddled against the bridge in harsh weather. It might have been a ploy to gain sympathy from innocent people. But their shivering was real. Annie would have liked to march them into the Shelbourne for tea and sandwiches. The porters wouldn't have allowed it. It was Dublin, dearie, and a decent hotel couldn't have beggars passing through.

But Annie wasn't helpless. Didn't the porters say *madam* to her? She was Dermott's lady, and she occupied a suite at the hotel. The

Shelbourne prepared huge mugs of tea that Annie brought out to the bridge. The children drank the hot tea with the same grizzled smile. Then, on her fourth day back in Dublin, they kissed her hand in the rain and led her over the bridge. They winked and touched the shallow part of her skirts. They weren't taking Annie by force. It was an invitation to follow them. She wouldn't desert the children now.

Up Gardiner Street they went, Annie and the beggars, to an old house in an obscure alley, off Mountjoy Square. There was the stink of fish and oily margarine. Did they bring her home to meet mum and dad? Doors shut behind her. She didn't remember climbing stairs. She was in a room that might have been a kitchen or a storage place. It seemed high as a barn to Annie. Jesus, there was a dead chicken on the wall, hanging by its neck. Piles and piles of clothing: shirts and vests and a hundred different trousers. A clothes barn it was, with a dead chicken to watch over it and scare away the wrong customers. She was crazy to come here. She shouldn't have crossed the Liffey with these beggar children.

They whirled around her in a cruel dance, pawed at her, as if she were a tourist lady. "Havin' fun?" they said. Her blouse came apart in their fists. They tore the skirts off her body. They held her bra and underpants. She was naked in front of the children. They tried to feel between her legs. Annie turned on them, became a savage of a girl. She was no dummy in the window that children could poke at and fondle with grime in the webbing of their hands. She threw lots of trousers at them, cursed the tea she had brought to O'Connell Bridge.

She might have won, but a man and woman stepped into the fight. They smacked her down to the floor and let the children have their way with her. Their hands were all over Annie Powell. She screamed for Saint Jude. The man kicked at the children and drove them off. Annie didn't care for his smile. He wore a beautiful vest, but his face was as marked as any beggar child. A runt in man's clothes he was.

"Pretty lady," he said. "You'll fetch us a price. Who owns you now?"

"Dermott Bride."

"Never heard of him."

"He's from America," she said.

"Indeed. What does he do, your Mr. Bride?"

"He bought into a castle," she said. "He works with the Fisherman."

"Explain that to me?"

"They plan to open the Paradise Hotel . . . out of Galway. It's for people who like to hunt for salmon. Hunt and fish."

"Does he have a Dublin address?"

"The Shelbourne, St. Stephen's Green."

"Ah, that's better," he said. "That's good. You'll write him a note explaining the circumstances, that unless he comes up with a thousand pounds . . . in English money, not Irish . . . he'll see you dead."

Even without her skirts, they couldn't threaten Annie in a clothes barn. She wasn't going to be bullied by a runt in a vest who managed beggar children. "My man's in Connemara," she said.

"Isn't that too bad. You'll have to wait with us until he comes to Stephen's Green." He nodded to the woman. "Ethel, don't bother tying her wrists . . . if she hollers, you can split her head with a grease pan."

Annie wouldn't give up her courage to a hag with a pot in her hands. This hag wore the same kind of vest. Was it Dublin, or another country they had lured her to? Her saint had gotten her out of the fog. Jude wouldn't abandon Annie Powell. The beggars scratched the chicken on the wall. They were happiest when they tweaked its neck. Annie heard a slight rumble outside the barn. The rumble repeated itself. She knew what that meant. Her saint had come in the form of a donkey. O'Toole was knocking over doors to get to her. The rumbles were growing loud. The beggars hid behind sacks of clothes. The man and woman hugged themselves as the door to the barn came down. Jamey hopped over the door with dust on his shoulders. He didn't even look at the man.

"Annie girl, put on some clothes."

Her own things were ruined. They searched for a vest and pants among all the heaps. She walked out with Jamey in a beggar's uniform.

"How did you find me?" she said.

"I figured you were tangled up with the gypsies when you didn't come back to the hotel. They've got competing families, you see. I paid one family to spy on the others."

"Why didn't you go to the police?"

"The gardai are a joke . . . they snore in Dublin Castle. They're as dumb as American cops. I should know. I was a detective until this son of a bitch Sidel threw me into the street."

They smuggled her around porters and clerks at the Shelbourne, with Annie naked under her vest. She wouldn't stop muttering about the beggar children.

"It's not their fault, Jamey O'Toole. Their parents train them to stick their fingers in your pocket."

"I say it's in the blood. They're born with a thief's eye. Once a gypsy, always a gypsy. Don't you ever go near Mountjoy again. They'll shave the hair off your legs and sell it to the feather merchants. There isn't a piece of you they couldn't barter with."

"You've a low opinion of human nature, Mr. O'Toole. Children can be taught *not* to steal."

"Fair enough. But it's a friendlier world inside this hotel. There'll be no more teas on O'Connell Bridge."

The donkey guarded her until Dermott arrived. He wouldn't snitch to the king about Annie girl. Never once did he mention gypsies, beggars, Mountjoy Square. Her man seemed preoccupied. The king mumbled to himself. He had a blackness under his eyes. He hardly noticed Annie Powell. It went on for days. Then he slapped his pockets and said, "Jamey boy, climb into your darkest suit. We're going to church."

The donkey couldn't believe it.

"What about me?" Annie said.

"Girl, any dress will do."

The king ordered up flowers from the hotel. Roses they were, pink, white, and yellow. The flowers had a perfume that made the donkey sneeze. Dermott was cross with him. "Will you recover from that fit? I need a man in a clean suit."

They took a cab out to Donnybrook, the roses in Annie's lap, and Dermott married her inside the Church of the Sacred Heart, with Jamey as a witness before God, the organist, two ushers, and the wedding priest. Jesus, couldn't you ask a girl if she was in the marrying mood? Dermott gave her a wedding ring that she wasn't supposed to wear. A silver band it was. She had to hide it in her pocketbook. "I don't want the Fisherman to know about us," he said. "It's a secret, understand?'

So Dermott's bride had to stay Annie Powell. It made no difference at the hotel. She was *madam* to the porters, whatever name she carried. They did have a wedding feast. Dermott booked a restaurant around the corner on Molesworth Place. You wouldn't have noticed this restaurant from the street. It didn't have much of a sign. You had to knock on the door to get in. A woman shook your hand in the vestibule. "Mr. Dermott Bride," Jamey said. "Party of three." It wasn't a restaurant where you had to eat on the ground floor, with the dampness sticking to your shoes. Annie climbed a flight of stairs to a dining room with six tables. Her man had reserved them all.

Jamey tinkered with his soup. The light from the candle fluttered on his jaw. There was a darkness between the two men. The donkey's jaw began to move. "Did you settle with the Fisherman?"

"I did."

"Well, am I to be banished or not?"

"Yes and no," her man said. "Our accounts are a disaster, Jamey. You'll go to New York and help my uncle Martin. He blunders when he's on his own . . . then you'll come live with us."

Jamey's eyes seemed to close inside his head. The candle couldn't reach into them. He had already shut himself off from Dermott.

"Ah, it's a grand country New York is. Perfect for little James. After all, murder is me business."

"Have you forgotten?" Dermott asked. "We're at a wedding party."

"Sorry, Derm. I'll finish my soup."

The donkey left in the morning. The porters carrying his luggage were like dwarfs around O'Toole. He had to stoop in the Shelbourne to kiss Annie's forehead goodbye. One lip went into her ear. "I'll wallop you, Annie girl, if you strut on O'Connell Bridge." Her man rode with him to the airport. She wasn't invited to come along.

It was lonely without O'Toole. Two of the Fisherman's people moved in with them. Then another two. Now it was Dermott, Annie, and four old men. They were careful with Dermott. They didn't get in his way. But he couldn't walk Annie through St. Stephen's without these old men. A woman she was, married and all, though she wasn't allowed to say it, and she had chaperones, four, with yellow teeth. It was bad enough living with them when her man was there. Then Dermott had to go to Americky for a little trip. "Close a few accounts," he said. "Give me the chance to have a pint with Jamey. A week," he said. "No more."

But he didn't come back in a week, and Annie had to survive with Coote's people surrounding her. Their cigars stank up Dermott's suite. Porters shuffled in and out of the rooms with sandwiches and jars of warm black piss that could have been scooped out from the boiling mud at the bottom of the Liffey. They were proud watchdogs, these old men. They loved to shadow Annie in the streets. It took up half her energies and the slyness in her head to shake the old men. She'd stroll into Gaiety Green, a shopping mall on West Street, try on a pair of boots, crawl behind a rack of dresses, and slip out into an alley near Cuffe Lane. They couldn't catch up with her, for all their yellow teeth. Then she'd turn corners and end up at Bewley's Oriental Cafe. She wouldn't sit downstairs and be served by waitresses who scratched your order on a pad and made you eat lemon tarts when you'd asked for scones. Annie went up a flight to the paupers' station, where you had to serve yourself. Oh, it was crowded in that room, and you were obliged to share your table with companies of strange men: if you didn't hold your elbows tight, you'd have the dregs of Dublin in your lap.

But a man protected her, cleared a space for Annie at the table, so she could chew her scones in peace. An American he was, a college instructor in a tattered raincoat and a crumpled hat, come to Dublin on a small grant. He was doing research on a gentleman called Jonathan Swift.

"Are you interviewing that man Swift?" Annie said.

The instructor laughed. "No, he's long dead. He wrote about a giant in the land of little people, *Gulliver's Travels*."

"I remember that book," Annie said. "The little people captured him. I would have bashed Gulliver, you know, when he was all wrapped up in thread." Annie grew quiet. Here she was with a wedding ring in her pocket. She didn't want the instructor to think she was a frivolous girl. She lied a bit. "My man's a professor too. He studies Mr. Faulkner and Mr. James Joyce."

"Where does he teach?"

"He's unemployed at the moment . . . but he doesn't really need a job. He's rich. He buys up castles and turns them into hotels."

The instructor's name was Gerald, Gerald Charwin. She saw that hungry look in his eyes. What should Annie do if a man was smitten with her? She could meet him by accident, sit and have her scones, but she wouldn't make an appointment with Gerald. He was waiting for her at Bewley's the next day, around three o'clock. He told her scraps of Irish history. There was a river under Dublin, he said. The Poddle.

"I don't believe it."

His man, Jonathan Swift, used to wade in the Poddle.

"Gerald, does the Poddle ever seep up when the weather is bad? Imagine a city drowning in the river under its streets."

But Gerald wouldn't encourage her. "The Poddle doesn't go very far. It follows the line of Little Ship Street. Dublin will never drown in it."

He would have liked to take her walking over the channels where the Poddle still flowed. They could touch the pavements, he said, and listen for the sound of water. It was only a block from where he lived. Annie was dying to *feel* the Poddle, touch an underground river with her feet, but she had to refuse. Suppose the watchdogs found them together on Little Ship Street? What would the old men think?

She stuck to Bewley's Cafe with Gerald Charwin. But she couldn't escape the old men. It took one more sit-down with Gerald to bring them into Bewley's. They hovered over the tables with their yellow teeth, sniffing peas, sausages, and chips. You would have figured they were the quiet type, angels off the street, harmless uncles of Annie Powell, looking for a meal of peas. They wore old men's sweaters and caps. They kept muttering, "Fine day," to people at the tables. "Nice, nice." They slouched behind Gerald, the four of them.

"Would you come downstairs with us, laddie? We'd love to have a word with you."

"He's nothing to me," Annie said. "Just a man in a cafe. We talk about rivers a lot. Leave him alone."

They seized Gerald by the arms, lifted him out of his chair, and banged him from table to table, excusing themselves as they did. "Sorry now . . . eat your peas and don't mind us."

They pushed him down the stairs and carried him out of Bewley's and into the street, with Annie pummeling their old men's backs. "Don't you hurt him," she said. "He's a scholar. He's reviving Mr. Jonathan Swift."

They ignored the girl. The old men stepped on Gerald's hat, punched him in the kidneys and the ribs, dropped him into the gutters of Grafton Street. It was over in a minute. The Fisherman's people knew how and where to punch a man without calling notice to themselves. Annie couldn't help Gerald out of the gutters. The old men caught her by the sleeves and shoved her quietly towards the hotel. "Fancy," they said, mocking her with tongues in the middle of yellow teeth. "The king's girl goes to Irish coffeehouses with a scholar boy. It's footsies under the table for Annie Powell. She's the clever one. She can love a boy without taking off an article of clothes."

"Shut your stupid mouths," she said. "Dermott will make you pay for what you did to Gerald."

They tittered under their old men's caps. "It's Gerald, is it? There's a level of intimacy, if you ask me. Don't torment us, Annie Powell. The king will knock you silly for playing with your Geralds."

They couldn't keep her locked in a hotel. The watchdogs grew dumb when it came to following her in the street. She could snake in and out of an alley before they had the chance to catch their breath. She wouldn't crawl back to Bewley's. Annie was ashamed. How could she tell Gerald that her man was a gangster who happened to love James Joyce and had four old idiots to punch your kidneys out of shape for the crime of having a cup of coffee with Annie Powell?

She disappeared into the pubs of Duke Street. The Bailey, or that other one across the road, with awnings in the windows. It made her laugh. Because the Bailey had stolen the door right out of Mr. Leopold Bloom's house on Eccles Street. It exhibited the door in its own parlor. The door had an Egyptian knocker on it. She could surprise her man. Annie understood a thing or two about Mr. James Joyce. The Bailey, the Bailey, and Leopold Bloom. A tourist attraction it was. Come sip your Irish coffee with Leopold's front door. The pub was deep enough for Annie Powell. She could hide in there, against the sunlight off the windows. Bailey's would get crowded close to five. Young executives from Dame Street would come piling in for their jars and pints and glasses of vodka and pink gin, and they nearly drove Annie off her bench with their smooth bodies and starched cuffs. They were a friendly lot. They would ply her with the best Irish whiskey and stick their hands under her skirts. Annie didn't bother with their names. It could have been Jack or Mick or Frenchy Pete. She would go home with none of them. At half ten Annie said goodbye and hobbled from door to door until she got to her hotel.

That was Dublin without the king. Afternoons at the Bailey, running from Coote's old men, while the lads from Duke Street tickled her thighs with the cuff links they wore. She guzzled Jameson's whiskey, drank herself into a terrible fog. Then, one night, with Mick or Frenchy Pete laying an elbow in her skirts, she looked up, because it was time to go, and she saw her man inside the Bailey.

Dermott it was. The king himself. His eyes were dark, and she would have warned Mick or Pete, whoever it was, but the lad was busy solving the different layers of Annie's underwear. The king didn't rush that lad. He had too much dignity to destroy a pub. He waited for Annie to fix her skirts and get up from the bench. He'd never punish her in the Bailey, not her man. She would have liked to point out Leopold's door. Bloom, Bloom at the Bailey, but she was too drunk to raise her arm. "Derm," she muttered into the wall, "why don't you buy that fucking door and take it home with us."

She didn't remember much after that. Dermott must have gotten her to the Shelbourne. She was lying in bed. The king sat next to her. She could feel his shivering leg. She was too embarrassed to stare at him with both her eyes. Her man had shadows on his face, as if the cheeks had been pulled out of him and he was left with hollows under his nose.

Oh, Annie heard the knife, the kiss of an opening blade. She didn't move her head off the pillow when that slash arrived. The strokes were very harsh. They hurt like Jesus, but she wouldn't moan or scream. She bit her tongue from all that pain. She would have tolerated it, *loved* the cut in her cheek, if Dermott had only stayed with her, nursed his wicked Anne. But Dermott went into another room. It was the old men who jumped about with the gauze and the cotton. They looked at her with open mouths. "Mother of God!" That was the comfort she had. Bands of yellow teeth. Coote's old men became her nannies. They dressed and undressed the bandages she had to wear. The king was on another trip.

They fed her soup, the Fisherman's people. They wouldn't let a porter near Annie Powell. When the bandages came off, they stuck a mirror up to her face. Annie knew without any mirror. The king hadn't cut her in a mad, purposeless fit. Drunk she was that night. In a stupor. But she was alive to him. She felt every turn of his wrist. He'd given her his own design. She'd wear Dermott's name on her cheek for the rest of her life.

Snow White she was, with a scar on her to spoil her complexion . . . and four benevolent dwarfs. They swept and did her laundry in the sink. They stood around her bed, waving a funny ticket at her. "You're going to Americky."

"Where's my man?"

"Well, the king, he's indisposed. He can't see you off. But he did pay for the ticket."

They took her to the airport, sat with her until it was time to get on the plane. They had their knuckles in their eyes. They were sniffling when they put those knuckles down. They were the same old men who had punched Gerald outside Bewley's. They could be so mean and so nice.

"Forgive us, Annie dear."

"There's nothing to forgive."

"We led the king to Duke Street. We thought he'd slap you a bit. We didn't figure on the knife."

"That's Dermott's way," she said. She kissed the hands and mouths of these old crooks who had mended her, and she went off to Americky.

Someone met her on the other side of the ocean. Martin McBride. He winced at the sight of her, but he didn't say a word. They wouldn't let her starve in Manhattan, no, no, no. The uncle had an apartment for her and a cash allowance. "Annie, you'll never have to work again."

She told the uncle to stuff himself. "Dermott can keep that apartment for his next lady. I owe him five thousand dollars and I intend to pay it off. I'm not his personal cow."

Martin shrugged. "Five thousand?"

"That's what he gave to my mother for the privilege of renting me. So long, Mr. McBride."

They didn't love the idea of Annie whoring in the street. She'd make that five thousand on her back, she would, with any man who'd have a scarfaced woman. The uncle tried to threaten her. "I'll get the cops after you, I swear."

But the cops didn't bother her. No one bumped Annie from her corner. The worst of it was having to see O'Toole. She was fond of that donkey, even if he still worked for her man.

"Do us a small favor now, Annie girl."

"What?"

"Can you pick a less strenuous occupation?"

"No."

"Then have a drink with me, for God's sake."

"I will."

The donkey looked after her, kept the most belligerent whores off her tail. But she didn't need Dermott's muscleman. She had a new benefactor. A bum, a *strange* bum. Father Isaac. He took her to lunches in his smelly clothes, mumbled shit about a daughter he had. Annie didn't want complications. The bum wouldn't pay her to undress. He lectured Annie, told her she wasn't for whoring. She should be somebody's wife. She was tempted to laugh and shout in his ear, *Mister, you're looking at the original Mrs. Bride,* but she couldn't give Dermott's secret away. A bum like that, where did he get the money to buy her champagne? She never asked. He had to be a special magician, because cops and pimps became ostriches around Father Isaac. They dug their heads into their shoulders whenever he passed. But it didn't always work in Annie's favor. The bum would scowl at her johns, and she had to get him to disappear, or she couldn't have made a penny.

It was a life for her, standing in doorways, smiling at idiots from New Jersey. She didn't care. She'd shove that five thousand into the uncle's mouth someday. *This is for Dermott, Mr. Martin McBride. Tell him he can brand a girl, but he can't make Annie into a cow.*

Oh, she was a big talker, she was. She began to see her dwarfs around the City. Jesus, it could have been the old men who had bandaged her, you know, washed her panties in the hotel sink, but she wasn't sure. All of the Fisherman's people looked alike.

They would come up to Annie and blow in her face. "Get off the street, little girl." But when she asked them how the king was doing, they ran from her in their brittle, old men's shoes. It was beginning to drive her crazy.

She would go into the Irish bars along Eighth Avenue and drink slugs of Jameson's whiskey, crouching on a stool. The whiskey couldn't help. The old men appeared in the window with their yellow teeth. She might as well have carried them inside her skirts, the way these old men clung to Annie. They followed her home. "Last warning, little girl. Invisibility, that's our advice. A certain gentleman would like to see you shrink a bit."

She should have told Jamey about the dwarfs. She didn't. They trapped her in her doorway the very next night. They struck her with the handles off a broom. It wasn't her body they were after. The dwarfs kept banging her face. She woke up in a fucking hospital. Father Isaac was there. She pretended not to notice him. She didn't want a sermon now. She must have been delirious. When she opened her eyes again, two of the Fisherman's people were standing around her bed. They didn't have their broom handles. They smiled, and then they were gone. She prayed to that saint of hers. Jude gave her the will to crawl off the bed. She went into the closet for her skirts and strolled out of the hospital.

The donkey found her wandering in the streets. He brought Annie up to her room. "Jesus, where the hell were you?"

She had bruises on her lips. It was hard to mumble. Her head was mixed up. "Coote, Coote the Fisherman."

"What's that?"

"He put his salmons in the window . . ."

She lay in bed for a week. The donkey came in and out of her room. "Jamey, who are those old men?"

"Retired cops," he said. "Ancient, hairy sergeants . . . they'll never hit you again. Not with O'Toole around."

"Was it Dermott who sent for them?"

"I doubt it, Annie girl."

She ate her bread and butter, and soon she was strong enough to go downstairs. She wasn't much of a whore anymore. Men would blink at her battered face and avoid Annie Powell. So she took to dancing at her corner as a way of attracting johns. She sang Irish songs. But the words didn't come out right.

> In Dermott's old city
> Where the boys are so pretty
> And the rivers run underground
> I met a fisherman
> A sweet, sweet fisherman
> Who cried, Cockles and cunts,
> Alive, alive all . . .

Oh, she did pull in a few customers with her songs, drunken Irishmen and Swedes, old sailors they were, who didn't seem to mind a bashed-in girl. But she had a bit of a problem at home. Jamey was shivering on her bed. He wouldn't tell Annie what he was hiding from. He grew a beard sitting in the dark so long. And he frightened the old sailors.

She had to learn how to live with Robinson Crusoe. It was an odd braying the king's donkey had. He spoke in grunts. It didn't bother her. She had nothing worth jabbering about. Was she meant to recall Dublin with Jamey O'Toole? Tell stories of Dermott? Coote? Cashel Hill? She was possessed with ideas of money. Five thousand, or she'd remain Dermott's cow. She'd buy her freedom, she would.

You couldn't take advantage of Annie Powell.

TWENTY

Did you ever see the man on Grafton Street, the sandwichman who holds a huge signboard near his chest, touting some miserable tourist pub, with his eyes dead to this world? He stands with his jaw in the rain, a giant in a shabby coat. Remember him? The signboard stays perfectly still. He never blinks or scratches his nose. The donkey in Annie's room looked just like that. His face wouldn't twitch for thirty hours. But Robinson Crusoe wasn't dead. He was dreaming of the fire escape behind his mother's house in Chelsea.

It was only twenty blocks from Chelsea to Annie's room at the Lord Byron. But Robinson Crusoe couldn't run or crawl those twenty blocks. How can you find your mother's window with holes in your head?

The Fisherman was watching the streets. He's not in Connemara. The salmon don't bite this time of year. The king should have listened to Jamey O'Toole. But Dermott was always the businessman. *Dermott, he's a rat bastard, he is. Didn't I work for him? He'd dummy up the evidence. Or get his lads to knock you on the ear. He poses as the quiet one. But he's the killer, all right. Don't believe him. If he puts us in two cities, he'll be able to pick us off.*

The king sent little James back to Americky. O'Toole had to help uncle Martin collect the rent. It all turned sour when Annie arrived. No one had to tell him the history of that mark on her face. It was Dermott who gave her the cut. Sweet Jesus, how did he lose his own wife?

Then the Fisherman got into the act. His cronies beat her with their sticks. The donkey went looking for Coote's little old men. He found three of those lads at the Kilkenny Inn on West Twenty-fourth. He shoved their skinny behinds into a booth. "That's lovely what you did to Annie Powell. It's kind of you to go for the face. I'll make you dumb in a hurry if you don't explain to me what it's about? I thought we had a bargain with Coote. Why did he attack the girl?"

"Jamey darlin'," the little people said, squashed inside their booth. "That's ancient history. The king threw her out months ago. Dermott doesn't want her on the street. So what's she to you?"

He pushed their flimsy heads all the way under the booth. "She's a friend of mine. Keep your bats and sticks to yourselves, understand? I'll leave your brains stuck to the wall if Annie has another accident."

"Dermott won't like his donkey boy meddling in Coote's affairs."

"To hell with Dermott, and to hell with you."

He tapped them once on the skull to give the lads something to dream about. Then Jamey walked over to the house where he lived with his mother. Two detectives were hunched in the park across the street. There was a third blue-eyed wonder in the alley at the back of the house. These blue-eyed boys were from the First Deputy's office. They belonged to Isaac the Pure. Was Isaac working for Coote? Jesus, the whole Force was under the Fisherman's net.

Jamey trudged uptown. Detectives followed him in their green cars. Coote's people loitered on every other block. They winked at O'Toole. There's a message in the crackle of an old man's eye The donkey had been sold out. He was an expendable item to Coote. They would get another boy to collect their black rent. It was silly to run from Manhattan. If Isaac had gone in with Coote, they would have their lads checking for him at all the depots. He could smash one or two of them, but he couldn't beat up the City of New York. Oh, it was a merry Police Department when one commissioner danced with the next. They'd be dancing on Jamey's head soon enough. He didn't have much of a choice. The donkey went to hide in Annie's rooming house, because it was a dark, ratty place where cops didn't like to go.

The donkey's instincts were correct. Isaac and the little people kept away from Annie's room. Jamey had a life of it. He drank wine and ale from bottles in the window. His jaw was gripped with patches of hair. His shirt cumpled on his back. He became Robinson Crusoe in less than a month.

It pained him to watch Annie scuttle into the room with her johns. Such geeky old men, sailors from two or three wars ago, rotting in their winter vests. The donkey was obliged to wait in the hall. He would curse the king on those occasions. *Dermott, you gave my ass to Coote and fucked Annie girl.*

He couldn't last in the dark forever, with the odors of Annie's clientele in his beard. The poor girl was always drunk. Whiskey drunk. The whiskey gave her the fortitude and the soft burn she needed to entertain those crumbling sailors, sing to them and part her legs. The donkey had a rage in him. He wasn't going to shrivel because of Isaac and Coote McNeill. He combed his beard. Robinson Crusoe was getting ready for the street.

Daylight hurt his eyes. He could have been indoors for centuries. He wasn't used to crowds of shuffling men and women. They seemed moronic to Jamey, with their hard, fixed faces and translucent ears. They were staring into some uneasy eternity inside themselves that made him want to pick them up and hurl them into the gutters.

Robinson Crusoe left them alone. His education had come in the dark. The king was dumb, swear to God. He'd allowed Coote to jockey him into a hotel wing that was more a prison than a home. Dermott had his Alcatraz in seven large rooms. Coote provided the jailers. Ancient cops with kidney stones, borrowed from the Retired Sergeants Association. Hearing aids and heart murmurs. But they'd served under good commissioners. They were trained to kick a man to death. Lovely boys. The king had given his guts over to them, when he had his Annie and his O'Toole.

Jamey gritted his teeth. The young dudes were out. They tried to feather him with leaflets from all the massage parlors. He knocked the dudes to the side. He stuck his face in windows. People shrank from him. But the cops couldn't get under his beard Those blue-eyed wonders who walked in and out of cafes scorned this Robinson Crusoe. They didn't connect him with their image of that strongman O'Toole. The donkey was free to cruise.

He traveled down to the Fisherman's territories inside the Kilkenny Inn and picked a table near the door. The little people, Coote's old men, didn't recognize him. They sat on their stools, looking past Robinson Crusoe. He sneered at them.

"Bring the Fisherman here."

The little sergeants squeezed their eyes. "What's this?"

"Never mind. Just get me that old fart."

They complained to the bartender. "He stinks, this bag of garbage. Who invited him in?"

"I don't need invites. I'm your loving friend. The O'Toole."

They smiled at Robinson Crusoe with cracked lips. "Is it Jamey? In the flesh? What makes you think the Fisherman would ever talk to you?"

"Well, would he rather have me knock on his door at Police Headquarters?"

They got up off their stools and stood near the pay telephone. Jamey whistled "Columbus Was an Irishman" and "Phil the Fluter's

Ball." Coote was at his table before he could turn his back.

"It must have been a long ride from Chinatown," Jamey said. "The traffic can get pretty thick in the morning . . . isn't that right?"

"What do you want, O'Toole?"

"Where's your bloodhound, Isaac the Pure?"

"Isaac?" the Fisherman said. He wasn't chasing salmon at the Kilkenny Inn. He came without his hip boots. "Isaac snores with the rats on Centre Street. I haven't said hello to that prick in months."

"Then why are Isaac's lads waiting for me outside my mother's building?"

"Maybe he loves you, who knows? . . . I could send a message up to him and find out."

"Don't bother. I'll ask him myself."

"I wouldn't do that, Jamey boy. It's best to leave Isaac out of it."

"Listen, old man, if you hit Annie Powell again, if your little helpers touch her one more time with their sticks, I'll scream . . . scream to Isaac, and if Isaac doesn't hear, I'll go to the PC himself. Tiger John isn't much, but he'll have to protect his reputation . . . he'll throttle you . . . tell me, how are all the McNeills? Has your clan inherited the earth yet? You might retire a bit too soon, and your ass will get shaved, just like mine . . . you're a fouler cop than I ever was, Coote McNeill."

The Fisherman left the table. He didn't motion to the little people on the stools. He walked out of the Kilkenny and got into his car, a blue Chevrolet. The Fisherman drove himself downtown, while Robinson Crusoe rocked at his table. He ordered whiskey in a bottle. He wasn't going to drink one thimble at a time. The little sergeants frowned at him. So he drank without their blessings. He didn't like his conversation with Coote. He was trying to protect Annie girl, but he hadn't jabbed the Fisherman hard as he should. He couldn't run to Isaac now. The bastards would be crouching in the doorways. Coote had people everywhere. They were too short to reach his head. Their sticks would clatter around his shoulders and break. The donkey would get past Twenty-third Street, all right. He'd have splinters in his back from all the sticks. But he'd go deeper and deeper into Chelsea, crawl on his knuckles to find his mother's house. He banged on the table to get the barman's ear. "Another bottle, you fat son of a bitch. Put it on Coote's bill. I wonder if a cheap old fart like that will give me a decent wake."

The little people began to smile. "We'll bury you fine, Jamey, we will."

"You'll be burying Coote before you bury me. I have a whole other bottle to drink."

PART FIVE

TWENTY-ONE

Fucking Isaac.

He was the freak of a Department that had been fed the Irish way: on loyalty, discipline, and devotion to the cause. Isaac had no sense of camaraderie. He was a commissioner who fiddled on his own. He wouldn't move into Headquarters. He sat in that old, dying box on Centre Street, a huge limestone hut that was beginning to crumble and sink into the ground. Give him another year, and the boy will be swimming in mud. No one could pull him out of his corner room. The First Dep was an ally of Mayor Sammy Dunne. "Hizzoner" had split Becky Karp's brains in the primaries, beaten the regular and reform wings of his own Party, and now everybody was paying homage to Sam. You couldn't touch Isaac because of him.

Isaac the Pure kept a blanket in his desk. He would sleep at the old building whenever he liked. The one janitor who serviced the place couldn't throw out the First Dep. Isaac was free to stroll the long marble corridors past midnight. The floors had weakened tiles that would break loose under Isaac's feet. He would trip in the dark and curse the old Police Headquarters. But he loved it, tile for tile, with its dented iron rails, the roof that leaked on his head, its cracked dome and useless clock tower. He'd made his house in these ruins.

But his triumph was small. A desk, a blanket, and marble floors weren't much comfort to Isaac the bum. He had a bad dream in his corner of the building. Three women were chasing him: Sylvia, Annie, and Jennifer Pears. Their faces would intermingle in Isaac's dream, twist into odd amalgams. Annie had Jennifer's green eyes. Sylvia had a mark on her cheek. Jennifer began to look like Isaac's dead angel, Manfred Coen.

He muttered "Blue Eyes" and coughed himself awake.

His room seemed clogged with a kind of soft gray smoke. It was dust, moving bands of dust. He poked into the hall. The dust was thick as Moses. Isaac could barely see. He felt his way to the landing. There were plasterers on the ground floor, teams of them. They stood on ladders and knocked through the walls. They wore masks with little nose cones and mouth protectors. They had a woman with them. Isaac recognized her under her mask. It was the fallen mayoral candidate, Rebecca Karp. She motioned to Isaac. They walked out of Headquarters and faced one another on the street. Becky took off her mask. She smiled.

"Cocksucker, I warned you to get with me."

Isaac slapped the dust off his shoulders. "Rebecca, Sam would have destroyed you without my help. This town loves a little man. It never votes for big, ballsy women."

"Isaac, you're such a baby. How did you survive so long? Schmuck, we've taken over this building."

Isaac stopped slapping himself. "Who says?"

"Don't you read the papers? I'm president of the Downtown Restoration Committee. We're turning this shithole into a cultural center. And we're kicking you out."

"The City owns the building," Isaac said.

"I know. We leased it from the Department of Real Estate for a dollar a month. Isaac, you can't win."

Isaac went to Broome Street and dialed the Mayor's Office. He couldn't get Sammy on the phone. "Tell him again . . . Isaac wants to see him."

He had to hike down to City Hall. He could never be anonymous in the Mayor's territories. Reporters sniffed him from "Room Nine," their closet near the main door. They ran out to grab hold of Isaac and badger him. Why wouldn't he give press conferences any longer? Was Sammy going to make him a super "Commish" in charge of all corruption?

"Children," Isaac said, "this is a private call. Catch me at my office."

They had their spokesman, a boy from the *Daily News*. "Isaac, don't bullshit us, please. You come in and out of your own whirlwind. Who can ever catch you?"

He got around them and entered the Mayor's wing. All that swagger he'd enjoyed with Sam was gone. He had to confront the Mayor's three male secretaries. He couldn't get past the third

secretary without snarling and rolling his eyes. The second secretary
was less afraid of him. Isaac's jaw burned from gnashing his teeth.
"Sonny, I don't make appointments with the Mayor." The first
secretary had Isaac by the seat of his pants. "Lay off. We're blood
brothers, me and Sam . . ."

The cops outside the Mayor's door laughed at the spectacle of
Isaac being chased by three male secretaries. They were a pair of
plainclothesmen who had sworn to guard Sammy with their lives.
They would have had to club the First Deputy Police Commissioner
behind the ear. But Sammy heard the commotion and peeked out of
his office. The vision in front of his eyes saddened him. "It's only
Isaac," he said. "Let him through."

Isaac got into that office on the heels of Mayor Sam. His Honor
wouldn't look at him. He stared out the window at City Hall Park.
His aides had bolted the window for him. Sam was frightened of
September drafts. He was a different Mayor now. That meek illiterate
who took to a hospital bed before the primaries had become the fierce
Old Man of City Hall.

"You made up with Becky Karp, didn't you, Sam?"

"Not at all."

"She would have broken your neck, and you're kissy with her. I
should have figured that. It's pinky politics. All the Democrats roll
out of the same barracks room. It's bite, bite at the primaries, and
then you lick each other's navel."

"Don't be so harsh. I hate the bitch."

"Then why did you make her a landlady over me?"

"I did not. You're accusing the wrong man."

"You gave her Centre Street. You leased *my* building to her
fucking arts committee."

"Jesus," His Honor muttered. "I only lent her one wing. She
can't abuse you, Isaac . . . it's your fault."

"How come?"

"I wanted to get rid of Tiger John and give you the PC's job."

"Give it to Chief Inspector McNeill. He's your best cop."

"McNeill's too old."

"Old? He's younger than you are, Sammy Dunne."

"But McNeill's not the Mayor of New York. The people won't
stand for a decrepit Police Commissioner."

"Sam, I won't be your Tiger John."

"Then help us out, for God's sake. Mangen is on our back. What can I do? He's the Special Pros. Come in with me, Isaac. Take one of my chairs."

"Is that some title you're thinking of?"

"*Yes*. An assistant mayor to watch the Police."

"A rat, you mean, a rat working out of your office. Sammy, it's not for me."

The Mayor turned glum and retired to the golden-knobbed desk that Fiorello La Guardia had used. "Isaac, Isaac, you know that job of yours. The First Dep is always a vulnerable man."

One of his inspectors ran up to Isaac outside City Hall. It was fat Marvin Winch. Marvin was out of breath. "Sir, we've been looking all over for you. Our boys found Jamey O'Toole. Looks like he was kicked in the face by a lot of people."

"Is he still alive?"

"No, sir."

"I hope you didn't bring Jamey to Bellevue? I don't want him in the morgue . . . not yet. Those medical examiners will chop his fingers off and put them in a jar."

"Isaac, he's in a yard behind his mama's place. They tried to stuff him in a garbage can. But he's too big."

Marvin Winch drove him up to Chelsea so Isaac could stand in the carnage around Jamey O'Toole. Broken sticks. Blood. Teeth. Patches of wool. A crushed eye-glass frame. A third of someone's sleeve. Jamey had done a bit of dancing before he died. The bastards had left him in an awkward position. He sat with his rump in a garbage can. Nothing more of him could fit. The donkey must have been punched and kicked a thousand times. His head was swollen with bump upon bump. You couldn't see the man's nose. He'd clutched at them in a blinded state. There were clots of blood where his eyes had been.

Isaac didn't examine the sticks and teeth near O'Toole. The lab boys could squat with their clippers and sensitive gloves and play Sherlock Holmes. Isaac left things to Inspector Winch. "Marvin, they'll accuse us of body snatching if we don't watch out. You'll have to bring Jamey's mother downstairs to identify the son of a bitch. You ride with him to Bellevue, hear? The kids from the ambulance like to steal a dead man's shoe. They think it's good luck."

He strode uptown with ambulances in his head. The logistics of getting Jamey to Bellevue were uncertain at best. It would take more than one attendant and cop to move that corpse. Four detectives, *five*, would have to squeeze him into a body bag. A normal stretcher would collapse under O'Toole. They'd be smart to borrow a dolly from a grocery store and trundle him into the ambulance. Isaac's love of detail had gone macabre ever since he returned from Ireland.

Annie Powell wasn't at her corner. Isaac asked the young dudes about her. "You mean the crazy one who sings without her underpants? She's on Ninth Avenue, with all the bag ladies."

He knew that spot. Three old women had built an enclave of cardboard boxes on Ninth and Forty-first. It was an open-air fort; the old women lived inside the enclave with their belongings stuffed in shopping bags. Isaac would permit no cop to drive them out of their fort.

They were Irish hags from Clonmel, Wicklow, and Dun Laoghaire. Annie was drinking coffee with them. Isaac approached that enclave of boxes. Annie's legs were crossed. Her brow wrinkled up when Isaac's shadow fell on her. The three hags said hello. Annie didn't have to raise her eyes; she could tell from the persistence of his shadow who it was.

"You're standing in my sunlight, Father Isaac. Do me a favor and shove your ass a bit."

The hags had a stove in their fort put together from pieces of tin. They were baking sweet potatoes in the stove, and they offered Isaac one. He couldn't hold the potato. He had to slap it and push the potato from hand to hand. Annie laughed at his clumsy routine. She was beginning to like him all over again. Finally he gobbled the bark off the potato and chewed the inside. It was an inherited trait. His crazy mother also loved sweet potatoes. She had a junk shop downtown, and she slept in it with her Arab boyfriend Abdul. Then a gang of kids beat her up. She lay in a coma for months before she died. Those kids had some wild grievance against Isaac, and they got at him through his mother. He was a dumb prick with a worm in him and a host of scars that stayed soft and wet. He bumbled through the City now like a wounded bear. Who was Isaac? The worm, or the bear that grew around it?

"Jamey's dead. Some people kicked him in an alley."

Annie blinked at Isaac. "How do you know?"

"I could take you to the morgue and let you have a look . . . they didn't leave him much of a face."

"Jamey's killers, were they little people with brooms in their hands? . . . then they work for the Fisherman." She couldn't say Coote, Coote, because she'd promised the king never to utter that name. "He's an old man with high boots. He owns a house on a yellow lake. If you get up early in the morning, you can watch the salmon jump."

"Did they have a falling out, Dermott and the Fisherman? Is that why O'Toole got killed?"

No matter how many times he cut her, she wouldn't give her man's secrets away. She'd mourn for the donkey without telling Isaac. "Don't fuck with the old man," she said. "You'll end up with a salmon in your mouth."

The girl spoke in riddles that Isaac couldn't connect. He'd have drawn her out of that enclave, removed her from the hags, but she might lift those skirts and show her quim to Ninth Avenue. Isaac couldn't risk that.

"Go to Castledermott," she said. "You can visit the yellow lake. If you pee in the water, God forbid. You'll murder all the fish."

He left Annie muttering and said goodbye to the three hags. His "angels" were across the street, watching Annie from the inside deck of a fruit and vegetable market. They were unfamiliar boys. His whole Department was shifting under him. Couldn't he get two fucking "angels" that he could recognize and trust? He'd have to call the *new* Headquarters, demand cops with kinder faces, like Manfred Coen. His "angels" were turning hard on Isaac.

TWENTY-TWO

He was beginning to shy away from Centre Street. He couldn't think with an army of plasterers droning under his corner room, tearing down walls to build a culture house for Rebecca Karp. They would bury Isaac under a curtain of dust. He'd have to spend his days with a handkerchief over his eyes. Sam was fucking him. But Isaac didn't intend to yodel in front of City Hall. Whatever the Mayor promised, whatever the Mayor swore, Becky Karp and her cultural committee would bump him into the street.

Isaac went to his hotel. The pimps were in a somber mood. They shouted at their black mamas. Younger "brides" were coming in, and most of them weren't black. They were runaways from Sioux City,

Bismarck, Pierre, and Great Falls, little snow queens, white girls who couldn't have been more than twelve, though their bodies seemed burnt-out. Isaac had a maddening drive in him to arrest every pimp at the hotel and bash them on the skull. These ancient young girls belonged in an orphanage, not a brothel. They were recruits from the prostitution mills of Minneapolis and St. Paul. But if Isaac revealed himself, if he came down on the pimps like a hammer, he'd lose his status as a bum. He wouldn't be able to wander through the hotel, half invisible, an old crock with black shit on his face and his fly unbuttoned.

Still, it hurt him to be near those girls and do nothing for them. They had the mousy complexions of frightened, wingless bats who couldn't stand the light. They thrived in darker places. The girls wore sunglasses inside the hotel. Isaac could hear them walk the corridors in their platform shoes. Was it Dermott or Sweet Arthur Greer who first made the Minneapolis Connection? Girls with pink eyes, skin that bruised at the touch of a finger. It was a monstrous imprisonment. Arthur and the king had helped transfer Isaac's hotel into a boardinghouse for squirrely twelve-year-olds.

He couldn't get to Dermott, so Isaac would have to try Sweet Arthur again. He jumped on the phone to round up detectives for a raid. He would destroy Arthur's penthouse if the "blues" didn't break that Minneapolis Connection and find a better home for these girls. His deputies had to interrupt him. "Isaac, there isn't an Arthur anymore." The "friend" of all Manhattan pimps had jumped from his penthouse roof.

"When did it happen?"

"This afternoon."

"Was he pushed?"

"Isaac, what do you mean? Arthur was alone. We checked with the doormen. They swear no one came up to the penthouse today."

"Dummies," Isaac said, "who gives a shit what a doorman swears? Doormen can tell lies. Like everybody else."

His own inspectors turned to imbeciles when Isaac wasn't around to stroke their wooden heads. Arthur wasn't the type to kill himself. He loved his penthouse too much. He'd been a hoodlum since the age of nine. He wouldn't have let a stranger close enough to shove him off a roof. He was with a "landsman" when he died. It was a familiar face that killed Arthur Greer.

Isaac wondered about that familiar face. He was being followed in the street. He'd had the same shadow a week ago. It was that ex-cop, Morton Schapiro, who used to fly from precinct to precinct in the Bronx. Captain Mort was supposed to be working for Arthur Greer. Isaac banged him into a doorway and grabbed Schapiro by the throat. "Your boss is dead. Schmuck, did you kill Arthur Greer?"

He seemed indignant, Captain Mort. "Isaac, let go of me. I got nothin to do with that boogie pimp. Honest to God. I have a kite for you . . . from Mangen."

Dennis Montgomery Mangen was the Special State Pros. The Governor had appointed him to ferret out corruption *everywhere* in New York. But Mangen was on a holy mission to clean up the City Police. The mention of his name could scare any cop.

"Mangen wants to see you."

Isaac still had Schapiro by the throat. "Are you one of Dennis' shoofly boys?"

"Yeah, I work for Mangen."

"Tell him I don't have time for him."

"Isaac, that aint too smart."

Mangen had his own investigators, his own stool pigeons, his own grand jury. He could slap an indictment on you faster than "Hizzoner" could blow his nose.

"Listen," Isaac said. "I don't like Dennis sending shooflies out to sit in my pants. If he wants to see me, he can come to my hotel."

"You're joking," Schapiro said. "Mangen doesn't go into the shithouses."

Isaac gave Captain Mort an extra squeeze on the throat. Then he threw him out of the doorway and went back to his hotel. Mangen appeared in fifteen minutes. He was much younger than Isaac, but they had things in common: Marshall Berkowitz and Columbia College. Mangen was another one of Marshall's protégés. He came to police work after *Ulysses and Finnegans Wake*. He was a tall, pugnacious Irishman who kept his old, battered "skeleton keys" to Joyce. He wore a coat with a fur collar in the middle of September. He sat with Isaac on Isaac's bed. The bum had no chairs in his room.

"Isaac, your Department stinks, right from the top."

Isaac smiled.

"I'm not talking about you," Mangen said. "It's Tiger John I want."

"Tiger John? The Tiger's pretty dumb for a Police Commissioner."

"I agree. But he still gets a nickel for every whore that has a pair of legs."

"Dennis, I've been scrounging at this hotel for three rotten months. I've watched the pimps and their women . . . the porno shops . . . the love parlors . . . and I never sniffed Tiger John."

"He doesn't come uptown to grab his nickels. He can sit at Headquarters. Tiger John owns a piece of the trade. He has nineteen different bank accounts . . . and aliases to go with them. You'd get a kick out of John's aliases. They have a deeper imagination than John himself. The accounts are in small bundles, that's true. But they add up to a hundred and fifteen thou."

"Dennis, if you're so sharp, tell me how much I have lying around . . ."

"You," Mangen said, "you're a poor man. You have nine hundred dollars spread in three accounts."

"I didn't think I owned that much," Isaac said. "I wouldn't care if Tiger John had himself a million . . . how do you connect his nineteen bankbooks with the whoring business?"

"Isaac, I can't give my sources away."

Mangen always had his "sources." He was known for the rats he kept on his payroll. If he couldn't buy information from you, he could bring you in front of his grand jury. A "call" from Mangen was enough to ruin a man's career. He would dishonor judges and cops, and make it difficult for bank managers to survive. But his "sources" were tainted with hysteria. A bank manager would announce whatever Dennis wanted to hear. He ran his two floors at the World Trade Center like a Gestapo jailhouse. Assistant prosecutors would bark behind locked doors, while you stood in the corridors waiting to be let in, with closed-circuit television cameras blinking pictures of your face from inside Mangen's walls.

"Dennis, if you chew off the Tiger's knees, you'll get flak from Sam. They were boys together in some Irish county. Sam's getting popular in his old age. If he gives a cry, you'll feel it. The whole Trade Center could begin to rock."

"Let me worry about Sam," Mangen said. "Just help me out with Tiger John."

"Don't mistake me for one of your shooflies. Me and the Tiger never had much in common. We avoid each other whenever we can . . . why did you hire Captain Mort? He may be a good legman, but he's a lousy cop."

"Morton's all right. He does favors for me from time to time."

"But I don't like to have him in my cuffs."

"Why? I put him there to protect your life."

"Who's trying to kill me?"

"Tiger John. He got to Sweet Arthur, and he'll get to you."

Isaac looked at Mangen with a bum's heavy eyes. The worm was waking up. That creature churned in Isaac's belly. "I thought Arthur jumped off his roof."

"He didn't jump. He was pushed."

Mangen had more sense than Isaac's own blue-eyed boys. But he was a little warped on the subject of Tiger John.

"Dennis, did you ever hear of a guy called the Fisherman?"

Mangen said, "No, Who is he?"

"I'm not sure. He's supposed to be partners with Dermott Bride."

"That one. He's a thug . . . and a police spy. He puts out for every cop in Manhattan and the Bronx."

"That's strange," Isaac said. "He never put out for me."

"The Tiger kept him from you . . . he owns Dermott Bride. And they'll fix you the way they fixed Arthur and Tiny Jim O'Toole."

"O'Toole was Dermott's man," Isaac said.

"That doesn't matter. The cunts know I'm onto their scam . . . they'll try to knock out every trail they left on Whores' Row. Isaac, you're a nuisance for them. They don't like the idea of having a commissioner in their neighborhood, pretending to be some kind of bum. They'd blow you away if I didn't have Mort watching out for your health."

The loose hairs on Isaac's mattress must have gotten to Mangen. "We're an odd lot," he said. "You, me, and Dermott. We all flew out of Dean Berkowitz's skull. The only fathers I had were Marsh and Leopold Bloom. Scan one line of *Ulysses* with Marshall Berkowitz and you can become the best prosecutor in the world . . . his wife ran away. Poor Marsh. It's his third marriage. Did you ever meet Sylvia?"

"Once or twice," Isaac said.

"She's a tart, if you ask me. I promised Marsh to help him find her, but the woman's disappeared."

What could Isaac say? That he was hiding her in his flat on Rivington Street? He was giving Sylvia the chance to reconsider her marriage. The First Dep hadn't humped her since his days at the

Shelbourne Hotel. That much was true. Mangen got off Isaac's bed. The fur on his coat stood crookedly around his neck.

"Isaac, whatever happened to that sweetheart of yours? Coen. Manfred Coen."

"He died on me," Isaac said. "Last year."

"He was a nice boy. Mr. Blue Eyes."

Mangen left, and Isaac heard a great clumping of feet on the stairs. The Special Prosecutor hadn't come to Isaac without his army of shooflies. He probably had men like Captain Mort stationed on every landing. Dennis was an "angel" with fur on his shoulders. The schmuck thought he was keeping Isaac alive.

Mangen shouldn't have mentioned Sylvia and Marsh. The worm burrowed with its armored heads, skewering Isaac. He walked out, went around the block to shake off Mangen's shooflies, and took a cab down to Rivington Street.

It was past dinner time on the Lower East Side. The knish stores had begun to close. You couldn't even get fried bananas, or yellow rice. Puerto Ricans, Haitians, and Jews were going home to their television sets. Isaac had no expectations that Sylvia would feed him and the worm. He was just looking in on Marshall's wife.

Isaac saw a cop's uniform on his chair. Sylvia was in bed with a patrolman from Elizabeth Street. Isaac had worked that precinct once. All the good, tough cops grew out of Elizabeth Street. You had to mend the little wars between a hundred different societies, gangs, and gambling clubs that surrounded the Elizabeth Street station. It was like being the white father in a cranky piece of Shanghai. Isaac was loved and feared on Elizabeth Street long before he became the First Dep. He wasn't wanton with his knuckles. If Isaac busted your head, it had to be something you deserved. He would protect small shopkeepers from rapacious cops and kids without asking for a free bowl of rice. He was Isaac the Pure. But that was twenty-five years ago.

This patrolman was sleeping off his tour of duty, "cooping" in Isaac's bed. Sylvia had opened her eyes. She wasn't disturbed at the prospect of a bear in the room. She pointed to the sleeping cop. "That's William."

"I wouldn't want to wake the boy," Isaac said.

"Don't be silly. Stay awhile. William never gets up this early. Isaac, would you like a cup of tea?"

"No thanks," he said, his stomach growling for ham, cheese,

lettuce, mustard, sweet Seckel pears.

"Then get out of your clothes, for God's sake."

"Sylvia," Isaac said. "William might not go for that."

"That's William's problem . . . not ours. Isaac, you look pale to me. Don't wait too long . . . you could freeze in your pants."

What the hell? Why couldn't Isaac be hugged near a sleeping cop? He'd had so many disappointments in the past few days. Green-eyed Jenny was having *his* child without him. O'Toole was beaten to death. Whore children were invading his hotel. Rebecca Karp had kissed Mayor Sam and secured a lease to Isaac's building. Annie Powell sat with three Irish witches in a paper fort, and wouldn't even nod to Isaac. Now Mangen pestered him with stories of Tiger John. The stories made no sense. Tiger John was Sam's creation. He didn't have the balls to push around a squad of killers from 1 Police Plaza. It had to be someone else.

The bear undressed and climbed in with Sylvia and the sleeping cop. William moaned from his corner of the bed. The cop was having a nightmare. He muttered, "Mama, mama," and pulled most of the blanket on top of him. Part of his leg was exposed. The skin was bitten down near the shank, and the calf muscles seemed to twist into the bone. The cop must have had rickets as a baby. Isaac entered Sylvia. Three in a bed. Three in a bed. She clutched his back and moaned louder than the cop. Isaac was in the middle of a slow despair. Men were dying around him. The Special Pros had more of a grip on the murders attached to Whores' Row than Isaac could ever have from his stinky hotel.

TWENTY-THREE

The bear had a troubled time. He couldn't tell where he was. Then he remembered that Sylvia lay between him and William the cop. The bear was still on Rivington Street, hugged by Sylvia Berkowitz in his own bed. Images of Marshall, Mangen, and Manfred Coen crept into Isaac. The worm chewed off lumps of him. His misery was complete.

He dressed without disturbing Sylvia and the cop. He watched the two bodies rub and make a creaky music. He wasn't jealous of the way Sylvia turned from Isaac's empty spot and reached for William in her sleep. Isaac had to get out of there.

He walked to Centre Street. Becky's carpenters wouldn't be

biting into walls at two A.M. The culture committee had made
enormous progress in a week. The bastards had reshaped the ground
floor. They were grooming the old Headquarters for a party that
would celebrate the beginning of Becky's lease. The pols admired
her. She'd stolen a building from the City of New York and was
ready to evict her only tenant, Isaac the Pure. All the bigtime
Democrats would come out for Becky Karp. Rebecca was
contemptuous of Isaac. She sent out invitations for her party to
everyone but him.

The phone was ringing in Isaac's office. Son of a bitch. "Hello,"
Isaac said, "hello, hello." It was one of Sammy's live-in aides. His
Honor was missing from Gracie Mansion again. Isaac shouted into
the phone. "Get Becky Karp. She owes the City a favor or two. She
can grab a nightgown to cover her tits and go looking for Sam."

His bitchiness began to gnaw at him. The Mayor was an old
man. He'd had problems with his memory before. He could have an
attack of senility and lose his way in the streets. Isaac took a cab up
to Cherokee Place. where he'd found His Honor strolling in his
pajamas two months ago. But there was no Mayor Sam on Cherokee
Place. He wondered if His Honor could have gone to an Irish club in
the area. Sammy must have belonged to twenty of them. His favorite
was the Sons of Dingle Bay, on First Avenue. The Sons had installed
a sauna on the premises, because His Honor loved the idea of a
Finnish bath. The club wasn't dead at three in the morning. Isaac saw
pecks of light behind the screens in the ground-floor window. He had
to knock and shout his name to get in. "Isaac Sidel . . . I'm here for
Mayor Sam." A few retired cops were playing poker in the game
room. Isaac didn't stall. He plunged into the sauna with all his clothes
on. The Mayor sat on the sauna's lower deck with a towel under his
bum to protect him from the heat of the wood. He was with his toy
commissioner, Tiger John. Two old men in a room built like a large
dollhouse with rocks burning on a crib that was placed in the corner.
"Laddie," the Mayor said, "you'll sweat like a pig if you don't make
yourself a little more naked." The Tiger agreed. Their raw bellies
moved up and down. They didn't seem surprised to have Isaac in
their room.

Sweat poured down from Isaac's eyes. He could feel a hot
blowing in his ears. "Your Honor, you ought to notify a few of your
aides when you have long hours at the club. They worry about you,
and then they call me on the phone."

"Jesus," the Mayor said, "you can't have a dry bath away from home without disturbing the peace . . . Laddie, you didn't have to come on my account."

"I thought you'd like to know something. Mangen visited me at my hotel."

"Ah, the great god himself. What did he want?"

"He had some crazy tale about whores and cops."

"Whores and cops?" His Honor said. The Tiger's belly continued to heave up and down.

"It wasn't important," Isaac said. "Mangen's on his usual crusade."

The bear had to get out. His coat and pants were boiling on him. He left Sammy Dunne and the PC on their wooden deck, with the rocks burning in the corner. The Dingle Bay boys cursed and flung their poker chips behind Isaac's dripping back. A blue Chevrolet was parked in front of the club. It had a curious chauffeur, Coote McNeill. McNeill shared the fourteenth floor with Tiger John at the new Police Headquarters. He had the longest tenure in the Department. He'd risen out of the youth squad twelve years ago to become Chief Inspector. His underlings called him "the McNeill," because he was supposed to be descended from a famous tribe of kings that controlled the lands of Galway until Oliver Cromwell beheaded the last McNeill. Isaac thought it was a lot of shit, but if the old man wanted to make up his own line of kings, who was Isaac to begrudge him?

The McNeill poked his head out the car window. "Sidel, where did you get such a red face?"

"It's my fault. I was in the bath with Sammy and John. I shouldn't have worn my socks . . . are you waiting for His Honor?"

"Yes," the McNeill said. "Somebody has to take him home. Sam's not the walker he once was. He's forgetful now. He could turn the wrong corner and lose that mansion of his."

"McNeill, did you ever know a boy named Dermott? Mangen swears he's a police spy."

Coote McNeill spit into his palm like any king of Galway. "It's a bit of a scandal, son . . . believing Mangen over us. You should come to Headquarters with your own kind. There's too much dust on Centre Street. Isaac, it's gotten into your eyes."

"The dust will clear," Isaac said. "Fat Becky is throwing me out . . . you'll have me for a neighbor sooner than you think."

Before the cops moved to Chinatown, Isaac was the strongman
of the Department. All the unsolvable items, all the mysteries, went
to him. His blue-eyed boys flashed in and out of the five boroughs,
grabbing for clues. But Isaac had gone to sleep. He crept among rats
and mice at the old Headquarters. Now Coote McNeill had sway over
Chinatown and 1 Police Plaza. With a fumbling PC like Tiger John
and an absent First Dep, McNeill had a house to himself. He owned
the new Headquarters. He was a little old man about to retire.

Isaac crawled back to his hotel. Sammy's hot box at the Dingle
must have smoothed the worm in Isaac and unstuffed his head.
Mangen wasn't daft at all. Some fucking dance was going on with
Mayor Sam and the McNeill. Tiger John shuffled between them. The
Police Commissioner was an errand boy. That senile old Mayor had
been stringing Isaac along, playing him for a goose. Herzog's
Bellow, His Honor had muttered at the synagogue in Queens.
Herzog's Bellow. Sammy was the shrewdest one of all.

Where did Dermott belong? Was he a silent member of the
Dingle Bay club? It was crazy to Isaac. Crazy shit. Should he mount
an investigation against the Old Man of City Hall? He couldn't even
marshal two good boys to protect Annie Powell. Things were
slipping past Isaac the Pure. Was the McNeill Annie's goduncle? It
was a happy family that Isaac was trying to bust. What did a few
corpses mean? The Mayor had his sauna bath. The world had to be all
right.

Annie Powell was lonely without her Robinson Crusoe. He'd
been a kind roommate to her. Jamey O'Toole. He wasn't a nuisance
in the end. He didn't have to climb into the hall when a customer
arrived. Annie had lost most of her trade. Even the decrepit Irish
sailors wouldn't come to her. She ranted at them, cackled songs that
didn't remind them of the Old Country. It wasn't Dublin she sang
about. It was a fish between her legs for somebody named the king.
She was serenading Dermott across an ocean, calling to her man. She
didn't believe in weather or the ravages of time. She refused to wear
underpants, stockings, and blouses in the fall. She had a coat, a
ragged slip, and one of the king's old undershirts to put on.

She was lonely, lonely, lonely without O'Toole. Tiny Jim was
her last tie to the king. She could smell Connemara on him, sheep
droppings, Castledermott—the house that wasn't Dermott's house—
salmon struggling in the water, the smoke of a turf fire, bananas and

cream, that dead cow in the road. Jesus, she was a girl in a jewelry store, selling her smile to customers, until Dermott pulled her out of there. But he shouldn't have bought Annie from her mother though. She didn't like a man to pay for her in cash. She could forgive the mad look in his eye, the twitch of his knife. A man could mark Annie Powell if he loved her enough. The king shouldn't have left her alone.

She sat with the three friendly witches of Ninth Avenue, Margaret, Edna, and Mary Jane. They had whiskey and hot potatoes that the witches chewed without their teeth. Margaret, Edna, and Mary Jane wouldn't live indoors. They hated the contraptions of a kitchen, pots and things, the flush of a toilet, radiators, windows, pipes. They couldn't have tolerated a roof over their heads. They needed the howls that came off the river at night. So they camped in the street. They had their home of boxes, crates, and rags strewn around them in a kind of haphazard open fort.

The girls welcomed Annie Powell. She had all the signs of a rag lady. She was a younger, more beautiful version of themselves, a witch with a damaged cheek. She muttered like the girls. She told obscene stories about the Irish male, who had to tuck in his balls for centuries because he was always on the run. She wore the same misspent articles on her body as they did. Nothing matched. One of her socks might be brown. The other green or yellow. The girls were natives of Clonmel, Wicklow, and Dun Laoghaire. They could accept a witch from Sunnyside. County Queens it was. A patch of the Old Country. She secured whiskey for them. They passed the bottle from mouth to mouth. They were widow women, girls who had lost their husbands forty and fifty years ago. They knew about love. They could remember nights under the quilt. Mother Mary, that's a man inside me sleeping gown! What's he doing in there? Those husbands had died young. When the memory of it shook them, they would raise a horrendous cry on Ninth Avenue. They could stop traffic for twelve blocks with their keening. They looked at Annie Powell and realized that she was a lovesick girl.

Annie didn't keen with Margaret, Edna, and Mary Jane. How can you mourn a live man? Oh, there were deaths aplenty. But her king was in Dublin town, having his sausages and marmalade with the Fisherman's people. What was a girl to do? A car passed near the fortress of boxes, a blue car with an old man hunched behind the wheel. The crook of his back wasn't unfamiliar to Annie Powell.

When did Coote the Fisherman get from Castledermott to Ninth Avenue and North Americky? She stepped over the boxes in her ragged skirts and called after the blue car, so she could interrogate the Fisherman, ask him about the king. "Coote," she said, "wait for me."

The car paused at the end of the block. Annie the witch went over and stuck her face in the window. "How are you, Mr. Coote?"

The Fisherman smiled. "Fit as a fiddle," he said. "And you, love? Have you been stuck in any fogs lately?"

"It don't fog much in New York," Annie said.

"It's a pity I can't help you the way I did in Connemara. I brought you down from Cashel Hill. Me and those lads of mine. But you shouldn't go on picnics in foul weather . . ."

"Would you like a sweet potato, Mr. Coote? I can ask Edna to bake one up for you."

"Thanks, love, but I've got the indigestion. Sidel must have given me his worm."

"Who's Sidel?"

"You know him. The boy who walks around in bum's clothes."

"Father Isaac," she said.

"Have you been talking to him, love? Did you tell him about Dermott and me?"

"I don't remember."

"He's a nasty fellow, that Father Isaac. Has he made any indecent proposals to you?"

"None. He likes to buy me champagne. He thinks I'm his daughter."

"You mean the famous Marilyn? That girl's been married seven times."

"She must have the itch . . . I wouldn't want seven husbands under my skin . . . how's the king? Does he have a new girl by now?"

The Fisherman said, "No, no. You're his sweetheart. He worries about you, love. He says, 'Why is my Annie on the street?' "

"I owe him money. I have to pay it off."

"What kind of money?"

"He stole me from my mother for five thousand dollars."

"Five thousand? You can borrow that from me."

"What's the use? I'd only push my debt around . . . if he wants his Annie off the street, Mr. Coote, tell him he has to come for me."

"I will," the Fisherman said. And he drove off, leaving Annie with the king awash in her head. She had a sweet potato with the girls. She guzzled Irish whiskey. She thought of Marilyn. How did it feel to be seven times a bride? Annie was only married once, but she was *twice* a bride. Dermott's bride she was. Bride's bride. It was all a hoax. Blame it on the king and his donkey. The donkey had given her away in the cool of an Irish church. She had to take the wedding band off her finger. There was small magic in that church. She was still Annie Powell, the same Annie. Dermott's secret bride.

She drank whiskey with Margaret, Edna, and Mary Jane. The three witches understood the restless agony of knees jumping under Annie's skirts. Like a cow she was, a cow gone wild in the head without its mate. The whiskey had maddened her with a hoarse fever. "Bridey," she muttered. "The bride of Little Bride Street." Ah, she had the hallucinations. She was counting the streets of Dublin in her wild talk. Annie climbed over the barricade. Boxes tore around her feet. Rags spilled out. "Good night," she said, with the sun shining in her hair. Even the girls had enough sense in them to declare the difference between night and day. "Night," she said, "good night," and she shuffled into the gutters. She didn't have a penny in her skirts. She was going to hop from bar to bar singing Irish songs like any street musician and collect pints of whiskey for the girls. But she never got to the south side of Ninth Avenue.

The girls had been watching the traffic for her. Housed in their fort, they'd developed a certain prescience. They could feel most disasters, the witches of Clonmel, Wicklow, and Dun Laoghaire. They would have yelled if the cars grew thick in front of Annie. But a cab scuttled out of nowhere to bump Annie Powell. It hadn't been part of the traffic. A willful, angered machine it was, that could throw a girl over a fender and disappear. The blood whipped from Annie's mouth in long, long strings. She shuddered in the air, rose with the force of that machine, her back nearly ripping into two separate wings as she fell into the gutter, with her thighs pulling loose from her shredded skirts. "Mother of Mercy," the witches shrieked, breaking through their barricade to get near Annie Powell.

PART SIX

TWENTY-FOUR

He'd killed the girl, *him,* Isaac, the big chief. He'd trusted Annie to pairs of strange boys from his office. He should have interviewed all the bodyguards he assigned to her. Only the schmuck couldn't even walk into Headquarters. He ran his office from an old dungeon that would soon belong to Rebecca of the Rockaways. He couldn't tell who was working for him anymore. He had to telephone his office to find out every piece of news. His blue-eyed angels should have been the scourge of the City. But these angels were falling down. They would bump into each other on various assignments and quests. They didn't have Isaac to pamper them and coordinate their attacks. They were disarmed without Isaac the Pure.

Their chief had a worm in him. The worm fucked his head. He'd gone into seclusion, lived in a ratty hotel, to lay bare the whore markets of New York. His bum's clothes taught him nothing. The pimps mocked the charcoal on his face. His hotel was a canteen for twelve-year-old prostitutes from the Midwest. The traffic in baby women flourished around Isaac. He couldn't make a dent. He scrounged here and there, and forgot to keep Annie alive.

Isaac grew active once she was dead. He couldn't locate the cab that ran her down, but he got in touch with Annie's mother. Mrs. Powell cursed him on the phone. She wouldn't come to the morgue and look at Annie. "My daughter's in Ireland. She went with a lousy thief. I wish I could say he's a Yid. But he's as Irish as Cardinal Cooke. Dermott Bride has my Annie . . . he has my girl. So don't tell me stories about this corpse you collected. I don't care if you're the commissioner to Saint Patrick. If you bother me again, I'll sue."

She hung up on Isaac. Should he give her daughter a Catholic burial? The worm wiggled no. He had to smuggle some kind of ceremony for Annie Powell. Apostate as he was, he still belonged to the Hands of Esau. This was the brotherhood of Jewish cops. Isaac had buried his Blue Eyes, Manfred Coen, through the Hands of Esau. He also tricked a grave out of them for Annie. "Jewish girl," he said.

"Never mind her name . . . I need a good plot."

The Hands of Esau hired righteous men to say the kaddish for Annie Powell. Isaac rode out to Queens in the funeral car. He threw bits of earth on top of Annie's coffin, as if he'd been a father to her. The gravediggers had mercy on Isaac. They offered him a cigarette. The First Dep wouldn't smoke near Annie's grave.

He returned to Manhattan and ended his apostasy for seven days. He camped out on Ninth Avenue with the witches of Clonmel, Wicklow, and Dun Laoghaire. He sat shiva behind their barricade, while the witches shrieked. They frightened merchants and cops with their long cries. When they grew exhausted from their keening, Isaac would stuff potatoes in their mouths. He wouldn't let the witches starve.

Sitting on his box, he stirred only for coffee and the needs of his bladder. He didn't wash. He didn't move his bowels. He didn't feed the worm. His chin darkened from the whiskers that were growing there. He got terribly thin.

After those seven days of mourning he stood up and walked to his hotel. He'd come home in the middle of a crisis. The black whores, girls of nineteen, had begun to rebel. They felt betrayed by their pimps, who were bringing twelve-year-olds into the house, white trash from the barns of Minneapolis and St. Paul. The black whores couldn't scare a gentleman off the street. Their trade had dwindled altogether. No one would take them but freaks. Everybody wanted the little snow queens with baby tits. So the black whores had to turn mean in the halls. They went after the little "whiteys," tore the clothes off their skinny backs. The snow queens couldn't scrounge for men in tattered underwear. They hid five and six to a room, trembling against the wrath of the black whores, who patrolled the hotel with hellish eyes.

It couldn't last. The "players" left their purple Cadillacs when they couldn't find one little "whitey" in the street. They marched into the hotel and finished off the rebellion. They freed the little "whiteys" from their rooms, dressed them in different clothes, and pushed them out like big ravaged dolls to draw the customers in. Then the "players" took their revenge.

They were beating and kicking the black whores just as Isaac entered the hotel. The pimps paid no mind to the old bum who had been sitting shiva for seven days and had dust and dark stubble all over him. Isaac saw bloody mouths everywhere. The black whores

gave up most of their teeth. It was as if Isaac had stumbled upon the
slaughter of twenty cows. The noise was the same. The moaning was
horrible to him. The pimps' assault on the black whores didn't make
him think like a cop. He couldn't produce handcuffs for every
"player" at the hotel. The moans he heard, that constant cowlike moo,
gripped Isaac in the belly and maddened him. Isaac was encouraged
by the worm. He trucked through the halls slapping blindly at each
pimp he met. He knocked off their hats. He bit them on the ear in a
show of fury. He ruined their fifty-dollar vests. The black whores
were amazed. They'd never had an avenger like this old bum. Isaac
muttered to himself as he threw down one pimp after the other. "Pray
to Dermott, you lovely boys . . . I'll close this fucking hotel . . . Annie
died because of me and you . . . the king can't protect you now."

The "players," the last of them, the ones who were still on their
feet, did the best they could: they called the pimp squad at Midtown
Station South. "Bring the cops, man . . . we got a maniac on the
grounds. He'll murder people, swear to Moses, he will."

Eight detectives arrived. They were part of the First Deputy's
office. Isaac himself had created them, a special squad to keep the
pimps of Manhattan from hurting their own women. But the pimp
squad suffered without any visibility from their chief. Isaac was only
a phantom to them. No one on the squad had ever seen the First Dep.
The squad's morale was low. Instead of protecting the whores, the
squad became friendly with the pimps.

The eight detectives were appalled by the blood and squalor
inside the hotel. They'd been sleeping in their squadroom for the past
two days. They despised anything to do with the ugly smells of the
street. They were on loan from the burglary squad. Some idiot from
Isaac's office had fucked up their lives. They were dangling men,
cops on a "telephone message." A phone call from Headquarters had
reshuffled them, thrown them in with the pimp squad. No orders had
been written up. Another phone call could take them away, parachute
them into the Bronx. You couldn't depend on shit when you were
doing a "telephone message."

They weren't in the mood to placate an old bum on the rampage.
They wanted to get back to their squadroom at Midtown Station
South, so they could sleep the rest of the afternoon. They caught
Isaac on the second floor, with a pimp's ear in his mouth. It was
dumb stuff. They couldn't smooth this out. They'd have to arrest the
crazy son of a bitch. Six of them fell on top of Isaac. The other two

grabbed his feet. They could either kill him, or handcuff him and bring him along to Midtown South. There were a lot of black whores in the hall. The whores were watching Isaac. Now the detectives would have to go through the entire rigmarole of collaring the bum. Their senior man, a detective-sergeant, shook the "rights" card out of his wallet and began reading it to Isaac.

"Hey, you glom, you're under arrest. You have the right to remain silent and refuse to answer questions. Do ya understand?"

Isaac growled up at him. "Eat your ass," he said.

"What's your name, you?"

"Moses Herzog McBride."

"Listen, McBride, anything you say can be used against you in a court of law. Ya understand?"

"Eat your ass."

Some of the detectives dug their knees into Isaac's groin.

"You have the right to consult your attorney before speaking to the police. And to have an attorney present for any questioning now or in the future. Ya understand?"

"My attorney's Tiger John. Go play with the Tiger."

"A clown," the detective-sergeant said. "And a fuckin' moron . . . you have the right to remain silent until you have the chance to consult with your attorney. So don't give me a hard time. Are you willing to answer our questions or not?"

"Eat your ass."

They dragged Isaac out of the hotel, sat him in one of their cars, and drove him to Midtown South. The pimp squad had autonomy over here. They were specialists, assigned from Headquarters. The precinct commander was nothing to them. They could ignore any cop who existed outside of their squadroom. They whisked Isaac past the desk sergeant and brought him upstairs. The bum refused to undress for a strip search. They punched him and shucked off his clothes. They took Polaroids of Isaac with his prick between his legs. They pulled him over a table, spread his cheeks, and looked up his rectum for suspicious foreign matter. This Moses Herzog McBride could be carrying diamonds or coke up his ass. The bum was clean, but he was riddled with pocks and many scars. You could tabulate the different warfares on Isaac's back and chest. The bum must have been knifed and gouged thirty times. He had a welt under his right nipple, a circular piece of raised skin, that looked like it had come from the plunge of an ice pick. The detectives began to finger Isaac's wondrous scars. "Hey, McBride, were you ever in Korea? . . . did the chinks do a job on you?"

"No," Isaac said, with his ass high on the table. "I got banged up at the Police Academy, wrestling with recruits."

They couldn't get a thing out of the joker. They locked him in the squadroom cage, and wouldn't give him back his clothes. Let the bastard shiver for a while. They would search through their pimp files for faces that resembled the old bum. Maybe he was a psycho with a grudge against pimps. If they could get his MO and his full pedigree, they might make a big score with this bum, and receive a commendation from the mysterious First Dep, who was everywhere and nowhere at the same time.

The bum began to piss in the cage. The detectives were furious with him. They were going to flip him upside down and use his scalp for a mop when they noticed another old man in the room. The man looked like a detective who'd gone downhill. His coat was shitty and he needed a shave. Isaac recognized him: it was Mangen's shoofly, Captain Mort.

"Hey," the detective-sergeant said, "what the fuck do you want?"

"I want your prisoner," Morton said. "Dress that boy . . . and give him to me."

The pimp squad yelled at Captain Mort. "We haven't booked him yet. This is just a friendly interview. We have to escort him down to Elizabeth Street."

The shoofly glared at them. "I wouldn't book him if I was you . . . you'll embarrass yourselves."

"Schmuck, how did you get into this room?"

"I always follow the pimp squad," Morton said. "That's my specialty."

The detectives' bark wasn't so fierce. "Who are you?"

"Schapiro. I work for Dennis Mangen."

Sleeping in the squadroom morning after morning hadn't dulled their minds. They knew all about the Special State Prosecutor. Mangen. The mention of him was enough to turn your testicles gray. No commissioner could protect you from the great god Dennis. But suppose this Schapiro was telling a lie? Anybody could bluff you with Mangen's name.

"Why do you want this guy so bad?" the detective-sergeant muttered with a little more respect.

"I don't want him," Schapiro said. "He's Mangen's baby."

The detectives peeked inside the cage at Isaac's scars and Isaac's prick. "Who is this fuckin' bum?"

Captain Mort showed his contempt for the pimp squad. He had a disgusting grin that almost swallowed his own two ears. "That's your boss. Isaac the Brave."

The detectives stood frozen in the squadroom. Their mouths were brittle and puffy white.

"Don't listen to him," Isaac shouted from the cage. "Take me to Elizabeth Street. I want to be booked without my clothes."

The pimp squad didn't know what to believe. "We frisked him . . . we didn't find a commissioner's badge."

"You think he's a dummy like you?" Morton said. "The First Dep don't wear a badge when he's on a caper."

The detectives were miserable now. Then the man himself, Dennis Mangen, came into the squadroom. It was the proof they'd been begging for. You couldn't mistake Dennis' fur collar and aristocratic Irish nose. They jockeyed with themselves to open the cage for Isaac.

"Boss," they said, "boss, we're sorry . . . you should have told us . . . we'd help you cripple every pimp in New York."

Isaac stepped into his pants. Who had assigned such sleeping beauties to the pimp squad? Not Isaac. No wonder the pimps and whores walked free on Times Square. Isaac had an awful desire to beat them around the ears and stick them in their own cage. Who would miss them if they were padlocked for a month? Their wives? Their daughters? Their sons? They had frightened, rabbity eyes. Isaac began to pity them. He would leave them in place. Was it because of Isaac's scarcity that they were impotent on the street?

He left Midtown South with Mangen and Schapiro. "Dennis, get rid of the shoofly, will you, please?"

"Isaac, you ought to be nicer to Captain Mort. He's been like a fairy godmother to you."

"Baloney," Isaac said. "You planted a pimp in my hotel, that's all. The pimp got in touch with Morton, and Morton hollered to you."

Dennis motioned to the shoofly with his jaw, and Schapiro scampered down the street.

"Mangen, I wish you'd level with me . . . are you looking for Mayor Sam under the Tiger's long johns?"

Mangen frowned at him. "I'm on good terms with Sammy. The

Tiger's my meat."

"What about the McNeill?"

"That old man? He's retiring in two weeks. What would I want with the Chief Inspector when I can have the PC?"

Isaac pushed away from him. "So long, Dennis . . . I don't like having my armpits licked by fancy prosecutors. If you feel like talking, give me a blow."

"Isaac, be careful. Those lads might turn mean on you. The Tiger has his private shotgun patrol."

"Oh, I'll be careful, Dennis. Believe me. I'll scream for Captain Mort when the shotguns start to fire. Goodbye."

TWENTY-FIVE

He was too fired up to go back to his hotel. He would have ravaged pimps again. Isaac the Brave, who was disturbed by the society he kept. He'd fallen in with a hotel full of whores, become a nanny to them. The black girls could lament their old age at nineteen. The little snow queens could drag their frail bodies in front of him. Damn the City of New York. Isaac was the First Dep. Couldn't he manufacture a holy writ, without judges and special prosecutors? Bite into Dermott's trade by shoving every whore and pimp off the street? It wouldn't be an official arrest. Isaac would store the pimps in some secret house, feed them with the petty cash that the First Dep had at his disposal. The Civil Liberties Union would climb on Isaac's back and wrestle him to the ground. Judges would hurl restraining orders at him. The pimps would have to go free.

Mangen should have left him in the cage. He could have danced with his prick out. It would have been a lovely thing to book the First Deputy Commissioner of New York. They'd have to throw a shirt on him for his arraignment. They don't allow you to go naked before a judge. What kind of bail would they set for Isaac the Pure? The bondsmen would titter at him. They'd call it a travesty. Isaac in handcuffs for attacking pimps in a foul hotel. The *Times* might make a wonder of it. City Hall wouldn't know where to leap. Should the Mayor get behind Isaac or the judges? The bitches would take his badge away. Dennis shouldn't have spoiled his fun.

Isaac decided to camp at his office. Rebecca Karp didn't have the power to lock him out of Centre Street. She'd have to send the

City marshals after Isaac. He could stall them for another month.

Centre Street wasn't dark tonight. The lights were on for Rebecca's coming-out party. Bunting flew from the windows and the gates. There were balloons on the old Police Commissioner's terrace. Isaac avoided the hubbub of Becky's people, all the little Democrats who had fastened themselves to her cultural committee. He got in through the Commissioner's private entrance at the rear of the building, and stole up to his office without being caught by Becky's spies. The party emerged around him. He heard the slap of kettledrums under his feet. Tubas came through the walls. Every motherfucker in New York was partying with Rebecca of the Rockaways.

Democrats prowled in the halls. There was lots of giggling. Isaac ground his teeth. The noise in his ears wasn't from the Democrats. The worm was communing with him. The bitch was singing to Isaac. Who can pull sense out of the babble of a worm? Someone drifted into Isaac's office. The First Dep dimmed his lights. He hoped this stray Democrat of Becky's would disappear. Isaac could see him in the shine from his window. It was a blue-eyed boy. A shiver tore through the First Dep. A spook had come to visit him. The boy was Manfred Coen.

Isaac blamed the worm. That piece of shit in his belly could drag out spirits from the dead with a nonsensical song. Isaac wasn't afraid to mutter to a ghost. "Blue Eyes," he said. "Manfred?"

The boy jumped. He hadn't noticed the man in bum's clothes sitting behind the desk. "Excuse me . . . I was looking for the men's room."

"Aren't you Manfred Coen?"

"No," the boy said. "I'm Scamotti, Deputy Mayor for Consumer Affairs."

Isaac bellowed at him. "Get the fuck out of my office." Scamotti ran away. Isaac cursed his fifty-one years. He had a worm to trick his eyes. The bitch could give him glaucoma with those squeezes of the belly. That worm ate from Isaac's blood. It thrived on sugar and other food. He'd lost his angel, Manfred. He had no one to play checkers with. Why couldn't the worm bring back Annie Powell?

The party began to irritate Isaac the Pure. He couldn't sleep with kettledrums and the smell of roast beef. The Democrats were devouring sandwiches in the main hall. Isaac went downstairs to join the party.

Men and women glared at him. The woman had waxed their legs and wore jewels between their tits. The men had tiepins and flared cuffs under their dinner jackets. They hadn't come here to mingle with a bum. Isaac went for the sandwiches. The worm had hungered him. He'd have to feed the bitch or go around with a pain in his gut that could bend his knees and cause him to whimper in despair. He put roast beef, ham, and chicken salad into his mouth like any pig of a First Deputy would do. He was standing near Marshall Berkowitz and his wife. Sylvia must have gone back to Marsh. The dean wouldn't smile at Isaac.

"Marsh?" Isaac said. The dean turned away.

Isaac brushed into the Police Commissioner. "Hello, John." Tiger John was supposed to be his boss. But he would hunch up and shiver in Isaac's presence. John was helpless without the Mayor of New York. His turkey sandwich fell apart in his fingers. Mustard dropped on his shoes. Isaac wondered how many bank accounts he had under his sweater. He was a doomed boy. *Run, Johnny, run, before Dennis pounces on you.*

"Did you have your bath this week?"

"What?" John said.

"The sauna at the Dingle . . . have you tasted the dry heat with Sammy again?"

"No," John said.

"That's good. Those bloody rocks make your heart beat fast. It's been known to kill a man . . ."

Isaac left him behind a pillar with his unraveled turkey sandwich and mustard on his shoes. Sylvia Berkowitz took Isaac by the elbow and didn't let him swing very far. She'd gotten away from her husband again. Isaac was trapped between Sylvia and a kettledrum. What kind of fucking music did Rebecca hire? Isaac looked and looked, but no band knit together in front of his eyes. Tubas and drums were placed around the stairs like a scattering of orphans. Each instrument breathed its own crazy line. Rebecca had a party where tubas talked to themselves, tubas and drums. It confounded the First Dep. He couldn't make peace with all those screaming melodies. Marshall's wife became a solace to him. He smiled, wanting to please her.

"I'm glad you went home to Marsh . . ."

But his words only angered Sylvia, who showed him her teeth. "I didn't need you to be my kidnapper," she said. "Two of your bulls ran me out of your apartment. They dropped me on Marshall's lap. You bastard, you could have been more polite."

"Hey, those bulls weren't mine."

"Then where did they come from? How many people knew I was living on your mattress?"

"Mangen . . . it was Mangen. He has his shooflies on my tail. Dennis kidnapped you, not me . . ."

The wife wouldn't believe him. "Don't lay it on Mangen," she said. "He wouldn't climb in with a lady and then desert her like that."

Sylvia went looking for canapés. Isaac wished he hadn't come downstairs. But he didn't want to sit with the ghost of Blue Eyes in his office. So he began to circulate. He pecked at different sandwiches. His luck brought him nose to nose with his new landlady, Ms. Rebecca. She didn't cackle at him, or scold him for crashing her party.

"Isaac, I heard a friend of yours died . . . a girl . . . Annie Powell."

"Who told you that?"

"The Special Prosecutor."

Did Mangen have a tube attached to Isaac's worm? It wasn't fair. *The fuck owns me.* Isaac was disgusted with himself. But he remembered to thank the landlady for her interest in Annie Powell.

"Isaac, how did you get so thin?"

"Seven days of mourning," he said. "I didn't have much to eat."

"You sat shiva for a gentile girl?"

"Why not?"

She kissed the First Dep on his cheek. She had wet lips for a landlady.

"Isaac, I didn't think you had a heart under all that fur. A cop who makes his own religion . . . that's a surprise to me."

Isaac had to get away from her, or she'd start waltzing with him to those crazy tubas. He saw that boy Scamotti again, the blue-eyed Deputy Mayor. Isaac shuddered hard. Who was this Scamotti? It had to be Coen. Manfred couldn't lie easy in the ground. He had a "kite" to deliver. *Himself.* He had to pay a visit to his murderer, Isaac Sidel. Isaac had used Coen, fed him to the Guzmann family as a kind of bait. Coen's reward was to get killed. Isaac was going to unwind this Scamotti, prove that he was Manfred Coen.

"*You,*" Isaac said. Half the Democrats in the main hall turned to look at the bum with a scowl on his face. Scamotti hid from him.

Isaac ended up with the Mayor and Mr. and Mrs. Pears. Melvin must
have patched up his differences with Mayor Sam. The lawyer was
chatting freely with His Honor. Democrats of every conceivable color
had crawled back under Sam's umbrella at City Hall.

"Mother of God," the Mayor said. "Isaac, what happened to
you? You're not the boy who went campaigning with me. Did they
trample on your skin somewhere? Laddie, put a little meat on you."

"It's nothing, Your Honor. I'm in mourning, that's all."

"Who died on you?" the Mayor asked.

"No one. Just the girlfriend of an ordinary thief. Annie Powell."

The name didn't seem to register with Sam. Isaac wouldn't
pump "Hizzoner" with Mr. and Mrs. Pears around. Jenny's green
eyes turned him gloomy. He recalled the live thing growing in her,
his child. *Lady, I've got a thing in me too, a worm that can twist up
into a cannonball, and outgrow any fetus in the world. The bitch can
scream and claw like Moses. I'll trade brats with you.*

Jennifer couldn't hear the whistling in his skull. Isaac was
attractive to her in his mourning clothes. She didn't enjoy him in
cop's pants, swaggering, with the mark of a commissioner on him.
She preferred him disheveled and unwired. Suffering and the right
kind of stubble brought out the character in his cheeks. He looked
younger to her, a boy with thinning hair. She was carrying this man's
baby. She had a sudden loathing for Mel. She didn't want to be
touched by him. Her husband was spending his afternoons with
Rebecca Karp. She wasn't jealous of that. They could smother
themselves in bear hugs if they liked. But Isaac shouldn't have come
to her with all the fat burned off. Mel became a chubby fool in her
eyes, a lawyer in cowboy boots sucking up to an old Irish Mayor who
hadn't gotten past kindergarten.

She would have rolled on the floor with Isaac among the
Democrats. Politics was a mockery to her. Two months ago this
Mayor had to move about the City after dark. His clerks rebelled
against him. He was received like an oaf at City Hall. His assistants
pirated all his files. New York had a shadow Mayor: Rebecca Karp.
Rebecca sat judges, bankers, Mel, and Sam's assistants on her knee.
She could rock the City to sleep, or create catastrophes with a howl
and a slap of her hand. But the old Mayor was shrewd. He brought
Isaac into the synagogues and stole the primary from Rebecca Karp.
Now the Democrats had to run and kiss the Mayor's ass. And Melvin
had gotten in line to kiss, kiss, kiss.

Only one man was aloof from Mayor Sam. Isaac the bum. A draft must have crept between them. Isaac begged nothing off the Mayor. He barely said hello to *her*. Who was this girl he mourned? Some gangster's moll. He walked away from them, left her with a husband who jostled her into Sam, so "Hizzoner" could peek at her tits.

Isaac was ready to go upstairs. He'd had enough of Democrats in the main hall. He couldn't live around Becky's people. They mumbled like the tubas and the kettledrums. But he was trying to catch Scamotti again. He wanted one last look at Blue Eyes. He got Dean Berkowitz instead. Marshall was without his wife.

"Marsh, I had to take her off the street, for Christ's sake . . . she was sleeping in telephone booths when I found her. I couldn't force her into your bed. What could I do?"

The dean was unforgiving. "Snake, you're nothing but a snake. You consoled me while you were eating my wife . . . and you used my office to get criminals into Columbia College. God knows how many other Dermott Brides I launched for you."

"Marsh, I wasn't Dermott's rabbi. Didn't you tell me how he took to Joyce? . . . he was your star pupil before he went to Yale."

"You primed him, Isaac, you taught him how to sniff for Leopold Bloom."

"You're crazy. I've forgotten every line in that book. It was burned out of me years ago, that shit."

"Cops don't forget," Marshall screamed. "And you're the biggest cop of them all."

Isaac was the snake of Rebecca's party. Democrats squinted at him. Wives lured their husbands out of his reach. Bread turned to cotton in his fist. He couldn't even chew on a sandwich. The snake was out of luck. He stumbled upon Dennis in a pack of young lawyers. Mangen had come to shake Rebecca's hand and wish her success in Isaac's building. Isaac grabbed him away from the lawyers. The lawyers were aghast. They couldn't believe the Special Pros would allow himself to be pawed by a bum.

Isaac's eyeballs were inflamed. He looked like some Ahab hunting whales in an old, dry building. A crease appeared in the middle of his forehead. His seven days of mourning had isolated him from all humankind. The hairs stood on his scalp like an idiot's knot.

"You cunt . . . *you* kidnapped Sylvia Berkowitz."

"I only took back what you stole. Where I come from a man's

entitled to his wife."

"Dennis, you've been living with subpoenas too long. You think you can scoop up a body and deliver it anywhere. To the courthouse, to one of your jails. Sylvia's a free agent. She doesn't belong to any dean of Columbia College . . . the next time you bring your shooflies into my apartment, I'll break them off at the neck. You've been collecting skunks and pissy old men. I'm not crazy about that rat's army of yours."

"Isaac, you ought to be. That rat's army has been keeping you alive."

"I'm sick of your fairy tales. God save me from protectors like Morton Schapiro . . . you love to play with history. Tell me again how little Dermott is a police spy."

"Ask the king. He can answer for himself."

"How, when he's sitting in Dublin?"

"Dermott's in New York."

"I haven't seen him," Isaac said.

"You will. He wouldn't leave the country without thanking you. You buried his woman for him."

Mangen disappeared from Isaac to mix with his young lawyers. Isaac's brain began to smolder on him. Why was *he* the last to get the news? Isaac had a mess of stoolies and cops clumping through the City. No one had mentioned Dermott Bride. Scamotti brushed into him. Isaac held on to Blue Eyes. "Manfred, don't fuck with me."

Scamotti laughed.

It was Coen's teeth that he saw. Coen's purple mouth. "If you hate me, Manfred, tell it to my face. I don't like to dance with spooks."

"You're hurting me," Scamotti said. "Leggo."

It was futile work. Manfred wouldn't admit who he was. Isaac would have to survive with a ghost around him. He went away from the Democrats and trudged upstairs.

TWENTY-SIX

The party boomed under Isaac. Becky's people seemed to exist without a place to sleep. Were the Democrats going to snore against the walls? Isaac heard strange nibbling sounds. Someone was eating the woodwork outside his office. Isaac didn't care. The fucker could attack his closets and his brooms. Isaac fell into a dream about Blue Eyes. Blue Eyes and Annie Powell. They were in Dublin together. It made Isaac whimper to see Blue Eyes and Annie wading with the ducks in Stephen's Green. It must have been summertime. Manfred didn't have a shirt. The blond hairs around his nipples were growing wet. Annie's dress was way above her knees. The ducks were hysterical about the condition of her thighs. They quacked at the scars that ran from her groin to her kneecaps. The impressions were deep, like miraculous birth scars, as if a woman could give birth to any creature through her thighs.

Isaac groaned in his chair. The nibbling sound had gotten closer. The party was asleep. The Democrats must have found somewhere else to go. Isaac could have his peace. He opened one eye and saw two little old men crouching in the dark. They wore derbies in October, and long neckerchiefs that could have been used to hide a man's face. The bits of light coming from the lamps in the street gave them fat shadows that humped up against Isaac's wall. The shadows wobbled because of what the old men were carrying in their arms. It could have been two long-headed babies. They're pros, Isaac muttered to himself. Only a cop or a hired killer would hold a shotgun with such profound gentleness. He ducked behind his chair.

The shotguns blasted pencils and cups off his desk. Wood splintered over Isaac's ears. The explosions could have made a fucking eternity around Isaac. The shotguns kept going and going. It was torture for what Isaac did to Coen. He'd have to live with the crump of two shotguns in his ears. They wouldn't even let the schmuck die.

Then the noises stopped. Isaac heard one of the old men say, "Shit." There was some scuffling. Isaac crawled into the foothole of his desk and came out through the other side. The shotguns were gone. He had no more old men with derbies to shoot pencils off his desk. Morton Schapiro was breathing over him, Captain Mort. "The pricks got away," Morton said. "I couldn't wrestle with both of them"

"Who were those guys?"

"Dunno. They looked like cops to me."

"You were in most of the stationhouses, Mort . . . didn't you recognize them?"

"I couldn't," Morton said. "They kept covering their mouths."

"Funny guys they were . . . with derbies sitting on their brains. Morton, what the hell were you doing on my floor?"

"Mangen told me to stay up here. He said you might have a few visitors tonight."

Dennis was his rabbi, all right. And Isaac had a new "angel," Captain Mort. He couldn't be sure if those two old men were serious with their guns. They damaged a lot of wood. But Isaac's skin was pure as ever. They hadn't even singed his hair. Still, Captain Mort had wrestled with them, faced up to their neckerchiefs and those wicked guns. Isaac had to pay his debt to the shoofly.

Morton was delighted with the stingy thanks he got, the mumble of words out of Isaac's mouth. "Now you can go home," Isaac said.

A gloom crept over Captain Mort. "What if they come again?"

"They won't. Morton, they're afraid of you."

He couldn't do much about the shattered wood. He'd have to work in a sea of splinters until Rebecca threw him out. He picked the shotgunned pencils and cups off the floor. Then he sat behind his desk. He was feeling snug as Moses ever could. The arrival of the two old men had been a preliminary dance. It was a bit of foolishness designed to scare the shit out of Isaac. He knew what would come next. He'd have to wait a little while. The main act would begin when the shotgun dust had settled.

A man appeared at the door. Isaac didn't have to blink. "Dermott," he said. "Don't be shy. Come on in."

The king stepped into Isaac's office. He was small, the way Isaac remembered him. He had a crow's black hair, and peculiar features for an Irishman. How did he get so dark? Were there gypsies in the Bronx that mingled with the shanty Irish of Clay Avenue and Crotona Park North? Or did his blood lines go deeper than that? He could have sprung from a hidden race of dark-skinned Irish, seafarers from the Levantine who had come down the Liffey four hundred years ago to settle in Blackrock. Isaac snapped on the lights. The king's eyebrows bunched on his face. Dermott had the right people to take Isaac apart. But no one seemed willing to murder him.

"That's a pair of lovely boys you lent me. Did you supply them with neckerchiefs and all?"

Those eyes beetled up at Isaac until they covered half the king's head. "Isaac, O'Toole is the only gang I ever had. And he's gone."

"What about the Clay Avenue Devils?"

"Christ, I ran from the Devils before I was eighteen. If you're going to make me spit out my past, Isaac, then at least let a man have his chair."

"Sit," Isaac said, and the king sat down across from Isaac in the room's only other chair. The First Dep didn't have a great need for hospitality. He preferred a barren room.

"Well, if the neckerchiefs didn't belong to you, then what was that joke all about? You're not a blind man, Dermott. You walked on the debris they left. Two old men in derby hats shot up my office twenty minutes ago."

"They're not mine, I said."

"Then why are you here? Did Tiger John send you? Are you supposed to warn me never to go near Mangen again? . . . you know, Dennis says you're a police spy. I told him he was full of shit."

The king laughed. "Since when are you so loyal to me?"

"Don't kid yourself," Isaac muttered. "I have eighteen special squads. I'd have known before now if any cop was carrying you on his lists . . . Dermott, I'm curious about something. It seems I got you into Columbia College. I read the report I wrote for Marshall Berkowitz. But kill me, I can't remember meeting you."

"We met. Many times. We had long talks, me and you, when I was with the Devils."

"I talked to Arthur Greer. He was president of the club."

"But Arthur didn't get into Columbia College."

Isaac still had that shotgun music in his ears. His head was a rubble of bones and blood. Why could he picture Arthur, who was pushed from his roof, and not little Dermott?

"What did we talk about?"

"Immanuel Kant."

The king was telling lies. Bronx thugs with black hair couldn't have gotten into Kant.

"You gave me books to read," Dermott said. "Dostoyevsky . . . Kant . . . James Joyce . . . it wasn't only literature. We talked about the South Bronx . . . the death of Crotona Park."

Isaac had to be in his dotage. Does senility strike at fifty-one? The Guzmanns had ruined him, those pimps of Boston Road. They'd given him a clever dose of venereal disease: a syphilitic worm that was eating away at Isaac's prick and Isaac's brain. He'd brought Kant and Dostoyevsky to little Dermott, and Isaac couldn't recollect a word.

"What other cops did you talk to?"

"Why?"

"Because a memo exists from my dead boss, O'Roarke, asking

me to put you into college."

"This O'Roarke never came to our clubhouse. I can promise you that. He didn't meet with the Devils."

"Then who could have told him about you?"

"Anybody . . . we were popular in those days. The Devils policed the Bronx."

"And you, you walked from Columbia to Yale, you said hello to Marshall Berkowitz and goodbye, you learned from Marsh about Shem and Shaun and the powers of the Liffey, and you graduated from Marshall's class to become the overlord of every pimp in Manhattan."

"And what did you learn from Marsh? To rush through the streets slapping heads? Big cop who grovels in the dirt and puts on disguises, so he can land in a crook's underwear. The trouble with you, Isaac, is you don't have some poet to celebrate all your deeds."

"I'm not dying to be famous," Isaac said. He was growing less fond of this dark-haired boy, this gypsy Irishman from Clay Avenue. He had an itch to take the king by his ears and shove him into the wall. "What's your secret, Mr. Bride? How did you stay invisible for seventeen years? A whoremaster without a face. Why didn't we have your pedigree in my files? We had pages and pages on Arthur Greer . . . I could have told you the grooves in his knuckles, or the size of his prick."

"Arthur wasn't happy unless he was at the center of things. He entertained judges and movie tycoons. I was the quiet one. I kept my nose clean."

"A pretty story," Isaac said. "But it's mostly shit. Some cop had to be fronting for you . . . you have bad habits for a king. A king ought to be gracious to his friends. He shouldn't sit still when they die."

"Isaac, what the fuck is in your head?"

"I didn't catch you grieving for Arthur and your man O'Toole."

"It's not your business how I grieve and who I grieve for."

"Your uncle, Bagman McBride. Where the hell is he?"

"He's safe," Dermott said. "The uncle is out of your hands."

"And Annie Powell? Once you discard a mistress, I suppose that's it."

Isaac smiled when Dermott reached into his pocket. He could predict the knife that would come out like a long tooth. The king's elbow made a perfect line. That line never wavered, never broke.

"Are you going to cut my face, sweetheart?"

"No," the king said. "I'm not interested in your face. It's your throat I want."

Isaac didn't move from his chair. He was gambling that little Dermott wasn't ready to stick him with the tooth. "Arthur lied for you the last time I saw him. He said you were the mediator for the Devils, and I believed him. The king made his rep with his tongue. No, no. You were his blade. The quiet boy who could scar you for life. That's how you talked . . . poor Arthur was only president of the club. You were the king."

The tooth disappeared with a snap of the king's wrist. "Where did you bury Anne?"

"Her mother wouldn't take her," Isaac said. "I had to find a plot. She's in a Jewish cemetery near Floral Park. Esau Woods."

Those black eyebrows began to rumple like mad, as if the king were having a fit inside his head, and nothing showed, nothing but the rumples over his eyes. He looked up at Isaac. "You shouldn't have let her stay on the street . . . I tried to get O'Toole to pull her into Brooklyn Heights. Jamey couldn't do it. *You* were around. The big rabbi from Headquarters, Isaac Sidel . . . how come you didn't ask me what I remember about you?"

The king was setting him up. Isaac could feel it in the shiver of his voice. Little Dermott had a harsh vocabulary. His words would lead Isaac into some ugly twist. "I didn't think you remembered very much. You wouldn't even nod to me in Dublin."

"Dublin was something else . . . Isaac, I always hated your guts. You were a pain in the ass from the beginning. You had to reform little Bronx boys. Save us from the wildlands of Crotona Park. How many of us did you ship to Columbia College? Savages who were taught to purr. We could mouth any sort of magic. We had Diderot for breakfast, Molière for lunch. Shitface, who told you to meddle? I'm not your rubber baby . . . why did you have to pick out Anne? Couldn't you reform another girl? Isaac, haven't you guessed? People die wherever you plunge. If you'd kept away from Anne, I wouldn't have to go searching for her in your Esau Woods . . ."

The king was through with him. He'd come to Isaac for the name of a cemetery. He hadn't shared a thing with the First Dep. "Isaac, I should have let those boys rip off your mouth in Dublin, when they had you in their car."

"Why didn't you?"

"I'm not inhuman," the king said. "I wouldn't hurt my old teacher." And he was gone from the room. Isaac was in the same bloody fix. He still couldn't remember the king.

There were dead balloons and slices of rye bread on the stairs. The king walked over the shambles of Rebecca's party. The place stank of Democrats: judges, lawyers, and clubhouse whores, men and women that Dermott had to smear with money. He'd bought the little Mayor and the Chief of Police. God knows, half the City lived off Dermott Bride. Manhattan would disappear without the girls of Whores' Row. The king put a tax on the girls that could carry a whole fucking island. The economy of New York lay with its whores, and what they could earn on their backs. He crushed party cups with both feet on his way out of the building.

The king got into a black Mercury. It was Tiger John's official car. The pimps had their Cadillacs, and the Police Commissioner settled for a black machine that was like a fat upholstered toy. It had gadgets hooked into the seats, telephones that could connect the Tiger with his men in the field. But he rarely used the phones. He was frightened of the buzzing they provoked. He preferred silences when he was in the car. Tiger John liked to think about the bankbooks in his pocket.

Dermott was abrupt with him. He didn't enjoy having to mingle with Sammy's toad. "Where's the Fisherman?"

"Are you daft?" the Tiger said. "McNeill can't be seen with you. Not in this country."

"Explain that, will you, Tiger John? Why you can sit with me, and McNeill can't."

"I'm the PC. I can do whatever I like."

This idiot had thirty thousand cops under his command. He could break a full inspector, knock him down to captain if he chose. Or drop a branch of detectives, decimate a squad. He was as gullible as a monkey in the Bronx Zoo. You fed him bankbooks once a month, like a banana in his mouth, and he was delighted with himself. He banged through Headquarters making mischief in the offices he entered. His rages were an enormous bluff. The PC had nothing to do. McNeill ran the Department for him.

"He's angry with you," the Tiger said, "for coming back to America without asking him first."

"Since when do I need Coote's permission to fly?"

"Boyo, that was the bargain you struck."

The Tiger had a crafty approach for an imbecile. Mayor Sam must have given him lessons in the art of Irish persuasion.

"Coote doesn't have to worry," the king said.

"You'll spoil his retirement if you don't get out of here fast."

"I'll be home in Dublin by tomorrow night."

The Tiger looked at him out of a pair of tiny, nervous eyes. "Boyo, tomorrow could be too late. Sheeny Isaac is crawling around. He followed me and Sam into the sauna room at the Dingle. He didn't have the decency to take off his clothes. All he did was talk about Dennis Mangen."

"He's your First Dep. Can't you quiet him down?"

"Jesus, I'd love to get rid of him. But he's the darling of the press. The newspaper lads bruise their own two feet begging interviews off the boy."

"Was that your shotgun party that Isaac was complaining about?"

"Not mine," the Tiger said. "McNeill's. The Fisherman sent over two retired sergeants to drop a neat kite on Isaac's room. But Mangen had his shooflies in the hall. The sergeants were lucky to get out of there alive."

The king laughed to himself. The cops of New York made a mad, struggling army. Mangen was biting everybody on the ass. Except for Isaac. Isaac was the great survivor. He could rise out of a curtain of shotgun smoke in his stinky pants. The First Dep was so smart and so dumb. Isaac had each point of Dermott's history in his heavy brain, but he couldn't pull them into a straight line. The Devils were a local club. They didn't have the firepower to terrorize a boroughful of gangs. They couldn't have gone out on rampages to enforce the peace without a little help from the cops. McNeill lent his youth squad to the Devils. The gang was a baby wing of the NYPD. Coote wouldn't deal with Arthur Greer. He touched Dermott on the shoulder, made him the king.

"Boyo," the Tiger said, "where are we going now?"

"To a cemetery in Queens."

"At this hour?" Tiger John bristled in his coat. "The harpies are walking about. Why are we going to a graveyard?"

"To meet a lady of mine."

Isaac had blabbered about a loss of memory. The poor demented boy couldn't picture Dermott's face among the Devils. The king remembered the old gang. They had to use a shack in Claremont Park as a clubhouse, the Devils of Clay Avenue. They didn't have the funds to buy colored jerseys. The Devils were nothing until the cops picked them up. They had to run to the cellars and the trees whenever the Fordham Baldies arrived on Clay Avenue. The shabbiest nigger gang could have destroyed them in an even fight.

The Devils were without a single patch of honor. They were the scavengers of the borough, mocked by other clubs. Only the worst pariahs came over to the Devils' side, outcasts and imbeciles. The Devils lacked the scars of open combat. They would fall upon the isolated members of some gang more craven than themselves. It took twelve of them to beat up one boy. They would whoop and scream, steal a pocket off the boy's shirt, and run back to their clubhouse in the park. They shivered summer and winter long, with the hysterical passion of cowards and invalids. They feared that an enemy might retaliate and burn down their miserable shack. But few gangs would bother with them.

Then McNeill wed his cops to the Devils. It was the only bunch of kids that the youth squad could control. He gave the Devils a bit of fighting blood. His motor pool would taxi them to different parts of the Bronx, so they could hit an unsuspecting gang and disappear. The Devils became known for these lightning attacks. They still couldn't have won if McNeill hadn't dressed his toughest boys in the Devils' jerseys to smack Fordham Baldies over the head. The king began to earn a reputation with his knife. He could slash out and rip a shirt sleeve, shave an enemy's skull, with Coote's boys behind him.

Things went according to McNeill. He could slap any gang in the Bronx through little Dermott and the Devils of Clay Avenue. But the king had ambitions of his own. He wasn't satisfied with his existence as Coote McNeill's knife and stick. He met in secret with the man. They stood outside the Webster Avenue shul, smoking cigarettes. No one would suspect an Irish captain and an Irish pug to declare new policies in the shadows of a synagogue.

"Ungrateful brat," McNeill said. "Haven't I blessed you enough? I picked you over that jigaboo, Arthur Greer. You're the goddamn lord of the Bronx. The Baldies piss on their toes when the king takes out his knife."

"I want more," Dermott muttered from the side of his mouth.

"That's grand. Should I pin a badge on your chest and call you Sergeant McBride?"

"No. You'd better gimme a college education."

McNeill had a laughing fit on the steps of the old shul. He wiped his eyes with a handkerchief. "They don't let donkeys into college. You're too old. You must be twenty, for God's sake."

"I'm seventeen."

"You never finished high school."

"So what? I want college from you, Captain McNeill. Or find yourself another baby."

They grinned at each other. The kid was bluffing. They both knew that. Little Dermott was stuck in his shack. He had nowhere else to go. But Coote liked the idea of a little gangster in college. The Department could raise up a lovely, educated pigeon. Coote went to see his boss, First Deputy O'Roarke. "Ned, that dark bitch will be useful to us. We'll have ourselves a cutthroat with a college degree." But even the great O'Roarke couldn't convince a college to take him. They had to groom him first. Only one lad in Ned's entire office could jabber about Karl Marx. That was young deputy inspector Sidel. "Ned, will you lend us the brain?"

"You can have him," O'Roarke said.

Isaac was a natural for them. The brain had ties to Columbia College. They could shove the king in that direction. But they didn't tell Isaac about their plan to educate little Dermott. They sent Isaac over to sit with the Devils. He brought Dostoyevsky into the clubhouse. Most of the Devils yawned. They wanted to go on a scalping party. The king took Isaac's prattle in. He had to make up for years of neglect. He memorized every murder in Prince Hamlet of Elsinore, and he got into Columbia College.

"Graveyards," Tiger John smirked into his coat. It took him and his driver hours to locate the cemetery at Esau Woods. John wouldn't step out of the car. He wasn't going to carouse near the tombstones in a Jewish yard, and let the harpies grab at him from the trees. Why was this Annie Powell buried with the Yids?

"That's an odd priest that would let her lie down in Esau Woods," he said to Dermott.

"The priest was Isaac."

Dermott walked over to the caretaker's shack and knocked on the window. The caretaker wouldn't come out. Dermott crumpled fifty dollars under the door. The caretaker smelled the money and stuck his head in the window. He wore a thick wool cap. "What do you want?"

"A grave," Dermott said.

"For yourself?"

"No. A girl was buried here."

"Under what auspices?" the caretaker asked.

"I don't know. She came with Isaac Sidel."

A sense of recognition grew out from under the cap. The caretaker smiled. "The Christian girl, you mean . . . they can't fool us, those big commissioners. She's in Lot Eleven, Row B . . . you'll find a marker with a red flag."

Dermott moved away from the shack. The caretaker shouted between Dermott's shoulder blades with genuine scorn. "What's the matter with you? You can't go in there naked? This is holy grounds."

He gave the king a skullcap to wear. He also put a huge flashlight in Dermott's hand. Half the graveyards in the borough of Queens could have heard those batteries knock. Dermott clumped through Esau Woods with a big, loud metal canister that couldn't light up his shoes: the bulb was nearly dead. He came to that marker on Lot Eleven, Row B. It was a stick on a smudge of earth, with a filthy rag knotted to it. That was all of Annie Powell. The king trembled near that grave. The cold burrowed through him. Why? It wasn't winter yet.

That rag knotted to a stick was the king's sign: a dirty sniveling crook he was, in a silk necktie, who rode out of the Bronx like a cannonball, with police money and police wit, and bribed a judge in Connecticut to shorten his name, so he wouldn't sound like a shanty Irish boy. Dermott Bride. Dermott Bride. Funny coloring for a mick. Dark the hair and dark the eyes. Would you believe it now? They have Irish niggers in the New Country. They live in a land called the Bronx. His dad couldn't explain this complexion of the male McBrides. The old man was a dark-haired janitor. He kept his family outside the Church. He wouldn't have child Dermott beaten by any bald witch of a nun. The boy went to public school. All the other micks in his class were so ruddy. Green-eyed girls. They grew taller than little Dermott. He fought those big Irish mules, boys and girls, biting, scratching, gouging with his thumbs, or he would have been eaten alive. They still wouldn't have much to do with him. He couldn't join the Salters, the Green Bays, the Emerald Knights. He had to go with the Devils, a mangy gang without a clubhouse, that took sheenies in, and had a nigger for a president.

The Devils couldn't smoke out his lineage for him. Dermott went to the history books. How do you look up *Irishman, Dark Hair?* He read about the Gaels, and the rude island that Caesar bypassed when he conquered the world. An island of savage people with bulls and cows. But where, where was the dark eyes? He read some more. The English conquerors, and the Pale they established around Dublin, where only Englishmen could tread. The Irish kings had to shiver in the booleys, with their cattle and their priests. And then little Dermott discovered his own history in the drowning of the Spanish Armada. A few of the ships were knocked into the coast of Ireland by a storm. It was 1588. Pockets of Anglo-Irish militia stood on the shore with clubs in their hands. The dark-haired sailors were beaten to death, one by one, as they crawled out of their ships. A handful escaped into the interior, and were hidden in some obscure Irish village beyond the Pale. Dermott's true fathers came from such a handful. He was a Spanish mick, an Irisher with eyebrows. He'd solved the obscurity of his line. It made no difference what his dad was doing in the Bronx. The boy was descended from Spanish-Irish pigherders, or something close to that. The McBrides had walked in pigshit for two hundred years. Dermott swore to himself that he'd climb out of the muck.

"Johnny, are you sleeping now?"

The king gave John a fright. The Tiger shut his eyes while little Dermott went creeping in the Jewish graveyard for his Anne, and Holy Mother of God, the lad returns before John could take a blink!

"Did you catch any harpies in the woods?"

"None at all."

"Too bad," the Tiger said. "If they pluck one eyebrow, it's supposed to charm you for a month. But harpies can be dangerous. God help you if they nest in your hair."

"The harpies weren't out tonight."

"It's the warmth," Tiger John said. "They won't come to you in October."

The Commissioner had an idiotic mythology for every beast that stirred in the woods. Let the harpies nest in Dermott's hair. He'd take them into Dublin and tickle them to sleep. Then he'd root them out with his knife.

"Did Isaac provide for the lady?"

"He did. A rag and a stick on a hump of dirt."

"Ah, that's the Hebrew law. You go to lots of Jewish funerals when you're the Commish. We have sheenies in the Department, you know. Thousands of them. It's years and years before they put a stone on a grave. So it has to be a rag for Annie Powell."

"I'll order a stone tomorrow," the king said, sucking with his teeth.

"The Jews won't deliver it. Not for six years."

"I'll hire my own deliverers."

"The rabbis will run them out of the graveyard."

"Then I'll buy rabbis to fight the rabbis of Esau Woods."

The Tiger chuckled to himself. "That will be a sight. Rabbis clawing each other's holy shirt . . . boyo, you don't have the time. No playing with rabbis. Mangen's not a fool. He'll wonder why you're here. You might never get to Dublin with Mangen around. His grand juries are notorious for latching on to boyos like you, so they can't leave the country."

"Dennis won't find me."

"That's good news," the Tiger said. "I'll pray for you."

You're the lad that needs praying for, the king understood. Someone would have to take a fall. It wouldn't be Sam. The bankers might cry over the prospect of a Mayor in jail. It could eat into the worth of municipal paper. But a crooked Police Commissioner wasn't that much of a liability. You could always put another toad in his place.

This one, John the tiger-toad, looked out at Dermott with a strange compassion in his eyes. He winked and blew his nose. "I can calm the rabbis for you. I'm the PC . . . you'll get your stone for Annie Powell."

The king nodded once. The old, dumb Commissioner meant no harm. Whose fault was it that he didn't have Sammy's wit or the Fisherman's brains? He could only bluster through Headquarters doing his Tiger dance. Dermott had already gone way, way into his Spanish skull. The bumping of the Mercury didn't register in his ears. The king despised himself. He was no better than a pimp who marks his woman for some small sin, like holding back five dollars, or daring to talk to one of the dudes at an after-hours club. The pimp would take a wire coat hanger and twist it into his main initial, heat it on the burner of his woman's stove, and stick it in her face. Dermott used a knife.

It was an old Bronx ritual that existed long before the Devils got their start. Girls didn't have an independent status in any gang, no matter how tough or beautiful they were. A girl was property, like an ice pick, or a tamed pigeon. And if she "wounded" you, if she roused your jealousy, if she shamed you in the eyes of the gang, you cut her with a knife, to show her and everyone else in the Bronx where the lines of your property ought to begin and end.

That was a dumb ritual for a king to follow. He'd been away from the Devils for sixteen years. He should have curbed his jealousies. Annie Powell. He'd left her alone in Dublin with those ancient bodyguards, while he sat in Connemara with the Fisherman, and established how many pieces they could get from a whore's pie, and where the pieces would go. What did he expect from Anne? Coote had pulled Jamey out of Ireland. She didn't have the king's donkey to watch over her anymore. It's a brave lad who gives his wife a scar and sends her back to Americky. Prick that he was, he should have cut his own face.

A noise blasted through the king. It was Tiger John's radiotelephone. It rang and rang from a niche in the upholstery. "Answer it," the king said. "Go on, Johnny. Scream your hello."

Dermott picked up the receiver and clapped it to the left side of John's head. John mumbled, "Yes . . . no . . . yes . . ."

Then he put the receiver into its place. But he didn't offer any information to little Dermott.

"Who was that? . . . Coote?"

"No." Tiger John took to whispering in the rear of his car. "It was Mayor Sam."

"Why didn't he talk to me?"

"Jesus, you're poison to Sam. The Mayor wants you out of the country on the next aeroplane."

"The Mayor can go fuck himself. I'm not leaving until I pay my respects to the mother of O'Toole."

John was certain the king had a draft in his head. "Mangen is closing in, and you can't leave until you kiss the mother of O'Toole? We'll send flowers in your name to that old hag."

"Don't send shit. The Fisherman killed my man."

"Swear to God, Dermott. It was sink or swim. Your man grew a beard and went crazy. He was going to run to Isaac and snitch on us all."

Coote was right about little Dermott. The king had lost his grip. A man with a nose for business wouldn't have come to New York to buy tombstones for an Irish bitch. Where's the value of it? The girl was already in the ground.

"John, are you driving me to the old woman, or not? If I have to walk to Chelsea, I won't be in Dublin until the day after tomorrow."

God forbid. "Hold your horses," the Tiger said. "I didn't say I wasn't driving you, did I now?" He'd have to get himself a castle, just like Coote. Then he could give the Mercury back, and retire to Kerry and Dingle Bay.

TWENTY-SEVEN

The king had never been a shylock, a *gombeen-man,* like Arthur Greer. He didn't have a countinghouse in Dublin or New York. His bagmen collected a fee from the pimps of Manhattan and the Bronx, and the king took this pimping money and scrubbed it the best way he could. He threw it into restaurants, bowling alleys, limousine services, and rare books. A good portion of it was churned back, so the king could stock a yellow lake with salmon for Coote McNeill, provide a secret pension fund for the Mayor, create bankbooks for Handsome John.

It was smooth and lovely work. The pimps would swagger in their long coats, because Mr. Dermott Bride had arranged a charter of principles for them with the Police. They were shrewd enough not to ask about the details of this charter. The sweetest mack always gave a dumb picture of himself. He had a harem to protect, a stable of "brides," little snow queens, and all his number-one ladies who broke their humps in his behalf. The macks realized that some of their nickels and dimes were going to the Police Commissioner. If Tiger John Rathgar lived off their bounty, what could happen to them?

But the Special Prosecutor arrived on Whores' Row. Mangen dropped a fucking siege around Headquarters. Cops bit their fingers and ran from him like a galaxy of cockroaches. Mangen had the power to subpoena bishops, whores, mayors, and pimps. The king couldn't peddle charters any more. He moved to a fancy hotel in Dublin town, and the cops began to pull entire harems off the street. Bail money was getting hard to find. The macks' own gombeen-man, Sweet Arthur Greer, fell off a roof. The king had to hide his old uncle Martin, or the bagman would have been dead. But he couldn't save his Irish bitch . . .

He got to Chelsea in Tiger John's car. Dermott was bringing a packet of money for Mrs. O'Toole, blood money it was, because he'd made a dirty bargain with Chief Inspector McNeill. The king had killed Jamey boy by sending him back to New York. There were no bugaboos in the hall, no cops from the First Deputy's office. *You're a gorgeous man, Dermott McBride, with your black hair and your knife. You can cut your name into a woman, give her your mark for other men to be wary of. He was the fool of fools. A thief shouldn't marry. He's like any businessman who has to neglect his wife for the silly bickerings of trade . . . Shouldn't have left her in Dublin with Coote's people . . . Prick that I am, playing Moses the punisher.* It wasn't the absence of her flesh that rankled the king. He could have bought and sold a hundred look-alikes to Annie Powell. Get another doll of a girl. But he loved that dumb banter she had, the way she could mourn a cow. His childy woman.

The mother of O'Toole had a metal plate on her door. It was open. The king walked in. Mrs. O'Toole sat in a rocking chair with a kind of bonnet on her head. She had big ears for an old lady. But the king hadn't come to criticize her looks.

He took out his packet of money, six thousand in hundred-dollar bills. "I'm Dermott Bride," he said. "I used to employ your son."

The old woman was made up like a whore, with lipstick that spread onto her cheeks in an impasto of purple moons. The knuckles in her lap were hairy and thick. Her feet stuck out of the brogans she wore. She had muscular ankles, this mother of O'Toole. Dermott picked the bonnet off her head. It was a curious scalp she had, with short white bristles on top. A Detective Special appeared from under her blouse.

"I'm Captain Schapiro," she said. "Stay where you are, you lousy crook."

The king didn't have to shiver. He had a blade on him that could carve up this beauty in the rocking chair. He heard the voice of a man behind him.

"Dermott, please don't go for the knife . . ." The man had a coat with a fur collar. He wasn't carrying a weapon, like Mother O'Toole. "I'm the Special Pros." He sent Schapiro into the kitchen, so he could be alone with the king.

"Where's the mother of O'Toole?"

"She's all right," Mangen said. "We figured you wouldn't leave the country without laying some gelt on her. You're not a careless man . . . we put her in a home on Charles Street."

"That's kind of you. Too bad I can't produce Jamey's ghost. He'd give you a shake of the hand for shuffling his ma around . . . Mangen, why did you dress Schapiro in women's clothes? Was it to entertain a Bronx boy like me? You needn't have bothered, you know. I would have liked Schapiro without his bonnet . . ."

"Forget that little trick of mine. I didn't want you to wrestle with an army of cops. You might have scratched them all, and I'd have to pay the bill . . . how could I thank you if we didn't have a talk?"

Dermott stared at this maniac in the fur collar. "Thank me for what?"

"For those names you put in Tiger John's bankbooks ."

"Ah, it was nothing. A bit of fun. I was hoping John would enjoy it."

"He did," Mangen said. "And so did I . . . I couldn't have traced his phony signatures without your *Molly Blooms* and your *Gertrude MacDowells*. I thought you were trying to tell me something . . . that you were fed up with McNeill and the whole rotten bunch."

"Hey Mangen . . . Molly Bloom wasn't any signal to you. It's a name, that's all."

He had a sad face for a boy millionaire. The king was stuck in two milieus. He was a hoodlum with a love for books. What could money get for him? He didn't belong anywhere. Not with Isaac, not with Marsh, not with Coote McNeill.

"Dermott, you don't have to go to Dublin. I could give you a suite in a good hotel . . . with bodyguards and everything."

"Sure, and then I'd be your canary. Thank you, but I'll take Stephen's Green." He bowed to the Special Pros and held out the packet of money. "You could do me a favor though, and give this bundle to Mrs. O'Toole . . . and my regrets for the life of her son."

Mangen took the six thousand. "I could confiscate this money, tag it and save it for my property clerk."

"I know," the king said. "But you won't." He went out of the door, and Mangen felt like an idiot, holding a bundle of whores' money in his hand. He called to Schapiro in the kitchen.

"You had to shove your Detective Special at him . . . never pull a gun on a man while you're sitting down. He could have chopped your nose off. Will you hurry up, Morton, and wiggle out of that skirt. Wipe the lipstick off, for shit's sake. They'll think we've been smooching on the stairs . . ."

PART SEVEN

TWENTY-EIGHT

It was the middle of October, and you couldn't find Sam in the streets. No one was alarmed. His Honor had won the primary. He didn't have to beg for votes. But where was the Old Man of City Hall? Was he on some kind of maneuvers in the countryside? Sammy would never leave town. Boys and girls from Dennis Mangen's office began to scuttle in and out of the Mayor's rooms. They didn't have a blemish on them. They arrived fresh from law school with pigskin briefcases and theories on the ways and means of smothering crime in the City of New York. The girl prosecutors were harsher than the boys. Mangen's girls wouldn't even smile at a deputy mayor.

They emerged from Sammy's rooms one morning, with the Old Man himself. He looked like a Mayor who was walking in his sleep. His eyes would focus on the ceiling and nothing else. He wore slippers rather than shoes. The slyness had gone out of him. Why was he captive to Mangen's girls, meek in their presence? The girls drew reporters out of their closet, and the Old Man held a news conference on the steps of the City Hall. "Misery," he said. "Lads, I'm in poor health. The Mayor can't have red meat. They give me grass to chew . I'll strangle on it if I have to run this City."

The reporters looked at Sam and rocked on their toes, trying to fathom his gibberish about grass and red meat. "Your Honor, does this mean you're pulling out of the race?"

"That's the rotten truth."

The reporters shoved a bit closer to Sam. "What will happen to the Democrats?"

"Ah," the Mayor said, "they'll survive."

The Democrats caucused on the same afternoon. Party chiefs spent an hour praising the Old Man. "Wonderful Mayor. The very best. We'll miss him dearly. We will." Then they went scratching for a new candidate. They didn't have to caucus very hard. The candidate had come to them like a thunderbolt. It was Rebecca of the Rockaways.

She arrived at the old Police Headquarters and hugged Isaac the Brave. Isaac was chagrined. "Rebecca, I'll get out soon as I can clear my desk."

"Stay," she said. "The Cultural Committee can spare one little room . . . Isaac, we have to talk. I'll need a good cop. I want you to stick with the Police."

Isaac grew more and more depressed. What Mayor renounces his candidacy a few weeks before November? Only Sam. The Board of Elections had to strike Sammy off the lists and print Rebecca's name. The Board was an old hippopotamus. It couldn't have roused itself. The Board must have known for a month that Rebecca would be on the ballot. That hippopotamus took its instructions from Sam.

Isaac dialed City Hall. It was a worthless occupation. You couldn't get Sammy on the phone. "What's your name, sir? Sidel, sir? We'll tell him that the First Deputy called." Isaac understood that most of this malarkey wasn't Sam's. The great god Dennis was behind it all. Mangen had gotten Sam to close his shop. They must have been bargaining while the hippo went to the printer with its ballots. Whom had the Mayor offered up to Dennis? It had to be Tiger John.

But the Tiger was still issuing memos out of 1 Police Plaza. The memos could have been for the cops of Peoria, Illinois. The Tiger mentioned riot batons, gas masks, all-weather shoes. Isaac grabbed at the memos in disgust. Cops were dying, and the Tiger wanted gas masks and a certain kind of shoe.

It encouraged a madness in yourself to interpret every line. John was hysterical over something. Isaac didn't have to guess why: Mangen's grand jury was in harness again. Twice a month Dennis would imprison twenty-three ladies and gentlemen in a secret room at the World Trade Center. He wouldn't let them out until they produced bills of indictment for him. When the jury doors opened, a twitch would spread from judges to lawyers and cops. You couldn't be sure where Dennis would strike.

The man had no shame. He walked into 1 Police Plaza with those girl prosecutors of his and a pair of City marshals. They went up to the fourteenth floor and arrested Tiger John. The PC had to wear handcuffs in front of his lieutenants and clerks.

He was booked at the precinct on Ericson Place. Officers had to search through his pockets and fingerprint the PC! They photographed him with his gray support hose dragging around his calves. He wasn't put in a separate holding bin. He sat with all the thieves. They were trundled over to Manhattan Supreme Court in a little truck, and he was arraigned before a judge who stared at the Commissioner with a crooked mouth. Tiger John was charged with extorting money from prostitutes and lending "his office, his title, and his good name" to help pimps and other vermin of the City. Bail was denied. The judge wouldn't set a vulture out in the street. John had to go to Riker's Island.

His Honor, Sammy Dunne, would permit no confusion among the Police. He stood before television cameras inside the rotunda of City Hall. The Mayor wore a dark green suit. His cuff links shimmered against the cameras and the lamps in powerful hues. He seemed recovered from his recent spell of witlessness. "I won't talk about Johnny Rathgar," he said. "If he's clean, we'll find out . . . and if he's guilty, we'll send him to the dogs!"

"Your Honor, who's the next Commish?"

"Only one lad could take on that job . . . with so much corruption smacking us in the face. Isaac Sidel."

The reporters were eager to know where Isaac was.

"Ah, he'll be here soon enough."

Isaac couldn't escape Sammy's call to become the next "Commish." Old shots of Sam and him, bumbling from synagogue to synagogue last June, appeared in the *Times,* the *Post,* and the *Daily News.* Television interviewers began to converge on Centre Street. The Mayor's office was phoning the boy every fifteen minutes. New York was still without a Police Commissioner. The Mayor had to swear Isaac in. Sammy's aides purred at Isaac on the phone. "Commish, His Honor needs you in the Blue Room."

The "Commish" had to run to Rivington Street for a tie, a shirt, and a handkerchief. The worm tugged at him while he changed his underwear. Isaac crossed the Bowery, cut through Chinatown, and showed at City Hall. The worm ate pieces of him. He might have swooned if the press hadn't come out of its closet to catch him in time. He blamed it on a lunch of bananas and cream. It was a big lie. Isaac hated bananas and cream.

The Mayor was in the Blue Room, near the portrait of Martin Van Buren. Isaac whispered into Sam's lapel. "You're a cocksucker in your heart, Sammy Dunne."

"Later," Sammy growled under his breath. "Laddie, why are you sweating so much?"

"Because I have a worm in me that says I shouldn't be your Commissioner."

"Wipe your forehead. You can't always listen to a worm."

Isaac took his oath of allegiance, muttering after Sam. The little Mayor had Tiger John's old badge, with its blue enameled face, and an eagle crouching on five gold stars. He pinned the badge on Isaac, and invested him as Police Commissioner. The press corps stood around Commissioner Isaac.

"Commish, what happens when Becky takes over from Sam? Will you be out of a job?"

"Probably," Isaac said with a moan. He could feel the worm gorging under his heart. "She has to win the election first." His mouth tightened. "Then we'll know. I serve at the Mayor's convenience."

"Are you going to help prosecute Tiger John?"

"Speak to Dennis. He hasn't asked me to cooperate yet."

"Commish, will you shut down Whores' Row?"

"I'm only a cop," Isaac said. "I don't make the laws."

Isaac nodded once or twice and walked out of the Blue Room with Sammy Dunne. His Honor was quiet in the halls. Isaac shook Sammy's arm. "You made a deal with Mangen, didn't you?"

"You've got bats in your ear."

He followed the little Mayor into his private office. "Pretty work," Isaac said. "Pretty work. You fed Tiger John to Mangen, just like that. What did you promise the idiot boy? That he could hold on to his precious bankbooks in jail? They'll tear his eyes out at Riker's, don't you know? They've got lads over there that aren't too enchanted with Police Commissioners. Sam, couldn't you have fixed a better bail hearing for little Johnny? Or did you conspire with Dennis and the judge to get him out of the way? Prick, I campaigned for you. I told lies in the shuls . . . and Becky gets it all."

"Ah, shit," Sam said. "A Mayor has to live . . . did you want me to go waltzing with John under the judge's bench?"

"No," Isaac said. "You're too dignified for that. But how did you get involved with Dermott Bride?"

"That crow with the black hair? He ain't even an Irishman. I wouldn't touch Dermott Bride."

"But you took his whore money."

"Not from him. You saw the press I had a year ago. My own Party was anxious to throw me in the river. Get rid of the old guy. He has a bad smell. I had to take care of myself. I don't have me a wife. I wasn't going to crawl on my knees with a pension from the City."

"So you went to Coote McNeill. The grand old tyrant of the Force. And he unleashed Dermott's money . . . nickel-and-dime shit. You're the Mayor. Why didn't you fiddle with the budget?"

"Jesus, man. I'm not a thief."

"Oh, you're too smart to grab with your own two fists. You found yourself a buffer, a go-between, Tiger John. He was your bagman, your messenger, your boy Friday. Then Mangen came along, and you got scared. McNeill had to dismantle his operation. He sent the king into exile. He killed Arthur Greer."

The Mayor had an ugly notch around his eye. "Don't talk murder to me. I never met this Arthur Greer."

"Of course," Isaac said. "His Honor doesn't mingle with nigger pimps. You're the good Irishman. But why didn't Mangen arrest Coote McNeill? It won't be much fun bringing Tiger John to trial."

"McNeill's gone," the Mayor said.

Isaac looked into that notch over Sammy's eye.

"Coote retired last week. He bought himself a house in the Old Country."

"The Old Country," Isaac muttered. "Everybody lands in the Old Country. But it doesn't make sense. Dennis could reach into Ireland if he wants . . . He'd rather have the idiot boy. He'll go the easy way and carve Tiger John."

Isaac developed a leer that dug into his chin. "Don't take me for granted. I'm not your suck. I don't exist to cradle City Hall. You cornered me into this job. You blabbed to the papers that I was your man . . . but you might get a little sorry."

Isaac walked out of City Hall. Clerks and typists stared at him. The new "Commish" didn't have a slouch like Tiger John. You could listen to the crunch of his body. He didn't patter away from the Mayor's office, as if he were a man without shoes. He went across the road to Police Headquarters. The cops had a plaza to themselves, a hub of concrete with terraces and rails, and a huge shithouse on top of it, a mausoleum of red brick.

They swarmed over Isaac soon as he entered the building. "Commish, Commish." No one had seen his hide for months. Now they had a Commissioner, all right. Not that pussyface, Tiger John, who had screaming fits in the halls, and would punish a borough commander for looking at him the wrong way. (What was the right way to look at Tiger John?) The State Prosecutor caught him with his pants down. They handcuffed the pussyface in front of a thousand cops. Disgraced the Department he did. Mangen made a home for him on Riker's Island. There he'll sit, without a postcard from the boyos at 1 Police Plaza. The pussyface can write his memoirs, describe how he stuck his fingers in a whore's pocket. But let Mangen come for Isaac the Brave! You couldn't drive the new "Commish" out of Headquarters. Never in your life.

He didn't go in to claim the territories of a Commissioner . He went to the First Dep's office on the thirteenth floor. The hair crawled on Isaac's head. Something was horribly wrong. He had an office choked with strangers. He walked from room to room; captains and clerks looked away from Isaac and stared at the walls. Who were these miserable people? "Where's Havisham? Where's Brodsky? Where's Marvin Winch?" The captains heard that roar out of Isaac. He picked on one of them. "What's your name?"

"Smiley. Captain Smiley."

"Who put you here?"

Isaac burrowed into the captain with his eyes. "Are you deaf man? Who put you here?"

"The Chief Inspector."

"You worked for Coote, you prick and a half?"

Smiley must have seen the devil in Isaac's face. His jaw dropped out from under his chin.

"And what did you lads do when I called this office?"

"We took the message upstairs. To the McNeill."

Isaac flailed the air with both his arms. "Out," he said. "All of you. Get the hell out of here."

Captains and clerks ran from him. They didn't know how to please the new "Commish." They stood in the hall, with their pencils, holsters, and gum erasers. Coote had smuggled a whole team into the First Dep's office. McNeill got rid of Isaac's men a bundle at a time. They were probably licking dust off fingerprint cards in the five boroughs.

One flight up and he was in the Chief Inspector's office. Coote's people hunched behind their desks. Isaac studied the walls. Then he cursed himself. He was stupid as a cow. McNeill had fishing paraphernalia tacked up all over the place: thin, beautiful rods that could whip into a perfect fisherman's arc, trophies with such tiny lettering, it would burn your eyes to read, fishhooks, maps of a hidden trout stream, photos of amazing salmon catches, pieces of an ancient lucky boot. Isaac had seen the bloody things before. McNeill had the same paraphernalia up in his old rooms at Centre Street. Isaac had to look at this shit on the wall to give his head a little shake. *Coote* was the Fisherman Annie had told him about. Cote, Cote the Fisherman. God, he might have saved that girl, if he could have remembered those hooks, salmon, and trout.

Isaac pointed to a fat clerk. "Take that junk off the wall and ship it to your old chief with the compliments of Isaac Sidel. No . . . tell him, Love from the Commissioner. He'll understand."

Cops were gathering outside the Chief Inspector's office: Stories had spread like a crazy fire in the building: the "Commish" would march into a room, breathing hell on his captains. You couldn't avoid the scrutiny of Isaac. He had a menace sitting on his brows. One wrinkle of his eye, and a man was doomed. Isaac snatched a lowly sergeant from the hall and brought him into the Commissioner's office, made him a master clerk. "Sergeant, I want you to take every cunt in the First Dep's office, every creature who worked for McNeill and Tiger John, and throw them to the Badlands. Give them precincts in the South Bronx."

That's how Isaac began his reign at 1 Police Plaza.

TWENTY-NINE

They drifted into Headquarters, blue-eyed boys rescued from the provinces. Their boss had come home. The boss seemed gloomy in his Commissioner's coat. His eyes had shrunk since they last saw him, months and months ago, when he sank into the ground and disappeared, in order to destroy the pimps of New York City. They understood part of his gloom. He missed his old sweetheart, Manfred Coen.

They talked about the worm in his belly. "It's eating him up. Soon there'll be nothing left of Isaac." But Isaac survived. He was teaching again at the College of Criminal Justice.

It was just before election time. People in the class were wearing buttons that Becky Karp produced in less than a week: VOTE MS. REBECCA. It was her war cry to women and men.

The buttons enraged Isaac. He built his lecture around them. "Flotsam," he said. "Politics. Ms. Rebecca Karp." The Commissioner had developed a machine-gun language. He shunned sentences, threw words and particles out at the class. He pounced in front of the room in a coat that hung on his body. He could have been a scarecrow, or any ragged man, with coal-black eyes.

"Buttonface. Whorehearts . . . lovely hour to vote."

He snickered on his feet. Then he turned articulate, muttered a complete sentence to the class. "They know how to fuck us, the lords and ladies who manage our lives."

His stalking near the blackboard had begun to mesmerize the student firemen and cops. It didn't matter what the Commissioner said. The class would have gone to hell with Isaac. "Those darlings have picked a beauty for us. Rejoice. The people's candidate, strong as apple cider. Our Lady of the Buttons, Ms. Rebecca Karp. How do you become a Mayor in such times? You step on an old man's back, that's how. You rise up on his shoulders and watch him sink. Then you manufacture a million buttons. You distribute them to the faithful. And you promise a lot. A white borough for the Irish, the Italians, and the Jews. Dental clinics for the Latinos and the blacks. A paradise in Far Rockaway for the over-sixty-fives. Boys, girls, it don't mean shit. The planet is running low. The subways are having a heart attack. You can't tell the difference between garbage and pennies in the street. But go on, pin Rebecca to your blouse. Who knows? It might do you some good."

There he was, insulting the next Mayor of New York. How many Police Commissioners are prophets and fools in one gulp? The worm drove through him with its many tails. There had to be a spy in the class.

Isaac hovered close to the door. He couldn't escape the green eyes of Jennifer Pears. He looked for signs of growth in her belly. Isaac wanted evidence of *his* child. He found nothing but natural curves.

"What month is it?"

Jennifer stared at him. "November."

"No, no," Isaac said. "For the child." He couldn't recall the pregnancy of his own wife. What was Kathleen when she was carrying Marilyn the Wild? Did she have a gargantuan waist by the second month? Blast an old cop's memory! He'd have to go before the Medical Board and prove he was a sane "Commish." He'd curtsy for the bastards and count the fingers on his left hand.

"It's the third month," she said. "You can see a little bulge if you pull my skirt apart."

She took Isaac by the elbow and led him out of John Jay.

"Have you decided to marry me?"

"Shut up," she said.

"We can't go to my hotel. The pimps would cut our throats. They're not fond of Police Commissioners and their girlfriends."

She brought him home in a taxi cab. Isaac could feel the doorman smirk at him. He never liked the East Side.

"Where's Mel?"

"He's working, you idiot."

"And the little boy . . . Alexander?"

"He's at school. Isaac, what's wrong with you?"

He was a lost, anxious child under his Commissioner's coat. He shivered in his socks. Jennifer had to unlace his shoes while Isaac growled at her. "Woman, I won't sleep with you until the husband goes . . ."

He crept into the coverlets, a frightened dog-boy with hair on his arms and a wild fur over the rest of his body. Nothing could sooth a "Commish." He had a foulness in his heart. The dead seemed to follow Isaac. They wouldn't lie still. He'd buried Coen, he'd buried Annie Powell. He brought rabbis in for them. What more could he do?

He made love to Melvin's naked wife. He touched that thickening belly. The fur smoothed on him as he pushed into Jennifer Pears.

He couldn't stay very long. Jennifer's digital clock blinked twenty to three. Alexander was coming from the Little Red Schoolhouse. Jennifer didn't wear any clothes to the door.

"Can I see you tomorrow?" Isaac said.

"Tomorrow's Election Day."

"So what?"

"Mel will be here."

"I thought the husband'll be out capturing votes for Ms. Rebecca."

"Isaac, don't be a prick. Rebecca doesn't need votes from Mel."

She went out naked into the hall and kissed Isaac on the wrinkle over one eye. "Come Thursday. For lunch."

He scowled in the elevator. Doormen couldn't intimidate him. He had the monkey at the plugboard dial Headquarters and ask for the Commissioner's car. A surly boy named Christianson, who'd chauffeured Tiger John, arrived in a black Mercury. Isaac could have

changed drivers. But he liked the boy's silences, his contempt for
every other vehicle on the road. Christianson swept around fire
trucks, pushed buses out of their lanes, challenged any police car that
dared crawl in front of the "Commish." The boy had a telegram for
Isaac. It wasn't in its usual cellophane jacket.

"Who opened this?"

Christianson shrugged his boyish shoulders. "Dunno, boss. I
found it on your desk that way."

"You," Isaac said. "Look at my face. I'm not Tiger John. You
tamper with my mail again, and you'll have to drive without your
kneecaps."

"Yes, boss."

Isaac unfolded the telegram.

POLICE COMMISSIONER
N.Y. CITY-N.Y.

SIDEL MET ME ST. STEPHENS WED
IO AM URGENT

THE KING

"Christianson, what does this say to you?"

"Sounds like crazy talk."

"Do you know where St. Stephen's is?"

"Could be a church somewhere."

John must have taught his chauffeur never to commit himself.
He'd have to sack the boy very soon.

"Christianson, take me to Aer Lingus. Right now."

Isaac left for Ireland on Election Day. He wasn't curious about
the results of Rebbeca's little pilgrimage to glory. She'd become
Mayor-elect soon as the polls shut down, and the City would have a
broken duck, His Honor, Samuel Dunne. Sammy deserved whatever
crippling he got. He shouldn't have grabbed at whores from City
Hall. But the Party wouldn't forsake its Old Man. Who can tell? Ms.
Rebecca might give him the gatekeeper's job at Gracie Mansion.

Isaac had his own problems. The "Commish" was rocking over
the water (in an Irish plane) on the strength of a miserable telegram.
He didn't trust the words. Little Dermott wouldn't have begged for

Isaac in such a bald way. He wasn't a showy man. He had too much breeding to sign a telegram with his pet name. *The King.* Someone else had signed it for him, and written the goddamn message. Whatever it was, Isaac couldn't avoid it. *Urgent,* it said *St. Stephens. Wed. 10 AM.*

He was at Dublin airport on Wednesday morning, around half-past eight. He wasn't Moses Herzog on this trip. Isaac had little use for camouflage. He didn't come over to kill a man. He was only the "Commish." He hadn't booked a room at the Shelbourne. He was returning to New York on the afternoon flight.

A cab brought him into Dublin. He hadn't bothered to convert his dollars into Irish pounds. The driver took his money without any qualms and let him off at the northwest gate of St. Stephen's Green. It could have been August. Isaac had the same chill about the ears. He strolled along the rim of the park. Men and women churned by him in their November clothes. It was a school day. You couldn't find laddies hunching in the grass. The white and brown ducks were gone. Isaac didn't see a bird in the old pond. He passed the stone bridge. A man was sitting inside the gazebo. His head was upright, under an eight-piece woolen cap.

Isaac could recognize a king by his ears. Aristocratic they were. Without points, or hanging lobes. But that dark Irish-gypsy face had a strange, unbending manner. A live man don't sit with a perfectly cocked head. Dermott's eyes were open. He had a Crotona Park grin. His neck was wired to the gazebo wall. His throat had been slit. The blood congealed under a napkin that had been thrust into the collar of his shirt. Isaac didn't have to guess. The king's bodyguards must have murdered him. They'd done a terrific patching job. His ankles and wrists were wired up, and you'd have to look down his collar to peek at the blood. "Ah, you poor son of a bitch, you shouldn't have come here. Dublin ain't for you . . ."

What was the use of unwiring him? His neck might drop off. The blood began to soak through that bib inside his collar. Isaac left the king undisturbed. A park warden would discover the dead man in the gazebo and call the Irish gardai. The cops would shrug it off. They'd hold the corpse at Dublin Castle for twenty hours and declare it a "painful case," altogether unsolvable, like any gangland killing, American style.

It was a fine touch to put that eight-piece cap on his head. The king's scalp of black, black hair might have brought attention to

itself. You can't be much of a killer without love for detail. Isaac
strolled back to the northwest gate. The king's bodyguards were
there, four old men in identical eight-piece caps. Isaac nodded to Tim
Snell, that old sergeant from the Chief Inspector's office.

"Morning, Tim . . . lovely work, that . . . wire a man by his
neck."

Timothy smiled. "We thought you'd appreciate it, Isaac."

"Did you cut him with his own knife?"

"Yes, we did."

"Then that telegram came from you."

"Naturally," Tim said. "I composed it with the king's fountain
pen. Took me half the day. To find the right wording you see . . . we
wanted to celebrate your new job. Congratulations, Isaac. It's not
every old bugger of a cop who can stand in Stephen's Green and talk
to the Commish."

"Don't let the title fool you, Tim. I'm the same lad you drove
through the quays three months ago. It's a bit crude to murder your
boss."

"Him? He was nothing to us. Dirt under your thumb, that's all.
Mr. Dermott Bride. A stoolpigeon he was that licked his feathers and
walked out of the Bronx . . . we work for a real king."

"The Fisherman . . . you slit throats for Coote McNeill."

"Shhh," Tim said, with that smile of his. "It's not nice to
mention names in a public park. Why don't you come with us, love?
We have the automobile across the road. We can continue this
conversation with cushions under your ass . . . and don't you scream
for the cops. They're good boys, the gardai. But dumb. They won't
be much help to you."

It was instinct that preserved Isaac the Brave. He caught
Timothy with an elbow and shoved him into the other old men. The
teeth clattered in their heads, and their caps fell to the ground as they
gave a little sigh. Isaac bolted out of the park like a rabbit in city
pants and shoes. The old men recovered their hats and chased after
the "Commish." You could hear them huff along on Grafton Street.
Isaac ran with his elbows wide. He could outwit four old murderers
who had a hard time breathing.

He took to the alleys, chose a crooked trail from Grafton to
Dame Street. He crossed the Liffey at Temple bar and Wellington
Quay. The river had lost its dirty color. It wasn't frog-green, like a
piss-pond or a spittoon. It was almost purple under the bridge.

November had cleared all the mud.

Isaac didn't keep to the south wall. He crept up to Mary's Lane and found a car-for-hire agency on Constitution Hill. He wouldn't get out of Ireland this afternoon. That corpse in the gazebo had interrupted Isaac's plans. He was going to pay a visit to Coote McNeill.

The "Commish" had done a bit of homework before he got on the plane to meet Dermott in an Irish park. His blue-eyed boys tore the Chief Inspector's files apart until they unearthed an address for Coote. The Fisherman's place was next to Screeb in County Galway. Screeb was where Isaac had the mind to go. The man from the agency lent him a map. Isaac bumped down Constitution Hill into the lower regions of Church Street. He was driving a little French car. The "Commish" was used to having his body chauffeured around. He had trouble with the steering column. It wasn't where it ought to be. It had moved from the left side to the right. Damn the French and the little cars they brought into Ireland. Didn't the Irish have their own make of wagon? A Phoenix Spark? A Donnybrook? A Cromwell Cadet? A Grand Drummartin? Holy Mother! He was on the wrong half of the road. The Irish were a mad people. They invented their own traffic laws to confound a man and tire him to death. Left is right, me boy, and right is left. The "Commish" had to reeducate himself on King Street North. *Isaac, stay left, left, left.*

He had a baby's crawl. He crossed the Liffey by mistake and got stranded in Dolphin's Barn. It took him three hours to break out of Dublin and find the road to Mullingar.

He drove thirty miles, then it grew dark on him. He stayed in a cottage that night, with an ironmonger's widow and her seven kids, near the town of Kinnegad. The children's whining came through the walls. It was a relief to Isaac. It kept him occupied. He didn't dare fall asleep. Coote's old men might be at the window. He had his bed and breakfast and crept back on the road early in the morning.

He wasn't dispirited on his second day in the Irish countryside. Teaching himself how to maneuver a wicked car on a wicked road had done remarkable things to Isaac. Pushed like a heavy thumb through the matting in his brain. Dermott didn't belong in an eight-piece cap. The king had to die before Isaac could remember him as a boy. Isaac's chief, First Deputy O'Roarke, had sent him out to tame a wild gang, the Devils of Clay Avenue. He traveled to the Bronx, a young inspector growing bald behind the ears. He couldn't understand where the gang got its reputation from. The Devils were a bunch of shivering boys. These were the lads who had conquered a borough? Their single property was a shack in Claremont Park. Who was it that led those raids into every corner of the Bronx? Not their president, Arthur Greer. Sweet Arthur always stayed at home. Isaac had to poke behind their idiotic grins. Only one other boy appealed to him. Little Dermott McBride. Short and dark he was. A cop's intuition told him *this* was the leader of the raids. He had a sadness around the eyes that reminded Isaac of his "angel," Manfred Coen, whom he'd pulled right out of the Police Academy. Isaac happened to need a sad-looking boy to infiltrate a gang of Polish thieves that was causing mayhem in the garment district. Coen was on special assignment to him. Isaac wouldn't give him back to the Academy. He liked having Blue Eyes around.

Twenty miles out of Kinnegad it struck Isaac that Coen and Little Dermott began to mix in his head. Isaac's batteries had crossed somewhere. It was his sorrow over Manfred, his own fucking guilt, and not that worm in his gut, that had eaten into Isaac's memory. He must have had a wish at the time that Manfred could enter into Dermott and steal away some of Dermott's intelligence. Then Isaac would have had an "angel" who was more than beautiful and dumb. It would have meant a reshuffling of brains, a lessening of the king to puff out Manfred Coen. But Isaac wasn't a ghoul. He wouldn't harm one boy to glorify another, just because they had the same sad eyes...

He got to Screeb. It was nothing but a fork in a road. He'd been traveling a good eight hours. He got lost in Galway City until a baker's boy led him out of that trapping of streets. He went along the coast. Isaac had the Atlantic under him. He had to stop for cows and sheep. He left the car and began to walk. Stones and trees weren't a proper landmark. You could have blindfolded him outside Centre Street and dropped him anywhere in Manhattan. Isaac would have felt his way. He had the gift. He could nose out the contours of a neighborhood. *Boys, I'm in the Heights. Around Audubon Avenue, I'd say. West of Highbridge.*

But a country road mystified him. Isaac walked with his teeth near the ground. God knows why he was traveling with a curl in his spine, like a hunchback? Was it to make himself less of a target for Coote's men? He looked up once and saw the corrugated roof of a house. He'd stumbled upon a castle in Screeb. *Castledermott*. That's what Annie Powell had said.

The castle had a yellow lake. Isaac heard a plop in the water. A man was fishing the lake, a small man with boots up to his arse. He would stare into that yellowness and grunt. "Come on up, me beauties." He was a fisherman without a fishing rod. He worked with a net and a plain billy club. He smacked at the water from time to time. But the net wouldn't fill. It was a senseless occupation. The man hadn't struggled with one lousy fish.

He stood near the rim of the lake. He was deaf, deaf to anything that didn't come from the water. Isaac could have plucked hairs off the man's head.

"Afternoon to you, McNeill."

An eyebrow knit for a moment. Then the face relaxed.

"Ah, sonny, I was expecting you . . ."

"Am I talking too loud? I wouldn't want to disturb the fish."

"But that's the point," Coote said, swinging his billy club. "I'd like to disturb them with this." He had a look of total menace as he bit into his jaw.

"Are you murdering salmon these days, Mr. Coote McNeill?"

The Fisherman eyed Isaac with disgust. "Not the salmon . . . I'm going after carp. They destroy a lake, sucking in the mud. Vermin is what they are, filthy animal fish. They can grow fat and live to fifty. So I club them in the head."

"You've been banging at the water, but I don't see many carp in your net."

"That's because they're tricky bastards. They keep to the bottom. They dirty the lake and drive out all my valuable fish."

"Why don't you hire Tim Snell to club the water with you? . . . you might get a few more hits."

"Sonny, I don't need Tim to clear a lake. He has other business."

"I know," Isaac said. "He had to write a telegram and wire up the king . . ."

The Fisherman continued to slap water with the billy club, The lake turned brown near his boots; no fifty-year-old carp came up from the mud.

"Was Tim going to wire me too?"

"You're daft," the Fisherman said. "Sonny, I could have had you killed ages ago."

"What about those shotguns you delivered to Centre Street?"

"That was nothin' but a tease . . . you're too precious to put underground. Jesus, the chances I had to get at you . . . the great Isaac roosting in Times Square with charcoal on his face. It's Mangen that kept you alive. Dennis' baby is what you are . . . and don't you get bright ideas about catching me alone in the water. I have lads in the house. If I whistle to them, sonny boy, they'll shovel out a grave for you . . . you'll rest with all the carp."

"Why did you summon me to Ireland, Coote?"

"To talk . . . Mangen was up on his haunches, so I had to get out."

"You didn't even have time to pack your fishing rods. It's a pity, but I had your office boys pick the rods off the wall. Have they arrived?"

"Not yet. You owe me something, sonny. Don't get comical with me." He thumped his chest with the billy club. "This old man made you Police Commissioner."

"Sure, you and Sammy fucked Tiger John and pinned his badge on me. It was a good cover for all of you. I come in and you ass off to your castle in Screeb and rid your lake of carp. A charming life. You gambled that I had enough affection for an old Mayor not to harm him. I couldn't prosecute Sammy if I wanted to. He's made his pact with Dennis. He won't starve when the money runs out. Rebecca will provide for him. That leaves you. Now what is it you need from me? You have your yellow lake . . ."

"I don't want my picture in the newspapers. I'm in seclusion here. I'll have me an angler's club. I'll start up a bit of a hotel. Lease my salmon rights to worthy fishermen . . . Isaac, the whore shit is dead. Why rake it up? Mangen has Tiger John. He's satisfied."

"Oh, I wouldn't disturb you, Chief. You're safe. You butchered everyone around that could do you harm. You were like a pope in New York City. The Mayor kissed your hand. And you took every boy from my office and farmed them out. They had to ride the ferry to work. You were smart. You left me a boy or two until the very end, so Isaac wouldn't know."

"Sonny, it aint my fault you didn't come to Headquarters. I couldn't have done a thing with John if you'd been there. But we could count on you. If you weren't sleeping with the Guzmanns, you'd be in some other filthy pile. You could never sit on your ass. And don't accuse me of butchering people. You butchered when you had to . . . like the rest of us. You killed your own boy, Blue Eyes, because that daughter of yours was crazy about him, and you couldn't stand the idea."

"The Guzmanns killed Coen," Isaac muttered into the lake.

"Indeed. Nasty souls they were . . . they made chocolate bars in the Bronx . . . and you had to declare war on them, Papa Guzmann and his five idiot boys."

"Papa gave me a worm."

"You deserved it," McNeill said. "Don't play Isaac the pure with me."

Isaac watched the billy club slap water again. The net dropped down and rose up empty.

"There ain't that much difference between us," the Fisherman said. "I took for myself, and you used the Department for your own imbecile cause. You killed, you maimed, you gouged out eyes, sonny boy."

"But I didn't wire a man to a bench, just to show off."

"I had to dispose of him, and one way's as good as another. He was getting to be a nuisance, you know. He falls in love with a shopgirl and we have to suffer for it. What kind of king is that? He was a gutter boy before I picked him up. The Department put him through college."

"I got him into Columbia . . . not you, or the Department."

"Piss on your brains," the Fisherman said. "You were always a little slow behind all that cleverness. Dermott belonged to me and Ned O'Roarke."

Isaac stood an inch out of the water, his toes collecting mud. He'd inherited his job from O'Roarke, the old First Deputy Commissioner. He was Ned's protégé, an apostate Jew among the Irish. Did O'Roarke hide Dermott under one knee without telling Isaac?

Coote grinned at that slump in Isaac's shoulders. "Ned made a Yalie out of him. It was a bit too close having him in town. So we groomed the lad in New Haven. A little gentleman he was. We let him steal. We let him have his books. We let him run the nigger whores with Arthur Greer."

"And when O'Roarke died, you stuck your hand in the pot . . . and pulled out a pretty penny."

"Would you have me chewing gumballs for the rest of my life? The king was my creation. Tell me why I shouldn't benefit from it? Him and the nigger got to be millionaires. Boys of thirty carrying hundreds of thousands in their pockets. Then he gets shopgirl Annie for a mistress and a wife. I sit him in Dublin because Mangen is coming on to us, and he neglects our business over Annie Powell. Imagine, going itchy for a stupid cunt that's nothin' but a whore, when he can have any woman on this earth. Him with education, money, and a gypsy's eye."

"*Annie*," Isaac said, "what did you do about Annie Powell?"

"Jesus, the girl saw my face . . . I couldn't let her whore in the street with Mangen's shooflies running everywhere. I paid a boy in a taxi cab to climb up on her back . . ."

Isaac's toes fell into the water. Coote wasn't an idiot. He could sense the rage that was coming over Isaac. The "Commish" 's forehead swelled out like a diseased melon with tiny bumps on it. "Mother Mary," the Fisherman said. "You didn't go and fall in love with that whore, did you now?"

He raised his billy club. It was a warning to Isaac. *Keep out of me lake*. But Isaac rushed at him. The billy club landed at the base of Isaac's neck. He felt a crunching in his scapula. His head tumbled down. But he shook off that motherfucking blow. The billy club whistled behind Isaac's ear. The old man had been too eager. He missed his chance to brain the "Commish." Isaac slapped the billy club away. He grabbed the old man by the roots of his scalp and shoved that head into the yellow lake. He kept it there without a touch of mercy, using his elbow as a fulcrum to dig between Coote's shoulder blades. Bubbles rose around Isaac's fist. Coote's arms jerked under the water. Then the old man went still. Isaac gave Coote's body to the salmon and the carp. He didn't see any signs of movement from the house. The chimneys revealed one lousy tail of smoke.

Isaac stepped out of the water. His shoulder humped up on him. Coote's old men could have ripped the nose off his face. But nobody ran after Isaac. He beat the ground with his shoes until he arrived at his little French car. He mumbled a benediction to the Irish. *God bless all little cars with the steering wheels on the right*. Then he drove out of Screeb.

THIRTY

He got past the customs booth at Kennedy. Where were the guys with handcuffs and the warrant for his arrest? No one touched the "Commish." It was a good year for murder. They let you strangle old men in the water these days.

The "Commish" got his chauffeur on the line. "Christianson," it's me. Turn on your sirens. I'll expect you outside Aer Lingus in eighteen minutes."

Christianson wouldn't disappoint his boss. Isaac was tucked away in his rooms at 1 Police Plaza before his hands could turn cold. A button lit up on his telephone console. It was the Mayor's "hot line" to Police Headquarters. Isaac could have let that button glow day and night. He banged on the console and growled into the phone. "Sidel here."

"Laddie, how are you?"

"Grand," Isaac said.

"Have you heard the news? . . . McNeill expired. The poor sod drowned in his own fishing pool."

"Did you say drowned? That's a terrible pity."

"Well, the Sons of Dingle are paying to have the corpse fly home. He wanted to be buried here, you know. We'll be having a service for him, Isaac. At St. Pat's." Isaac had been rubbed in Kelly green. He knew all the rituals of Manhattan Irish politicians and cops. They always sing their prayers for the dead at St. Patrick's Cathedral.

"Ain't he entitled to an Inspector's Funeral?"

Only Isaac could call out the color guard to honor a dead cop. The PC plucked his chin. He wasn't sorry that he'd pushed McNeil's face into the water. *I'd murder him again and again.* But why should he forgo the honor guard for Coote? Thieves had to be laid to rest like any other man.

Isaac said goodbye to the Mayor and rang up Jennifer Pears. He excused himself for missing lunch with her. "I was out of the country. Swear to Moses . . . had to make a short trip."

"Trip?" she said.

"To Mother Ireland."

"Isaac, is that where your people are from?"

"They might as well . . . I'm Irish to the bone."

Jennifer laughed at him. "Come for lunch . . . right now."

Isaac screamed for Christianson, but he couldn't escape from Headquarters so fast. His mentor, Marshall Berkowitz, was in the vestibule. The PC wouldn't run out on Marsh. An aide brought him in to Isaac. Marsh stared at the furnishings of a Commissioner's office: the flags, trophies, pictures, drapes, the huge desk of burled oak that had belonged to Teddy Roosevelt when he was Commissioner of Police.

"Marsh, you'll have to forgive the décor. It's Tiger John's. I haven't had time to move in." Isaac looked at the dean's broken shoes. "Is it the wife? . . . Marsh, has she disappeared again?"

The dean nodded to Isaac. He had bubbles on his lips.

"Why didn't you let Mangen know? His shooflies kidnapped her out of my living room . . . don't you remember that?"

"Mangen says he can't help me now that you're the Commish."

Isaac put the keys to his apartment on Teddy Roosevelt's desk. "Go to Rivington Street, Marsh. She's probably there. I can lend you a few boys and a squad car. I'm as good as Dennis when it comes to kidnapping people."

He didn't like betraying Sylvia, but he had to give her over to Marsh. *That fucking dean is the father of us all.* He taught Isaac, Mangen, and little Dermott the tyranny of moocows coming down the road. Marsh was a different man when he had his nose in a text. He could tear your lungs out with a few words on Mr. Joyce. *Did I ever tell you about Joyce's eyepatch? Don't believe his biographers. That was a perfectly good eye under the piece of cloth. He wore it to impress the beggars of Paris. So he could squeeze pennies out of them. Joyce was the biggest sponge in the world.*

He was late for Jennifer. They had to rush through nibblings of hollandaise sauce. Jenny's boy would be home from school in half an hour. It was curious business. In and out of bed, like a squirrel in the trees. Do squirrels have mistresses too? What did it mean when you could feel a child in your *mistress'* belly? And how come the worm was lying so still? It hadn't stirred since Isaac touched ground in New York City. Did the motherfucker pick up some Irish disease that was shrinking its head and tails? That little purring monster used to adore Jennifer Pears. Now the monster wouldn't purr.

Isaac could hunger for Jennifer without the participation of a worm. She kissed the bruise on his shoulder, but the Commissioner couldn't come. He stayed hard inside Jenny until the doorbell rang. "It's Alex," she said. She got into her panties and a blue robe to greet her little boy. Isaac dressed and walked into the parlor. Alexander peered at him from the long prow of a rain hat.

"Remember me?" Isaac said. "I'm Dick Tracy."

Jennifer laughed and unzipped the rain hat. "He's a liar. Call him Isaac. He's the Police Commissioner."

Alexander pulled on his nose. "Do you have a gun?"

"Not today," Isaac said. "Commissioners don't have to wear a gun."

Isaac seemed to diminish for the boy. He went into his room to play, while his mother was stranded in the parlor with Isaac the Pure. The robe dropped to Jennifer's belly. Isaac sucked on one nipple with a mad concentration. His pants were suddenly on the floor. He lost his inhibitions with that boy a room away. He clung to Jennifer and was able to come.

"How did you hurt your shoulder?"

"It's a gift from Ireland," Isaac said. "I had to kill a man. He was a thief and a son of a bitch."

"Do you often go on business trips like that? . . . I suppose it's all right. They'll have to forgive you. We can't have *two* Commissioners sitting in jail. The City would fall apart . . . who are you going to murder next?"

"I'm not sure." He kissed Jennifer on the mouth, and it was like that first kiss they'd had near the elevator, with his tongue down her throat. A girl could hardly breathe.

"What's going to happen to our kid?"

"Nothing. I'll have it and it'll stay with me and Mel."

"Can't I be one tiny portion of its father, boy or girl?"

"No."

Isaac left with a scowl on his face that could have eaten through a wall. Jenny grabbed him by his good shoulder. "Weekends are out," she said. "But you can come on Monday . . . and the day after that."

Isaac crept into the elevator with Monday fixed in his head. Jennifer locked the door. She gathered the ends of her robe and pulled them close to her until she was ready for her boy. She strolled in and out of mirrors, catching the little puffs under her eyes. A lady of thirty-three. She had a husband who lusted after fifty-five-year-old mayoresses. Would he move into Gracie Mansion after Ms. Rebecca got rid of Sam and rolled her carpets in? They could have their politics on a Persian rug. Jenny walked into the toy room to be with Alex. He was almost five, her little man. He had a set of Lionel trains that wound across the room like the territories of an unfathomable world. Tracks snaked into one another. Tunnels bloomed. Alex presided over every switch. He could make bridges collapse, have engines explode and spit out their parts, and torture a caboose with his system of flags and lights. You didn't need a mother when you had Lionel trains.

She stooped over Alex with Isaac's seed dripping out of her. She mussed his hair. "Want an Oreo sandwich, little guy?" Alex was too busy attending all his different tracks to think about food.

Isaac was on the steps of St. Pat's, surrounded by his own Police. Fifty captains had come out in uniform to honor the great McNeill. The Shamrock Society had black handkerchiefs and mourning bands. The Irish would never disappoint their dead. Isaac could hear a murderous gnawing behind him, a gnawing of many throats. The sons of Dingle stood in their eight-piece caps. They were with Timothy Snell and the Retired Sergeants Association. Old Tim mashed his throat as hard as any Dingle Bay boy. His eyes were shot with blood. "Timmy," Isaac said, "did you fly in with the corpse? It's a pity he went and drowned himself."

"Murderer," Tim pronounced under his breath. "The best Chief we ever had. He meant no harm to you . . . Isaac, you better not stand in the open too long. You might twist your leg and fall. You'd have a lovely time bumping down St. Pat's."

"Quiet, you prick. This aint a castle in Screeb. I rule here. The Irish sit under me. You know, Tim, I keep having this dream. It's about little Dermott. He's still wired up in the park, just the way you left him. He says, 'Isaac, do me a favor. If you catch Tim Snell, wire him to Delancey Street' . . . go on back to your funeral party before I shut down the Dingle Bay and steal your fucking sauna. You won't have a room to piss in. Move, I said."

Old Tim shrugged at Isaac and joined his fellow mourners. He marched up the stairs and went into the big church with the Shamrocks, the Sons of Dingle, and the Retired Sergeants Association. Earlier Isaac's honor guard had raised the bier out of the funeral truck, struggling with it on their shoulders until they got it into St. Pat's. Isaac didn't go inside. He'd lend his honor guard, but he wouldn't join the Requiem for Coote. He remained on the steps with his hands in his pockets.

He whistled to himself. The melody cracked on him. Isaac couldn't blow air. His cheeks contorted and his mouth turned grim. He had the shakes. Something was diving near his groin. His guts twisted in and out. The "Commish" had a corkscrew in his belly. Mother Moses, that worm had been lying in wait. The monster picked its moment to get at Isaac. What did it mean? Was Isaac in some kind of heavy labor? The worm was going to give him twins. A gypsy and a blond Jew. Baby Dermott and baby Coen.

Ooooooo! His knees waltzed out. Isaac had to sit on his bum. Celebrants ran up the stairs to be with Coote McNeill. Cops were arriving a little late. They saluted their Commissioner, paused, and went in. It was funny seeing Isaac with his knees in his face.

Another lad arrived. It was Tiger John, handcuffed to a "screw." Isaac had bullied the Corrections Department into letting John out of Riker's for an hour so he could come to the funeral.

"Morning to you, Isaac."

Isaac's mouth puffed like a dying fish.

"That man needs a glass of water," John told the screw.

The screw wasn't concerned with Isaac. He shook the handcuffs. But John refused to walk. "Isaac, should I get one of the priests for you? They must have a glass of water somewhere in St. Pat's."

Isaac pushed on his ribcage like a bellows and brought up bits of air. He belched out a few words to Tiger John. "You can go in, Johnny . . . I'll be fine. How are they treating you over there?"

"So-so," the Tiger said. "I get the Commissioners grub. Piss and black pudding . . . They let me teach the fundamentals of banking to all my little brothers."

The screw yoked on the handcuffs with one fist, and John had to crawl. Jesus, they were a funny pair, that Corrections officer and the old "Commish" with their rumps climbing together. Isaac was going to tell the screw to ease up on poor John, but the worm gathered under Isaac's ribs and uncoiled itself with a squeeze of its tails. Isaac tore his collar away. His windpipe rattled. His fingers turned blue. The little bastard was out to choke Isaac the Brave.

He couldn't rise up from the stairs. Isaac had to lull that creature to rest. He started to hum.

There was once a Commish
Who lost his mind
On the steps of St. Pat's.
He'd killed one lad too many.
He went to Ireland
To cure himself
But he couldn't break that habit
Of getting people killed.
Isaac the Commish
He brings carnage
Wherever he goes.

The worm must have liked the humming it got. It began to let go. The tails disappeared from Isaac's ribs. He was still too weak to get off his ass. He sat with his ruined collar, while the Fisherman had his Mass.

Two bodies came out of the church. Mangen and his shoofly, Captain Mort.

"Boyos," Isaac muttered. "Are they finished in there? Why are you hurrying the dead?"

Mangen continued down the stairs.

Isaac held out his hands. "Arrest me, you son of a bitch."

Mangen stopped and turned to look at Isaac. "Do you have to make a spectacle of yourself outside an Irish church?"

Isaac appealed to Captain Mort. "You're my witness, Cap. I killed a man."

The shoofly wouldn't speak. Mangen crept closer to Isaac. He sat on the steps with him. He was wearing gorgeous red-and-brown socks. He motioned to Schapiro, and the Captain went to the bottom of the stairs.

"Isaac, what sort of killing have you done?"

"*Him*. The guy in the coffin. I made him drink his yellow water . . . well, are you going to arrest me or not?"

"Isaac, I'm no magician. I can't arrest you for a crime that didn't take place . . ."

The "Commish" had a violence in the chips of his forehead. "What the hell do you mean?"

"McNeill drowned, may that old man rest in peace . . . his own boys saw it. He was in the lake, slapping for fish. And he fell. They ran out of the house, but they couldn't revive him."

Isaac slid with his bum to a lower step. "Are you happy now? The Tiger's in jail, McNeill's dead, and Sammy's over the hill . . . you even have me working for you. I sent out two cops to steal Sylvia Berkowitz from my own apartment."

"The woman's a little nuts. She can't make it alone. She has her flair of independence, and then she falls apart."

"Dennis, if you're going to play the wise man who brings together husbands and wives, what about old John? Will you furnish a wife for him at Riker's?"

Mangen stood up. "John doesn't need a wife."

The Special Prosecutor abandoned Isaac on the stairs. He jumped across Fifth Avenue with Captain Mort. Isaac wasn't done. He'd sit until the funeral was over. Then he'd ride down to Headquarters with his honor guard and those captains of his who were in mourning for Coote McNeill.

THIRTY-ONE

It was a house of ragamuffins, cell block 5, where inmates wore jogging suits, fedoras, Navy fatigues, cashmere sweaters with holes under the arms, silk scarves with mousy rents in the lining, odd pieces of prison clothes. No two men had trousers that matched. It could have been a training camp for clowns. But the clowns never smiled.

There had been two attempted hangings last month. The block had its own suicide squad, volunteers who would go from cell to cell and reassure brooding inmates. The suicide squad was the only touch of sanity on Riker's Island. The screws were crazy here. They would rush through block 5 with gas masks and billy clubs and shout "Geronimo." God forbid if you got in their way. More than one prisoner had been trampled upon and left in a gallery to moan and bleed, until the suicide squad appeared with an impoverished medical kit.

When Tiger John Rathgar heard "Geronimo," he would hide in a corner of his cell and wait for the gas masks to finish prancing through the block. He began to talk like everybody else. Rastafarians, Latinos, blacks from Bushwick Avenue. "Cocksuckers. Motherfucking screws." But John was the former PC, and that gave him a certain cleverness over the prisoners of his block. He understood the reason for gas masks and billy clubs. The screws would have been eaten alive if they'd come unarmed. They were frightened to death of John's block. There were cannibals among the population, according to them.

John was shown all the amenities that were proper for a "Commish." The screws sneered at him, but the Rastis, the Latinos, and the blacks would nod quietly and leave John alone. They wouldn't break into his cell and harangue him for contributing to their destruction. Only the white prisoners were uncivil to John. These men would stick out their tongues and cry like lunatic apes. "Tiger, Tiger, we're gonna burn your ass."

They didn't lay a finger on the old man. But the threat was always there. John had to chew his carrots in the mess hall with his ass off the edge of the chair and his eyes searching for hostile spoons and forks. You couldn't tell where an attack would begin. John stayed out of the recreation room. He didn't have to weave baskets and look at a ping-pong ball. He sat on his bunk most of the time. He pulled a blanket over him so you couldn't see what he was doing. Then he would take the bankbooks out of his pocket and remove the worn rubber band. John wasn't greedy. He didn't hunger for the amount registered in each book. What he liked best was to leaf through the different names. *Simon Dedalus. Gabriel Conroy. Leopold Bloom. Gertrude MacDowell. Anna Livia Plurabelle. Nosey Flynn. . .*

A screw was knocking on the bars of John's cell. The nose valve of his gas mask was open, and he was able to shout at John. "Are you deaf?" John gathered the bankbooks under his knee. Then he came out of the blanket to acknowledge the screw.

"You have a visitor, Mr. John."

Tiger John shrugged. It was after dark. Riker's didn't let visitors in at such an hour.

"Come on, you. Out of that fucking corner."

John stuffed the bankbooks into his pocket and climbed off his bunk. He followed the screw into the gallery and across block 5. A few of the prisoners winked at him and made friendly grabs at his shirt. "Freedom, man . . . you blowing out of here."

John grew into a frenzy. A pulse started to beat in his neck. His mouth was dry. It had to be an important guest. They wouldn't open Riker's for an ordinary stooge. The Mayor had come for him. The Man himself. The Honorable Sammy Dunne. Who else? Ah, they'd show these lads what a Mayor could do. Him and Sam, they'd be in the sweatbox at the Dingle before midnight.

He entered the visiting room and found nothing but dumb gray walls. He was put into a grimy cubicle. He stared out at the spook on the other side of the Plexiglas. It was only Isaac the Brave.

John frowned. "Jesus, I was hoping for Mayor Sam."

"Forget it," Isaac said. "Sammy couldn't even show up at St. Pat's. He's as much of Mangen's prisoner as you are . . . only Sam gets to sleep outside. Do you have a lawyer, John?"

"The best. He screams at me on the telephone twice a day."

Isaac saw the bulge in Tiger John's pocket. Bankbooks. They couldn't have been worth a penny to John. Mangen must have frozen the accounts. He's use them as evidence at John's trial, if a trial ever took place. Who could tell what was in the great god Dennis' mind? He could quash the indictment in another six months and let John slip out of jail with a pack of foolish bankbooks. Hadn't he shamed the Police? He'd gone into Headquarters and arrested the PC. Mangen forced the Department to clean house. He could advertise this when he ran for Governor next year on the Republican ticket. But Dennis had other means to turn John into a ghost. He could push back the trial and have Tiger John sit like the Count of Monte Cristo, until his sideburns covered his nose and he became the invisible man of Riker's. Who could say how many poor, shrunken devils schlepped through these galleries at the House of Detention?

"Can I get you anything, John?"

Isaac's lips seemed to swell through the Plexiglas. "No," John said. It was a ludicrous sight. Laughable. The old "Commish" and the new with a glass wall between them. "You should have taken better care of me, Isaac. You were my First Dep . . . now go away. You bring a man bad luck."

John walked out of the cubicle. The screws would remember that Isaac the Brave had summoned him from block 5, and they'd torment John for it. He wouldn't be able to flip through his bankbooks in peace.

He heard a strange, soft pluck from the roof over block 5. It couldn't be anything like a drizzle. The house gang would have gone ape by now, cursing, mopping floors with the blankets they swiped from the cells, measuring the leakage, so they could put garbage cans under the worst holes. White puffs trickled down from the roof. You could catch them with a finger. Mother Mary, it was the first snow of autumn. John touched the white puffs to his face. November snow was a godly snow. The flakes could heal. *Simon Dedalus. Leopold Bloom.* What more could a man need? John patted the little books in his pocket. Then he winked at the screw behind him and waltzed back into his cell.